I0748391

WILD

THE BEAUTIFULLY WILD SERIES

LEESA BOW

This book is a work of fiction. Any references to real events, real people, and real places are used fictitiously. Other names, characters, places, and incidents are products of the author's imagination, and any resemblance to persons, living or dead, actual events, organizations, or places is entirely coincidental. The use of psychedelic drugs is illegal in many countries. The author does not advocate the use of these substances. It is mentioned for fictional purposes only.

Editing by Swish Design & Editing

For Shauni,
Your strength and fight to live made me view the world through different eyes.
I love you and am thankful for small blessings every day.
To the friends you met at the Adelaide Children's Hospital who lost their battle to childhood cancer, this book is also for you.
To Jenna, Will, Michael, and your parents, your emotional toughness in the face of fear will stay with me always.
Writing this story gave me the strength to cope.
A mother—afraid, finding hope.
My beautiful family and friends showed me the way.
Lynden, Jamie-Lee, Ashleigh, Demi, Mum and Dad, and Vickie were always by our sides.
Fear remains. How we cope is our strength.

BEAUTIFULLY BROKEN

PREQUEL

1

EDEN

HAPPINESS IS DIFFERENT FOR EVERYONE, yet at only twenty-two years of age, I feel like I'm living in a contented, loved-up bubble of bliss. Some days I wait for the universe to strike because how am I this happy in love when many of my friends are still searching for the right guy?

My boyfriend, Ethan, and I met in high school. With our families being close, love was destined to blossom. We have the same circle of friends, and our lives, our world, is simply perfect.

Simply is a word I do not use lightly.

Our love is effortless.

Uncomplicated.

He still manages to surprise me, like today when he arrives at my office with flowers. "Thank you, babe. They're beautiful." Pushing onto my toes, I place my lips against Ethan's before taking the peonies and lilies to place in a vase. "I love you."

He smiles at me—it's a combination of cheeky and sexy. Even after all these years, he makes me gooey on the inside.

"Do you have plans tonight?" he asks, following me into the kitchen with his hand on my ass.

Dropping the flowers on the sink, I move into his arms as he leans in to kiss me. It's deep, loving, reassuring. When we break apart, I'm grinning as I run my hands over his suit jacket because this man knows how to make me feel wonderful.

I reach up and rub noses with him, "My plans are to make love with you all night long."

Tenderly cupping my face in his hands, he kisses me again. "And there's nothing I want more than to spend all my nights with you. Only there might be this work thing. I'll know more when I get to my office. I'll let you know, okay?" He hugs me tight before heading out the door.

I'm so freaking proud of how far my man has come.

After graduating, he branched into real estate law while working in HR. I'm slowly working my way up in our family business, running a beachfront holiday hotel in Southern Australia. My father always wanted me to follow him into the family business, and since I enjoy making him happy, I'm the one continuing the family name in Monte Hotels. Dad hopes that Ethan and I will someday take the reins so he can retire.

My elder sister and younger brother are not interested in working for the business. It hurt Dad, and I didn't have it in me to inflict more pain, so here I am.

"Can I get you anything while I'm out?" I ask Dana, Dad's Executive Assistant. Dana has worked the past twenty years for Monte Hotels.

"I'm good, Edes, unless you pass the bakery with the gluten-free donuts dipped in chocolate."

I laugh at her comment while wrapping a woolen scarf around my neck. "You know they still have fat and sugar?"

"The way I'm wired, my brain tells me they're better than the usual donut." She grins. "Say hello to your friends for me."

"I will."

As I step out into the wintery wind, I hold the scarf close to my mouth. We might be on the beachfront, only in June the ocean is gray, and the waves crash into the shoreline with a force showing mother nature's fury.

The wind is equally wild and whips hair around my face. I duck my head as people rush past to get out of the blustery weather. With my head lowered, I bump into an older lady and apologize. It jolts me immediately out of my daze. The woman reminds me of my Gran just before she passed. "Are you okay?" I take her arm.

"Yes, dear." She holds her coat tight around her neck. "I'm sorry I ran into you. My sight isn't what it used to be."

I ensure she's steady before releasing her. "I wasn't paying attention.

Have a good day." I wait until she is safe in her car. Her similarity to Gran is uncanny, and causes my chest to feel hollow, as though I'm in a time warp. It took years to stop missing her before I could start appreciating the things she had taught me.

Dad stopped talking about Gran after she died. I couldn't put a finger on whether it was grief or if he wanted to forget. I never asked, as we all deal with grief in our own way.

The wind picks up a notch forcing me to focus. Upping the pace, I turn the corner to enter the café where my friends are waiting.

"How are you, Edes?" my friend Yasmine asks.

"Windblown." I laugh and swipe at the lock of hair that's stuck to my face. Yasmine always checks in on us. The conversations between us are more about life and what makes us happy, although it is often over a glass of champagne, and at our age, we admit to drinking too much.

Taking the chair beside Amy, I unwrap the scarf from my neck. "I'm great. How are you both?"

"Glad it's Friday," Amy groans. "Do you want to meet at the Shores tomorrow night for a drink?"

The Shores is a nightclub on the corner of the esplanade where we hang out. It's been a meeting place of ours since we left school.

"I ordered your coffee," Yasmine says as three coffees are placed in front of us.

"Thank you." It tastes divine. I set my phone on the table, the screen lights up with a message.

Ethan:

> Sorry but the work thing is confirmed. You
> should meet up with your friends. Don't wait up.
> Love you xx

"Ethan just canceled our dinner plans." I can't help the disappointment in my voice. "Do you girls have any plans for tonight?" I wait for Amy to make a remark as it's no secret she isn't a fan of Ethan. She knows we've discussed a future. I'll never choose a guy over my friends, but it has been awkward defending him for years. Her animosity dates to when we were teenagers.

He kissed another girl.

It happened once.

A mistake.

I forgave him.

Amy never has.

We have been together long enough for me to trust him.

"Ugh." Amy flicks her blonde ponytail over her shoulder. "Before I go on placement with bratty eight-year-olds, I'm all for going out," she pleads.

"Count me out. I have a date." Yasmine winks. "And I was going to ask if I could borrow your floral dress? The camelia print one."

"Of course. I'll drop to you on my way to get Amy tonight."

"Come to mine straight after work," Amy suggests.

I check the time. "I have time to shoot home now and grab what I need then I'll drop off the dress to Yasmine before coming to yours tonight," I tell her.

I down the remainder of my coffee before saying goodbye.

Dark, angry clouds roll in over the ocean. It's a short walk back to the office, yet I break into a jog, not trusting the weather. I jump straight into my car and drive the ten minutes to Ethan and my apartment.

After taking the single flight of stairs, I unlock the door. The apartment is quiet, and while checking around, I can't help but smile. Ethan takes as much pride as I do in keeping our apartment tidy. This morning, he must have spent extra time cleaning. Even the cushions on the couch are fluffed and positioned perfectly. How did I get so lucky to find the love of my life while in high school?

Thank you for cleaning the apartment. Enjoy your night. Show them why they should give you a raise. I hope they know how amazing you are. I'm spending the night out with Amy at the Shores. I'll text you later to see if you need a ride home. I love you xx

I drop my phone in my bag, then riffle through my wardrobe for the dress, which I unhook, and head back to the car.

The rest of the afternoon flies by, and by five I'm tidying my desk, ready for a night out with Amy. When I arrive at Yasmine's, she greets me with a smile. Her eye makeup is seductive lines, and it suits her. "You look amazing."

"Thank you. Oh, how I love this dress. The vibrant colors and the way it flows, it's freeing." She twirls the dress before hanging it over the bedroom door.

"Freeing?" Yasmine has a unique way of describing everything in her life. Her positivity to the world is like a magnet pulling you toward her. Around her, I feel calm and alive.

"Maybe it's my mood." She grins at me, tucking tight black ringlets behind her ear. "This guy I'm meeting up with..." her smile grows, "...there's something about the way he talks that warms me. We have a connection, and I can't help feeling happy in his presence."

"Sounds like someone I know." I wink at her. "Maybe he's your perfect match."

She shrugs, and it surprises me. "Maybe. It feels right for now. I have plans to travel, so I don't want to be tied down in a relationship."

"You can travel if your relationship is solid," I state.

She tilts her head. "Would you travel the world for months at a time and leave Ethan home?" She gives a slow blink when I hesitate. "You'd want to travel with him, right?"

"I guess. We've been together so long it would be weird to leave him for months at a time."

"It's not, if your relationship is as solid as you believe." She raises her eyebrows. "It's a mind trap we fall into, and I don't want to harbor any emotions of guilt or pity if I leave a boyfriend home. I know the places I want to see and explore, and if he doesn't have the same aspirations as me, I don't want him ruining the experience."

I nod slowly. "You've never told me about the places you want to visit."

"Are you interested?"

"Of course, I am. If you're inspired, then I'm sure I'll want to go."

"It would be a girls-only trip, Edes. But I can share my ideas with you sometime. Not now, because I need to get ready for this date."

I hug my beautiful friend. "Have a fun night."

Yasmine squeezes my back as she rests her chin on my shoulder. "Thanks, Edes. Enjoy your night."

A half hour later, I arrive at Amy's. "Are we foolish heading out when it's freezing?" I joke as she climbs into the car.

Could we just stay in and chat over a bottle of wine?

"The things we do for a good time," she says excitedly. Amy thrives in clubs where she can drink booze and dance the night away. Since Ethan and I stay in more Friday nights than not, I don't want to let my friend down, as it's been a while since it was just Amy and me.

A half-hour later, we are inside the Shores nightclub and the loud music thumps a rhythm against my ribs. Is it lame that I feel like I'm too old for this? Give me a quiet bar anytime. Amy is single and most single guys our age hang out in nightclubs, but some of these guys are not boyfriend material. After a few drinks, it's all about the night, to live in the moment, the rush of adrenaline when the lust sets in. One night and bang it's over. I'm not judging—I only want to help my friend find a guy that will be kind to her.

"I'll buy the first round of drinks. See if you can get us a table," Amy yells over the music. She's wearing more makeup than usual, and it makes her eyes pop. Her blonde hair is curled and falls over her bare shoulders in waves. I should have listened to her and wore layers as the heating is cranked, and most girls are in skimpy clothes. I'm still wearing a formal sweater dress that hugs my body with long sleeves. Before I overheat, I need to find a window table furthest from the speakers so we can talk.

A group of guys wanting to chat surround Amy. She points in my direction, and I cringe. I keep weaving until I find an unoccupied table away from all the action.

Random guys lift their chin in a weird nod. Others wink. Ew. I focus on the window even though I can't see anything outside. The reflection of what's happening around me plays out, and I don't have to make eye contact with strangers looking for a hookup.

Amy drops into the chair opposite me and slides a wine across the table. "I just ran into Cleo."

"Really?"

"Yeah, we were talking about Yasmine's date. She said she likes this guy."

I laugh. Yasmine's younger sister, Cleo, is as worldly as Yasmine. While her protective attitude is admirable, Yasmine is smart and needs the least protection out of all of us.

"Cleo's heading to the east coast to see her friend, Ava."

"Oh, that's awesome. I can only imagine how much they miss each other. I would hate for you to move away."

"Yeah, but Ava went into hiding. That's the tough part. I couldn't imagine not being on social media except for a few close friends. And no one knowing where you are."

I stare at Amy. "Yeah. If I had a baby, I'd want my friends to be part of my child's life. Ava must feel lost without Cleo."

Amy takes a sip of her wine slowly like she is pondering something. "I'll probably have to move to the country to secure a teaching position, but I'm not moving interstate. A few hours' drive in the car is my limit." She downs the rest of her drink. "I don't want to think about the future tonight. Can I get you another?"

"No, I'm driving, but I'll buy you another wine." Attempting to snake around the crowd is more like squeezing between hot bodies as I make my way to the bar. One of Ethan's work colleagues is sitting there, and I wave at him in hopes Ethan is also here. His brow furrows, and then he turns his back to me.

Rude prick. I struggle to like half the staff Ethan works with. Most have their noses high in the air, and I feel so unimportant around them. *That's fine, mate, because I didn't want to talk to you, anyways.*

After ordering Amy's wine, I head back with a bottle of water for myself and tell her what went down.

"Ugh, what a dick." She pulls a face.

"Yeah, but I feel off as though I'm missing something."

"You've missed nothing," she emphasizes. "Those guys are just rude dicks."

A smile tugs at my lips. "Yeah, they are. He's the type of guy I don't want you to end up with."

After sipping her wine, she gives me a confused look. "I've never been interested in those guys."

"I know, but you do end up with guys that are not interested in anything more than one night. You need someone who is one hundred percent in it for you. A guy who brings you flowers for no reason at all. A guy who cuddles you on the couch and watches *your* favorite shows. A guy who you can be comfortable around."

"Comfortable? Is that what you are?"

Before I can answer, a guy drags a chair over and sits at our table. "Ladies," he says in a smooth voice. His good looks match his tone. "How's your night going?"

Amy's face lights up. "Eden, this is Ford. The guy I told you about."

My mind is blank before I recall Amy talking about a guy she met on

Tinder—she's been out with him twice. She liked him, though he wasn't looking for a relationship. By the expression on her face, I can tell she's happy he's here, and for the next half hour, they talk and laugh, trying to include me in the conversation wherever possible. It's clear I'm a third wheel right now, and it's the perfect opening for me to leave.

"I'm going to go," I say to Amy. "Let me know if you need anything. I can give you a ride home if you need one later. Text me."

The way Amy and Ford stare at each other, she has no intention of calling me.

On the drive home I think about messaging Ethan, only I don't want to sound clingy when he's out with his work colleagues. Instead, I'll watch a movie and contact him later to see if he needs a lift home. Rain is forecast, and the last thing he needs is to be standing out in the weather waiting for an Uber.

I unlock the door to my apartment and throw the keys on the side table, freezing when I hear a bang.

The door was locked. I checked it before opening it with the key.

Bang.

A groan comes from another room.

Get the hell out of here, I tell myself.

My feet stick to the tiles.

If someone has broken in, they can have everything. I need to tiptoe back outside and run.

More groans cause my thoughts to misfire.

My heart is pounding in my chest.

I pick up the ceramic vase from the side table and creep around the corner toward our bedroom.

The moans become a sequence of heavy breathing. My gut instinct is preparing me for the worst. The bedroom door is slightly ajar, and the moans get louder as a female voice cries out, "Ethan!"

I push the door open.

The world tilts.

Ethan's white ass is on show, his trousers at his knees. A female is on all fours on my bed, moaning as he thrusts into her.

I stop breathing.

She is completely naked.

Long red hair falls over her back and around her like a curtain, stopping me from seeing her face. Her ass jiggles as he pounds into her, and I can't look away.

A thousand thoughts smash through my brain.

The shock fills my head with white noise.

I feel faint.

I gasp in a breath.

While a cocktail of emotions hits me, a wave of anger boils in my chest.

And before it even registers, the vase in my hand hurtles toward them. It smashes on the wall above her head. Ethan dives onto the bed, pulling her into a ball beside him.

"Eden!" Ethan yells, his eyes popping out of his head. "You're home."

Now that they are lying side by side, I get a good look at the face of the woman who my boyfriend has obliterated our future with all within a matter of seconds. Or has this been going on for some time?

"What the hell," she whines as she wriggles out of his arms, reaching for the sheet.

Ethan pulls up his trousers, his pathetic semi-hard cock pushed into his boxers before zipping his fly.

"Stop there." I hold up a hand because if I could reach anything else, I would throw it at him. "Don't you dare come near me."

"Eden, I can explain." His face screws up, pleading with me to hear him out.

"This..." I make a circle around the bed, and the redhead, "...is all the explanation I need." I back away before turning and striding toward the door. I want to get out of here faster than I can run.

Ethan follows behind me.

The first thing I do is rip off our friendship ring and throw it at him. "I *never* want to see you again," I scream. He ducks and turns momentarily to watch where the ring lands. It's not enough, even though it signifies he ruined the bond between us. I grab the keys from the side table and throw them harder, the metal clangs hitting the wall.

"Next time I won't miss," I warn.

"Wait." Ethan stands there, his face pale. He lifts two hands and drops them to his side.

I shake my head. "Pathetic." I yank the door open, slamming it behind me. Taking the stairs faster than I have in my life, I sprint toward my car. Once I'm behind the wheel, I screech the tires and veer the car into traffic, then scream, "Why!" loudly, as the tears fall.

With my heart pounding so hard, my chest hurts. My throat burns as I sob and sob, releasing all the anger and sadness into an angry ball of emotion.

Why?

Why?

WHY?

I smack my hand on the steering wheel over and over.

Where the hell am I even driving? I have no place to go.

Amy is living with her parents until she finishes her teaching degree, and tonight, she's with Ford.

Yasmine doesn't have a spare room, and she is on a date, so I can't go back to hers.

It feels like a step backward to go home to my childhood home, but where else can I go?

My sister has a new baby ... I can't go there either.

The tears cascade down my cheeks like a river. Ethan has ripped my heart from my chest. A knife twists inside the gaping hole like I've never felt before.

Love might hurt, but hate hurts more.

I pull into a free space on the esplanade and turn off the engine. Staring at the dark ocean, the place I usually find happiness, I curl into a ball and allow myself to unhinge. I sob and sob until I can't cry anymore.

WHEN CAR LIGHTS shine into the window, I wake. *What time is it?*

It's three a.m.

While trying to stretch the kinks out of my neck, I straighten. I can't stay here. I'm so cold, yet I'm numb. So I start the car and drive a few blocks to my parent's place. Unlocking the door, I creep inside. The whistle of dad snoring comes from behind the door of their room as I tiptoe down the hallway to my old room, shutting the door behind me. Once I climb into my bed, I curl onto my side and will my eyes to close.

The image of Ethan's bare ass pounding into the redhead plays on repeat in my head.

The tears well again, and I end up crying myself to sleep.

THE FOLLOWING MORNING, I wake to muffled voices outside my room. I stare at the wall until my brain catches up. *I wish last night was a bad dream*. Yet I'm in my bed at my parent's home, so I know it's not. My chest aches as though a hundred elephants are sitting on top, crushing me. It's crippling every thought, so I don't know what to do next.

What do I say?

I replay the night.

What did I do wrong?

What will I do now?

All I can do is take things hour by hour until I make sense of what happened.

I check my phone, hoping for something from Ethan.

Fifteen missed calls.

Ten messages.

Yet it doesn't ease the hurt. Nothing he can say will fix what he broke.

Nothing I do from this moment on will repair the gaping hole in my heart.

I recall my grandmother's words.

Time heals most wounds.

Time will help me survive, but I'll never forgive him or take him back, that I know with certainty.

Two missed calls from Yasmine. Did Ethan call her?

There's a gentle knock at the door. "Eden?"

"Come in," I croak. *How am I going to explain to my mum without breaking down?*

"Honey, is everything okay?" She's already dressed in jeans and a classy coat, ready for their traditional Sunday brunch.

I nod and sit up. "Yes. I lost my key to the apartment, so I came here. I hope it's okay."

Mum looks warily at me. "Of course, it is. Only Amy is here looking for you, and we didn't know you had come home."

I force a smile. "She probably wants to tell me about last night."

Mum frowns. *I haven't convinced her I'm okay.* "Sure. I'll send her in."

I can't relive it over again. I'm partly to blame and the humiliation of failing fills me.

Amy steps into my room, dressed in a sweater and track pants. Her hair is tied back in a ponytail. She doesn't look like she had a late night. She closes the door behind her, coming to sit on the side of the bed. "You look like shit," she whispers.

My eyes sting with more tears. "My night sucked. How was yours?"

Reaching out, she takes my hand, reading between the lines. "What did he do?"

I shake my head, and my throat constricts as I reach for the bottle of water on my bedside table, guzzling a few mouthfuls, hoping to dissolve the grapefruit-sized lump growing in my throat.

"One guess," I croak.

Amy's eyes grow dark. "The fucker."

"You had good reason not to trust him," I admit. A sob escapes my mouth, and I suck it back. I can't allow my parents to know what went down.

Her arms wrap around me, holding tight. Amy doesn't ask me anything more as she swings her legs onto the bed, lying down beside me. She's always had my back and knows not to push when I'm at my lowest.

After a while she strokes my head before sitting up. "I'm going to get us some coffee." She heads out of the room, and I hear her tell Mum that we are both hungover and in need of coffee. I hate that she had to lie for me, but I love her all the more for it.

When she walks back into my room, she hands me the mug. I sip it, and it soothes my throat.

"I don't think your mum believed me."

"No. I drove here, and she knows I'm not irresponsible."

Amy nods. "What are you going to tell them?"

"The truth. That we're on a break. No details required. If he wants to tell people why we broke up, then it's on him."

"He's too gutless," she almost growls out the words. "He'll probably play the bloody victim."

I shrug, too tired to care how he's going to deal with it. "If anyone asks, I'll say our relationship ran its course, and we mutually agreed to have a break. Only the break will be permanent." I clench my eyes closed as I swallow the dry lump of emotion threatening to undo me again.

I want to go to someplace where nobody knows me.

"I need to be anywhere but here."

Amy pulls out her phone. "Yasmine is asking about you. I'll call her back later after I text that I'm with you. Ethan called her last night and left a voice message asking if you were there, claiming you had a fight. She told me earlier this morning. He obviously didn't have the guts to call me."

"He knows you would call him out on the pathetic person he is."

"That's putting it nicely," she snarls.

After I finish my coffee, I flop back onto my pillow and cover my eyes with my arm. "I don't think I can leave my room for the next year."

"You don't have to go back there, Edes. I'll go grab your things."

I lift my arm and stare at my friend. "You'd do that? You need to get organized for tomorrow."

"I'm already organized. Have been for weeks."

I manage a smile. "You pretend you hate kids, but you're going to be the best teacher."

Amy's lips turn up at my compliment. "What's important now is helping my friend. Let me go and face him. He won't argue with me."

"No, he won't." I think about all the things we shared in the apartment. "I want nothing that will remind me of us. So, only my clothes. He can keep everything else. I don't care." The thought of my favorite dresses I wore on dates with Ethan is likely to undo me. "I'll probably donate half of my clothes, anyway."

Amy nods. "I know which ones not to bring back here. I'll mainly grab your office clothes. We can spend the afternoon shopping online for new clothes."

The idea of a girl's shopping day usually excites me. Not today.

"I have a better idea. Let's plan a holiday soon just to shop. We could go to Melbourne. Or what about Bali?"

"Bali." I nod. "Could we go somewhere far away and never return?"

Amy pats my hand. "Bali first. We'll plan the best girl's trip ever. But we'll need to arrange a few months away, so it won't be spontaneous."

"I could hand in my resignation letter now." I'm not joking.

"Edes. I'm going to get your stuff. Do you have your key? I'll call Yasmine on the way and tell her to free up a weekend soon to go away."

I shake my head. "I threw it at him before I stormed out."

Amy stares at me, and I can see the cogs turning behind her eyes at the possibilities of what went down between Ethan and me.

"You threw your key at him. No punch?"

A sarcastic noise comes from my throat. "I wish, but no. I had to get out of there."

"Well, I'm not promising anything about shutting that smart mouth of his. If he tries to make any excuse—"

"Don't give him any of your time. He's not worth it. Just go in and get out. I'm not making excuses for him, but what happened between us is our relationship ran its course. I just wish I'd seen it before last night."

Amy pauses by the door. "I'm not promising anything. I have your back, and if he says one word about you, I'll quieten him *my way*."

"Ames. I love you, but I need to move on. I'll never forgive him or go back to him. I promise you, we're over."

"I'm going to make sure you remember that promise." She stalls with her hand on the doorknob. "You will get through this, Edes." Then she's gone.

She is my gatekeeper.

Like *Heimdall,* protector of *Asgard.* I only wish she had the power to heal the gaping hole in my heart because even protectors can't stop the pain in my chest that's tearing me apart.

BEAUTIFULLY WILD

INTRODUCTION

Fear (noun)
Feeling of anxiety
A frightening thought
Terror

Fear (verb)
Be afraid
Be apprehensive
Be frightened
Feel reverence for somebody or something

Fear often stems from one's past, the unknown or something bad happening in the future.
My journey is about conquering fear.
The challenge lies in taking risks to remove the power fear holds.

PROLOGUE

SAMUEL

Undisclosed location in the rainforest of Venezuela

LARGE DARK LIPS pucker around a bamboo pipe. Tattooed cheeks puff round.

A tiny smoke cloud momentarily blocks his view of the shaman's face. When their eyes meet, Samuel lowers his gaze. He knows his place. The upper-class society he was born into holds no ground here.

Words are spoken in a foreign language, one he had to learn and isn't taught in any educational curriculum. Many indigenous tribes inhabit the Amazon and other rainforests, only this one is unique. Their laws are a stark contrast and incredibly extreme compared to his California lifestyle. Yet he's chosen to remain here to live a primitive lifestyle for five years and build trust with every passing month or every full moon, as time is perceived differently.

Trust.

Another measure he had to overcome to substantiate his manhood. Every time he leaves the village and returns, he places the entire village at risk of disease. It strains the trust between him, the shaman, and the elders.

Samuel's ventures beyond the village boundary have lessened over the years. By remaining in the village, the shaman's trust in him grew.

This year, old friends demanded he make an appearance. They were worried about his mental health.

He reciprocated the same opinion of them.

Kneeling before the shaman asking permission to return to the village reminds him of his younger years at an expensive private school. Only here the repercussions could be life or death.

"O'win nuno." *One moon.* One month. Wrinkled fingers rise toward the sky. A prayer follows the spirits living among them, a divine power in the tree vines and beneath the soil.

"Waküpe-küruman." *Thank you.* Samuel understands that if three full moons pass, his re-entry will be rejected. A new sacrificial ceremony will be required, and Samuel isn't sure he has the strength or stamina to endure the interrogation of another initiation. When he first came to the village, he was a driven, younger man with a pharmaceutical scholarship. Finding a cure to terminal illnesses fueled his passion for science. Now the only person who holds answers sits before him, a library of knowledge captured inside the mind of the shaman.

The shaman scoops red paste with his finger and wipes it behind Samuel's ear to where the chief had tattooed him. Another line is drawn across his forehead, representing how the shaman will follow Samuel by his thoughts. He lowers his gaze and nods once, rising to his feet only after the shaman walks away.

He strides to his hut, grabs his backpack, changes into cut-off cargos and a t-shirt, and slips on his sneakers. Outside his hut, the sun is directly above him. He waits until he passes the village perimeter before breaking into a jog, ignoring the pining gaze of a young female native American. He makes his way along a narrow dirt path between thick shrubbery, careful not to touch any spikes on unruly vines. Some needles can cause paralysis in minutes, and thanks to the shaman, Samuel's now wise enough not to take on the overgrowth in these parts.

He stands on a sandy embankment where tree limbs overhang the water's edge on either side. Asoo will pass the river fork soon. A weekly occurrence. He's alerted to the faint roar of a motor, a sound similar to a Yamaha motorbike. He waves to the driver of the dug-out motorized canoe.

"Ciudad Guayana?" Asoo asks. Asoo is of *Pemón* descent—a similar tribe to the Ularans.

Samuel shakes his head. The cities north of Canaima are collection points for parcels and letters about his research. Places where he posts exotic plant species to a professor in Caracas. "Rio for a couple of weeks."

Asoo's black eyebrows lift. "Rio? For Carnival?"

Samuel curses under his breath. It's the last thing he wants to do. The hundreds of thousands of people lining the city streets are a threat. Being in Rio can jeopardize the health of the indigenous people he has grown to love. Even a common cold threatens their survival.

"My friends are traveling from California and New York. We're meeting up in a matter of days."

Asoo breaks into a song, chanting "*New York*." Samuel shakes his head. A fairy-tale city to many. A place where dreams come to life.

Living in a large city no longer interests Samuel. He has found his destiny by trying to escape the one his father had set up for him in Los Angeles.

He considers his sacrifice. Like a priest married to God, he too has dedicated his life to a divine power. Here he learned about ayahuasca, the vine of the soul, while living primitively and in the name of medical research. From a Western medicine perspective, Ulara is a world that made little sense to him, a perspective he has learned to overlook, for Ulara preserves secrets, which potentially can save lives.

1

EDEN

Adelaide, Australia

EVERYONE IMAGINES the moment you tell your boss to shove the damn job. Some create composed and reasonable exits, and others are much more dramatic with extensive cursing.

To me, it's merely a dream because I work for the family business, and my father is the boss. I'm not whining, especially since I'm not unhappy. To be honest, it's a great job with an opportunity for an upcoming promotion. Did I mention the location is by the beach?

I'm often distracted and gaze out of the window of our small office. Days like today, the ocean is simply mesmerizing. The water is flat, barely a wave, and like glass—the perfect day for paddleboarding. Waves drift in and out as quiet as the office, except for the subtle tapping on the keyboard. It's quite serene, and I can't visualize anything to make me angry enough to want to quit despite the feeling in my gut telling me it's time.

Time to make my own choices.

My father walks out of his office, and I turn from the window to meet his glowering look. "I trust you're smart enough to stay out of the jungle." His tone holds a warning, and I'm guessing he finally read the email with the attached itinerary of my upcoming holiday.

Angling the monitor from his view, I minimize the email on

vaccination schedules—specifically, yellow fever, rabies, and our options on malaria prevention.

"Of course," I say in a level voice.

As if someone upped the cooling, the temperature around us turns icy, reminding me of the winter wind blowing up from Antarctica. Where we live, vineyards lie to the east, north, and south of the city. Adelaide is no jungle.

His executive assistant coughs. I assume she senses the tension between us. "I have the December report you're waiting on, Mr. Monteford. I'll forward it to you now."

"Thank you. I'll run over the figures in my office." Blue eyes reminding me of my own, hold my gaze in a warning that this discussion will be continued.

When the door to his private office closes, I swivel on my seat. "Thanks for the distraction. I have no idea why he's so hung up about this holiday?"

"At least he didn't make another underhanded comment about letting him down. Remain calm because you'll be there in no time and leave all this behind," Dana says, extending her arms wide. She lets out a gentle laugh. Her brown eyes crinkle at the corners as we share an understanding.

I smile at the sound of her laughter because it quickly warms the mood in the small room. "Guilt-tripping isn't going to change the fact he'll need to hire someone. I mentioned my sister could help out, only he wouldn't have any of it."

Dana pushes short strands of hair behind her ears. Her classy-styled bob-cut never has a hair out of place. Her mascaraed eyes are always perfect. "No need to hide your true feelings to me. For years I've witnessed a different set of rules for your sister than you."

And my younger brother, I want to add. Only I keep the thought to myself.

OUR OFFICE IS LOCATED on the bottom floor of the apartment building where I live. It's ideal in the sense I don't have to worry about time or expense in getting to work. Not so ideal when it comes to the time before or after work to clear my head. When I clock off at the end of the day, I've made a habit of walking along the esplanade to level my thoughts, and breathe in the clean ocean air. I love this time before twilight when everyone is capturing 'me' time. Skaters whiz past. Cyclists ting their bells and call out, "On your right." The Bay is one of Adelaide's popular beachside suburbs, and we need an extra lane on the path for this amount of foot traffic. I pass groups of fitness enthusiasts doing star jumps on the grass. Further along, families picnic on rugs spread out over the grass and wicker baskets within reach. Others prefer fish and chips enticing the seagulls to behave erratically.

Before entering our apartment complex, I stand out front and admire the white stone building. Built in the early 1900s, my grandparents purchased it in the late 1950s and passed it onto my father. Part of me is proud he trusts me to handle business matters, but the other part is regretful I didn't seek my own adventure.

The white façade has several cracks in the faded paintwork weathered by the ocean climate. The popular hotel a few buildings down —all modern glass and steel—gleams in the sunlight. Our smaller building has weathered some tough times and regained popularity, mainly for the renovated interior that has incorporated the vintage appeal crossed with a crisp bohemian design. We manage the eight apartments. The hotel on the corner has one hundred and eighty rooms. We are no threat, and yet we're fully booked until Christmas next year.

The external flights of stairs are stringed with tinsel and fairy lights. I love this time of year when everything sparkles. Choosing to take the internal staircase, I make my way up the three flights of stairs to the penthouse.

The front door creaks as it opens. The cry of a child comes from another room.

"We were just talking about you," Faith says as she stands.

My sister is visiting. *Fantastic.*

"Why?" I focus on my father sitting opposite my mother at the kitchen table. A few seconds is all I need to acknowledge Mum has been to the hairdresser—freshly colored mocha hair sits motionless under a can of lacquer.

"We were discussing suitable applicants to replace you while you're gallivanting in another country." Faith's tone is condemning. She doesn't wait for a response before heading toward my parents' bedroom, where her sleeping toddler has awakened.

"Let me get him. I haven't seen him in weeks."

Faith crosses her arms. "He's not the happiest when he wakes."

I ignore her and open the door. My nephew raises his arms for me to pick him up. So adorable. I lift him out of the portable cot and love how he curls into my chest. "How long have you been sleeping, little man?"

"Two hours," Faith says. She leans on the doorframe. Brown hair borders her face before falling to her shoulders. She's the clone of our mother with her alluring eyes—pools of melted chocolate.

They're both extraordinary businesswomen—go-getters in life, confident, and resilient. Our parents named us, as though in hindsight of the future. They always had faith in my sister to succeed and do the right thing in life. My name, Eden, has a meaning of pleasure and delight. My father keeps a close eye on me as if I'm going to become a bohemian hippie if he turns his back. Ironic when I have an average personality and life.

"Are you sure it's not possible to shorten this holiday? Instead of taking all your leave at once and leaving Dad in a predicament, you could split your leave and travel to Europe next year?"

"I'm not interested in Europe at the moment. And you fail at being subtle." I stride past her. "Why don't *you* work a couple of days a week, and Mum could look after Seb? You always say my work isn't that difficult."

"You can't expect Faith to work in the office when her morning sickness is at its worst."

I blink several times at my mother before turning to Faith.

She raises her hands at Mum. "Not how I was going to tell her."

With my free hand, I hug her. "Congratulations. You'll be busy. Have you extended your leave from work?"

"I didn't expect to fall so quickly. I'm thinking of resigning and returning to work when the kids are at school. Jake has always wanted three kids, so..."

I gape at her. Our parents funded her university education to study law. It's where she met Jake, whose parents own a law firm, and subsequently employed her to work alongside their son. She took her career seriously until they married. Has she forgotten what my parents gave up for her? What I gave up?

I wasn't 'allowed' to study full-time—only online because our father needed *me* to work for him. I also worked weekends while at school and did anything to save my parents money by not hiring extra staff. For the last few years, the business has turned over substantial profits, so I'm taking extended leave to work out what I want to do with my life. My father has created a new position in the company in marketing and building development. The position is mine if I want it.

"My leave isn't debatable. I suggest you hire a temp for the eight weeks I'm away." I take a breath. "I'm going out to meet my friends for a couple of drinks and to discuss our upcoming trip." I kiss my nephew on his cheek before handing him to my sister and make my way to my room. Before I reach the door, I pivot to meet my father eye to eye. "Why are you hung up on the jungle? If I take precautions, is a small tour so bad? It's part of the Iguassu Falls tour we have booked."

Scarlet heat rises along his neck, masking his pale skin.

"Eden, this also isn't debatable." Mum's hand rests on her chest. "You have no idea of the possible danger."

"I told you she's *just* like her grandmother," Dad grunts under his breath. Only we all hear, and by Faith's expression, she's as confused as I am.

It's not the first time he has related me to Gran. But I'm twenty-four, not sixteen, and thankful to be moving out on my return. Even if it means moving in with Yasmine and listening to her daily meditating chants and spells and taking all the herbal concoctions she swears by.

"For once, I wish you'd trust me like you do Faith and Will." The door closes with a thump behind me before giving him a chance to respond.

2

EDEN

"EVENING, EDEN," Dave says when I reach the doors of The Shores bar. We're on a first-name basis since the bar is only a half a block from our apartments, and I'm here most weeks. The Shores is a trendy hotel, including a nightclub, cocktail bar, and restaurant. "Your friends are already inside."

"Thanks," I say and offer him a smile. I weave around the booths and tables to find my girlfriends sitting in the usual seats by the window with an ocean view.

"Sorry I'm late." I plop down on a comfortable lounge chair and stretch my hands over the padded armrests.

Amy stops mid-conversation and stares at me. "What's pissed you off?"

I sigh loudly and shake my head. "Nothing. Just my father trying to guilt-trip me again."

"Here." Yasmine pours a glass of sparkling wine and hands it to me. "Medicinal bubbles always help."

"Medicinal?" I smile at Yasmine.

"Good for your heart, your skin, your cognitive brain, and it will improve your mood." She beams her white teeth at me. "Bottoms up." She raises her glass to me and takes a sip.

"Cognitive thinking?" Amy muses. She runs her fingers through her long blonde ponytail and adjusts it to sit over her shoulder.

I down the glass in one go and let out an appreciative sigh. "I'm feeling better already." I wipe any residue from the corners of my mouth.

"Only three glasses a week to improve your memory," Yasmine adds as though we all need educating.

"You don't need to sell it to me," I say. "You had me at boosting my mood. As for improving my memory, I'd rather forget some things. Tell me, if I drink more than a few glasses a week, does it reverse the effects and wipe out my memory?"

Yasmine shakes her head, and dark spiral curls bounce as she does. "If you lived with me already, then you could use my essential oils and have access to my motivational books."

"Be careful." Amy smirks. "She only wants to practice her spells on you."

Yasmine rolls her eyes. "You need to have an open mind."

"I do. Just with other things," she says. Her eyes fix on the dark-haired, handsome man walking past our table. "I'd be willing to be open with him."

Ugh. "You don't even know him. He could be someone waiting to spike your drink and then have his way with you." God, I sound like a prude. I'm not. Because of a certain someone, I now have my own trust issues after he stomped all over my heart.

She gives a devilish grin. "And I wouldn't object."

"This is why we need to talk about our holiday," I say to Yasmine. "We need to be sensible and have group rules. We can't be going to an exotic part of the world where crime is high and think it won't happen to us."

"Bree will have it covered," Yasmine says as though she's undeterred. "We need to talk about what we want out of this holiday because we all have different needs."

"Men," Amy blurts out and sits forward in her seat as though we're now discussing a topic that interests her. "Those gorgeous Brazilian men. I want to know if there's any truth in the stories."

God, did she just wink? "Seriously?" I roll my eyes, yet I'm not surprised. "You can get laid anywhere, Ames. Don't you want to visit the old churches and see the architecture of another culture?"

She shrugs her shoulders. "I'm not objecting to those things. I'll go with you if that's what you want, but I also want the party. You can't go to Rio and be like, 'the architecture is wonderful, darling.'" She says the last few words in a high voice and as if she has the olive from her empty martini glass in her mouth.

"I wouldn't say it like that."

"This is good. We're talking," Yasmine adds. "I want it to be a spiritual journey. Come back wiser and stronger for it."

My phone rings, and I glance down at the screen.

Bree.

I swipe the screen and press speaker. "Hey. You called at a good time. We're all here at The Shores."

"Drinking medicinal bubbles," Amy adds with a smile.

"Hey, girlfriend," Yasmine pipes in. "We're talking about the holiday. I think we need to consider what's important to each of us so we can cater to everyone's needs."

"Good point," she says in a serious tone. "I've been thinking about our first-aid kit and collecting items from the hospital."

"Bree, are you stealing from your workplace?" Amy teases.

"No. I'm paying for everything."

Amy grins, well aware Bree would never do anything dishonest. "How's Sydney?"

"I wouldn't know. All I do is work and study."

"That sucks," Amy groans.

"It's why I can't wait to get away. Are your vaccinations up to date?"

"I have one more," I say. "When you get a break, text the group what's important to you in case we need to make any last-minute amendments to some tours."

"Honestly, I'm so exhausted I'm happy to lay on a beach and drink cocktails, so long as we're safe."

"Safety is your priority," I conclude.

"Absolutely. Sorry, I have to get back to the ward. I'm so jealous of you all there, together. Have a drink for me."

"Bye, Bree," we all say in unison.

"Talking about safety, my father is giving me a hard time about staying safe."

Amy's eyes round. "Seriously, when is he going to treat you like an adult?"

"He does treat her like an adult. It's obvious he has trust issues," Yasmine adds.

"Yet he's not like this with Faith and Will." I shake my head. I have never done anything for him not to trust me.

"For fuck's sake, it goes further than that. He's pissed you split up with that dickhead. In his eyes, you and Ethan were meant to be together, and I wouldn't be surprised if he believes you'll get back with him."

"Not going to happen," I say firmly. "Although his behavior of late has nothing to do with Ethan. He's worried about the jungle, of all the places."

Yasmine smirks. "Not Rio and getting shot or at the very least mugged for your purse?"

"Oh, he's already warned me of those dangers."

Yasmine blows air into her cheeks. "I'm glad my mother stays out of my business."

"You have the privilege of not living at home." After living with Ethan for eighteen months, I found it difficult to adjust to living with my parents again. I was distraught and desperate and needed somewhere to live after throwing the key at him and storming out. "If I weren't saving every last cent for this holiday, I'd be out already." I refill my glass, emptying the bottle, and then signal the waiter to get us another.

"Same. I mean it's great to save money, but my little sister's drive me crazy. The other day Alex used my expensive nail polish on her bloody dolls," Amy exclaims. "As soon as I receive a permanent teaching contract, I'm moving out, hopefully with my new Brazilian boyfriend."

We giggle at Amy's optimism and clink our crystal flutes.

"On that positive note..." Yasmine says, "... I want to talk about our first days in Salvador. There's something that interests me, and I don't want you to feel uncomfortable."

"I'm interested in what would make us uncomfortable because I'd be surprised if anything does."

"Butting in there, I've booked my last laser and then a tan appointment. I. Am. Ready." Amy angles both hands toward her pelvis.

"It's a wonderful thing to be comfortable in your own skin." Yasmine smiles at Amy. "I want to point out our holiday will be an adventure, and we're filling it with wonderful experiences, and not all experiences are good." She shrugs. "Not bad either. Some could make you uncomfortable. What I'm saying is if an experience isn't enjoyable, it isn't reason enough not to do it. It's all about opportunities and trying different things. Some we love, some we don't. The important thing is to do it. Try everything and give your inner courage a chance to bloom."

3

EDEN

Salvador, Brazil

Three weeks later…

We arrived on the first day of February in time for the Candomble tradition. Attending the festival of Iemanjá is a tick off Yasmine's bucket list. It reminds me of the times we celebrated Yemaya back home.

"What time is it?" Amy moans. White foiled strands of hair fan over her pillow, giving an angelic impression.

"Eight thirty."

A steady drumbeat creeps closer, accompanied by unapologetic singing.

She pushes up onto her elbows and stares toward the window. "Sounds as though the festival is underway."

"Yeah. I can't wait to be part of it tomorrow." Plucking a brochure from the table, I flop back on the bed.

"Pelourinho," I say. "It looks interesting."

"I'm keen," Amy says, now upright.

"You sure? It's the historical center of the city, and I don't expect you to obsess over the architecture with me. I can take a bus."

"We don't go out alone," she reminds me. "Bree's rules."

I smile at Amy because I know she's making an effort for me. This isn't her thing. I already knew Yasmine and Bree were staying at the hotel for Yasmine to prepare for the offering. Preparation for these ceremonies brings out Yasmine's creative side, and she enjoys doing it. So, I expected to go out alone. Shit. It's only day one, and I'm contemplating breaking a group rule. Who the hell am I?

A short time later, Amy and I are squished like sardines in a bus, our skin similarly smeared with sweat since there's no air conditioning on the bus. Staring out the open window, her blonde hair blows wildly around her face, uncaring about knots when it's the only source of air. As the bus chugs up sloping hills, pastel-hued buildings snare my focus, the mismatched colors beautiful in their uniqueness. I'm enchanted with the people and their bright clothing.

Baroque churches are our first stop on my list of tourist sights, and here, it isn't a case of 'you've seen one, you've seen them all.' Even the photos I take on my phone are jaw-dropping. The Cathedral Basilica, trimmed with gold, is considered one of the finest examples of the wealth of Portuguese Baroque architecture.

"There's something about the beauty of a church," I say from the street and turn to take one last shot with my phone. "It's inspiring and calming."

"Architecture... inspiring and calming." Amy holds out a hand as if weighing something on an imaginary set of scales. "Working for your father and slaving away at the family business... busy and demanding." She tips the scales and pretends to overbalance, and I laugh.

My chest warms, knowing I have eight weeks to discover the beauty and thrills of this country and learn a little more about me.

Time gets away as we wander through walls of art, mesmerized as though we have time-traveled to another world. Here in Salvador, I sense I'm going to lose track of time every day.

We make a final dash along a pebbled road and then come across Foundation House, a place where the famous Brazilian author, Jorge Amado's book covers are housed in his honor. Four floors inside the blue colonial building hold the entire archive of his work. Discovering small treasures like this adds to the adventure, although we are unable to stay long for already the sun is descending toward the horizon.

We pass a museum for African-Brazilian art and artifacts. We have enough time to wander inside before the bus arrives. The exhibits reflect the African cultures of the region and deities. I lead Amy to a carved wooden statue of Iemanjá.

Amy fixes her gaze on the statue, then reads the inscription. "I'm beginning to understand why it means so much to Yasmine, knowing it's part of her heritage."

"Yeah." I've always understood Yasmine, and yet right now, I'm a bit jealous of how she's in touch with her spirituality in this exotic place. I've followed her lead because she offers the best advice and is always feeding us girls with word porn that's healthy for our souls.

We arrive back at the hotel to find Yasmine has purchased frangipanis and other white knick-knacks to divide amongst us. She instructs us to tie them to our letter when offering it to Iemanjá. Tomorrow, if the ocean swallows our offering, it means the deity has accepted our gifts.

All our wishes differ. My friends have written long lists, but mine is simply asking Iemanjá to guide me in finding happiness and a sense of purpose.

Lord knows I need it.

4

SAMUEL

Salvador, Brazil

THE WEIGHT of meeting his friends plays on Samuel's mind. Unable to sleep, he shaves and cuts his unruly hair to appear more civilized before wandering out to buy breakfast.

A sea of white packs the street, blocking his path.

Dressed in a red t-shirt and cargos, he stands out like blood on a chef's white apron. He'd forgotten about the ceremony when he decided to stay in Salvador overnight before flying on to Rio.

He's witnessed it all before and respects their belief. It still intrigues him, so he decides to mesh with the crowd. Pulling his t-shirt over his head, baring his tanned chest in an attempt to blend. He follows the mob toward the beach, watches them load small boats filled with gifts—gifts to please the Iemanjá so she'll grant a favorable fishing season among other personal blessings.

The chanting continues, repetitive singing and white flowers adorning hundreds of offerings. The people follow wading and jumping the waves to leave their tributes and asking for blessings.

A voice with a sweet accent catches his attention.

Laughter.

Blonde hair that's whiter than his.

The crowd parts momentarily, and he allows his gaze the luxury of lowering. Subtle curves in a white swimsuit knock the wind out of him. The swimsuit style is cut to her navel, revealing the swell of her breasts. He forces his gaze to lift and meets the most beautiful blue eyes as rich as the ocean's color.

Caught in her spell, he's unable to look away. His entire body hums, and for a second, his world tilts. He's quick to shut it down and blames lack of food and sleep. He resists the urge to take a step toward her and wills his feet to remain in the sand.

Her friend steps forward and severs the pull between their eyes.

He lets out a breath and wills his heart to slow. Samuel turns in the direction of the hotel, his place of refuge. For too long, he has denied the feeling that shook his core, the pull of need reminding him he's still a man—*desire* from a single glance, an understanding of lust.

Years of constraint incinerated in seconds.

He blames the Brazilian sun and seeks shelter behind the walls of his hotel.

For him, safety is *not* in numbers.

5

EDEN

"WHAT IS IT?" Yasmine takes a step closer and blocks my view.

"Nothing," I say quickly and sidestep around her to wade through the ocean to the sand. Only it wasn't nothing. In those brief seconds, I was walking on clouds.

I search the crowd after losing sight of the shirtless blond with the intense stare. For a few seconds, my balance wavered with the pull of lust. Only it wasn't just lust. On another level, I felt more, which is odd for me since I don't know him. Heaven forbid I mention for the first time in countless months that my libido came alive. I imagine my friends celebrating the resurgence of my sex drive by dropping to their knees and giving thanks to whatever deity is a sex goddess. Hmm, maybe this is something I should know about. I could be praying to the wrong god.

"Eden!"

Ignoring Yasmine calling my name, I wade out of the shallow water only to stop on the sand, finding myself caught in a group of people repeating a mantra over and over. Did I imagine him? Am I that desperate to find happiness that I'm now hallucinating? Suddenly, I'm shuffled forward, and I am feeling out of sorts with the constant singing messing with my head. I am more of a silent worshipper, usually concentrating on a prayer for longer than a few minutes makes me fidget. In the moment, overcome with emotion and in a strange country, I'm struck with uneasiness being out of my comfort zone. Seriously, and what's with the humidity here? Coming from a city that feels closer to the rim of sea ice in the Southern Ocean than the tropics, extreme humidity is a quiet hell, heating from the inside out.

A man standing before me flops to the sand. His eyes roll to the back of his head, and the rest of his body shakes. A hand lands on my shoulder, and I jump. Yasmine gives a subtle head shake.

She knows me well, as my first instinct is to drop to my knees to assist him. I glance around. Other followers keep chanting and praying.

My gaze shoots back to the man who has collapsed near my feet. I'm scared he'll choke right beside me, and the crowd is overlooking him. Bree appears on the other side of Yasmine, and Yasmine presses her hand on Bree's stomach to stop her from going to him. Bree is a medical student. If something goes wrong, at least she'll be able to help.

The imposing sound of a hundred people chanting out of sequence clouds my thoughts. Drums echo from the street. What the hell is happening?

The guy stands, brushes sand from his clothes, and smiles as though nothing happened, or something has, and he now feels the better for it. To my surprise, he raises his arms toward the sea with gratitude in his expression.

Amy is now standing on the other side of Bree, and by their expressions, they have the same concerns as me.

Yasmine whispers, "He believes the queen of the ocean has freed him from whatever demon kept him captive."

I nod and take a step back. In a bid to stay out of the way, I take another step back when other followers hug him and pat his back affectionately. Questions sit on my tongue. I itch to ask Yasmine, only the look she gives me yearns for understanding. I respect her belief and so remain quiet and attempt to push out my own insecurities.

I'm not denying I am completely out of my depth. It makes me nervous, and I'm attempting to embrace it. My father taught me being uncomfortable is the first step in learning something new. Funny, on this occasion, his advice echoes Yasmine's words. Immersing ourselves in different cultural experiences is all part of why we came to Brazil. This ceremony is the beginning of us encompassing it.

Still, I need to down a few caipirinhas, regardless of the time.

6

EDEN

Rio de Janeiro, Brazil

Two days later...

Bare golden shoulders shine with a film of sweat, a combination of one's own perspiration and that of strangers from pushing through the crowd on Copacabana Beach. At twilight, the heat is somewhat more bearable. Yet, the air remains thick and makes it difficult to breathe among the hundreds of thousands of partygoers along the shoreline.

Despite the heat, happiness is contagious. Yesterday my heart settled into a quicker beat from the time the plane descended, and the Christ the Redeemer statue came into view. The memory is etched into my brain—a false sense of security, maybe with the protector overlooking the city, arms open wide embracing every living soul.

The drums.

The singing and dancing.

The vibrant colors.

Rio de Janeiro has met our expectations and more. Salvador prepared my mind and body for the deluge of excitement buzzing inside of me.

Swallowed up by the crowd, my reticence dissolves. My hips sway to the beat—the drums demanding it—and I hum to an unfamiliar song in a foreign language.

Yasmine returns with caipirinhas to pep up our mood. We down the cold liquid in minutes. Amy and Yasmine return to the bar for refills.

Bree wipes her face. "Argh, I don't know why I bothered with bronzer."

I snort a laugh. "You're tanned. Your skin's flawless. And in this heat, why bother?"

Seriously, every guy would want her to be his doctor. She's tall and slim, long dark hair, and the most caring brown eyes framed with long lashes—the ones where you don't need mascara.

She shrugs. "Part of the getting-ready-to-go-out process."

I rub the skin along her jaw to blend powder where she rubbed off the color. Over her shoulder, my gaze locks with a guy with dreamy dark eyes. Not the same eyes that captured my attention in Salvador, the blue-eyed hottie who stole my breath. Instead, this guy's eyes hold a familiar look and one I recognize from the men looking for a hook-up back home. Here, it feels soul-boosting.

Tanned. Sculpted shoulders. Dark hair shaved close to his crown. His lips curve, and I swear Rio is under a spell. Apart from the flattery of him checking me out, I still find it uncomfortable. I inhale a breath.

You don't know him, and it's absolutely fine. It's acceptable, so chill.

When I glance up at Bree, there's a flirtatious twinkle in her eyes. A tall, athletic-looking guy is smiling at her. He has the same olive skin, dark eyes and hair, and a heartbreaker smile like most of the guys in Rio.

"A linda garota gostaria de dançar comigo?" the hot guy says to Bree. He takes her by the waist, his pelvis connecting to hers.

She smiles at me, eyes wide. "He said, 'Does the beautiful girl want to dance with me?'."

Of course, Bree has already picked up the Brazilian Portuguese language. I wave her away. "Go."

I do my best to ignore the guy who's eyeballing me, and before an uncomfortable feeling of being alone settles in, Amy and Yasmine return with four Caipirinhas.

"I see Bree is making progress." Amy grins at me. I nod while sucking my cocktail down. Swift sucking through a straw is my new superpower.

"Slow down, girl." Yasmine takes my empty cup. "I volunteer to refill again."

It finally clicks. "What's the attraction at the bar?"

"Same attraction as here." Yasmine nods in the direction over my shoulder.

I look to the guy sending me his best let's-fuck look. He raises his chin and gives me a you-know-I'm-sexy wink. Ugh, could he be any more obvious? He's now getting on my nerves. In the open air on the beachfront, another band takes to the stage.

"Let's dance," Amy says. She takes my hand, and we create space allowing our hips to move to the beat like our bodies are charmed by a musical spell. Soon, it's simply us four girls dancing, and for the next hour, we barely give our feet time to rest.

By the time the next band comes on stage, my friends are grinding hips with random males. I dance alone. The quick samba step tests my coordination, especially after downing several Caipirinhas.

It's a click to midnight, and my thoughts are in another zone where my head is light, and my heart is brave.

Watching my friends, I pray the rest of our holiday isn't about hooking up with hot guys. Visiting an exotic country is about much more. Or is it because my heart is scarred from the last guy who destroyed my faith in men?

7

EDEN

"UNREAL," I squeal at the top of my voice to the instructor as we glide off the mountain into the air and fly toward the city. With a bird's-eye view, I pinpoint Christ the Redeemer where we visited yesterday, Sugarloaf Mountain the day before, and the white stretch of beaches where we lazed other days. The night is all about the beach bars. We have already been in Rio for one week, and I have loved every minute.

"What's next for the Aussies?" the pilot asks. His voice is lost in the wind.

"Iguassu Falls and the Carnival," I yell back.

He veers the pole of the hang glider like a steering wheel. The surrounding mountains and vast rainforest are as beautiful as the city. My insides spark with excitement thinking about Iguassu Falls and being in the rainforest, enjoying the natural beauty of this country. "You're lucky to do this every day. The view is breathtaking."

"Yeah. I appreciate the tranquility," he says in a thick accent.

Below, there's a vibrant city. From up here, it's a whole other world. "I love all the green of the forest. It's appealing to the eye."

He chuckles. "Nature's trap to lure you in. Many don't find their way out."

"From down there?"

"No, we have walking trails down there. If you visit the Amazonia rainforest. She's beautiful, but if you're thinking about a trip to the jungle like many tourists, you need to understand what it takes to survive. Foreigners come looking for adventure, thinking they'll find it in the jungle and aren't prepared for mishaps or deviations to their plans. The weather can change rapidly. Everything looks the same, so you need an experienced guide to find your way out. Numerous animals and insects are a threat, so getting fast medical aid becomes a bigger problem."

"Are you speaking from experience?"

He nods. "Banana spider. I lost my daughter at three. I prefer to admire the beauty from up here."

My gut turns thinking about his loss.

Thank God we have Bree and her extensive medical supplies.

NOTHING EXCITES Amy more than a music festival. The blocos, or street parties, are popular during Carnival, and this is one reason why Amy wanted to visit Rio during Carnival. I'm sure party-'til-you-drop is her middle name. With more than four hundred to choose from over the carnival days, there are blocos on practically every corner.

Choosing which bloco to attend even has Amy overwhelmed. Bree suggested we head out to the shops to buy costumes as part of the fun in Rio is dressing up. The receptionist at our hotel recommended a street market for cheap costumes and accessories, so after a quick dip in the pool—because it's the only way to combat the heat—we head to the Saara market.

In a matter of hours, we're back in our cramped apartment dressing into our colorful animal-print outfits. And by colorful, I mean neon pink, yellow, and blue with a black background.

We decorate our faces in a dark bronzer before applying the glitter and colorful eye makeup to match our costumes.

"You know this makeup isn't going to stay on once we head out into the heat, right?" I say as I stroke mascara to my lashes.

"You should have fake lashes. Foolproof," Amy quips. She bats her synthetic ones to make a point.

"If I were to glue any now, it would melt in this humidity, and by the end of the night, I'd probably find it on my cheek."

"She has a point," Bree adds.

Amy ignores Bree. "Done." She twirls in front of the mirror. "Girl, we'll be picking up tonight."

I stare at her in the reflection, my hand frozen mid-air. "Here? In this tiny apartment? Do I need to remind you we're sharing a queen bed?"

Amy shrugs, causing Yasmine and Bree to grin at me.

"Hope there's room for three in your bed," I remark to their reflections.

"There is. I'm not that big," Amy replies.

I roll my eyes.

Yasmine smiles at me. "I'm popping the champagne now."

"I'm glad we have only two more nights here." I bump Amy with my shoulder. All four of us trying to use a single bathroom mirror isn't ideal.

After popping two bottles of champagne, we head to Ipanema Beach. With the alcohol pumping through my veins, combined with the excitement of partying with fifteen thousand other revelers, I swear I'm close to wetting my pants.

Forty-five minutes later, I clamber out of the taxi holding my stomach because I spent the entire ride squeezing my pelvic floor.

Amy appears by my side. "If it makes you feel any better, I was scared for my fucking life!"

Bree joins us. Her face is also pale. "That ride was an experience."

Ignoring us, Yasmine walks past with a spring in her step. "I can hear the band."

We don't question, only follow.

"I have to pee," I tell Yasmine. "I need to find some form of restrooms first."

"C'mon," Amy yells from outside the cubicle when I'm taking the longest pee in the history of urination. "I'm dying of dehydration out here."

"Okay, ready," I say when I join my friends outside. There's no doubt where the action is. The crowd is thick along the beach, and we have no clue where to even look for the bar.

It doesn't take long for us to infiltrate the membrane of the crowd.

"How the hell are we supposed to get drinks when we have to snake around partygoers, and all I see is people dressed in drag with twenty-inch heels, or they are propped for the Samba parade with a ten-foot headpiece?" Amy whines.

I chuckle because we have always teased Amy about her height.

"That's why Bree is leading us," I say and wink. Even though I'm almost as tall as Bree, I fall behind because this body on body and being surrounded by sweaty skin isn't as fun as it looks.

We get to a point, and no one moves to allow us through. We can't see beyond them or where in the crowd we're stuck. "Can you point us in the direction of the bar?" Amy asks a group of guys.

A guy stares at her with a confused look.

"Bar," she repeats and mimes drinking from a cup.

"Sim." *Yes*. "Bar," he points toward the beach further along.

"Thank you," she says.

"Obrigada," Bree adds. *Thank you*.

"Seriously?" Amy says to Bree with her hands on her hips. "You didn't think to help me then?"

"Babe, you had it under control."

We all laugh and head in the direction the guy pointed.

Periodically, I catch the scent of salty air drifting from the ocean. It's a welcome relief from the musky human odor hanging in the air.

Half-naked, exposed skin glistens, and toned bodies move to a rhythmic beat. The laughter, singing, and positive vibe are contagious. Never have I been so overwhelmed with emotion, and learning to ride it is a new skill I'm yet to master.

After buying two caipirinha's each, we make our way toward the beach side of the stage. Too far away to see the band, we dance in our little group and enjoy the music despite not understanding the foreign lyrics. Two drag queens dance beside me. After downing both drinks, my hands are free, and I have the confidence to dance with them. Bree and Yasmine head to the bar again. Amy joins us, and the dance moves up a tempo, and our new friends take the challenge. I'm laughing at Amy's competitiveness. She grinds her hips and drops to the ground, and with a quick rebound, she springs up showing her hip-hop style. Taller, and with bigger breasts and longer lashes, they just do sexy better. I stand back and clap at the three of them when Yasmine taps on my shoulder and tilts her head for me to follow.

"We have found some American guys," she says. "They asked us to hang out with them."

"Sure." After waving goodbye to our dance competitors, we weave a short distance to four guys standing together, dressed in plain street clothes.

"We met them at the bar," Bree explains. "This is Michael." I nod and smile at the guy a little taller than me with dark hair. "And this is Sean." I wave at the blond guy with a beard. Bree is smiling at Sean, and I already sense a connection between the two.

Yasmine jabs her thumb toward the next guy. "Harrison," she says, and he smiles. His eyes, skin, and hair are a darker shade like Yasmine's. Harrison nudges the fourth guy who's looking toward the ocean and disinterested in the bloco and apparently also in meeting us. He's tall, with beach-blond hair, lean, and tanned. Beneath the sleeve of his t-shirt, defined muscles contract with his movement. I take an extra look. His physique is different—strong, not bulky like a gym buff but more natural or earned from hard labor.

"And this is Samuel," Michael announces. Michael steps to the side as though he's not going to force his friend to interact.

Samuel turns, his big beautiful blue eyes lock with mine, and my stomach flutters—not of butterflies but the bloody uncoordinated flapping of an emu trying to dance.

"Hey, I'm Yasmine," Yasmine says in a polite voice. "This is Bree, Amy, and..."

I sense Yasmine staring at me.

"Eden," I finish. I force the blue haze of a spell his eyes cast over me to clear.

It's him.

The guy I saw in Salvador.

The guy who made my body hum like I was having an out-of-body experience and floating on the clouds. From the way he's staring at me, I assume he remembers me also. Something passes between us. The air crackles with physical electricity, and even in this heat, my insides warm. Something zings low in my stomach, reminding me of the joy I've deprived myself. I force myself to look away and check on my friends. They're chatting with the other guys, unaware this man—without even touching me—has awakened my female organs.

I smile at Samuel. "Nice to meet you. Are all four of you from the US?"

He nods. His brow pulls tight as though I've given him a vibe. Going by his expression, he's not pleased. His scowl flusters me.

"As you can tell, we're Aussies..." I pause, yet he gives me nothing.

"We're here for Carnival and then heading north. What about you? Are you here for Carnival?" Damn, I keep tripping over my words.

He closes his eyes in a slow blink, and by the way his shoulders slowly rise and fall, he's either taking a deep breath, or it's a sigh.

What. Am I boring him?

"Please excuse me," he says in a smooth, deep voice. His gaze leaves mine. "Michael, I have to go." He waves at Michael before turning and disappearing into the crowd.

My mouth gapes. I push up onto my toes to find him, but it's useless. What did I say?

I turn back to the group and stand next to Samuel's friend. "I don't know what I said to upset your friend, but he's gone," I say to Harrison.

Yasmine looks at me, and I shrug.

Michael glances from Yasmine to me. "Don't worry yourself," he says. "Samuel's not one to stay out."

I nod as though it's nothing.

Did I say something to upset him?

I shake my head, hoping to find some clarity. I mean, who walks away from someone you just met? It wasn't like we didn't have chemistry. I felt it and know he did too—what a rude jerk. Well, Mr. Rudey Pants, it's your loss. I huff to myself and decide to think nothing else of him.

Only I can't stop thinking about him.

Bree must notice my mood because she grabs my hand and dances with me in the middle of the group.

We continue dancing late into the night.

Samuel.

I say his name over and over in my head.

In Salvador, I thought I imagined him and didn't believe I'd see him again. Yet here we are in Rio, and now my friends are hooking up with his friends. My alcohol-fueled thoughts are telling me I can be anyone I want to be. Rio is the city of love, after all. I raise my cup and stare into the liquid as though it holds answers. If I could have that time over, what would I say to him? I need to be prepared for the next time I bump into him.

Now my friends are with his friends, there will be a next time.

8

EDEN

TWO DAYS LATER, I'm throwing summer tank tops in a case and sorting through dirty clothes, even sweaty clothes from the clean ones. I zip up my case, and simultaneously on the floor beside me the phone brightens with a notification.

Ethan.

The jerk who broke my heart and one of the reasons I needed this holiday. I'm even more pissed my father hired him to replace me.

Since there's a slight chance it could be work-related, I open the message.

> Hey...
>
> Hope you're enjoying your holiday. It's weird working here. Sitting in your chair. Using your computer. I keep staring at the frame on your desk—the one of you and your friends. You're everywhere. I'm waiting for you to walk through the door and kick my ass and tell me to get out of your seat.
>
> Dana's grumpier than I remember.

Your dad looks sad like he misses you even though you have only been gone two weeks. I'm grateful he's given me this position while you're away. It gives me a chance to work out what's next for me. When my internship ended, I thought the law firm would keep me on. My second biggest mistake. You think I'd have learned not to take things for granted.

I still regret what I did and hope one day you can forgive me. I do appreciate you saying we're friends. So, as a friend, I'm grateful to be working with your dad and seeing constant reminders of you, even though it hurts.

Stay safe, possum.

A storm of emotion tightens my chest.

The hurt.

The anger.

The embarrassment.

I toss my phone on the bed as if it's the cause.

Possum!

"Bree and Yasmine will meet us downstairs," Amy says, emerging from the bathroom.

I retrieve my phone and drop it in my bag because nothing will dampen my mood. The Copacabana Palace Hotel awaits us. We're living it up for the last two days of our stay in Rio. It's a highlight of our holiday, and the idea of experiencing the grandeur is enough to dismiss Ethan's text. Even more exciting, our new American friends secured tickets for us to attend the Magic Ball—standing tickets only. So, we need to shop for masquerade masks. Yesterday we ventured out and hired long gowns and shoes for the evening. Something we didn't pack since we never expected to attend. We were simply happy to be staying in the thick of the celebrations.

Hours later, with glittering masks packed in our cases, we head to the Belmond Copacabana Palace Hotel. I'm clinging to the seat of the taxi with every corner taken too fast and too hard, the Samba music blaring.

"Holy fuckeroni," Amy whispers when we pull up out the front of the hotel.

"It's even better up close," Yasmine says, eyes bulging.

"Ladies." Bree's sharp tone pulls us back. She coughs and nods to the doorman standing near the taxi. It appears most guests arrive in Mercedes, BMWs, and other luxury cars.

"*Obrigada*," Bree says, handing cash to the driver. *Thank you.*

Standing outside, I stare up to the hotel's imposing cream façade—a representation of elegance and sophistication. The doorman guides us inside to an opulent lobby. The sparkling chandelier grabs my attention first before a white-gloved hand lifts prompting us toward the reception desk. There are walls of fine marble and floors in mosaic. I consider the rich and famous footsteps we're following in as we're led toward the elevator.

We take the elevator to the third level. I stand at the door with Yasmine and smile in anticipation. Bree and Amy walk a little further along the hall to the room next to ours.

We open the door to polished antique furnishings, a marble bathroom, and chocolates on a period desk to welcome us. In unison, we drop our bags and stride to the double doors opening to a Juliette balcony facing the beachfront.

Yasmine exhales dramatically. "Just wow."

Salt air assaults my senses. The view is enough to make me forget the humidity.

Yasmine opens her arms wide like she's impersonating Christ the Redeemer statue. "I'm never leaving."

"Neither am I." We giggle, then slip back to being mesmerized at the sight of the cerulean ocean, watching surfers and swimmers.

"Want to check out the pool?" Yasmine asks.

"Hell, yeah." Exploring the hotel is an adventure on its own.

We hang our ball gowns in the closet, change into swimsuits, then don the white bathrobes and slip-ons provided. After notifying the other girls, it's only a matter of minutes before we're all sunning ourselves on the loungers surrounding the pool.

Stretched out on the sunbed, the sun warms my ochre skin. The waiter delivers champagne in crystal flutes, and I feel like a friggin' superstar.

I take a quick dip in the water to cool off and then lie back on my navy and white striped towel.

"Look at us living the life of the rich and famous," Amy sings.

"I could get used to it, I guess," Bree says and chuckles.

Slowly, people vacate the pool area, and I assume it's to prepare for the ball tonight.

"Hey, I'm going to head up and shower first," I tell Yasmine.

I slip on the white robe without bothering with the ties and hesitate at the winding marble staircase when I hear the elevator door ding. I stride past staff speaking anxiously in their foreign tongue. I assume the fuss is about tonight's ball.

The doors open, and I rush in then hit the button for the third floor without looking at the guy leaning on the back wall. He steps beside me, so we're both in line and ready to race through the doors. Awareness shoots along my spine. A forest scent combined with earthy male hits me. I tilt my head toward him, and fire flares inside of me when Samuel's pure blue eyes lower to meet mine.

A dent forms between his brows. "It's Eden, right?"

"Yes." I look away, doing my utmost to ignore the pull between us.

"Water refreshing?"

"Uh-huh." I keep my focus straight ahead.

"I understand my friends have purchased tickets for you and your friends to attend the ball tonight."

Is he serious? This is his first thought after what happened between us the other night. "We're paying Michael back for the tickets," I say quickly. "Will you be going?" I turn to gauge his reaction.

His eyes rise to meet mine, and we both know I've caught him checking me out.

"Under sufferance." He turns and stares directly ahead at the elevator door as though wishing it would open.

"I'm sure no one is forcing you."

The sarcasm in his chuckle matches my tone.

The elevator dings. The door opens, and I walk out without even a goodbye. Somehow, I managed to act cool around him, but the way my heart is pounding in my chest, I'm anything but calm.

My eyelids are artfully painted with powdered glitter. I've paid extreme attention to detail even though a lace mask will conceal half my face. I down another glass of bubbles, and joy pumps through my veins making me lightheaded with an understanding of what freedom is.

Not wild as my father believes.

Brave and free.

I pour another glass. This time, I sip it slowly while waiting for my friends who are still in the bathroom adding finishing touches to their makeup. My white gown fits like a glove, and I almost didn't choose it in fear of looking washed out with my fair hair. Here, with sun-kissed skin and a holiday glow radiating from within, I feel anything but washed out.

"It's time," I say, urging my friends along. I pick up my phone and take a selfie.

With alcohol fueling my thoughts, I tap out the reply to Ethan I had been avoiding.

> Rio is epic. I don't want to come home. So, go ahead and get comfortable in my chair.

> Btw, we all make mistakes. You need to learn from each one and not repeat the same shit. So, please stop calling me possum. The sweet taste of hearing you call me that soured a long time ago. Don't feel guilty about us because I don't. We are friends. That is all. Oh, and thanks for working for me.

I hit send and drop my phone in my bag, smiling from one jeweled ear to the other. I drain the last of my champagne and promise myself that tonight I'll prove that I'm over Ethan, once and for all.

9

SAMUEL

On entering the ballroom, Samuel makes his way to the balcony. He finds a space in the far-right corner and remains there. The position allows him to inhale the clean ocean air, keep his distance from the crowd growing inside the French doors, and be prepared for when *she* arrives.

He tugs at the bow around his collar and loosens the button beneath. It's been years since he wore this attire. It's a vast difference from the grass skirt he dons in Ulara.

He pulls at his shirt. The need to dress appropriately is impractical when the humidity is much the same as in the rainforest. He shakes his head. Society conforms many to unrealistic rules.

Samuel turns away from the ladies standing within arm's reach of him and clicking selfies on their phone.

He stares out to the ocean.

It's the one thing he misses, the one thing the rainforest doesn't offer despite the clean running water streaming from the tepui—crystal clear water unpolluted by man. He smiles, thinking about his *home*, and yet looks longingly to the sea. He makes a silent promise to swim before he leaves. He bows his head, his duty to his friends fulfilled for another year. He has proved his well-being. As for his sanity, they believe his anti-social behavior stems from living in solidarity. They know little of his life in Ulara.

Except Michael.

He's privy to more.

"What can I get you?" As though summoned, Michael appears and lands a hand on Samuel's shoulder, a crystal glass of beer in his other hand.

Samuel raises his glass of water. "I'm good, thanks."

"Sam, it's your last night. At least have one for old time's sake."

Old time's sake.

In college, he and Michael survived on booze, parties, and sex, usually all three in unison in the house they shared. And even now, he's cautious with Michael trying to pry more from Samuel about his lifestyle. There were times when Samuel wanted nothing more to do with him. Only he's a family friend and stood by Samuel when his parents were infuriated with his decision to throw away his career.

Samuel looks away to gather his thoughts and conceal his expression while pushing out judgment of his former self. "I'm honestly fine drinking sparkling water. In this heat, and wearing a tux—"

Words stick in his throat at the sight of her. Black lace covers her eyes, yet he recognizes her. She's laughing with her friends. It's as though his body has tuned in to the tone of her voice, the sound waves float across the crowd and, like a homing pigeon, find him. Every nerve ending is on high alert.

He's avoided the Western world's alcohol for years. Tonight, he needs it more than ever to calm his erratic thoughts. Tonight, he should avoid it more than ever to keep all wit about himself.

"Maybe one, then," he says without taking his eyes off Eden.

"That's my man. The old you is in there somewhere." Another slap to his back is hard enough for him to step forward.

Michael calls out to Harrison, who has already waved the girls over on the balcony, twenty feet away from where Samuel stands. A group of a dozen men and women close the gap between Samuel and his friends. His attempt at keeping a safe distance from people is pointless. The corner position allows him to watch her from a safe space and decide whether to retreat quietly back to his room after one drink. His brain tells him to do the latter. He has managed to shut out lust for years. Tonight, he struggles to control his attraction. A chemical overdose streams through him after being deprived for too long. He glances down at his hands. His veins bulge, and he understands why. The chemicals fueling his bloodstream are now controlling his bodily responses.

She speaks to her friends, and he hisses out a curse at the sweet sound. He closes his eyes and wills his heart to slow. No female has had this effect over him, ever. What the hell is wrong with him? She's another human only of the opposite sex, and he sees half-naked women in the village every day. He shakes his head, chuckles quietly to berate himself, and turns back to the ocean. He leans his elbows on the rail while he takes in the vista. To think he not long ago believed he had lost the urge, and now he's acting like an experienced fool.

"Michael said to bring this over to you."

At the sound of her voice, he spins awkwardly, almost knocking the glass of beer from her grasp.

"Shit, I didn't mean to spook you." Eden flicks beer droplets from her fingers and wipes the material of her dress.

"I apologize." He leans in and brushes droplets from the white fabric clinging to her hips. Her skin warms his fingers through the thin material. He yanks his hand away, takes the beer from her grasp, and nods. All rational thought is lost as he inhales her fruity scent.

"Okay, then." She fidgets seemingly lost without anything in her hands.

"May I get you a drink?"

Eden smiles, elevating Samuel's desire to touch her, a need his body longs for, and instinctively, he takes a step closer.

"Amy is getting me a glass of champagne. So..." She takes a step back. "You should come over and join us." She nods toward his friends.

"I need a moment." He pulls out his cell as an excuse. "I'm expecting a call."

"Right. Well, I'll catch you later." She turns and glides in her heels back to the group. His gaze roams over her bare shoulders, down a back crisscrossed with spaghetti straps. He watches her hips sway and makes out the swell of her rear beneath the white satin. He assesses the lines and realizes she's wearing a thong and imagines her naked in nothing but that thin piece of material.

Samuel has succumbed to the power she has over him. He leans over the balcony and closes his eyes. The way the band of his trousers has tightened around his hips, he'll need more than a moment.

For one night, he'll divulge in the pleasure of being close to her.

Tomorrow he'll head back to Ulara and far away, not to be charmed by her presence.

He waits until he can straighten without embarrassment before finding his friends. Harrison is talking to Eden. His hand rests on her shoulder, and Samuel's pulse surges. He fights the urge to storm over and smack his hand away. He downs the cold liquid in three gulps and places the empty glass on the tray of a waiter passing by. Jealousy was never part of his makeup. He feels possessed and uncomfortable with how he's reacting. Panic builds in his gut in not having control of his emotions.

He starts for the door, weaving around guests.

"Hey." Sean pats his back and hands him another beer. "Wondering when you were going to join us."

He bumps Samuel in the direction of the group. "Got this for Michael, although you could use it more." With a hand on Samuel's shoulder, he walks beside him. Being close to Eden is like being on a high and craving the pleasure of dopamine to be rewarded with euphoria. It's a warning for him to remove Sean's hand from his shoulder and call it a night. Instead, he accepts the beer and walks toward *her* as though he has lost all control.

When they join the group, Eden turns and makes space beside her. "Did you take your call?"

"I did." He looks to Michael.

Michael gives him a smug smile. "Not so bad after all, is it?"

10

EDEN

My stomach cartwheeled the moment we entered the ballroom, and I'm still amazed we secured one of the hottest tickets in town.

Decorations sparkle on the walls and ceiling. Under the lights, a band plays a catchy jazz tune, and the smile hasn't left my lips. Along with every guest, I talk at a higher octave, my voice joining the hum of excitement in the room and on the balcony.

"Thank you," I say when Yasmine hands me another glass of champagne before she stands beside Michael. I don't miss the way she looks at him, hanging off every word he utters. He has dark hair and brown eyes with *that* look and a muscled physique—a tell-tale sign he works out. And I know Yasmine's thoughts are tick, tick, tick. I understand as I'm doing the same standing beside Samuel. My heart is racing, yet I'm doing my best to act cool around him. When Michael convinced me to take him a beer, the change in him could give a girl whiplash. For some reason, I now feel like I have the upper hand.

Michael makes another joke about his travels in Peru.

Yasmine pulls a face. "I call bullshit."

"I kid you not. Have you been there?"

Yasmine shakes her head. "We will be in a couple of weeks."

"Michael." Samuel has barely uttered a word, and yet this sounds like a reprimand. My breath catches momentarily.

Michael frowns at Samuel. I'm not sure what's happening between the pair but note the silent message conveyed.

"Well, I'm up for an adventure in Peru because I fell in love with Iguassu Falls and the rainforest," I say to lighten the conversation.

Michael rolls his eyes. "You haven't experienced anything until you venture into the heart of the jungle." His gaze flicks to Samuel, and he shrugs. "Just saying."

Samuel stiffens beside me.

"You don't like the rainforest?"

His brow arches at my question. "I'd like to hear more about your trip to Iguassu."

I smile as I recall the details of our trip only days before. "Invigorating. Breathtaking." I shake my head in wonder. "Seriously, you have to go there. It was two hours by plane and well worth the journey." His lips curl a little at the edges. "I'm not joking. It's been a highlight so far."

"The humidity and oversized bugs didn't bother you?" He grins at me as though he's waiting for me to concur.

I wave my hand acting blasé. "You don't even notice because you're in another world. The power of the water surging over the cliff. The rainforest surrounding you and all the noise of the creatures fade because the roar of the water is deafening."

His eyes lock with mine. After a moment, he smiles all perfect white teeth, and the joy reaches his blue eyes. Damn, he needs to smile more. "You like waterfalls?"

"Yeah." I smile back. "It was different than anything I've experienced. When we walked through the rainforest, we even saw a toucan."

"Impressive. Where are you headed next?"

"After the Samba parade, north along the coast to Ilhéus. Then a short stop in Caracas before Margarita Island. From there, on to Peru and hopefully, Galapagos, although we haven't booked the last week in case we decide to extend our days in Peru or head to Colombia." I didn't sound like someone who lived a sheltered life and was afraid of change. It feels good not to be that person and be adventurous. I raise my chin and look into those beautiful eyes with newfound confidence. "Have you traveled to any of those places?"

"A while ago." He loosens his collar beneath his bowtie, takes several mouthfuls of his beer before looking sideways at me. "How long will you be in Ilhéus?"

"About a week to explore the coast and have some downtime."

He nods while looking into his beer. "There's this place. It's quite a bus ride to get to, but it's worth it for the caves, smaller waterfalls, and a mystical lake."

"A mystical lake?" I grin at him. "I must remember to mention it to Yasmine."

"A non-believer?"

I snort quietly. "I'm a visual person. I like to see things with my own eyes. Though some things…" I pause, thinking of when I found out my ex had cheated on me. "Some things I believe if the information comes from a good source." I glance at Yasmine, thankful to her for having my back.

His eyes never leave my face. Under the heat of his gaze, I'm reminded of the first time I saw him on the beach in Salvador. I'm sure it was him, except the way he acted at the bloco—

"Can I get you another drink?"

I glance down at my empty glass. "Were you in Salvador a few weeks ago?"

"What?"

I glance up. "In Salvador. At the Iemanjá ceremony?" I watch his Adam's apple bob. "We saw each other, didn't we?" I'm thankful for the alcohol fueling my courage.

He takes the empty crystal from my fingertips and turns toward the bar. In perfect timing, a waiter walks by with a tray of beverages. Samuel takes a glass of champagne and a beer, swivels back, and hands me the crystal.

"Yes," he says and takes a swig without looking at me.

I knew it.

"Why were you rude to me at the bloco?"

"Not to you. I didn't want to be there."

"You were a grump."

He smiles into his glass. "I've been called worse."

His gaze lifts and meets mine. There's something about the different shades of blue in his hues that mesmerizes me, and I struggle to look away. In a moment of contentment, I know Samuel has come into my life for a reason. Judging by his expression, he senses a connection as well.

He leans in. I lick my lips and lean closer. His lips are so close to mine—a whisper, a kiss away. What would they feel like on my skin? My neck? My décolletage? I raise one hand to touch his face—

He jerks back.

Freezes.

His eyes dart up to his friends as though he requires backup.

What just happened?

"I'm sorry if I gave you the wrong impression." He holds one hand up at his friends in farewell.

Shit. He's not into me?

"Night, man. Sleep well," Michael shouts.

His friends don't seem surprised Samuel is leaving.

"It was nice meeting you," he whispers.

Before he turns away, there's a flicker of regret in his eyes.

What the actual heck?

"Yeah." I want to say much more, only the shock of him bailing has words stuck in my dry throat.

I withhold from turning to watch him walk away.

Michael is watching me curiously. "I know his room number if you're interested."

Yasmine catches on and gapes, then a smirk creeps over her face. "Go on, Eden."

"He's not interested," I manage to rasp out.

Michael laughs. "I'll ask you again at the end of the night."

11

SAMUEL

THE LAST TIME Samuel checked his cell, it was close to midnight.

Laughter echoed behind his door with tipsy guests bumping the hallway walls heading back to their suites.

He rolls over, stares at the window, and groans. At this rate, he'll get no sleep. It's not the noisy guests he blames. His thoughts are relentless of Eden and what could've been. Ecstasy for one night could open the gates of desire. More of what he can't have. He'd forgotten the buzz of lust and attraction and the thrill of pleasure hormones circulating and fulfilling certain areas. Now he's suffering and unable to sleep, wanting a release.

He reminds himself of the promise he made years ago—not to get involved with a woman while he was committed to the Ularan people. It's not their way to divulge in casual relationships, and he's now one of *them*.

A bang on his door has him listening for revelers. Another, and he realizes it's no mistake. He jumps up, pulls on shorts, and steps closer to the door.

"Samuel. Open the door."

His heartbeat soars at the sound of her voice.

The knocking grows louder.

"It's Eden."

He flicks on the light before opening the door. "Is everything okay?"

"No." She strides past Samuel before he has a chance to object. He catches the sweet aroma of wine on her breath. "Michael and Yasmine are getting it on in my room. I'm not into watching. And Amy has hooked up with Harrison, and Sean with Bree. So, it leaves you. I know you're not into me, but I need a place to sleep."

A better idea would be to pay for another room for her to sleep because he won't get any rest with her so close. He locks the door. Her hips sway beneath the white gown as she moves toward his bed. She looks even more beautiful than she did a few hours before.

Eden unzips her dress. He struggles to breathe, yet he can't look away. He should tell her to leave. Tell her she's right, and he's not interested. Only it would be a lie.

"Stop," he hisses.

"You can't expect me to sleep in this." The dress loosens and slides over her curves to pool around her feet. She pauses and looks longingly at him. He holds her gaze, and yet he sees all of her. His peripheral vision is outstanding—rounded breasts bounce freely, and the skin-colored flimsy piece of material on her hips barely covers anything.

His chest expands in a greater need of air. He's aware of other parts of him expanding too.

He retrieves a t-shirt from his case and hands it to her. "You'll be more comfortable in this."

There's a glimmer of sadness in her eyes.

He slides under the sheet to hide his attraction. "There's toothpaste in the bathroom if you need it."

Under the safety of Egyptian cotton, he watches her bare rear as she pads to the bathroom. Hell, she's truly perfect.

"Hinting about the toothpaste..." she calls out from the bathroom, "... could mean you want to do something," she mumbles with the toothbrush in her mouth.

He sits up, but she's out of his sight. "Are you using my toothbrush?"

"Is it the little white one in a pack?" she says with a mouthful.

"No." He flops back onto the bed, remembering his is in a bag, and the complimentary brush remained next to the basin. The back of his wrist rests against his forehead, and it does nothing to ease the sexual thoughts tormenting him.

"Stop avoiding my question." She gargles water. "Are you intending to kiss me?"

"Being a gentleman and providing you a place to crash, and then offering for you to freshen up isn't an invitation to hook up," he mumbles, even if it's what he craves. He inhales a breath, and all he smells is the sweetness of Eden, and the scent is enough to send his thoughts into overdrive.

Moments later, she clambers in beside him. "What is it about me guys don't like?" she whispers.

"I have no idea what you're talking about?" Keeping a safe space between them, he slides onto his side, so he's facing her.

"It's Rio, for God's sake and not one kiss."

"You want someone to kiss you?" His voice cracks on the words.

Eden nods. "It doesn't have to mean anything."

Only it will, and knowing so, Samuel ignores the warning in his head of the commitment he has made. He wants to reach out and touch her cheek and tell her what he truly feels. She's a beautiful woman, and yet the pull between them is beyond physical attraction. The short time he has spent with her has given him time to see the colors of her aura. The kindness and passion of her heart emanate from her soul. How he sees and senses it is beyond explanation, and it's getting harder for him to resist the burning attraction between them. He leans in until his lips are inches away and hesitates. Her eyes hold him captive, pools of blue capable of drowning him. He stops fighting what he wanted to do the moment he saw her on the beach.

He starts slowly—a gentle kiss. Soft, moist lips reciprocate. She sighs into his mouth. It triggers a reaction, and he presses his lips harder to hers. Her tongue finds his, and he loses all coherent thought. *How long has it been since he has kissed a woman like her?* If he is being truthful, he's never met anyone like her.

His body presses against hers as he gives into lust. His hands move over the swell of her hips and higher to find her soft breasts. He pulls back and stares into her eyes.

"Don't stop."

He doesn't want to. Only he remembers how much she has had to drink, and if anything happens between them, it will be under the influence of alcohol. Reeling in emotion, he rasps, "Not tonight when you've been drinking."

She flips up, throws a leg over, and lands on his hips in one smooth action. She settles where he feels it most. Eden smiles down at him. “You do like me.”

“More than you’ll remember tomorrow.” He grabs her hips to keep her from moving deciding to speak honestly—there is a high chance she won’t recall anything he says when she wakes. “You’re right. I did see you on the beach, and I wanted you then. I’ve been fighting it the entire time. Right now, I want nothing more than to be between your legs.” Her eyes widen. “But it won’t happen. I’m not taking advantage of you. You’re killing me right now, so please…” he grabs her hips tighter, “… don’t move, or we both might do something we regret.”

Eden hasn’t taken her eyes off of him. She frowns as if her thoughts have caught up. “I wouldn’t regret it. I should be angry with you. You were an ass.”

He wishes she were. He could handle her anger better than her advances. “You have every right to be.”

“You’ve liked me all along?”

He nods while assisting her in lying beside him. He strokes her face, runs his hand along her neck and shoulder. “You’re truly a beautiful woman.”

She smiles, and he likes how it reaches her eyes. “So not tonight,” she whispers. She closes her eyes. “I’ll see you in the morning.”

“I’ll be looking forward to it. Are you heading to the Samba parade tomorrow night?”

She makes a purring sound. “Uh-huh, then onto Ilhéus. I’m looking forward to staying at the resort on the beach.” Samuel continues to stroke her face until her breathing slows, and she sounds like she’s asleep. He kisses the tip of her nose, knowing he won’t be resting anytime soon.

12

EDEN

"Desculpe." *Excuse me.*

"What?" I moan and roll over in bed.

My eyes open, and I gasp. A maid is standing by the door. I jerk up and realize I'm not in my room, and snippets of last night flash in my mind. I'm staring at the maid.

"I'm sorry. Did Samuel order breakfast?" I straighten the t-shirt over my chest and stroke my hair, wishing it would behave.

We exchange confused glances. "Mr. McMahon checked out," she manages in broken English.

"Pardon." My stomach tightens, trying to comprehend what she's telling me.

She bows her head and takes a step backward to retreat.

"No, no." I scan the room for my clothes. "If you give me a minute, I'll be out of here." I hold up one finger. "One moment."

She nods. We stare at each other for a brief moment before she leaves—long enough for pity to settle in her eyes.

I clench both fists and want to scream. "Fuck you, Samuel McMahon." I take a deep breath. Who does that? Who bloody checks out while I—whatever I am to him— am still in the room? I pull off his t-shirt and slip into my white satin gown.

I gather my shoes and purse. I glance back at his t-shirt on the bed. I'll claim it too. With the Brazilian soccer team logo on the front, it's like my personal souvenir.

Waiting at the elevator, I have no idea what floor I'm on until the number above the door lights up.

"Asshole" plays over in my head like a mantra.

I tap on the door before I use my room key to open it.

"Yasmine," I whisper and peer around the corner. Two heads are on pillows with sheets covering their bodies. I sneak in, grab some clothes from the closet before heading to the bathroom.

Yasmine lifts her head. "Edes." Her voice is thick with sleep. "What are you doing? The plan was to sleep in, remember? We're going to be up all night at the Samba parade."

I glance at the clock. It's just gone seven in the morning. Oh, for heaven's sake. "Well, we didn't explain that to Samuel before he decided to check out at some ungodly hour, and the maid woke me believing the room was vacant," I spit.

Michael groans. "He what?" He sits up, and the sheet falls away to reveal a tattooed muscled chest.

I swallow down the ball of hurt once more. Tears sting and threaten to spill out the corners of my eyes. "Samuel checked out."

"Are you sure?" He rubs his hands over his face and sighs.

"Yep."

"The jerk." Michael reaches for his phone, but the screen doesn't light up when he touches it. "It's dead." He tosses it back onto the bedside table. "I'll find out what the hell is going on later. I'm not surprised, though. He's… different."

"You don't say." I fold my arms.

"He does this. It's not you." Michael rubs the back of his neck and shakes his head.

"Is he married?"

"Not to a woman." He chuckles when he sees Yasmine's and my expressions. "Or a man," he adds. "To a way of life." He pauses. "It's hard to explain."

"You better start trying harder," Yasmine threatens in her best tone.

"I'm going to shower." I raise my hands in the air. "Please find a way to explain it because I'm feeling pretty shitty."

Behind the door, I ignore the murmurs of Yasmine and Michael in a discussion.

Under the water, my thoughts clear. Memories of last night flash back. He wanted me. He did from the moment we saw each other. I sob into the water spray remembering his words, his touch.

What's wrong with me?

13

EDEN

Ileus, Brazil

Two days later...

Under the Brazilian sun, I roll my shoulders and stretch my neck from side to side. I'm grateful that Yasmine discovered the coastal town and booked the beachside resort so we could rest after Rio. Only now, with what happened in Rio, busy is better to keep certain thoughts at bay. The brochures are spread out on the sand so I can plan my days. My thoughts wander to the mystical lake *he* mentioned. Now, I'm determined to find it —to take something positive out of our negative interaction.

"There's a chocolate factory. And we can go on a tour of an old cacao plantation," Bree says beside me.

"Oh, and look. You know *Jorge Amado*, the author we saw in Salvador? He came from around here." Amy hands me another brochure. "There's a bar, the *Vesuvio,* named in one of his books. It looks popular."

"I can rely on you to find a reason to go to a bar."

Amy winks at me. "I've had enough of the beach. I'm heading up to the resort pool. Anyone keen?"

"I will." The wind has picked up, and I'll find it easier to read through the pile of brochures in a sheltered area.

Amy hands me the brochure on the *Vesuvio* bar and gives me a pointed look. "We need to go out and let loose."

"You know, you're right."

THE FOLLOWING MORNING, Bree rolls her eyes at Amy. "Someone go a little hard on the Caipirinhas last night?"

Amy plucks the straw from the glass and sucks the acai smoothie in a slurp. "I had fun. Oh shit." She glances down at the purple spots on her white tank top. "I need to change."

"You have ten minutes before the bus arrives," I warn her. "And we're not missing it."

When Amy races off, Yasmine piles the laminated menus on the table. "I'm going to brave the Dourada tonight."

"You're going to try catfish?" Bree asks, her voice a higher pitch.

"Yep."

"I'm not sure why we're discussing dinner at breakfast." I laugh. "If we're eating lunch at *Vesuvio,* I might not need dinner."

Bree starts in on the nutritional value of the exotic fruits available here. "They are a rich source of Vitamins A and C and minerals calcium, iron, phosphorus, magnesium, and zinc," she says and continues on until Amy returns.

"Okay. Let's get this tourist stuff out of the way for Edes, so I can get back here to the pool," Amy says, out of breath.

"I found more churches as well." I ignore the eye-rolling. "Don't you find the architecture interesting?"

"I guess." Amy shrugs. "I find *other* things more interesting. We have five weeks left, and it's about meeting guys, adventure, and fun."

We make our way to the front of the resort in time for the bus.

"Michael and I are staying in touch," Yasmine says, taking a seat beside me. "We message several times a day." She bows her head as though she has a secret. Or maybe she's embarrassed. "He gets me... like really gets me. I think even more than all of you." She peers up. Her eyes convey an apology.

"What do you mean more than us?" I whisper, my voice cracking on the last word. I'm not sure whether it's hurt or anger that she believes a guy she has just met has a stronger force of understanding than a decade of friendship. What did he say to her? I can't help thinking he has an agenda. I'm overcome with wanting to protect her, except it's Yasmine. She has always looked out for my friends and me. She's the one who's strong in her beliefs and convictions, even more so than Bree because Bree still doubts herself and her ability even though she's borderline genius.

"It's like we're searching for the same thing." She shrugs. "There's more to our personal being. More to this life," she says in an even quieter voice. I tilt my head, so my ear is closer to her face. "We talked a lot in Rio about life and our individual journeys. He wants to meet up again before we get to the island."

I had noticed she was spending more time on her phone, which is also unlike her. "What makes you think he knows you better than me?"

Her eyes scan my face, and I know I'm failing at hiding my concern.

Her head tilts to the side. "I'm different."

"In a good way," I say.

"If I tell you what I want to do, you'll get mad at me."

"Why would I? You're my friend, and I trust you."

Her shoulders rise and fall. "I'm considering meeting Michael in Peru."

I nod quickly to portray I understand. "Peru is part of the itinerary."

"I want to go further than the outskirts of the Amazon. I want to travel deeper into her heart. Experience what she has to offer."

"If you've considered it, then I know you have weighed up the facts and know the pros and cons. I'm not sure why you thought I'd be mad."

"Because I'm going to experience it all. You know I believe there are more dimensions to our world. The Amazon is a place of life. The people, their simple way of life, their beliefs... it's a multitude of everything... race, color, plants, diversity. The jungle holds the secrets I've been searching for, and I want to try the medicinal plants. I know you're freaking out, but Michael will guide me."

Admittedly, I'm a little scared for her. Hell, Bree *will* freak out because she understands what could possibly go wrong and will do all she can to deter Yasmine.

"It's what my soul craves, and I want to do it with Michael. I don't want negative thoughts to block my spiritual journey or you all telling me what can go wrong, not how wonderful I'll feel after."

"Okay, then," I whisper. "If you feel this strongly about it, then I'll have your back." I reach and touch her arm. "We go together," I emphasize. "I'm not going to let you do this alone, but we need to learn more because we definitely have to be cautious, and I'm not being negative."

Yasmine smiles, then turns to gaze out of the bus window. Her smile doesn't fool me. She's lost in her thoughts, and I sense she isn't telling me everything. We're traveling together yet embarking on our personal journey, which might mean doing some of it alone. It's not what we promised each other before this holiday. Nor my father. I push out the thought because right now, I need to do what it takes to look out for my friend.

THE FOLLOWING DAY, I'm sitting on a hot bus while my friends hang at the beach. I promised them I'd be fine and needed some time alone. A tour inland to a mystical lake—the one Samuel suggested—and to waterfalls didn't interest them, especially after they hit the bars again last night. Amy insisted on coming until Yasmine told her to give me space. When I didn't go out with them last night, my friends realized I was still upset about Samuel. I used the time to call my parents, reassuring them I was fine.

"Fishing is a means of survival here." The sound of the tour guide's voice brings me back. Pressing my nose closer to the glass, I make out small fishing villages dotting the edges of a large lake. Canoes line the shore. The tour guide speaks about folklore and the floating islands on the lake. Tales of an underwater kingdom and mystical beings—hence, why it's known as the Enchanted Lake. He tells a story of how fishermen never returned if their boats sailed near the floating islands at night. It intrigues me as to how some small communities have a strong belief in folklore and how these myths influence their lives and cultural tradition compared to our dependency on science, fact, and statistics. I struggle with the legends since I'm a visual person. I snort, thinking how I'd be the fisherman venturing out because I didn't believe and possibly never return. If only Yasmine had come with me. She'd enjoy hearing about the folklore.

I close my eyes momentarily and wish for some things in my life to change.

The bus bounces along the dirt road. “The first waterfall is Salto de Apepique,” the tour guide says. “This waterfall is popular for rappelling.”

The cliff edge isn’t high, so a dozen of us are taken through the steps of a quick safety instruction before rappelling the rock while the others relax with morning tea.

The rope supports me when I push off the rocky edge. Water sprays my face, refreshing and awakening the fact my life is in the hands of one rope. No sooner do I reach the bottom, I’m clambering up the rocky cliff to do it again and again.

“We now have a short walk, so I apologize to those who have wet shoes,” our guide calls out.

My feet are squishing in my sneakers. Ugh. Blisters will not be fun, but after an experience like that, it’s worth it.

“Where are you from?”

I smile at the middle-aged lady beside me, both of us stumbling as we trample over pebbled rocks.

“Adelaide, South Australia.”

“We’re from Sheffield in the UK. By the way, I’m Kim.”

I’d picked the English accent. “Hi, I’m Eden.”

The guide stops and points to a cave. He talks in Portuguese first, then Spanish, before addressing us in English.

“Please gather in, people. We’re to enter the cave. I’ll explain the next activity. In the cave, I’ll give a command. Then everyone is to remove their top and swap it with the person closest to them.”

What?

I look at Kim, wide-eyed.

“You won’t be able to see inside the cave. When we exit the cave, you’re to find the person wearing your top. This person will be your partner for the remainder of the tour.”

Surely, there are occupational health and safety issues with sharing clothes? This is worse than any team-building and trust exercise I’ve ever done.

I withhold my grumbling and offer a fake smile when laughter sounds through the group. I look around at the couples and consider how awkward it is for some. Hell, I don’t have a partner. I follow one couple in, afraid to turn and check who's behind me. I don't want to establish what top they're wearing or if there are any sweat marks.

I remember Yasmine's words about not all experiences are enjoyable.

C'mon, Eden. It's an adventure, so try and roll with it.

Chatter and laughter echo as we approach the opening of the cave.

"Watch your step," our guide warns, shining his flashlight into the cavern. "Find a rock to sit on." I stumble on loose stones before regaining my balance. I walk about thirty steps in darkness, a dim light reflecting the outline of the stones. Taking a seat on the cold, moist pebbled ground, I rest my forehead on bent knees then lift my head when the guide speaks. I strain my eyes when he turns off the flashlight.

In the dark, fear creeps in. I've always been afraid of the unknown, of what I can't see. I remember being a little girl afraid of spiders, unlike my fearless gran. Her words echo in the back of my mind. What if I'm sitting next to a scorpion right now? I re-curl and place my head on my knees and wrap my arms around my thighs to block out the world and concentrate on my breathing.

"Sorry... sorry." Whispers come from behind me as someone stumbles to find a seat.

In the dark, our guide continues with his folklore stories relating to the Enchanted Lake. The musky air tastes wet, and with only blackness around us, it creates an eerie presence. Goosebumps prick up along my arms, and an unnerving tingle runs down my spine. Yet, I visualize his words. I see the calm waters of the blue-gray lake and the boats sailing across the water without a motor and feel the serenity in the stillness of night and of a single breath while watching these slow-moving islands drift into another dimension.

A weird sensation rolls over me. In the darkness, I'm reminded of nights I've cried myself to sleep. How in those times, Gran's spirit talked to me in my dreams. It's weird I'm thinking of her now.

The guide claps his hands, and I jump. "Now is the time to swap your top."

Would anyone know if I didn't play along? After all, it is dark, and no-one knows me...

I jump again when a hand rests on my shoulder. *Shit.* I close my eyes, which is pointless really, except it helps me suck up what has to be done—remove my tank top. Soft material lands on my shoulder. I hold my tank out until it's yanked out of my hand. I fiddle with the top, trying to find a tag, not wanting to be the person everyone laughs at because her top is inside out or the back is the front.

When I reach the cave opening, my eyes burn in the light. A green t-shirt falls to my hips. I don't recall anyone wearing it. I search for the person wearing my yellow top. Laughter erupts from the group as people discover their surprise partner. The giggling continues as tops are turned from back to front and inside out. Some men have squeezed into their female partner's clothing.

In the distance, I spot a guy sitting alone with his back to me. A topless figure, a rock with yellow material thrown over his shoulder. The stranger is wearing a hat. He's facing away from the group looking out toward the rainforest beyond the cliffs. I look back to the group as I walk toward him, checking no one else is wearing my top. Everyone else appears to have paired up.

With every step, awareness zips up my spine. I recognize those shoulders. I want to believe it possible and curse myself for showing vulnerability.

I'm pulled closer by an invisible whirlpool.

When I reach him, I gasp.

What the actual hell?

Samuel's gaze is lowered as though giving me a minute.

My eyes laser in on him. I'm holding my breath waiting for him to say something.

His eyes lift slowly to meet mine. Gone is the confident asshole. His eyes hold apology as he searches my face.

"Is this a sick joke?"

His brow pulls tight, then he shakes his head.

I fold my arms and glare at him. "Then why are you here?"

"It's not something I can explain in a couple of sentences. First, I wanted to apologize."

"For what? You just checked out early. It was your room, after all."

His mouth opens as if my nonchalant response surprises him.

"Oh right, for your shitty behavior. I remember now. In fact, I remember *everything*."

He stares at me, and his silence pisses me off even more. He nods to the group. "We should join them." He holds out my tank top. "I believe this is yours."

In a swift action, I pull his tee up and over my head. His gaze lifts to my bikini. "And I assume this is yours," I say bluntly.

He takes it from my grasp and doesn't put it on. He pushes up and uncurls to stand. Like dominoes, his muscles contract with movement from his arms, down his chest, to the ripple of his abs.

I'm dead.

I close my eyes momentarily before forcing my feet to move. I need a moment because my every cell crackles like live wires craving him. I hate myself for wanting him when right now I need to remain angry and hurt him like he hurt me. It's immature maybe, but my thoughts are all over the place. Mostly, I'm surprised as to why he's here.

Our guide points to the door of the bus. I take a seat at the back, and Samuel follows in silence, sliding in beside me. The window is now my focus, my shaky hands pushed under my thighs.

"Our next stop is *Saltos de Almada.* Here you can relax and take a swim," the guide announces.

The other tourists cheer.

My gaze doesn't falter from the glass. I don't want to be on this bus and this close to him when all I want to do is scream. "Why would you promise me morning and then leave before I wake?" I turn to meet his gaze. "You're nothing but an ass."

14

SAMUEL

SAMUEL DIDN'T THINK she'd remember the words he spoke in Rio.

"You'd been drinking," he says gently.

"Not so much that I forgot."

He looks out the window to what has her interest and sees their reflection in the glass. She's watching his every move.

He sees the indent between her brows, and yet there is sadness in her eyes. "You're angry. I understand." He witnesses an eye roll. "The other night..." He closes his eyes momentarily with the memory. It was only five nights ago, yet it feels longer. "You surprised me. It put me in a position, and I needed time to consider my action."

She turns and glares. "Most guys would jump into bed with a naked woman given a chance," she hisses under her breath. "Especially the one I gave you. Unless I'm—"

"I'm not most men," he says. "I don't indulge like our friends."

She stalls as though comprehending what he's saying. Her expression softens, and he hopes she's considering his words.

She turns again to the window like it's a safety barrier even though both of their expressions are visible.

"Did you know I was on this tour?"

He nods. "Wait for the next stop, and I'll explain..."

As best he can.

How does he tell her the truth?

He can only explain how she has haunted him from the moment he first saw her.

Even from the time she took a seat on the bus, her scent filled the small space, and he knew it was her before he caught sight of her long, blonde ponytail flowing from the base of her cap, the same fruity, floral scent on her skin she wore to the ball. It taunts him with the memory of her lying close to him, and the soft curves of her body beneath his hands.

She obliterated his armor in Rio, armor he had built up over the years to resist women so he could focus on his work. His duty. He has never expected anyone to understand his way of life or his choices. Years of restraint and the willpower to get to this point in his life all vaporize when he's around her. He doesn't know why he gravitates to her like a bee to a flower. Not any flower. She has evolved from all others. Her scent and beauty attract him in a combined complexity, controlling his thoughts and manipulating his behavior. She's his weakness, and now he has her scent ingrained in his memory—his brain has selected her. The overwhelming need to understand *why* was enough for him to change his flight and head to Ilhéus to find her.

"I wanted to say hello before you hurried off to climb the waterfall, only I didn't know how you'd react seeing me—"

She turns her head in a snap-like action. "You've been on this bus the entire time?"

"At the back," he confesses.

Eden removes her hands from beneath her bare thighs and wipes her palms on her tank top. "I don't know what to think."

The bus pulls to a stop, and the guide announces they have thirty minutes for a quick swim at the rock pool and to stay close by. Samuel stands when the rows before him file out. He glances at Eden and holds out his hand to help her slide across the vinyl. Her gaze remains fixed on the glass, and she stays seated. He leaves her to walk ahead. When he reaches the stream, he finds a smooth boulder to sit on away from the group.

He observes the other tourists splashing in the water to cool down. He catches her in his peripheral vision. She strips down to her bikini and wades into the water only several feet from him.

Tossing his t-shirt on the rock, he sits on the edge so his feet can dangle in the water.

For days, he contemplated what to say when he saw her again. His heart and mind have endured a battle since the morning he left her lying in his bed.

He grits his teeth when a voice tells him *you're weak*. He is threatening everything he's worked for, endangering the lives of those he now calls family. Simultaneously, his gut tightens the moment Eden rises from the water and takes a step toward him. Water drips from her sleek body, moisture glistening on golden skin in a goddess form. Right now, he believes she's one. It's the only explanation for the hold she has over him. The dark shadow of weakness consumes him.

Lust.

Desire.

And more.

It has sparked and ignited his soul. He had tried to ignore it and disregard the voice calling to him to do what he shouldn't. A voice reminding him of the one he hears in the dark of night when he sleeps on the jungle floor, a voice more powerful than any living being.

He sucks in more air as she approaches. She's six steps away. He braces himself for the impact. Their eyes lock. He sees her and is aware the moment her nipples peak beneath thin nylon. She squeezes moisture from her hair.

Three steps...

Two...

She sits beside him.

Her floral scent crashes through his barrier. He moves slightly to give her more room, ensuring her skin doesn't brush his. The slightest touch threatens his thin web of restraint. His manhood shifts a gear to drive his thoughts. He closes his eyes to give himself a moment.

For hours, he has prepared several short excuses as to his sudden appearance. Now she has infiltrated his senses, his composure flails. Yet hers has strengthened. Her strength impresses and nevertheless weakens him further.

"How did you know I'd be on this tour?" she asks without looking at him.

"I noticed your name on the booking sheet for the bus at the resort."

Her head snaps to face him. "You're staying at the resort?"

Samuel nods, hoping she doesn't make an assumption. "I'm not trying to scare you. After all, I did tell you about this tour. Yasmine revealed the resort where you're staying to Michael. I wanted to see you, so—"

"Then why did you leave Rio?"

"I can't explain it here. We need to be away from everyone."

"Do you hear how crazy you sound? You have stalked me, you treated me appallingly, and now you're asking me to be alone with you so you can *try* to justify your actions?"

A smile pulls at his lips. She thinks he's crazy *before* he explains.

15

EDEN

I NEED to keep a level head.

It's not easy to do when he slides into the seat alongside me, and inside the confines of the muggy interior of the bus, I'm overcome by his manly forest scent. His heat radiates too damn close, inciting desire, and it's building quicker than I can control. I wage an internal battle—the thoughts of *what if*? My face warms thinking of the night in Rio. Physically, my body craves him, but hell, he pursued me, and I'm in an unfamiliar country where laws differ from home.

A half-hour passes before I level my thoughts and ask one of many questions. "So, what do you do for work?" A question a stranger could ask on a greeting, and it's less intrusive than my other thoughts. I turn to catch his expression as though I have an internal lie detector.

"I'm a doctor."

I nod. "Where did you study?"

"Stanford."

He didn't hesitate.

His chin lifts slightly. "What do you do, as you put it?" His eyes flick over my face like he's assessing me. If I lie, he'll know it.

"I… work as a marketing coordinator for a hotel company."

"Where?"

"Adelaide," I reply. "And you? Where do you work?"

His brow lifts. "Now?"

"Yes."

He nods ahead, and I peer through the large glass windshield of the bus to the road. "This is my stop."

We're in the middle of nowhere. I shoot him a blank look. I thought he was staying at the resort.

"The path here leads to the beach. Would you like to take a stroll with me so we can chat?"

The resort must be at least a half-hour drive away. "Walk?"

He nods, then stands. He holds up a finger at the guide.

"I don't know you?" I rasp.

"I'll answer your questions as best I can if you come with me."

I stand, ignoring my father's voice in the back of my head, and allow my gut instinct to guide me. Generally, it's on point, and I hope this is a time when my intuition doesn't let me down.

The bus slows, and we both walk the aisle. When we reach the guide, he places a mark beside our names on his notepad.

While we wait for the bus to pull to a stop, I reach for my phone and send Yasmine a message.

> I'm with Samuel. Samuel McMahon. Can you google him? He studied at Stanford. We're taking a walk along the beach. See you later!

Before stepping off the bus, I shoot a look toward our guide, hoping he'll remember my face.

Here goes nothing.

When the bus pulls away, I'm met with unruly green overgrowth on both sides of the narrow road.

"Where are we?"

"Not far out of town," he says before we turn onto a dirt path wide enough for a car to navigate despite the green wall of the forest threatening to swallow it up. Apart from the blue strip of sky directly above us, the forest walls impede vision, so I see nothing else.

"Is this someone's land?" Hell, you'd never find a body here. The way the plant life grows, you'd swear it rained steroids.

"It is. I met the owner several years back. He doesn't mind people using this track to the beach so long as you don't trash it."

"Trash it? I think it would win. Digest anything you threw at it."

He chuckles lightly, and damn, it ignites a beautiful emotion deep in my chest.

He picks up a piece of dead wood and smacks the overgrowth, allowing us to pass with ease. The vines are literally freaking me out as I'm torn between second-guessing my decision and simultaneously looking out for snakes and spiders.

"How long is the walk back?"

"Three hours."

What? I glance at my Fitbit. "It will be dark before we get to the resort."

He nods, then directs me to the right when the path forks. The path is narrower, and at times, branches and vines block it. Samuel pins down wayward stems for me to squeeze past. I can hear the ocean, and it's enough to calm my thoughts because the notion of being trapped in this overgrowth is beyond unsettling.

Every time I brush past him, warmth envelops me, melting my fear. This time his eyes connect with mine as I slide past.

"Wait up," he says, smiling. Naturally, I smile back because one thing I've learned is Samuel rarely smiles. "I want to watch your reaction."

"My what?"

Samuel steps ahead of me and pushes another clump of vine aside. I step past onto white sand to meet the ocean. I inhale a deep breath to fill my lungs with clean, salted air. "Wow." I take a few steps and look from left to right—what a sight. The ocean is a bright azure blue meeting white sand, bordered by a green rainforest. Never have I seen anything so beautiful. Untouched.

Samuel points, indicating the direction we'll be walking. "We need to keep moving."

"Because it'll be dark before we arrive back?"

He stares down at me. "And the tide leaves little space to walk."

"Right." I pick up my pace. *Holy shit.* "You didn't think to mention this before?"

He smiles at me. "We'll be fine and maybe have time for a swim."

"I'll wait and see because this tide thing is freaking me out a little."

We keep walking at a steady pace. There is barely a wave, and even from here, the water is transparent in the shallows. The whole setting is serene, yet when I glance up, there is seriousness behind his eyes. "You look like you're carrying the weight of the world on your shoulders."

This man has me curious, and I want to know what's going through his mind.

His gaze is fixed ahead. "Some days, it feels that way," he says in a softer tone.

"Is it your work?"

"Relatively. It's more when I'm not at work I feel the pressure to return."

"Ah, a work-a-holic."

With his eyes trained to the path ahead and a serious expression, he doesn't confirm or deny it.

"Do you work in a hospital?"

"Not anymore."

"A private practice?"

"In a way, yes."

"What state do you practice in?"

"As in the United States?"

I nod. "Where did you say you're from?"

"California."

"I've always wanted to visit LA and San Fran."

"Why?"

I shrug. "It's exciting. I've watched heaps of shows and—"

"Tourists believe it's like what you see on television and in the movies? It partly is, but there's a whole other side."

"It's not exciting to you because you've always lived there."

Samuel drops his backpack and retrieves a water bottle. "Would you like some water?"

"No thanks. I have plenty." I find my bottle while he guzzles several mouthfuls before placing it inside the backpack.

He wipes his brow with the back of his hand before continuing. "Have you always lived in Adelaide?"

I nod. "Apart from a quick trip to Bali, this is my first serious overseas holiday."

He peers at me sideways. "Serious?"

"Well, it's a risk coming to a strange country. We received a shitload of vaccinations. And there's crime and guns and—"

"So not for work. Serious enjoyment." He smiles down at me, and although I'm sensing a touch of sarcasm, I like seeing him smile.

I bump his side with my hip. "Enjoyment is a serious matter, don't you think?"

Our eyes meet. For a few seconds, we allow ourselves to assess each other before he drags his gaze from mine.

"You're yet to explain *why* you're here. So... did you follow me?"

"Since I was here first, I don't believe it's following you."

"You knew I was coming. Don't make me categorize this as stalking."

He chuckles. "Fine."

"After Rio, what changed your mind?" I quicken the next few steps, so I'm ahead of him, then turn and walk backward so I can observe his expression as he answers.

He slows the pace. "What is it you want to hear?"

"I don't want you to tell me what I want to hear. I want to know what changed for you?"

He glances to the ocean as though it holds answers.

I slow up, and it forces him to stop in front of me. "No lies," I whisper, and our gazes meet once more.

He takes a step forward, and I lengthen my neck to maintain our connection. We're so close, his breath tickles my face. "You've been under my skin since Salvador."

It's a moment of weakness, a moment when he should kiss me, only he steps back.

"You make me sound like I'm an irritation."

He chuckles. "You have a way with words. Unfortunately, if we don't keep moving, we'll be forced to leave the beach." His hand lifts to caress my cheek. I close my eyes and take pleasure in his touch for a brief moment and tilt my head toward his hand before opening my eyes. "A little further, and we'll reach a bay. There we can swim. And chat." He turns, links his fingers with mine, and like that, we're walking hand in hand.

It surprises me since only hours ago he was guarded. Yet we continue on in silence, and I use the time to mentally prepare more questions.

The coastline changes, and a bay comes into view.

"Over there." He nods ahead. "We'll stop for a rest."

In the distance, the colonial buildings of Ilhéus and residential houses rise from the shoreline. Although I feel somewhat safer, my stomach sinks in disappointment.

The physical attraction I have for him doesn't change the fact that Samuel is a stranger. So why am I breaking my own safety rules and hoping he seduces me?

16

SAMUEL

Gray storm clouds roll in over the ocean, blocking out the blue sky. Samuel considers the possibility of rain since it's not uncommon in the afternoon.

He slows his pace and unlinks his fingers from hers. "We should swim now before twilight."

"Finally. I'm so bloody hot."

Samuel smiles at the sound of her Australian accent, his grin fading when she pulls her tank top over her head and adjusts her bikini top. He notices more than he should since he can't keep his eyes off her body.

After wiggling out of her denim shorts, she runs toward the water. He watches her rear as she rushes off. Her bikini barely leaves anything to his imagination, and the way his body is zinging, it's best he visualizes her in a onesie.

He makes his way to the water. Are onesies still a thing? He has no idea, no idea of where the world sits in the fashion industry. He's in tune with the planet yet out of touch with society. It concerns him if their conversation is guided by modern-day trivial news since he has no idea what's happening and what is current.

Eden dives into a wave, surfaces, and swipes her face. She straightens, and the seawater streams over her curves. "The ocean is different here. Warmer," she says as she wades closer to shore.

He dives beneath a wave. A safe fluid membrane lies between them.

When he surfaces, he feels the pull, caught in her current. It's like she's created her own riptide. She glides closer, barely making a ripple in the water.

Soft hands land on his chest.

"Kiss me. I want you to kiss me," she murmurs. Her hands slide to the back of his neck, and she guides his lips to hers.

For years he's fought the release of what men need, trained his mind not to be tricked by desire and lust.

With her, he feels every sensation tenfold.

He doesn't fight it. He knows the kiss will be different from when she was drunk, even though he remembers how she tasted and how much he wanted to take more.

She moans into his mouth the moment their lips touch. Her kiss is delicate and slow. He follows her lead, and it turns frantic and needy.

Eden cups his face. Her tongue finds his. Her hands slide into his hair and grip the ends. In response, he lifts her until she straddles him.

She gasps as she slides down against the length of him.

He dips beneath the water and adjusts her position so she's not riding his groin. Hell, that will send him over the edge quicker than he could control.

She breaks the kiss, gasps for air, and offers him her neck. He dots kisses along her moist skin. Dizzy with the taste combined with salt, he craves more. Supporting her back, he sucks his way to her breast. His nose moves the flimsy material aside so he can take her breast in his mouth. She moans in pleasure, the sound causing him to thrust against her.

"Yes," she whispers.

He moves to the other breast, her whimpers goading him on. He flicks her nipple with his tongue before taking her breast into his mouth and sucking until she moans, "More."

More.

Samuel chose a secluded beach. The younger version of himself would be on a home run, taking her on the sand. "Not here," he whispers. "I want you to know who I am. And I'm not a guy who has sex with women on a beach."

She leans back. There's sadness in her eyes. "Okay. We'll talk first."

He nods. "We need to make our way to the streets. It'll be dark soon, and I don't want you on the beach."

"I'll be with you."

"You will. I'd be more than happy to spend the night alone with you on the beach, a fire burning, only I wouldn't be getting any sleep."

"You say it like it's a bad thing. What are you afraid of?"

"It's more what you'd be afraid of. Snakes? Thieves? Or if the police found us? This isn't the place."

"The police finding us? Doing what? It sounds like you've thought it through."

He leans in and plants another kiss on her lips. "I have. Unfortunately, we need to leave. Not far ahead, there is a path leading to a quiet street. From there, we can arrange for transport back to the resort."

"And then?" she whispers.

"We'll have dinner and talk."

Yet, in his mind, he has already surrendered to her.

17

EDEN

My stomach tightens when the taxi pulls into the resort. "Give me a half hour to shower," I say quickly. "Wait. What room are you in?"

"Twenty-four. You go ahead. I need to talk to reception about something."

I hesitate.

"Eden, I'll come to your room in twenty."

"I'm in room eight." I let go of his hand and move briskly along the path. Hell, thirty minutes to wash my hair and apply makeup, and what am I going to wear?

I reach for my phone. "Amy, I'm back. Come to my room. I need a dress for dinner," I say, puffing out the words. My heart hasn't slowed since the cave, and now I'm beyond remaining calm.

"Eden, what the hell's going on?"

"I'll explain soon," I say and end the call.

I pull out my key, and before I get a chance to unlock the door, it swings open.

"Girl, what's happening?" Yasmine's brow pulls tight. She steps aside for me to pass.

Bree is standing near my bed, arms folded.

Amy is going through my cupboard. "Nope. Nope. Nope," she says as she pushes dresses aside.

"Yeah, there's not a lot to choose from. I was hoping you had something."

"Hers are undersized and too short for you," Bree adds.

I shrug. "It's *that* kind of dinner. I want to... you know..."

"Impress him?" Bree's eyes round.

"Entice is more the word." I step closer to Amy. "Do you have anything? I don't want to look like... *me*."

Yasmine sits on the bed before me. "Edes, I've spoken to Michael about Samuel. Going by what he said, your clothes are fine. He likes you because you're different. And he's different. Don't overthink this."

"No," I shoot back. My stomach is in knots, and I barely have time to explain. "Tonight, I need to do this. I can't afford to let him 'get away' without knowing... argh, trust me, okay?" I spin back to my closet and throw clothes aside. "I have nothing."

Yasmine strolls to her side of the room and reappears holding one of her dresses on a hanger. "How about this?"

I take it from her and smile. A white, lacy boho dress, ankle-length with a low cleavage cut to the waist. "Perfect."

"I'm hitting the shower. I want to tell you everything except I don't have time. I'm meeting him in a half hour," I say as I head to the bathroom. "I can explain tomorrow."

I shower and wash my hair with mango-scented shampoo and finish in record time. With a towel around my head, I open the bathroom door to find my bed dotted with jewelry. Amy's makeup is spread out on the table.

"We can help." Amy sings. "Since you're the only one with a date tonight, we're all helping to make it perfect."

"And we can chat about what you're getting yourself into," Bree says in warning.

"Bree..." I say, searching for understanding, "... not tonight. Let me enjoy it."

"I googled him like you said," Yasmine says.

"Should I be worried?"

"If you were me, no. But you're you, and—"

"Then I'm not. We'll discuss it tomorrow."

18

SAMUEL

Samuel raises a hand to knock and hesitates when laughter echoes beyond the door. He smiles, liking the sound, taps twice, and hears hushing.

The door opens. His entire body stiffens taking in the sight of her. Her eyes remind him of the Brazilian ocean, framed with long lashes, and the sweeping lines of kohl accentuate her beauty. Straightened blonde locks fall over slim shoulders to caress her breasts.

Breasts.

He pauses a moment too long. He sees the pretty white dress, only his gaze is drawn to her chest.

"Hi." She gives him a knowing smile.

"You look beautiful," he says honestly.

"Thank you. Shall we go?" She pulls the door closed behind her and links her fingers with his.

He glances over her shoulder to the window and nods to her friends peeking through the blinds, then he glances down to his board shorts and polo and feels underdressed beside her. Eden deserves him in a tux. The one he rented and returned to reception in Copacabana. He didn't count on being away this long.

He never saw her coming.

The ultimate distraction.

The ultimate threat.

"Your friends—"

"Can talk to you later. I'm not willing to share you yet. Though it wouldn't surprise me if they rock up at the restaurant." Her fingers tighten around his. "Would it bother you?"

He smiles. "Spying isn't beneath them?"

"Amy would resort to worse." She laughs as though it evokes a memory. His insides tighten with the sound of her laughter.

Parrots zoom past to roost. She ducks as though she's on their radar.

Is she superstitious? Spiritual? What would be her opinion be of him if she knew the truth?

He can't ignore the idea he was meant to find Eden. He closes his eyes, knowing whatever they have will end in a few days, so why does it matter?

Yet he *is* here, with *her,* allowing a male instinct to guide him.

She squeezes his hand, bringing him back. They stroll along the path to the resort's open-air restaurant. It reminds him of his jungle home—his place of belonging with a peaked ceiling and no walls. The breeze flows in from the sea.

The waiter leads them to a small table where they overlook palm trees and the gentle swinging hammocks connecting them.

"I like it here. I mean, I loved Rio, but here I feel more at home."

The breeze catches her fruity scent, and he takes a deeper breath, closing his eyes momentarily. "How long are you staying in Ilhéus?"

She pulls a face and grins. "Your stalking skills disappoint me."

"I didn't plan anything beyond seeing you on the tour. I believed you'd send me away."

Her eyebrows rise. "After telling you how I felt in Rio?"

"You were drinking. We had mutual attraction except..." He shakes his head.

"Are you having second thoughts?"

He holds her gaze. "No."

Her nod is gentle.

There's a sense of caution, which he respects.

"Where are you headed after here?"

Her sentence holds a question as to 'what happens' next. It's subtle and wise to ignore it at the moment. "North."

"Same. We're heading to Margarita Island before Peru."

Samuel nods. "To meet up with Michael, Sean, and Harrison?"

"I was hoping you were also heading there."

He decides on some honesty. She deserves some truth as it may help with understanding when the time comes for him to leave. "My vacation has ended for now. I was heading north to return to work."

"Where?"

"It's not well known."

"Are you working in medicine or doing some work to help pay for your travels around the country?"

He raises a brow.

"You know, like bar work or living in backpacker quarters."

He stifles a chuckle. "No. This is medical work and with..." he pauses, "... another scientist."

Further explanation is saved when the waiter approaches to take their order.

Eden picks up the menu and points. "This pizza is amazing." She smiles at the waiter before her mesmerizing eyes meet Samuel's. "Have you eaten here? I can vouch for the wood-fired pizza. Best in the world, in my opinion."

"Sim." The waiter grins. *Yes.*

Samuel nods at the waiter and raises two fingers. "Make it two since the lady recommends it."

"It's a safe choice. Some things I'm just not ready to try. Although, all the fresh fruit and vegetables are fine."

Samuel takes a mouthful of water. "What foods have you tried and dislike?"

Eden pulls a face. "Cuttlefish in its ink." Her hand goes to her throat. "Amy found a restaurant, and we tried a few dishes like eel stew." She shivers as though the thought repulses her. "I didn't mind those snacks made with cassava flour."

"So, no dishes like buchada?"

She shakes her head.

"It's made of the animal's internal organs."

Her eyes widen. Samuel doesn't react. If she lived like him, would she be open to trying the food he survived on?

"No more talk about food. Tell me about you. Do you play sports? Follow any teams? Are you an artsy guy?" she asks.

"I played basketball in high school. Then my studies became a priority. Although I like to run... I competed in track in college." His physique was suited to long-distance running, and the activity facilitated his hunting skills. "What about you?"

"I played some basketball socially. I was never a sporty person. Although my ex..." she hesitates and meets his gaze. "He played football. I didn't fit into his world."

Hairs rise on the back of Samuel's neck with someone taking advantage of her good heart. "I imagine you'd fit in anywhere. Where is he now?"

She sighs. "In Adelaide working for my father." She rolls her eyes. "He loves Ethan. Hoped we'd end up together." She shakes her head.

Samuel picks up the knife and twirls it in his fingers like it's a spear.

"Even thinking about him makes me angry, and that my father has employed him. But it's a story for another time."

A story Samuel wants to eventually hear.

No. He can't invest in the emotion.

The pizzas arrive.

"What are your plans for the rest of your stay here in Ilhéus?" Samuel asks before taking a bite.

Eden swallows a mouthful of pizza. "What are yours?"

"I asked first."

"Okay... to be with you."

He nods. "Then I'll see you tomorrow."

Eden's gaze flicks over his face. He senses doubt.

"I'll see you tomorrow," he promises. "Tonight, I need sleep as I barely slept last night worrying about today and how you'd react. We have the rest of the week to be together."

It's all he can offer for now.

19

EDEN

"I FIND it weird he has no social media presence," Amy had said last night.

"I find it refreshing," I'd replied, although it did spook me a little, almost to the point he doesn't exist. When Yasmine googled him, the searches popped up from ten years ago detailing his medical achievements at Stanford and around six years ago at a hospital in California. We found images of his father, a renowned hematologist. He possessed the same fair hair and blue eyes as Samuel and an identical browline.

The nerves in my stomach haven't settled at the idea of us sleeping together. Yet I sense him holding back, and it confuses me for most guys I know sprint to third base for a home run.

Even the way he dresses baffles me. From our internet searches, his family has money. Except for the tux he wore to the Copacabana ball, his fashion choice indicates he's barely getting by. I'm not being judgmental, only trying to understand his character.

I step out of the bathroom to Yasmine waking with a weary moan. "So, you're meeting him for breakfast. Then what?"

I shrug. "Last night he mentioned the beach."

Yasmine pushes up onto her elbow. "I can head into the town center, so you have the room to yourself." She offers a smile, although I know she senses my uneasiness.

“No need. He has his own room if it comes down to that.” I turn to the mirror and pull my hair into a messy bun to keep it off my neck. I adjust several strands ignoring the way her eyes study my reflection.

Dressed in denim shorts and a white tank, I leave my friends for the day. And, the night, hopefully.

“Hey,” I say and smile when I meet him on the path outside my room. “How did you sleep?”

He scratches at the whiskers along his jaw. “Not as well as I’d hoped.” He takes my face in his hands and kisses me. Warm, soft lips caress mine, conveying why he didn’t sleep. “You hungry?” he says against my mouth.

A double entendre.

“Always.”

He takes both my hands and gazes down as if our linked hands hold answers. His expression retains anguish behind happiness.

“How cute.” I point to a domestic cat on the path, crouching and staring into the tropical garden.

Samuel releases my hand and steps between bromeliads and leafy heliconias. He bends and scoops up a baby parrot. It squawks and flaps its wings. Samuel envelops it with both hands, the cat meowing. “I’ll take this guy to reception before he’s lunch.”

He strides off, and it takes a moment for me to register and follow. “What’s wrong with it?”

“It looks like it has an injured wing. It may have fallen out of the nest. They can notify an animal rescue shelter.”

“Can I see it?”

He stops, smiles at me, and opens his cupped hands to reveal a calmer chick with blue and green feathers.

I smile and look up at him.

“You go ahead and grab us a table in the restaurant. I’ll meet you there soon.”

After finding a table, I keep looking at the entrance anticipating his arrival, and expecting he’ll do a runner. The warning in my gut tells me not to fall for this guy. This is a holiday romance, and I know it will inevitably end, but my heart is all in ready to embrace the thrill of the ride.

Samuel returns, and we share a platter of exotic fruits.

“Are there any foods you don’t like?” He holds a piece of seriguela between his fingers.

"I love all the exotic fruits here but reluctant to try some of the fish dishes, and battered foods never sit well with me." I scoop pitanga berries onto my plate and pop one in my mouth. "What about you?" I stare at his lips.

With every word coming from his beautiful mouth, I didn't hear a word he says. I'm mesmerized by watching him. He has to be one of the most handsome men I have ever met in my life. Points to him for acting like a gentleman by getting to know me better before wanting to get me between the sheets. Only I'm dizzy with the pent-up need inside of me and wish he'd take it down a notch because all I want to do is fast forward to tonight.

WE HEAD to the beach and lie side by side on a mandala towel. I'm supposed to be relaxing under the sun, only every cell is on fire being this close to Samuel. I sneak glances at his rippled abs. Our fingers brush, and the zing shoots to my toes. I trace the contour of his sternum, and I can't help ogling his bare, broad chest and defined shoulders. I visualize those arms framing me. I run my fingertips lower and rest my hand on his taut stomach.

His eyes meet mine with the familiarity of someone who knows what the other person is thinking. A hunger burns behind his blue hues. "I'm going to take a swim," he rasps. I follow him into the water, wading through calm seas until I reach him.

"Come here." Without hesitation, he pulls me into his arms. Large hands cup my face. "I want you so much it's nearly killing me."

My chest flutters hearing words I've longed to hear. "Then why are we waiting?" I whisper.

"To be sure."

"Sure of what?"

"We're doing the right thing."

The right thing?

I'm not going to say *it's just sex* because, for me, it won't be. I've never been that girl. Yet, he's bringing out a different side of me.

"Does this feel right?" My mouth hovers close to his. Our eyes connect one last time until our lips touch. It was going to be a gentle kiss.

In seconds, he switches to wildfire, the kiss broken with breathy gasps, and we can't get enough of each other. He tastes of saltwater and the sweet melon he ate earlier. "We need to leave," I moan against his lips. "Take me to your room."

"I'm going to take you in my room," he says. "All of you." His fingers link with mine as he leads me out of the water.

We collect our belongings from the sand and wander along the path lined with coconut palms back to his room. He unlocks the door and dumps everything on the floor where we stand, and kicks the door shut with a bang.

He holds my face in his large hands and kisses me hard. "You're right. This..." he murmurs against my lips, "... feels right."

"You taste like the beach." I lick my lips and savor the saltiness. A taste that will forever remind me of him.

"Taste," he murmurs. "It's another thing for us to explore." He leans over and sucks my neck, my ear lobe, and then my lips are his once more. Our kiss heats up, and I moan against his lips. Samuel pulls away, and a cold space surrounds me. I open my eyes to seek reason, only to find his eyes flicking over my face.

"Eden... I," he stammers. Then he takes my hand and leads me to the bathroom. Samuel steps out of his boardshorts, and I can't look away.

Samuel is gloriously perfect.

All of him.

I strip fast to match his readiness. There's a hint of a smile on those sensual lips. Samuel flicks on the shower and adjusts the water temperature. I step in first and wet my hair. It's cool. A little too cool, and I'm not sure if it's for his benefit.

Under the spray, his hands glide effortlessly over my curves while his mouth tracks along my neck to my breasts.

"You're a beautiful woman," he murmurs against my skin.

"Samuel..." I moan. His name sounds like pleasure the way it rolls off my lips.

He makes a rumbling noise in his throat, and then his fingers caress the spot that yearns for him. Using his shoulders for support, I circle my hips, enjoying every sensation whipping through my body and making me weak at the knees. Right before I come, his lips find mine, smothering a scream, and then my knees buckle at the right moment of pleasure.

The shower turns off.

And I'm awakened from my moment of lust.

A towel is wrapped around me.

Samuel dries quickly.

I should dry off, only I'm still coming out of the haze and questioning why we stopped. This can't be all that's happening? If he gives me the gentleman's speech, I'll lose my shit.

He pulls me close, so I feel his length, and there's no denying he's aroused. I go to drop to my knees, only he stops me.

"We're not done," I say gently.

"I know." His smile reaches his eyes. "I need you in my bed."

He whisks me off my feet and carries me to the wooden framed bed. A slight scream escapes my throat in surprise because I can't remember the last time a man has carried me like this.

I link my arms around his neck and admire his handsome face. The slight dent between his brow deepens. "What is it?" I whisper.

"You." One word, yet I hear the torment.

"I want this." I keep my voice low, but I let him know there's no mistaking my intent.

He lowers me gently to the white sheets, then crawls and hovers over me, his eyes fixed on mine.

"As do I. It's been a while since I've felt the longing of how I want you."

I wiggle my ass down the bed. "So let's not waste another second."

"You make me feel like a young boy again. In, that there are no repercussions."

"Repercussions?" I let out a snort. "I use contraception if that's what you're worried about. And I visited a doctor for a check-up after the last time, which was years ago."

He frowns, then his eyes glaze as though he's lost in his thoughts. What other repercussions is he talking about? Finally, he closes his eyes, and when he opens them, I feel the heat as his gaze tracks over my face.

His lips crush on mine. His hands are between my legs, moving and shaping my body to fit his. He eases into me with gentleness, and yet the air rushes out of my lungs. I moan the first sigh of pleasure of having him inside of me, and as each movement gains momentum, so does my breath. Our breaths and sighs mix with the rhythm of our bodies.

He builds, and the lust climbs higher and higher. "Faster," I moan, almost there. The sound of my heart races in my ears. His pulse races equally with mine—the spot on his neck pulsates with every beat. "Samuel," I cry out, and then my body melts into the sheets as my orgasm waves over me in a delicious sensation.

The dent between his brow deepens as he pumps faster, shudders, and collapses over me. He dots my shoulder with kisses, finding his way to my lips.

The table lamp provides a mellow light, creating a shadow against the wall. I sigh with every touch and kiss as though he has awakened the part of me that has been dormant for over a year.

I never imagined being fulfilled to the point beyond speaking. We catch our breath as Samuel lies beside me. We both stare at the ceiling in quiet appreciation. His hand reaches for mine—a gentle squeeze. "I need to be inside you again," he whispers. "I want to make love to you over and over."

I turn my head, and even the simplest look has electricity sparking between us. "And I don't want you to stop."

Leaning against Samuel's chest, I take his hand and study it. The bathwater has softened his skin. I run my thumb over the whitish outline of calluses on his palm.

"Did I hurt you?" he whispers, dotting my neck with kisses.

I roll over, so my body aligns with his, and my chest is pressed to his. The scented bath water cocoons us. "No. In fact, I'd like these hands to keep exploring." I guide his palm to my rear and crane my neck so our lips meet. "First, tell me what you did to get hands like you've been wielding an ax all your life?"

"Maybe I have," he whispers.

I kiss, then bite his lip. "I'm serious. Can I ask you a question?"

He slides up. Bathwater spills over the edge with the sudden movement. "What do you want to know?" A tell-tale dent forms between his brows.

"Where do you work? I know you have to eventually return, and I want to visit you." I push away to put space between us, hoping I can accurately read his expression.

"Visiting is... difficult. I work in a remote area in Venezuela."

"As a volunteer?"

"Not really, although I do volunteer some of my services."

"What's your favorite thing about it?"

"I'm questioning your employer's credentials. It's clear you can't count."

"This is conversation."

He smiles at me. "More like an interrogation. Hmm, one thing? The waterfalls. Have you heard of Angel Falls?"

I shake my head.

"Maybe you should visit there if you and your friends have time. It's the highest waterfall in the world. The locals know it as Kerepakupai-merú."

"Really?" He pronounces the unusual phonics easily. "And you get to go there often?"

"I try to."

A few seconds pass before I speak again. "Your turn to ask me something."

"One thing? Hardly fair," he says and chuckles. "Although there is one thing not sitting right with me. Why do you allow a past relationship with a douchebag to control the way you see yourself?"

"Sorry?"

He takes both my hands. "The moment you mentioned your ex, something changed in your expression. I saw a glimpse of unhappiness, not for loss of love but more the loss of self-appreciation. What did he do to you?"

"You mean what did I allow him to do to me? I'm a wiser woman now."

"A wise and beautiful woman who deserves much more." He pulls me close and kisses me until I forget what we were talking about.

20

SAMUEL

Samuel holds the lock until he barely hears the click of the door. His gaze shoots to his bed, to Eden lying beneath the white sheet. Her hair splayed over the pillow blends with the crisp cotton. He closes his eyes, remembering last night. Even a day and night with her isn't enough to cure the insatiable desire pumping through his veins.

More than anything, he wants to crawl back under the covers, allow her to ruin him over and over, and remind him what he has sacrificed. Show him paradise. Her paradise.

"You have coffee?"

He nods, coming out of a daze. He goes to her, sits on the bed, and hands her the other cup. "I thought you might need this."

"Thank you." She rises, the sheet slipping. She catches and secures it with a hand under her breasts. The white linen sits low over her tanned breasts revealing enough cleavage for Samuel to lose focus and remember how his mouth had claimed each one equally last night. Or was it this morning? Either way, it's the reason he rose early and hired a Kombi at the receptionist's desk. He needs to get them both out of his room before he loses all coherence.

Every minute spent with her last night sparked something within him to question his future. His commitment. Yet he wants her by his side for every second until his inevitable return.

The Ularans know nothing of selfish ways. He *should* leave. Save them both from heartache. Only the incredible power she wields, or perhaps selfishness on his behalf, is allowing her to control him.

"It's a good brew."

He smiles at her accent. It's thicker on different occasions. "I have a surprise for you today."

Her eyes light up, and his chest expands knowing he gives her happiness. "Tell me."

"It requires you to wear clothes and sneakers. Pack your swimsuit in case."

"In case?" She takes another sip of coffee.

"There's a river you can bathe in after I show you the surprise."

Eden throws back the covers. "I can shower here, and you could join me."

He sucks in air. "I need to make some calls, and you need to be quick as I have a booking at a certain time. If we shower together, it won't be quick."

She smiles, knowing what he infers, then frowns, comprehending. "You have a phone?"

"Doesn't everyone?"

"You never use it. I assumed you borrowed one in Rio."

"I use it when I need to."

She nods as though she's thinking about his words while she slips into her shorts. "I'll head back to my room to freshen up and inform the girls where we're headed. Which is?"

"Nice try."

She giggles, and it fills his heart with warmth. Swiping her key from the table, she says, "I'll be back soon."

It surprises him when she taps on the door twenty minutes later. He assumed most women took longer. He reminds himself Eden isn't most women.

Taking her hand, he guides her to the front of the resort, where a pale blue Kombi awaits. He jingles the keys. "Our ride for the day."

She lets out a little squeal and bounces on the spot.

He chuckles at her reaction. He opens the passenger door and takes her hand as she steps up to the seat.

"Where are we going?" she asks before the keys are in the ignition.

"Did your parents ever explain what a surprise entails in order to keep it one?"

“Of course.” She fiddles with the radio dials, and Brazilian music blares from the small speakers. The sound is distorted except for the signature quick drumbeat, and on cue, Eden wiggles in her seat.

He indicates to pull out onto the road. “For your own safety and mine, I’ll ask you to refrain from dancing.”

She raises her arms and jiggles her chest while tapping her feet. Samuel lets out a sigh and is thankful he hasn’t yet veered onto the road.

Heading south, they pass beachside resorts and endless fields of coconut trees.

“You know I’d hoped to watch the Samba parade with you.”

“I apologize again for my behavior in Rio,” he says. He glances at her and notes her attention is to the window. It reminds him of her sad face a few days ago on the bus tour. “My decisions aren’t rash, and yet sometimes I make bad choices.”

“Sometimes?” She grins, and he hopes it’s to lighten the mood.

With Ilhéus behind them, the scenery changes to the blue ocean on one side and green vegetation on the other.

“If practicing your Samba in the car makes you happy, then do it. I want you to be happy.”

For now, small talk works well between them. He points ahead. “Did you know much of the coastline had thriving cacao farms, and this area was known for producing some of the biggest traders in the world?”

“Do they farm cacao beans now?”

“Not to the same extent.”

“It’s a beautiful country.” She smiles at him and continues humming to the music, their conversation now about the landscape.

“What’s this?” Eden points to the sign ahead, her focus away from their conversation.

He smiles. “Your surprise.” When her eyes light up, so does something inside him.

He thought the Uno Ecopark might bore her. To Samuel, this part of the Atlantic rainforest is similar to his ‘home.’ A sanctuary for wildlife and rich in biodiversity, it’s one of the most endangered ecosystems in the world. He believes the park stands to nurture as does his home village. He told himself it wouldn’t be a test, only now he wants to observe how she reacts to the things he loves.

He takes her hand and leads her into the park to a walkway bridge suspended one hundred feet high among the treetops.

"We're going up there?" Her hand rises to her throat.

"We are. Are you afraid of heights?"

"Now I am..."

"I'll be right beside you."

She looks up to meet his gaze. A tingle forms at the base of his skull and travels down his spine, and like an electric force, shoots to his arms and down his thighs to his toes.

He closes his eyes.

He's falling for her.

"My palms are sweating."

With every step, Eden grips onto the bridge's rope. Netting below her waist is the only thing to stop them from falling through the barrier. The bridge is held by ropes overhead and nearly wide enough for one person. With every step, it sways a little.

Resting his palm on her shoulder, he remains one step behind at all times and reinforces their safety.

"I didn't believe I was afraid of heights until today," she whispers.

"Rest a moment." He points into the distance and places a finger on his lips.

She stares at the green treetops, her expression blank. Samuel wraps his arms around her shoulders, leans in and whispers, "A golden-headed lion tamarin. Do you see it?"

"I do."

"You'll only find them here."

"It's so cute."

He hears the fondness in her voice. Every moment they share, he's learning a little more about Eden. He leans down and kisses the side of her neck, wraps his arms tighter, so her back presses against his chest. Whatever way he holds Eden, she molds into him like a perfect fit. He closes his eyes with contentment filling his core.

Underneath the happiness, he worries she'll consume him, and he'll never want to go back.

21

EDEN

"You're all packed," I say to Yasmine when I arrive back at the resort. Her case is by the door, and the room is the tidiest I've seen it.

"Yep. I'm going to wear this tomorrow." She indicates to her skirt and an off-the-shoulder top.

"Where are you going for dinner?"

"We're heading into town. We didn't think you'd be joining us since it's your last night with Samuel."

Our last night.

"I'm hoping it's not. I intend to talk to him about getting more time off from his work and joining us on Margarita Island."

Yasmine nods. There's something amiss in her expression as though she knows something I don't.

"What?"

"Nothing. I want you to be careful, that's all."

"I am." I file through clothes deciding on what to wear tonight. "I'll chat to you tomorrow because I doubt I'll be coming back here tonight." I throw a wink her way.

"I didn't expect so. Be contactable, okay? We need to leave here by ten."

"I'll pack up my gear now. Tell the girls I'll see them tomorrow."

When the door closes, I throw clothes into my suitcase. Time is scarce, and I need it to prepare myself for the sweetest night with Samuel.

I told him I'd meet him at the restaurant.

When I make my way along the winding path, I can't ignore the thoughts in my head warning me not to get my hopes up. This is only a holiday romance.

I want it to be more.

By the way his eyes sear me when I walk into the restaurant, I know he feels the same way.

"Wow," he says, standing to greet me. "You're stunning."

I give him an easy smile. "What are you drinking?"

"The local beer. What can I order for you?"

"A white wine."

Our conversation remains safe, and we continue to banter about trivial things as though we're catching up like long-lost friends.

Coldplay's "Viva La Vida" sounds through the speaker, and I smile. "I've always loved Coldplay. Watched them perform live in Adelaide."

"A great band."

"What's your favorite song?"

"A "Sky Full of Stars.""

"Same," I say as though we're playing a card game of Snap.

Only his expression is serious. His eyes hold mine captive as though he's searching for more. "Where's your happy place?"

"Depends. There are many places that can relax me. Back home, I love nothing more than sitting out under the Southern Cross and looking up at the stars. No building to block my view, only the sound of the ocean as a reminder I'm not in heaven."

"You live by the ocean?"

I smile, sensing it pleases him. "I do. Have all my life and can't imagine not living there. It has a sense of calm and excitement, depending on the time of day and the seasons."

"I know what you mean."

We're interrupted when our food is delivered.

"What's your favorite food?" Samuel continues.

"Depends," I say with a mouthful of pizza. I wait a moment before answering. "If I go out, I love Greek or Thai. Japanese, too. At home, I snack on avocado and tomato on toast and other times fruit."

"What fruits?"

"Anything really. Depends on what's in season. We have some of the best stone fruits in the country. Apricots are one of my favorites."

"Do you like exotic fruit like acai, pawpaw, and dragon fruit?"

"Absolutely, but they can be expensive. What about you?"

He holds my gaze when he answers, "I live mainly on fruit."

"Ah, that's why you look so fit." His brow pulls tight. It seems he missed the compliment I intended.

The waiter places the dessert menu on the table, and Samuel declines and asks for the bill.

"You don't want dessert?" Damn, I could go for something chocolaty tonight.

"I'll be having dessert in my room." The seriousness behind his eyes has my insides tightening with anticipation.

Dropping the napkin on my plate, I push up from the chair. "Ready when you are."

WALKING hand in hand to his apartment, it seems like we've been together our entire lives. I was meant to take this holiday and find him. Even from the moment I saw him in Salvador, I knew he had come into my life for a reason. My gut tingles with a strange sensation—anticipation and acknowledgment equally. I'll be getting to know him better once we reach his room, only I can't help thinking what happens after tomorrow. I don't want this to be the end of us.

I used to mock people who fell in love at first sight. Lovers who thought they found their soulmate after a couple of dates. I believed they were fools, yet here I am, feeling the same pull of need to be with someone beyond a few weeks. I need more time because after moping around the last eighteen months, I've come all this way to discover someone who's everything I have wanted in a man.

Samuel opens the door and stands aside like the gentleman he is. He follows me into the room, and the door lock clicks. He takes my hand and tugs, so I'm pressed up against him. He kisses my neck and sucks gently on the nape. "So sweet," he murmurs. "One taste, and you could put chocolatiers out of business."

"Ha." I smile at him. I overlook the excitement growing between my thighs for a moment, so I can talk to him before we spend all night making out. "Can I ask you something?"

He pulls away and stares down at me as though he's missed something. "Sure."

"You seem familiar with Venezuela and Peru."

"I have traveled there..." He steps back and gives me a quizzical look. "Why is that?" He pours two glasses of cold water from the fridge and hands me a glass.

"You seem to know the best places to visit, so I hoped you might like to be my personal tour guide?"

His arm freezes with the glass halfway to his lips. "I thought you were going straight to Margarita Island?"

"Well, yes. But with the latest protests, we're avoiding Caracas and instead flying to Guayana City for one night before heading to Margarita Island. I'm hoping you could show us some of the sights and then come with us to the island?"

"Guayana City." The crease relaxes between his brows. "It's the gateway to the tepuis and a great river system. Pity you're not staying longer. You'd love the Angel Falls tour."

My stomach flutters with a window of hope. "If I stayed longer, would you take me?"

"Eden, I—" His lips are on mine. His kiss has me losing my train of thought. Strong arms tighten around me as though he doesn't want to let go. "Let's talk in the morning. I'll glance over my plans then. I don't want to waste tonight with us going back and forth."

"So, you'll try to come to Margarita Island with your friends?" I rasp against his lips.

"I will."

Then his open mouth claims mine. The kiss is needy, and I can't shake the feeling it's a last kiss.

A goodbye.

He walks me back until my knees hit the bed, and I'm lifted onto the mattress, losing my clothes and my thoughts to his passion.

I shiver despite the tropical air basking us in a light film of sweat. His touch is gentle, his eyes unwavering except to study my body in appreciation. Running my hands through his fair hair, I grip the ends and whimper when he sucks on my breast.

He lifts his gaze and stares at me as if he sees me for the first time. "I want you so badly."

I bring my mouth close to his, so we share the same breathing space. "And I want you. Now. So please don't stop."

"I'm not going to stop," he says in a low, deep voice. "In fact, I intend to make love to you all night long."

Everything about him feels so right. We can't end after tonight. When we're together, it's like nothing else in the world matters. The feeling of freedom I have with him is like nothing I've ever experienced, and tonight is even more of a reason to absorb everything he has to offer.

"Fine by me," I murmur and bring his lips to mine.

22

EDEN

As I roll over, my arm reaches out, searching.

It takes a moment for me to acknowledge its morning and the empty space beside me.

I sit up. Like yesterday, I assume Samuel has slipped out to get us morning coffee.

I pad my way across white tiles to the bathroom and notice the absence of his toiletries. I let it absorb for a moment. A heavy feeling grows in my chest. We're both leaving today.

After washing my hands and splashing water on my face, I head back into the bedroom, deciding whether to wait for him in bed or get dressed so we can have breakfast together. The closet door is ajar. I have no idea why, and yet I open it, and every bit of air rushes in and then out of my lungs.

I spin and find no sign of a packed case. "Not again," I moan.

No, this can't be happening.

My heart is thumping in my chest as I open and close every closet. Every drawer. I look to the kitchenette, and on the bench is a note.

My chest tightens, knowing what it says without even reading it. The hopeful side of me whispers it's a note explaining he's getting me a coffee. I read the first line and *hope* can go to hell.

I don't get past the first three lines before I screw up the letter and throw it at the wall. "You bastard," I scream.

A note, a text message—it's all the same.

Gutless.

I dress in the same clothes from last night, grab my clutch and key, and dash out without closing the door behind me.

Passing families on the path as they head to breakfast, I keep my head down and swipe at my tears, hoping I don't look like the fool I am. I swallow down the emotional lump scratching the back of my throat before it explodes inside my chest.

I need my girls.

Then it dawns on me.

Did Yasmine know?

My gaze shoots up to the door in sight, and I run, ignoring strange looks as I gasp for air. In one smooth action, I turn the knob and push the door open with more force than usual.

Yasmine stands from the end of the bed and throws her phone on the crumpled sheets. Her eyes pop, her mouth opens, but she says nothing.

My body trembles in a combination of hurt and anger. I grip the door to balance myself. "Did you know?" The words fall out in accusation.

"What did he say?" she asks. Her voice is calm, yet her eyes tell me otherwise.

I flick the door closed and take a step closer to her. "Did you know?"

"What happened, Edes?" Her voice holds the worry I'm holding in my gut.

I make an exasperated sound in my throat and throw my arms in the air. "He left," I shout. "I mean, what did I expect?"

Yasmine rushes to my side. I stumble, and she wraps both arms around me, guiding me to the bed. She pushes strands of hair away from my eyes, stuck with tears to my cheeks. "What happened?" she says with a familiar warmth that's consoled me many times over the years.

"I woke up, and he was gone. Not even a goodbye." I turn and bury my face into her shoulder and let the tears flow.

"He couldn't, babe. He's fallen for you, too."

"Then why didn't he give me something? Like a phone number, email, anything? Not an *I'm sorry* note."

The door swings open to Bree and Amy mid-conversation.

"Who's up for breakfast?" Bree sings.

Amy stalls. A panicked expression flitters across her face. "What happened? What did he say?"

"Nothing." I run my thumb under my nose and sniff hard. "It's the whole problem. Nothing."

Both girls' gazes flick to Yasmine as if they're waiting for her to say something.

I do the same. "You do know something."

"He left a note," Yasmine says to Amy.

"But you were talking to Michael last night. What did he say?" Amy's voice holds blame.

I gape at Yasmine. "What did he tell you?"

"I'll grab us some coffees from the restaurant," Bree says quickly before leaving the room.

"To be fair, I didn't know what Samuel would do." Her eyes seek understanding because we have always believed in honesty with our friendship. "Michael told me Samuel wasn't joining them on the Island. He never was. And he already pushed limits on his work contract to meet up with you here. In truth, he said he never expected him to come to Ilhéus. Work has always come first for him."

I nod. "And you didn't think to mention it to me?"

"Did you want me to barge into your room last night? C'mon, Edes, you both knew it was your last night together."

I let out a sigh. "You could've warned me."

"It was up to Samuel to tell you. I'm pissed off at him like you are. He should've explained it himself."

"Yasmine's right. He did a shitty thing." Amy tightens one arm around me.

I appreciate their hugs, only it's not enough to numb the pain in my chest.

"And now I'll never know anything more about him," I rasp.

"You could talk to Michael when we get to the island," Amy suggests.

My gut sinks knowing it will be for nothing because Samuel will have already returned to his work. If he wanted to see me again, he'd have mentioned it. I need to let it go and understand it was merely a whirlwind holiday romance.

It's not a simple act of letting it go because I'm furious I had no say in this. He had all the control over how we said goodbye. I hate how he ended us and didn't give me a chance to show him we could try a long-distance *friendship*. Because the idea of never seeing him again cuts through to my fucking soul.

In perfect timing, Bree returns with four coffees. "Girls, we should go check out," she says as she passes us all a disposable cup. I down it in one shot and wish it contained something harder.

"I have to shower first and get his scent off me," I snap.

Bree nods like she's a bloody dashboard doll, her head bobbing continuously.

Under the shower, I let my frustration go. I cry uncontrollably, the water washing away tears of heartbreak. I trusted him to let me go gently, not leave me alone with a fucking note to end us. It's not as bad as the breakup with Ethan, yet it hurts more. I expected more because he acted like a gentleman and not a twit like my ex.

We weren't together-together.

Still, I trusted him to do it right this time since he left me the same way in Rio. My chest heaves with hurt, a stab wound to my heart, and for the first time, I wished I had never met him.

On the drive to the airport, I barely speak.

We board the plane, and I'm seated beside Bree.

I lock away my hand luggage, and before sitting, I lean over the seat and look Yasmine in the eye. "Can you find out from Michael where he works?"

Yasmine nods. "I'll do my best, babe."

She's not to blame, and yet I can't help the anger and disappointment inside me believing she could've probed Michael more since she didn't seem surprised that Samuel up and left me this morning. Is she hiding something? I know Yasmine is good for her word, and if she promised Michael, then there's no way I'll get her to reveal anything without his consent.

I let out a sigh.

It's her relationship with Michael I envy and how she trusts him despite our friendship spanning a decade. I glance out the window and, at the moment, acknowledge I'm the same as her. I trusted Samuel just as quickly as she did Michael, only Michael has proven himself not to be a douchebag like Samuel.

Halfway through the flight, Bree digs into her pouch and holds a crumpled piece of paper folded in an attempt to smooth out creases. "I went to his room. The door was unlocked, and I found this on the floor."

My heart skips a beat, realizing what she's giving me. I look down at the piece of paper.

"I can't." I shake my head. "Not here. Can you hold onto it until I'm ready?"

"Sure." Bree tucks the letter under the top to the pouch holding her passport.

"Did you read it?" I whisper.

Bree's eyes hold mine. "Only the first few lines to make sure I had the right piece of paper." She squeezes my hand, then lets it go.

I look out the window at the clouds. We have begun our descent, and beneath the clouds are vast stretches of green. The tight ball of anger in my chest softens. Rivers are like snakes, winding and dividing the land. I'm filled with an inner calling.

I can't help thinking Samuel is down there.

Somewhere.

The question is, am I capable of letting him go?

23

EDEN

Ciudad Guayana, Bolivar, Venezuela

Guayana City isn't like any other place we've visited. It's a river city with modern architecture and pretty patterned lawns.

We checked in to a Euro Hotel. While the receptionist organized our rooms, I browsed through the rack of brochures on display. It turns out we're in the heart of the city and close to Llovizna Falls. The truth is, regardless of what this city has to offer, I want to stay in my room, be alone, and hide under the covers. I need time to process why I fell hard and fast after months of locking away my heart.

"I hear there's a nightclub downstairs." Yasmine smiles, and I'm aware it's her way of trying to pull me out of a dark place. I smile back at her, and yet it holds no joy. Out of habit, I grab a handful of brochures before following her and the others, who are chatting excitedly about how to spend our two days and one night here.

"I need food," Yasmine says.

"And a swim in the pool," Amy adds.

"What do you have there?" Bree nods at my hand holding the brochures.

"I might go exploring rather than stay in and wallow." I can hear the sarcasm in my voice.

"Cool. Let's get settled, and we can check them out," Bree says, sounding upbeat as we walk into our room next door to Yasmine and Amy's.

I'm checking out the minibar when Bree says, "This is fascinating. Let's head there now."

I spin around to ascertain what it is she's talking about. "Look. Two rivers combine here. The confluence has distinct colors of dark and light. There are heaps of information about the importance of the rivers and a tributary leading to the Amazon."

I smile at Bree's excitement. Science is her thing, and although she took the medical field, she has David Attenborough's passion in her voice when discovering something unusual.

"Now?" I ask.

"Why not? We're not here long, and we can check out Llovizna Falls while we're out."

A waterfall. I smile at her. "Okay. You message the others."

Waterfalls remind me of him, and I'm still hanging onto hope.

The minibar can wait.

WE ARRIVE BACK at the hotel and order a cheeseburger for dinner at the restaurant downstairs. After downing it with a glass of sangria, we head up to our room for the girls to shower. I close my eyes in a false sense of calm while they thicken their lashes and style their hair. They don't question my decision to stay in.

God, what must they think of me?

When the door closes, I rise and head to the minibar. I pour straight scotch into a glass and down it then shiver when it burns my throat. I don't want to think about the next couple of days. The island no longer has the same appeal knowing all three girls will pair up with Samuel's friends.

Yasmine had messaged Michael. He told her Samuel was back working and in an isolated location. He couldn't tell her more other than it involved medical help with an indigenous group.

I pour another shot of scotch and throw it down my throat. I groan, wishing it had the same effect as it seems to in the movies.

I'm drawn to Bree's bed, where she has fanned the brochures over the covers. They showcase beautiful beaches toward the coast, zoos, and a range of botanical gardens. The brochure on Canaima catches my attention—it's a national park south of Ciudad Guayana with tours to Angel Falls.

I stare at the brochure and recognize the name. I read it front to back then repeatedly flick the piece of paper in my hand. What am I thinking? I can't do this tour. It requires at least two days. I can't be traveling south when my group is heading north. And it's Bree's last days before flying home. I shake my head, only I can't stop thinking I need to take this trip.

The letter from Samuel sits on my bedside table. I stare at it, wishing it would burst into flames.

With a quick swipe, I grab it and walk to the corner of the room, slide down the wall, and curl over as though it will help in some way to shield my heart by hating the words he wrote. Tentatively, I unfold the piece of paper.

Eden,

Last night when you drifted off to sleep, I thought about our goodbye kiss. It was difficult to imagine kissing you one last time because I don't want to leave you.

Over the past week, I've thought over and over about how we could make it work, how we could be together. We could if we could visit each other because that's what couples in a long-distance relationship do, right? They survive on phone calls, so they can hear the other's voice until they can see each other again. They plan when they can next visit, depending on their work and finance restrictions.

My work involves a greater depth of limitation when it comes to visits and phone calls. There is no internet service. And visitors are forbidden. I can leave to meet others in a nearby camp, but it's risky, and I'm committed to work for at least another year with no breaks.

I was hopeful until I considered how everything will change when we return to our normal lives. You'll be in Australia and so far away. In another year, so much can change, and I'll be just another memory of your holiday.

I have been awake for hours watching you sleep, and I know I have fallen for you. I want to wake you and hold you, listen to your voice one more time, kiss you one more time, only I can already feel the pain of goodbye. I'd be the source of your pain, and seeing you hurting because of me would crush me even more.

So, I'm choosing to leave quietly. It's the only way even if it means you hating me because I can deal with your anger more than heartache.

Believe me when I say, I'll think of you every day.

You're the best thing that's happened in my life for many, many years.

I hope you'll still want to be friends when I visit Monte Hotels on the esplanade of Glenelg in another year or so...

Yours truly,
Samuel

TEARS FALL, blotting the paper.

He knows where to find me.

Yet it means nothing because my heart hurts with more than the pain of an ended holiday romance and knowing they are just words. He has one thing right. So much can happen in a year, and I'm not going to live with the hope that maybe he'll come find me.

Liar.

Ugh, I'm frustrated he believed leaving quietly would be best for both of us. I shake my head. I know what we had was right, and we could have worked through anything.

Why doesn't he want to be found?

Work commitments—I won't accept it as a reason we can't be together.

My father always said, *if there's a will, there's a way.*

And I have the will.

I need to find the way.

Before boarding the plane to Canaima, I check my yellow fever vaccination certificate is in the back of my wallet. After sending apologetic messages to my friends, I turn off my phone.

Apart from not joining them on Margarita Island, I broke important group rules. I'm traveling alone to somewhere unknown and not on the itinerary in *Venezuela*. In the current economic and political climate, we made rules about staying safe. The risk is now intensified with limited internet and poor communication channels.

No roads lead to Canaima. You can only travel there by plane. And it's the smallest plane I've ever traveled in.

I take in a deep breath and blow air out slowly.

Who the hell am I?

If my father taught me anything, it's to follow through with a plan.

The texts I sent him and my sister are unread—a message informing them I've changed my travel plans and won't be with the girls for a few days. I know exactly what he'll say before hearing or reading his response.

This is the most erratic decision I have ever made. My heart is thumping hard in my chest, and it's not at the sight of the small aircraft as we walk out onto the tarmac with the sun rising on the horizon, ready to board.

At least my friends know where I'm headed if I don't return.

Hell, what am I saying?

I'm following a strong instinct to visit a remote area on the edge of the Amazon jungle. Shit, my father will freak. At least he doesn't know details—only that it's a national park.

I remind myself it's *my* journey.

"Este camino por favor." *This way, please*. A uniformed woman smiles at me. "We're boarding now."

I nod at her before taking a step forward into the unknown.

My sole resource—courage.

Flight time is over thirty minutes.

"I'm doing the right thing," I murmur when we're above the clouds.

The brochures portrayed the landscape below as stunning, and on attempting to peer out the tiny window, I'm hit with nausea and a wave of lightheadedness.

I close my eyes, hold onto the armrest, and pray for the next twenty minutes.

24

EDEN

Canaima National Park, Bolivar, Venezuela

Canaima base camp's dirt landing strip did nothing to reassure me that my decision was a safe one. But a jovial man with a strange English accent greets us, and my erratic heartbeat—matching my decision-making—slows. Maybe it's reassurance in knowing someone here speaks English.

"I'm Victor, and I'm taking some of you to your accommodations." He points to an oversized yellow jeep. For a moment, I'm stunned because the body is painted with large random spots like a jaguar, and we're heading into the wilderness, thus requiring camouflage.

"Eden Monteford."

My name is read out loud, along with a few others. Out of the five passengers on the plane, three of us are staying at the lodge.

We board the jeep. There are no windows or doors. There are four rows of bucket seats, face to face like the other passengers and I will be seated on a train.

I take a seat along with a middle-aged couple.

"What brings you to Canaima?" The woman's broad smile is unwavering.

"It was a last-minute decision. I decided to tick Angel Falls off my bucket list before traveling on to Margarita Island."

"A good decision. I've been waiting years. When we traveled, I promised myself to return and visit Angel Falls. My husband is wary with the political tension, so we avoided Caracas." Her American accent thickens the more she speaks. "Are you taking the aerial view or by foot?"

"Um, by foot." Only option with my budget. "Canoe, I believe."

"Curiara," she corrects. "It's the indigenous term."

"Right."

"Are you taking the Sapo Falls tour?"

"I believe it's part of the package." I shrug.

"Helen." Her partner interrupts, and I turn in the direction he's pointing.

Wow.

Flat-top mountains rise through the vastness of a green forest breaking through the heavy clouds. I've entered an emerald world. It's like the heavens have poured green paint as thick as lava from above, and it has coated everything it touches. As we head closer, a lake comes into view, and our accommodations sit on the edge of the water with the waterfalls in the distance. The jeep slows, and the squawking echoes around us. Birds and monkeys overpower everything else.

I'm fixated by the beauty of the lake blending in with the surrounding landscape and the low-lying fog hovering above the water.

While checking in, we're offered refreshments and informed about the morning tour to the waterfalls and lagoon ride.

Every step toward my room I'm besotted with the beauty of nature surrounding me. I step onto a terracotta-tiled patio that joins each hut, all facing out to the lagoon. A hammock is tied to posts outside the door, an invitation to relax and take in the magnificence. Before unlocking my door, I pause for a moment to take in the view of Canaima Lagoon and the waterfalls in the distance.

My room is nicely decorated and cool despite the humidity. There's no phone, and I have no reception reminding me of our isolation. I change into sneakers, apply Deet because the mosquitoes are already making their presence known, and head to the restaurant for breakfast.

Walking the tropical gardens, I spot a macaw on a low branch. Its head is tilted, watching me, and I it. It hits me how the bird symbolizes paradise, and looking around, I realize I've found it.

BREAKFAST IS a smorgasbord of exotic fruits spanning a table in the dining room. Exotic fruit, one of the things I told Samuel I enjoy, and right now, there are some I fail to identify. Regardless, I try everything. I want to taste every piece of fruit on offer. With every bite, I think about our conversations during our days together, trying to remember if he hinted at where he could be.

A voice brings me back to the room, and our small group is guided to a seated lounge room where we're briefed about the ecology of the area and being mindful of leaving a footprint.

Our host, a local indigenous man, is dressed in cut-off cargo shorts and a loosely buttoned khaki shirt. I'm surprised he's wearing solid boots in this heat. He fiddles with a sturdy broad-brimmed hat in his hand.

"Hello. I Asoo. I ask you respect our culture and land. Twenty thousand Pemón live in Gran Sabana," he explains. Thick lashes frame his dark eyes, his straight black hair is long enough to cover his ears, and his skin is a deep bronze. "Treat environment with care, it's a fragile ecosystem." I nod, barely understanding his pronunciation even though it sounds rehearsed like he's trying to remember the correct words. "Bring your trash back to lodge and dispose appropriately."

The 'respect and be mindful' mantra demands reflection, and I'm already glad I decided to take a risk and explore this area.

Asoo leads those of us on the tour to the lake, and we begin by boarding the *curiara* anchored at the muddy edge of the lagoon. After seeing our mode of transportation, I'm a little nervous. The canoe serves a purpose, and it's not designed for comfort. It's a long, narrow shell of a tree trunk, carved and hollowed out with wooden planks as seats. A portable outboard motor sits at the back of the canoe.

Asoo revs the motor, which sounds more like it belongs on a motorbike, and we jerk backward with the absence of support. With a burst of nervous laughter, I grab hold of the plank of wood under my rear.

We make our way across the lagoon, and I exhale quietly in gratification. The breathtaking scenery alone makes it worth the effort to get here. I'm filled with awe and know *this* is what my soul seeks.

The waterfalls come in full view. In the background, three table-top mountains hover in low-lying clouds. Asoo explains these are tepuis, and the word is from the Pemón language meaning 'House of Gods' significant to Pemón mythology.

We reach the shores of the main island. "Anatoly Island, where the river system splits coming down from the mountains," Asoo says, using his hands to emphasize his words. He nods at me. "My English ... Victor say... rusty."

"You're doing fine," I tell him.

We disembark for a fifteen-minute hike across the savannah to reach the first waterfall. The air is heavier with moisture, and we pass rocks, moist with slime. It's the end of the wet season. Large red ants scurry near the trail, so I tread cautiously and don't know whether to look up or down.

We reach the first waterfall, Sapo Falls. From the top where I stand, it gives me an uninterrupted view down the length of the waterfall.

Asoo instructs us to tread carefully as we take the trail down the side of the waterfall. "Down is another path leading behind waterfall. Everyone wait. Ground slippery."

We follow the wet, rocky path behind the waterfall, and the spray makes visibility difficult. I'm completely soaked, and then I skid in the mud. "Shit." I reach for a rope strung on the side of the path. The man in front of me turns and wipes water from his face.

"Are you okay?"

"Yes," I say and shoot out a nervous giggle. I stop and absorb the energy and acknowledge the water's power as it surges over the cliff. I remind myself why I'm here, remembering only a few days prior how I decided to shed the skin of the old me, take a risk and go on an adventure, and just maybe find a trace of where Samuel is working.

My concentration reverts to the man ahead as I follow him along the path leading to the base of the waterfall and to a small pool of clean water to swim and escape the heat.

"The water safe to drink," Asoo tells us. Still, I opt for the bottled water in my bag.

We move on to the next smaller waterfall. The water is significantly pinker, and I wonder why.

After a quick lunch break of sandwiches, we begin the return journey, retracing our steps and head back to our accommodations.

It's late afternoon when the curiara hits the sandy shore of the resort.

With weary legs, I tread the path and clamber into the hammock on the porch. I close my eyes and simply listen to the constant noise of the jungle. I have no idea how much time passes before the mosquitoes force me to retreat indoors.

After a quick shower, I collapse on the bed, not bothering about dinner. The information about tomorrow's trip to Angel Falls is on the bedside table. I read over it again, paying particular attention to the paragraph on Pemón communities. Dotted on the map are the known communities around the Gran Sabana. I keep reading the lines of *funding by international aid.*

Specifically, *the help of volunteers, medical supplies, and visiting practitioners.*

I sit up and stare out into the distance toward the tepuis.

He's out there.

How in the hell am I going to find him?

25

EDEN

Low in the eastern sky, brushstrokes of yellow, pink, and orange break the horizon. I barely make out the lake for the dark shadows. I follow the silhouettes of a few tourists walking the path toward the main building.

I'm early for my tour, so I take the opportunity to send Amy a message while I'm close to reception to use Wi-Fi. I send a quick text because I don't expect any of my friends to be awake at dawn, especially now that they are on Margarita Island with Samuel's friends.

I'm safe and will call you later.

Seconds later, my phone buzzes in my hand.

"Are you completely insane?" Amy screams into the phone.

"Maybe..." I whisper. "I don't know how to explain it, but something has drawn me to this place."

"Shit, Eden. You have broken all our rules, and I thought you were the responsible one?"

"I'm sorry—"

"Bit late now to apologize. We're worried about you. You shouldn't have gone alone. Why didn't you mention it to me? I could've come with you, for fuck's sake."

"Would you really have come?" I murmur.

There is silence for a few seconds before she responds, "We probably would've talked you out of it."

"Exactly. I can't justify my gut instinct to stay, except there's something about this place I need to explore more."

"Stay? C'mon, Edes, what are you saying?"

"I'm doing another tour today, and then there are these indigenous communities along the river I'd like to visit—"

"You're looking for him, aren't you?"

I let out a sigh. "I might not make it to Machu Picchu, so I'll meet up with you in Arequipa or Lima. Definitely before you get to Iquitos."

"You were the one who was keen to tour Peru. So, you've just wasted your money?"

"It's not about the money, Ames. I'm following my heart."

"I don't know what to say to change your mind. I'm scared for you."

"Don't be. I'm having the best time. It's like I'm meant to be here," I say, now smiling. "I'll keep in touch, but for most of the area, I won't have coverage."

"Have you spoken to anyone else?"

"No. Please tell the girls I'm okay and say goodbye to Bree. I'll call and message when I can. I love you, and I owe you."

"I don't want to end this call not knowing when we'll next meet up." I understand her apprehension, and yet I can't give her an answer until I know myself.

"I'll be in contact and will send the contact details of the lodge in Canaima where I'm staying. They have email and a landline."

"That's hardly reassuring."

"It's all I can offer for now. Bye, Ames. Don't worry, I'm truly fine."

I press the end button and stare at the screen while going over the conversation in my head.

Am I insane?

There's warmth flowing through me as if I have suddenly developed the freedom to be courageous. Holding onto the sensation, I scoop up my pack and follow the path around the lake until I meet at the sandy beach with the other tourists.

A few more travelers had arrived overnight requiring two *curiara's* to transport us. I climb aboard Asoo's boat, taking the same seat position as yesterday.

My backpack is wrapped in plastic and sits at my feet. It contains a bottle of insect repellent, sunscreen, snacks, bottles of water, and a towel along with a change of clothes and shoes. My phone is for the purpose of taking photos. Stuffed at the bottom is a mosquito net in case things don't go to plan. If not viewing Angel Falls by plane, there are two parts to the ground tour. A day trip—my choice—so it will be late when I arrive back at the resort. Others chose to stay the night and sleep in a camp at the base of the falls, not in a hotel but a wall-less hut with hammocks strung from poles. Local Pemón assist the tour guides and provide the traditional dinner and breakfast. In energy-sucking heat, no further bedding is required except a mosquito net. Although I'm taking anti-malarial medication and regularly applying personal repellent loaded with DEET, the mosquitoes and I have already developed a close relationship, and it's one I don't appreciate.

Banter fills the air as we chug across the lake taking a similar route as yesterday. The sun rises, and the sky turns blue, and again, I'm awestruck at the backdrop of three tepuis jutting up through the clouds. The plateau of the flat-top mountain is invisible. Asoo spoke about the myths of these mountains yesterday. Myths aren't what attracts me to this mystical place, and yet there's something eerie, a warning looming in the clouds.

"Are you taking the tour by plane tomorrow?" the woman seated in front of me asks.

"No, only today's tour."

"Are you staying overnight?"

I shake my head.

"I thought most of us were."

I shrug. "I'm on a tight schedule."

She turns to her partner, no doubt realizing I'm of no help. "Did you pack extra snacks and water? I'm not sure I'm going to agree with the food on offer."

I smile at her and consider asking to trade places. Only it's not part of my plan.

We sail into the Mayupa rapids and disembark to cross on foot. Asoo and another helper ride through the rapids to meet us on the other side. Two guides lead us through grassland, a safer journey than trying to navigate the rapids.

We board the curiara and sail upstream. It's more what I imagined in my dreams with thick tree growth bordering the river's edge, overhanging into the water. Walls of green vegetation block the world like a never-ending jail cell locking us into her heart. My trust is now in two strange men to get us safely to our destination regardless of what the river, jungle, or Mother Nature throw at us. There's not a cloud in the sky. We're not fooled after Victor's warning about how weather conditions can turn in the blink of an eye and how downpours can turn calm water into raging currents.

Monkeys howl, and it sounds like an alert to our presence. I'm engrossed, looking beyond the vines choking the branches trying to see one. I imagine snakes, spiders, and scorpions inhabiting the thick growth of the jungle floor and other dangers residing in the trees. I shouldn't be focused on trying to see a monkey. How anyone could survive in the jungle is beyond me. In a moment of truth, I realize the life jackets strapped to our bodies are useless with anaconda, piranha, and dangerous parasites inhabiting the murky water below. All would threaten my safety before I could make it to land. Or have I watched too many horror movies?

We approach a sandy river beach and disembark for morning tea on Orchid Island. Colorful wild orchids line the forest doorway intertwined in the trees and vines. The purple, pink, and white flowers growing near the sandy river beach almost trick me into believing we're in a wonderland. We don't venture far. After a quick break, we board the canoes and continue our journey along the Carrao River. The river forks, and Asoo explains the new route along the Churun River, preparing us for the smaller rapids.

A woman seated at front squeals when the canoe thumps the water while another guide helps navigate the rapids.

"*Auyán-Tepui* is origin of Angel Falls," Asoo says. "Water produced on top of tepui has no land water source. All water comes from clouds and squeezed out of the cloud onto tepui. It pools and feeds all waterfalls."

"Incredible," I murmur.

He shoots a smile over his shoulder before focusing again on navigating through the rapids. "*Pemón* named Angel Falls *Kerepakupai Merú*, waterfall of deepest place."

I remember Samuel telling me this. Could I be on the right track to finding him?

"*Pemón* myths say tepuis are home of gods. The *Mawari* spirits of dead, and people forbidden," he continues.

The mountain is associated with spirits of the dead. Well, that just confirms its eeriness.

The rapids ease, and Asoo signals an end to our river journey. After leaving the canoe behind, we find several man-made base camp shelters, structures where hundreds of hammocks can be hung from its many poles. Asoo had mentioned over five hundred visitors used to come to the waterfall daily. Now it's a handful of people every week. My heart goes out to the people here, knowing from our own family business the importance of tourism for survival.

Unusual flowers reminding me of red luscious lips and orchids line the path as I wander back to the group.

Our small group makes the uphill trek. It's more difficult than I anticipated, and I find myself falling behind, tripping on ribbons of exposed roots and slipping on dead foliage coated in mud. I stop to look ahead, tilting my head to gather my bearings on the steep hill. The largest palms I've ever seen fill any void. Thorned bamboo towers so high it bends at the peak, further growth obstructed by leaves of the taller trees. Small shrubs and new growth sprout everywhere I look. Thorned leaves on vines weave around trunks and branches or dangle down like rope searching to attach and attack anything solid. Yellow moss covers most tree trunks. Dampness thickens the air. I have to take deeper breaths, which worsens the higher we climb. Keeping my gaze low to maintain my balance, I spy mushrooms sprouting beneath the decaying foliage. Even though I'm following the person in front of me, I remind myself to glance up occasionally in case I need to duck away from a web, with what I imagine might contain an abnormally large spider. Ugh. I shudder.

Swiping sweat from my brows, I blink through the salt burning my eyes.

"You stay?" Asoo asks me.

"I can't."

"Omar, my helper, will stay night. I go with you and meet group in morning."

"How do you find your way around here? I mean, everything looks the same."

White teeth glow against his dark skin. "I live here many years. Your home in city scary. I get lost."

I laugh. "We all do at times."

I stop in my tracks before bumping the guy in front. Omar has his hand in the air signaling for us to halt and remain silent. Asoo points to a colorful toucan in a nearby tree. We take more photos before moving on to an unfenced lookout to view the falls.

I let out a sigh of achievement.

With my phone in my hand, I click away admiring the waterfall streaming over the cliff edge more than a mile high, so it's impossible to capture its entirety.

The steep rocky decline leads to Angel's Stream and a pond fed by a second cascade. We moan in unison at the disappointment of the cloud hovering above and blocking our view to the peak. Asoo encourages us to hike down to the pond for a swim, and no one objects in the sweltering heat.

Following Asoo's lead, I scamper down the rocky drop and strip down to a swimsuit, which is now like second nature to wear under clothes. I shower under the second fall and climb slimy rocks to walk behind the cascade. After a swim and feeling significantly cooler, I clamber out of the pond and sit with Asoo.

"It's breathtakingly beautiful. I only came here because a friend recommended it, and I'm glad I took up the offer." We exchange smiles of appreciation. "My friend, he also talked about the Pemón communities around here. Their traditional way of life interests me."

Asoo frowns. "Most have European influence." He gazes up without elaborating, and when I do the same, I'm amazed how the clouds have dispersed, and Angel Falls is now in full view.

"Unbelievable," I whisper. The sheer height of the falls is mind-blowing from the ground.

Asoo and I sit back on the rocks, and in a trance, I realize I'm on the adventure my heart seeks so desperately. It's only now my journey has truly started. I stare at the falls for I have no idea what length of time, and my thoughts drift, wondering if my past has led me to this day. The clouds pass by overhead, slowly thickening, and in a short time, our view is blocked once more, as if white-out has removed everything above the green.

"Eden," Asoo says, bringing my head out of the clouds. "You lucky. You see her beauty. Now, we head back."

The way down, I assume to be quicker, only I slip even more on the tangled roots than I did before. Asoo maintains a good pace, the gap between us widening. By the time we reach our curiara, I'm out of breath. Asoo waits for me to board and pushes the canoe out into the river. I scramble over seats to sit with him at the back and chat while straddling my seat to observe our approach and him because he's been frowning for the past half hour.

"Something is bothering you," I say, more of a statement.

Asoo points to the sun.

I nod. "We don't need to stop for breaks. I have fruit in my backpack."

"My helper say rapids safe. We travel alone."

"If it's faster, then yes. It'll be quicker than me walking."

I turn to admire the view of the river snaking through a never-ending garden. The awareness of danger dissolves with an inner peace of being here in the Amazon. Her gardens are the lungs sustaining all life. I take in a deep breath and smile.

We turn the bend, and Asoo takes a tributary river, the fork disguised by overhanging tree branches narrowing the entrance to twenty feet wide.

If I ever considered my mind and gut could work in unison, it would be now. My thoughts race knowing this isn't our route. He's focused on navigating the canoe, but nothing in his expression hints not to trust him.

Sensing me staring, he nods to a package at his feet. "I deliver parcel to friend."

I draw my gaze from studying his expression to the river ahead. The current is significantly slower with a narrower river and sharper bends. Retrieving my water bottle, I guzzle down a few mouthfuls. Pushing my drink inside, I stumble on my seat at the crack of thunder directly overhead. Asoo shouts in a language I don't understand. Clouds roll and thicken, and it's as though I'm watching a storm on film in fast forward. In a matter of minutes, the skies open and cry heavy tears on us.

The rain pelts my shoulders and back. I'm all for getting wet to cool down, only the sting is like a high-pressure hose.

Asoo points to a small bowl and indicates to bucket it out. I do it quickly with the water pooling around my ankles, not watching ahead.

"Stay low," he warns. I fall forward when the boat hits an embankment. "Stay low."

Before I respond, he's out of the curiara and heading toward a figure. Positioning myself on the seat, I look up to the rainforest surrounding the river's edge except for the narrow bank of sand stretching for approximately one hundred and fifty feet.

I squint through the rain. Asoo has met with a man. He's naked except for something covering his groin. His skin is a golden bronze. Not of indigenous heritage—skin changed by the sun.

I stand and raise a hand to shield my eyes. Like a switch, the rain stops. Blue sky peeks through the gray clouds dispersing as quickly as they formed. My breath hitches on hearing a familiar voice. The boat rocks with my ungraceful moves to clamber to the front. Ignoring Asoo's warning, I jump onto the sand. With every step, the conversation between both men becomes clearer.

Asoo looks sideways and holds up a hand. He's standing several steps away from the man as though it's a safe distance between them.

The stranger's head snaps in my direction.

His eyes pop.

I still.

As though in quicksand and further movement will thwart my safety. My heart pounds in recognition.

Samuel takes a few steps toward me, and I do the same.

I want to run to him. Only my thoughts don't line up.

I want to scream at him for leaving me. Something holds me back.

I'm caught in his gaze, struggling to believe it's him.

Asoo places a hand on my shoulder to turn around, only something in me fights the delirium and refuses to obey.

Samuel shakes his head, bewildered. "How?" he rasps.

"You left me clues," I blurt out.

"Eden, stop," Asoo demands.

I push past him and march through the sand until Samuel's strong hands grab my shoulders, keeping us an arm's distance apart. His gaze roams my face, searching, as though answers will magically appear.

Before he speaks, the branches rustle. An oversized headdress catches my attention first. Red and black grass strung high in a semicircle. One glance, and fear hits me with an unfamiliar world beyond the trees. A long, decorated stick thumps the ground demanding attention. Bones and beads rattle with the force.

"Don't be frightened," Samuel says gently and falls to his knees. "Follow my lead," he whispers, head bowed.

I kneel beside him. "What's happening?" Samuel doesn't look up, only stares at the indigenous man's feet and waits.

"Eden," Asoo shouts from the boat, its motor revving.

Samuel speaks unrecognizable words and sounds.

Peering over my shoulder, I foolishly wave Asoo on. He throws my backpack onto the sand. "I come back tomorrow," he shouts.

"Keep your head down," Samuel instructs.

Long, rough fingers wrap under my chin and tilt my head until I'm forced to look into the eyes of the man before me.

"What do I do?" I whisper.

"Nothing." Samuel glances at us before lowering his gaze once more.

Dark eyes lock with mine. The aging lines around his eyes deepen as he studies me. White paint slashes each cheek. Beneath each slash are shadows of old tattoos. Thin strands of gray hair fall to his shoulders, camouflaged by the grass and feathers framing his face. He speaks words not intended for me.

Samuel responds, and my chin is set free.

"Follow me."

The man waits while Samuel leads me to a small A-frame structure made of branches and palm leaves. Samuel glances over his shoulder. I don't need to look to know we're being observed. I sense it, along with Samuel's concern. I take his hips, wanting to pull him close. His hands land on my shoulders, firm enough to keep us apart.

Worry lines crease at the corners of his eyes. "Remain here until I come for you."

He bends and scoops up his backpack and the package, and walks toward the man. I'm a little stunned as to what's happened. Yet I can't pull my gaze from his near-naked body as he walks barefoot over the sand. When he reaches the native American, they disappear into the trees.

I cough after inhaling the smoke from a small fire. Near it is a canopy of dried palm fronds, and it's high enough not to catch alight. It protects the flame somewhat from the downpour of rain, although the fire smokes as if rain has seeped in. Wood is piled under the cover, so I place another chunk on to burn. Not because I'm cold, but more to warn off insects and other things I don't want to think about.

The sun is getting low. I have no idea where Samuel has gone and how long I'm to wait here. I remember my backpack and sprint down to the water's edge to retrieve it. I stare toward the direction Asoo traveled in. There is no sign of him or anyone else. Monkeys howl in the trees above. Insects screech with impending nightfall. I unwrap the wet plastic from my backpack and shake it to rid it of the water.

Under the shelter, there's a hammock and a log. Then I notice string tied to a stick and fish bones scattered in the dirt. Beside the bones are pieces of dried skin from some type of fruit or vegetable. Through the branches, a vine grows bearing fruit reminding me of passionfruit. Knocking the vines and branches aside, I take a few steps into the overgrowth checking for webs and other creatures living in the trees. After choosing several pieces, I retreat and take a seat on a log under the shelter. There's a sense of safety here in the clearing where I'm able to observe my surroundings. Splitting the fruit with my nail, I break it in half. The yellow flesh with black seeds is familiar and safe. It's sweet. With every mouthful, I gaze up into the distance awaiting Samuel's return.

More time passes.

I stand, pace, glance to the river, and allow reality to set in.

I found him. No matter what joy and accomplishment I feel, I acknowledge this is his place of work.

The place he tried to keep a secret.

Going by his lack of clothes and the strange man's tribal headgear, this isn't one of the Pemón communities Asoo had mentioned.

Asoo. My gut tightens remembering his hasty exit and how overwhelmed I was with finding Samuel to care.

Sticks snap, and I look beyond the trees.

"Who's there?" I shout.

Did I expect anyone to answer?

Visibility is poor through the maze of green and failing light. I kneel behind the small fire, peer through the smoke, and add a few more pieces of wood, not wanting the flame to burn out.

My chest tightens.

Don't be scared. You are fine. Samuel knows you're here. You're not alone. My thoughts steamroll like a checklist accounting for my actions. *Shit.* There was no kiss. In my head, I deliberated how I'd react when I saw him and contemplated the million questions I had. Mostly, I imagined the kiss.

What if he doesn't return?

And what was with him falling to his knees bowing to the strange man like he was some kind of god?

I turn to the hammock. Is this where he's been sleeping?

I reach for my water bottle. My hand trembles, and water dribbles from the side of my mouth as I gulp down mouthfuls, trying to swallow the dry lump in the back of my throat.

Yes, I found him, and he's disappeared, again.

The reality is night is falling, and I'm *alone* in the middle of the damn jungle.

26

SAMUEL

Ulara

BEYOND THE HUT, Samuel looks to the leaves glistening under the moonlight shining through the tree canopy. Trapped droplets from the rain shine like tiny diamonds, the rainforest's unique jewelry store. His surroundings have always calmed him, only tonight he feels something else.

Samuel places a gloved hand on the young girl's forehead. She groans and rolls over crinkling the twine mat beneath her as she does. Her fever is easing. The shaman had spent hours grinding plants for her medicine and placing wet palms on her body. Occasionally, their medicine fails, and that's when the shaman asks for Samuel's help. A seizure caused the shaman to panic. His niece's daughter has never suffered seizures in the past.

A simple over-the-counter Western medication eases her temperature. It doesn't help with knowing the cause, though. He expects a bad gastric virus, hopes it's not measles as it would mean community transmission. The latter is of concern because the village is hidden from the rest of the world.

Until he speaks further with her family to account for the past week's activities, he can only treat her symptoms.

Samuel stands when one of the Ularan warriors approaches his hut.

He creeps out and nods to the young man. He has estimated his age to be around twenty, and he's yet to find a wife. Rare, as most men here find a partner after initiation—a celebration when a boy becomes a man. Samuel assumes Tïmenneng wants to learn from the shaman. He hopes he doesn't take a page from Samuel's book—thirty-two years and no partner. The shaman has no partner, a pattern of devotion. And yet, the shaman has a daughter. Samuel has never asked about her mother. Asking is taboo. One day he expects the shaman will tell him the story, like many other stories he's privileged to hear.

Samuel speaks to him in the language the Ularans understand, a dialect similar to Pemón.

"Safe?" he asks in their native tongue. The dialect is clear even with the mask covering his mouth and nose for their protection. He couldn't be more thankful for a bright moon, knowing Eden is alone.

Tïmenneng tells him Eden sleeps. The other warrior, Wayara, remains on watch, hiding in the rainforest, a request by Samuel to the chief after the shaman requested the girl to remain.

He didn't expect it. He'd been overwhelmed at the moment. His heart had been torn, wanting to speak to her and ask her to leave, for she didn't belong. No matter how he feels about Eden, the latter is the truth. The shaman had surprised him by permitting her to spend a few days but only on the outskirts of their community. Maybe the shaman sensed what she meant to him or if he rewarded Samuel for returning and required his immediate help. Could the shaman's dealing with Eden's arrival be a rash decision? He didn't believe it. The shaman never acted on impulse.

"Is she afraid?" he asks.

The warrior remains silent, a strange word to them. Their world knows only personal growth, along with survival and acceptance, mostly coming to peace with your inner emotion and thoughts. Her isolation is a health and safety measure and a test. One Eden was unprepared for.

Her safety is what matters.

Samuel nods to dismiss the young warrior before returning to the young girl's side.

On first arriving in the village, Samuel learned his social status. His family's wealth and expensive college education were insignificant to the people and useless as a means of survival.

Eden will also learn her place.

Time isn't regarded here in the same way it is in the outside world. There are no clocks—only the sun and moon to guide hours, days, and years. Yet the tick-tock of the clock fills Samuel's head with how much time he can spend with Eden.

Never has he expected any woman to live the way he has chosen. His gut tightens fighting desire- fueled thoughts, threatening all logic. Eden *can't* be here. Yet his imagination fills with hope of her staying longer than a few days.

Gathering his thoughts, he checks the niece once more before taking a mat near the far wall to get a few hours' sleep.

A WHIMPER WAKES HIM, and shards of sunlight streak through the trees.

The young girl is sitting, holding her stomach. Her mother stands outside the hut, her dark brown eyes plead to his. He nods for her to enter and stand at her daughter's side. The niece indicates she's hungry. Samuel smiles. He was told for many days she has suffered and not eaten. Last night was the second seizure. After administering an antispasmodic medication, he suspects the worst is over, and their indigenous medicine can replenish her energy.

He tells the mother she's to remain here for another day. The mother can feed her tea and *oo*—cassava bread made from yuca—and remain by her side. He points out the wooden bowl of water for her hands.

Samuel leaves them alone and makes his way to a nearby stream to wash before visiting the shaman and chief. It will give him time to consider his words when asking the chief to grant Eden a longer stay.

He doesn't want to think about the alternative and if he's refused permission to see her again.

27

EDEN

I ROLL ONTO MY SIDE, curl into a ball, and continue dreaming. Only this morning a slight roll causes the bed to sway beneath me. I jerk up remembering where I am. In the process, I tangle my arms and legs in the mosquito net wrapped around me. Alerted to buzzing above, I kick harder to untangle myself, forcing my eyes open and to focus.

"Oomph. Oh, for God's sake," I say when I land on the ground. I bounce back up onto my feet, shove the net aside, and look around me for anything crawling at my feet.

Rubbing my eyes, I groan and stretch out the kinks in my back. I had more energy and got more sleep after a hard night of partying than I did last night. Stumbling across the sand, I head to the river, scoop handfuls of water and wash my face. I stand and search the river bend for any signs of life. I'm grateful for the absence of movement in the river in the form of *caiman*, a smaller alligator found in these parts because that would send me over the edge.

Birds squawk high in the trees, and the monkeys squeal. I quickly glance over my shoulder to the vines and strangler figs choking the trees. The river divides the jungle's domination apart from the stretch of sand below my socked feet. I can't help my overwhelming sensation of vulnerability and consider how many souls are lost in here. The water before me isn't so much an escape—rather a potential death trap misleading you as a path out. No one knows what lies in those muddy depths.

"Why did I allow Asoo to leave me here?" I mutter. Oh, that's right, for the man who left me alone *all* night in the wilderness with nothing more than a smoldering fire.

"Why am I so surprised?" I say with sarcasm.

My stomach growls needing food, preferably the type prepared and ready to eat. Already I'm missing the luxury of Uber Eats—even a fast-food drive-through seems like a treat. Unzipping my backpack, I pull out nut snacks, a banana, and my anti-malarial meds. I take a tablet and guzzle water from my spare bottle, then peel down the banana skin and savor every piece then I head back into the forest edge to pick more.

Standing beside the vine, I'm on alert for bugs near my feet or movement above. I snap off a piece, then gaze ahead past the foliage while splitting the skin. I feel like I'm in a tunnel, the vegetation surrounding me is so thick. Yet through the web of green, I spy a man. Dark hair catches my eye first. It's cut like a basin framing his face. His skin blends with the rotting leaves on the forest floor. Strangely, I'm not alarmed, only aware. He's grasping a stick to balance, or it could be a spear. Squatting on his heels, he's as still as the tree trunks surrounding him. I have no idea how long he's been watching me. I recall Samuel telling me not to be afraid, so I take a tentative step toward him and then another.

He doesn't move until I take a few more steps, winding a path around trees until we make eye contact. His long legs uncurl in a slow, controlled movement. He holds his ground, maintaining his stance the closer I come. Then he shoves his stick forward, the base remaining on the ground. I'm not sure if it's for his protection or in warning.

"Where's Samuel?" I ask in a low voice. "Samuel," I repeat when he says nothing.

The piece of wood rises. He pulls out a small spear from his grass skirt. It's the size of a dart, and he places it in the hollow opening and blows hard. I shriek and jump on hearing a thump behind me. The man runs past me. A huge snake slithers on the ground, and I scream as loud as my lungs will allow. The native American drops to his knees, hands over his ears before turning wide-eyed to stare at me. I'm still panting when he snaps the head of the snake, and its long body falls limp.

Gathering the length of it, he slings the creature over his shoulder. Words stick in my throat as a vile taste coats my tongue. Without thinking, I run, pushing vines out of my path to my camp and sit by the smoking fire.

"Eden." Samuel runs toward me from further along the river, and I sprint to him. He takes me in his arms and holds me close. Stroking my hair, he whispers, "What happened?"

"A snake," I croak. I point toward the trees and hold back the tears threatening to undo me. I thump his chest in blame. "Why did you leave me here alone?"

His expression wears the same sleepless mask as mine. "There was no other way."

"I was afraid," I rasp.

"I know," he says, stroking my hair.

"Iwoi." *Snake.* The indigenous man appears wearing the reptile wrapped around his shoulders like a necklace and a wide smile.

"I see you've met Wayara. He watched over you all night."

I cringe knowing there were times I had to pee, and unaccustomed to bush squatting, I removed my shorts to do so. "Where did you go?"

He takes my hand and leads me to the place I slept, and Wayara follows. He points to the fire, and Wayara throws the snake in the cinders.

"First, we eat."

"The snake?"

"You'll be surprised by the taste."

My hand rises to my mouth. If I ever considered being a vegetarian, now is the time to speak up. In perfect time, my stomach grumbles.

"Pretend it's chicken. You'll need the energy."

HUNGER CAN PROVIDE the mental strength of visualization of what I wouldn't even attempt under normal circumstances. Choosing an alternative on a menu isn't an option here, so tricking my mind into believing I'm eating chicken is easier than I thought.

Sharing a meal of smoked snake with Wayara and Samuel, dirt on my face, my rear on a log, is far from any version of glamping I had previously imagined.

Wayara stands, and Samuel nods. “He needs to return to the village,” Samuel tells me.

For a brief moment, I anticipate we’ll have some time together to talk.

“I have to go with him, explain to the chief that Wayara has been in contact with you, although not closer than five feet. And I need to check on someone.”

I glance down at my crinkled clothing. His words startle me as though I’m dirty and contagious. The men stand, and I do the same with only the fire dividing us.

“Please don’t leave me again?” I plead.

He stops, and his brow furrows. “I’ll be back soon. Does it help to know someone is always watching?”

I look toward the trees. “In a way…” I’m confused and have no idea what I’m doing.

“Did you bring repellent?”

“Yes, and I’ve enough Doxycycline to last me a while.”

“Good.”

It’s his final word before both men run into the forest and disappear beyond the skyscraper trees.

“Wait. Why do you want to know?” I call out. High in the trees, the monkeys shriek and drone out my voice. “What am I supposed to do now?” I shout to the forest and then plonk my rear back on the piece of log with a huff.

28

SAMUEL

"Oko Weju." *Two suns.*

On bent knees, Samuel closes his eyes and quietly thanks the universe.

The chief has granted her another two days but no contact with the Ularans.

Samuel lifts his chin and meets the chief's gaze. Deep wrinkles exacerbate the scowl in his expression. His reasons for not wanting Eden to stay are understandable. For anyone else, he'd send them away.

Wings take flight in his stomach, and he pushes through the excitement to find reason. What does a few more days achieve? She cannot stay—wouldn't *want* to stay. And he can't *be* with her. Unmarried and sleeping together, he'd risk banishment.

Scarlet, hyacinth blue, and yellow feathers of the macaw point up to the heavens, secured by an embroidered band around the chief's crown. Red paint slashes his cheeks and dots his nose and chin. The dotting art continues along his bare arms, chest, and midriff.

Trophies in the form of teeth hang around his neck. There are several strands, including some from caiman and jaguar. The size of the incisors indicates a larger breed. Samuel has no doubt the chief himself won a battle with each.

What surprises him is the shaman's support. He senses fear, as with any outsider, there's the risk of disease, including yellow fever. Any virus is a threat when there is no built-up immunity in a community. The Ularans avoided the Spanish invasion and associated diseases. The original village resided deeper in the jungle. The decision to migrate was made because of tribal war before the shaman was born. The newer community remaining untouched thanks to the mountains and the hidden waterways behind the village to hide. In southeast Venezuela, myths of their folklore hold warning, and fear has kept intruders out.

Samuel rises to his feet and brushes dirt from his knees and then from his hands. The shaman watches him with intrigue. Since his arrival, and after proving his worth in a useful element to the shaman, Samuel has emphasized the importance of clean hands and wound care. His ways still fascinate the shaman. One scratch from a vine has infection potential. The Ularans have a plant for almost every ailment, except the common cold, a virus that could kill many.

The thought takes Samuel back to Eden in quarantine. He can't see her tonight with the first of many celebrations in preparation for their upcoming expedition. A special dinner and sacrifice to ask the gods for a safe passage and return and to find the plant Samuel seeks. The journey will begin in several days on the next full moon phase to light the jungle at night.

The shaman gives Samuel a knowing look. Samuel bows his head to both the shaman and the chief before following the shaman to the outskirts of the village and into the rainforest, keeping a safe distance between them.

They walk a short distance before vines, trees, and low vegetation engulf every space. To an outsider, it's a jungle requiring a machete to make a path. To the shaman, it's a medicine cabinet where every plant is beneficial to his people.

Today the shaman's entire face is painted white. The horizontal lines over his chest remind Samuel of an x-ray exposing ribs. The shaman's long thin fingers reach out and touch a vine growing abundantly among the trees, the vine, the mother of all healing plants.

To the Ularans, ayahuasca is a plant that heals the body and cleanses the blood. In order to heal, the mind must be open and cleansed of past traumas and emotions to allow the body and mind to work in unison in healing. For this to happen, the third-eye chakra needs to be open, to experience a celestial realm. Ayahuasca is controversial in the Western world, and yet it's part of the Ularan existence.

Samuel refused the ceremony ayahuasca for many months. A scientist and non-believer, he tried other healing plants on himself and on the younger children with good effect. When a child in his care nearly died, and the shaman introduced the same medicinal plants with the help of ayahuasca, he witnessed a miracle—an understanding as to how it opens the body's energy for other medicinal plants to have a purer effect.

Tonight, the warriors will drink the brew made from the vine. Samuel's body remains *poisoned* by the Western society foods after his trip to see his friends, and he needs to detoxify before drinking it in a shamanic ceremony.

The shaman cuts the ayahuasca vine and the chacruna plant and sings a harmonic tune in words Samuel is yet to understand. He comprehends words of gratitude and hope, and Samuel quietly thanks the vine. The spiritual power astounds Samuel, and over the years accepts that some things can't be explained.

The rumbling of a motor carries through the trees. The shaman gives Samuel a nod, and he dashes toward the river, surmising Asoo has returned to check on Eden. When he reaches the forest edge, he remains behind a rubber tree and listens to their conversation before making his presence known.

"Did you spend night here?"

Eden stands near the boat. Her backpack remains under the shelter. He lets go of the air in his chest.

"I did. Not as scary as it sounds."

Asoo chuckles. "You're acquainted with the jungle."

"Not really. I'm to wait here for Samuel."

"For how long?"

She shrugs. "We haven't had much of a chance to speak. I guess I can go with him soon."

"Where?"

"To the village where he works."

Asoo shakes his head vehemently. "Ulara no place for you. Come to Canaima." He holds out his hand for her to climb aboard.

Panic tightens Samuel's chest, so he steps out from the trees.

"Eden. Wait."

29

EDEN

"SHE'LL BE safe here with me." Samuel gives Asoo a stern look. Something passes between them—a silent warning.

"Why wouldn't I be safe?" I ask Asoo.

"Will she stay with you?" Asoo asks Samuel.

Samuel frowns at him. "I'll look after her."

Asoo nods. "Then I return tomorrow."

"Thank you, Asoo. I appreciate it," I say quickly.

It will give me time with Samuel before returning to Canaima and contacting my friends to check in before making alternative arrangements to travel to Peru.

I remain on the bank and watch Asoo's curiara sail away. I'm not sure I made the right decision, but I didn't come all this way not to discuss *us* with him. Turning to Samuel, I ask, "Am I safe here?"

"As long as you follow the rules."

Rules?

"You left me alone. How did you know I was safe? And don't say you had those men watching me. They don't understand English, so how could they know if I was in trouble?"

"They have eyes and ears, Eden."

I dig my fists into my hips. "Oh, please. They don't know what I'm feeling. Or how scared I am. What if I ate the wrong thing and was poisoned? Or a snake or spider snuck into my shelter? They are too far away to see it. I don't want to be here alone."

He leads me into the rainforest to the place I picked the passion fruit. He points to several trees bearing berries and fruit. "You can eat these. It's safe to wander here."

Stepping over mangled tree roots, I follow him to a vine choking a tree.

"This is poisonous." He points to a shoot dangling from the branches high in the canopy, searching for another host. "The spikes can make you ill within minutes. Even the tiniest scratch can cause severe vomiting and diarrhea. Please watch where you're walking."

I want to plead my case. This is a reason not to leave me alone, but it raises another concern—the lack of bathrooms. Pee squats are fine, only the day is ticking on. "And if I were to become sick?" I cough. "As in requiring extra assistance in hygiene..."

His lips curl up. "The jungle garden has everything you need."

We backtrack toward the river and then off to the side, and he points out two plants growing near the bank. "This one." He picks a leaf and hands it to me. It's soft and wide enough to use like paper. "You can squat in the river downstream or find a rock to dig a hole."

"What?"

"I usually pick a few leaves and have them ready, so I don't need to go searching."

I cringe, ignoring his smirk.

"This plant." He picks a leaf, and I follow him into the shallows. "Wet your hands and rub it between your palms."

The leaf foams, my hands filling with a forest fragrance. "Amazing," I say before washing the foam from my hands.

He heads toward my shelter, and I'm quick to follow. I watch as he adds another log to the fire. "Keep the fire burning at all times."

I nod.

"And keep up your repellent spray and malaria meds."

I nod again.

"Can you fish?"

I tilt my head at him.

"I'll teach you."

"What? No. Not now. I just want to be with you. Talk to you. Why aren't you taking me to your village where you work?"

A muscle ticks in his jaw. He looks to the river. "It's not that simple." He bends to pick up a long stick with an attached line lying in the dirt under the shelter. He unravels the line, muscles contracting in his forearms. "Come."

I follow him down to the river. "Why are you showing me this. You're going to be with me, right?"

"In the jungle, everyone needs to be capable and self-sufficient. You need to know what it takes to survive." He points to where I slept the night. "I weaved the hammock where you sleep. I constructed the shelter that protects you, started the fire, and chopped the wood to burn. There is an abundance of fruit to pick. The river provides a source of protein, and the forest a source of water. I'll teach you how to get both."

I gape at him. Is this how he lives?

I'm not sure what I expected, but it wasn't this. Not luxury but hell, he's talking about survival tactics. "You told Asoo I'd be safe," I rasp.

"And you will be. You need to learn how to stay safe."

"You're talking as though I'll be alone again tonight."

"I keep a few things here." Samuel unhooks some netting from one of the bamboo poles and focuses on attaching it to the line. He walks a short distance to some shrubs and grabs some sort of large beetle. Eww. He traps it in the net and throws it out into the water. I watch in curiosity before realizing what his silence means.

"Are you bloody serious?"

"There are rules I need to explain after I show you how to catch your food."

I want to scream at him and ask him why he wanted me to stay. Instead, I stomp up the sand to the shelter, grab my bag, and secure the strap over my shoulder. Samuel watches me for a few seconds before turning his focus to the water.

A ball of frustration grows inside me with him ignoring my little spit by continuing to fish.

We both know I'm incapable of going anywhere.

Dropping my backpack, I sit on a log by the fire. There's barely a flame. Only hot embers smoke. After finding a smaller branch, I place it on top of the others, watch the flame build as blue fingers wrap around the wood, and smoke dances and twirls toward the sky. The longer I watch, the slower my breathing becomes.

What did I expect?

Admittedly, I had no expectation—only to find Samuel.

Naïve *and* stupid, really.

Dammit. I shouldn't have devoured all the fruit. I need a restroom without an audience.

I stride forward to stand beside him and look out to the river to where his gaze lands.

"What were you saying about the restroom services here?"

He gives me a sideways glance and points down river. "Follow the river for thirty yards. You'll find the same plants growing there I showed you, and you're screened more so than here."

I nod and scurry off, picking some of the wide, soft leaves on my way.

Removing my shorts, underwear, socks, and shoes, I wade into the shallows and squat, all while focusing on the trees before me and checking behind me for anything untoward in the river. Nerves could slow the process, so I praise the jungle garden.

The leaves are soft, I muse before tossing each one into the river.

Finding the foaming plant, I pick a few and wander back to wash my hands.

I hear giggling and freeze. Thankfully, it's not at me. Two children frolic in the water, splashing each other in the shallows. I take a few steps closer and hide behind a bush to dress.

Black hair is cut around their mocha faces, which are dotted with red paint. Naked, the kids play without concern. I smile, hearing their excitement, and yet I'm unable to comprehend a single word they say. Nevertheless, their smiles and laughter tell all.

I push through the low foliage along the embankment to Samuel standing by the fire. Tiny fish on the palm leaves are cooking in the embers.

He smiles without looking at me. "Found the way okay?"

"I did. And saw some children playing in the river."

His gaze shoots up.

"I didn't approach them."

He nods and points to a log opposite him. "Take a seat. It's time we talk."

"Finally," I huff. "Because you're sending mixed messages. I hoped you'd be happy to see me. Be surprised, and, well, a little impressed with my effort in finding you since you disappeared without a goodbye. And hell, don't get me started about that. Piss weak to just leave. *Again*. If I were a fling, then you should've manned up and told me so, but we both know I wasn't, and that's why I'm here. This misbelief I couldn't hack your life is bullshit. We do have a future."

I stand and point a finger as though I'm jabbing him in the chest. "You're wrong not to believe in me. We're so right for each other. And I... I'm full of surprises. Hell, I've surprised myself every day on this holiday. And I *can* hack it. Just give me a chance to prove it to you." I stand with my hands on my hips, out of breath after ranting on about every little thing that popped into my mind. There's much more I want to say, only I need him to respond to the first fifty questions.

"Please, sit." A command, yet his voice is gentle. "First, we eat."

30

SAMUEL

"THEY ARE VEGETARIAN PIRANHA," Samuel emphasizes after her concerned glance. Since piranhas have minimal flesh, the meal ends quickly.

Eden expects an explanation.

He focuses on clearing his thoughts. He couldn't start at the beginning—there's not enough time. More importantly, he doesn't want to scare her. Leveling his gaze with hers, he straightens his shoulders, hoping she'll understand why he left her in Ilhéus when she still owned his heart.

"When I saw you yesterday, I thought I was hallucinating. I have dreamed about you every night since the day in Salvador. So, it wouldn't have surprised me if I imagined you on the beach because I hated myself for leaving you without saying goodbye."

He raises a hand when she attempts to interrupt.

"I need to say some things. Let me explain without offending or breaking my vow. If you don't understand, I'll try and explain it later. For now, allow me to speak." Her eyes round. "I'm not going to explain why I left my family and the luxurious LA lifestyle. I'll only say that I received a pharmaceutical grant to work with the missionaries in indigenous communities by providing pharmaceuticals to promote companies and offer better medical care in the community. Along the way, the companies heard about plants native to the areas, some rumored to hold substantial therapeutic benefit. After some time in these communities and working with a professor in Caracas, where I send the plants I find, the pharmaceutical company considered me finding other rare plants unique to the areas near the tepuis, which could provide medical breakthroughs, especially to certain diseases like cancer and diabetes."

Eden gapes at Samuel in a combination of surprise and adoration. She nods for him to continue.

"I was privileged when a renowned rock climber and local Pemón native American familiar with the Auyán tepui took me up the mountain in search of a plant they talked about in their stories. I'm sure Asoo has mentioned some of Pemón mythology."

"A little," she says with a fixed expression.

"These other communities have a Spanish influence, including adopting the Catholic religion. They also dress in Western clothing. We had ropes and all the climbing gear, and we tackled the easiest path up the tepui. It still took a few days to reach the top, and we found the unusual carnivorous flowers. On our trek home, I saw one of the Ularans in the jungle. His red body paint caught my eye. My guide was oblivious, and yet I knew he was from another time. Untouched by any other human influence in the way he dressed and the concern on his face, we assessed each other momentarily before I caught up with my guide, not speaking a word.

"A month later, I decided to search for these native Americans, curious as to how they lived. The shaman found me after my canoe ended up on their river beach, where I slept. He treated me for dehydration, and my relationship with them grew. Naïvely, I believed I could help by treating them with Western medicine. Over time, I have helped only when their medicine failed. Mostly, they have taught me more of who I am than decades of studying at the world's best universities."

He stands and indicates for her to follow him. More than anything, Samuel wants her to understand his life here, yet he can't allow his demeanor to crumble. He's confused because she wasn't part of the plan *now*. God, he wanted her, more than anything, only he can't afford the luxury of a lover until his work here was complete. When she learns the truth and the reality of his world, he expects her to run far away from him. In his note, he wrote how he wanted to be with her, come find her at her family's hotel when his work here was done. He meant every word.

After learning of the man he is here, he doubts she'll want him to come for her.

Behind Samuel, Eden treads loudly over the forest floor scaring any nearby tiny animals. He's thankful he's not hunting. He points to a vine and smiles. "The forest garden supplies everything you need to survive. You only need to be educated on what and how to find it. Ulara is kept from the rest of the world, hidden behind thick foliage with tiny tributaries from Angel Falls supplying fresh water and fish. These people don't need anything else or anyone for their survival. In fact, people like you and I carry disease." He hopes Eden understands this was a major factor why he discouraged her from visiting him.

"A common cold can wipe out families as their immunity differs from ours. They have plants to help heal, except viruses from the outside world are a different threat. As a rule, I quarantine myself every time I return to Ulara. I remain on the outskirts until enough days pass to ensure I'm not a threat, or I remain a safe distance from them. I also wait for Asoo to ascertain from the surrounding communities that no travelers have fallen sick after leaving Canaima. It's not just here. The surrounding Pemón communities are also vulnerable to tourists and international volunteers. It brings me to why you're here and why I can't be with you as much as I want to..."

He stalls, his eyes hold hers captive. Even looking at her sends him wild with desire.

He swallows hard and reels in his thoughts—the memories of their time together. He glances at her fingertips and visualizes the way she touched and caressed him. Only now, her skin is smeared with dirt, and her pretty nails are chipped. Samuel bows his head, remembering his place here is far from the freedom they had in Ilhéus. "We aren't at liberty to do what we please." He tilts his head and seeks understanding. "There are rules I must obey. Hugging and kissing aren't allowed unless a couple is married. Your unexpected arrival changes things. If we're to gain the trust of the chief, we need to show constraint."

"What?" she rasps. "I'm only here for two days. I have to leave and catch up with the girls."

He nods, breaks a piece of wood from a tree, drinks the water trapped inside, and offers her some.

She shakes her head. "It's fine. I still have some bottled water."

He nods, understanding her apprehension. "I don't expect anything of you or for you to understand why I do what I do. Even when my contract ends in a year, I might not return to my home in LA." Her eyes glisten with moisture, and he bows his head. "It's why I didn't tell you anything to encourage you. This is no place for someone like you." Her shoulders stiffen, and he hopes she didn't misinterpret his words. "I should've known not to underestimate you." He offers her a smile and shakes his head, still astounded by her efforts. "If anyone were to find me, I'm glad it was you. Although, I trust you'll tell no one, only that I work with the missionaries. There is more at stake than I can tell you."

"Of course, I understand. And I'm glad I found you, too," Eden whispers and dips her chin. "I'm frustrated with you because I thought I'd see more of you," she says in a louder voice. She sighs and takes a moment before her gaze settles back on his. "Although I shouldn't complain since I'm lucky to have such a luxurious place to sleep." A grin slowly creeps across her lips. "I'm alive, so, hey, it's not all bad." She shrugs.

"Eden." He stares at her, hoping she understands the extent of his words. "I want to be with you more than *anything,*" Samuel's voice cracks on the last word.

She reaches out, brushes her fingers across his. It's a gentle brushing of the tips of their hands.

He takes hers and squeezes it. "I wish there was another way."

31

EDEN

MORNING SUNSHINE BREAKS through the canopy. I open my eyes and see the white and yellow circles of sunlight as the rays reflect off leaves and dewy fronds.

Damn this heat. I was hot and bothered all night despite the absence of the sun. With a foggy head, I stand and stumble to the river holding my back.

Stretching my arms over my head, I attempt to iron out the kinks. It's going to take more than a couple of nights to get used to the hammock. And to be honest, it could do with a wash. I groan, thinking about bubbles and water. What I'd do now for a bath or shower. Even the river looks appealing, although I'm not yet brave enough to strip down and wash, especially here on a river beach and out in the open. Besides, I'm not convinced the river is safe, even with the children I saw yesterday frolicking in the water. I glance upstream. Slashes of red and purple color the Eastern sky. The current is slow along this tributary compared to the Churun River and more so the Carrao River to which it flows. I smile, thinking how Bree would be impressed with my geography knowledge of the area.

A wave of sadness hits me thinking about my friends. What are they doing? I glance down to my feet in the river sand and imagine it to be the crisp white sand of Margarita Island. What do they think of me? I close my eyes at the realization of my erratic behavior.

If only I knew.

It's why Samuel didn't want me to come after him. I understand that now. If only I weren't as stubborn as my father. I let out a long sigh, the disappointment still with me.

Asoo will be coming downstream from the north. I'm not sure when and only know to listen for the motor.

I wander back and sit on a log to slip on my socks and shoes. The fire is almost out, so I carefully lay another log over the top. I jump back when it hisses at me. Now hungry, I meander through the vines—with more shoots sprouting in the two days I've been here—to pick as much passion fruit I can hold in the material of my tank top. After collecting what I can reach, I head back and sit by the fire.

I pierce each piece with my nail. Good god, my hands are filthy. Thankfully, I don't have to touch the flesh I eat. With each mouthful, I stare into the trees. Will he come and visit me this morning? Or will he allow me to leave without a goodbye? I'm so exhausted, I don't have the energy to be optimistic. Samuel explained everything as best he could last night. I don't have a choice and have to accept he has a commitment to uphold. It is what it is. There's no happy ending. I just wish I had the patience and waited for him to come find me in a year or so. I could've kept working with my father, go back to my boring, dull life, and wait for the day when Samuel walks back into my life.

I blow out the air between my cheeks. "Yeah, right," I mutter. I bite into the gooey flesh of the passion fruit and keep eating it until each piece is halved and the skin is lying beside the fire.

I gather my belongings and roll the mosquito net into a ball and stuff it inside my pack. The plastic to cover my bag is rolled up in a ball in the corner. I unravel it and wrap it around my pack. In the distance, there's a muffled sound. I gasp realizing it's a motor, and I haven't spoken to Samuel.

I head down to the beach and wait. My breaths come fast, and I look to the trees. I want to run in there and call out to him.

The curiara putts around the corner. My shoulders slump, and I drop my pack onto the sand. I never got the kiss I wanted when I found him, and I sure as hell won't be getting a kiss to say goodbye. It hits me how he's going to let me leave because we both know I never belonged here.

"Eden," Samuel's voice comes from behind.

What? He's here?

At the far end of the beach, he strides toward me. I smile, knowing he's come to say goodbye. I want to run to him but know I can't. Oddly, he's wearing cargo cut-offs and a t-shirt.

He gives me the same smile that reminds me of how he used to be in Ilhéus. "Good morning. Have you eaten?" He hands me a banana. Steely eyes hold mine captive.

"Morning," I say quickly. "And thank you." I take in his clothes and backpack. "What are you doing?"

He waves out to Asoo. "Taking you to Canaima."

"I don't need a chaperone." I want to kick myself because, more than anything, I want time with him, but if we're going to move on without each other, prolonging the pain isn't going to help me.

"I know. I want to monitor the questions Asoo asks." He doesn't look at me when he says it. A muscle ticks along his jaw.

"I won't say anything to anyone," I whisper.

"I know."

"Then why are you really coming?" I'm not sure he hears me with the motor now revving closer.

He points to direct Asoo to the shore and then gives me a sideways glance. "We both know why."

I don't have time to respond before Samuel is guiding the canoe to the sand and throwing his sack aboard.

"Eden. Samuel." Asoo raises his hands in the air. "I happy to see you."

Samuel nods, jumps aboard with more grace than I ever could, and takes a seat in the middle of the boat. He points to the seat in front for me to sit. I do so after taking some water from the bag Asoo has packed for us.

"Keep your eyes peeled on the river. Asoo needs assistance to steer, and you can point out small boulders further along he may miss."

"Sure." I nod, remembering how the guides helped navigate the canoe through the rapids. And let's pretend nothing about this is weird at all.

"I appreciate you making the extra journey," Samuel says to Asoo. "I can pay you when we reach Canaima."

So, he has money even though it's useless to him in the village.

I turn around so Asoo can hear me. "I haven't booked a room."

"It fine," Asoo says over the rattle of the motor. "Samuel has room. Rooms for everyone."

Keeping my eyes trained ahead, I smile to myself, knowing Asoo might have a case of loose lips.

Samuel has his own room. I mull over his words a while.

"Your English is a little better," I tell Asoo.

"I practice," he tells me. "Victor has book and CD." He gives me a proud smile.

"LEFT," I call out. Both my hands clasp the wood under my rear as I hang on to stop myself from being thrown forward or back. Samuel stands to push us away from the huge boulders, several feet tall, while Asoo navigates us through a narrow path to dodge the smooth rocks protruding out of the water.

I barely speak to the men. Samuel communicates to Asoo in Spanish or Pemón, whatever it is, and it gets on my nerves. I understand communication between them is easier this way, yet I can't help the paranoia creeping in and questioning my sanity. Like a pendulum swinging back and forth, my thoughts alter from *I'm brave and did the right thing coming here* to *what the hell was I thinking?*

Fearless bordering on stupidity.

What did I achieve by having a couple more days with Samuel? Do I hope to find out a little more about him? Am I waiting for him to promise he'll come find me when his contract is finished? All I know is something inside my heart led me here, and it's like the instinct to find him overpowered every other logical thought. Every day with him has to be viewed as part of my intended journey. Otherwise, I could possibly be going mad.

Not every experience is enjoyable.

Yasmine has told me this many times.

It's not a reason not to do it. It's all about opportunities and trying different things. Some we love, some we don't. The important thing is to do it. Try everything and give your inner courage a chance to bloom.

I smile, thinking about her words. Thank you, my friend.

I grab my bag to find my phone and wait for it to power on. Twenty percent battery life is sufficient to take photos. I click away, taking snaps of the tepuis in the distance and the jungle overhanging the river's edge. It truly is an experience I'll never forget. I turn, and Samuel frowns when I point the camera at him and Asoo. I turn back and sneak in another with myself at the front of the curiara in the group selfie. I check the image and smile seeing my friends in the background. Hell, I look like shit. I pop the phone back in the plastic before we pass through the rapids.

By the time we reach the other side of the plains not far from Canaima, my thoughts are in a better place.

I'll have Samuel to myself.

Except he never clarified whether he intends to return immediately or stay the night.

32

EDEN

Wakü Holiday Resort
Canaima, Bolivar, Venezuela

THE WATER SPRAY dances over my face like tiny fingers massaging my forehead, temples, and cheeks. After the last two days, a warm shower hands down equals that of a luxury spa treatment. I'm going to make an appointment as soon as I get home, and right now, I don't give two fucks of the cost.

Home.

My stomach drops.

I owe my family and friends a call.

Lathering soap over my body, I cringe when soap stings the small scratches on my shins.

Securing one towel on my head and another around my chest, I check if my phone is still charged. My room is closer to the reception area than the previous one, and it picks up the Wi-Fi, albeit slow. I flop on the bed and send a text to my friends to confirm my safety. While I'm waiting for the little blue line to cross the top of my screen, I open the last message I sent to my father. It will probably take a while for all the replies from my previous texts to come through.

"Eden." Knock. Knock.

I spring up to open the door.

Tormented blue eyes lock with mine. A slight breeze carries his freshly showered scent into my room, and it jolts my memory of us together in Ilhéus. His Adam's apple bobs. "May I have a word?"

"Sure." I widen the door for him to enter.

"I see you've showered." He turns in a slow circle as though assessing my room.

"I did. There was room for two."

When his gaze shoots to mine, I turn away and casually towel dry my hair. "Are you heading to dinner? I'll be ready after I call my friends and arrange my flight out for tomorrow." I hate talking about leaving him, especially not knowing where we stand makes the effort in finding him somewhat pointless. I understand his commitment, but it doesn't have to be forever.

I push the comb through my hair with extra force. "Ouch." My knots are glued together since I haven't used a brush in two days. The wind factor from the river ride was a formula for hairspray.

"Is it what you want?" he questions and takes a seat on the edge of the bed.

I stop combing. "I'm sorry, what?"

"To leave?"

I shake my head. "I don't have a choice."

He stands and walks to the door. "I'll wait in your hammock while you make the calls."

I'm gaping at the closed door. He walks by the window and slides into the hammock on my porch with the slightest rock. He folds his hands behind his head and stares out at the lake.

I yank open the door. "Don't put this on me. You said I wasn't allowed in your village. There are restrictions, and you can't touch me."

He flies out of the hammock and pushes me inside. "Yes, we have limitations." He spins me. His lips caress my bare shoulder. His hands wrap around my waist, so I feel the length of him pushing into my back. "We don't have any here."

"Here," I repeat.

"What did you expect when you came searching for me?" His lips are close to my ear, hot breath caresses my neck.

"To find out if you cared about me as much as I you," I rasp out.

"You knew I did. I showed you my feelings in Ilhéus. You've complicated everything in a way I've never felt before." Hands tighten around my stomach and travel down and touch me where heat builds. "I don't want you to go. Is that what you want to hear?"

"Yes," I grate out. "Of course, it is."

"Then, you've won. You drive me crazy. I hope you're satisfied that I'm a mess."

I attempt to turn because I want to take him in my arms and kiss him. Only he halts my action, his strong arms keeping me still, my back to his front. We're both peering toward the window to the view of the rainforest beyond the lake and waterfalls.

"You honestly believe you could survive out there?" He raises an arm and points. "Live like me?"

After my short experience—no. I couldn't do it. If it meant giving us a chance, an instinct tells me it's a place where I could find myself and truly question my happiness, challenge my abilities, overcome fear, and grow. It's what this trip is meant to be—a journey of growth. Finding Samuel and love was a bonus. Then it dawns on me why I wanted to find him so much. By finding him, I also found my strength.

"I'd like a chance to try," I whisper.

He stiffens behind me. His chest expands and releases faster with every breath. His forehead touches the top of my head.

I listen to him breathe for a while before his arms loosen around my waist. "I want to kiss you. We need to be careful, and you haven't been in quarantine long enough to—"

"Stop talking. If I do this, I'm not living on the outskirts. I'm coming with you into the village."

"We can't sleep together."

"I know. Wait. I thought the chief said no?" I push his arms off me and turn to face him.

"Turns out the shaman sees something in you." He smiles at me. "He has granted you time, and I'm going to request for you to stay longer." A dent forms between his eyebrows. "That's if you want to—"

"Longer, as in the rest of my holidays?" What's he saying? Shit, I have four more weeks.

Samuel's expression softens. "If you think you can handle the four weeks, then yes."

Pfft. If I can handle it. Does he even know me?

I'm smiling like an idiot.

Four weeks.

It's enough time to form a solid bond and see if we have a future together. Our initial connection can't be ignored, and now that I've made all the effort to bloody get here, I'm not going to walk away wondering *what if*?

"Yes, of course, it's what I want. Give me time to make those calls, then we can head over to dinner."

He shakes his head. "We don't associate with anyone, only Asoo, as he knows to keep his distance. No handshaking or embracing tourists. We eat in our room. I'll pick some fruit from Victor's organic garden and bring it to you."

I nod. Damn, I was looking forward to a schnitzel or steak and a glass of wine at dinner.

A small sacrifice, really.

"Do you have everything in your larger case to cover you for that amount of time?"

"Not malaria meds. I'll need more."

He nods. "I have plenty. Anything else? Lady products? I have bags for trash."

I gasp. What do the Ularan ladies do? "It's fine. I have an implant. I haven't menstruated in years."

I take his hand and step closer and look up into those serious eyes. I'm ready to challenge him and make those eyes sparkle with lust. "You and I have some catching up to do. Less limitations," I remind him.

When he doesn't tell me to stop, I untie my towel, throwing it aside on the bed. His eyes bore into mine, then lower and glaze over. I watch him take his fill as I take a few steps toward him.

When I reach him, he spins me, takes my hands, and places them on the bed. "I'll take it from here," he whispers in my ear.

Moments ago, the world beyond my room was alive with nature. Monkeys howling, animals screeching, and the insects clicking. With Samuel's every touch, the sound fades into the distance, and all I hear is the excited throb of my heartbeat in my ears.

Samuel's lips trail along my back as his fingers glide over my slit. He teases and caresses me before sliding his fingers inside.

I sigh loudly and tilt my hips toward him. "I want you," I say urgently.

For once, he doesn't argue.

He slips inside of me, thrusts deep and hard, and moans my name. "Keep your hands on the bed."

Samuel adjusts my hips, and his thrusts turn fast, deep, and erotic. His willpower is lost to animal instinct. Sexual desire is strong enough that neither one of us can fight.

I'm going to enjoy the bliss while I can, and since I'm already breaking all the rules, I intend to break a few more tonight.

His hand reaches around, rubs, and presses my clit. The excitement thrums through my body, rising and rising, and little orgasms explode inside me as I build to climax. My knees weaken. His cock is pounding me, yet I want more of whatever Samuel can give. Lust has taken over our minds, especially knowing I can't touch him like this when we are in the village.

"Harder," I rasp out between breaths.

"I hope you know what you're asking," he warns under his breath, and then he slams into me until I'm incapable of uttering another word.

My body aches in a desirable, sexy way. My clit's swollen, and there's a steady throbbing between my legs. I'm sore, and I couldn't be happier. Rolling off the bed, I push up to find my phone and finish sending the messages before I was beautifully distracted.

I owe my family a call and not a text, and since Samuel might be a while *gathering* dinner, I have time on my hands.

Flicking my fingers nervously, I decide to call Yasmine first.

It goes straight to Yasmine's voicemail. I hope they're having the time of their life, then I won't feel as guilty for leaving them. I try Amy next and pace the length of the room waiting for Amy to answer.

"Eden," Amy screams. "Are you okay?"

"Hey." I let out a long breath. "More than okay. I'm with Samuel."

"You found him?" she asks in a higher pitch.

A smile spreads across my face like a victorious child finding all the hidden eggs at Easter, anticipating the joy to come. "Yeah. It's why I'm calling… to apologize again. I'm not coming to Cusco."

"What?" she gasps.

"I'm staying here. You can go on without me. I'm staying for as long as I can, so I'm changing my flights."

"Edes." Amy makes a sound like she's going to cry. "I'm worried about you, and I miss you. It's not the same without you here. Bree left early. She changed her flight for work reasons, and Yasmine spends all her time with Michael since he has taken your spot on the tours. They're acting weird, whispering and going off alone. I'd rather be a third wheel with you."

I snort. "I doubt it. I'm staying in a remote village."

"Canaima looks great on the map."

"I'm not in Canaima," I whisper. "I'm closer to Angel Falls." I really had no other clue to Ulara's location. "If you need me, call the reception at the lodge and ask to speak to Asoo. I'll send you the number. He can get a message to me. I'll be all right, I promise."

"I feel lost here without you. Can't Samuel come here with you? Do the trek? Because Yasmine is talking about heading into the Peruvian jungle with Michael."

I remember my conversation with Yasmine on the bus. This is part of her journey—something I understand better now. "I know she wants to. She mentioned it to me in Brazil. Listen, if you don't want to go, then wait for her at the hotel. Call me to leave any messages."

"I can't believe your father has agreed to this."

"He didn't." I twist a lock of hair around my finger. "I'm about to make the call."

"He's gonna lose his shit."

I know.

"I gotta go, Ames. Talk soon."

"Stay safe, babe."

"I will. Love you."

I end the call with a heavy weight in my gut, knowing how alone Amy feels. I'm torn between going to her or doing what my heart tells me—staying here.

I pull up Dad's name and wait for what feels like forever for Dad to pick up. It goes to voicemail.

"Dad, it's Eden. A quick call to let you know I'm okay. I'm staying in Canaima, as I really love this part of the world. I'm not traveling any further with my friends. I know you'll be mad, but please trust me on this as I'm doing everything to stay safe. I love you and will check in regularly, so you know I'm okay. Bye."

I need to speak with someone from my family, so I call Faith.

"Are you fucking serious?" Faith yells, sans any greeting.

"Hope your kid isn't around to hear your potty mouth."

"Whatever. Focus," she chastises me like I'm her child. "Dad's been beside himself. He's spoken to Bree now that she's home, and she said you're in a remote area of Venezuela. Of all the countries... do you know the Canadian embassy closed, so there's nowhere for Australians to go? If you get into trouble, you're seriously fucked. You'll need to get to Colombia."

I hadn't paid attention to the news considering it's in Spanish. "Thanks for the update. I'm calling to let you know I have a new itinerary because I've met someone, and I'm staying with him." I go on to tell her some things about Samuel, mainly his medical experience.

"And this is supposed to make me feel better. You're seriously out of your goddamn mind."

There are times I agree with her, but I also don't expect her to understand. Love came easy for her and Jake. Their lives fell into place like a fairy tale, and years later, he still idolizes the ground she walks on. Even when I was with Ethan, I still felt alone because he never treated me like I was a priority.

"I need you to explain a modified version of what I told you to Dad. Tell him I'm fine, and I'm messaging you regularly. I'll call in a week or two, or at least get a message to you. If you need to get in contact with me, then either send a text or leave a message at the resort's reception with Asoo. I'll text you the number."

"You know he's going to freak out, right? You're going *into the jungle*."

I remain silent a moment.

"Yeah. I need you to weave your magic. I owe you."

Faith sighs into the phone. "Yep, you do. He had an early morning meeting, so you could call him in an hour?"

Right now, I don't have it in me to listen to his disappointment. "I can't. I'm heading to bed."

"You're lucky Ethan and Dad are getting along so well. Another reason why Dad wanted you home sooner rather than later. He has Ethan's desk set up next to yours."

"Ugh."

Another reason why I'm *not* rushing home.

MY PHONE BUZZES on the bedside table, and it's enough to wake me. My thoughts are whirling, and I've barely slept even though Samuel is in my bed spooning me.

Samuel.

Lying beside me.

Maybe it's because my heart is beating too fast to rest. I'm grappling with how everything has unfolded over the last few days. Trying desperately to understand, I keep questioning my decision and doubting his and my sanity.

Lying on my side away from him, I read the text.

I blink twice to focus. There are four messages from Ethan.

> I know you're probably sleeping and hope it's not too late. Not time wise. I hope there's something I can say to change your mind about putting yourself in danger and adding stress to your family. Bree said your decision to stay is because of a guy. She said he's odd and he lives in the jungle…

> I'm struggling to believe you would want to be somewhere like that and stay in a third-world society. Didn't you want to advance your career and step into your father's shoes? You like the beach. There'll be no football on weekends, hanging with your friends, and heading out to bars at night and cafés during the day.

> Seriously, Eden. What are you achieving? And for a stranger? No wonder we're all worried. You heard about that last cult, where people ventured into the jungle and then the leader shot everyone. Please tell me you're not part of one. And yes, I'm worried. I understood this holiday would be about fun, and I thought you would come home refreshed with clarity to where the hotel business is headed and hopefully ready to assess our relationship again. I love you. I always have.

I know I messed up. Give me a chance to make it up to you. To work for you, beside you every day. To show you how much I have changed. Your father knows how crazy I am for you. Every day I see how stressed out you've made him. Please come home. I'm scared for you. Scared of not having you in my life x

I release air from my lungs with a sigh then check if the shine from my phone has disturbed Samuel. The dim light reflects onto his beautiful face. His gaze lifts from my phone and meets mine. He doesn't say anything, and yet there's apprehension in his eyes. I wasn't going to answer Ethan until my fingers start typing.

Hey, Ethan. Thanks for your message. I'm lucky to have so many people who love and care about me. I assure you your concern is unwarranted because I'm fine. Very happy and on the adventure of a lifetime. Yes, I have met someone, and I'm learning so much about life from him. I miss everyone! I'll be in contact soon.

I place my phone on the table and roll onto my side. My face is close to his, and my lips tingle with the light breeze of his every breath. I kiss him, so our lips barely brush. He doesn't retreat, and I take it as a green light. My mouth slowly caresses his, and I shudder with need, a slight tremor to my touch. A hand takes my shoulder, and our bodies align. His kiss becomes frantic, the air zinging between us.

"I need you to make love to me," I whisper against his lips.

He rolls onto me and sinks between my thighs.

To hell with the rules tonight.

33

SAMUEL

What was he thinking?

In one week, Samuel is to embark on a journey to the top of the tepui in search of a purple flower, one to heal the cells of the body. He learned about the unique plant from the shaman, knowledge gained during an ayahuasca ceremony where the vines and trees communicate to reveal secrets of the forest.

The pharmaceutical company believes the purpose of his stay is to find plants to cure disease. Samuel's stay in Ulara has developed into something far more valuable. The people here have taught him the meaning of a soul, healing yourself from within, and connecting with all living things on earth in a way he never thought possible.

He has grown in character, in mental and physical strength, and learned to accept some things that can never be explained. His science-based thoughts questioned how and why with every miracle the shaman performed. Over the years, he understood some happenings have no justification by way of his education. He didn't believe in magic. Happenstance in the jungle is far more powerful and connected him with other worlds his former associates mocked.

He understands the jungle more so than his previous privileged society. And by leaving that society, he became a different man, one indebted to the Ularans.

So why did he entice Eden to return with him?

It seems his selfish ways remain with him.

Eden sits ahead of him on the curiara, pointing and smiling toward the endless green when a monkey or colorful parrot catches her attention. He and Asoo laugh at her excitement, his gut tightening, hoping she maintains her cheerfulness during her stay.

Her acceptance into the Ularan community is yet to be decided.

Samuel recalls his initiation was more like torture, his mindset then the strongest of his life. Yet during the last forty-eight hours, he has portrayed weakness and jeopardized the health and safety of the people he has grown to love.

Part of him is ashamed of his selfishness.

Yet there is no fighting the adrenaline soaring through his body, knowing someone will be by his side for the first time in years.

His heart beats in a quick Samba rhythm and not from excitement alone. There's an underlying fear in the chief rejecting his request. Asking permission is the biggest risk Samuel's taken in years, and his shaky hands know it.

Hours pass, and he hasn't prepared her. He leaves Asoo to navigate alone as he climbs over the wooden planks to sit beside Eden. She places her head on his shoulder, and a contented sigh escapes him.

"If you see a girl eating alone and keeping her distance, it's not that she's unwell. She is being ostracized as a way of social control."

"What?" Her forehead creases with a frown.

"I'm telling you, so you don't go and sit with her because I know how you think."

There's a glimmer of defiance in her eyes. "You think you do..."

He smiles at her before continuing, "It's only for a couple of days. I need you to follow their rules. Otherwise, you'll be the one who's excluded."

Did she roll her eyes at him?

"I'll do what I have to if it means I'm with you." She pats his leg reassuringly.

He'll be there beside her when tested to her limit. He goes on to tell her other things. "The village is divided into a series of huts. Families sleep in separate huts. The shaman has his own hut. The young men, the warriors, sleep together in another hut. Girls sleep with their families."

"Where do you sleep?"

"I have my own hut. It's connected to my treatment room. I'll make sure you're with me. New huts have been built as the village is preparing for the upcoming wet season and another for ceremonies."

"Like weddings?"

He laughs at the twinkle in her eye. "It's a similar celebration of two souls uniting."

Her hand squeezes over his. "I'd love to witness one. I guess it's all the same, only without the hefty wedding costs. Wait, does the bride wear a dress of some sort?"

Samuel shakes his head. "It isn't a wedding celebration."

His fear rises with her curiosity.

He's said enough.

A JOG TURNS into a sprint as Samuel takes the path, swiping at unruly vines and smacking low branches, his pack bouncing on his back.

He reaches the village perimeter and slows to a walk to catch his breath.

He emerges from his hut in a grass skirt and a beaded necklace strung over his shoulders. He inhales a long breath and then a slow exhale to calm his thoughts before finding the shaman, passing the women leaning over mud pots, smoke rising from the fire beneath. He nods to Kaikare. Years ago, he believed she was an outcast. Like him, she'd found no partner. In those early days, he'd find her sitting with the shaman listening intently to his words. The two were close, and initially he thought they were a couple, only she was many years younger. Then he discovered she was his daughter and an apprentice, like him, who understood sacrifice.

She nods in the way of the garden. Samuel snakes around more hut clusters until he reaches the village perimeter's farthest point from the river.

A song leads him to the shaman, peaceful sounds of vows repeated in a tune sung to the trees in gratitude.

Dropping to his knees, eyes closed, Samuel concentrates on the words and allows the tune to fill his thoughts. The melody calms his heart, and he bows his head and simply absorbs the sounds like medicine healing the soul. He opens his eyes when a hand rests on his crown, and the singing stops.

Samuel speaks first, his head bowed. He tells him Eden waits near the river.

Nothing more.

No explanation.

Consequences are understood.

The shaman asks Samuel to wait outside the chief's hut until a decision is made.

Samuel does so, and elevated voices carry through the village. It's not the usual calm way the Ularans communicate.

White fluffy clouds roll overhead and block out the sun. The sun breaks through momentarily before clouds shut it out again. It's Samuel's only way of knowing, at this moment, time is passing by.

Kaikare mimics his pose, sitting cross-legged beside him, mere feet from the chief's doorway.

She nods to the river and, in her language, tells him the children saw his Tamu'ne Akare.

He holds back a smile at the name the children have given Eden—White Tortoise. He assumed her white hair—like his—would garner attention. And after the warriors watched over her those few nights, they thought her to be a slow learner of their ways.

Kaikare's name is a combination of a jaguar and a tortoise, and he wonders if, in her younger days, she was also a slow learner of the Ularan way. Or someone they wanted to protect like the tortoise when it came time to lay its eggs in the sand on the riverbank. The jaguar part he didn't question for it's the most feared animal in the jungle.

The rattle of beads and bones on a walking stick indicates movement. Samuel rises to his knees. Kaikare is a little stiffer than he remembers. She ambles to her feet. He considers her to be in her late fifties. He'd thought arthritis restricted her movement at first, yet it's not a condition he often sees with the forest offering herbs as treatment. She hobbles away when larger mud-coated feet come into his vision. Cracked nails require taming. A bang on the ground and a rattle of animal teeth and beads demand his attention.

With his head bowed, he listens to the chief's disapproval of an outsider. His obligation is to protect his people, the location of the village, and how they have lived without the influence of outsiders to keep the spirits happy—no new sickness, no evil weapons, or their forests burned down. More importantly, no evil spirits known as Kanaima have entered the village in many moons. The stone mountains are satisfied.

Samuel's thoughts drift to the tepuis—the stone mountains—and to his upcoming journey where warriors will also accompany him to the base as they venture out on their hunt.

Samuel realizes his mistake.

Eden isn't welcome.

He'll be away from the village for possibly weeks. He nods, thoughts racing. His gut aches, torn between respecting their law and fulfilling his own selfish thoughts.

His demeanor is weak. His time here is waning. He nods, and before he signals obligation, the shaman speaks for him and places Eden on trial.

"Kapeá töuking enya." *Five full moons.*

Five months.

The shaman's lenience surprises him.

She can only stay weeks with the government's rule on visas, but now isn't the time to explain the outside world restriction.

The chief thumps his stick. "Uarati." *Man.*

Samuel is fully aware of his place here and his duty as a *man*. His initiation into the community established his manhood and a responsibility to be a better person.

The chief dismisses him, and the shaman motions for Samuel to follow.

They approach the women preparing the yuca and stop for the shaman to wave his stick at Kaikare. All three walk into the forest. The shaman takes Kaikare's hand and juts her swollen finger joints toward Samuel.

Samuel asks her if she has suffered any fever over the past weeks like the young girl he had treated—dengue fever, yellow fever, malaria, Mayaro virus, ross river, swine, zika. So many viruses come to mind and none should have made their way into the village. It gives him cause for concern.

"Pupai?" *Head*. He indicates pain in his expression like a headache.

Again, she shakes her head.

He glances down to her abdomen. Beyond the paint and dirt, there's no hint of a rash.

The shaman is a healer beyond Samuel's explanation. Yet there are times he seeks out Samuel's guidance. When it comes to Kaikare, his daughter and apprentice, Samuel understands her importance to continue his work. He thinks the shaman to be around his mid-seventies and expects he'll make the century.

The shaman and Samuel walk further toward the unruly vines. Samuel points to plants, and the shaman snaps leaves and flowers from a variety of plants. Samuel is careful not to touch anything and maintains a safe distance from his friends. He tells the shaman to give the leaves to Kaikare to boil and drink in tea. It will purify the blood and has an anti-inflammatory effect.

With gratitude, the shaman informs Samuel that Kaikare will look out for his Tamu'ne Akare. So, this is now Eden's name.

In a slow nod, Samuel thanks him and dashes toward the river to find his *white tortoise*.

He slows to a walk when he reaches the jungle edge and takes the narrow path to the sandy beach. Eden stands and slings her backpack over her shoulder when he comes into view—there's no running into his arms.

He allows her time to peruse his bare body to assess the red and black beads around his neck, the string of caiman teeth, his trophy. Tonight, his body will be painted again and reapplied the night before the hunt.

Her gaze lowers to his grass skirt.

He speaks before his body reacts. "The chief has granted you permission to stay. Although you'll be on trial, so I'll make sure you're aware of all the rules before I—"

"There was a chance I wasn't allowed to stay?"

She doesn't allow him to add he's going on an exploration in a week. Seeing her reaction, he deems it best not to mention it now.

He nods, answering her question. "I wanted to take the risk. I'm sorry, it was selfish of me. Now you're here, you need to obey—"

"Obey?" she repeats.

His jaw clenches. "You're free to change your mind."

She reaches for his hand, her fingers skimming over his. A tingle pricks his fingertips, and new energy sparks. Yin energy soars up his arms and through his body. She links their fingers, and he savors the warmth.

"I want to do this. Only... here I get somewhat rebellious. I can't help it. Maybe it's because you're dressed like this." She gives him a cheeky smile.

He holds her gaze. "Everything is black and white. There is no confusion. Please don't risk being sent away—"

"I won't," she promises, stepping closer to him.

Keeping hold of her hand, he leads her along the path he walked moments before, pushing branches away from her face, allowing her to pass. With every step, he leads her closer to the village, to a world where he belongs and the center of his universe. His axis tilted four weeks ago. Samuel hopes Eden's presence will realign his universe, seal the hole in his heart he never knew existed until the day he first saw her on the beach.

The chief expects her to conform and behave in an acceptable way—eat what they eat, work the fields, cook alongside the women, and dress like them. His gut tightens imagining her in a palm skirt with only beads covering her breasts. Remembering her in a swimsuit in Salvador, he understands the effect she'll have on the young men and what he must do to protect her.

34

EDEN

"Welcome to Ulara." Samuel grins at me, and we both turn and gaze at the village before me.

The excitement rushing through my body is like a *Welcome to Hollywood* movie set. We're standing in a clearing where several thatched huts form a circle, and more of the same huts can be seen in the distance. Smoke rises in the air above the grass structures, and I catch the scent of food. It smells good, whatever it is. Until now, I didn't realize my hunger. With only fruit for dinner and breakfast, I'm craving anything that can be cooked.

Following Samuel, I walk a dirt path at the back of a smaller circle of huts. Between each hut, I get a glimpse of a central fire pit. It's dry, and no one tends to it. Around us, the jungle squawks, the only applause for my arrival. The further we walk the snake-like path, the more the air steams. The hum of mosquitoes circling above my head never ends. I wipe my hands on my denim shorts before swiping my brow.

Samuel leads me to a long hut with open walls and windows. Here, several fires burn. Some women lean over huge mud pots stirring the contents with a long stick while others squat, grinding or mashing.

The same carbon hair borders their round faces. The color matches their eyes. Slowly, the women uncurl their bodies naked, and take a step back. A soft chatter grows among them. I'm not sure what I expected, but fear wasn't one. From behind me, the children giggle. "Tamu'ne Akare."

Samuel says one word I don't understand, and they laugh back at him.

"At least the children like me," I say.

"They're fascinated by your clothes."

With legs like pogo sticks, they jump in front of me, pointing and laughing.

Samuel makes a noise, and they stop. "They have never seen long white hair."

"Right." I drop to my knees to give them a better view. Faded paint covers their dark skin, a combination of Vs and long lines on limbs and chest. Sneaking a glance at the ladies, they're all watching me with a little more curiosity.

A crack on the ground has them running, although the giggling continues. Samuel drops to his knees beside me. On our left, two older men with similar feathered crowns stand before us.

"Look down," Samuel demands.

I do, although not before my eyes meet with the man holding the decorated stick. My gut tightens seeing conflict in his dark eyes. It's a look that tells me he doesn't trust me combined with an expression of power.

A conversation takes place between Samuel and the two men. One of them is the man from the river—the shaman—the one who's on *my side*. I slowly raise my chin and sneak a glance. The shaman is watching me, staring at me as though he's mesmerized. Maybe it's my hair? The other guy is more interested in speaking with Samuel.

"Is there a problem?" I whisper.

Samuel hushes me.

He nods repeatedly.

"Stand. Follow me," Samuel commands.

I do as he says and nod to both the older men. "Thank you for having me," I say.

"They don't understand English."

"I know, but I feel like I have to say something. Show gratitude."

"They'll be expecting gratitude in other ways."

"How?" I ask and keep up to his pace as we walk the snake-like path again.

"Showing your worth. Not being a liability."

I let out a sigh. "Oh, right. Because my survival skills suck. Wait, where are we going now?"

"To cleanse. There's a stream behind the village. It's the best place to bathe. The water flows from the tepui and leads to a pond before flowing into a cave."

"I'm not complaining because I'm bloody hot, only we both showered today, and we have less dirt on our skin than everyone else here."

"It's not about dirt, Eden. We need to be purified."

"Okay. I'm not going to comment."

"I find it hard to believe."

I'm not going to object to a swim in this heat. And swimming with Samuel.

"Tonight is a celebratory dinner. After I take you to your hut, you need to help the women prepare the food."

"What sort of food are we cooking?"

"Fish, potatoes, bread, and fruit. They call the bread from yuca, oo. I'm not sure if you've heard of it. It's only prepared by the women, not you."

"You think I can't cook?"

"Eden." He gives me a pointed look. "It's laced with cyanide and takes special preparation before you can eat it."

"Oh." Shit, even the food can kill me. The perils of the jungle tick over in my mind until we stop at a stream.

Samuel unties his skirt. "Take off your clothes." He wades in before I get a good look at his front, although Samuel's rear is just as pleasing.

After kicking off my sneakers, I peel off my sweaty top and bra before removing my shorts. I wade in, allowing the cool water to swirl around my legs, walking slowly toward Samuel. He doesn't look at me until I'm waist-deep and in the center of the stream. He turns slowly, keeping his gaze averted.

"The stream is relatively safe. There is no caiman, only the occasional snake, so keep a lookout."

I grin and wiggle my eyebrows. "A snake?"

"Focus. You're safe in the village, only there is danger around you. I'll teach you to understand the jungle and use it, so your surroundings become a way of survival."

Monkeys scream from the treetops, and birds squawk as though being attacked—noise pollution replacing the horns and loud V8 motors of my city jungle. In this moment I miss the city—home. Then I watch Samuel dive beneath the water, and a memory jolts my thoughts—my grandma telling me, "*Home is never in one place, dear. Home is where your heart is.*"

If I cancel the rest of my tour, then for the remaining four weeks, my *home* is here with Samuel.

ORNAMENTS HANG from the walls inside Samuel's hut, reminding me of the beads around my neck.

"I'd feel more comfortable with a few more strands." I glance down to my exposed breasts, the strands of beads covering less than that of a bikini top. It's going to take time for me to appear in public wearing my birthday suit like many of the others here chose to do.

"I agree. I'll ask Kaikare for more strings of beads," Samuel says.

I nod, thankful for small things, including the two grass skirts around my hips for the extra layer of concealment. I roll my shoulders to ease the weight of the long, beaded threads, especially since some are doubled for a graded appearance from my chest to my waist.

My hair is tied back in a braid, still wet from our swim that was interrupted when the women delivered my *clothes.* I drip-dried while they dressed me, Samuel watching from the stream. Although by the look in his eye, I was well aware he liked my new adornments.

Every minute, we're tested to keep our hands off each other. I agreed to it, and even though I'm mildly uncomfortable with my new attire, I'm not afraid to be part of Samuel's life and to understand why he has chosen to live this way. For me, it's a matter of sucking it up and not being self-conscious about my body.

I slide into the hammock and stare up past the mosquito net at the peaked thatched roof. This is a special hut with the walls made of clay, not thatched grass like the other huts. The windows are an open space, and there's an open doorway. It's more private than others and sectioned into two parts. In the smaller section, I clamber in and sway in a hammock. The larger section is a treatment area. In the corner, a wooden table is piled high with books and notes. On another table some sort of equipment and a microscope. A locked case is on the floor beside a long wooden bed.

"Do many of your patients sleep here?"

He pushes off the wall. "Sometimes. Mainly the children." He takes a few steps closer to me. "Do you know how euphoric I feel right now, seeing you in my bed as though it's the most natural thing for you to do?"

The intensity in his eyes warns me we're stepping on shaky ground. I'm not going to risk anything on my first day, even in *his* hut. "I wish you could join me on your bed, although I understand it's not possible, for now."

"Trust holds power to change," he says before walking through the doorway.

I scramble out of the hammock and fall on my knees. "Where are you going?" I spring up to my feet and follow him.

"To find Kaikare and ask for more beads."

TWILIGHT FALLS EARLY with the jungle blocking eighty percent of the sunlight. Long, dark shadows creep over the village, indicating its dinnertime. Kaikare leads me to the cooking fire in the village center. She demonstrates how to gut a huge fish the men had caught earlier in the day. My stomach turns squeamish, and I want to cover my mouth and nose, so I don't inhale the stench. But I can't act like a liability when I'm supposed to be an adult in terms of skill.

Harden up, princess.

A dozen more fish lay on banana palms and are covered in fresh herbs waiting to be cooked. How many do we need to prepare? I finish one without heaving and place it among the others. Every time I glance up, I catch the other women staring oddly at me, or maybe it's at my technique.

Kaikare smiles at me, one of the few women who seem to believe I'm not here in the form of a bad spirit. She has a different look about her—her skin is a shade lighter, her eyes are a honey color and not the usual black, and her dark brown hair falls over her shoulders in waves and different from the jet-black dead-straight hair of everyone else.

Her body is marked with red paint on her extremities and abdomen, a pattern of Vs lines along the length of her stomach with more dots on her chest. Red, white, and black are the standard colors of embellishment, be it the beads or paintwork, except for the blue and yellow feathers in the crowns of the chief and shaman.

I'm given potatoes to chop. The object I'm handed is a fine, thin stone tied to a thick stick. It takes a few attempts for me to chop one potato, and I miss the ease of a sharp knife. The smiles and nods of other women after I achieve the simple task is strangely gratifying.

"I'm Eden," I say and jab myself in the chest.

Kaikare says, "Tamu'ne Akare." She smiles at me and repeats it to the other ladies. I have no idea what it means. I smile and nod as it seems to please them.

More fires ignite from posts around the long hut lighting the cooking area. I wave my hand over the food, although the best repellent is in the form of smoke that wafts our way.

"Shoo." I wave my hand madly, realizing ants have made a trail toward the fish. I cough out a choke when I inhale the smoke.

The women laugh, enjoying my antics. In bare feet, I squish a few black ants with my heel in a quick action, trying not to get bitten.

Kaikare waves her hands at me to stop.

"No?"

"Besides being a source of protein, they add flavor." Samuel stands on the other side of the fire, grinning, arms folded, enjoying the entertainment.

"I'm to let the ants get to the fish?"

He chuckles at my response. "When the ants come, they slide the fish onto the fire, ants and all. You'll be surprised by the taste."

"I'll treat them like anchovies on a pizza and pick them off," I say and groan.

"I should warn you about the entrée, although I'm looking forward to seeing your reaction."

"Why?"

Excited screams come from children running out of the jungle.

"Ah, right on time," he says.

Each child carries a palm leaf curled into a handle. From this side of the fire, I can't make out what has incited their joy. Long thin sticks are handed to every child. Each child holds a twig, extended low and away from their body. Something black wiggles on the end. They run toward me to the fire dividing us and form a circle around the flame. Recognition hits me, and I stumble back, knocking a clay pot of chopped potatoes over.

"Christ," I yell, trembling at the sight of two dozen black tarantulas gored by sticks being cooked over the fire like bloody marshmallows.

The collective sound of laughter pulls me out of my frozen haze of fear, goosebumps pricking at the realization I'm the center of attention, not the giant spiders.

More men have gathered near the fire wearing toothless smiles, fingers pointing at me.

"They taste like chicken." Samuel chuckles.

"Everyone says that about shit you shouldn't eat," I snap. He's grinning when he should be consoling me.

Geez, I can hear the squeal as the spiders cook on the heat, the stench of burned hair filling my nose. Samuel walks around the fire to stand with me. The sound of popping is like corn in a pan.

"Hear the pop? They're ready. They'll offer you a leg."

"No bloody way," I say to him.

"I understand," he says, yet I sense him holding back a smile. "There'll be times you may need to eat something you're not comfortable with."

"Yeah? Well, it won't be a bloody tarantula."

In perfect timing, I turn to the kids gnawing on spider legs exactly like we would a chicken wing, and I wonder to myself if they are really so different from us? Maybe we're all products of our society. Taking my seat near Kaikare, I smile and shake my head graciously when she offers me a spider limb.

"Maybe another time."

THE LONG HUT is divided into sections. The furthest part from the river is open walls with only the cone-shaped thatched roof to protect us from the elements. The smoke from the fire warns off airborne insects, and here, the mosquitoes aren't as troublesome. Most of the people sit cross-legged on the ground or in a squat position. There are a few pieces of logs lying around, so I use one as a chair with Samuel squatting beside me.

When everyone gathers around to eat, I don't know where to avert my gaze. In the shadowy light, there is no mistaking testicles hanging in the dirt as men squat on the ground. In curiosity, I lean forward to check Samuel.

"What are you doing?" he says between clenched teeth.

I ignore him and glance up, my instinct right. I'd assumed the young girls opposite us were staring at me.

No.

In a squatting position, Samuel's bits are in full view to those across the room. Here, a man's testicles on view aren't an unusual sight, only I assume a white man a good foot taller than the average guy here and exceptionally well-endowed is unusual, and teenage girls are curious.

"You're turning the girls on," I remark.

"Don't be ridiculous," he hisses. "They've known me a long time."

"Really? And I bet some have come of age recently, and they notice certain things more so. Take a look for yourself."

He glances across the room, quickly changing his position to cross-legged, so his skirt fans out over his thighs.

"There are some things I just know," I whisper.

He stands and collects food from near the fire and brings it back to me—unusual bread, potatoes, and fish on a palm fronds. It's placed in front of me on the ground, and with each piece, I chew slowly despite the hunger gnawing at my stomach. After some time, I notice Samuel not eating.

"You're not well?"

"I'm only drinking the tea."

"Why? I mean you told me it's okay to eat."

He chuckles low. "It is. In fact, the fish is my favorite meal. I'm... detoxing."

I frown at him. "For what?"

His smile fades. "I need to tell you something."

Hearing his tone, I stop filling my mouth with food. "What?" Like seriously. What the hell now?

"In a week, I'm leaving to go up the tepui on an exploration. It will be one of my final journeys and—"

"Am I coming with you?" I whisper, already knowing the answer.

He shakes his head. "Kaikare will look out for you. I should only be gone a week, maybe two."

I choke on the last piece of food sitting in my mouth. "I'm only here for four weeks."

"I know. It can't be avoided. If I find the plant, then my contract may end earlier, and that would benefit us both."

I turn away from him with tears stinging my eyes. He knew this before he asked me to stay. I press my fingertips against my forehead with the beginnings of a headache.

Being here alone will change everything.

"I feel nauseous." I close my eyes as betrayal settles into my chest. Again.

He takes my hand and squeezes it. "I'll walk you back to my hut, and we can talk some more."

"Väi Uarati Kún-imá," the shaman says to Samuel. *Sun man with long leg.*

"He wants to speak with me. I'll meet you back there."

"Take your time," I snap.

Right now, I want to be alone.

35

SAMUEL

SAMUEL ASSUMES the raucous clicking of insects mere yards from his hut will hinder Eden's sleep. Stepping inside, he sees her silhouette in the hammock, the mosquito net twinkling under the moonlight like morning dew on the leaves.

She had walked on ahead when the shaman had asked to speak to him.

"Are you awake?" he whispers.

"Of course. It's not exactly peaceful."

Her banter is better than silence. "Do you need me to walk with you while you—"

"I was busting. So, I went alone."

He nods. Before dinner, he pointed out areas where she could relieve herself and didn't believe she'd venture out in the dark.

"I used the light on my phone. Not that I'm going to be able to do it much longer since it's barely got any battery left."

"Your eyes will adjust."

The hammock grinds with her movement. "In four weeks, I doubt it."

"Can you see me?"

"No. My eyes are shut," she snaps.

"Open them. Now, can you see me," he asks in a calm voice.

Her dark outline adjusts position. "Kind of."

"Close your eyes." He stands beside the hammock and waits. He hears a sigh pass her lips. "Can you sense me?"

"Your voice leads me."

"Concentrate." His fingers hover over her body.

Electrical energy pricks his fingertips with heat radiating from her body to his hand. He wiggles each finger lightly, imagining the energy flowing back and forth joining them as one force. He pads in a slow motion, each foot lifting as though weighed down with concrete in an effort not to stir the air. Hand flexed, it follows the contour of her body as he moves.

"There's a warmth rolling over me. I'm craving to be touched," she whispers.

"Only focus on the energy between us, not how it makes you feel. Allow it to seep into your skin," he says in a gentle tone.

He homes in on the sound of her breathing—slow and audible.

"It was selfish of me to ask you to stay, knowing I'll be gone for a while. I'm sorry, Eden. I know my apology doesn't mean much right now, but I promise to make it up to you when I return."

"It does mean something," she whispers.

He reaches for her hand. "I want you to try something... focus and remember this energy, how it flows between us. Feel me when I'm not around. Knowing you're here gives me a source of vibrancy I've never known. Your spiritual force will guide me home."

Soft fingers brush his hand before linking them in an unbreakable chain. "I feel you, Samuel. In my heart and all around me. Even when you left me, I could still feel you. Even though I'm not happy about being alone, I'll do it. Know I *can* do it. Your spirit, or whatever you want to call it, guided me here. I'm not going to run away now." Her grip on his hand tightens, "It's odd because I haven't felt this way about anyone, not even Ethan. I've been lying here sulking. Yet I know what we have is real even though it'll be challenging. Part of me wants the challenge because I need it. So, while you're gone, I'll be okay because I'll be finding out a little more about myself while I'm here."

In a moment of truth, he forgets rules, lowers his head, and brushes his lips over hers. "Here, you'll find a sense of power within and develop an ability to control your environment. Unlike the outside world, where material catastrophes happen every day and people feel they have no control over them, you can build what you need, and it changes your sense of value. Your sense of importance changes."

Soft lips silence him. "My journey has already started."

Fingertips skim the length of her body. Her breath catches in a sharp inhale.

"Good night, Eden," he says before finding the treatment bed to stretch out on until dawn.

Securing the mosquito net around him, he listens to her breathing, the sound taking over his mind. Every breath giving her life offers him meaning. Eyes open or shut—it didn't matter. He focuses on emptying his brain of useless images and on connecting with the sounds around him. The jungle screech is his mantra, and he imagines his own wings flying through the forest, the trees whispering, guiding him to the tepui, high up on the rocky mountain. It's here the whispering stops, and he finds himself alone, no spirit to guide him on the tepui. At this point of his journey, it's important he focuses on Eden. Her energy will guide him to the flower and back to her.

SAMUEL SPENDS the morning in the long hut with the older men who basketweave. He's drinking the tea, another day of fasting, and a day to weave a new hammock, the one he is making for Eden.

Samuel catches a fleeting glance of her while she cooks alongside Kaikare. He smiles at her and nods. After he checked on her several times this morning, the women shooed him away. It brings him joy knowing they are warming to her.

Tonight is another ceremony, one he hopes she understands. In a world where less is more, he's not to explain matters. Her journey is her own to understand matters when they happen in the moment and not by preparing her mind for prejudgment to learn their ways. It's the way he learned, and he wants her to experience it all like him.

Fascination has grown among the children. The girls want to learn to braid Eden's hair. After lunch, the women paint her limbs with long red lines. He grins when they lift her beads to paint her chest and abdomen, her head shaking and her hands moving in a stop action. She settles on her back to be the surface for a temporary tattoo, the women eager to paint lighter skin and showcase their skill.

By evening, everyone gathers near the fire, the children up front close to the shaman to listen to the stories about their ancestors and the land.

Wide-eyed, the children huddle closer as the next story explains the anaconda.

"Is this really a bedtime story for children," Eden says under her breath when Samuel translates the shaman's words.

"He's building up for the chief's story."

The shaman raises both hands to the night sky. "A-pantoní-pe nichii." *May you take advantage of this story.*

The shaman nods to Samuel. A cue to meet him on the other side of the long house. "I have a private meeting with the shaman. Kaikare will look out for you now. Don't wait up for me. These meetings can go into the early hours of the morning."

"I'm happy to wait for you," she says when he stands.

"I'd rather you sleep. You'll need your energy for tomorrow. I'm going to show you around." She chuckles with him, making it sound like it's another Hollywood tour.

Samuel walks the outside of the story circle to Kaikare, sitting with the women. He explains his absence for the next few hours and tells them to watch over Eden, making sure she doesn't wander to the ceremonial side of the long house.

In a thatched-walled room, Samuel and a dozen warriors kneel before the shaman. Trying to find inner peace, Samuel closes his eyes and listens to soft harmonic tunes, the shaman calling to the forest, asking her to accept her children kneeled before her and connect their souls to guide them in their upcoming journey.

The shaman's song drones out the screech of the jungle. The warriors hum a low 'mmm,' a mantra Samuel connects to and sounds out along with them. The shaman sucks the wooden pipe, blows smoke into his face, a different tune for each warrior, a new request for a spirit connecting to each soul.

These are men who, for weeks, have sacrificed meat, sugar cane, and any substance capable of hindering the absorption of the brew. There's been abstinence of sexual orgasm to preserve energy and align thoughts to focus on the spiritual dimensions ayahuasca demands. Samuel has failed to refrain for the required weeks, only days, and hopes his experience of training his thoughts on this occasion will be enough.

He allows thoughts of Eden's safety to melt away, knowing Kaikare will safeguard the ceremony. Men join the room, a support for each warrior. It's time to leave the quiet room and congregate in the *waipa*, an open-air round house where celebrations take place.

In two lines, the men walk in silence, the receiver and the protector side by side, ready to begin the journey of the mind.

Silence has fallen within the village perimeter, except for a steady drumbeat by an elder to remind one's thoughts to remain in the circle of the shaman. The fire beyond their walls flickers in the distance, no longer maintained by those who gathered hours before.

A quiet normality fills him. The usual shrill of mosquitoes circle around his sweaty crown. The thick, moist air forces extra effort on inhalation, almost a natural way for him to breathe.

The serene voice of the shaman prepares him for his volatile body reaction. His protector passes him a bowl of ayahuasca tea. Samuel downs it, shudders at the bitter taste, reminding him of tequila and lemon. He's handed another, and another, and another. Focusing on keeping the contents in his gut for as long as possible, he hums, eyes closed, his body trembling as the indigenous medicine is absorbed by his cells. The first sign of his stomach contracting forces Samuel onto his hands and knees, and he fills the large bowl before him. He swipes his mouth and settles back into a cross-legged position and is handed more brew. The slight tremor in his arms intensifies. The quaking in his gut radiates out until his entire body convulses, leaving him curled on his side, his protector lifting his cheek for vomit to flow freely.

"Water," he screams out, only in his head.

The brew can't be diluted.

Every synchronized vowel from the shaman's throat drones out the moans and puking of those around him. Irregular purple shapes form before his eyes, then turn into slow-moving lava blobs, switching to pink, red, and orange and morph in a kaleidoscope of color, mesmerizing his vision. He allows the colors to take control of his body, lulling him into a false calmness until the probing tickles his hands, tracking the veins along his arms. Long intrusive fingers find his innermost thoughts and sort through every memory like a filing system searching for the crippling memories haunting him most. Every ayahuasca experience rakes through memories and addresses different files of the brain. Emotions overboil until he sobs like a young boy denied his most favorite toy, only the energy is tenfold.

As a sixteen-year-old, he visualizes friends bullying a girl, and he *watches on*. He experiences pain through *her eyes*, not his privileged upbringing in wealthy Trousdale Estate in Los Angeles. The taunting, the teasing as though she was inferior, and then until she could take no more, his soul cries for her soul. He has carried the burden of letting her down along with the promise he made to her all those years ago to be a better man and not follow the same path as his friends.

His thoughts switch to sexual infidelities through his university life, then to rebelling against his parents and their attempt to influence his career. Every piece of his past has led him on this journey.

Why does he exist at this time, in this place, in the universe?

He sees the plants with extraordinary powers to heal. His work is to find meaning in his existence, the euphoria of finding the essence of *why*. He sees Eden's face, a sign she belongs—with him. In a flap of wings—turquoise, red, and yellow feathers—he finds the space above the trees and soars through the jungle, *his forest*, a place of belonging. Below him is a map lit up like New York at night. A satellite view of every tree, branch, and root interconnecting with the next like a nervous system, each trunk a spinal cord, blue neon lights pulsing with electric energy. The effects of the ayahuasca vine guide him, lighting a path through the forest floor, a network of roots coming together in a giant web of the Amazon. With the wind in his wings, he recognizes river systems, crossing into an unknown section, and his concentration intensifies.

A black jaguar sprints the same path below, joining him on the mission, intimidating predators daring to cross his path. A second black jaguar joins them, a surprise. His confidence soars as he approaches the tepui, a dark shadow rolling like thunder clouds inside the giant stone. He has heard of the bad spirits residing there—*Kanaima* and the *Mawari*, spirits of the dead. He has the shaman running below protecting him, and now he has another black jaguar, and something tells him the shaman's mate could possibly bring extra enforcement against the spirits of this mystical world.

Could it be Kaikare? Only she's not part of the ceremony.

Eden's cry sounds in the distance, bringing him catapulting to the ground. The black jaguar growls. The shaman's voice tells him to focus and continue. The second black jaguar is attacking, not in fight but more in reprimand. Feathers beat. He soars up the side of the tepui to the plateau, the network now highlighted in electric yellow dotted with red. His flight path is low. He searches for the purple flower among the red, the pull to find it overbearing. He stops when a third black panther dashes beneath him—a younger cat and not as fast as the other two. His focus is challenged by curiosity, *her* voice breaking through the vision in cries and screams, yelling abuse. He falls and tumbles. The cat padding toward him, a predator ready to pounce. It bounds past him, pulls up a few feet away beside a miniature lily-shaped purple flower.

The shaman's voice pulls him through a funnel of color, recalling him into his own body, the present, the round house. He moans in disappointment, the exhilaration of flying forged to his memory. A map of the tepui is ingrained into his brain. Getting there will not be easy, especially without flight.

36

EDEN

SAMUEL RETURNS to our hut at first light.

It's a little after sunrise, although it's difficult to interpret the exact moment the sun rises with a canopy of tangled green blocking most of the light.

He tiptoes around, and yet he wakes me since my head is thick from barely sleeping. I'm still haunted after finding Samuel curled up like a fetus in the shaman's special ceremonial hut. The stench of acid lingered in the air, his stomach contents in a bowl by his side.

I had cried, tried to wake him, yelled profanities knowing the meaning would fall on deaf ears. It felt good to release my frustration until Kaikare took me by the shoulders after the shaman shooed me away.

His broad, muscular back tenses as he kneels to open his suitcase, busying himself with a map.

"What was wrong with you last night?" I ask, trying to hide concern.

He freezes, although he doesn't turn. Instead, he dips his chin. "I can't explain now. I need you to go to the fields with Kaikare and learn their ways."

I clamber out of the hammock. "But—"

"Eden, *please*, not now. You shouldn't have come. I'd asked you to stay here. Please go to the fields." He points to the doorway, and sure enough, Kaikare is waiting.

He hands me two bananas and a clay mug filled with water. "The women will cook something more substantial soon."

I down the water and hand the mug back to him. "Promise me we'll talk later."

He places a hand on my face and rubs his thumb on my cheekbone. "Okay. So long as you stop worrying about what happened last night." He leans in with a quick kiss to my forehead. "Kaikare will teach you today."

Kaikare and I walk side by side just as friends do, except the entire journey is in silence.

We keep walking beyond the village until we stop at a small clearing and join the other women dotted among the rows of prickled shrubs. I turn in a circle, assessing the fields. Some plants I recognize like sugarcane, capsicum, and potatoes. Toward the jungle edge is a cluster of pineapples and banana palms. Unfamiliar are the rows of woody branches dotted with small thorns and fanning leaves. Samuel had mentioned yuca as a main source of diet, so I assume—since no-bloody-one can enlighten me—these are the source, and it's our chore for the morning.

Kaikare tilts her head, holds out a long thick branch with a stone fastened by twine at the end. She points for me to dig the root. Remembering what Samuel had previously mentioned about the root containing cyanide, I crinkle my brow at Kaikare.

She points to her mouth and eyes, shakes her head.

I turn and observe how the other women harvest the root, a technique without using garden gloves or protective clothing. My core switches on, and I suck in my bare stomach as much as possible because of the tiny thorns. Swaying the man-made pick over my shoulder, I whack the ground. Vibrations shoot up my arms to my neck and back. I let go with one arm and rub a point at the base of my neck beneath strands of beads that are becoming heavier by the minute. Ignoring sideways glances from the other women, I heave and take another swipe, barely denting the soil.

I can do this.

Several blows later, Kaikare nudges me aside and extracts the plant pulling out the entire root. She smiles at me before throwing it on a pile. She nods to the next plant growing beside the one I previously mined.

Two more plants are added to the pile. I wipe my brow, my attention captured by the giggling of young girls reaching for banana bunches. To my left, a pregnant woman plucks capsicums, and I can't help the pang of jealousy that she doesn't have to wield a blunt axe. I stop to inspect a blister on the thumb line of my palm. Kaikare points to the next field. Potatoes. I smile, although I need to relieve myself first.

Pointing to the jungle, I leave her and wander to the edge of the field. I weave around tree trunks, dodging the unruly vines, all while maintaining my balance on the black decay covering the tangled roots. Yellow butterflies erupt before me, the cluster forming a cloud. It's no surprise since the butterflies are everywhere, and even still, I smile every time it happens.

Inside the green walls, the sunlight tightens, and I'm thankful for the added privacy. A moan comes from the distance to my right. A younger voice. Female. I walk the opposite way even though defecating with an audience doesn't seem to bother these people as much as it does me. I stop walking and hear a deeper masculine moan. I turn and spy two figures leaning on a tree for support, one leaning on the other's back. Realizing what I'm witnessing, I still in shock. In seconds, the boy sprints away weaving through the wide trunks until he's out of sight. The girl straightens. My position makes vision difficult though she seems calm. She grabs a handful of leaves and attends to herself. She adjusts the beads around her neck before strolling toward the jungle edge of the fields.

Her hair is short in a bowl-cut like many of the other girls, so I wouldn't recognize her anyway. I have figured out the girl's hair is cut when she first menstruates, as the young girls in the village have longer hair. The older women have long, gray-streaked hair with thinning ends, longer because they are menopausal, maybe.

I keep walking, stumbling in my sneakers, my concentration hazed thinking about the young couple. There would be consequences if they were caught. When I find a palm adequate for my hygiene, I squat, checking the ground for poison ants, snakes, and anything moving.

In a vulnerable position, I hurry through the paces and rethink the path I took to get here.

I leave and walk back. The fields are near empty. On the far side, the last of the women with baskets on their heads disappear into the trees.

Feet barely touching the ground, I sprint through the potato rows reminding myself not to be a dependent child and be mindful of the tasks of the day.

I reach the younger girls at the back of the rank, catch my breath, and follow the procession of baskets to the long hut. The men sit cross-legged on the ground weaving baskets and fishing line. The children play with a coconut, rolling it along the ground, jumping out of the way as though it's an object of tag.

Kaikare finds me and leads me to a space on the hard ground beside her. She coaches me to chop potatoes. She wraps the vegetables in palm leaves or chops others to boil. Curiously, I watch the women prepare the yuca root. Kaikare sees my interest, points to me, and shakes her head. "I know," I say, nodding. Aware I don't have the skill.

Damn, I nod a lot.

I continue to observe the process of grating the root and soaking it in a clay pot of water. Outside the hut, there's an area consisting of beams and ladders. I first presumed it to be a child's playground. The overhead poles are used to secure a long, tightly-woven tube where the root is stuffed inside and left to drain the deadly juice. Kaikare joins some of the ladies to empty the contents of the twine- woven tubes hanging for, I assume, several days. The vegetable is now flour-like and placed on a long clay tray spread out to cook on the fire.

"Heating it removes the last of the poison," Samuel says. I sigh, hearing his voice. "Next, it will be turned into bread."

"How are you?" I search his face.

He nods to Kaikare and answers me at the same time, "Fine. Have you finished your chores?"

"I don't have a list, but I've helped some."

There's a hint of a smile when he speaks to Kaikare.

"What did you say to her?"

"I asked her if you were productive. She said you're learning."

"I am," I say, indignant. "Without any orientation."

He chuckles low. "Let's take a walk."

We reach the far end of the village, and he continues along a well-trodden path of tree roots. "I thought you might want to bathe."

"I do because I worked up a sweat in the fields. And I have to ask why the men don't help?"

"They prepare the soil and grow the new crops from cuttings and seeds. Their job is to hunt, fish, weave the baskets, nets, and hammocks, make the darts, and harvest the poison for the arrows and darts. The women tend to the fields and cook the meals."

"And tend to the children. Which reminds me, I spotted some of the women with babies strung to their backs as they worked. Surely, the fathers who are basket weaving could watch over the young ones to save the mother's back?"

"The men don't help much at a young age. They tend to show their sons how to hunt and fish, and the girls follow their mother's ways until they marry. By early teens, they are promised to someone, and when it's time, the guy shifts his hammock into the girl's family hut. He then learns from and works alongside his new father-in-law."

I gawk at him. "Simply like that. No wedding."

"The only ceremony is for new warriors heading out on their first hunt, like an initiation or a celebration as told by their folklore or ceremonies as you witnessed last night."

"Are you going to tell me about last night?"

"I know you're concerned for me, but your being there could've ruined everything."

"Or I could have helped. You were in a bad way. Vomiting. Crying out. Moaning. Seriously, I couldn't leave you like that."

"I knew what was happening. It was part of the ayahuasca process. Next time, please do what is asked of you. The shaman might not be so lenient if it happens again." He stops short. "Are you going to bathe?"

I hadn't even realized we'd reached the stream. I wade in while Samuel fetches the foaming leaves to wash myself.

"Am I going to be punished?" I ask, taking the leaves from his outstretched arm. He sits on the bank and watches, his masked expression showing no emotion.

"I only heard him say you didn't belong."

"At the ceremony?"

"No. In the tribe." He kneels in front of me. "My heart sank hearing his words. It broke me because more than anything, I want you here."

"Tell me what to expect tonight. I don't want to stuff-up again." I clamber over rocks wishing there was an Egyptian cotton towel to greet me. Useless really because, in minutes, the sweat will bask my skin and gleam like a wax coat.

Samuel offers his hand to hoist me up. He holds my gaze, and I see a glimpse of the longing inside of him.

"If you follow Kaikare's lead and do what I ask, you'll be fine."

"What happens tonight?"

"We eat. We drink. More stories. New warriors are initiated."

Something tells me it won't be that simple.

37

EDEN

THE STEADY BEAT of a drum and the soft notes of a flute filter through the air. It's the most relaxed I've ever been while eating dinner. The people sit quietly, smiling at one another. No excitement, and yet there's a sense of gratitude even though the makeshift wooden spit is absent of an animal. The fish and vegetables are still satisfying, and I find my fill easily. What's surprising after nothing except fruit all day, my stomach is adjusting to this lifestyle. I'm not even craving chocolate.

The fire is stoked, and the flames climb toward the dark sky. The shaman utters a few words. Young and old gather closer to form a half-circle around the shaman. The blue, yellow, and orange flames glow behind him creating his own theatrical stage.

There are more sticks, reminding me of cat whiskers, protruding from his cheeks tonight. He's wearing a smaller headdress with more teeth and bones than feathers. Raising his hands, he looks to the heavens and tells a tale about *The Tree of Life*.

Samuel whispers the translation. The touch of his lips near my ear is more gratifying than any story. When it concludes, I recognize the shaman's last words.

"A-pantoní-pe nichii."

"What does it mean?" I ask.

"May you take advantage of this story."

"Right. Like a lesson learned." I glance back and catch the shaman staring at me—again. "The shaman keeps looking at us."

"If he makes eye contact, don't look him in the eye. He'll take it as a threat."

"I looked him directly in the eye last night when I shouted at him. It's a good thing he doesn't understand English," I say under my breath.

"You hope he doesn't."

"Does he?"

"I'm not sure. He doesn't speak it to me, although he may understand certain words. He hinted at being offended by your actions."

Shit, I called him a bastard.

"I was scared for you and wanted to help. And before you say I shouldn't have been there, I was, and you were in a bad way, so what was I to do? Leave you lying in your own vomit?"

"Yes," he says firmly. "I know what happens, Eden. You have to purge to get to the next stage, which is the most important part of the ceremony. Knowing you caught me in an exposed position, well I..."

"What?"

"Did you ever consider I was embarrassed by you seeing me vulnerable?" He looks down at me, his gaze mellow. The reflection of the fire flickers in his pupils.

"I'm here for you," I whisper. "I was scared I was going to lose you. Then you didn't come home." *Home.* It's weird I'm thinking of his hut as our home. "I only wanted to hold you and make sure you were okay."

He slides his hand under my elbow and along my arm until our fingers link. I want to lay back and melt into him until I glance around and note no one is showing any public affection. No arms on shoulders. No handholding. No teenage girls on boy's laps. No children nestled into their mother's chest for a cuddle. All private people.

The dom-dom of drums breaks my train of thought. Five young men march into the center of the large circle, their lean bodies freshly painted in long black lines and red Vs. Tonight's audience appears to be a full house. There are one hundred Ularans, Samuel, and me.

The shaman stands in the center of the young men, now on bent knees. Kaikare walks to the shaman and holds up a thick piece of bamboo. She pops the wooden plug. One ant crawls out, and she replaces the plug. The shaman takes it by the thorax and places the ant on a young guy's shoulder. He cringes a little, and I understand why.

"Jesus," I murmur, seeing the ant's body raised in the air, its pinchers latched onto his skin.

"Say nothing," Samuel whispers.

Kaikare pops the lid, and ant after ant is attached to his skin on both shoulders and down his back. The boy's expression remains stoic. The process is repeated on the next boy. When the last ant is attached, the shaman returns to the first guy. Kaikare gives him something small and holds a leaf.

"It's a piranha tooth," Samuel says.

The boy bows his head when the tooth is placed behind his ear. The shaman carves the skin, his mouth gapes a little, and his gaze is focused. He sings a melodic three notes. Dabbing a stick on the leaf Kaikare holds, he then blots it where he cuts.

"A tattoo?" I whisper.

Samuel nods. "He's ready for his first hunt. A step in becoming a warrior."

"He didn't make a sound," I say in awe.

"No. It doesn't help, and noise upsets others. They need to find the strength within. The ants helped."

"How?" I choke out.

"Apart from guiding them to find their inner strength, the burning sensation diverts the pain away from the tattoo."

"Well, I'd rather the tattoo," I blurt out.

His mouth leans close to my ear. "The tooth is sharp and stings like a bitch, yet nothing compares to the poison burning like a million hot irons."

I move Samuel's hair away from his right ear. It's there—an X with a line through the center. I'd seen the symbol on the baskets. "What is it?"

"Their symbol for a butterfly."

"Why a butterfly?"

"A representation of life. Endurance. Hope. Change for the better. Resurrection." He glances down and smiles at me as the thought gives him inner peace.

"I see them everywhere, and today I came across heaps of them like a cloud of yellow."

"It's called a flutter."

"Okay... a flutter of butterflies. Does it mean anything? I mean everything seems to hold significance here." My gran had told me butterflies were someone special we once knew, or something good was going to happen, except my father told me never to believe what she said about those things. Now I'm finding myself wanting to trust her words.

An arm slips over my shoulder. "It means you're on the right path." He kisses my forehead and then releases me as quickly.

The drumming stops.

The chief stands and holds his arms in the air. He gazes up to the night sky and speaks to the heavens. Or maybe it's to their god or ancestors. Wait. Are their ancestors the spirits in the tepuis?

Everyone stands, and the circle falls away.

There's no cheering. No congratulatory slaps on the young boys' backs. The ants are plucked from their skin and dropped safely inside the bamboo tubes. Families disperse in groups and return to their huts. Once again, I hone in on the monkeys' mindless chatter and the birds' piercing squawks as the background music. A near-full moon lights the way to our hut. Samuel slips his fingers in mine when we walk past a group of young men. My lips tingle with a smile at his ownership.

"This moving your hammock-wedding thing. I hope the men don't want to do this to me while you're away."

He squeezes my hand in warning. "That's not even funny."

Stifling a giggle, I snort and laugh at myself. "How do you stop it? I mean it sounds too easy, yet we're not allowed to *be* together."

He gives me a sideways glance, expression unchanged, not seeing the humor at all. Maybe he caught a more serious tone to the last few words I said.

"The shaman has to approve it first. Then the father-in-law."

"So, a couple has dated a while then."

"Not always."

Turning my body, I walk sideways so I can read his face when he answers my next question, "Are you telling me the girl has no choice?"

"Not always."

"Do any of them believe in falling in love, first?"

"Some. Only the decision lies with the shaman and the father-in-law. My intent is known to the shaman if it's what you're worried about."

I remember some international couples who I'd met in our hotel. They had told me they were married by an arranged marriage, which is common in their culture. Their love for each other is as strong as any other couple I knew. They told me their bond and love grew with time, and they couldn't imagine themselves with anyone else. What concerns me is the young couple I saw earlier today and if it's a secret love affair for a reason? Is one of them promised to another?

"I don't see couples holding hands and being in love."

Samuel glances at me as we reach our doorway. The light flickers across his tanned, muscular chest. "Like us."

"Yes. Like us"

Without an audience, he whisks me up in his arms and carries me through the doorway in a declaration of making our own rules.

"Our time will come," he promises.

Arms linked around his neck, I slide down his body and close my eyes with the sensation of warmth being close to him and stand a moment longer, making out his expression in the shadows. He leans down and kisses me hard. I didn't expect it. The need overtakes every thought, and I link my leg around his hips to bring our bodies closer.

Large hands grab my cheeks, bringing his forehead to mine, and he breaks the kiss. Sensing his torment, I slide my leg down his body putting space between us, my desire screaming in defeat.

At this angle, his face is hidden, but there's anguish in his labored breaths. "Every day you're here, I'm struggling to keep my hands off you."

"Do you want me to leave?"

He shakes his head, his forehead sliding on mine.

"Can you talk to the shaman?" I rasp.

"It requires *more* than a green light to sleep together. It's a commitment, an expectation we'll stay together. Be married here. I know that might not mean a lot to you at the moment, but for me..." he hesitates, "... I'm one of them now." He backs away from me until he's standing in his treatment room. "Could you live with me here?"

"Indefinitely?" I gasp. "I thought you had a contract?" My throat turns dry, so I walk to the bench and scoop out a few cups of water from the clay bowl on a narrow side table.

This is a conversation we need to have, so I ease my rear up on the hard wooden table, my legs dangling. "Have you changed your mind about eventually leaving? I mean, I assumed my being here meant there would be an *us* in the future when your contract ends?" An unspoken understanding when we were in Canaima.

He stands opposite me with both hands on his hips, only his gaze is lowered as though he's deciding on how to respond. "I thought you might understand that I don't fit in with society. I hate all the materialistic bullshit and drama. It's not a world where I want to live."

A ball of panic grows in my chest. "And you're mentioning it now?"

"You saw how I struggled in Brazil."

"There are many awkward people in the world. You were a different guy in Ilhéus."

"Ilhéus was different because I was with you." He smiles at me. "You have a way of settling me. Now you're here, it has made me think about the days leading up to the end of my contract and what I'll do. I want to think about a future with you, only I'm afraid to go back to a world where I was unhappy." He glances at me. "I was depressed for some time."

Samuel places one foot slowly in front of the other as he moves quietly around the room. "Years ago, when I was still living in LA, I watched a documentary on a young dentist who became an explorer and lived with the indigenous people in Venezuela. He helped them, as a dentist, and over time, they taught him how to live by means of using his surroundings. The idea appealed to me. So, I lodged an application and found a position in a Pemón village not far from here and worked as a volunteer physician. It felt like nothing else I've experienced. I learned more about myself during that time, so when I returned to LA, I searched for more volunteer work. My wealthy parents were appalled at the direction my medical career had veered toward, so they pulled strings, and I was offered several paid positions. I found a physician and botanist contract located around here. Of course, I jumped at the opportunity and stayed with different communities. The more remote, the more joy I found."

Questions sit on my tongue, but I don't want to interrupt him.

"When I found something unusual like a plant the shaman used, or one considered to be rare, I documented it and sent a sample to Caracas for analysis. Sometimes it was a new species." He stops and places both hands on the bed beside me. "Do you know how exhilarating it is to discover a plant never found anywhere else in the world and with medicinal value?"

"Wow," I whisper.

I sense his need to release all this information pent up inside of him for years. "For short breaks, I'd stay at Canaima. I bought my own room, so I could go there whenever I wanted. Back then, it was hard to get accommodation. Now with the political unrest, only a handful of tourists visit." He shakes his head. "It took me a while to adjust and live by these ways, so I don't have an expectation for you to cope in a matter of days."

"Is that a compliment?"

"It is. You're doing better than I imagined." He brushes hair from my face and offers a warm smile. "I'm proud of you. Even so, we still need to be careful. One thing I want you to promise is to keep an open mind. There's a mystery to their stories, but it's also powerful. Do you understand? Don't shrug off their tales as fairy tales."

"Okay," I say, nodding repetitively.

He walks to the doorway and peers out. "Living here has become a natural way to exist by using the environment and not money for food. There's no dependency on the internet, water, food, money, or where I'm ranked in society, and especially, not what university I attended. None of it matters. What does matter is my ability to survive. To make a fire. To make my own bed and shelter to protect me from the weather. To make lines and nets to fish and arrows and spears to hunt. To make a tool to cut your kill. Know where to find water in the plants and where not to drink because as much as the jungle provides, she can kill you in seconds if you're ignorant." He looks over his shoulder to me, I assume to see if I'm catching up, but my god, I'm having trouble comprehending it all. "I'm rambling now," he mutters. "I apologize. The tea is getting the better of me."

I didn't want him to stop, except there is a change in the air, and I'm not sure if it flows from him or me. I don't want to think about the jungle or what lurks out there, or the days he'd be gone, and I'd be alone.

Unlike him, I miss my family, my friends, the comfort of home, sunsets on the beach, and admittedly, I like the internet.

I wanted an adventure, and I'm living it. I wanted to find love, and I've found that too. Caught up in the excitement, I went beyond my comfort zone for *him*.

Do I want to commit simply so we can bang each other in the village while I'm here? Surely, it's not a promise to stay.

The Ularan stories are not fairy tales.

If Samuel doesn't want to leave this place, and I can't stay, then maybe I need to stop believing we'll have our happy ending.

38

SAMUEL

Two days later...

SAMUEL and the shaman stroll through the garden of healing. The shaman sings as they walk, words only for the forest to understand. His song instills an inner peace within Samuel like no other.

They stop to examine the plants infiltrating the soil of the medicinal ones, every shrub vying for space. Here, only the quality vines are allowed to survive. Weeds and toxic thorned vines slashed. Occasionally, a new plant surfaces, one Samuel has not seen, and the shaman takes a sample, and in a private ceremony, asks the tree spirits if this plant will heal or take life.

Samuel picks twigs, leaves, and flowers all necessary for his upcoming journey. Some are best dried. Even so, the list of what he'll need for medicinal use and first-aid purposes is extensive.

He's to drink the brew of ayahuasca and chacruna before he leaves in a ceremony the night before—one without interruption.

He picks a little extra for Eden so she can rub the insect repellent leaves on her mosquito bites, more spots visible since she ran out of repellent. He stashes it into his animal skin pouch that's secured with twine around his hips.

The shaman touches his hand.

"She distracts you," he says in his stilted language. "She distracts me."

Samuel frowns.

He tells Samuel she's like the sun and the moon together, her light ever-present. He waves his arm in an arc—Eden the golden light over the rainbow.

Samuel tells the shaman he is focused. Before the shaman has a chance to speak of her, he confesses he relies on her presence like one does air. To his surprise, the shaman's expression is unchanged, as though he already knew the depth of his feelings for her. He tells Samuel he was once distracted in his early days of training and almost chose a path with a woman instead of medicine.

Samuel acknowledges his words, disguising his surprise. He emphasizes Eden will know her place and not interfere with his work and asks for the shaman's blessing.

The shaman holds his gaze with fierce intensity, so much so, Samuel bows his head. He tells the shaman there is no risk, and if it comes to a choice, he'll choose the safety of the village.

The shaman's face lights up, an expression Samuel's rarely witnessed. He hears footsteps and follows the shaman's gaze to the one who treads heavy on her feet.

"Kaikare pointed this way, so I thought I'd find you here," Eden says in a tone indicating she's pleased with herself.

Samuel spins to the shaman expecting him to be distressed with Eden in their sacred place. Instead, his eyes hold a twinkle, and it takes a moment longer before he holds up a hand.

"Stop," Samuel orders. She stills and looks around her. "You shouldn't be here."

She raises her arms and drops them to her side. "You need to give me a list because there are no warning signs to stay out."

He goes to her and leads her back over her tracks. "I assumed you were with the women in the field. I was coming to find you after I finished here as Asoo is due to visit today. Do you need some supplies because we could give him a list of things to collect in Canaima? Another thought, he could charge your phone and return it to you in a few days."

"Really? You trust him with my phone?" Her eyes round.

"I do." Samuel takes a path past the round hut toward the treatment hut. "You could give him your phone to read messages and let you know if anything is urgent."

"Good idea because I need to send messages to the girls and my parents. If they reply and my phone is in Wi-Fi, Asoo can bring it back to me."

"Grab your phone. I have paper and a pen in my case. I'll also ask him to get some insect repellent." They reach his treatment room, and he stills her to inspect the bites on her shoulders, arms, and back. Samuel pulls leaves from his pouch. "Rub these over your bites. It will help ease the itch and stop any infection. I'll get some sap for you to use on your skin to act like a natural repellent until Asoo returns."

Eden smiles, the relief hinting at her exhaustion. "You know I hated the rash I got from the repellent, only these bites are bloody killing me."

"You have plenty of malarial meds?"

"I do."

He flicks open the case and grabs the paper and two pens. "I'll arrange for Asoo to grab some supplies from my room at Canaima. Write your message for Asoo along with names, and I'll make a list of supplies."

Minutes later, he leads her toward the river to wait for the sound of the motor.

The tapping motor alerts them to its presence before the curiara putts around the bend, the gray-brown water streaming in a wide 'V' behind it. Asoo doesn't wave out like he has on other days. Sensing his concern, Samuel waits on the bank, putting distance between him and the canoe when he mounts the sand. With balance and grace, he glides over the edge and lands only feet from Samuel.

"My friend needs you in Camp Sundown. A measles outbreak. Some children have pneumonia."

"Are the people vaccinated?" Eden asks, her eyes filled with desperation.

"No." He ponders his risk, the Ularans risk of contracting it. "Are the volunteers issuing antibiotics? Quarantining those who are sick and their families from the community?"

Asoo shakes his head. "My friend, I messenger. I sent to ask for help."

"I can give you some of my supplies as I ordered more when I last visited Canaima. Is Doctor Robert still in the camp?"

Asoo closes his palms in a prayer gesture. "Yes."

"Give me some time to gather my supplies. If he needs anything else, let me know. Unfortunately, I can't help as I leave for an exploration tomorrow."

"Already?" Eden asks.

"It's a day early as we're leaving with the warriors at the beginning of the hunt. I'm sorry, I'll talk to you about it later. Give Asoo your message and explain what you need him to do." Samuel takes off to the treatment hut, his thoughts whirling between Eden, his journey, and the news from Asoo. He hopes the outbreak is contained and not spread further into the jungle.

TWILIGHT. Night. Dawn. Daylight. The time in the jungle never alters in the constant heat and humidity. The wet season exacerbates the humidity and the balance of life, with the challenge of finding sufficient food if the river floods the village.

He ponders how the Ularans believe this is in the hands of the gods.

This season the Ularans dodged upsetting the gods, the river only creeping near the outskirts of the village. The elders fear the next wet season to be worse. Plans are underway to build huts further away from the river and high off the ground in the trees. Samuel overheard an elder mention the spirit of the Kanaima in their village lives in the white sun god. He hopes the others don't believe Eden's presence will bring them bad luck.

Tonight, at twilight, he's to prepare for the ceremony.

Eden has barely spoken to him since meeting Asoo. He can't afford to be distracted by her now. She doesn't understand the importance of his upcoming journey, especially tonight's spiritual one with the guidance of the shaman to lead him to the rare flower. In truth, as much as his own journey has led him to this day—the pinnacle of why he is in Ulara—Samuel also wishes for it to be over so he can only be with her.

NIGHT HAS FALLEN over the village.

The jungle choir on the highest volume barely distracts Samuel from his purpose. Small fires flicker in the round house, creating enough light to see the bowl of fluid handed to Samuel. He drinks the brew made from the ayahuasca vine. He gulps down several bowls, waits for the moment his stomach turns inside out to rid itself of the vile tea. The purging begins, a severe headache takes hold, and he loses the ability to stay on all fours. Curled in a ball, he holds his temples, the pain taking over until he moans and cries, his voice overbearing the harmonic song of the shaman.

Two soft hands cup his rough fingers. The voice of his angel whispering in his ear. "You're safe. Go where you need."

In his mind, his thoughts connect with the voice, psychedelic colors purging his brain when he feels his soul, and his spirit travels beyond his childhood memories into another dimension—a tunnel of bright neon light, a kaleidoscope of dreams.

He visualizes his life in rewind, and it quickly switches to fast forward to the future where he spreads his yellow, turquoise, and red feathers and takes flight on a path he has already traveled. An inner peace fills him knowing his body is in safe hands with not only a protector, more so with love surrounding his aura.

With her, he's ready to take the journey into the unknown.

In the early hours of the morning, Samuel returns to his hut, passing Eden sleeping peacefully in her hammock. She disobeyed him again. He touches the side of her cheek and kisses her lips. "Thank you for your support," he whispers. "I was grateful to have you there to look after me." It was the first time he came to without any vomit on his cheek or shoulder. The shaman had revealed everything, including her washing him while he slept off the medicine. "I know you're worried about my exploration. Afraid to be here alone. You'll be safe. Kaikare will take care of you. Knowing you're here will guide me home because you own my heart."

She doesn't move beneath his touch. Her breath is heavy with sleepy sighs.

Sighs he wants to hear when he sleeps beside her. He now longs for the day to hold her in his arms every night.

Sometime after dawn, Samuel gathers his containers and kit to hold the plants and fills his bag with food and bottles of water. Sources of water can be found in the jungle, but with the length of their journey, he needs to carry extra and have a bottle ready to collect it from the trees and bamboo.

Around his waist, a twine belt holds a pigskin pouch. Hanging from the twine are handmade darts, a knife, and in his hand, a long blow pipe doubling as a walking stick. A hammock is rolled into his backpack along with a mosquito net and Western medicinal supplies. For this exploration, he wears his sneakers because his feet haven't adapted to the long miles, the damp jungle floor, and the torturous rock they'll climb over for many days.

A small group gathers to send them on their way. Eden rises early to be with him. He kisses Eden on the lips for the second time in a matter of hours, knowing the shaman has witnessed their affection. "You'll be fine," he says, meaning every word. "I'll come home to you as quick as I can."

"I know you will," she croaks and swipes her eyes. They stand a moment assessing the other, both stiff-lipped. She watches him join the warrior circle, chanting and waving their spears, mentally preparing themselves for the hunt. Samuel and Tïmenneng will separate from the others after a day's journey to begin their exploration. Other men aren't so eager to enter the home of the spirits.

The green membranes pulsate with life. He turns before the green cavern swallows him up and nods to the only woman brave enough to experience this world with him.

He gives her a subtle nod, an unspoken promise of love.

39

EDEN

My chest is tight with a ball of panic growing inside it, threatening to unleash all my insecurities. The composed expressions of the women make it worse. They may live in a peaceful place without the stress of first-world issues, only this isn't my world, and being here *is* stressful. I'm not skilled in their ways, and I'm struggling to find water in the plants like they do. I snap plants the wrong way, and the couple of mouthfuls stored in the stem gushes out before I get my mouth to it.

Heaving my ax above my head, I slam it into the ground near the yuca. In a few sharp blows, I've excavated the earth and dug out the roots. I glance up to a young girl picking bananas and watch as she leaves her duties to wander into the forest with some other girls.

Getting Kaikare's attention, I point to my mouth, indicating I'm hungry and head to the palms hoping to find one yellowing banana. Since most are picked green, bunches strung to beams in the long hut to ripen, I don't hold out much hope. Reaching up, I move a clump to the side to inspect the skin and jump back when a large brown spider unfolds and emerges. I clutch my chest gasping. Willing my heart to slow, I remind myself not to panic. *It's only a spider.* Although this one doesn't look like the tarantulas the children brought back to eat. It's almost as large, hairy, and brown with a smaller thorax and abdomen. With spindly long legs, it moves fast over the bananas, and its red fangs flare. An outstretched arm lands on my stomach and pushes me back a few steps. Kaikare is by my side shaking her head.

We take another step back. With her axe, she flicks it to the ground, and it scurries away. She looks at me and shakes her head. Points to her throat and gags.

"It could've killed me?" I rasp. She tilts her head. I place my hand to my throat and gasp for air. She nods twice. "For fuck's sake." I want to cry. "Why didn't you kill it?"

Kaikare places a hand on my shoulder and strokes it gently.

"Thank you," I croak out. "Thank you for saving my life. I know you can't understand me, but—" I turn and look around. I want to curl up in a ball and feel sorry for myself, only where? A few tears spill out—from fear, disappointment, and second-guessing my decision in coming here. Most of all, the disappointment is in me.

I point to my throat and mime a drinking action. Kaikare nods and takes my hand, showing unusual affection as though she understands. Something I've never witnessed among the others. She leads me to the stream and where the water runs clear. There are clay bowls nearby filled with water, leaves floating on the surface. Hoping the leaves serve as purification, I scoop out some water with a clay cup and drink three full scoops. *Why didn't Samuel mention these large bowls?* Maybe he did. Admittedly, I haven't taken on everything he'd told me as it was a lot of information to comprehend at once.

Further downstream, the children frolic in the area where we bathe. Finally, it makes sense. Upstream we drink. Downstream we bathe. The same rule applies with the river—closer to the mountain they fish while downstream is used for personal hygiene. She drinks a cup herself and rises to her feet. We backtrack through the jungle to the fields. Passing over the tangled decay of the jungle floor, I glance up at hearing a low moan. A flash of skin between the trees catches my attention. Kaikare touches my hand and shakes her head. I can't help but look back and realize it could be the same young couple. Kaikare leads me to rows of capsicum and spinach-like plants called aurosa. We pick and slice leaves, and when I place the vegetables in a woven basket on the ground, I catch sight of the young girl emerging from the jungle. I take in her features, the beads around her neck. I'm not the only one who notices. Kaikare lifts her gaze at the same time before returning her focus to her hands at work.

I can't help the curiosity and know better than to show it in front of Kaikare. I'll ask Samuel about the girl when he returns.

Come twilight for the past five days, I'm overwhelmed with nausea, knowing I'll be spending the night alone. Today is no different, and inevitably dusk descends.

The days pass quickly by working in the fields and cooking around the fire. I have company, but with limited communication, there's loneliness even when surrounded by people. At dinner, I eat the vegetables and bread on offer. Hours earlier, I had walked past the fire and saw a pile of headless monkeys—dark blood pooling on the ground—and covered my mouth to smother a heave. The pong of charred hair sent me rushing to Samuel's hut to hide out for a moment and reel in anxiety. It's all too much for my first week alone.

The moment I've dreaded is upon me. I wave my hand, refusing the meat, knowing it's a sign of rudeness. The deep lines around the chief's eyes almost join with those in his forehead. I glance down at the monkey paw on a palm leaf, rub my stomach, and shake my head again.

I accept the flat bread Kaikare hands to me, and I'm left to be insignificant once more when the shaman rises from the ground and stands in front of the fire. Bright-eyed, the children shuffle forward, and despite not understanding their language, I detect the excitement in their voices as they scramble toward the inner circle.

The shaman raises his hands and stares toward the heavens before beginning his story. His words capture everyone's attention. I gaze around, watching their reaction. What makes them believe these stories?

Fear?

Respect?

The sound of night creatures echoes from the tangled knot of green and black surrounding us. The squawking, clicking, and chattering never eases. Tonight, the sound magnifies, taunting me, a warning not to relax. My heart beats at a quicker rate, on alert after my close encounter with a deadly banana spider. I stare toward the pulsating gloom. Why did I ignore the advice of the people I love to risk my life in the jungle?

Answers I don't find before I hear the words, "A-pantoní-pe nichii."

The shaman's tale is incomprehensible for me to *take advantage of the story*. More importantly, I need to understand my journey.

And why I left my closest friends to come here.

Every night since Samuel has left, I've peed right here outside my hut, too afraid to venture into the green.

Wrapping the mosquito net around my hammock, it's difficult to ignore the deafening raucous beyond the walls, my so-called jungle lullaby. Only it doesn't lull me into sleep. Now that I am alone, I'm listening more so to specific sounds, an awareness to which are warnings. Without Samuel to guide me, I have to rely on my own instinct since there is no one else I can ask for help. It exaggerates the notion of being alone, and it scares the crap out of me.

40

SAMUEL

THE DAYS the journey took Tïmenneng and Samuel through the jungle were familiarly dangerous. He knows the signs, the sounds of possible threats, and can identify a poisonous plant with a single glance. He understands where to find water and which fruits to eat. The forest garden offers an abundance of food if you know where to find it, and it means he can keep the food in his sack for the days on the tepui. Still, he can't risk sleeping in certain parts of the jungle with only a hammock and small pocketknife for protection. He won't use it unless absolutely necessary so as not to reveal the knife to his warrior companion. Considering Tïmenneng has poisonous-tipped arrows in the animal-hide sack he carries on his back, he hopes no danger will come close enough for him to wield a steel blade. He packed it even though Tïmenneng knows nothing of knives or the metal objects from Samuel's world. Carrying the weapon isn't an insult to Tïmenneng, more a reason to live with the promise he'd return to *her*.

Yesterday the jungle led them up a steep slope toward the tepui wall, a constant battle through thorny vines and over mangled muddy tree roots. It rained most of the previous day, and Samuel hopes it holds off while on the rock face of the tepui. Rain and storms aren't ideal when free-climbing a dangerous mountain, most of it unknown to man. Tïmenneng leads the way, and although Samuel has faith in his navigation, it was the shaman who conveyed Samuel's visions of the location of the purple flower to Tïmenneng.

They wake at dawn and clamber down the tree where they rested. They continue their trek and are soon face-to-face with the rocky wall of the tepui. Samuel and Tïmenneng gaze up to the clouds, a sandstone barrier overhanging toward them. To Samuel, the tepui appears unclimbable without the special ropes professional mountaineers used for safety.

Tïmenneng places one hand on the rock, his gaze lifted as though studying every crevice and crack in a game of chess. He places an ear on the rock, closes his eyes, and listens.

The House of Gods.

Samuel's common sense tells him it's a myth, only now he's wiser, a believer, and it's possible the spirits are guiding his warrior friend. If so, he hopes the gods steer them right.

Tïmenneng wanders for another thirty minutes keeping a hand on the rock as they wrangle past the trees growing close to the rocky wall, competing for space and seeking sunlight. Tïmenneng stills, assesses the rock, and with one hand, he then reaches up and hoists a foot, the other hand, and then the other foot into the tiny crevice. His limbs spread out like an insect, and as light as a six-legged creature, he scrambles up the wall.

He doesn't ask for Samuel to follow, and he doesn't direct Samuel to stay put. Samuel's not surprised since their culture expects you to understand matters when they happen in the moment—learn and adapt to being a warrior. Yet, the vertical path on the sharp, flat rock seems ludicrous.

Samuel searches the rock for a crevice strong enough to take his weight. He's slim but not built like a stick insect and uses his core to lift and then spread his weight, so it's distributed evenly between his limbs. His movement is slow and calculated. Periodically, he glances up to ensure his path is the same as Tïmenneng's, as one wrong move could be perilous. There's an overwhelming feeling of blending into the rock, like slow-moving creatures barely visible from the ground. Each time Samuel stops to catch his breath, he peeks over his shoulder to the sun on the horizon to check for clouds as a storm can roll in quickly with barely time to find cover. On the ledge would be a death wish.

"Konopo?" he shouts. *Rain.* Tïmenneng has a better view and is more agile to turn and assess their situation than the fleeting glance Samuel takes over his shoulder, so he doesn't overbalance and fall.

"Weju," Tïmenneng replies. *Sun.*

He sucks in a deep breath of relief that the sky is clear. Yet he can't relax when the sun will sink below the trees in a matter of hours, and they need to make the first rocky ledge to set up their camp before nightfall.

Above him, Tïmenneng calls out. "Ero po." *Here.*

He offers Samuel a sweaty hand, and he scrambles onto the narrow cliff. It's a ledge wide enough for them to stand and rest for the night. He lumbers to his feet, turns, and inflates his lungs with clean, crisp air as he admires the view with the last minutes the day has to offer before the golden orb sinks below the green horizon.

In a race against time, they pitch their hammocks to the sapling trees growing out of the rocks. They eat the food in their packs and drink from the bottles Samuel has supplied. His muscles ache, and the scratches on his fingertips sting. Samuel can barely keep his eyes open, so he clambers into his hammock, eager to fall asleep to the sound of the jungle hundreds of feet below them. Eyes closed, his thoughts wander across the treetops searching for her essence. The notion of her remaining alone in the village, waiting for him to return, gives him a sense of purpose and self-appreciation with a woman sacrificing as much to be with him. He drifts off to sleep, imagining the soft sighs of her sleeping beside him.

THE FOLLOWING morning both men wake at first light.

Tïmenneng rolls up his hammock, and Samuel senses his eagerness to move on. Securing his own pack to his back, he prepares his mind for the mental strength to keep going despite every muscle in his body screaming in pain and his toes blue from the climb.

Tïmenneng points a finger to walk sideways across the rock. Green moss coats the rocky surface above them, making it slippery and unclimbable.

Samuel's nails are chipped, his fingertips battered and covered in cuts. His calves burn from side-stepping, all his weight bearing through his toes. His fingers splay, searching for a cleft in the rock to dig his fingers in before moving his leg. Rocks break and fall beneath him, the clash unnerving as neither men wear helmets. Tïmenneng calls out to him, and out the corner of his eye, Samuel sees an object approach. It's a vine Tïmenneng has swung toward Samuel. He grabs it without levering his weight from his extremities and gives a tug to assess its safety. He winds it around his wrist before he takes another step to his left and then sees Tïmenneng standing on another rocky ledge waving to him. He clings to the vine, his feet gripping like a monkey, and uses momentum to swing toward the protuberance to join his friend. Tïmenneng grabs and secures the vine as Samuel lands and stumbles on the edge. He crouches on all fours and takes a moment to gather his thoughts and regain his mental strength to push on.

He pants out of breath. Wait, is that—

"Tuna." *Water.*

The sound comes from a small opening. Is this what Tïmenneng was listening for?

Both crouch onto all fours to enter the cave, eventually sliding on their stomachs over smooth boulders into the unknown. It takes a moment for Samuel's eyes to adjust and for his hearing to guide them toward the underground stream. The cave widens enough for them to stand, and then he finds himself in a damp cavern, a stream to their right and a cathedral-shaped dome ceiling above. Tiny potholes of light shine in from all angles casting enough light to make out the ground beneath their feet. Tïmenneng holds up a hand, points, and says a single word in a hushed breath. They follow the stream, walking opposite the current in an upward spiral path. Samuel can't help feeling an overwhelming notion of being an intruder to a sacred place where many myths originate about the spirit world.

Soon they come across a boulder wall, and Tïmenneng directs Samuel on what boulders to slide his body over so as not to disturb the supporting boulders as the structural balance relies on a fine thread of cohesive sand.

It seems as though they are going in circles, for every hour or so they stumble across another opening blocked by boulders, and they slide through a tiny space to get to the other side. Only the punctures of light in the rock above grow brighter. Previously, Samuel had only ventured to a smaller wall on the other side of the giant tepui, to an area more assessable to climbers. He's barely capable of this climb. Over the past couple of years, the area close to Angel Falls has become popular with professional rock climbers, and helicopters and planes zoom over the top with curious tourists every day. The journey to find the medicinal flower has brought them to a treacherous section of the tepui, away from adventure seekers.

Climbing the rock from the inside through unstable sandstone columns in the caves is a better choice than the unclimbable rocky walls of the tepui. Only he has no clue of time inside the cave, and it's messing with his sanity. Tïmenneng remains composed. Time holds less significance to the Ularans, as night and day are all that really determines their behavior, and his duty is to guide Samuel in finding the flower. He will do so until his body tells him to rest. As light streams in, Samuel can see more of his surroundings, including the giant-sized cockroaches scrambling near his feet, and he doesn't even have the energy to flick them away.

Finally, they scramble through an opening. "Whoa," Samuel yells and stops at the edge. They are surrounded by walls of a large sinkhole, the opening above them around one-hundred feet high. Circling below from where they stand is a miniature forest, home to unique and varied species. Above, a waterfall cascades over the tepui summit to a lake pooling hundreds of feet below.

In minutes, the light dims with the sun already low on the horizon. Tïmenneng points to their bags, and Samuel couldn't be more delighted to sling his hammock on the edge of paradise.

41

EDEN

It's BEEN fourteen days since Samuel left.

Fourteen days of hard work in the fields, and this morning the blisters on my palm have finally popped. Every day I have completed the chores expected of me and follow the lead of the other women, our routine unchanging, until now. Instead of heading to the cooking pot with the other women to prepare lunch, Kaikare waves for me to follow her, leading us to the stream. She removes her skirt and beads before wading waist-deep into the water.

"Tamu'ne Akare." She repeats, laughs, and waves me in.

Throwing my costume aside, I follow her in and submerge myself beneath the cool, clear water only to surface and find her climbing the bank. She gathers leaves from different shrubs before splashing as she lands beside me. She foams a leaf and rubs the soap through her hair, handing the green waxy leaf to me. I use it to wash my hair, forgetting how wonderful the sensation of clean hair is, and the scent is remarkably better than any product I know on the market. She laughs like a child, even though I presume she's thirty-plus years my senior.

The humidity makes it impossible for our skin to completely dry naturally. We replace the black and red beads over our necks and loop the tweed ties of our skirts around our hips. I catch a whiff of my socks and groan before slipping on my sneakers. I still refuse to walk barefoot.

If only I could rewind time and contemplate what I could squeeze into my pack, like an extra pair of socks.

Rewind to when I was with my friends.

Following the footprints of Kaikare along the narrow path to the village, I'm surprised when she leads me to another hut. She stands at the door and smiles.

Inside, animal skulls hang on the walls. Trophies of teeth are strung in a necklace with incisors large enough to be of jaguar or caiman. She opens a small woven basket with a lid and pulls out something with a handle. She hands it to me, both hands outstretched like it's precious. Taking the object, I turn it over and catch shards of my reflection in the dirty glass.

"A mirror. It's beautiful." I turn it again, several times, rubbing the glass tainted by time. I scrub the back with my fingers and catch the flower decoupage under glaze that has worn away. I hesitate. It's otherworldly, old, and only an outsider would have gifted it to her. Before I hand it back, I catch the bird-nest hairstyle I'm fashioning. Holding the mirror higher, I check myself in an unstained piece, running my fingers through tangled strands endeavoring to tame my mane.

Kaikare laughs again and takes it from me, copying my action with her hair. Hearing voices outside, she hastily replaces the mirror in the basket, tucks it under a woven mat, and leads me to the village center. Before we reach the fire, the children run up to her shouting and pointing to the river. The children bounce near my face, grab my hand and drag me a few steps until I'm forced to follow. The shaman appears out of nowhere, and there's a discussion between Kaikare and him. I kneel to allow the children to touch my hair yet manage to keep Kaikare and the shaman in my line of sight.

Kaikare shakes her head and comes to stand beside me. Even I can make out the warning in the shaman's voice. She leads me toward the river, and I'm surprised to find Asoo waiting on the sandy bank.

"Asoo." I run up to him and throw my arms around his waist, eager to speak with someone who understands me.

He nods at me, his eyes full of sorrow.

"Is everything okay?"

He hands me my phone. "You have a message. I bring it to you."

My stomach drops before reading the message, then settles when I understand the message from Yasmine is informative, nothing bad.

We finished the Macchu Piccu trek and are heading north to Iquitos.

Fantastic! Text me and let me know your plans. Miss you all. Stay safe x

Stay safe. I want to laugh at my advice, thinking touché.

I hand my phone back to Asoo. "Please ensure it sends when you're back in Canaima."

He takes my phone and wraps it in plastic before slipping it into his bag. "I need to ask a favor of my friend, Samuel. Is he here?"

"No." I hear the disappointment in my voice.

His chin dips to his chest. "It bad. Children dying. Doctor Robert ask for more supplies until his arrive."

"Of course. I'll search Samuel's bag to see if I can find anything of use."

I run into the bushes and almost scream when I bump into Kaikare, forgetting she led me here and clearly couldn't reveal herself. "I need supplies," I say as though I need to announce my good intention despite the language barrier. She remains on my heel the entire way to the hut and watches while I forage through Samuel's case taking needles, alcohol solution, saline, and antibiotics in vials. I find antibiotic tablets and dressing packs. Samuel mentioned more supplies were being sent to him, and I assume his medicine is rarely used. Emptying the contents of my backpack on the table, I shove the medicines into the bag and jog the path to the river.

"Here." I hand my pack to Asoo, puffing like I ran five miles even though it's only one.

"Come. Help the doctor," he pleads. "Help the children. Put wet cloth on face." He acts out the action with a hand to his forehead. "They have fever."

"What?"

I have been vaccinated.

I glance over my shoulder toward the village. "I can't." My thoughts whirl remembering what Samuel said about the Ularan people's vulnerability and how he quarantines himself for days when he leaves.

Asoo places a hand on my shoulder. "Please." The way his eyes plead, I know he wouldn't ask this of me unless the situation was desperate.

Shit!

"How far is it?"

"Half day."

Listening to my raspy breaths, I focus on doing what's right. "Okay," I say, knowing I might not be allowed to return to Ulara.

Kaikare appears from the bushes. Asoo stumbles back, turning his body toward the canoe. She speaks in a calm tone, her eyes and focus on Asoo. To my surprise, he understands her, and they talk to and fro as though they have met before. Kaikare gives me a long stare, guilt eating at my stomach. She speaks to Asoo in an elevated tone, and I hope she's not demanding I stay.

"She wants to come and help. Her medicine can help."

"What? No, she can't. Kaikare isn't vaccinated." I shake my head, my eyes begging her.

"She says she had needles. A baby. She wants to help."

I'm shaking my head, confused and torn on what to do. "It's her decision, but please ask her more questions as I need her to be safe."

"She's gone for her medicine," he says when Kaikare retreats to the vines and disappears beyond the trees. I anticipate the shaman's reaction knowing I'll probably be blamed.

My thoughts are whirling, second-guessing, and now I'm worried for Kaikare. "The camp, do people wear Western clothes?"

Asoo nods. "They own clothes on their back."

"Give me a minute to grab mine."

When I pass the village center, I notice Kaikare talking with the shaman. Both wave their hands, neither raising their voices. I keep my head down and make my way to Samuel's hut, grabbing a skirt, two tank tops, shorts, my mosquito net, and doxycycline tablets, then I head back to Asoo.

We wait for Kaikare on the sand, my stomach in knots, knowing she has placed herself in bad favor with her leaders. I look over my shoulder every few seconds and almost tell Asoo to go without her because her coming with us isn't the right thing for her safety or the entire community. Only the decision isn't mine, and I've never seen her so determined.

If anything happens to her because of me, then my erratic behavior would be unforgivable.

42

EDEN

THE RIVER current assists our journey downstream.

Kaikare sits at the front of the curiara, her back straight, looking out to the water, ready to tackle anything we greet. Asoo and I can't see her expression, yet I wonder if it's her first time sailing down the river away from her home.

What's Kaikare thinking as we sail away from the only place she knows? Her courage amazes me, especially with the shaman forbidding her to leave. In direct light unfiltered by the canopy, her scars in straight lines and Vs shine on her naked back.

What honor do the scars represent?

After retrieving my phone, I check the time. Something I miss even though there isn't any service. If only I remembered to pack a wristwatch and kept it hidden in my hut.

An hour passes, and we have mainly traveled in silence.

"Do you think you could talk to her?" I ask Asoo. "I'm worried."

"I understand some," he tells me. "Her language a combination of all Pemón languages."

"Can you ask her if she feels safe?"

He nods. "I will sit with her and no shout over motor. Come. I show you how to steer."

We swap seats. I take the stick and wrestle to hold it in place for a moment. "Stay here." He points to the left of the river. "Middle, the current stronger. Not close to edge. Away from floating branches and vines."

Asoo settles in the seat behind her, slightly to her right, so he's in her periphery.

I hear nothing of their conversation with the motor in my ear. Occasionally, Asoo bows his head as though words escape him.

We reach a fork in the river, and he points for me to veer to the right, the girth twofold, requiring a firmer grip on the stick to steer us out of the center. There are more sandy beaches and less overhanging jungle, and soon Asoo climbs back and retakes control in time to guide the canoe onto a small beach. He says nothing of Kaikare.

"We walk now. You can dress." Asoo jumps ashore and stands with his back to us. In the canoe, I pull on a tank top, shoving the beads in the front pocket of my pack. I slip into shorts and untie my tweed skirt. Curiously Kaikare watches. I clamber over wooden planks and hand her another tank top. Her chin raises, she shakes her head, refusing my offer. She stands and finds Asoo. Admittedly, her skirt covers most of her bits, and the beads fall over her breasts. She's proud of who she is, and I respect that. Covering her body with Western clothing is more about my insecurities.

We cross a grassland before seeing the brick and clay structures before us. One building is a makeshift church with a cross on the top. It catches Kaikare's eye. She says nothing, yet I can't help wondering what's going through her mind.

Some children approach us in dirt-covered t-shirts and shorts, all barefoot. Three dogs of no particular breed follow the children like friendly mutts.

Kaikare grabs my arm and freezes. "Asoo, the dogs," I call out. "It's okay," I tell her and reach to pat one with my free hand.

Eyes wide, she watches, although she steps away when it bounces toward her.

"Down," I demand.

Asoo chuckles. "The locals speak Pemón or Spanish. Some learn English. Dogs no understand your words."

I take Kaikare's hand and shoo any other dogs in our path until we enter a small brick dwelling.

A thin man sits behind a desk. Asoo speaks in Spanish first, then turns to me. "Eden."

The man nods. "I'm Robert." He runs his fingers along the length of his beard and eyes us through gray bangs.

"Nice to meet you. I've come with supplies." I place my backpack on his desk and empty the medical kits. "I believe you're in need of some help. My sister has a toddler, and I've cared for him when he's been sick. It's not much, but I'm willing to assist where I can."

"Your friend?"

"Her medicine is from the jungle."

Asoo reverts to Spanish so fast, and the only word I catch is *Kaikare*. He turns to her, and his language becomes stilted, speaking in her native tongue.

Kaikare nods slowly, leaning forward in a slight bow.

"I'll show you ladies where you'll sleep, and then I'll take you to some of the huts where the children are isolated," Dr. Robert says.

Thankfully, our room has a door and hammocks. Kaikare watches as I open and shut the door, the handle fascinating her. I point to us both and the hammocks before placing my hands under my ear and close my eyes. Surely, it's a universal sign. We head out, Kaikare refusing to let go of her basket, and meet Asoo. The dogs are tied with a rope away from us. The children shout and laugh innocently, and the adults shoot wary stares. They seem unsure who they trust least—the native American or the privileged white girl.

The doctor is inside the long hut. From the moment I step inside, I'm greeted with chesty coughs and sniffles. The children's faces and bodies are covered in a red rash.

"Most of the children and adults only have the cold symptoms although many are compromised with poor hand washing and now have pneumonia." The doctor takes the temperature of a girl. "Some of the children have suffered seizures, and the older generation believes it's the work of a bad spirit." He points to a bowl of murky water with cotton cloths cut in strips beside it. "I don't need all my shirts, so I'm using pieces to help cool them."

He pumps a bottle of sanitizer and wipes it over his hands. I look around. There's no running water. "We have one tap that pumps water from beneath the ground. The whole community shares it. We have electricity for three hours a day from a generator. Most of the volunteers come for eight weeks and leave. One brought the measles virus with him. It spreads like wildfire in a community with no vaccination. I treat them for malaria and parasites, diseases known to their community for years. We can't afford communicable diseases from outsiders."

"What do the volunteers do here in only eight weeks?" I ask him.

"They help with the fields, gardens, cooking for so many mouths to feed. The elderly people are tired, some sick themselves."

"I want to help in any way I can." I walk over and examine a rash on a boy no more than three years old. He moans and barks out a cough.

"Thank you for these antibiotics. The packs Samuel sent have helped a few of these kids. We've had nine deaths in two weeks."

I gasp. "Tell me what I can do now."

"Strangely, I need no one to visit for a few days. Their families want to come in and check on their children, only they are taking the virus back out to the community. I can't keep watch here all the time. They can stand in the doorway and no closer. And you can wash down their bodies with wet cloths to help stop the febrile convulsions."

The humidity is still rife and thick in the air. Even I want to wash just to cool off. No wonder the children struggle with high temperatures. I find a bowl and wet some cloths and wipe one small boy's forehead, chest, and shoulders. I glance up to Kaikare watching me.

She speaks to Asoo. The conversation goes back and forth.

"I show Kaikare the women. She needs water and pot for fire."

"Wait. Does she want me to come with her?"

Asoo shakes his head. "I stay and help if she needs anything."

"Okay."

They leave me with the doctor, and I continue assisting him administering medication. My thoughts wander to Asoo and Kaikare with an inkling they are keeping something from me. Maybe they believe it's something I wouldn't understand.

By dusk, we sit around a fire in a way no different to Ulara.

Kaikare is on alert, her eyes permanently round like saucers. She holds a dinner plate in her hand and utensils I assume she's never seen before. She eats with her hands from the plate, watching out for the dogs.

There are many similarities to Ulara, and I'm comfortable knowing

I'm not out of my element. Tonight, I eat everything on offer—meat, vegetables, and yuca bread. I didn't question the type of meat. Could it be my mindset because I didn't witness what was killed before it was cooked? I'm not sure I'd ever be comfortable consuming monkey, and yet I understand the need for meat when these people have little choice when it's about survival. "Asoo," I whisper. "Is the meat dog or monkey?"

"No," Asoo says sternly. "Fowl. Dogs are treated well. If you harm your dog—"

"Then when your fifth soul goes to the heavens, your dog will be waiting and kill you," Dr. Robert finishes for him. He gives me a knowing smile.

"Good to know," I say with relief.

This piece of knowledge surprises me. The surprises keep coming every day. The little things bringing joy on this holiday have led me on an adventure of wonder.

THE HAMMOCK beside me is empty.

I consider Kaikare has gone to pee, then enough time passes for me to comprehend this is not the case.

I check the time on my phone, a luxury for a few more days, and realize it's not quite seven. Throwing off the mosquito net, I head out to find Kaikare.

Eventually, I find her with the doctor, spooning mouthfuls of her tea into gaunt-faced little mouths. Oh, my heart. She's a natural with these children, and I have no words to describe the admiration I hold for her. She is warm and caring, risking her health and respect from the Ularan elders to come and help. Not just to any place, to one outside the safety of her world, where I assume she's out of her comfort zone. Yet here she is, her head high, doing what she can to help these children survive.

"Morning," I say and smile.

"Morning, Eden." Dr. Robert nods toward Kaikare. "Your friend has a great brew. We gave it to one of the children last night, and this morning when I listened to his chest, there was minimal wheezing."

"Already an improvement?"

He raises a brow at me. "We were as surprised as you. Whatever

Kaikare has going on here, we'd appreciate more of it. And another child has less mucus secretion than yesterday. Do you know what plant her medicine is derived from?"

"No, but I can find out. When Samuel returns, he'll be able to show you." I watch Kaikare's face light up when each child finishes their cup and babbles away, thankfully. "I think she's happy to help."

"If there's a way of getting that plant to us with instructions on how to boil it, for how long and with what combination of other plants, we'd appreciate it. My appreciation extends to your generosity in providing the supplies Samuel had in stock. You're very kind."

I nod. "It's the least we can do. What can I do to help now?" I ask him.

"Continue spoon-feeding the children the brew." A child coughs repeatedly behind him. It sounds moist and hacking. He turns and assesses the little boy. "You could start with Amos."

"Right." I scoop out a cup of the tea, and with a spoon ready, I kneel beside Amos. "Hey." With a hand behind his head and back, I help him to sit. I keep one hand behind to support him, and with the other, I scoop a teaspoon of the river-colored brew and sit it next to his lips. Dark eyes stare up into mine, almost questioning if he can trust me. I give him a gentle smile and nod. "It will help you feel better." I know he doesn't understand my words. There is one thing I have learned in the weeks of my stay, and that is the tone and body language communicate understanding more than our foreign words.

By late morning, Dr. Robert has arranged for Kaikare to show the women how she prepares and boils the brew. When she has finished preparing the next pot of medicine, it's time for us to leave the camp. At midday, we're on our journey back to Ulara. I know it not from my phone but by the sun directly above us. Kaikare glanced over at me with a smile from ear to ear. Like her, I'm filled with gratification in helping others—the best kind of joy. Only I'm preoccupied with ideas of fundraising when I arrive home in Australia to support communities like this. With Dr. Robert's business card in my backpack, I promise myself I'll research organizations and other indigenous villages in the Gran Sabana.

My fondness for Kaikare and the village has grown, only I can't see myself staying in Ulara forever. Yet, I don't want to just give up on Samuel and me and some kind of future we could have. Maybe we could combine our homes, live a mixed life. At least when I'm home, there are things I can do to help even from the other side of the world. Money might not hold status in Ulara, but for these communities, it can buy pharmaceuticals and medical supplies. Yet, after what I witnessed with Kaikare's brew, no doubt a recipe from the shaman, our worlds need to share all our secrets as there is a place for both to heal the sick and vulnerable.

43

SAMUEL

"LET'S DO THIS," Samuel mutters to himself the following morning. The snacks inside his pouch are low, and the water in his bottle is almost gone. They need to find more sources and fast. They make their way up the steep wall to the surface, using branches for support as they clamber over rock and slippery moss. Hours pass, pausing only to sip mouthfuls of water from the drink bottle. Samuel swishes the water around his mouth before swallowing. Everything is now about preserving the energy, so the two barely talk and only focus on getting to the top. They use vines to climb or propel them upward.

The moment Samuel lifts his leg onto the plateau, he lays there a moment in amazement. The tepui surface reminds him of an alien planet. Black rock with a volcanic appearance similar to totem poles or dangerously long, horizontal fractures around a half-mile deep like narrow craters, slice into the plateau. It's like nothing he has ever seen on earth. Walking over the treacherous surface is another challenge but hopefully the last before finding the flower.

In his mind, he visualized the journey, only he underestimated the demand on his body and has to dig deep to pick himself up and keep moving. He finds Tïmenneng kneeling on one knee assessing a bromeliad, his feet bloody and covered in cuts.

"Pyjai," Samuel tells him. *Medicine.*

He drops his sack beside him and pulls out the leaves that clean and disinfect wounds. Samuel understands if bacteria gets in his wounds, the challenge of combating the infection is tough without giving him antibiotics.

Water sits in the rocky crevices beside them, not a lot but enough for him to dip the leaves and rub over Tïmenneng's feet. Tïmenneng winces a little before regaining a stoic expression.

Samuel pulls out the last of the dried berries for them to nibble. They need a moment's rest.

Sitting cross-legged on the jagged rock, Samuel closes his eyes and meditates for a few minutes to gain his energy. At first, his thoughts are blocked, and he sees only darkness. He curses, ignoring the lethargy weighing down his body and his mind. Visualizing the flower and the song of the shaman, his thoughts clear, and Eden's voice finds a way into his head. "I love you," she tells him in his dreams. Finding the flower will complete his purpose to the pharmaceutical company, and more importantly, free him from his demons so he can be with her. He looks to the sky with gratitude. "Thank you," he murmurs.

Tïmenneng stands beside him and places a hand on his shoulder. He nods, ready to begin the last leg of the journey.

They trek over the rocky landscape, pushing thorny bromeliads and orchids aside to search for the purple flower. The sun moves across the sky above them, and he stands and leans back, his hands on his buttocks to stretch out his lower back. They push on, and he can't help thinking his visions were misleading. Tïmenneng points to a cluster of flowers, the striking purple color is squished between the pink orchids. He runs to the plant and moves the orchids aside to examine the quality of the plant—the roots of the purple flowers clinging to a rocky crevice.

This. Is. It.

Samuel takes a single breath, and time stills. His past has led him to this moment—his destiny of finding what he has searched for, for many years. With shaky hands, he extracts the flowers with roots intact before sealing it in a weatherproof bag inside his sack. He turns in a full circle, stunned by the bleak, windswept summit where the rare exotic plant survives. There is minimal plant life near the fractures, and he understands water is responsible for the harsh erosion. He follows Tïmenneng to a rocky meadow abundant with more bromeliads, pitcher plants, and other carnivorous insect-eating plants. The bright red color catches his attention, the same as it would to insects that become prey and respects the plants' diversity to survive. In the distance, green forests line the rocky edge of the mountain, and a river divides the land that feeds Angel Falls. The looming gray clouds tumbling toward tepui is enough for him to cease further admiration.

Time is suddenly of importance being as high as the clouds. They race against Mother Nature to seek protection from lightning and before the temperature drops dangerously low with an upcoming storm. Without clothes or blankets, the men run the risk of hypothermia if they don't make it back to the cave before night falls upon them. Even with the flower in his possession, his duty isn't complete. He made Eden a promise to return to her.

His body aches and his hands shake from exhaustion. The downhill climb is just as dangerous, yet he wants to push harder and lessen the days on his journey home because every minute steals valuable time away from Eden.

His mission, a success.

In his mind, a new goal blooms.

His heart is no longer divided.

All he visualizes is *her.*

44

EDEN

I REMEMBER what Samuel had told me about quarantining outside the village and ask Asoo to explain to Kaikare our need to be cautious that we're not carrying any viruses.

She agrees to stay with me in the small campsite Samuel erected, and I can't help thinking like me, she's not ready to face the shaman yet. After watching Asoo sail away with my iPhone, insecurity creeps back in. Stupid, since it could only take photos, provide time, and a light while the battery lasts maybe a few more hours. The photos were memories and a connection to home and my friends. With every passing day, I'm missing them more.

Alongside the river, Kaikare gathers Piri-Piri, a reed-like grass Samuel had explained was used for some basket weaving yet also had medicinal value. She digs up the rhizomes, carries them back to our camp, and grinds them with a rock. In a fast-twirling action of a stick on rock and dead matter, smoke sparks, and her hands cup to protect the small flame. She hands me a dirty clay pot and points to the river. First, I wash it, then return with it filled with brown water, hoping we don't have to drink it. The ground rhizomes are scraped into the pot and placed on the fire. She rubs her stomach, and I nod, understanding her underlying nausea or nerves. While we wait for it to boil, she walks a short distance to bamboo, which appears to have grown overnight. Snapping several pieces, she hands me a piece, a source of clean water. I have no idea how far we are from the stream on the other side of the village. If I venture too far from the camp, I'm afraid I won't find my way back. So, I take it, and she continues to snap more until we have quenched our thirst.

Sitting around the fire, she sings quietly to herself, the sound calming my erratic thoughts. Immediately, I'm thinking about Samuel.

Is he safe? I try to imagine what it's like being out there, climbing a tepui with minimal assistance, catching your food at the same time as being the lower echelon of the food chain. She jabs a cup at me. I sip the earthy-flavored tea and pretend it's coffee, ignoring the gurgling in my gut.

Dusk falls upon the forest, and I remain by her side, only to add fallen branches to the fire, knowing it's the one mechanism of defense I understand.

Our smoke-perfumed hair and skin deter the number of mosquitoes circling our heads. When darkness falls, she stands as though cued and waves for me to follow her into the jungle.

"Really. We wait until it's almost dark to go in there?" I question. I am finding I'm talking to myself more and more because the silence is beginning to frustrate me, and hearing my voice speaking English offers some sanity. "I'm really not a fan because well, you know, there's this thing I'm conscious of... nocturnal predators... spiders and snakes. Oh, and we don't have a flashlight."

Kaikare stops when enough light from the night sky breaks through the canopy and shines on the fruit several steps inside the denser growth. *More passion fruit*. She picks several pieces before being disturbed by a shower of Brazil nuts falling from above, knocked to the ground by monkeys screeching as they swing from branch to branch. She gathers nuts that have landed by our feet, hands them to me, and proceeds to reach up and snap several sprigs of acai berries from a palm. I follow her lead, and we weave through vines to our camp. I'm hungrier than I realized.

No sooner do we finish, she stands again, waves for me to follow her back into the forest away from the safety of our fire. "You know, I'm full and don't need seconds," I tell her, especially since it's somewhat darker. She stares at me, so I push up from my log seat and moan with some reluctance. "I'll come with you because it's the safety in numbers we should be considering."

Even I question my sanity following her deeper into a black jungle, stumbling over swollen roots and slipping on leaf decay even while holding her hand. Arrows of moonlight provide enough light for Kaikare to weave around the giant tree trunks of kapok trees. Monkeys screech louder with our approach. The click and chatter of insects stop and start, depending on our movement. She pulls up, and I stumble with poor coordination, her hand under my chin guiding my focus to the ground.

The leaves glow, their veins lit up like a green x-ray image. Mushrooms dot the floor like a network of Christmas lights. The jungle flaunts bioluminescence across its decayed floor. The forest's night music now has party lights, and even though I'm smiling in awe, I can't help feeling we're uninvited gate crashers.

"It's beautiful," I tell her, hoping she hears the appreciation in my tone.

We return to our site, and my feet welcome the relief of being elevated in the hammock. Side by side, cocooned in a mosquito net, I fall asleep to the Amazonia lullaby.

LAST NIGHT, I woke several times in a sweat from bizarre dreams. Unexplainable dreams making no sense, only my heart raced so fast it put the fear of death in me, and I re-evaluated everything. How the hell did I end up here in a hammock hugging a woman I barely know and with no medical facilities for days? Where's the responsible Eden? If I died, what would happen? Would they send my body down the river or be cremated?

I take it as a sign the sensible voice of my conscience is warning me the adventure is coming to an end. As much as I've appreciated stepping outside my comfort zone, opening my mind, and living in a world I never believed existed, I have to go home to family and friends.

As we wash our faces and hands in the shallows of the river, Kaikare stares at me with concern. Whether she senses my indifference or it's her own, I'm relieved there's been no sign of the shaman.

Then he appears as if silently summoned.

Jesus, there isn't any rustling of foliage to warn us. He simply steps from the jungle onto the sand. My heart jumps to my throat. He didn't approve of our leave.

Kaikare nods to him, her poker face unreadable. I want to stand behind her, then stop myself. We're in this—trouble—together. He stops a distance away from us, and she plods a few paces closer yet a safe distance as though she learned the distancing rule from Samuel. He speaks to her, and she lowers her head. I follow her lead. Their conversation goes back and forth several rounds, and not once do I detect heat in their words. By the time I glance up, he's disappearing into the jungle once more. I follow her back to the fire, dying to know what was said. She picks up my bag and holds it with an outstretched arm.

I nod and take it. Her expression changes as though she's struggling inside, and I take it as a sign I'm receiving marching orders.

"It. Time," she manages.

My heart leaps hearing her words. I want to hug her until I realize what she's saying, and my excitement falls flat. Leave on foot? The ball of panic—always present—slowly grows. "I should wait here for Asoo."

She frowns at my words. A hand reaches for mine. "Come."

Slinging my backpack over my shoulder, she leads me into the jungle, pushing past vines and weaving around some of the thickest tree trunks I've seen. I stop to rest momentarily, gripping the narrow trunk of one of the more common trees. Kaikare waves her hand, shaking her head. I let go, and on closer inspection, realize the tree is unlike others. Fire ants swarm the branches. "Shit." I brush my hands and shake myself. She gives me a long look before leading me into the sunlight of thinning overgrowth to a garden of sorts with an abundance of orchids, hot-lips flowers, and heliconias.

A distant song halts my step, mixed vowels of no meaning yet harmonic and mesmerizing.

The voice of an angel.

45

EDEN

WHENEVER MY HEEL hits the ground, I focus on trying to be lighter on my feet, now aware the plants hold value. With every snap of a twig, I wish I had more grace. Maybe if I did ballet lessons as a child, I'd be less of a lead foot.

Standing by a kapok tree, the shaman sings a harmonic tune. His eyes are closed, and both hands are on the tree, fingers splayed over the bark. The size of the tree is so imposing, it consumes most of the sun's rays. I didn't notice Kaikare slip out of my sight until she comes to me holding a prickly heart-shaped pod. This time, I realize she's leading me to the village.

Keep your distance. Samuel's words play over in my mind as I follow her to the cooking fire, where she breaks open the pod to reveal dozens of reddish seeds. After scooping them into a pot of water, she then places it over the heat.

A loud crack has me jumping. The heavens open, and heavy rain drenches me in seconds. With my backpack over my head, I sprint to Samuel's hut.

Everything is like we left it.

I strip out of my wet clothes, not for being cold as the rain is refreshing, more so my clothes need to dry before musk seeps in.

Kicking off my sneakers, I heave at the smell of my socks. I peel them off for the first time in days. Come to think of it, lifting my arm, I get a whiff of me. Ugh. The socks and I both require a good scrub. It's weird I didn't notice until I thought of how society has an expectation of body odor. The subtle musky odor of the Ularans isn't offensive, and I guess it's grown on me. Even still, I'm washing because my feet reek.

Laying my soaked clothes on the wooden table, I tie the skirt around my waist, slipping the beads over my head and shoulders.

My stomach growls, reminding me I've barely eaten. Remembering Samuel left a note to help with some of the foods' nutritional value and what is safe to eat, I scour through his case. "What's this?" It's a handwritten piece of paper. No, a wad of notes on medicinal uses of some of the plants. I flick through the notes reading the descriptions. Many of the plants aid in killing bacteria and parasites, and I understand now how everyone remains relatively well. It's why Samuel reiterated foreign viruses were a threat. Anti-inflammatory, anti-cancer, digestion, blood purifiers, cough relief, bronchitis, diarrhea—there is a plant for almost every known ailment.

Rain continues to pound the palm roof. At times, I worry it's not going to hold. I curl into the hammock with a handful of notes and read more about Samuel's findings, staring at his neat handwriting, imagining the passion driving him to do this.

My gut tightens the more I reflect, missing the man who led me here.

I hold the paper to my chest, close my eyes, and imagine him talking to me. I allow his imaginary voice to envelop me like a warm blanket. Until realization hits—my being here has tortured him. I don't want to be the reason he fails his obligation, knowing the extent of his study and how close he is to finding what he needs for pharmaceutical research. Is love a strong enough reason to be together at this point in time?

Before I come to a conclusion, the rain stops, and Kaikare is at the door waving for me to follow her. I want to hug her when she leads me to the stream.

A pot of red liquid sits on the embankment. She raises a finger, and without hesitation, I wade in, grabbing a handful of scented leaves to wash as I go. Minutes later, she waves me out of the water. "Already? I could lay here all afternoon." She smiles at me, and yet I know it's not a sign she comprehends my words.

Clambering over the edge, she hands me a handful of leaves to dry myself. I'm still not accustomed to being naked in front of people and push down my inhibition and insecurities. She glides the leaves over my back like a squeegee cleaning glass. After drying where I can reach with the leaves, I squeeze the remaining water out of my hair and secure it on my head in a messy bun.

Wrapping the straps of the reed skirt around my waist, I tie a knot while Kaikare bends and scoops red paste from the pot. She adjusts my shoulders, so I'm standing upright and proceeds to paint my back with a sequence of strokes and angles. Freshly washed and painted, I sense it's in preparation for something. I pray it's not an initiation like the one I witnessed with fire ants.

Kaikare continues to paint my front. I close my eyes when she touches my chest, although this time, I don't stop her. I focus on breathing and tell myself it's not weird. At all. The strokes extend to my limbs. I open my eyes and admire the long lines along the length of my legs. Do they stand for more than simple decorative body art? She takes my chin in her palm, angling my face in assessment. My forehead, chin, and temples are dotted. I smile as I look into her eyes, eyes holding understanding, honey-colored eyes different than everyone else's here. She holds my gaze. Seconds pass, and it's like time stands still with no judgment, only understanding of the things we have learned about each other. Her lids close and open in a slow movement, and then she smiles.

UNTIL TODAY, I was ignorant of how rain and tropical rain differed.

Back home, we would say, *it's bucketing down*. Although the worst of the rainy season has passed, Mother Nature decides otherwise, and the rains have paved a small stream past Samuel's hut to the round house. Kaikare keeps me under the cover of the long house where the fires are protected by high makeshift palm roofs and small moats to lead the water away. And this isn't even the wet season.

A faint sound of cheering comes from the jungle. My eyes are unaccustomed to seeing anything through the blanket of rain falling in sheets rather than drops. Peering into the gray, I make out naked human figures waving spears in the air as they approach.

"Samuel?"

I stand and walk toward the edge, stopping myself from running toward them. Shit, would I have to keep my distance from him? I can't think straight with the sound of my heartbeat in my ears. I'm smiling ear to ear as the warriors emerge from the green carrying animals attached to long sticks of bamboo on their shoulders. Not caring about the deluge of water, the women run to them cheering and jumping about, leading them toward the fire. How long has it been since they left on their hunt with Samuel and Tïmenneng with them for part of the journey? Sixteen days? It dawns on me the excitement extends from the men returning to their loved ones. The meat is much-needed food, and everyone was waiting for this hunt. Strung up by the feet are a wild pig, two small deer, and the largest snake I've seen.

"Is it a boa?"

No one answers since I'm a good distance from the other women. Even if my words were understood, I doubt I could be heard over the applause. Immediately, the animals are prepared before being secured over the fire pits.

Everyone's bellies will be satisfied tonight.

TWILIGHT IS BARELY noticeable under a canopy of gray.

It reflects my mood, and I'm going stir crazy. We're stuck in the hut, and I am away from the others, not knowing what to do with myself. My stomach rumbles at the aroma of spit-roasted meat. God, I could eat a full animal on my own. Sitting on the ground, I pick up a rock and make squiggly lines in the dirt. Kaikare leans in, and her brows pull tight. "I'm doodling," I tell her.

She gazes up at me. "Doo-lin."

"Yes." I want to hug her. "Yes." I smile at her like an idiot and point to the meat, then rub my stomach. "I'm hungry. Hungry."

Kaikare shakes her head and points to the meat cooking over the fire.

"What? I can't eat anything?" I ask in desperation.

She brings her hand from her shoulder to her hips in a fast ax action.

"I take that as a no." Ugh, what's their word for no? "Awarö?" *Bad?*

She tilts her head at me. The meat isn't bad, I already know that. I wish she could explain why I can't eat it.

She stands and leaves me a moment before returning with yuca bread and potatoes on a palm leaf. She shoves it in front of me, and I take it. Without waiting for permission, I down it quickly and look for more. Kaikare stands and gestures for me to do the same. I guess it looks like seconds are out of the question.

The rain has eased to a drizzle, and we walk through the sludge to the round house. Inside, in the far back corner, the shaman kneels, smoking a pipe. A massive-feathered headdress sits on his head. Small fires dot the dirt, and it's light enough to make out the blue, yellow, and scarlet feathers on his crown. Across his cheeks are strokes of red like mine. He glances up and nods. Is he expecting me?

A woven mat lays on the floor in front of him. It hits me—I'm being prepared for my own ayahuasca ceremony. "God help me," I mutter as I remember Samuel's reaction after ingesting the tea.

A bowl is placed to his left, feathers tied to strings of teeth and bones to his right. He lifts the twine holding feathers, bones, and teeth and shakes it like a musical instrument before breaking into song.

"I'm not sure I'm ready for this," I say to Kaikare as she assists me to kneel before him. "I mean what if I have a reaction? I know I'm going to puke my guts up, and hell, maybe lose control of my bowels, which I prefer not to think about, but it's the racing heart and shit that scares me most. I could have a heart attack because we all react to drugs differently. Your people probably fall in the body of the bell-shaped graph of a desired drug effect. Some fall on the lip of no effect, yet knowing my luck, I'll fall in the minority where it's probably fatal..."

Shit.

I go to stand, only she stops me and wipes the tears I'm oblivious to. She places a hand on my cheek and smiles, a finger circling between us as though she's telling me she'll be here for me. "I hope you know CPR," I murmur. "So, this is it. I die in the rainforest, and my father gets to say, 'I warned you' at my funeral."

I shut up when a cup-sized bowl is handed to me. *I'm already crazy*. I shoot Kaikare a worried look before downing it in one go.

I gag and cough on the vile taste, handing her back the cup. "It's disgusting," I say. It reminds me of a night on tequila. Spluttering, I try to spit the bitterness from my mouth.

She lets go of my hand to refill the bowl by the shaman's side. He blows smoke over the bowl from a pipe and returns to his song. When I down around seven cups, I hold up my hand to refuse anymore. The shaman blows smoke into my face and chest. The ground seems to move beneath me. I fall back onto my rear and close my eyes. The room spins as if I'm intoxicated, lying in bed and can't sleep—the very worst part of being drunk.

Breathe.

You can do this.

My heart thuds behind my ribs, a quickened beat as though in a race, and I'm sprinting to the finish line. My breaths quicken, and no matter how I try to calm my thoughts, it's helpless to slow my vital organs' reaction to the brew. I'm guessing my heart wants this shit out of me as much as I do.

After a series of flips and turns, my stomach gurgles in warning, and I say, "I'm ready."

Lying on my side seems natural, and I'm not sure how many minutes —or hours—pass before I shoot up on all fours ready to puke.

Beneath me, I sense a clean bowl right before the regurgitated tea finds its way out. I sweat profusely, heave and cough, while my gut continues to twist and contract. Wiping my mouth on several occasions, I sit back on my heels, saying, "Okay. I'm done," until a demon possesses me once more, and I throw myself forward in an exorcism on my soul.

Burning wood overpowers my senses. When smoke hits my face, I'm forced back onto my butt as though a ghost pushed me. The shaman's harmonious tunes fill my head, and I'm swaying back and forth, handing control over to him. A shiver leads to trembles quaking over my body. A warm hand guides me to lie on the mat. Each vowel echoes as though my brain is trying to find meaning in a dark cave. My lips tingle. Spots form before my eyes, a kaleidoscope of brilliant color in the most unusual patterns and brightness I could ever imagine. The brightness is in my head, and before me, as though I could reach out and touch the rainbow on steroids, something alien reaches in for my soul so that it can witness the astral show. Colors twist and turn, slow to almost nothing before returning to their former brilliance. I don't want it to stop for it's not only the color, I'm overwhelmed with emotion and pure joy.

The nausea builds again, only I manage not to puke. The tingling travels up my arms and over my body, and my thought processes unravel as if something is inside of me, coursing through my veins until its fingers probe the lock to my brain. The doors to my world open to allow this alien intelligence to rifle through my thoughts. The spirit is stronger and more powerful than me. I sense its strength without fear, only endless love. Memories flash before me, and along with them, emotions undo my resolve—my time with Ethan and the moment he killed my soul and my life being controlled by my father, never being free to live the way I choose. Tears come with more images morphing to my friends, their faces appearing and disappearing, a movie on fast-forward until I'm visualizing a life-size image of Samuel.

He stares back at me as though searching for my life force, blue eyes holding my focus. My chest rises as though my heart reaches for him. My grandmother's face appears, her beautiful smile telling me I'm doing fine and to reach for the stars. She morphs into a black jaguar, and I sense I'm looking at a mirror image of myself. My soul or whatever part of me is connecting with this higher intelligence glides into dark nothingness in a universe surrounded by stars and other souls. For a moment, I believe I hold knowledge for all there is to know. If anyone were to ask me a question, I'd have an answer. Colored wings coming from the stars soar toward me in the form of beautiful butterflies. They speak to me in the voice of the shaman, and I understand every foreign word. *Evol* is whispered. One word. I don't know what it means, but it shoots emotion into my head. Rain falls in the form of butterflies all whispering to me, nothing comprehensible yet full of meaning.

Life.

I feel life.

The click of insects has its own language as does the chatter of animals. I hear everything differently and feel connected to what lies beyond the border of the jungle. Gone is the fear I held inside. Fear of the unknown. Fear of what could harm me. I understand now we all have a place. A chance to live harmoniously together by respecting each creature and their purpose on earth.

My eyes open to darkness, the shaman's song, and a hand on my shoulder. The trees rustle their leaves, speaking to me. I turn to the jungle, the trees glowing green, their bioluminescence like we saw last night. Each tree is lit up in a network of nerves, and a web penetrates beneath the soil to the roots. It's as if my face is to the ground, and I'm seeing what lies beneath as you would when in the ocean and staring beneath the surface. A central nervous system connects one tree to the next, electric energy firing between each, silently communicating with one another, and tonight, me. I feel every vibration of life. I hear the whisper of the trees, the energy surrounding us, emanating oxygen to the world in clouds of green.

Our lifeforce.

EVERYWHERE I LOOK IS as though we have two suns shining bright light upon us. Before my experience, I perceived the world through a cloudy lens, a heavy fog clouding my thoughts. Today, I woke with more clarity than I've ever experienced in my life. Even now, out in the fields with the other women, the ax is light in my hands, and there's a sense of purpose that I didn't have before.

Looking into the jungle, beyond the trees, I have clarity. A connection. Maybe I'm still high? I don't care because I have found everything I was searching for—my eudaimonia—and I don't want to lose the feeling of infinite happiness.

Kaikare smiles at me, knowing my secret despite no words exchanged between us. By lunchtime, I'm starving, and despite the new sense of energy soaring through my veins, I am shaky after puking equal measures of my body weight last night.

I stop to wipe my brow, the sweat even drips from my chin with my body trying to eliminate the toxins after the ayahuasca cleansing. I have no experience in microbiology, but if I was carrying a disease, I think the tea destroyed it.

Heavy gray clouds loom overhead. Hurrying along, we carry the produce in woven baskets and head back to the village center, dumping our day's work on the ground near the fire to keep the insects at bay.

I'm eager to learn how to prepare the yuca since I'm more in tune with their ways. Before I consider my words, the children come cheering from the direction of the river. Kaikare listens before waving for me to follow.

I want to run to the river. It could be Samuel, and there's a chance he could be sick after being away for so long. We reach the sandy beach, and I stop to catch my breath, the lightness in my chest fades.

"Hey, is everything okay?" I say to Asoo.

Asoo hands me my phone. "Your friend, Amy, say it urgent."

"What?" I take my phone from him and read her messages.

Skimming over the words, my thoughts racing to the worst possible scenarios.

> Eden!
>
> I hope you get this message soon. I'm so scared. I don't know what to do and need you here to help me. I'm in Iquitos alone because Yasmine is with Michael. I don't care that I'm alone, but I'm worried about her, and you're the only one who seems to get through to her when she refuses to listen. She's about to take a tea with a shaman, only this shaman isn't reputable because I have asked around. Some people have died in his ceremonies!
>
> She won't listen to me, and what's weird is Michael asked for you and Samuel to come. That made me panic because he sounds worried. I don't know what to do, and when I tried to talk her out of it, she got angry with me. She's due to take the ceremony in two days. Please hurry!

I GLANCE UP TO KAIKARE, the well of tears in my eyes blur my vision. "My friends need me. I have to go." I blink the tears away and swipe my eyes. "Asoo, please give me a moment to grab my things, and please explain to Kaikare the need for me to leave. Tell her I'm going to miss her."

I don't think, I just act and leave my friends on the bank to sprint to Samuel's hut. My throat burns as I gasp for air. This is possibly the last time I'll see Kaikare, the shaman, and the smiling faces in this hidden village. After last night, my perspective has switched. Even though I couldn't live here forever, the notion of staying for a few months is appealing. Now, I understand Samuel's desire to live here and be connected to every living thing.

Denied of that choice, my decision is made for me without a chance to say goodbye to Samuel.

I hope the universe knows what it's doing.

46

EDEN

BENEATH THE SCATTERING OF CLOUDS, the broccoli jungle fades, and with it the very place I left my heart. Looking away from the window to my hands, I trace the outline of red Vs no amount of soap could remove in a day.

Yesterday when I entered the resort in Canaima with a painted face and limbs the looks from the staff were priceless. Did they think I was innocent? A grin spreads across my face. The sense of belonging and the memories will stay with me always.

When the plane touches down and I regain Wi-Fi, I'm searching for the next flight to Iquitos.

The airfares are double the usual fare, and thankfully, I have enough savings since I've barely spent a cent these past few weeks.

In the hub of the airport, people bustle around me. I have a few hours between flights, and it gives me a chance to grab some food. I'm craving meat, yet I decide on fruit—a banana and an apple since my stomach has been in knots since I first saw Asoo by the river. Security and the police are everywhere I look. The news flashes on the television, the presenter speaks in Spanish, and I have no idea what's being communicated. Living in a village sheltered from the rest of the world, I'm clueless to world events, although the political world is volatile, and I could be headed straight into a shitstorm. Keeping a low profile, I stick to myself and remain in the terminal for my flight. As much as I want to put it off, I have to call my father. Thankfully, I'm seated away from other travelers as they'll hear him roar. Inhaling a deep breath, I mentally prepare myself for a dressing-down.

"You have reached Winston Monteford, CEO of Monte Hotels. I'm not able to take your call, so please leave a message regarding the nature of your inquiry."

I let all the air go out of my lungs. Shit, it must be around midnight in Adelaide.

"Dad, I didn't want to send a text. Only a quick call to let you know I'm fine. I know you heard I separated from the girls, and you're disappointed with my decision, but I'm safe. I'm meeting up with my friends tonight, and we'll be heading home in a few days. I'll call you from the airport and let you know our arrival time and if there are any delays. Looking forward to seeing Mum and you, and of course, Will, Faith, and little Seb. Love you all."

Pressing my hand to my chest, I feel the measure of my heart being torn between missing my family, leaving Samuel and a jungle village I have grown to love.

People around me have joined a queue to board the plane to Iquitos. Following the line, I walk the aisle, take my seat, and sink into my chair. I relax into the headrest, close my eyes, and refuse to open them as the plane soars along the runway. Finally, I'm a step closer to seeing my friends.

I arrive in Iquitos around nine at night and am required to pass through customs with my luggage. My suitcase is full of stuff I now consider unnecessary.

Amy is waiting in the airport terminal somewhere. When the crowd disperses, she waves her hands at me, then she sprints and leaps into my arms, almost knocking us both to the floor. I regain my balance, and she lets out a sob, her face nestled into my chest. "I've missed you so much."

"Me, too," I tell her, squeezing my arms around her shoulders.

Arm in arm, we head outside, humidity smacking my face, a reminder I'm back in the jungle.

"We get around on tuk-tuks," she says. "I'll get us one to get to the city. It's like Canaima here, you can't access it by car, only plane or boat."

I nod. "So, you researched Canaima?"

"Yep. I almost came to you." She turns and waves down the three-wheeled motorized vehicle. Amy tells the driver of our destination, and he helps me with my luggage, putting it at our feet in the squishy cabin. He veers into the traffic without looking, and I grab Amy's arm.

She ignores my anxiety and instead nods at my face. "Is this a new form of makeup?"

"I can't concentrate right now, so it's a story for another time." Her brows pull together, and before she says anything else, I ask, "What's important is you tell me everything that's happened with Yasmine."

She shakes her head as though she's exasperated. "She only talks to him, not me, and if I'm around, she bloody whispers. I mean, what the fuck is that about? You'll barely recognize her. Can someone change in a matter of weeks?"

Reflecting on my journey, I nod. "Sometimes, yes."

We stop out front of a colonial-style hotel wall to wall with the other buildings. The hall is beautifully tiled with historical black and white pictures lining the long passageway.

"This is mine," she tells me and opens the door to a quaint room with one queen bed. "It's just you and me, *ba-by*."

I laugh and yet head straight to the bed and flop backward. "I have missed the luxury of a mattress."

Amy screws up her face. "What have you been sleeping on?"

"A hammock." I kick off my sandals—my smelly sneakers dumped in a bin at the airport—and lift my legs onto the bed. "And as much as I want to talk about my adventure first, you need to tell me what the plan is for tomorrow because I'm not going to keep my eyes open much longer."

Amy lands on the bed beside me with more energy than necessary. "Yasmine is in preparation, apparently."

Linking my fingers behind my head, I stretch my elbows wide. "How do you know?"

"Michael calls me. He keeps asking if you and Samuel are coming? He mentions *Paulo* and how Samuel would understand."

Asking for Samuel and me doesn't sit right with me. I'm her friend. I can talk her out of most things if warranted, and besides, Michael is aware of his friend's commitment. "Why is Michael allowing her to go through with it if he's concerned?"

"They both went to some sort of shaman festival. You meet around thirty shamans and choose the one who's right for you. This guy is from New York. We're not sure why she chose him, but he convinced her to go down the river to his little camp. His fee was close to double the others. I mean, I saw some of the shamans. They looked like spiritual, beautiful people, but this guy appeared fake. I don't trust him, and there have been whispers his brew has killed people, although no one has proved it. I hope it's all whispers."

"Wait. You pay?" I'm so naïve.

She nods. "It's a commercial thing here. Part of the reason many come to visit. Camps are set up even for corporate businesses from around the world. And there are women's groups as well as professionally organized ones, yet Yasmine decided to go with this Paulo from New York who could sell ice to an Eskimo."

It doesn't sound like Yasmine. She's smarter than this.

"Do you know where the camp is?"

"Yep. I have a map with directions from Michael."

"You said he calls you. How would he if he's in the jungle?"

"Michael has a satellite phone."

"Oh, right."

Does Samuel have one too?

After texting Asoo that I'm here safe at the hotel and mentioning Paulo's name, I climb under the sheets and curl into a ball. "We'll find her tomorrow," I murmur. My eyelids shutter closed as the energy drains away.

THICK, moist air in the tropics isn't the easiest to breathe at any time, and if you combine it with pollution from the tuk-tuk and motorcycles, it's even more difficult. Amy and I wait on a landing for a boat to take us along the Amazon River. At least the air is cleaner here.

"I've booked us on a tour boat," Amy informs me. "It's large enough for thirty people interested in visiting a small river village."

I wipe my forehead with the back of my hand. "Oh really. A small village."

"Yeah. I thought it might interest you since the help in these villages comes from missionaries and volunteers."

"Right. It does, but you know my interest before was simply to find Samuel, right?"

She gives me a long look. “I didn’t want to mention his name.”

Giving her an easy smile, I shrug my shoulders. “I miss him for sure. I also believe when his work is done, he’ll come looking for me. For now, we both have to live our lives until that day comes.”

“God, you sound mature and so confident.”

I laugh once and yet say nothing because we are interrupted by the tour guide, and we’re directed onto a boat. It’s a civilized means of travel, everyone with their own seat and a canopy to protect us from the sun.

“This is cool, right?” Amy says as the boat picks up speed, and we sail along the water.

I smile at Amy. “Yeah, this is cool.” We point out birds as they fly overhead and chat about the rainforest bordering the river, although it’s nowhere near as majestic or towering as the jungle where I’ve lived these past few weeks.

I sit in awe, staring out at the impressive Amazon River. I’m not sure how many miles wide it is. The current and body of water are more powerful than the smaller rivers I voyaged near Angel Falls. A pink dolphin surfaces and swims alongside the boat. We laugh and call out to the dolphin as though it were following us.

After a couple of hours, we arrive at the small village. While everyone disembarks for a village tour, we cross through on tuk-tuk to a tributary river on the other side. Traditional and Western structures line small, sealed pathways along with a church. Children play, dogs wander, and we interrupt a football game with enthusiastic barefoot teenagers yelling as the ball passes sticks for goal markings. The overland segue is waiting for us, and it then takes us fifteen minutes until we board a motorized canoe. I smile at Amy’s glee. It’s a little more streamlined than my previous canoe experiences, yet it still features a plank of wood as a seat.

My focus is to chat about Yasmine, and yet I’m more relaxed than I should be in the thick, uncomfortable heat. Sailing along the river, the breeze in my freshly shampooed hair, and surrounded by rainforest, it’s almost natural for me to seek comfort in this environment. It gives me a sense of awareness to honor myself. Do what’s right for me. Enjoy the little things and stop stressing about the future, especially the fear of being loved. It has taken me all these years to realize love is more than something found as part of a couple. It has to start from within. In Ulara, I learned to love myself.

In my heart I know Samuel and I will be together one day. It makes leaving him and his work okay because I'm being true to myself as well. I found how helping others as I did in the Pemón camp is rewarding and important to me. It helped me to understand him better. I'm not sure I understand the level of Samuel's commitment, although over the last couple of weeks, I understand why, as I too have grown to love the Ularan community, the people, and the place.

The jungle has grounded and lifted my spirit. During the tea ceremony, I felt harmonious to the earth, to every living creature, and I developed a tangible unity with the universe. I'll never lose that bond.

"It's not too far ahead," Amy says after speaking with the driver. She carefully steps over the planks to sit beside me. "What are you going to say to her?"

We didn't speak much on the previous boat ride with other people sitting close to us. "Besides what I mentioned at breakfast? I have a few things I've mulled over that might help her rethink her decision. If taking the tea is what she desires, we'll help her find a reputable shaman. There are hundreds of experienced shamans, so I'm curious why she chose a guy from New York. When we find out why, then we can negotiate with her."

The driver pulls into a poorly constructed small pier, and I realize by the buildings high on stilts, this area is susceptible to extreme flooding in the wet season. There are only a couple of structures reminding me of the Ularan village, only sturdier with the assistance of modern tools. I now understand the need for rubber boots that are provided when we booked this trip. The driver waits for us in the boat. We slip on the boots, leaving our flip-flops on the boat, and walk through the muddy water pooling ankle deep.

We only have minutes to convince Yasmine to leave with us.

"Can you imagine wanting to stay here?" Amy whispers while watching me peruse the palm-leaf thatched roof and open walls of the two huts.

I ignore her comment, my senses alerted to a herbal aroma hanging in the muggy air. I cough at the unpleasantness. A small indigenous woman dressed in a green t-shirt and pants approaches, almost camouflaged by the surroundings. She speaks to us in Spanish.

Amy talks over her. "We're looking for Yasmine and Michael."

Lines deepen on the woman's forehead. The hand behind her back reveals itself as she takes a cigarette to her mouth and sucks while giving us a once-over. She puffs out smoke in my face as though my facial paintwork offends her.

Doing my utmost not to cough, I follow her past similar structures with walls reminding me of log cabins. She points to a treehouse. Amy and I step up the ladder, my feet slipping in the rubber boots, and I grip the side in case I misjudge a step.

On reaching the top, we scramble onto all fours before standing to find Yasmine in a hammock with Michael. My entry isn't delicate, so surprise turns to suspicion when both remain sleeping, especially since the small room reeks of smoke, musk, and sex.

"Did you really come here to sleep?" I snap.

Michael jolts. The hammock sways and both scramble to be upright.

"Eden? I mean, how? Why are you here?" Yasmine croaks. Her hand clasps her throat.

"You sound terrible. Are you sick?" I ask. She shakes her head. "Okay, well, I'm here because our holiday is almost over, and it's time for us to meet up and go home."

She shoots me a warning look with narrowed eyes. Yet I sense she doesn't have the energy to argue. "This is the last thing I wanted to tick off before we leave," she says, with her hand remaining on her throat.

"I know," I say in a calm voice.

"Did Samuel come with you?" Michael probes.

"Why would he?" I snap.

Michael glances at Amy. "Did you give her the message?"

Yasmine scowls at Michael. "What message?"

"I was concerned about you, babe, that's all." His hand slides across her forehead and down her cheek.

Yasmine slaps his hand away. "What message?"

"He told me to tell Eden and Samuel to come as you were putting yourself in danger being here with Paulo," Amy states.

Yasmine glares at Michael. "Danger? You recommended him."

"Babe. You chose him. You were adamant. I know you've been high for days, but this was your decision."

"We're taking you back to Iquitos," I tell her. "I know you want to do this but not here and not today. You're sick, and you need to get well first. You have to cleanse and be healthy. In your condition, it could be dangerous to take the brew."

Her eyes widen.

"Quite knowledgeable, Eden. Just where is Samuel?" Michael asks in a low, deep voice.

"He had an exploration. I know you understand his commitment to his work, and besides, I haven't seen him in almost three weeks."

"Where did you stay while he's away?" He stalks closer to me.

"In Canaima. I told Amy where I was."

"I've been to Canaima. These markings aren't from there," he says, holding my chin and turning my face.

I push his hand off me. "I went to help in a Pemón village. The doctor needed some extra hands, and most of the volunteers had left."

He raises a single brow. "Right. Nice try."

We both turn when Yasmine groans and Amy wraps a hand around her back.

"I can't believe you kept her here in this condition?" I gasp. Right now, I wish I had some medical knowledge. I wish Samuel were here.

He crosses his arms and juts out his chin. "She refused to leave. It's why I sent for you." I push past him and assist Amy with Yasmine. "She's still high. Give her some time for the drugs to wear off."

"What drugs?" Amy yells at him.

"It doesn't matter. We're leaving now," I tell them both. "There's a driver waiting for us."

"Eden, but I want to—"

"Not here and not today," I repeat. "Michael, you need to help us get Yasmine down the ladder."

I make my way down onto the muddy ground and take Yasmine's arm to balance her landing.

"What's going on here?" I swing around to a man with straggly blond hair falling around his shoulders.

"We're taking our friend," I tell him. "And don't worry, she doesn't want a refund. Keep the money, only there'll be no ceremony."

He looks at Yasmine. "Is this what you want?" he says in an American accent.

"You know what I wanted. Now my friends are here, and I'm not well, so—"

"I have stuff that will help you get better. You have to talk to me, girl. I can't fix what I don't know."

"If..." I say in a stern voice, "... you're the shaman you claim to be, you could heal without instruction. You would simply know as the forest would talk to you." I slip Yasmine's arm over my shoulder and take a step past Paulo, ignoring his glare.

"You and I need to chat," Michael whispers.

"We do," I say but not in the same context.

WE ARRIVE at the small village, and a tuk-tuk takes us to the missionary's office as we've missed the boat back to Iquitos. It's a silent ride because I'm too angry at Michael to calmly discuss anything and equally worried about Yasmine.

The door opens, and a middle-aged nun in a traditional long, white dress with a white veil concealing her hair and part of her face steps forward. "You welcome to stay, boat can take you in morning. We have beds for you," she manages in English, her Spanish tongue thick. "Young man can sleep in other room. No see ladies with ring."

"Is there a doctor here?" I ask her when my friends leave to find their room. "My friend has a sore throat, and I'd like him to take a look."

"Yes, child. He go to you after dinner," she says in her broken English.

"Thank you. We appreciate your kind hospitality."

"Would you like some tea?"

Knowing Yasmine is safe with Amy, I take a chair at the table. "Do you mind telling me about your work here, Sister?"

She opens a tin to reveal cookies inside. "You like Alfajore? You call them shortbread."

I smile, my mouth already watering. "I would very much. Thank you."

It's something to sweeten my thoughts before I question Michael.

THE FOLLOWING MORNING, I tap gently on Yasmine's bedroom door. "Can I come in?"

"Not if you're going to lecture me," she groans.

I open the door and peek in. Yasmine is still in bed. "Hey." I stride to her side and sit on the single wooden bed, lean in, and hug her. "It's not a lecture," I whisper.

"You're lucky I'm too sick to yell at you because I told you my plans in Ilhéus," she starts.

"I know. And I respect that. Only he wasn't the right shaman for you. I know what Michael said..." I add quickly when she opens her mouth to interject, "... because I've also experienced the tea."

"You have?" Her eyes round, and she pushes up onto her elbows. "With Samuel in the jungle?"

I nod slowly and not in an excited way. "It was part of my journey, and the ceremony wasn't with Samuel."

"What did you see and feel?" Her words come out fast.

"All our experiences are different, which is why I want you to benefit from it and not fall sick." I slide tight, dark ringlets away from her face and smile at her. "How is your throat?"

"A little better. The antibiotics are helping some."

"There'll be another time for you, I promise, and it won't be with Paulo. As for Michael, I'll be questioning him because things could've turned out far worse if you went ahead."

"Why did he want Samuel to come?" she asks, her hand resting on the base of her neck.

"I'm not sure. It's another thing I'll be discussing with him. Right now, we need to get you up and showered, so we can catch the next boat back to Iquitos."

47

SAMUEL

The plane descends, and the Amazon River widens far more than the one he calls home. His eyes are fixed on the window, and he looks below as the plane approaches the runway. He should've relaxed more on the flights to regain his energy. The thought of not seeing Eden for many months caused his chest to tighten, and he couldn't breathe. He closes his eyes when the wheels screech, his shoulders less heavy. The voice over the speaker talks in Spanish. He listens to directions and waits for the time to be mentioned—*6:31 p.m.*

He rushes through customs, the first in the line, and takes the first tuk-tuk he sees into the city, praying he has not missed her.

His exploration was a success, despite him not eating anything substantial for days. His critical thinking directed him to what needed to be done. He pushed through hunger, hiked miles with only acai berries to eat, found water amongst the plants with flowering plants in his pack.

The down trip was harder. His thoughts went to her. She was the best and worst distraction. The image of her ingrained in his brain guided him *home,* knowing she was waiting for him.

He was weak and tired, but it didn't matter, but then he found her backpack missing. Kaikare filled him in. He'd missed her by a day. Asoo came by the next morning, mentioned Paulo, and Samuel has since been on plane after plane.

He hopes she's at the same hotel that she mentioned in a text to

Asoo. If not, he doubts he'll find her in a city of half a million people or if she's in one of the water villages dotting the river.

He dreams of holding her, making love to her, yet he can barely remain upright. He pays the driver in American dollars and is grateful the hotel reception is open.

"No reservation? I'm sorry we're fully booked. There's a hotel up the road," the receptionist says in Spanish.

He places one hand on the desk to balance himself. "I'm looking for Eden Monteford," he tells her. "Is she staying here?"

"I'm sorry, sir, we can't give out confidential information."

"Samuel?"

He turns at the sound of her voice.

She runs to him, almost knocking him off balance. Her arms wrap around him. "You're okay."

"Barely, but now I've found you, I'm more than okay." He kisses Eden holding her tightly, wishing he didn't have to let go. He breaks the kiss and leans in so their heads are huddled together.

"You're safe that's all that matters," she rasps.

Safe in each other's arms they allow themselves a quiet minute to process their emotion. Tears stream down Eden's cheek. His heart is near bursting. His resolve cracks and he cries quietly with Eden in his arms. Gathering some strength, he takes in a deep breath, and inhales her scent.

She's all he needs to survive.

Eden leans back, her eyes flicking over his face. "You're thinner." She runs her fingers over his cheeks. "Come, let's get you up the stairs."

Stairs.

One arm hooked around his waist, she guides him up each step and unlocks the door with one hand. She leads him to her bed and grabs her phone. "I'm sending Amy a text to bring extra food back for you. She's with Yasmine and Michael."

"What was the message about Paulo?" he croaks.

Eden curls up beside him on the bed. "It's a story that can wait." Her hand is under his t-shirt, stroking his ribs. "How much weight have you lost?"

"It happens on these trips, although it's not as concerning as the thought of losing you."

She pushes up so their lips meet. His walls are down. Everything about her arouses him—her scent, her touch. The warmth radiating from her calms him like no other. And the memory of him between her legs. His fingers curl around her hair. She owns his heart and soul. He kisses her with more passion and need than he believed possible. She fuels his energy. In minutes, they are naked, their legs intertwined.

With frantic breaths, he sinks into her, rasping, "I love you," against her mouth. Unlike the last time, he moves slowly, lovingly, inside of her.

Delicate hands hold his face while blue eyes demand his focus. She waits for his breathing to slow and whispers, "I love you, too."

He collapses onto the sheet beside her. His eyes heavy and overcome with exhaustion. "When do you leave?"

"Tomorrow," she whispers. "I'm sorry."

"Don't be. It was inevitable. It's not goodbye. I'll come and find you. I promise."

Knowing his words to be true, he closes his eyes, his heart finally finding peace.

"Where are they now?" Samuel asks Eden while sitting at the table after eating breakfast.

"In Yasmine's room, I assume. He managed to worm his way out of any blame and said he was doing what Yasmine wanted. Yet he knew you would come. Why is that?"

Samuel crosses his arms and leans back in the chair, his gaze rising to the ceiling while he constructs his explanation. "Michael knows about the shaman in Ulara. Well, bits and not as much as you... only that their ayahuasca recipe is pure and more effective than any other brew. He wants me to divulge what plants are used and the secrets of the village. He's been using subtle blackmail for years. And yes, I stupidly told him some things when I first decided to stay in the village as I needed to report to someone my whereabouts for safety. He has tried different teas with shamans over the years. We met Paul, or Paulo as he's now known, when he first arrived in Peru. He stated he wanted to become a shaman and learn their ways. To be a healer takes many years and a special skill to connect with the forest. It's not a job you apply for and can be trained in a year. Yet Paulo was determined and thought he could make a living if he remained here. He married a local from one of the villages, and it's worked out for him. Only he's not a true shaman. I believe he can be dangerous because he doesn't take anyone's past medical history into account or any underlying symptoms. To him, it's a fix-all brew. He mixes too much caffeine into it, and it not only makes you sick and gives palpitations, but for someone with an underlying heart condition, it can be potentially fatal."

"Amy said people have died in his care."

Leaning forward, he rests his weary arms on the table. "Two deaths. The first happened years ago when someone stood while still high from his concoction and fell and hit their head. He said it was beyond his control and not his fault. The second had a stomach ulcer and died in Lima a few days after leaving his ceremony. He denies both were any fault of his. It's upsetting because the shamans here pride themselves on their work, and sharing it with people who need their help is important. They didn't want bad publicity from a—"

"What? Fraud?"

"That's almost a correct assumption. Although Paulo has studied some, just not enough."

"Can you speak to Yasmine? She wanted to experience a ceremony. I told her I wouldn't stop her, only she couldn't do one with Paulo."

"Understandable, and you did the right thing for your friend. I'll deal with Michael after you leave. You need to care for Yasmine. I'll tell her how to prepare properly and provide a diet to follow if she wants to come back. And strictly, no alcohol. At certain times, Iquitos is busy with tourists searching for the right shaman and willing to pay extraordinary amounts of money to find direction in their life or help them with depression. I know the benefits, and now..." He runs a finger along her cheek. "May I?" He takes out his phone. "Smile." He takes a picture. A memory of her embracing his world so he can look at it any time he wants.

"Your phone?" Her eyes round. "Can I add my details?"

"Of course."

Eden taps in her number and address. Then she calls her phone before handing it back to Samuel.

A grin spreads across his face. "Now, do you want to share what the markings are about? Kaikare mentioned some, but I was in a rush to leave and come find you."

Eden's chest rises and falls as her lips part with a smile. "I understand why people pay if they get to experience what I did."

He links his fingers with hers. "I didn't want you to experience it without me there to help you. Kaikare said you found your spirit."

"Maybe I allowed my walls to come down knowing you weren't there?"

Samuel chuckles. "Ayahuasca is the vine of the souls. She has no barriers. She'll go where she chooses. She reminds me of you," he says, his forehead crinkling.

"Me?"

"It was a long boat ride with Asoo, and so he told me what Kaikare and you did. I'm proud of you, and I'm also upset you left me no supplies."

"Aren't all people your priority? You have your herbs as well. These people needed your medications and Kaikare's help."

He rubs his hand over hers. "I *am* proud of what you both did. In fact, it shocked me a little. Have you considered studying medicine in some form?"

She squeezes his hand. "I've learned a lot about myself these past weeks. When I found Yasmine with a fever, I had to help her. Maybe I was a nurse in another lifetime." She grins at him.

Without a second to lose, he leans in and kisses her. "You'd make a wonderful nurse."

SITTING beside Eden in the tuk-tuk, he's aware of every minute passing before her flight home. Ulara will not be the same without her, although he'll enjoy hearing the stories of Tamu'ne Akare.

He squeezes her hand tucked securely under his. "Kaikare will miss Tamu'ne Akare."

"And I'll miss her. Wait." Her eyes round. "What did you call me?"

"It's your name." He manages to keep a straight face.

She smiles at him warmly. "I had a name?"

He nods, holding back a smirk. "White tortoise."

Her brow crinkles. "White I understand, but... they thought I was slow?"

"You did take a while to pick up on things." He chuckles at the noise of surprise coming from her throat.

"All right, then what was your name?"

"I have two. Everyone is given a name at birth. One is sacred, private, and not to share. The other is what everyone knows you by. After I was initiated as a warrior, I was given a birth name. My other name is Väi Uarati Kún-imá."

"Oh. It's quite a mouthful."

He chuckles.

"What does it mean?"

"Sun man with a long leg."

She bursts out laughing, and he frowns, not understanding why?

"Because you have a big dick?"

"No." He shakes his head in exasperation. "Because of my fair hair, and I'm tall. You might have noticed the Ularans are smaller in height."

She's still giggling. "Yeah, let's go with that. What about Kaikare?"

"Her name is a combination of tortoise and jaguar. She can be both."

"I'm going to miss her," Eden whispers. "She was like a mother to me."

He holds her gaze, pushes wisps of hair from her eyes. "You're a lot like her in some ways." He wraps his arms around her, smiles leaving both of their faces when the tuk-tuk arrives at the airport.

They stand on the side of the pavement. Her suitcase divides them while she waits for her friends to arrive. Silence shrouds them, afraid of the words to come. He links his fingers with hers, fighting an overwhelming urge to ask her not to leave.

"I forgot to mention something," she whispers. She waits until his gaze meets hers. "When I was under, *dreaming*, I saw butterflies. They spoke to me." She hesitates when his expression changes, a combination of fear and concern. "It was euphoric. And I understood every word even though it sounded Ularan."

"It's not the Ularan language, Eden. It's a universal language of the jungle known by all their ancestors across the Amazon."

"Oh."

"What did you hear?"

"It's hard to explain, although one word was repeated over and over. *Evol*. At first, I thought it was evil until I felt this amazing connection with the jungle. Well, to everything, really."

He takes her in his arms and holds her tight. "I wish you didn't have to go. The jungle has embraced you. The spirit of the jungle has accepted you." He kisses the top of her head before resting his nose in her hair. "*Evol* backward is *love*. You're as one. And now you're leaving..." The words claw his tender heart apart. He wants to tighten his squeeze and never let her go.

"You promised you would come find me," she whispers.

Samuel leans back and meets her gaze. "I did."

"Well, one day I'll come back to Ulara. It's *my* promise to you."

On tippy-toes, Eden kisses his lips, wraps her arms around his neck, and deepens the kiss as though it's their last.

48

EDEN

Adelaide, Australia.

Two weeks later…

"Twenty-five percent of modern pharmaceutical ingredients are derived from sources in the Amazon rainforest today. But only one percent of its medicinal potential has been discovered."

I CLOSE the newspaper after reading about illegal forest logging in the Amazon and how it affects the environment. I move the paper to the corner of my father's desk, wipe my eyes to compose myself, and walk out of his office. The past two weeks he's been on a business trip in Sydney, and since my homecoming, we've only spoken on the phone. I've teared up anticipating the questions he'll ask face to face because the only thing he has said on the phone is, "*Are you sure you're okay*?"

I don't want to lie to him, and I don't want to disappoint him either.

Since opening my eyes this morning, I've thought only of Samuel and how much I miss him. Maybe it was my dream about being back in the rainforest. Or that I keep reliving our last night together, the love and the longing for each other, and how we connect on a physical and spiritual level when we're together.

How can the universe be so cruel in letting me find my soulmate and yet keeping us worlds apart?

Still, I'm grateful to have grown and discovered things about myself. Like the strength I knew was inside me and kept hidden in fear of hurting those around me.

"Thank God, it's Friday. That's all I can say." Dana stacks her pens in a container and then closes down her computer.

"Are you doing anything special on the weekend?" The weather forecast predicts the rain will clear by the evening, so it should be fine."

"We're heading to the Barossa for a wine tour. What about you? Or are you still recovering?" Dana stands and wraps a silk scarf around her neck.

I glance out of the window. I don't think I'll ever recover, nor do I want to.

"I'm no clairvoyant, but something tells me it's not jetlag why you're still lethargic. Could it be something or *someone* else?" She gives me one of those looks she must have learned from my grandmother.

"You could say it's both," I say. I haven't shared much about Samuel with my family. I won't until I'm strong enough to talk about him without any tears.

"If you're smart, you'll tell me about *him* on Monday while Ethan is around."

I laugh at her. "You haven't *really* told me what it's been like to work with him."

Dana shrugs. "Can't complain because he does what's asked. He's your father's robot. But if you ask me, he has an ulterior motive for being here. I know a rat when I smell one."

Dana has never forgiven him for breaking my heart. "Maybe I have one as well, so be *nice* to him."

"What are you not telling me?" Her eyes fixate on me while adjusting the collar of her coat.

I smile. "If the pieces line up for me, then you'll be one of the first to know."

"You're going to leave me to deal with him, aren't you?" she asks, pointing the curved handle of her umbrella in my direction.

"I'm not saying anything. Have a good weekend. Enjoy your wine tasting."

"By the sounds of things, I'm going to need it."

Being back at work is harder than I anticipated. I miss you so much. I don't want to be here. I want to be back in the jungle with you—it's something I didn't think I'd say, yet I miss everything about it. Love you with all my heart. E xx

IT'S the fifth text message I have sent Samuel.

Each message lines up below the other with zero replies in between. I have no idea when he'll respond. Yet, I'm thankful to keep in contact and have a form of communication with him, even though it could be weeks or months before he responds. For now, it's enough.

Grabbing my coat, I head out the door to Faith and Jake's house. She arranged the Friday night family dinner party to hear about my travels since we only caught up briefly last weekend. Mum is picking Dad up from the airport and driving directly to Faith's house. I'm not sure Dad wants to know everything, so I placed *safe* photos in an album to share on my phone.

Faith lives twenty minutes from my parents' beachside residence and only minutes from the city. As much as I admire the Edwardian architecture of her luxurious home, I carry some envy in how everything has come easy for her. It only lasts momentarily because I'm happy for her, and right now, my heart warms knowing I get aunty cuddles with my nephew.

I hesitate before knocking to appreciate the old stained-glass panels surrounding the front door. Beyond the door, there's the patter of tiny feet on the floorboards. My brother, Will, unlocks the door, and before I have a chance to respond to his surprise visit from college, Seb jumps onto my leg.

"Edes," Seb says excitedly and leaps into my arms.

I reach to Will with my free hand to pull him in for a hug. "This is a nice surprise. Are you on a semester break?"

"Good to see you, too, sis. Yeah, a brief break before mid-year exams. Have to say I like hearing stories about your trip. For once, I'm not the one stirring trouble."

I laugh. "It's not intentional. And you've grown again," I say, tilting my head back more so than I remember.

Seb grabs my cheeks with both hands and turns my face, so he has my undivided attention. I kiss his cheek and plant my nose in his hair and inhale his freshly bathed scent. "Aunty Eden's missed you." He raises his head and nods at me. "And you're going to be two soon? You're growing up so fast." Sebastian holds up two fingers. "That's right." I kiss his fingers and carry him into the kitchen, where my sister is placing a lasagna in the oven. The roundness of her stomach is now evident beneath her jersey.

"He's missed his Aunty Eden, too." She smiles at me. "Like your other surprise?"

I smile at Will as he takes a seat at the table and scoops a handful of cashew nuts from a bowl. "She didn't recognize me."

I roll my eyes. "You might be taller than me, but you still have the face of a little-shit brother."

Faith laughs. "Have to ask, though. Are you ready for tonight? You know Dad will fire questions at you—"

"Yeah," Will interrupts. "I want the popcorn ready for that show."

"Shut up, Will," Faith says. "You haven't been here to see how crazy Dad's been acting."

Great. Now I'm more nervous than I was before I arrived.

Will taps away on his phone. "Looks like I'm gonna miss the show," he says and stands. "Brock's out front, and I'm heading to his to watch a footy game."

"You're supposed to be here for the family dinner," Faith rouses. She's already perfected her 'mother' voice.

He pushes up from the table. "It's not going to be a happy one." He glances at me with an apology and sympathy in his expression. "I'll see you both over the next couple of days."

Before Faith has a chance to respond, he's walking the hallway toward the front door. "Good luck, sis." His voice echoes from the hall.

"Thanks," I yell back.

"I don't know why Dad's so worked up about you when Will is so erratic. He just doesn't give a shit what anyone thinks."

"He's a teenager." I shrug, although I wish I could be more like him. "About tonight. I've placed the photos in an album. I'll show you the other ones I mentioned when I come over tomorrow."

“Yeah, thanks for babysitting on short notice. Jake has another business dinner in the city. In a few more months, I won’t feel up to going.”

“Honey, I’m home,” Jake calls out when he walks through the front door.

Faith rolls her eyes. “He says that every time he arrives home.”

Jake strolls into the kitchen and drops his briefcase in the corner. He takes Faith in his arms and kisses her dramatically until she pushes him away. I can’t help giggling at his antics. He comes to Seb and gives him a kiss on the top of his head.

“How’s my favorite sister-in-law?”

I shake my head at him. “You’re such a suck. Yes, I’m good.”

He holds out his arms for Seb to go to him and I’m surprised when he curls into my chest.

“We’re still catching up on cuddles.” I tighten my arms around Seb, and kiss his cheek with a smack of my lips.

“He did ask for you a lot while you were away,” Jake says warmly. “And thanks for babysitting for us.” He loosens the tie around his neck and unbuttons the top button.

“Not a problem.”

He glances at Faith, then at me, and then at Faith again. “Do I have time for a shower before dinner?”

“Make it quick,” Faith says. “Mum and Dad will be here soon.”

“And I don’t want to miss the main act.” He winks at me before striding toward the door.

Ugh.

I nuzzle Seb, the perfect distraction, and laugh when he giggles. “That sound…” I tell Faith, “… makes my heart swell. I love it.”

She smiles fondly at her son and rubs her stomach. “I hope he’s okay when this little one arrives.”

“Of course, he’ll be fine. He’s bound to have some jealousy, though. But I’m sure it’s natural. You’re a wonderful Mum, and he’ll never feel unloved.”

“You mean like us?” She raises a brow.

“We were loved. Mum and Dad were busy, but we had Gran. And then Dana helped out when Gran traveled. Then if Gran got sick, we always had someone who was here for us.” Seb wiggles, and I lower him to the floor. He runs off to play with his cars scattered across the living room.

"Gran was always *sick*." She makes imaginary inverted commas with her fingers. "You know Dad never fully trusted her to look after us."

I stare at her. "No. How sick?"

"Mum said she had mental health issues. She was never diagnosed, although Mum mentioned postnatal depression to me because she wanted me to know the warning signs, especially since Dad said he was aware she was depressed growing up, although she never took medication for it. He remembers when he was little, she was always crying, and he held some resentment to her in his upbringing. He never knew why, and I think he blamed himself."

I had no idea about any of this.

My memories of her are all happy ones. My gran was one of the kindest and most loving people I knew. "Before I went away, Dad mentioned I was like Gran."

"Yeah, I remember it. Weird. I don't know why he said it."

"He seems to have more power over me than he does Will or you. I've always done what he's asked, and you both do what you please, and he supports you."

Faith wipes her hands on a towel before coming to me and pulling me into a quick hug. "While you were away, I really missed you. It got me thinking how Dad expected too much of you compared to Will and me. I have no idea why." She shakes her head before returning to wash lettuce under the tap. I sit at the table and chop cherry tomatoes and cucumber for a salad. "He'd say stuff about keeping you in check when you returned home because he didn't want you getting this travel bug and becoming 'side-tracked' in life. And how everything will change now Ethan's working for him."

"Ugh." I shake my head. "I thought as much. I'm not going to date Ethan again just because he's working alongside me. If Ethan thinks he can win me over with his sexy, bloody smile when he waltzes through the door on Monday, he can think again."

"Can he? It sounds as though you have given it some thought."

I give her a long look. "Not anymore now that I've met someone."

She gives me a knowing smile.

"I believe he's my soulmate…" I shrug. "It's going to be complicated for a while."

"Bree didn't paint a great picture. I know she gets concerned easily, but damn, I've been waiting too long to get you alone to talk about him."

"Yeah. He's been working in Venezuela for years, and the fact he's in the jungle didn't sit right with her."

"Don't tell Dad, he'll only stress more."

A knock on the door stops our conversation. "Hello," Mum coos, her voice echoing down the hallway. The heavy door closes with a bang. I stand as though it's a command knowing who has arrived.

I walk to the hallway and stare down the long passage.

"Look who's here," Mum announces.

I rush to Dad like I did to Mum at the airport and wrap my arms around his waist.

He leans down, and his hold is tight like a bear hug. "Edes, my girl. I have missed you." He pats my back like I'm a child in his arms.

"I missed you all," I rasp because my throat burns with new tears forming in my eyes. "Argh, I don't know what's wrong with me?" I swipe the tears because I'm feeling foolish.

"Nothing wrong with missing your father," he says proudly. "I'm just glad to have you home safe."

I smile as though it was never a concern, and yet I know some of my decisions were not thought through.

"I'm happy to be home, too."

Over dinner, we all laugh and chat about old times until it's time for me to show the photos of my trip. My phone is passed between Mum, Faith, and Jake, my father shaking his head.

"I'll look through them when you're all finished," he says.

I know it's his way of saying I need time to assess her trip.

"There are places I never got to visit, so I plan to go back," I say in warning to him.

"Because you thought it smart to leave your friends and travel alone in one of the most dangerous countries in the world?" He raises both brows and gives me one of his looks, which intimidated me as a child.

"I never felt unsafe. In fact, the people were some of the kindest I've ever met. The media make things out to be worse than they are."

"Right." He laughs sarcastically. "Like all the protests and troops in Caracas are a façade, and the warnings not to travel there should be *ignored*."

"No. We avoided Caracas for that reason. I'm saying other parts of the country are suffering when they rely on tourism. It's not unsafe in all areas."

"And where's that, Eden?"

"We saw some beautiful photos in Canaima," Faith interjects.

"Yes," Mum agrees. "Here, I'll show you." She swipes my phone and holds it in front of Dad's face. "Oops, I'm sorry I got out of it." She presses away. "Oh, what are these?"

Faith's eyes round before she looks past Mum's shoulder with an expression indicating I should panic. I reach for my phone, only Dad takes it before I get the chance.

"Dad, I think you should give Eden back her phone," Faith says politely.

Dad swipes a couple of times.

There were several images of Ulara and the people I kept in a separate album. The memories were for me and are not intended to be shared.

Dad's expression falters. Deep lines ingrain his forehead. He slides my phone to me without uttering a single word. He drags his hands over his cheeks to the back of his neck. "I've seen enough."

"Enough of what, Dad? To judge me?" I rasp.

He pushes his half-full red wine glass away. "Grace, I'd like to go."

My mother drinks her sparkling water and stands.

"Please don't," I croak. "I don't want the night to end like this. I'm not a bad person. I'm not sure why you're so upset."

"Let it go, Eden," Mum says gently. She gives me a nod in understanding, and I hope it means she'll explain what just happened when we're alone.

"Eden, I know you're not a bad person. But there is much you don't know about our family, and you went against my wishes when I asked you specifically to stay out of the jungle. Those photos were not taken on a tour." Dad stands without looking at me.

"No, but—"

"I've been up since four this morning, and it's been a long couple of weeks in Sydney. I'll talk to you about this later. Thanks for a lovely meal, Faith. I'll see you all on the weekend."

Faith stands and walks my parents to the door while I lean my face into the palm of my hands. Why is he so hung up on the jungle?

"Are you okay," Jake whispers. "Can I get you a glass of water? A full bottle of shiraz?"

My hands fall from my face, and I chuckle. I forgot Jake was even sitting at the end of the table. "Sorry you had to witness that."

He looks up as Faith enters the room.

"That was *interesting*." Faith drags a chair and sits beside me. She pats my back in a calming way like she would Seb when putting him to sleep.

"As much as I want to stay and listen because dinner parties with your family are always much more interesting than mine..." Jake says. "I'll leave you two girls to talk alone."

"I know she'll tell you everything, anyway."

"Yeah." He grins at me and walks past patting my head. "Night." He kisses Faith on the top of her head. "I'll check on Seb and then head to bed."

"Night, babe." She turns to me. "You want to explain what those pictures were?"

I sigh. I need to talk to someone without divulging all the secrets of Ulara. "It's where Samuel works as a volunteer... sometimes." I go on to tell her about my experience helping in another community alongside a doctor and see it as a future job for me.

"Actually... there's more to it." I meet her gaze and wait a moment.

"Go on," she says, her eyes rounding.

"I need to know I can trust you because I want you to know the truth about Samuel." I reach for her hand.

Faith squeezes my fingers and gives me a nod. "I'll always have your back."

"Remember when you came home from college and said you can't help who you fall in love with?"

Faith smiles. "And you told me to follow my heart."

I nod because Faith fell in love with Jake when he was dating her best friend. She felt guilty about her feelings, and they never got together until he broke up with her friend. "Well, when my heart decided on Samuel, his circumstances are a little more complicated. It's why I'm going to return to him. Maybe at the end of the year."

"What?"

I blow out the air between my cheeks. "I miss him, and I don't want to feel like this any longer." Her eyes round. "But it will only be a short holiday..."

SUNDAY NIGHT, I meet Amy and Yasmine for a drink at our local hangout at The Bay.

"Have you spoke to Bree since you've been home?" Amy asks.

"No, only by text. She's coming to Adelaide to visit her parents, so I assume we'll all catch up then."

"She'll be asking questions," Yasmine says and places a glass of sauvignon blanc in front of me.

"I wouldn't be telling her what you told us," Amy quips and takes a sip of beer out of a bottle. "Ah, I've missed the taste of Aussie beer."

I chuckle at her content expression. "So, how's the new job?"

Amy shrugs and flicks her ponytail over her shoulder. "I signed another contract leading me up to the Christmas break. I'll be teaching grade four for the rest of the year."

Yasmine grins. "Poor kids."

"Poor me," Amy replies quickly.

"What about your work?" I ask Yasmine. "Did you have great sales while you were away?"

"It appears many of my online customers followed me on Instagram and were inspired by our holiday. Boho dress sales are through the roof, and I have a huge backorder. I'm thinking of putting someone on to help with marketing."

"I can help you set it up," I say.

"Damn lucky you're moving in with me then." She gives me a wink even though we haven't yet settled on a date. I take another sip of wine and push it away. I'm not in the mood to drink alcohol tonight.

Over the next hour, we reminisce about our holiday. It's the thing about holidays—as soon as you're home, everything goes back to normal, and it barely feels like you were away at all.

Except for my heart. A piece of it is still missing, and I'm not sure the ache will ever go away.

"I better get going. Big day tomorrow," I say and roll my eyes.

"Call me tomorrow night," Amy states and takes another sip of beer.

"Call *me* on your lunch break. I want to know what Mr. Slimeball is up to."

I chuckle at Yasmine's description of Ethan. It's the same description she used for Michael. She has barely spoken to him since arriving home and can now see why we were worried about her.

It's a short walk back to our apartment complex, and I take the esplanade path even though the icy wind is whipping my face. When I open the door, the penthouse is in darkness with Mum and Dad already asleep.

I can't shake the loneliness of missing Samuel even when I'm surrounded by friends. Even worse, tomorrow I have to work alongside the guy who once upon a time I trusted with my heart. After stomping all over it, he thinks he can win me back.

Loving Samuel has helped me to forgive him even though the memory of seeing his naked ass pumping *her* against the wall is still ingrained in my thoughts.

When I'm alone in my room, I close my eyes and replay the memory. I threw his key at them before slamming the door. Seeing his name come up repeatedly on the screen of my phone and rejecting his calls of apology and refusing to discuss it with him even though he told my father he messed up, I can still hear my father saying, "*How bad could it be*?"

Everyone believed he *kissed* someone else. I never ratted on him but simply told my family to let us work it out—meaning for him never to contact me again.

As usual, my father had other plans.

When I stop taking the malaria medication in a few days, hopefully, the vivid dreams will stop because it's a memory I don't want to think about. Or is it the fact I'm worked up about working with him?

A CRACK of thunder wakes me. I toss for about twenty minutes and can't go back to sleep, so I shower and dress, then I creep down the stairs. When I unlock the office door, it's still dark, and I'm the first to arrive. An hour later, Dana strolls in, mumbling something about Mondays when she walks past my desk.

"You ready for this?" she asks as she slips off her coat and places it over the back of her chair.

"You know how I asked you to be nice? Well, scrap that," I say and swallow the last of my coffee. My second cup. "At least for today."

"Consider it done," she says, firing up her computer.

By the time Ethan waltzes into the office, both Dana and I are well into the day's work with most emails addressed.

"Eden," he says with the warmth I remember from happy times. "It's good to see you."

He's wearing a lilac shirt and black tie that matches his pants. The way his dark hair is swept away from his tanned face accentuates his beautiful brown eyes even more. Their beauty was the first thing that caught my attention when we met ten years ago.

I stand and hold out my hand. "Thanks for all you did while I was away."

Ethan takes my hand, and he reaches in for a friendly kiss on the cheek. "Glad to have you back."

It grinds on me how he says it as though he's got this covered. I remind myself it's not a bad thing even though this company has been my baby since I left school.

"Do you want coffee while I go over everything I've ticked off your list?"

Raising my mug, I smile. "On my second cup already. Heads up... in my father's eyes you're late even though you technically haven't clocked in. And I worked through your list last week while you were in Sydney. I'm sure Dad will cover everything in his Monday morning meeting." I raise my arm to check my watch even though I'm not wearing one—only to make a point. "Which is in one hour, so best you check your emails now."

The space between his eyebrows creases, only slightly yet enough for me to notice.

"I replied to most of mine yesterday except for a couple that may have come through early this morning."

Working on a Sunday would impress my father.

"He has placed me on the pool and guest house reno."

My gut drops. It was my idea. I even had architects draw up my design.

"With you," he adds.

"Okay..." I'm breathing faster in a combination of relief and pent-up anger. Some projects are my babies. If I'm planning to move on, I need the reassurance everything will be handled in a way that's best for the business.

"Did you peruse my plans?"

"They look great, but I have a couple of ideas to add."

"Yeah," I say, tapping my fingers on the desk. "Same. I've been inspired by the architecture from my holiday. Perhaps we can brainstorm over lunch." I want to kick myself the moment the words fall out.

I give myself a moment and accept I'm capable of working alongside Ethan. Until *that night,* we got on well. We told each other everything. He was my best friend. It would make my father happy if we can work alongside each other.

As an added benefit, it would allow me to get the wheels in motion to gain freedom for myself because that's what I crave—freedom and a certain someone hidden away in the jungle with a tight hold on my heart.

49

EDEN

On Saturday, I hand my mother a cup of coffee and wait for her to take a sip before announcing, "I'm moving into Yasmine's apartment."

She tilts her head, and for a moment, I see a hint of sadness in her expression. "When?"

"In a month or so." I shrug. "After I save a little more to pay my share of the deposit and up-front rent.

"Honey, you don't need to move out if you want to save for something important."

I take a seat beside my mother on the balcony lounge overlooking the ocean. The esplanade is busy with people donning beanies and coats and walking their dogs. I snuggle my chin into the woolen scarf around my neck. "There is something I want to talk to you about. Besides saving to go on another holiday, I'm thinking about studying something different."

"Really, love? What?"

"I always thought it would be architecture, but after my holiday, I'm considering a complete career change. Maybe nursing, although I'm undecided."

Mum peers over the rim of her mug. Her expression is unreadable. "You know your grandmother was a nurse."

I pull a face. "Your mum?" My mother was adopted, and her adoptive parents both died when she was in her early twenties.

"No. Ivy."

"Gran was a nurse?"

"There's a lot you don't know about her, and it's time I filled you in." She stands and indicates for me to follow her inside. She leads me to her bedroom and their expansive walk-in closet, the décor in rose gold. She hands me her mug, then pulls out a small stepladder and reaches for a wooden box on a shelf. It's the size of a shoebox. I place both mugs on the carpet near the wall, so I can take it from her before Mum steps to the floor.

The cedar wood is patchy where the color has faded, and there's some flaking on the side. Still, it's stunning. Four carved timber legs and three letters are embossed on the lid. Fancy swirls are cut into the corners like a frame surrounding the initials.

I.M.M.

Ivy Maisie Monteford.

"Albert had it made for Ivy," Mum says. "It contains memories and some of her belongings. She asked me to give this to you on your twenty-fifth birthday."

"Why then?"

"Most of us have a better understanding of ourselves by our mid-twenties and know what direction we want our lives to take."

I nod. Even though my birthday is only a couple of months away, I'm aspiring toward personal growth. Only, I'm unsure if I am following the right path. "Am I allowed to see it now?"

"This is why your father has been stressing all year. It's time I explain some things to you. You deserve to know what upset him, and perhaps it will help you to understand him better. I really hate seeing you both like this. You have always gotten on well. The stress isn't good for him."

"It's because I did what he asked and never argued. Only I'm not sure if..." the back of my throat burns before I say it, "... if I want to keep working for the hotel."

Mum places a hand on mine. "You'll work it out. We all need a break from time to time." She finds a key taped to the bottom of the box. "Shall we?" She wiggles the key until the old lock cooperates. Opening the lid slowly, we both peer in as though waiting to be surprised.

The first thing I pull out is a notepad or a diary with a faded tan leather cover and a tiny lock. I press the tarnished brass lock, but nothing happens.

"Your father hasn't unlocked it, and we don't know where the key is. He decided never to unlock it, believing some secrets should stay with his grandmother. I think he was afraid of what he might discover, and back then, he wouldn't have coped if it dragged up sad memories." Her eyes hold empathy and a touch of sadness.

"I understand." I place the diary aside as there is much more to discover.

Underneath the diary is a pile of family photographs. I look closely at each one before passing it to Mum. "We looked so happy. Yet Faith tells me Gran had a history of depression. She never showed it around me."

"Well, you were her favorite," she says with a sigh.

"I never noticed and played on it. I mean, if it's what you're implying by this box being left to me..."

"She saw something in you when you were born that Faith and Will never had. She blessed you when she came to the hospital to visit you as a newborn."

"Blessed me?"

Mum lifts the photos and takes out a photo frame, a lock of blonde hair, and an old brush. "Over time, most of her friends stopped talking to her... said she was a witch."

I laugh because it sounds insane. Mum's gaze lifts, and I realize she's serious. "Oh, how awful for Gran. Was she ostracized? Wait, you believe it, and you think she... what? *Performed magic on me*?"

"It sounded that way as it wasn't a religious prayer she was quietly singing. Ivy told us you were like her, and it has haunted your father ever since."

I shake my head to unravel my confusion. "She loved us and both of you. She helped out when you needed her to take care of us when you worked late hours. I don't understand. She was nothing but kind."

"Ivy was always kind, Eden." She finds a picture of Pop and hands it to me. "I'll tell you what your grandfather told your father and me. He met Ivy when she was seventeen, and they fell in love. He knew the moment they met he'd marry her even though she was different than the other girls her age. Everyone wanted to find a nice boy, get married, and have kids. It's what they did in their era. Only Ivy was always helping someone. She had a kind soul like you said. She was also a little *wild* for those days. She studied nursing, and her shifts during her training meant your grandfather and her were apart for long stints. So, they set up rendezvous weekends. She'd sneak out of the nursing quarters and would visit him. She ended up pregnant with your father, and they had a quick wedding. Only in her heart, she wanted to continue nursing. She had told your grandfather she'd always wanted to travel and volunteer overseas as a nurse."

I run my fingertips over the matte surface of the photograph. Only now, I note the musky scent coming from the box, as though it hasn't been opened in years. The image of my pop holds more than just a snippet in time—it's the beginning of a world of secrets.

"She developed postnatal depression, and so he let her go," Mum continues. "She was gone for almost three years and returned before Winston started prep school. She said her place was with her husband and her son, only she had this sadness about her, and they fought a lot. Eventually, she confessed she'd had an affair during her travels. Had a daughter, Dawn, and lost her at twelve months old. She came home brokenhearted. Although she promised your grandfather she was in love with him, not the other guy."

I gasp and cover my mouth. "Oh, Mum, I had no idea. It's so sad for everyone."

Mum nods. "Your grandfather set some ground rules. She was to give up nursing to be a mum and wife one hundred percent. It turned out she had complications and had a hysterectomy overseas, so they couldn't conceive any other children. She almost died by account. Anyway, she never spoke about her travels. We only know about it from what we found in this box when she passed. The sad thing is your father partly blamed her for your grandfather's death. He became an alcoholic and drank himself to sleep every night. He had a massive heart attack and died at fifty-five. Winston had already thrown himself into our business with a vision of making the building we inherited to be something special. He thought you could also be part of it since you wanted to help out from a young age, even when you were at school. Faith had her heart set on law and had no interest to work in tourism on any level, and besides, he couldn't handle her stubborn nature."

Pride warmed my heart. "Part of why... did it stem from keeping me in close check because Gran thought I was like her?"

"He saw something in you, which also reminded him of your gran, but also reminded him of himself. I don't believe it was so you wouldn't become wild like your Gran."

"*Wild.*" I roll my eyes. "I wanted to travel and see the world. You both have traveled."

"Eden, it's the jungle." She flips through images and scrambles through the box until she finds a picture. "This is Gran. She's in the jungle surrounded by native Americans with spears. None are wearing clothes except for grass skirts, including Gran."

I study the image. Blonde hair falls over her shoulders covering her breasts. Gosh, she looks like me. My heart races. I know where this was taken. Only I don't recognize any faces. One of the ladies holds a white baby.

"Is this...?"

Mum nods. "Apparently, it's Dawn."

My chest tightens. My thoughts race. What would giving birth in a village like Ulara be like? Without the Samuel's of the world, things would've been harder. Then, I remember Kaikare protecting me from that deadly spider. Perhaps they wouldn't have been that much harder after all.

"Now you know why your father gets upset."

"Yeah, I do." I release a breathy sigh.

Our eyes meet, again an understanding passes between us before Mum restacks the photographs. "Apparently, there's a journal about her time in the Amazon, but she gave it to her friend as your pop banned her from talking about it. I think if she hadn't got rid of it, Albert might have burned it." She tilts her head as though recalling a memory. It sounds like an extreme measure, only now I understand why Pop would've been angry. "Brenda and your Gran both nursed together, and the last I heard she was in a retirement village. Your father isn't interested in what happened in the jungle, and we haven't spoken to Brenda since the funeral."

I pick up the diary. It's light, and yet the emotion inside it gives an illusion the pages are lined in mercury. After a quick scrape around the bottom of the wooden box, I'm a little relieved not to find a key. No one has read Gran's diary. The discolored cover arouses curiosity as to when she started writing in it.

I place the diary at the bottom before Mum packs the remainder of the contents into the box. She does it slowly. Is this hard for her? Does she miss Gran too? She pushes the box over the carpet toward me. "It's all yours."

I CAN'T SHARE what Mum has told me to anyone until I process everything. Until then, the box will remain in my closet for when I'm ready to absorb everything. I understand the joy my gran felt while living in the jungle, yet the pain caused to her husband and my father is so messed up that my heart hurts for them all.

The box can stay locked until I'm ready to inspect her memories with an open mind. I make myself a cup of tea in a china cup like the way my gran used to drink it. I fire up my computer to the open documents from yesterday. After speaking with Mum, there's a weight off my shoulders. Hoping the universe is guiding me right, I click and send on my nursing application and quickly close the computer before I second-guess my decision.

50

EDEN

One week later...

I miss you xx

I PROMISED Samuel I'd message him every week, and I'm keeping my promise.

51

EDEN

One week later…

I love you xx

I STARE at the screen with a list of messages, all from me. My thoughts snowball to panic. I hope he's safe. Damn, I wish he'd respond. Just once.

52

EDEN

Ten days later…

"THESE ARE GOOD," I tell Ethan and trace my finger over the design on the desk in front of him. His ideas for a Bali-inspired resort pool would suit our complex.

"I've always liked the relaxed setting," he says. "The garden is a mix of Mediterranean and Bali if you know what I mean."

"It's unique in a way. Anyway, we can talk on Monday." I stand and head to the bathroom. I've cut back on tea and coffee the last few days because all I seem to do is pee.

When I emerge, Dana is waiting for me. "Everything okay?"

"Yep. Ever since I finished all the meds from traveling, my body is up and down."

She nods slowly. "You have a good weekend," she says as she enters the cubicle.

"You, too." I walk back to the office and finish packing up my desk.

"Any chance for Friday night work drinks?" Ethan winks at me.

"I can't, sorry. I have other plans."

Please don't wink at me.

Shoving everything into my desk drawer, it can wait to be sorted on Monday. I rush toward the door leaving Ethan to lock up.

I don't bother changing out of my office clothes. It's a short drive to

Yasmine's apartment. Finding a parking spot on the street, I grab my bag and walk the path to her apartment door and knock twice.

Yasmine answers, and the aroma of herbs and rice wafts into the night air.

"Come in," she says.

"We ordered you a Thai red curry." Amy wipes her hands with a cloth. She points to an Uber Eats bag. "It should still be warm."

"I'm sorry I am late. Ethan and I were going over some drafts."

Amy stands and doesn't respond. She cracks open a bottle of wine. "If you're going to talk about him, I'll need more of this."

"I'm not. When I mention him at work, think of him like you would Dana."

Amy rolls her eyes.

I grab my food and take a seat next to where Amy is sitting. Her phone lights up next to me—she left it open on Tinder.

I check out the guy posing on her screen. "Want me to decide for you?"

Amy snorts. "Our taste differs."

"Oops, I super-liked him."

"You didn't!" She puts down her wine glass and grabs her phone to check. "Hilarious." She closes the app, and I laugh. "I have a date on Wednesday night, and I want your opinion on what to wear."

Amy disappears out of the room.

Yasmine hands me a wine glass and takes a sip from her half-full crystal glass.

"Have you been chatting about Tinder dates waiting for me to arrive?"

Yasmine rolls her eyes. "Her list is insane. For every minute we waited for you, she cursed Ethan. I don't like the guy, but Amy despises him."

"I'll chat with her. She doesn't need to worry. There's no chance of us getting back together. Besides, if I've moved on, she shouldn't be so worked up about him."

"I need to tell you something," she says. "Michael is messaging me again. He called a few nights ago and apologized over and over. He wants to remain friends and plan a holiday together somewhere else."

"What?"

Amy waltzes into the room holding four tops and a black mini skirt. "What do you think?"

I give Yasmine a look that our conversation will be continued, and then smile at Amy.

"It's a Tinder date, right?" I hold up each top to decide if it's suitable. "I like this one."

"That one's for you. It doesn't suit me." It's a low-cut navy top with frills along the bust line.

"Thanks." I love receiving clothes from Amy. She often buys them, then changes her mind and sends them my way. Amy strips to try on the others, and I do the same to check if the navy top fits.

"Stop buying online and come into my shop," Yasmine tells her. "I'll fit you out properly, so there are no rash purchases."

"I know. I love your store, but I do most of my shopping at night when I can't sleep. Damn, girl." Amy stares at me wide-eyed. "Check out your tits."

"What?" I glance down to my ample cleavage and clutch both breasts. "You know, they've been sore the last week. It's like I'm getting my period, except I haven't had one in years because of my implant."

"Does it need changing?" Yasmine asks, holding one of the other tops against her chest.

I stare at Yasmine, my mind ticking over. "Shit." I reach for my phone and scroll through my calendar. "April," I murmur. "I forgot to make an appointment."

Yasmine stares at me. "Sore tits. Anything else?"

"Apart from the crazy dreams from our meds, I want to pee all the time now that the weather has turned cold?"

"I don't want to pee," Amy says.

"Same," Yasmine adds. "You better get a pregnancy test."

"Don't be ridiculous." Only, I have a gut feeling something's not right, so I push the wine away.

Amy grabs her keys. "Right. We're all going for a ride to the pharmacy," she says, leaving her glass of wine untouched.

ON MY RIGHT, Amy stares at the stick on the table. On my left, Yasmine's gaze is fixed on the same spot. Elbows on the table, we wait the three minutes as directed on the box. I keep looking away as though it's all a joke, and it will read negative.

"I see a second blue line," Amy says, and our heads dip closer.

"I don't see anything."

"I do," Yasmine quips. She grabs the stick and holds it up to her eyes. "There's definitely another line, Edes."

"Show me." I take it from her fingers, and sure enough, it's there. Two blue lines. "Shit." I drop the stick back on the paper. "This isn't good."

"Home tests aren't always accurate. You need a blood test, so make an appointment with your GP," Amy says, trying to calm me.

"I need a check-up as I need to have my rod removed anyway. So, I can mention it then."

Yasmine rubs my back, and my face falls in my hands. "I really can't be pregnant. I'm still living at home, for fuck's sake."

"Not for long," Yasmine says and smiles. "We're going to be one happy family here."

I smile at her kindness. We're jumping to conclusions, yet I panic every way I look at it. How do I tell Samuel? Christ, he doesn't even reply to my texts. It's something I'd have to say and not in a text.

Ugh, how do you tell someone over the phone?

Surely, I can't visit him while pregnant.

"Don't worry unless you have to." Amy removes my glass and pours the wine into her glass. "Go to the doc and take it from there. To be on the safe side..." she raises her glass, "... no more alcohol for you."

I sigh because right now I need a drink.

I SET the *National Geographic* magazine on the chair beside me when my phone vibrates. I have every intention of ignoring it until I read Asoo's name on the screen.

> Samuel misses you. Good you left Ulara. Samuel followed from his exploration by warrior from Watache tribe. Some cannibals. Shaman's magic scare them away.

He was followed. What does that mean? Is another tribe angry at them? I had read somewhere that cannibalism still existed, only I thought it was deeper in the Amazon. There are tourists and helicopters visiting Angel Falls not far away. Why can't he just leave if his safety is jeopardized? There must be some clause in his contract. Honestly, I think he enjoys the element of danger when he has to ramp up measures for his safety. I shake my head and try to picture him here with me. I want to believe we could live happily together, but I have no idea how long he'd survive in society without it depressing him.

He'd have me.

"Eden Monteford."

I look up to the doctor calling my name and follow her along a hallway.

After another urine test and physical examination, she tells me I'm pregnant and writes a referral to an obstetrician. She removes the rod from my arm and sutures the incision.

"Malaria medication can be detrimental to the fetus. You also ingested ayahuasca, and my knowledge is limited regarding these teas. You can discuss this in more detail with the obstetrician." She peers at me over the rim of her glasses with a tight, serious expression. "My calculation is a January baby, although it's a broad guess considering you haven't menstruated in some time, and the times of sexual intercourse were spread over a couple of months."

I nod. The rough lump in the back of my throat burns, and I'm afraid to speak. The moment I open my mouth, I know the damn tears will come. I've cried more since I returned from South America than I have in a long while. I should've picked up that it was a sign of hormone overload.

"Good luck," she says as though I'll need it.

On the drive home, my thoughts race to Samuel and my father and how to break the news to both. Or do I?

The photo of Gran holding a baby in the jungle is like a snapshot of my future. I can't shake the image out of my head, and I can't help believing it means something more.

Is Dad right... am I like Gran?

I let out a sigh. I don't want to disappoint anyone. If I decide to visit Samuel and tell him about our baby, I have to be aware of the many things that can go wrong. Shit. Is it how Gran lost her daughter? Or was it the malaria prevention medication? Did they even have those meds in the 1960s?

I have to take each day as it comes.

Making my way up the stairs, I head directly to my room to be alone and process everything.

"Eden."

I turn to my father stepping out of his bedroom.

"Do you have a moment?" His brow pulls tight, and his eyes flick over my face. "I don't want us fighting anymore. I haven't properly apologized for my reaction at dinner. Your mother has informed me she has enlightened you on why I felt strongly about you avoiding the jungle."

"Yes, she—"

"It's still no excuse not to trust you. I apologize."

"Dad, I understand."

He runs a hand over his head. "I may have earned myself a few more gray hairs in the meantime." He chuckles low.

I go and hug him. "I'm lucky to have you always looking out for me." I take a step back. Now is a good time than any. I clear my throat. "Though it's time I do what's right for me, and right now, I need a change, and I'm not sure the hotel is my future." I twist my fingers waiting for him to say something.

"My girl, I knew this day would come. I hoped it wouldn't be yet, although your mother did forewarn me. I want you to be happy, so I'll support you on whatever you decide, even if it's nursing. Just promise me if you're unhappy, you'll consider coming back to the hotel."

"Oh, Dad."

"Don't say anything." He pops his arm over my shoulder. "I'm proud of you and know you'll do well wherever life takes you."

"That's because I have your determination," I say and laugh once.

"That you do. That you do."

I give him another hug before heading to my room, my shoulders lighter than a few minutes ago.

Below my bedroom window, the ocean crashes onto the foreshore rocks with a force of energy, creating a boom with each wave. The wind howls against the shutters. I shut my blinds and block out nature's anger.

While wrapping a blanket around my shoulders, I slide onto my knees then pull open the closet door to find the locked wooden box. Something has been playing on my mind. Flipping through Gran's belongings, I locate the brush and turn it to the tarnished decoupage of flowers decorating the back. Even behind the rust color, I recognize enough of the design to know it's similar to the one Kaikare showed me.

Impossible.

Photographs, trinkets, jewelry lay sprawled around me until I find the black and white image my mother pointed out. My grandmother is standing beside a young man wearing a small ring of feathers around his head. The image is old and not taken close enough to identify anyone. Only the blonde hair of my grandmother contrasts with the dark heads surrounding her makes her identifiable.

Nothing is impossible—I learned that in Ulara.

I reach for my computer. I open it to a website on visa applications, knowing what I have to do.

53

EDEN

Canaima, Venezuela

Three months later...

FROM THE SMALL window of the Cessna aircraft, I peer out to the mountains of green vegetation. It's stunning and unchanged. A sea of green seen from the air, the beauty conceals the danger lurking below.

After a few bumps on the landing strip, the pilot pulls up the plane, brakes screeching.

I'm one of two passengers and surprised the flight wasn't canceled, although I assume Canaima tourism will do everything to encourage visitors in light of what's happening in the country.

My interest in obtaining a visa was questioned, especially in light of certain embassies closing. The closest is Colombia, and God forbid, anything goes pear-shaped, and I can't get there. The visa took eight weeks to arrive, allowing me to save more cash in the meantime.

Victor greets me and drives me to the resort lodging. It appears I'm the only guest arriving today. We chat about Australia and his desire to travel there.

"You tell your friends to come visit Victor's resort," he says enthusiastically while wheeling my small case to reception.

"Of course." I smile at him. "Is Asoo here?"

"He's at a camp. Returning tomorrow."

I wonder if it's the same camp Kaikare and I visited, although there are hundreds dotted along the river and around the Gran Sabana. "Have many of the volunteers and medics returned to help?"

"Yes. Some." He nods, not saying anything else, and I assume some may have re-evaluated their travels with visa problems.

"I'm so happy to be back here." I inhale the clean, fresh air already heavy in my lungs and glance out to the vista before us. I'll never tire of looking at the waterfalls on the other side of the lake. In the distance, three tepuis push toward the clouds.

I swat at the annoying buzz above my head. There's not a guest in sight, and despite wanting to take a stroll since I have the entire resort to myself, I retreat inside to apply more repellent.

Here, mosquitoes are the enemy.

EARLY THE NEXT MORNING, I make my way across the grass toward the sandy beach of Canaima Lake. Asoo waves out to me, and I smile at his enthusiasm even when it's just after dawn.

"Samuel doesn't know Miss Eden coming."

Not a question. "No, he doesn't. I wanted to surprise him."

"I visit once every two weeks. Now you here, I visit more."

"Thank you. I'd appreciate that."

He takes my hand and assists me to step into the curiara. "You're welcome."

"Your English has improved," I compliment Asoo.

"Yes. When I visit Samuel, we speak in English, not Spanish or Pemón. He teaches me."

"I noticed it's quiet around here. It's good you're using your time to learn."

Asoo shakes his head. "Victor not say much, but everyone sad no tourists come."

I understand their concern when tourism is their livelihood. I settle in the seat in front of him and gaze out to the mountains beyond the lake. It still astounds me when I imagine Samuel climbing the tepui to find a particular flower. The rocky face juts up straight toward the clouds, and to my naked eye, it looks unclimbable. The indigenous believe these mountains house the spirits of the dead. It's why only one Ularan warrior volunteered to go on the journey with Samuel. It's a reminder to me I'm returning to another world where mythology influences their daily life.

We take the Carrao River deeper into the jungle. Beyond the trees, I catch movement. It could be a wild pig, and then the monkeys sound an alert from the trees. Macaws fly overhead from one side of the river to the other. It all feels strangely familiar, like home.

"You know I traveled along the Amazon River in Peru," I tell Asoo. "The width is several miles wide in some parts. The current is substantially stronger."

"She's beautiful wherever she flows."

I smile, loving how he sees joy in everything.

"Have you seen Kaikare again?"

He shakes his head. "Ulara quiet, especially with Watache man spying. It's dangerous now."

"Dangerous how? You have your boat."

"They very good hunters. Every spear strikes pig." He makes a whistling noise, and with his free arm, mimics a spear in the air. "They make bad poison. I could die in minutes."

I stare at him, aware I'm gaping. "And Samuel remained there?"

"They scared of shaman. He has secrets. They scared to die like us. Now they mourn their chief who's same age as the shaman. Watache have shaman's young son, and he still learning. He has gone back to old ways believing if you eat a man, you'll inherit their knowledge and power. They know Samuel a different medicine man, smart with no magic. You tell Samuel to stay with shaman."

I'll be asking why he's still there.

"And bad people cut down the forests for money. Big money," he says. "They forced the Watache from their homes and north toward us. I believe they are passing through toward Colombian jungle where it safe to hide."

"I hope so."

We don't speak much for the remainder of the journey. As the hours pass, I'm finding the seat uncomfortable, having to lean back on my hands clutching the plank of wood. I straighten my spine as much as possible to ease the ache, thankful to finally reach the junction to follow the Churun River.

A helicopter flies high overhead. It's the first one I've seen all morning. "Is that a tourist chopper?" I ask Asoo.

Asoo stares at the base of the helicopter because it has a symbol painted on the bottom that I don't recognize.

"No, it's going to the mines."

His face is solemn. Does this upset him? Before I ask him anything else, he guides us to the entrance of the small tributary river that leads to Ulara. The current isn't as strong as I remember. In fact, the river is low for this time of year. We glide past overhanging branches, thicker than I remember, that protrude like long tentacles into the water.

Asoo kills the motor early and guides the canoe onto the sandy embankment. I take my small pack, the remainder of my luggage is with Victor in Canaima.

"I'll keep my phone on me for now," I tell Asoo. "I'll give it to you to charge when you next visit."

"Do you want me to wait? Samuel not expecting you."

I shake my head. "No need. "I'm sure he'll be alerted soon. I'll stay over here at the small camp for now."

He pushes the boat out into the water. "See you soon, Miss Eden."

I wave goodbye and tread to the camp. Fresh new growth almost conceals it. It seems untouched in months. Pushing vines away, I walk to where I remember the passion fruit grows. Plump fruit covers the vine, and I pick several and tread back to the log seat where Samuel first took me.

I'm unsure of the minutes or hours that pass. I'm not prepared to remain out here alone with no fire or even with fire, now I'm pregnant. Isolation, I understand, only it needs to be in his hut.

Beyond the shades of green and brown, a rustling of leaves alerts me to a visitor. Slowly, I pad back toward the river in case it's not human because I remember Samuel telling me jaguars have been sighted in the past. With my back to the water, I scan the green wall trying to see behind the trees.

Maybe I was imagining a presence. I walk up the small embankment to the camp to retrieve my phone. The sun is low, and I estimate another couple of hours before it's sunset. Looking around, I search for sticks in preparation to make a fire, even though I'm not entirely sure how to create a spark.

"Shit." I throw the sticks to the ground, glance up, and notice him standing by a tree watching me. In warrior stance, legs apart, balance equally distributed, arms by his sides near a spear in his twine band around his waist.

I meet his gaze, hesitant at first. I see it, *feel it,* the emotion where words aren't needed for me to understand what he's feeling because I feel it too.

54

EDEN

SAMUEL DOESN'T MOVE AS THOUGH he's processing. His knees flinch. Those long, tanned, and muddy legs don't hide the faded red artwork that decorates his lean muscles.

When Samuel takes the first step, I forget all the rules and run to him, jumping into his arms kissing him hard.

"I told the kids to stop messing about," he says against my lips. "I thought they were teasing me."

"How are you?" I say in between breaths. My fingers catch in his knotted fair locks. "Asoo told me another tribe was after you."

"I'm fine, even more so now." He breathes heavy sighs into my mouth.

His earthy scent jolts me back in time. I slide down his body until my feet hit the sand. "I know I should be in quarantine, but honestly, I haven't come all this way to remain out here. I'm happy to be isolated in your hut, so please don't make me—"

"Not a chance." His calloused hands frame my face, and he holds me there for a moment and just takes in every detail.

"I'm sorry. I should've warned you. I thought it would be a nice surprise."

He shakes his head in disbelief. "It's a surprise. I'm just having trouble believing you're here. That you came back to me."

"We promised each other, remember?" I push up on my toes and kiss his lips. "I've had time to think, and I am sorry I'm breaking your quarantine rules. I'll be mindful and keep a distance—"

He silences me with another kiss. "Don't you worry. I can take extra measures." He takes my hand and starts to lead me away.

"Wait." I pull my hand from his to fetch my bag, run back to his side, and match his stride over the mangled roots and decaying leaves. "Will it be a problem with the shaman?" He takes my bag from me and throws it over his shoulder.

With his other hand, he takes my hand and squeezes it. "You're my family."

Family.

"You look well." A little on the thin side, yet he still looks healthy. I smile at Samuel and instantly know I made the right choice in coming here.

"You look radiant as always." He stops walking and pulls me in for a kiss. "I can't believe you're here."

I've waited months for his kiss. I run my hands up his back, his muscles contracting beneath my palms.

"It will be different this time," he tells me and leads me toward the village at a much faster pace.

When we reach the outskirts, the children run to me and bounce up and down. They giggle and shout to me with big smiles across their beautiful faces. I laugh along with them, waving enthusiastically. "Hello, hello," I say to them all.

Samuel is frowning at the kids. He raises a hand in a gesture to stay away. "Senke awarö," he repeats. *Near, bad.* "They have to wait before they can touch you."

Inside the village barrier, there's a change in my sense of gravity. With every step, I'm light on my feet, so light I'm walking on air, and at the same time grounding me to the earth. I match Samuel's stride with the grace of his step. We take a path around the outside of the village, avoiding as many people as possible until we reach his hut. He's still holding my hand as he takes the steps inside. He lets go and places my pack in the corner. It appears the same but different. One striking change is the whiter twine of a second hammock strung next to his. "This is new."

"I began to weave it while you were here. Finished it months ago and hung it in hope... want to give it a try?" He lifts me onto the edge, and it swings with my weight. He holds it steady before he slides on and settles beside me.

"Hoping for a wife?" I rasp, remembering how simple it is to be married here.

"Hoping the person I intend to marry returned."

I stare into his beautiful blue eyes, my heart thumping in my chest. "I promised I would one day, but you also said you'd come find me. I thought I'd see you in Australia before I visited again."

He stares into my eyes, and his eyes flick over my face.

I reach out and touch his cheek. "Luckily, I had a change of heart."

He nods once, kisses my lips, and slides off the hammock. "Give me time to speak to the shaman and chief."

When Samuel disappears from the doorway, I scramble out of the hammock and walk the length of the hut, noting a new string of red and black beads, animal teeth, and bones hanging on the wall. I question the significance—is this a promotion of sort? My hand lowers and rests on my stomach, a habit that's a reminder to myself and a protective touch to my unborn child. A fluttering makes me smile. Sensing another presence, I turn to the door to a figure watching me. I gasp at *his* presence, and in the few steps it takes for me to reach the doorway, the shaman has disappeared from sight.

Admittedly, he still freaks me out a little. I'm surprised he didn't say anything, or maybe he didn't know I was here. Seeing him unsettles me, and I'm glad Samuel has gone to talk to him. At least he kept his distance, although I don't expect any affection from him like a hug. Come to think of it, I have never seen the shaman embrace anyone, not even Kaikare.

Unsure how long these discussions will take, I climb into his hammock. I inhale so that his scent fills my head, and I'm transported back several months in time. I close my eyes and imagine my time here will be different. I've returned a wiser woman.

Samuel returns and stands in the doorway holding a wooden type cup. God, the sight of him has my ovaries exploding. There is a little dirt around his shins and knees. His hair is a messy bed-sex style. I can see every outline of muscle when he moves. Those blue eyes lock with mine. "The shaman wants you to drink this in case you're carrying any viruses."

Oh right. I scramble up, and my hand goes to my stomach out of habit when I get up.

"Is your hammock comfortable?" He raises one eyebrow and hands me the cup.

"Yes. I just wanted to lay in yours for old time's sake." I smile at him and then take a whiff of the tea.

Ugh. I grab my stomach and heave. It doesn't take much to make me nauseous. I cough to get the vile smell out of my throat. Over the months, I've been careful about what I eat and drink for the baby. Staring into the cup, I ask, "What is it? What if I react?"

"Eden, I don't make the rules, and please be thankful for the leniency they're already showing you."

"I can't." I shove it toward him. "I can't risk it."

For a moment, our eyes lock before his lower to where my hand rests under my naval. His eyes widen, studying me. His mouth gapes, and he stumbles back a step.

"Mine?"

I take a step toward him. "Of course."

Samuel takes the cup from me and places it on the ground, then he wraps his arms around me. His kiss is hot like wildfire. Warm lips dot my cheeks and neck before finding their way back to my mouth.

Samuel pulls away, out of breath. "I'm sorry I wasn't thinking straight. You must be hungry since it's dinner time."

"A little." I shrug. More for him.

"I can't wait for Kaikare to see you." His voice holds the excitement like a boy meeting his idol.

"Shouldn't I remain here?"

"You can keep your distance. "I'll tell her no hugging."

"What about you? You're with me and then—"

"I can keep my distance from the people. I have meds and a bottle of alcohol hand wash. I'm not leaving you alone at night." He walks briskly toward the center of the village.

Twilight never scared me. The dark hours past midnight freaked me out more, and I'm thankful to be in his hut and not alone in the dark at the campsite.

"There's an immune-boosting tea I'll have the ladies make you. It's safe for pregnant mothers. It will also help fight any viruses you may be carrying." He points to a log at the side of the fire, a good distance from the others as they eat dinner.

Heads turn, curious eyes meet mine, and a whisper spreads through the group. A new person visiting can be unnerving to them, and apart from Samuel, no one returns to the village. Yet after seeing Kaikare's trinkets, I know people have visited before Samuel's arrival. My interest is with one particular visitor, and I need to approach the question with sensitivity.

I glance over to Samuel, who is standing away from the ladies cooking over another fire. One hands him a cup, and he drinks it. They give him another, and he holds on to it. Our gaze meets. The fire casts a flickering light, and I catch his expression—a look of relief, joy, and desire. The sight of him takes my breath away. Shadows highlight pectoral and abdominal definition, and I'm already imagining running my fingers along each contour tonight.

Turning away, I'm still smiling when my gaze meets the shaman. His expression is serious and questioning. I nod, lower my gaze, and dip my chin. When our eyes meet again, I sense the probing, like ayahuasca's fingers in my thoughts. Standing before the fire, his headdress is stunning with long feathers and more beads around his neck than I remember the last time.

Samuel appears beside him. They exchange a few words, and he holds up the cup in his hand. The shaman waves his hands over the top while Kaikare appears on his other side. Samuel speaks to her. Our eyes meet, and Kaikare beams a smile at me.

The shaman hands him the cup, and he walks around the outside of the congregation and slides in beside me.

"Everything okay?"

"Yes." He hands me the cup. "Drink this before your dinner."

I take the cup and peer into the dark liquid, hoping it doesn't come straight back up. I knock it back like a shot and cough at the bitter taste lingering on my tongue. "It tastes like poison," I groan. He chuckles and speaks to one of the women who places a huge palm with roasted vegetables on the ground in front of me. She bows her head once before walking away.

"What did the shaman say?"

"He envisaged your return and knows you carry a secret."

I place my hand on his knee and find joy in the way his eyes sparkle. "So, you told him?"

"He already knew, and it's not the secret he was referring to."

The shaman's voice breaks our attention. The shaman raises his arms, holds them wide, encompassing his audience. I never thought of it until now, but he reminds me of the Christ the Redeemer statue in Rio—a bigger-than-life protector overlooking his people, arms open wide, embracing every living soul.

"I have something else to show you," I whisper. "I think you'll be as curious as I am."

"Let it wait for tomorrow. Enough surprises for one day." Samuel's arm snakes around my back, and I snuggle into his shoulder while he translates our bedtime story.

55

EDEN

AFTER BATHING IN THE STREAM, I change into my newly woven grass skirt and take Samuel's hand to tread through the forest. We stop for him to explain a certain vine or flower or point out the strangest of insects. The passion in his voice is different than my last visit. He's more relaxed, and it's like everything is sugarcoated, and he's not warning me about the dangers.

Smoke from the village fire lingers in the breeze, helping to guide my broken compass. The path to the stream is identified by others where a cut vine or branch guides them. I'm starting to pick up on identifying marks to lead me even though it comes naturally to Samuel and the Ularans. The jungle grows rapidly, even overnight, and I don't trust my instinct to walk alone until I can rely on my sense of direction.

We arrive at his hut, and I flop into the hammock. Nothing is simple. The walk to the stream is an equal distance from the village to the river only in the opposite direction. I stretch out the kinks in my back since last night wasn't about sleep. There were times I doubted the strength of the hammock could support us both with Samuel demonstrating how much he had missed me.

Samuel climbs in to lay alongside me. We both need to catch up on rest. Snuggling into his side, I glance up at him wide-eyed.

"I thought you were tired?" I murmur.

"Lying here beside you is restful," he says, and he takes my hand and squeezes it. "We talked about not keeping secrets. Do you want to tell me what's in your pack?"

Oh, that. "I can't be sure..." I roll off the hammock as ungraceful as I was on my last trip here. I open my bag and pull out the waterproof zip-lock bag containing photos and my grandmother's brush. The diary is packed in a separate compartment and double-wrapped. "I want to explain the story from the beginning." I climb back in to lie beside him.

First, I explain how my sister and brother have lived under different rules than me and how my father asked me to stay out of the jungle. Then I relay the stories my mother told me about my grandmother, her postnatal depression, and her work as a nurse. When I reach the part where she volunteered, met someone, and lost her baby, I show him the photos. We peruse the image for a while before I bring out the brush. "Kaikare has the mirror to match this. It could be coincidental for that period, but..." His face changes when he understands what I'm telling him.

"You believe the photo was taken here?"

"Kaikare told Asoo she's had needles when we went to help with the measles outbreak in the small Pemón community. Do you know how old she is? I mean, measles vaccines released in the mid-sixties, right? My father is fifty-nine. Do you think she's a few years younger than him?"

His eyes widen. "You believe she's your father's sister? Your aunt?" His voice is skeptical.

"Well... my gran's baby died. So, I don't know, but don't you at least think it's strange that Kaikare has the mirror to match? Because I believe the shaman had something to do with Gran."

He holds the black and white photo closer to his eyes. "It's taken too far away to identify anyone. Did your grandmother travel to Papua New Guinea?"

"I don't know the details of her travels. There was another journal, although she apparently gave it to her friend."

"Is her friend alive?"

"My parents haven't spoken to her since Gran's funeral. I understood the hurt it caused my father, so I've worked with what I have. Could you ask the shaman some questions?"

Samuel raises both hands. "It's a delicate matter. Ularan shamans don't marry. They commit their energy to the forest and her medicine.

It's why Kaikare never found a partner as she's following in her father's footsteps."

"Like a priest?"

"There have been partners but no marriage. His work comes first."

"Like you when we first met."

He gives me a look. Behind his eyes, I sense the cogs of time turning. "Yes, and yet here we are." He pulls me into his arms. "I'm sorry I haven't messaged. I didn't want Asoo to visit, and I couldn't risk my phone being lost because we've had torrential rain."

"I heard about the cannibals, which is another thing I want to talk about."

"I didn't want you to worry. I'm fine and know what I'm doing. Your being here changes everything."

56

SAMUEL

"Can we show Kaikare my brush?" Eden hands the brush once owned by her grandmother to Samuel.

Samuel understands Eden's enthusiasm, although he's aware of the fragility of the Ularan people's emotions by searching for answers and being intrusive. Over the months, Eden was gone when the lonely nights merged into one long, dark night until he realized she was living *her life* without him. They loved each other, this he knew and made promises, knowing time holds the power to erode the chains of promise. He'd learned that cruel truth from his parents.

He had tried to go back to how things were before her. Tried to forget how she made him feel by spending countless hours in the garden with the shaman. He ventured out beyond their boundary in search of a miracle despite the danger, to bring testament to why he is there—the reason to his life choice.

The pain he suffered *before* coming to Ulara resurfaced and found cracks in his armor. His strength weathered like a rock battered by the ocean, anxiety seeping into tiny fissures. With his shield weakened, he had to eliminate debilitating thoughts and focus on why he is here, not his own selfish desires.

Each day he woke focused on small wins in progress.

Nothing made sense without her.

Eden had changed him.

"*Yes.*"

The answer he wants to give to every question she asks of him.

But this question is lined with warning.

Lives may change.

Hearts might break.

All for a secret shared by two lovers, forever apart.

He makes a silent promise that the same fate will not be repeated for him and Eden.

Samuel flips the brush in his hands, studying the detail. "Kaikare will be curious. Consider the repercussions. Anger is unacceptable here. Please remember their ways."

Eden wraps her arms around his waist and leans back, so her beautiful eyes capture his. "I know. I've thought it through, and it's not right to put it off because it's like I'm keeping a secret. They deserve to know of the possibility..."

He sighs loudly. "I have no idea how either one of them will react."

He allows her to guide him out the door toward the shaman's hut.

Mid-morning, he expects the shaman to be singing in the garden and is surprised to find him in his hut. The shaman steps through his doorway and greets them with an open hand. No headdress. No beads. Gray hair drooping over his shoulders, bloodshot eyes hinting at wariness.

Eden looks to Samuel before holding out the brush. "It was my grandmother's. Ivy."

Samuel translates her words. The shaman's focus is on the brush, turning it over in his hands. He brings it to his nose, closes his eyes. His serious expression gives nothing away. He points to his hut, and both follow him inside.

Samuel watches Eden's expression as she looks around, taking in the decorative ornaments and trophies lining the walls of the shaman's private space. The shaman crouches and draws a circle in the dirt between them. From a clay bowl, he pinches something in powder form and sprinkles it to form three piles—a triangle over the circle. He bows his head and sings to the jungle, lifts his gaze to Samuel, and nods.

In a brief conversation, Samuel explains how Eden thought it coincidental the brush matched the mirror Kaikare owns even though these brushes were popular in a certain era. He chooses his words carefully so as not to offend him.

The shaman asks about her grandmother. Samuel relays what Eden had told him, although where Ivy volunteered is a mystery. Eden pulls out the photographs from her pack before Samuel can stop her.

The shaman gazes at the black and white image with no alarm in his expression. Samuel asks if he had seen a photograph before, and he nods, explaining many, many moons ago. A few minutes later, he hands the photograph to Eden without another word.

Samuel apologizes. Bowing his head, he excuses himself and asks for forgiveness.

The shaman nods. "I knew be-fore."

Samuel and Eden gape at his broken English. "Ivy come here. I see spirit. You."

Samuel responds in the Ularan language to clarify his words.

Eden gasps. "Is it why you allowed me to stay?"

The shaman nods to Eden.

"Did you have an affair with my grandmother?"

Samuel places a hand on hers, shakes his head in a gesture not to overstep their place. "Perhaps you should head back to the hut. I'll take it from here. You can't interrogate him with questions to satisfy your curiosity."

"We're talking about my grandmother here. I have a right to—"

"And he has a right to keep a secret. Let me speak with him without anguish in my voice."

"There are many things I need to ask."

"I know. We need to tread carefully. Otherwise, you'll learn nothing more. I'll ask him the important questions now."

Eden lowers her gaze and chin before leaving Samuel alone with the shaman.

Free to speak openly, the shaman tells Samuel about the day Ivy landed in his village, and like Samuel, the shaman knew the moment those blue eyes met his, everything in his world would change.

He contemplated giving up his shaman training to be with her without considering her time being numbered in days. He fell in love with the white-haired woman who took away his words of speech. Samuel smiles, understanding infatuation. Their baby became sick, and she left the village to travel elsewhere when she didn't believe their medicine would help. It angered the shaman, yet she had a will as fierce as her jaguar spirit. When she returned, she was different. Something had changed in the many, many moons she was gone. Kaikare had grown. He told her Kaikare belonged with him in the village. Her tears, he remembers. He touches his heart, and there's a heart-wrenching look in his eyes as if he is reliving the memory. He tells Samuel Ivy's spirit remained after she left. Samuel questions him, thinking he means death. The shaman's hand rests on Samuel's shoulder. The spirit of the blue-eyed jaguar that runs with Samuel in his dreams. The other jaguar is Ivy.

The younger jaguar is Eden.

Eden cannot remain here.

Besides the new danger of the Watache tribe, he can't risk a claim made on their baby. Before reaching his hut, he sees her pacing near the doorway.

"So, what happened?" she says, eyes wide.

"You were right about the affair. He loved your grandmother very much and didn't want her to leave. Kaikare is the shaman's and your grandmother's daughter."

"You know I already knew it," Eden says, her hand resting on her chest, the other hand wrapped over her stomach. "Deep down, there was something about Kaikare that drew me to her. I just can't get my head around why Gran didn't bring her home."

"It concerns me as well. The shaman told me Kaikare became sick at some point, and Ivy disappeared for some time with her to get treatment at a hospital. It could be when she received vaccinations."

"Oh my God," she rasps. "It's really sinking in that she's my aunt."

"He knew." Samuel stares at Eden. "When you first arrived, he knew who you were. It's why you could stay."

Eden's eyes round. "And he didn't say anything." He senses anger whirling within her. "I have to go speak with her."

"No." Samuel takes hold of her hand, his eyes pleading for understanding. "Enough for one day. We'll both speak to Kaikare tomorrow."

Again, Eden has managed to shake up his world. Only this time, the secrets have him questioning whether the shaman saw *him* coming long before Eden?

57

EDEN

AT SUNRISE, my energy levels are ridiculously high, so while Samuel sleeps, I roll out of my hammock and pad to my bag. I'm staring at the photo of my grandmother and the shaman and several photographs of my father and grandmother over a twenty-year span. At first, I hesitated in packing Gran's belongings, and now I'm glad I did. Will the shaman want to see the pictures of my grandmother, learn about the life she lived after Ulara? Or will it hurt too much? I glance up to the window and peer out to the rainforest, my view blocked by a silhouette.

Before panic builds, I realize it's Kaikare. She waves for me to come, so I keep hold of the photographs and creep past Samuel toward her. I follow her along the path until thick one-hundred-feet-high kapok trunks obscure us from view.

Kaikare's eyes study mine, questions whirling behind her honey-brown hues.

"Do you know?"

She says nothing. With only her eyes to guide my decision, I hold out the photographs.

I allow her to study each in silence, and like her father, her expression is unreadable. What I'd give to know what she's thinking. I hold out my hand for the pictures. Her fingers wrap around mine, and I'm pulled along the path before asking where we're headed. She leads me to her father's hut, and I know I shouldn't be here, but fate has led me to this moment, and I have to follow my gut instinct in doing what's right for Kaikare. The shaman nods to me and gestures for me to sit.

Cross-legged, the three of us sit facing the other. Kaikare hands him the images, and he speaks to her in a gentle tone, pointing to the man beside my grandmother in the jungle photo. Not once do I detect anger or any emotion. She responds with a nod of the head. How can she be calm? How can he? I want to tell them both how important this discovery is and ask why they aren't upset or excited. I'm about to say something, hoping the shaman will understand part of my words, only I notice Kaikare wipe her eyes.

"Eden, what are you doing?" I spin to Samuel standing outside.

The shaman points to the door, and I take my leave without the photographs.

Samuel isn't as practiced at hiding his concern.

"I asked you not to do this without me," he whispers. He takes my hand and leads me away toward the northern end of the village. "I wanted us to do it together, so I could communicate for you. Causing disruption to peace in the village can mean you being sent away and not allowed to return."

"I only wanted them to learn the truth."

"I know. And I want what is best for you. For us. Please understand our views differ when it comes to harmony and breaking their rules. Kaikare needs to focus on her training. If something happens to the shaman, it's like a library burning down, decades of knowledge gone."

"What do you mean? I'm not hurting him," I rasp.

He leads me to the garden, picks fruit from a vine, and hands it to me. "Please eat. You're my concern like the shaman is Kaikare's. He is old. He could have a heart attack or stroke like any elderly person, and she still has some to learn. They hold emotion inside, and although he is healthy, stress of surprise can lead to a stroke."

My gut tightens, and I want to go back to apologize. In a moment of my thoughts being read, the shaman and Kaikare appear.

"Oh, hi," I say like a dork.

Samuel ignores me and bows his head. He speaks to them in words I don't understand.

"You're now considered family," he says, the dent between his eyebrows deepening. "It seems both are happy about your photographs."

Yet Samuel doesn't seem as happy. In fact, the deep lines on his forehead tell me everything but happy.

"IT'S ALL I WANTED," I say to Samuel when we're alone. "For them to be happy about the truth. For them both to see pictures of my grandmother and know she arrived home safely. And for Kaikare to see her mother and my father, since he's her half-brother."

"Since you arrived I've witnessed a change in the shaman. You have shown them another world. One that's frightening to them, and that has possibly created a problem for us." He swipes the side of his face.

"Us. How?"

"You are family as was your grandmother. I don't want the same fate for our baby, so I'm sending you home. You have to remember, in their eyes, the people of the rest of the world are fueled by greed. Forests are destroyed and burned for land. We bring disease, use guns, and our emotions aren't intact as the Ularans."

"But I have almost three months," I croak out. "I want to be with you."

Samuel takes me in his arms and kisses the top of my head. "I know. And I want to be with you. I also want our baby to be safe."

My hands tighten around his hot skin. "Please don't make me leave. When I'm with you, I'm stronger. I need to stay."

"Eden," he croaks. "I feel the same. More than anything, I want you here by my side." He holds me, so our gaze meets. "Before I met you, I believed I was happy. The day you left, I realized you took a part of my heart and soul with you. I'll never be the same. I've changed for the better."

"Then don't make me leave," I beg.

He runs a finger along the side of my cheek. His kind eyes are filled with love, yet his lips press tight in a straight line.

"Say it. Say I can stay. Please..." I stretch out the last word. "What if something goes wrong with our baby, and I can't reach you. What if—"

"Stop." He exhales slowly, the heat of his breath hitting my face. "If." He leans his forehead against mine. "If you stay, you have to promise me something—"

"Anything," I croak.

"You remain here only if there is no danger to you or our baby. The moment anything escalates, and it includes word from Asoo about border security with rebels outside the village, you are to leave. No questions asked."

"Agreed."

I tilt my head to meet his eyes, watch as his lips meet mine. There's urgency in his kiss like it could be our last. I ignore my gut and allow him to melt away all my thoughts.

"I love you," I say against his lips.

Holding both my cheeks in his large hands, he tilts my head. "And I love you more than anything else I value in this world."

I have eleven more weeks.

It will bring me close to the term of my pregnancy, and I need to consider the risk of flying while in the last trimester of my pregnancy. Do I leave before the airline refuses travel, or stay and *somehow* extend my visa and have my baby here?

Yasmine would understand.

Dad will take more convincing.

Faith has my back, so she'll be able to talk to him.

It's not forever.

I smile, knowing this man who led me on this crazy journey will protect me because I chose to take a risk, take steps outside my comfort zone, and embrace fear—to be here with him.

I only hope the shaman doesn't see me as a threat. My time here is in his hands. Though my gut tells me not to let down my guard because Samuel's love might not be enough to protect me.

HOPELESSLY WILD

1

EDEN

THE RAINFOREST IS DYING.

A scent not born from fire—instead, it's a distinct stench of death like decaying meat.

Wet and musty.

Rotten wood.

Mold.

A smell I can't escape since it's rained nonstop every day for the past two weeks.

When I arrived in mid-September, we had sunshine and occasional drizzly rain.

"You brought the sunshine with you," Samuel had told me. "At least you missed the worst of the rainy season."

What the hell is this?

Never have I seen so much rain.

A blanket of water falls from the sky every minute, and I can barely see ten feet in front of me. I'm a prisoner in the hut, only venturing out to visit the jungle toilet, and I hold off as long as possible. My soaked, muddy shoes remain near the hut entrance. I shifted my belongings away from the open windows, even though there's barely a puff of wind to blow the rain anywhere except directly downward. The grass-thatched roof overhangs the structure, directing rain runoff to form a waterfall imprisoning us in a fluid fence. The overspill creates small rivers throughout the village. A moat-like trench surrounds Samuel's hut, and the past few days has seen the water lap at the entrance, concealing the two wooden steps below the doorway.

Everything smells damp. There's no escaping the mildewy aroma. Only the raucous insects distract your thoughts, and I wish they would shut up.

During the day, I'm left to go stir-crazy while Samuel attempts to save some of the precious herbs. He pots the plants and lugs the clay pots into the long house. Many of the plants thrive, being acclimatized to this weather. Only the shaman is afraid of losing the rare ones, and considering we've had around twenty inches of rain in a short period, the water isn't draining away fast enough, and the plants sink in a deluge of muddy water.

Fungus is a threat, and after Samuel's story of how fungus can grow inside an ant until it bursts out of its thorax, I know the jungle has the power to control every living species that lives in her womb. No single species will dominate, and the balance can be horrific.

It's why I need to protect the one that grows in my womb from the unseen dangers lurking in the green cavern on the edge of the village.

Opening my sack, I retrieve the plastic bag from the bottom and unwind the tightly wrapped package. It's the one thing I have avoided for months. Only today, I'm unsettled and need to divert my thoughts from the miserable weather and the fact I may as well be in a prison cell.

I push on the tiny brass button before yanking at the flap binding the diary to the lock.

Shit.

Scurrying through some instruments on Samuel's workbench, I find a small steel-pointy object he has used on wounds and poke it at the lock. It doesn't fit. I rustle through his bag, and at the bottom, I find a random paperclip. Pulling the sharp end away, I jab the lock and twist several times, using more force than necessary.

"Give me a break," I yell and toss the book against the wall. Reflecting my patience, the flap snaps on impact and lands open on the ground. I let out a gasp and scoop it up, brushing dust from the pages and cover. I slide into the hammock, curl into a lazy C-shape, and open Gran's diary at the beginning.

To My Darling Ivy on your 18th birthday.
All my love,
Albert xx

I SUCK in a breath and turn to the first page.

18TH JANUARY 1956

My first entry in my new diary from Albert.
He surprised me, and I think he understands me better than I understand myself.

I didn't expect us to last since I plan to move away from him for at least three years while I live at the hospital. Albert claims to understand, but three years is a long time apart.

It's the start of my new life after working at the local delicatessen since finishing school two years ago.

Two years. And I've been with Albert for almost a year. Tonight, I'm heading to his house because his parents are out playing cards with his relatives. He said the card games can continue into the early hours of the morning. I know what he's implying.

I'm not afraid. In fact, I'm excited knowing we will be alone.

I turn the page back and forth, but that entry doesn't continue. Hell, was that my grandparents' first time? My breath catches, and guilt fills me knowing I'm reading my grandmother's private notes, only I can't look away.

19TH JANUARY 1956

Last night wasn't as bad as I'd thought it was going to be—not after the stories I'd heard from the other girls. Maybe it's because we have come close on other occasions. This time he was prepared. The latex hurt a little, so I need to find an alternative, and I'm not sure who to ask. I'm not telling anyone I have lost my virginity because I don't want them to judge me. And they will judge.

Last night, Albert accepted my decision about nursing.

6th February 1956

Do they really expect us to wear these starched uniforms? Matron has a ruler and measured the length of my tunic. After one day, I can predict we will not get along. But I want this more than anything, so I will have to abide by the rules. At least my room in the nurses' quarters is near Brenda's room.

"Hey."

I drop the diary and scramble out of the hammock.

Samuel runs his fingers along the netting covering the doorway and adheres the mosquito net to the edges. Leaning forward, he shakes water from his hair as though he has just stepped out of a shower.

"How are you feeling?" He wipes his hands over his face and flicks water from his fingers before checking the net remains secure on our open windows.

"Good. I'm..." I hesitate. His gaze lands on the diary in the hammock. "I have Gran's diary, and up to now, I was too afraid to read it. The jammed lock didn't help, but I picked it. I found a paperclip in your bag, and I think it loosened the clasp." I fail to mention the impact of the diary landing on the wall resulted from my frustration of acting like a caged animal. He wouldn't know it now, for in the short time reading Gran's words, it feels as though I'm embarking on a journey with her. I'm in her time warp, and it's almost serene.

He raises a solitary brow. "My only paperclip?"

Is he seriously concerned about one paperclip?

"So you're not concerned about the fact I foraged through your stuff or that I'm learning about my grandmother?" I fold my arms over my chest and release them with a sudden ache. Every week my boobs are growing and becoming more uncomfortable.

"You're reading about her past. Something we can't change. So, no, it doesn't concern me. The only thing that matters to me is you. It's the first thing I asked when I stepped inside." He takes me in his wet arms and rubs his hands up and down my back. The moisture left on his skin gives some relief to the muggy heat, so I rest my cheek on his chest, hoping to cool my face. "So, how are you?"

I turn to hide my face in his hard chest. "Hormonal," I murmur. "I'm sorry if I've been narky these past few days, but I am going stir-crazy. I mean, if you were here with me then—"

He takes my shoulders and pries me off him. "I'm here. I told the shaman I need to focus on you. I can't do much more until the rain settles."

"Which is when? I can't believe how much I miss the weather app or the news. I mean, even if I could play my Spotify list, it would help. There's nothing to do." A mischievous smile tweaks my lips. "I thought about reading your notebooks, but when I picked up one of them, I didn't even get through the first page of not understanding half of it. The medical terminology? I'm not even pretending to know what you're talking about." I throw my arms in the air. "So, I decided today was the day I faced my fear and open Gran's diary."

His lips curl into a smile. "Face your fear." A light chuckle bursts from him. "You're in the jungle. You traveled here alone, and your fear is in a small book with words of the past?"

"You wouldn't understand." I turn and scoop water from the bowl in the corner and cover it again with weaved twine.

"I think I'd understand, considering my past. You're lucky I have all day for you to tell me what spooks you most." He comes over, bundles me in his arms, and carries me to the hammock. He curses when he lays me down and swats at the buzzing above his head. A small clay dish on the bench holds the balm he uses to protect us from the mosquitoes. Samuel grabs it and stops the hammock from swaying before lathering it over my face, arms, and legs. I could do it, only it's like a relaxation massage by the one person whose touch I crave. Flicking my hair from my shoulders, I expose my breasts. I close my eyes, relishing the way his hands make circles over my skin, over my stomach, around my breasts, to my shoulders, and my neck. Warm fingers glide down to my breasts again, the action slower with a gentle squeeze. I open my eyes and meet the fire in his blue hues.

"Did you say you had all day?" I rasp between moans.

"I do." He places the tub of balm on the ground. "I'll do your back after."

"After?"

He leans in, lowering his lips to mine. I sigh into his mouth, and it's enough for him to lift a leg onto the hammock. A giggle passes my lips when the hammock sways.

"You're losing your touch."

He lifts his head and frowns at me.

"Your balance. Not your touch with me." Do I have to explain everything to him? I know my Aussie lingo confuses him at times, but Samuel has been away from society so long that he misses the joke.

"Just kiss me already," I say. Wrapping my hand around the back of his neck, I guide his lips to mine.

The hammock rocks a little more when his entire weight is beside me. He lifts my knee, and since I'm only wearing a grass skirt, he arouses me with ease. "Have you been thinking about me?" he whispers.

"Yes." Our kiss intensifies, our tongues entwine, and my body craves him inside of me. "I'm always ready for you." My hormones have me wanting him all the time. Every hour if I could.

He climbs over me with the balance of a cat, hovers until the sway of the hammock is minimal.

"How are you going to cope when we're back in society, and I wear underwear?" I smile before my hand guides him to my entrance. The look he gives me is a touch unsettling, as though he hasn't contemplated us both returning any time soon. I don't have time to dwell. His mouth covers my lips, his tongue seeks mine and he tastes me as though he has been starved for weeks. The butterfly sensation of fluttering in my stomach transforms to the wings of a hummingbird hovering. Lust streams through every part of me. Samuel loves me slowly, intimately, the hammock barely rocks. His thrusts are deep, and I feel all of him. He builds slowly, the hammock moving with him. A gentle sway while making love is my new favorite thing. A romantic motion and I'll take it as there are no red roses or romantic private restaurant dinner dates. His hands glide smoothly over my oiled skin. His fingers caress one breast, my nipples harden and then he finds the other. Eyes closed, I savor his touch, moan his name as my orgasm builds. Samuel thrusts faster, and faster until the bliss overwhelms everything else, and I sigh his name, exhausted with pleasure. Exhausted as my labia remain swollen from last night. Not a complaint, I'm happy to have an orgasm more than once a day. My hormones demand it. Yet we remain discreet about our sex life not wanting to offend the Ularans which is why our special times are when no-one else is around. The last thing I want is to be sent away.

So, I'll take every opportunity to love him, blind to what tomorrow brings. My limited time is like a bomb ticking away inside my heart.

2

EDEN

Sun blooms over the treetops—an invitation to a new day. The raw light streams into the hut and onto the empty hammock beside me. Absent of any breeze, the choking heat makes me crazy in my dreams, and last night was no exception.

Beyond our hut, life pulses with new vitality. The squawk of insects and screeching monkeys echo from the thriving jungle. I stumble out of my hammock to peer out the netted doorway and sense the jungle has crept closer to the village overnight.

Steam rises from the leaves of the low-lying vines, threatening to strangle everything in its path. My shoulders fall with every sharp breath of thick air. It's early morning, and yet the layer of sweat covering my bare chest glistens in the filtered light.

Samuel said he'd be back by lunch. Many hours remain to amuse myself, and although the rain has eased, I'm not enticed to leave the hut until some of the mud hardens. When I have to relieve myself, the mosquitoes circling above my head sound like a swarm. The horror stories of all the mosquito-transmitted diseases spook me enough to be mindful.

I swat at one buzzing near my ear. In defeat, I fasten the protective net and retrieve the balm to cover my face and limbs. During the long, lonely hours while Samuel works, I question my sanity in being here, risking my and my baby's life for him.

A banana and a basket of berries sit on the bench near a bowl of clean water—my breakfast. I eat the fruit as slow as possible to pass the time until more light filters in. Today, I have a date with my grandmother.

I retrieve her diary and the family photographs from my backpack. I take my favorite one of Gran and slide it inside the diary's cover. Clambering into the hammock, I'm ready to be transported to 1956.

4th June 1956

Last night Brenda and I snuck out of the nurses' quarters window when the matron's bedroom light went out. Mary kept watch, ensuring the window remained open around midnight for when we returned.

We giggled as we ran across the wet path, holding each other's hand so we didn't slip over. My other hand was supporting my bra where I hid the sheath. Mary put me on to it, and I know she won't tell. It felt weird against my skin, a jellyfish texture.

Brenda was more concerned about the rain flattening her curls. She wanted to impress Jonathon far more than I did Albert.

She told me she knew Jonathon was the one for her. It made me a little envious how she knew what her heart desired before getting to know a man properly. A quick wedding, a baby straight away, and to give up nursing? I couldn't fathom not nursing. Women stop working when they marry or fall pregnant. Here, it's enforced without a choice. I've worked hard, and I'll not give it up because it's expected all women want is to be married and have children.

The idea of helping others gives me much more happiness.

My mother had told me happiness is all that matters.

Every time I think about traveling and discovering new places, I get a tingling along my spine. It's the rush I thrive on, and it's why I want to work in the emergency department.

Like tonight. The rush of sneaking out to meet Albert was half the fun. He makes me laugh, but I wonder if it's enough? Sure, he's tall, dark, and handsome. He's got eyes the color of whiskey and a heart so kind. How could I say no to him? Ever?

Not even in the back of a car.

It's kind of fun.

Brenda wants to wait until they're married.

It's why she wants to rush into a wedding, especially after I told her how good it feels. The secrecy doesn't bother me. I know he loves me. I guess I love him too. But I'm not sure if I want to marry him... yet. There's so much more I want to do.

Travel.

Nurse overseas.

Live!

One page and it tells me so much about my grandmother. I turn the page as though I'm reading a great book. Only the next few entries are about my grandfather and her private times, so I skip those.

I'm surprised by the time lapse between her entries. There's no mention of special times like birthdays or her parents.

17TH DECEMBER 1956

> *Today I met a doctor who told me all about his travels. It wasn't the discovering unknown places or staying in luxury hotels that impressed me, but his time volunteering in Africa and South America.*
> *It sounded so exciting, and listening to him, I know, in my heart, it's what I want to do. Ethiopia is where I want to travel. Africa, the mother country. The large animals, well, I wish I had enough money saved so I could leave now. I'm having lunch with him in the cafeteria tomorrow.*
> *I have many questions I want to ask. First, I need to set a plan for my savings. Not only to get there but how much I'll need to live on if I'm away for twelve months or more.*

I take a moment to absorb my grandmother's words. No mention of Christmas. Only her dreams and not a word about my grandfather. Is she still with him? I flip the page and realize she is because the next few lines are about intimate times. More private times follow on several pages, but on skimming the words, not once do I find mention of the word *love*.

13TH SEPTEMBER 1957

Matron hates me.

I wonder if she knows I've been sneaking out at night?

Maybe she likes Dr. Anderson? That could be it since she didn't stop staring at me when I sat with him at lunch. When I giggled—well, laughed loudly—at his story, she came over to the table and stood over me and said, "Nurse, isn't it time you went back to the ward? Your lunch break is over."

She didn't like that I had a reply and told her I was on the afternoon shift.

"Then keep it down," she said like I was a child. "You're disturbing the other staff."

She is so prim. I bet she's frigid too.

Shit. My gran is a bad ass.

I'm not ready to stop reading so I turn the page.

18th December 1957

Albert's grandparents died last month. As sad as it was, his cousin inherited money since they were the next generation of first-born males. The concept angered me, knowing the daughters of his uncles got nothing. Albert is an only child, so there were no siblings to feel sorry for because I'd be speaking up if I were his sister.

Family. I'm glad I'm not close to my parents. But there are days I'd be grateful for some support because I worry about where I'm going to live when I finish nursing. Without even asking, I know what my dad would say. "Marry Albert."

Albert is always thinking of our future even though I never bring it up with him. How can I when the unknown scares me?

He has a surprise for me for Christmas.

I'm nervous because I hope it's not a proposal.

My poor Pop. Even reading between the lines, I can tell how much he loves Gran.

2nd January 1958

Albert has bought a motel complex. Three levels on the esplanade at Glenelg. He said we could run it together, have a family, and set up a future for them. On paper, it makes sense. He purchased it at a bargain price because the building needs repair. Only I never envisaged this as my future. He didn't even ask me if it's what I wanted.
It's 'my' Christmas present, and now I feel bad for being ungrateful.
I'm so confused.
He hasn't spoken to me in a week.

Shit. I can imagine them fighting. I turn the diary and look at the cover as though it's more valuable than any diamond. I'm glad to be on this journey with them. To think this is the beginning of my family's business. Monte Hotel's birth. At some point in time, my parents changed it from motel to hotel.

19TH JANUARY 1958

Albert is talking to me again.
I knew it wouldn't last because he can't keep his hands off me.

I stop reading and flick the page, then double-check the dates. It's been more than a year since her last entry. What happened during that time?

18TH FEBRUARY 1959

I intend to undertake a further year of study and do the Heidelberg Infectious Disease Course at Heidelberg Hospital.
It's the only place that offers the course, and it's in Melbourne.
I don't know how to break the news to Albert.
Brenda wants to study midwifery because she wants a family and feels like it would help her. If Jonathon proposes beforehand, then she's quitting.
Eight more weeks, and I'll be a qualified nurse.
My father said I'd never finish.
I can't wait to wave my certificate in his face if I see him.
They haven't visited in over a year, so I won't hold my breath.
The last thing he told me was just to be a good girl and marry Albert.
My guess? That's the worst thing her father could've said.

29TH APRIL 1959

Mary smuggled in bottles of beer for Brenda and me to celebrate our graduation. We were so drunk that she had to keep coming to our rooms and shushing us as she could hear us all the way down the corridor.
Mary is mentoring Brenda because Mary has almost finished her midwifery course.
Brenda keeps crying about me leaving. She said it won't be the same without me. Giving in to emotion, I allowed myself to cry because she's more like a sister to me than a friend. I'll miss her more than anyone.
Albert has finally come around to accepting I'm leaving. He admitted it might be for the best as he spends most of his time at the motel, getting it up and running again. In a way, it has been perfect for him. He finished his plumbing trade and can fix any of those issues in the building. We've barely seen each other with my studies and Albert working two jobs, so it won't make a world of difference by my being in Melbourne. We'll work out special times when he can catch the bus and visit on weekends, and his parents can manage the motel. His parents spend most of their days helping him, anyway.
I guess I'm a little jealous of the support of his parents. I know he's doing it for us. I'm just not ready to commit to him. Some days I see him as the one. But when he becomes frustrated by my ambition to have a career, I wonder if he's the right person for me.
Yet, I can't imagine myself with anyone else.
Or anyone at all.

I CLOSE the diary and take a deep breath. I know how this story ends, and yet I'm nervous to read on. Pushing up, I find the bottle of folic acid tablets and down one with water. My bladder is ready to burst. I slip on my shoes and trudge through the muddy soil in slow, exaggerated steps. I want to bathe. Hopefully, I can get down to the stream with most of the flood water filtering in the opposite direction toward the river.

Scanning in all directions before I squat, I let out a sigh because this baby has me peeing far more frequently than I want to.

Something rustles in the undergrowth nearby, so I rush back to the hut, kicking my shoes off, and doing my best to reseal the netting around the doorway. Mud flecks dot my calves, and I don't care because I need to know what happens next.

. . .

11TH NOVEMBER 1959

One of the few weekends I returned to Adelaide, Albert proposed, surprising me with a ring and flowers. He got down on one knee and asked me like you would ask someone if they wanted a cup of tea.

I saw it coming because he keeps asking me what I'm going to do when I finish. Where will I work?

On his last trip to Melbourne, I cried, saying how confused I was and didn't know where I was going to live.

He told me I didn't have to worry as we had the motel.

I guess he misunderstood.

My career is in nursing, not running a motel.

He had set the whole thing up with Brenda and Jonathon, so they were waiting at the pub for us. Brenda and I drank champagne until our cheeks hurt from giggling.

I can't stop staring at the diamond on my finger.

Only I can't wear it in Melbourne. You're not allowed while you're studying, so it will remain locked in my safe.

I'm still in shock, yet somehow, I know I made the right decision.

He loves me.

It's a weird feeling because it's like I'm lowering a wall and agreeing to let him take care of me. He didn't say those words, but marriage is confusing.

I'm scared I'm going to lose who I am to be with someone who loves me.

I also love him, but I'd never ask him to give up anything for me. Yet it's expected, as a woman, my dreams and life are now ones I share with a future husband.

I'm making a promise to myself—my happiness will not be compromised by marriage.

I take a moment to absorb my grandmother's words. I didn't get to know my grandfather like I did my gran since he died when I was a child. My heart is torn. I'm reading a love story and vying for the couple only to know the sadness in how it ends.

The next few pages show how much she loves him because it's only an account of each night they get to share because my grandfather took a week's holiday to visit Gran in Melbourne. So, she snuck out of the nurses' quarters every night for a week.

Dad was born in 1961. So I can safely read on knowing my grandparents were still happy.

29TH NOVEMBER 1959

I never believed a nursing subject would excite me like microbiology and pharmacology. I'm excited to be living in the 1950s. I'm spending many hours reading textbooks in my room. It distracts me from getting angry when I think about Albert's parents. They told Albert I couldn't move into the motel until we're married. As if they have a right to tell me what to do. Albert spoke up for me, and his plan is to have separate rooms until then. The nights they don't stay over, they'll never know if we're sleeping together. All I can think about is sleeping in a double bed with Albert and not in this hard single bed. It will feel strange in a good way.

2ND DECEMBER 1959

Dr. Anderson visited the hospital to give a talk on mosquito-borne diseases. I was so excited to speak to him after the lecture. He informed me he's leaving for England in a couple of weeks, so I asked him to send me his address and direct it to Albert's motel. I told him I was still interested in volunteer work. If he has any contacts to please send me their address so I can apply.

The look he gave me made the hairs stand up on the back of my neck.

"But you'll be married by then," he said.

"Are you telling me they won't take me as a volunteer because I'm married? God forbid a woman leave her husband to help the poor. Why am I studying bacteria and diseases if I'm not able to use my skills?"

He smiled and patted my shoulder and told me, "You'll do just fine."

I close the book and smile because I know where I inherited my determination and maybe some of my stubbornness too.

MY EYES flicker open to a soft touch on my hair and forehead.

Squinting and only half awake, my vision clears. It's Kaikare, my beautiful aunt, not Samuel touching me. She smiles, resting her hand on my shoulder.

"I'm okay," I tell her. I take the diary and put it on my other side, away from her. Ridiculous when she can't read it. Yet I'm filled with guilt reading words about her mother when she's entitled to the truth more so than me. When I finish reading Gran's diary, I'll ask Samuel to translate parts for Kaikare. A filtered version, depending on how the story pans out.

She points to the bowl of water. Her hand goes to her mouth as though she's scooping water from the river to drink. She makes me smile, and even though we have been apart for days, something has passed between us. She's my family, and while our societies and communities have raised us in different ways, an understanding that we're of the same blood subconsciously makes us closer. Even when I first came to the village, we both connected quickly. Maybe the universe was telling me something.

I scramble out of the hammock. The last thing I need is for her to report back to her father that I'm tired, weak, or not coping.

Is it why she's here?

Samuel said he'd be back by lunch. Maybe he sent her?

I walk over to the water bowl and scoop myself a glass of fresh water. When I turn around, I find the manual sphygmomanometer on Samuel's bench.

Surely, a week hasn't passed since I had my blood pressure taken. Days pass slowly when trapped in a hut, but when I think of how much time has already passed, I want to panic, knowing every hour is one closer to the day I have to leave.

When I turn, Kaikare is by the hammock looking at the diary. She picks it up and flicks over the pages, studies the leather cover, opens the pages again, and the photograph of Gran falls into her hands. She studies it a moment, then her eyes meet mine. Placing my cup on the bench, I go to her.

All I can do is nod and offer a gentle smile. I lower my gaze to where my hand rests over hers, holding her mother's—my grandmother's—life in words. I wish she could also read it. Although I'm not sure she could or would understand our lifestyle.

A privileged life.

I open my mouth and look her in the eye, ready to say something. Anything. Only words catch in my throat when a single tear cascades down her cheek. Not knowing what else to do, I throw my arms around her and squeeze. With trapped arms by her side, she lays her forehead on my shoulder.

"I'm sorry," I croak.

Sorry for not being able to communicate with you about what your mother was like.

Sorry for upsetting you because as an Ularan, I'm sure she shouldn't be feeling emotions as strong as sadness or anger.

Sorry because I came into your world uninvited and turned your life as you know it upside down.

"What's going on?" Samuel asks from behind us.

I release Kaikare and spin to him. He's covered in mud up to his thigh. With one hand, he leans on the doorway for support, and the way his shoulders slump, I want to ask him if he needs a hand?

Kaikare nods to him, then tosses the diary onto the hammock before rushing past him and out the door.

"What did you do?"

"Nothing. She came in here and saw the diary. She knows it's about Gran because she saw the photograph and shed a tear," I say, exasperated. "You should go after her."

He pushes through the mosquito net, and it floats like a parachute back to the doorway.

It feels like I'm in trouble, yet he can't blame me for Kaikare feeling all this new emotion. It all comes back to secrets.

Kaikare deserves to know about her mother.

3

EDEN

CLUELESS TO TIME, I pace the room for what seems like hours before the netting separates like a curtain to reveal Samuel's presence.

"Is she okay?" I blurt out before he has both feet inside the hut.

"Yes. Put on your runners. We'll take a walk to the stream." He holds the net wide for me to pass through the doorway to sit on the step and slip on my shoes.

The water is slowly seeping into the earth or making its way to the river systems. In the wet season, new tributaries are temporarily formed. The ground is now muddy with decaying leaves dumped everywhere, along with puddles of water that have nowhere to go. These puddles can also breed more mosquitoes. I turn to the plant I notice out of the corner of my eye. It's a vine in a pot near the doorway and the window. There's another placed on the other side of the doorway, and it reminds me of home—decorative pots of plants strategically placed to make a house more appealing. Only these will not be for decorative reasons.

"These are new."

"The vine is to deter mosquitoes." He walks away, so I plod along after him, consciously lifting my feet with every stride.

"What did you say to Kaikare?" I swat insects away from my face. Macaws shriek from above as if they find my words offensive. If the bloody monkeys can just shut up for five minutes, then I might clear my head.

“Mind this puddle.” He points to a shallow pool of water. “It’s deeper than it appears.” He waits a few seconds before answering as though he’s assessing what’s ahead. “I told her you only started reading words about her mother’s life, and when you understand the words, you’ll tell her about it. We chatted about her emotions and how she is feeling things she has never felt before. She’s confused as to why she’s feeling sad about a woman she never knew.”

“I understand.”

“It’s not about your grandmother. It’s not their way. Kaikare is feeling like she doesn’t belong in some way, and those feelings of trust and sadness are confusing her as the elders have taught her not to succumb to those emotions. She’s feeling not like a failure but almost an intruder. It’s like another personality is coming out in her.”

“She has our genes.” I give an empathetic sigh as I step over tree roots and concentrate not to slip on the decaying leaves and bark forming a layer over the earth.

“No. She has her father’s genes, and environmental influences are what she has learned here. You and I…” he motions his finger between us, “… we need to be invisible and not bring our ways to confuse the Ularans. All you know isn’t to be revealed here.”

I second-guess what I wanted to achieve by coming here. Obviously, I wanted to inform Samuel I was pregnant with his baby. I also wanted the joy of being with him wherever that was because I love him. He loves me too, yet I can’t shake the feeling he has no plans to leave Ulara soon.

“I’m still learning, and if we’re honest, I’m the intruder. Our baby is due in a matter of weeks. I have to go home soon. I can’t keep living day to day waiting for you to say I’m coming home with you, and we live happily ever after.”

He stops walking and takes both of my hands in his. “You’re no longer an intruder. You’re doing great learning their ways, but it will take time.” He leans in and kisses my forehead before brushing wayward strands from my eyes. “You can leave at any time. I’d never make you stay. I can’t leave until my contract is finished and—”

“What?”

He looks into the jungle as though it holds the answers he seeks. “There’s enough evidence the flower from the tepui is a success in cancer treatment.”

“One flower. They’ll need more than one.”

When he nods, my thoughts become thick like fog. "You'll need to make another trip?"

He takes my hand, and we keep walking. "I don't want to assume anything. They can search for other tepuis by helicopter. While I'm here, I'll continue to learn from the shaman and help the community where I can."

"The Ularans mean more to you than a community, right?"

"I know you find it hard to understand, but they are my family now." He hesitates. "Until I met you, they were all I had."

It's an opening for me to say something about his parents, but I decide to focus on us. "So if they find the flower on other tepuis, your contract will end quicker, and you'll be free to leave with me?"

"I intend to be with you and our child. I can't give you a date or time frame until I hear more about the research findings."

"So, we wait?"

He squeezes my hand and smiles at me. God, he doesn't need to say another word because his smile does all sorts of things to my insides.

"Yes, my love, we wait. Like we're waiting for that beautiful baby to grow inside of you, some things can't be rushed."

My hand lifts to rest on the swell of my stomach. "I don't want to have this baby alone. I want you there."

He turns and pulls me into his arms and kisses me. "I love you," he murmurs against my lips. "I want to be there with you too. Please understand I'll do everything in my power to make sure you're both safe."

I wrap my arms around him and rest my cheek against his firm chest. "Thank you."

Samuel drapes an arm over my shoulder, and we walk the remainder of the way at a slower pace.

We arrive at the stream, and small beams of broken sunlight stream through the trees. Everything seems quieter here in our special place.

Samuel kicks off his shoes, then drops to his knees to assist me to slide mine off. I lean both hands on his shoulders, grateful not to bend over because my stomach is already getting in the way. He unties his skirt, and I do the same with mine.

Inspecting his back and long legs, I can tell they are thinner than when we first met. When he turns, his eyes lower to my naked body, and he holds out a hand for me to use as support. I step to him, and now closer, I see the fire burning in his eyes.

"I love you," I tell him. "Everything I do is because I love you."

"I know," he rasps out. "I love you too."

The moment our bodies submerge in the water, I wrap my legs around his hips, my arms around his neck, and I kiss him, knowing it's the one way to simplify everything between us.

His lips meet mine in need. I still feel like an intruder despite Samuel's words. The only way I could explain to the shaman and the chief my being here is like being a drug addict, and Samuel is the euphoria. They wouldn't understand, but they may understand him as my ayahuasca. He heals me, takes me to a better place where our hearts are one.

THE CUFF of the sphygmomanometer tightens around my arm. Samuel listens through the stethoscope, then releases the valve and smiles. "All well."

"I expect it to be. There's no past medical history to think otherwise, and I eat healthily," I say to minimize his concern. "Those watches and modern devices? Well, if I had one, I could check it myself."

He writes the results on a notepad and closes it. "This is reliable. It only needs to be calibrated every five years. And I'm not relying on batteries or other energy devices for it to work."

"Right."

He stacks the notepad and the sphygmomanometer in a corner. "I want us to take a visit to Ciudad Guayana. You need to have an ultrasound and have some blood taken."

"I had an ultrasound before I came. And blood. Everything is fine. I made sure of it first." He gives me a look that says not to argue with him, but when he slips into doctor mode with me, I want to do just that—argue. "I have a good doctor. Or is it me you don't trust?"

His eyes meet mine, and today he's failing to hide his frustration even though only hours ago we made love. "I'm safeguarding *our* baby."

"What do the women do here?" I know the answer and want to hear him say it.

“You’re not Ularan.” He folds his arms over his chest. “They are used to giving birth with no medical intervention.”

“I’m here with you. I know you’ll look after me. I don’t want to waste time leaving for a few tests, then having to go through your self-enforced quarantine out there.” I point to the jungle where we hide out for days anytime we return to the camp. “That scares me. It’s unhealthy.”

His eyes widen. I should take his blood pressure.

“And you think your being here isn’t a risk to our baby? To you?”

“Maybe, but here women do it all the time, so I’m staying with the man I love,” I say with emphasis, almost desperate.

Samuel runs a hand over his cheek. “Your being here concerns me. I’m distracted, and so is shaman by Kaikare’s emotions that have stirred since you’ve arrived.”

I slide off the table and stand before him, so he has to look me square in the eye. “Fine. Blame me. Do you want me to leave?”

“No,” he says the word so I barely hear him. “No, because I need you here more than I realize. I have purpose and feel like a person again.” He leans his forehead against mine. “I’m sorry. I didn’t intend for my words to sound like you’re a problem. Only I’m surprised by how stressed I am about you and our baby’s well-being. I’m afraid if something goes wrong, I’ll be incapable of helping you. And the idea of failing you both will destroy me.”

I wrap my arms around his middle and rest my cheek on his hard chest. I let out a sigh when his arms snake around my back, pulling me closer to him. “I didn’t come here for you to protect me. I came here because it was the right thing to do. I need to be with you and will adapt and do whatever it takes to stay.”

For how long, I’m unsure. All I know is I want to be with Samuel as I’m a stronger person when I’m with him. Today, I’m brave, and I’m ready to take steps to remain in Ulara and have my baby here just like my grandmother. I blow out air slowly.

Shit. Is that a commitment I’m ready to make?

“Are we having dinner in the long house tonight?” I ask, ready to change the subject.

Samuel kisses the top of my head. “We are. The shaman will tell a story about a Kanaima spirit and why some crops were lost.”

“Well, they can’t blame me for the weather.”

When Samuel says nothing to reassure me, I squeeze my arms

tighter. Maybe there's more to his concern than he's letting on. Maybe I look to him to protect me.

"PLEASE STOP," I whisper to Samuel.

I didn't want Samuel to translate the story further. It began in a roundabout way with the mountain spirit of the dead being unhappy, and the rain resulted from his unhappiness. I sit between Samuel's legs with my head resting on his chest. I look around the gathering of Ularans, all eyes on the shaman, the star attraction wearing his red-feathered headdress like a king would a crown. They believe every word that comes from his mouth. He's a healer, so they have no reason to doubt his word when, as Samuel has told me, he has performed miracles beyond what Samuel can medically explain.

Tonight, the shaman's voice is louder than his calm, talking voice yet not theatrical. His tone has picked up an octave but not in emotion. He's always cool-tempered. I don't know if it's the herbs because I seriously don't understand how these people can be so calm all the time.

Acceptance.

This is how it is, and they accept it.

I feel sorry for the pregnant women and teenagers with raging hormones. Glancing around the semi-circle, I find the young girl who I saw with a boy beyond the field all those months ago. I assume it's her because she's staring at the boy sitting across from her in the circle.

The shaman lifts both arms and looks to the heavens after finishing his tale about a Kanaima. "A-pantoní-pe nichii." *May you take advantage of this story.*

People stand from a seated cross-legged position. The families regroup and file toward their huts. I watch the teenage girl head off alone. The boy watches her as well.

"I need to pee," I tell Samuel.

"Do you want me to come with you?"

"No. I'm okay."

She walks in, and I follow a few steps and stop, afraid to venture further. Unlike the Ularans, my night vision sucks.

Rustles shift the leaves ahead of me.

Their moans are so quiet anyone further away wouldn't hear it over the jungle squawks and clicking insects.

I remain deathly still, listening for any sign of—

What am I listening for? The sound of lovers having sex? Because it's none of my business. It's against the rules, and like me, this couple is taking a risk to be together in a forbidden love affair. What I guess I'm listening for is if he's forcing her to have sex with him because she doesn't look much older than fifteen. Maybe both are underage by Western society standards, but not here. They accept love when it's done the right way. And I'm sure his hammock isn't hanging in this young girl's family hut.

I guess it proves that not all Ularans agree with the rules set by the shaman and chief. It mightn't be my business, but if they are caught, I *care* about the consequences inflicted upon them.

4

EDEN

TODAY I DIDN'T WAKE up in a film of sweat.

A small win.

It's late October, and the rainy season is hopefully over, and to think Christmas is only eight weeks away.

Christmas.

My mind works around the date out of habit as it's the hotel's busiest period. Only I had planned on staying here for Christmas with Samuel and leaving immediately after, only days before I was thirty-six weeks pregnant. There's an underlying urgency in booking a return flight as my travel requires permission from authorities after that date. Unless I have special permission from an obstetrician to certify I'm low risk.

There's no indication of a complicated pregnancy, and I intend to stay as long as possible. I miss home, but leaving Samuel isn't something I want to think about, so I open Gran's diary and read the words of her past. She taught me to be grateful for small things, and right now, her words connect me to home.

30TH JANUARY 1960

It has to be one of the hottest months ever. I can't think straight in my room. No air conditioning. No breeze. No wonder people have died in this heatwave. The thought of wearing that stiff uniform to work this afternoon makes me want to say I'm sick. Only it's more comfortable on the hospital ward than in my room.

I have one more month before I'm heading home to Adelaide to be with Albert.

15th May 1960

Today is the best day of my life, apparently, and yet here I am vomiting up my guts. My fault since I wasn't careful when I first arrived home in Adelaide.

Brenda is by my side to help me get through the day. I need her to tell me I'm doing the right thing.

I know I'm doing the 'right thing' for everyone else and my reputation, only is it what I truly want?

Brenda told me not to panic because everyone gets cold feet.

Shit. Was that my gran's wedding day? Her *reputation*. I inhale hot air and allow myself a moment to absorb her words.

She was pregnant.

It seems she writes in the diary when she's troubled or unsure. It's not an account of happier times except for the times she and Pop made out. Only I want to see those happier times. I want to know my grandparents were happy together, at least for some of their lives. If not, I'm unsure if I want to keep reading.

16th December 1960

Our baby is due next month. I can barely walk from the kitchen chair to the bedroom, and all Albert is worried about is the fact the Aussies drew with the West Indies in a test match in Brisbane.
When he was yelling at the television, I wanted to cry. Why can't he be that supportive of me?
I let out a sob, understanding her frustration. "Oh, Gran," I murmur and rest my hand on the swell of my stomach. If only I could hug her one more time.

11TH APRIL *1961*

I barely sleep.
Winston cries all the time.
I've tried everything for colic, and nothing works.
Winston and I sleep in the same room since we know Albert is tired from working the motel and needs to be up at five every morning.
I've never felt more alone, even more than on my first day arriving in Melbourne and knowing no one. This is much worse, and I feel like no one cares.

If only I could tell her that Pop cared. They didn't expect men in those times to help around the house, but he did love her.

I can't read anymore today. Placing the diary in my sack, I slip on my runners. There's been no rain for three days, and I want to go for a walk, maybe to the fields, even though Samuel insisted I stay in the long house and help prep the vegetables. At twenty-eight weeks, I'm still capable of helping some, although the rate my baby is growing has surprised me. I smile and run my hand over the swell of my stomach. I'm not short, and Samuel is more than six feet, so our baby won't be small.

Kaikare stands when I reach the long house. She says something to the lady squatting beside her stirring a pot of water before coming to my side. She takes my hand, and we walk to the other end of the village. The lack of communication is getting to me—an annoying barrier between us.

Does the shaman prefer it that way?

I know he loves Kaikare, and in the community, love is important.

No matter the curiosity eating at her about her mother, she grew up loved and in a safe environment. It's more than some of my affluent friends.

It dawns on me it could be why Samuel has spoken little about his parents and his life in LA. I know they are wealthy, yet he refuses to talk about them.

He deflects all his energy to Ulara and is in denial about his previous life. Before now, I didn't question it, I abided by the rules, and my reward was to stay longer. Only now, I have a ticking time bomb inside me.

Why is he scared to leave?

What happened for him to come here and hide away?

I'm not accepting that he's a workaholic or career-minded or that it's his contract, and he wants to find a cure for some disease. Something happened for him to be like this, and I'm so mad at myself for not seeing it sooner.

I let out a little sigh with the realization.

Kaikare stops walking and lands a gentle hand on my shoulder with a questioning look on her face.

"I'm fine," I say quickly, even though she doesn't understand. So, I smile and keep walking, despite not knowing where she's taking me.

We reach the village edge, and she leads me into the jungle. Vines choke the trees that are so tall they almost touch the heavens. We pass a tree crawling with bullet ants before she leads me into a garden of orchids and other brightly colored flowers.

I've been here before.

We continue along a narrow path where the vines reach out like fingers as though trying to touch us. Then I hear the shaman's song. His voice thrills me with the sensation of life. It's a sound that wraps you in a secure blanket, and you feel safe, relaxed, and euphoric. We continue until we find him and Samuel in a herb garden. I walk past strategically placed wooden signs, all an arm's length long with identifiable names painted on the wood.

"Eden." Samuel comes to me. He smiles from ear to ear. "How are you feeling?"

"I'm fine. If there's something wrong, I'll tell you." I squeeze his hand. "Please stop worrying about me." I point to the garden. "Did you make the signs?"

"Yes." He takes my hand, and we walk a few steps to the first sign.

Banisteriiopsis Caapi. Underneath it reads *Ayahuasca vine*.

Next is *Psychotria Viridis.* Underneath reads *Chacruna DMT*.

I smile at him. "This is where you grow your plants for the special tea?"

"Some, yes." He takes my hand and leads me to a deep purple flower growing on top of stones with minimal soil. "This is the flower I picked from the tepui when I left you…" he stalls on the last word. "I sent samples away and kept some. Despite the rain, it has survived. It's a breakthrough." His gaze is fixed on the plant as though it's a million dollars left on the ground for someone to find.

The shaman continues to sing from behind us, and I turn to see Kaikare picking the vine. "Another ceremony?"

"The warriors are heading out on a hunt. They haven't eaten meat in weeks."

"Will more boys be initiated?"

"Not tonight."

"Good. I don't have the stomach to sit through that kind of ceremony," I murmur.

"Are you nauseous?" His beautiful eyes study my face.

"No more than I was back home in the first trimester." My hand lifts to my stomach and rubs gently as though to calm my child. Samuel's gaze lowers and lands where my hand rests.

"Have you thought any more about taking a visit to Ciudad Guayana?"

"We can chat about it tonight among other things."

"About a hospital visit?"

"No." I steel myself, ready for his reaction. "About your family."

His eyes meet mine, and there's a fury there I've never seen before. "I told you before my family isn't up for discussion."

"And since our child has your family's blood pumping through his or her veins, it's up for discussion. I don't want to skirt around this anymore."

I follow Samuel's gaze over my shoulder. Only now do I realize the shaman has stopped singing.

"Here isn't the place," he says in a softer tone. "We'll talk later."

"Yes, you will." I give him a look that my father used to give me when I needed pulling into line.

Kaikare walks over and takes my hand. A smile is on her face. I know she smiles a lot. Is it because I'm standing up to the men?

I'm in the hammock, clutching my grandmother's diary when Samuel enters the hut. He creeps around, seemingly unaware my eyes are open and watching him. His blond hair is ruffled like I have run my fingers through it, and I imagine him doing just that as he concentrates or right before he decides on something. I'll never tire of simply looking at him. Admiring him. Even the way the muscles in his back contract when he moves those glorious arms. His long legs, muscular but lean thighs and calves like a marathon runner—they are so lickable.

It would be an effort to get back up when I'm on the ground, but still, it would be worth it.

Samuel rearranges objects on the bench before turning, creeping a few steps, and freezes. "I'm sorry, did I wake you?"

"I wasn't asleep. Only resting before I help with dinner. I was appreciating the view."

"Are you up to it?"

I raise my eyebrows. He misunderstood the view as meaning beyond the hut to the jungle.

"You don't have to help if you're tired."

"I do what I'm allowed to prepare." Which isn't a hell of a lot since I'm still earning their trust. "Come here." I pat the hammock where I lie. "I want to ask you something."

"Does it affect you and me?"

"It could in the future." My gaze travels down his sun-kissed body from his hard pecs to his washboard abs where his grass skirt sits low on his hips and the indented 'V' points below the band of the skirt.

"If you keep looking at me..." he clears his throat, "... we won't be talking."

"No. We talk first." I lift my arm to motion for him to come beside me. "Lay with me."

His expression is apprehensive, yet he comes to me and slides into the hammock with it barely swaying.

"Tell me about your life."

"My life?" he rasps on the last word. "Why?"

"Because I want to get to know the father of my baby."

His brow pulls tight. "You already do, more so than anyone else alive."

"I only know Samuel, who gives everything he has to make others happy. The man who has dedicated his life to work in a primitive community whose inhabitants don't know the world beyond the jungle."

"This is who I am... now." He kisses my cheek and snuggles into my shoulder as though he needs to rest. "You don't need to know anything else."

But I do.

"What if I ask a question, and you answer it the best way you can? If it's too hard, then you say pass. That way, you don't have to start any conversation."

He grumbles something, and I swear it's a curse in another language. "I'll make a deal. You get to ask questions if I can take you to Ciudad Guayana."

"Fine," I say, even though I have no intention of leaving here unless it's absolutely necessary. I take a deep breath and then start with something easy—something I know will get him talking.

"Who were your best friends in college?"

It must have hit a chord because he remains quiet for a moment before answering, "Carter. Brant. And you already met Michael, Sean, and Harrison."

I want to groan at the sound of Michael's name. We haven't discussed him since I have returned, and I want to remind him he's barely a friend after the stunt he pulled in Peru. "First girlfriend in high school or college?"

"In high school, it was Sienna. I didn't have girlfriends in college." He stiffens beside me.

"No dates, or did you just have friends with benefits?"

He remains quiet for a moment.

"It's okay. We've all done things we regret."

He gives me a dark look, one that implies I wouldn't understand. "What mistakes did you make?"

"You know about Ethan." I stare up at the bamboo beams supporting the thatched grass. "And my trust issues. Coming here to be with you was a big step for me." I pause for a moment and swallow the lump at the back of my throat that grows with the memory of when Ethan killed my faith in guys. A part of me died that day. "But I trust you." I swivel so I can see his eyes. His eyes tell me what he's thinking, so I need to see how he reacts when I say the next sentence. "It was one of the most challenging things I've had to do. I took a risk, hurt others, yet in my gut, and even though I was scared of so much going wrong, I knew I had to take a giant leap and be with you."

His eyes hold mine, and in those bright baby blue hues, appreciation swirls. Only I can sense he's holding back.

"You were always a good person, Eden. No matter what shit went down or how hurt you were, you were the good person."

"Well, yeah—"

"I wasn't," he says it bluntly as though I wouldn't understand. "I was the guy you'd hate."

"I doubt it."

He brushes my cheek with the back of his hand. "If you attended the same college as me, then we wouldn't be together. I'd probably be doing my damnedest to hit on you because back then, all I did was fuck girls."

My breath hitches at his harsh tone. Only I don't react because he's waiting for me to do just that. Show the shock on my face. "I was familiar with fucking," I whisper. It's a white lie as I've only been with a couple of guys.

He chuckles lightly as though he knows it's not true. "You weren't familiar with my type. If you were, then you'd have run far away from the likes of me."

"But many didn't..."

"No. Many didn't," he says in a strangled voice.

His eyes become distant as though he's recalling a memory.

"Did you have any feelings for some of them? Want it to be more?"

He squints with a hint of humor in his eyes. "Feelings? Only the sexual kind where I'd fuck them again. I recall Michael and I having a limit. Ten times with a certain girl, and then no matter how good she was in bed, ten was a hard limit. Then, with no explanation, I'd stop talking to her."

"That's rough." I tilt up and search his face for a sign of remorse. Only he's a closed book, wearing the mask he wore when I first met him in Brazil all those months ago.

"I was more than rough," he says in almost a growl. "And I never *slept* with any of them. Trust me when I tell you, you don't want to know the younger version of me."

He pushes up, throws his leg over the edge of the hammock, and I reach to stop him. My hand tightens around his wrist. "Please don't go. I want to know about the young Samuel McMahon. He's still part of you even though you have... transformed." I couldn't think of a better word.

"I've worked tirelessly not to be that person." His elbows rest on his knees, and I'm forced to release him. Samuel brings his hands to his face and rubs like he's expelling a memory.

"I'm sure they forgave you."

He groans into his hands.

"It's only sex, Samuel."

"I made a promise to one girl, and I never had sex with her." He pushes off the hammock and strides away. "It was a point in time I was lower than life. I had the blood of a demon in my veins."

"Wait." I scramble out and go to him.

Samuel hunches over the bench with his back to me.

"You're not a bad person, so what is it that has you putting space between us?"

His head hangs low between his arms, outstretched on the bench. "I'm disgusted with myself when I think back to what I did. And I don't want to talk about it. Can't without feeling nauseous." His voice is cut with a rasp.

I rub my hand in circles over his back. It's progress, and I know there's something stopping him from wanting to leave Ulara. For my sake and our baby's sake, I have to dig deeper. "Did you sort it out at all?"

"Not before she took her own life," he murmurs.

My hand stalls on his back before I consciously continue in a slower action. "You can't blame yourself."

"No. My friends and I were to blame. Now, can we please stop talking about this? As I said, I'm no longer the same person." He glances over his shoulder but won't turn to look at me.

"It's healthy to talk," I say gently.

"You mean repent. And I have done it over and over when drinking ayahuasca. I don't need to do it again." He straightens and pushes off the bench before striding past me toward the door.

"Where are you going?"

He freezes with his back to me. "In the garden to fucking cry. And no, I don't want you to come with me. It's something I need to do alone."

"No one has to cry alone." My heart breaks for him, especially that he believes he can't cry about this in front of me. I wrap my arms around his back and rest my cheek on the spot where his heart beats inside his chest. "Please stay with me."

He doesn't move. His entire body is stiff, so I take his hand and tug gently to guide him back to the hammock. Keeping hold of his hand, I clamber in, and he follows my lead. He curls up beside me, his head on my shoulder. I take his hand and place it on my lower stomach. "No matter what, we will always love you."

"I buried that life a long time ago and refuse to be that person," he croaks. "I know what you're thinking, though I'm more disgusted with myself than anyone else could be. Telling you, the one person who loves me for me..." his voice cracks. "With everything else going on in my head, I'm not ready to tell you everything."

I keep stroking and holding him, but my mind is whirling. How can I do this—give birth to a child with a man I'm still getting to know?

Closing my eyes, I force the thought out. Of course, I can do this. I don't need years behind us to know he's the man for me. His past will not dictate our future. I also refuse to go back in time to being the weak woman I was before I met him. Together, we're stronger, and I can handle all he has to reveal. I need to if we're to move forward—together.

5

SAMUEL

Eden has bewitched Samuel.

He always knew the power of her love. Only tonight, she unearthed a crippling memory of his former self he'd kept locked away for years. Eden tried to pry it from him with loving tentacles, and the metal walls surrounding his heart melted like mercury. Raw and exposed, he wanted to run to his safe place in the shaman's garden and curl up in a ball until the sound of the shaman's voice released him from the hell playing over in his mind.

A time will come when he'll need to confess the horror of his past and why he was so screwed up living in his entitled world. He'd like to think he was brainwashed, but it wasn't so simple. He made choices and openly followed his friends and acted just like them without remorse for the consequences.

Until *Inesa*. She opened his mind and heart. Only it was too late to make it up to her. His apologetic words were meaningless. Her friends called her Nessie, and he had no right to call her by an affectionate title known to a select few. Yet, he hears Nessie's voice over and over in his head. He relives the tears and hears wails when her friends mourned her name. It took every ounce of his courage to attend her funeral alone. Samuel's friends declared their innocence to fuel any thoughts of her mental destruction. In the brief time he got to speak with Inesa, he could see how wrong they were.

Inesa instilled the power in him to change.

Eden has greater control over his soul, more so than anyone, including himself. Her power scares him more than any danger that lurks in the rainforest, not even the jungle herself.

"STAY WITH ME TONIGHT. I'm not up to eating any more yuca. Can I just have pizza?"

Samuel chuckles. "Capsicum and pineapple on flat yuca bread?"

"Funny." Her hand lingers at the curve of her pregnant body.

"Is everything okay?" He lifts her chin and directs her gaze to his.

"Yeah. I'm tired." Her hands wrap around his body. Her soft cheek presses against his chest, so he's forced to release her and rest his hands lightly on her shoulders.

"Would you like to lie down? I can fetch some fruit so you can snack on some food here."

"I'd love some fruit, please. And can you check if Kaikare has some of her special tea?" She walks to the hammock. Samuel assists her by lifting her feet for her to settle in the swing.

Samuel leaves to gather the fruit and bread and finds Kaikare. "Eden is eating in our hut and asked for some of your special tea," he says in their native tongue.

Kaikare's eyes convey concern. Samuel places a hand on her shoulder understanding the two of them are close and explains she's tired, and it's natural for her to be so.

He returns with loaded palm leaves, including one carrying warmed fish, yet he can't shake the concern at the back of his mind that Eden isn't getting enough nutrition with her body being unacquainted with the rainforest. He's proud of her determination to be like the other Ularan ladies. The moment it conflicts with her well-being and their baby's safety, he'll intervene.

Eden pushes up in the hammock and uses her stomach as a table to rest some of the food on. "Do you remember the young couple? The lovers I told you about?" She bites pieces of fruit and waits to swallow before continuing, "I've noticed them together on several occasions and yesterday saw them holding hands near the fields. I think she was crying."

"Kapeá Tapire was crying?"

"Is that her name?"

Samuel slides in next to her, holding the palm leaf with the fish. "Yes, it is. And you should eat this."

"I don't think I can stomach it." She lifts a hand to her mouth.

"You don't have to eat it, although you haven't eaten protein in a while, which furthers my argument about us taking a trip to Ciudad Guayana for blood tests."

"There's a story about the young couple, isn't there?" she asks, changing the subject.

"There is." He takes the palm leaves from her and springs from the hammock.

"Wait." Eden pushes up onto her elbows, and the hammock wobbles. "I want to know."

Samuel chuckles and throws the palms outside. He seals the netting and takes his place beside her, curling in so he can take her in his arms.

Eden lifts her head to get comfortable and sighs. "I thought you were going to leave and not tell me."

He kisses her cheek and smiles. "There's nowhere else I'd rather be."

"Ha." She slaps his chest. "Tell me about the secret lovers."

"It's not so much a secret. Everyone simply turns a blind eye."

"I knew it."

"Okay, Detective Monteford, let me know when you're ready to hear the story."

Eden rolls her eyes. "Go ahead."

Samuel can't hide his smirk. "Her lover, Mari' Iwoi, was from the Watache tribe."

"Wait. Isn't that the bad tribe? The cannibals everyone fears?"

"Yes, and yet the real power is here. In the parameters of the village, you have nothing to fear, and you'll most likely never see a Watache warrior."

"Warrior? Are they the only ones who venture out?"

"Yes, usually to hunt."

"How did he come to be in Ulara?"

"By circumstance after a sacrifice. He was brought here by one of the women when he was left in the rainforest as a newborn. A sacrifice to their god, but our shaman and chief debated on what should happen to him."

"Really?"

He pulls her close to his side and kisses the crown of her head. "Mari' Iwoi translates to 'dancing snake,' a name the women gave him. At first, he wasn't to be trusted, and yet he was a content baby. Kaikare told me he moved his limbs a lot and giggled at the sound of their voices."

"Such weird names."

"Says the tortoise."

She punches him in the arm, and he chuckles. "What about the girl?"

"Kapeá Tapire was born on a red moon. It's what her name translates to."

"It doesn't explain the secrecy."

"Kapeá Tapire was promised to someone else. A jaguar attacked and killed the young man a few years back."

"A jaguar," she croaks.

"Again, it's something we rarely see, yet they do venture close. Everyone turns a blind eye, so to speak, as they believe their physical attraction is the spirits' doing. A Kanaima messing with the Ularans. Kapeá and Mari' are... cursed in their minds, and many believe what happens between them is the business of the gods."

"They hide their affair, and yet they probably don't need to?"

"They need to out of respect until the shaman gives his blessing, and then Mari' Iwoi moves his hammock into Kapeá Tapire's family hut."

"When will the shaman give his blessing?"

"Not until the jungle speaks to him. It's why he wants another ceremony as he says the jungle is talking about an unhappy balance."

Eden rests her cheek on Samuel's shoulder. "I'm glad the jungle approved of us."

Samuel closes his eyes and nods. He can no longer imagine his life without Eden.

THE FOLLOWING MORNING, Samuel wakes early and creeps around the hut so as not to wake Eden. He understands her fatigue and the need for her to get adequate rest. He'd love nothing more than to lie with her, pretend it's a lazy Sunday, and spoon her until she stirs.

"Hey," she murmurs.

He stills and turns to check on her. "I was trying not to wake you."

"Our baby has been moving all night and kept me awake."

Samuel goes to her and places his hand on her abdomen. "Do you feel okay?"

"Ah-ha." She places her hand over his. "It wasn't just our baby. I had a dream last night and need to know about the Watache tribe, so I won't fabricate my own version of cannibalism."

Samuel takes Eden's hand in his, raises it to his lips, and kisses her knuckles. "I'll let nothing happen to you. Now come." He eases her up and out of the hammock and then guides Eden to the treatment table. "I'll tell you how it was explained to me." He takes the clay pot containing the balm and rubs it over her shoulders and neck. Her little moans remind him how much he loves her. He massages circles, his need building with each one, more and more.

"Were they always bad?"

Eden brings him back to the present, and he takes a moment to compose himself. "My interpretation is the stories originated in the early 1700s, but I could be wrong. The shaman described the Watache tribe as being descendants of an ancestral tribe known as the Kariña—famous for their violence because they were not good communicators. The Ularans are descendants of the Pemón, and the Pemón, Macuxi, and Kariña tribes are all descendants of the same tribe from hundreds of years ago. But the folk tales say the Kariña didn't develop the peaceful characteristics of the Pemón people. The Kariña believed they were the only 'true' people, and outsiders were considered unintelligent, animal-like, and inhuman if they didn't speak the same language. The phonics differed between tribes, and this language barrier gave reason for the Kariña to believe other tribes were not human and were therefore dangerous and should be hunted. They hunted foreigners like animals and ate the flesh of people outside their tribe."

"Oh my god." She shakes her head.

He rests a hand on her shoulder for reassurance. "They believed eating their victim was magic, and it gave them a sense of spiritual power. The Kariña believed the person's soul would remain in their body after consummation. Feeling indestructible, the Kariña would attack other tribes, accessing the villages by river. All tribes in the surrounding areas feared the Kariña, which, in return, gave them more power. In their mind, they were not eating other human beings as only actual people spoke the same language as them."

"I can't imagine ever having to eat another person," she murmurs.

He moves to her front and massages the balm along her arms. "My point is they didn't intentionally eat humans."

She shrugs. "They decide someone isn't human because they talk differently and yet they have the same appearance. It's messed up."

"No more so than anywhere else. We have more monsters in what we think is a civilized world. This happened centuries ago, and stories are interpreted by the listener. Fear stems from what you want to believe."

Eden remains quiet for some time before she speaks again. "I'm thinking I should learn more Ularan words. Just the basics to help me get by when you're not around. I tried before, but I struggle to get my tongue around some phonics."

He chuckles lightly, and yet he's delighted she wants to learn their dialect. "I'll teach you a few more while I walk with you to the long house."

Beneath his delight, a dark thought lingers in her wanting to learn the language for safety reasons. Until now, his concern for Eden's well-being centered on her and their baby's health. He's aware their lives swing in a balance jeopardized by the things they can't see. It goes without saying dreams play a major role in this unique world, and maybe he should listen to Eden as her dreams could be a voice alerting her to the future.

Because he'd never forgive himself if anything happened to her.

6

EDEN

Two Days Later...

SWEAT DRIPS from my brow like a leaky tap.

I lean the axe on the ground while I flick beads of sweat from my forehead. The sun has shone all morning, and in the field's small clearing, I've relished the rays on my bare skin. I've removed the necklaces except for the one strand Kaikare made for me since all were too heavy for my shoulders and neck, especially with the added weight of Baby McMahon. Instead, I rely on my tangled locks to cover my breasts, but it fails, considering they have grown equally in size with my baby. How much I still care has surprised me. I'm fine here in the fields where many of the ladies, pregnant or not, don't cover-up. Yet when I'm around the men, I feel exposed, so I wear the beads at dinner but not out here.

Kaikare and I follow the line of women with woven baskets on their heads. We gather in the long house for lunch. There's a wild hunger in their eyes, and I hope the men will return with game to feed everyone in the village.

The teenage boys have caught a few monkeys over the past two weeks by hiding out in camouflaged cubby houses. Palm fronds built like a miniature tepee around their body conceals their presence. Inside the tiny space, they are armed with poison blowpipes and sit motionless for hours, hoping for a kill, providing a meal to prove they are worthy hunters.

When some teenage boys shout and kick a coconut along the ground, I recognize them as the young hunters. My shoulders fall in relief, happy they have returned empty-handed today. I'll never get used to the thought of eating monkey.

"Kuwata?" I ask Kaikare. I was quick to learn the word for monkey so I could decline the meat if offered.

"Awarö." She bows her head. *Bad.*

Wakü, I think to myself. *Good.*

"Oo?" She hands me the bread made from yuca.

"Waküpe-küruman." *Thank you.*

Her slim lips turn into a broad smile.

In the dirt, I draw a snake with a forked tongue and stripes. She studies it a moment. I tell her, "Snake."

"Iwoi," she replies. I repeat the word in my head.

Next, I draw a spider, remembering my encounter with a wandering spider in a bunch of bananas. "Spider."

"Spi-der," Kaikare repeats, and then adds, "Mojowai."

I say it over and over in my head. "Mojowai awarö." *Spider bad.*

"Are you asking for a list of everything you fear?" Samuel stands close by with a grin on his face. Damn him and his stealth skills that let him appear like a ghost.

"Did I tell you about the time a wandering spider almost bit me? It happened while you were away on your journey."

"Almost?" His eyes widen, and he crouches to listen to my story.

I tell him how Kaikare saved me and how freaked out I was to have my hand close to its fangs.

"I'm glad she was there, especially as we don't have an anti-venom here."

"Jesus, Samuel." I shake my head to rid the stressful thoughts coming to mind.

"The venom is toxic to the nervous system, and in men, a bite can cause a painful erection for days as the venom boosts nitric oxide, which increases blood flow. Then, sexual dysfunction can be for life if the poison doesn't kill you first."

"Seriously, what the hell am I doing here?" I raise my arms and act more dramatically than I intended.

Samuel raises a brow and waits a moment before I drop my arms to my side. "Do you have poisonous spiders in Australia?"

"Well, yeah, of course. It's Australia." Duh.

"No different from here, Eden."

My shoulders heave with a sigh. Every day I wait, and it's not with sugar-coated hope for Samuel to say he'll leave Ulara to be with me. It's glazed with fear that something bad will happen. Samuel's journey to the Ayuan Tepui hasn't gone unnoticed among the Ularans. I see it in their eyes. Only one warrior was brave enough to travel with him to the house of the devil—the home of Mawarí spirits. Will there be repercussions for upsetting the spirits?

"Hey." He waits for me to meet his caring gaze. "I think we'll take that trip to Ciudad next week, okay?"

"Okay," I say without argument. Kaikare is turning her head every time one of us speaks as though she's at a tennis match. She places a hand on my back, and I rest my head on her shoulder.

"Tamu'ne Akare wakü," I tell her. *White tortoise is good.*

"You're doing fine," Samuel says in a low, gentle voice. I don't miss the concern in his eyes. "You don't have to go back to the fields this afternoon."

"I enjoy spending time with her. Besides, I don't know how much longer I can work, and I want to prove my worth. The rate our baby is growing, I might be basket weaving with the men."

"That will be a first since it's not women's work." He grins. "Though, with you, anything is possible."

AFTER A COUPLE of hours of working in the fields, the girl who sneaks off with her lover, Kapeá Tapire, catches my eye when she wanders past the banana palms and into the rainforest. I grab Kaikare's attention, point to the trees, and then follow the girl since I also need to pee.

Vines slash my wrists as I forge a path in an attempt to be out of sight. My name suits me now as I move almost as slow as a tortoise, which is why I lost sight of Kapeá Tapire. Finding a large Kapok tree, I squat beside it and watch the ground for anything that crawls near my feet.

"Ahh." The wail doesn't sound far away. Is it Kapeá Tapire? Is she okay? I finish peeing and weave around a few trees, walking as fast as I can toward the sound. She crouches, one hand on the ground, the other holding her stomach. There's movement behind her, but I don't see who it is.

She continues to weep, so I make my way to her and rest my palm on her back. "Kapeá Tapire wakü?" *Kapeá Tapire good?*

She raises her chin so her eyes meet mine. My heart sinks at the tears in her eyes. The Ularans don't feel emotions and not to this degree.

I asked if she was good, and knowing she's not, I'm lost as to how to communicate further.

"Are you hurt?" I ask, hoping my tone conveys meaning.

I'm barely capable of maneuvring to a full squat, so I lower myself with one hand on the tree for support. Her gaze lowers to my rounded stomach. She bursts into tears and runs the opposite way to the fields crying uncontrollably. Overhead, the sky turns dark, and a rumble sounds in the distance. This isn't good. I follow her, but I'm too slow to keep up.

"Kapeá Tapire," I call, pushing past several palm fronds. A loud crack and I scream, bobbing for cover. Within seconds, heavy sheets of water fall to blur everything beyond a few feet in front of me.

Bloody hell.

I raise my hands to my brow and try to work out which way to turn to find my way back to the field. I pivot a full 360 degrees and move to stand under the largest tree closest to me. Useless when the branches act like a waterfall, and I near drown when I look up. The already saturated ground has barely a chance to soak in the water, and it's pooling everywhere. I slush through the murky puddles with my head down and no idea if I'm walking toward the village.

"Samuel," I scream at the top of my lungs. Another *crack,* and my voice is smothered by thunder.

"Ahh." I turn in the direction of the scream. It has to be Kapeá Tapire. I need to find my way back to the village for safety—to Samuel. But I can't leave her out here. Not alone. Not like this. I keep my head down, concentrating on every step so I don't slip and fall.

"I'm coming," I call back when the rain eases as quickly as it fell.

They appear out of nowhere like ghosts from behind the trees. Dark-skinned bodies with red-painted faces, so I can only see their eyes. The red paint continues down to their torso. A stick is pierced through each nose like a trademark to what tribe they belong. Long arrows point at my throat, a warning not to scream. Behind them, I make out Kapeá Tapire on the ground, her hands and feet being tied to bamboo, then three men lift the bamboo to their shoulders, and she's carried like a wild animal.

"Stop!" I scream and raise my hand.

Spears jut closer to my throat.

A taller man steps forward and eyes me. He speaks a different dialect and waves his hand to the men carrying Kapeá Tapire. She moans with the impact when they drop her to the ground. I turn toward the movement I see in my peripheral vision.

I hear the thump of stone on my skull before I feel it.

7

SAMUEL

After working in the shaman's medicinal garden, Samuel makes his way to the long house to search for Eden. He assumes she's resting in the hammock as the downpour ceased work in the fields. He intends to tell her not to overdo it to prove her merit when a high-pitched wail and more wails in a chant-like sequence have his feet moving quicker in the direction of the chief's hut.

Kaikare runs to him with panic in her voice, her words tripping over the other in near hysteria. His heart speeds up. She's not previously acted like this, not even when a jaguar stole one of their own. He raises his hands, trying to calm the alarm spreading in the village.

Kaikare pants as if she's hyperventilating. Samuel places a hand on her shoulders. "Awarö?" *Bad?*

She nods. "Watache Tamu'ne Akare."

"Jesus." He runs his hand through his hair and turns a full circle. He doesn't know which way to run. Why? How? None of it matters. He takes a few quick breaths to clear his thoughts. He points to the river.

She shakes her head vehemently before pointing to the jungle and then to Kapeá Tapire, who's huddled in Mari' Iwoi's arms by the cooking fire.

Samuel sprints over to her and asks what happened.

She stops sobbing and nods. "Areku wokyry." *Angry men*. She shakes her hands and points to her feet, showing Samuel how they tied her to a pole. "Konopo Tamu'ne Akare." *Eden appeared out of the rain.*

"Watache topu upùpo." She acts out being hit in the head with a rock.

Samuel's eyes widen. "Tamu'ne Akare's upùpo?" *Eden's head*?

She nods and tells him it was under the two rubber trees.

Confirming the area, Samuel takes off into the jungle, swatting unruly vines and sharp branches aside. Is she unconscious? He turns when a chant comes from behind him, several warriors on his heels, jabbing spears to the heavens.

An old wound opens with the memory of failing someone when he is in a position to help. The scar will always be there.

Wayara meets Samuel's stride. With longer legs and his elite track training in college, Samuel is the fastest of the Ularans. He struggles for every breath, his throat tightening in fear—still, he wills his body to run faster, to find the strength.

He slows to a walk as they approach the two large trees that tower high amongst the canopy. Wayara holds out his hands to stop further movement and leans over to inspect the ground. Samuel spins and listens for the jungle to alert him of alien movement.

"Pona sakùne," Wayara tells him and points to the puddles. *Seven men.*

There are signs of a struggle—several muddy footprints and scattered yellow beads that were around Eden's ankle.

Samuel does not know where the Watache village is located, and although the Ularans are peacemakers and keep to themselves, the warriors are spies for the chief. "Do you know where the village is?" he asks Wayara in Ularan.

Wayara tells him to follow the river path for two days and walk west for one. If they haven't moved camp.

"Fuck," Samuel screams to the trees. He falls to his knees and stifles a sob. "No, please, no."

The men circle him, chanting the same syllables he's never heard sung before. The spears shake toward the tepui, but the Mawarí spirit isn't to blame. Eden was in the wrong place at the wrong time, and Samuel wasn't there to protect her like he'd promised he would be. He closes his eyes and visualizes her face. In his mind, he searches for her soul in the depths of the jungle. His third eye sees his outstretched hand reaching into the darkness, his every nerve on alert seeking her energy. He needs a spark of hope. The black jaguar with the blue eyes growls only inches from his face. He topples back onto his rear.

He may have disappointed her grandmother, and yet it's the hope he seeks. Ivy's spirit is in the jungle.

Wayara gets up in his face, bringing him back, telling Samuel he thinks they can follow their tracks.

The one thing they have going for them is Eden will slow up the Watache men unless they don't care about her well-being. He pushes out the thought before his mind is trampled with images of them hurting her.

The men head back to the village to gather supplies and form a plan along with advice from the shaman.

"Wayara," Samuel calls out, and he won't apologize for his overbearing tone. He points to the ground inside the long house and draws a map of the tepuis, the rivers, Angel Falls, and Ulara. The men lean in, expressions of wonder on their faces at his knowledge of the land that stretches for hundreds of miles. He hands Wayara the stick and asks him to mark where the Watache village is located.

Samuel studies the location and rushes back to the paper map he hides in his briefcase. He spreads it out on the treatment table, and hope allows his chest to expand as he runs his finger east along the Carrao River. It's a slow journey using paddles with no motor but quicker than going on foot.

He stuffs the map into his pack, grabs a first-aid pack, including antibiotics and some bottled water before meeting the warriors by the long house. The women shove bowls of food in the warriors' hands, their backs laddered with arrows, spears, and blowpipes. The shaman sings a song, one so sweet as though it will calm any anger, promote clear minds as to what's the right behavior, and remind the warriors that killing for revenge isn't wise. It could start a war—one they have avoided. They've experienced centuries of peace by remaining hidden from the world, including other Pemón descendants.

What has Samuel caused?

He lifts his gaze to the chief. Deep lines are etched around his eyes. The young warriors chant before him, testosterone unrestrained compared to the calm, older, and wiser men.

A dozen children carry a long curiara, one Samuel has never seen or used in fishing. Its faded paint looks decades old. The warriors carry it to the river, where they are out in the open exposed to the rest of the world. His heart weighs heavily at the cost of this journey to the Ularans. When out of sight of the chief, Samuel joins in the chant, his voice louder than any other.

He knows what he needs to do—fight for the one who owns his soul.

8

EDEN

WHEN MY EYES SHUDDER OPEN, I reach for the side of my head to where it throbs. Then the nausea hits me. I cringe with every jolt coursing along my spine as though I'm on a poorly engineered rollercoaster.

Treetops pass and the clouds roll by.

I lean onto one elbow and, for a moment, think I'm in Asoo's curiara, only smaller and with no planked seats. But I'm not smoothly sailing on water as I'm swamped by trees.

Squinting in pain, I want to call out to put me down. The bumpy ride creates a sharp vibration in my skull. Before I do I make out three figures ahead, their red-painted bodies, and then recall following Kapeá Tapire before being surrounded by these men.

A whimper escapes my throat, and I quickly smother it before I scream. *Shit. Shit. Shit.* Are they Watache?

I'm so bloody scared right now.

What am I going to do? My thoughts cloud as fear builds inside of me.

How am I going to escape? My gut is tight with panic and I'm breathing so fast it feels like I'm not getting any air.

My hand goes to my stomach and rubs reassuringly over the reason why I can't lose my shit.

I need to protect my baby.

Closing my eyes, I focus on slowing each breath. At this rate, I'll soon need a paper bag.

A single sob blurts out of me, and one of the men jogging ahead turns, and I duck before he sees I'm awake.

Thump.

Did someone just punch from underneath me?

God, my head is killing me.

I gently touch the side of my head and check my fingers for blood. It's sticky, and after dabbing my hair, I hope the bleeding has slowed. How long was I unconscious?

I should have stayed with Kaikare in the fields. No matter how scared I am I can't change the fact I'm in a situation and I need a plan.

To save my baby, I have to stay alive.

I can't escape. I couldn't take them on, and if I tried, well, then what? Even with a million-to-one chance of defeating these trained warriors, I'd be left to find my way home.

Think.

Assess.

As rough as the journey is, it's better than being slung like an animal to a pole or forced to walk endless miles. The only reassurance is Samuel *will* come looking for me. Until then, I need to stay alive and not do anything to provoke them.

Cannibals.

The explanation Samuel gave comes back to me.

Jesus.

Fear bubbles to the surface and disperses in waves over my body. A single quiver, then one after the other, and I can't control it. I'm curled on my side. My head bounces on one arm, the other under my stomach for support. My vision blurs with tears. Trees pass, one by one, nothing out of the ordinary, and nothing noteworthy to identify my location.

In a slow movement, I raise my leg to assess a sting on my calf. It's red from a graze, and my beaded anklet is gone.

Beads.

I touch the single strand of painted yellow and red beads on my chest.

Slowly, I rise onto an elbow and look around. Three men walk ahead of the men carrying me on their shoulders. No one walks behind.

Lifting the beads over my head, I pry the knotted ends apart with my teeth, slide several beads off the twine, and in a subtle movement, I throw one high in the air behind the canoe the men are carrying me in. I wait for the sound of it hitting a tree or the ground.

Nothing

And I couldn't be more grateful to the squawking creatures surrounding us. I wait for what seems like minutes before I toss another. It needs to be more strategic, so I count to five hundred before throwing the next and visualize Samuel finding the bead.

Clouds roll like a tumbleweed above me.

Shit.

If it rains, the beads will be washed away or be covered in muddy soot. I clamp my eyes shut and hug my baby. The negative voice in my head tells me this is in vain. I'll most likely die out here alone.

No. I make a silent vow to protect us.

My god, when was the last time my baby moved?

Rolling my palm over my stomach, I prod a couple of times and wait.

Please move. Please, please move.

Squeezing my eyes shut to stop the tears from coming, I try to clear my thoughts because I'd never forgive myself if anything happened to my unborn child. My only plan is to outwit these people because physical fighting or running is futile. I open my eyes to more sky from a clearing of trees. A potent stench of smoke makes me woozy for a moment. I cover my mouth.

Burned monkey fur. Ugh.

It doesn't smell like one or two monkeys. It's so strong it must be the whole damn howler monkey family.

Children scream with excitement.

I sigh in relief because I've always believed children are innocent until taught otherwise. And I hope they haven't watched someone die.

Yet.

The bounce in the capsule intensifies with the men running and screaming out a weird sound. With every reverberation of wood to my torso, I'm hit with another wave of nausea. My head continues to thump like a drum, so I wrap my arms around my head to protect my skull moments before I'm dropped to the ground.

The thud startles me, and I make an oomph sound combined with a groan, then reach for my stomach. Black hair framing red-painted faces block out the sky. Rounded white eyes peer down at me.

Several men shout in anger. "Stay calm. Stay calm," I murmur to myself. I refuse to speak loud enough for them to hear my alien words. Because of Samuel's story, I know I have to act as an equal but not disrespect them to stay alive.

Their eyes hold fear and curiosity. I lift my head in the slightest movement, and they jump back. I freeze when spears are jabbed at my face, back and forth in warning. Fear, I assume, is what provokes their anger—or maybe it's a protective reaction.

The Ularans were curious by my white hair, skin, and blue eyes. They had some reservations about my spirit and whether I was evil even with Samuel in the village. These people have no outside influence and could believe I'm a threat.

Shit.

What do I do now?

The one thing the Ularans admired was Samuel's height. Willing my legs to move after endless hours of being curled in the same position, I unfurl my limbs until I'm crouching. The women and children stumble back. The men hurl unusual sounds in abuse, and tone is all I can go by. I continue to unroll, one vertebra at a time until I'm standing, looking down on the crowd. The women are tiny compared to the men, and if not for their breasts, quite difficult to distinguish from one another. The man closest to me yells, his venomous yellow eyes appear possessed, so I crouch to be less threatening. I'm at eye level with his naval and can't help a gasp at how his penis is stretched and flattened against his stomach. Red twine is wrapped around his hips, securing it almost in strangulation.

Appearance. First impressions.

My thoughts cluster into one mess. A bead of sweat falls from my forehead. I will my heart to slow and concentrate on each breath to control the fight-or-flight response. I clench my fingers to hide the tremor, only it draws more shouting, and spears are raised toward my face. I imagine what Samuel would do, how he'd work through this. He taught me not to fear, to use my surroundings to my advantage.

"Upetoy," I say in a loud voice. *Friend.*

The women mumble something to me. Broken vowels spoken too quickly to comprehend. I focus on one lady with the least paint on her body.

"Waküperö." *Hello, how are you?*

She steps away from me as though I have singled her out, and the man standing beside her shouts, "Tamu'ne woryi awarö." *White woman bad.*

"Tamu'ne woryi wakü," I reply. *White woman good.*

A sudden movement at the back of my audience has them stepping apart like a zipper. Red, blue and yellow feathers strewn into a crown bob toward me. A leader. A shaman or chief. Either way, I know to stay on my knees and bow my head. I sneak a glance when the last man steps aside. A dozen long sticks protrude from the leader's cheeks like whiskers.

My throat tightens.

His face blurs as the tears well in my eyes.

Don't show fear.

I lower my gaze without bowing my head to keep him in my peripheral vision. My heart thumps in my chest. It beats so hard the pain in my head worsens. I'm doing what I can not to let the fear bubble to the surface, knowing he's staring at me, determining my fate.

Focus on one thing.

Feathers are sewn together in a cape, draped over his shoulders and falls to his knees. One red and one yellow feather threaded through each ear lobe protrude at odd angles.

Is he a bird spirit?

The shaman.

My baby moves inside me.

My shoulders slump in relief.

"Thank you," I murmur to my god, the universe, the jungle, or whoever is watching over me.

I yearn to touch my stomach in comfort but know better than to bring attention to something vulnerable inside me when I could be perceived as a demon. The majority of the tribe have protruding stomachs like me only not all are pregnant.

My grandmother's face fills my thoughts. I pray for her to give me the strength she found in the jungle.

"Tamùne woryi wypy," he says to his audience along with other incomprehensible words. *White woman mountain.*

Shit, he thinks I'm a bad spirit from the tepui. Or is it because I'm taller than his people? Please let it be the latter. I've never been so happy to be called a mountain because of my size.

I close my eyes and keep praying to God or anyone who can hear me.

Samuel.

I focus on his spirit—his love. Picture his love protecting me like a colored aura. I open my eyes to black eyes close to my nose. I stifle a scream and fall back onto my rear.

The raw belly laughter rises in the air and incites the monkeys to squeal from the treetops. Confirming I'm not a threat, I bow my head not only in respect, but the throb near my temple is getting worse. I raise a finger and touch the goo of old blood. When I meet the shaman's gaze, there's a hint of a snicker behind his painted expression. He waves his hand and shouts to the crowd, then grabs a handful of my hair and leans down to sniff it. He yanks hard, so I'm forced onto all fours, and he turns to walk away, my hair acting like a dog chain.

I scramble out of the capsule and stumble behind him, hunched over with my face to the ground. When I lift my chin, the feathers of his cape block my view to where he's taking me. I have an awareness of no one following.

From the force of him pulling and a sudden release of hair, I stagger into a hut and fall onto my knees. Dirt puffs up around me, and I close my eyes and cough, one hand protecting my stomach. His voice comes from behind. I adjust my hair to fall over my chest and sit on my legs, my head bowed. Words are shouted. He's lost the cape and no longer appears threatening. Mid-thirties maybe, he's young to be a shaman. Skinny, with paint covering every inch of his skin. Like the other men, his penis is tied around his waist, only he has a bamboo-like tube to protect his package.

With dust coating my throat, I need water. I cough and make an action like drinking. Regardless of what's offered if I don't hydrate soon, I'm putting both my baby and me at risk. He stands and grabs a stainless-steel cup and scoops the water from a bowl. In the corner is a collection of foreign items, including a machete and gold jewelry hanging from a pot.

"Sweet Jesus," I murmur. Did the people who offered these gifts survive? Are they trophies? At least the Watache have seen civilized people. He hands me the cup, and despite the cloudy appearance of the contents, I guzzle the water down, then hand it back. He refills it. I take it without hesitation and cough again when it hits my empty stomach. I have no idea how long I was out or how long we traveled, depriving my body of food and fluid. The chance of Samuel finding me is slim, and the reality hits me like another blow to the head.

I slide onto my side, resting my head on my arm in case I pass out. The Watache shaman squats and fixes his gaze on me as though he doesn't trust me to look away. I close my eyes, ignoring the female voices at the doorway.

I did what Samuel advised. I stayed out of the jungle at night when predators hunted. Daytime is supposed to be relatively safe. Only these people aren't nocturnal hunters. They do what it takes to survive, and I'm a means to an end. I'm unsure as to how I'll benefit them, be it food or bargaining or pleasure. The thought eats away at my soul, and I do my best to shut off my mind to the world and seep into the earth.

A shaking of my shoulder rouses me. He shoves bananas and passionfruit in my face. I sit and nod, taking the food from him. Backing away, he squats to watch me eat. Twilight has filled the hut. Through the door space and in the distance, a fire flickers. Again, I'm hit with the smell of meat. The jungle shrieks with life, a warning on high volume as though the trees are talking to me.

A woman enters the hut, full-rounded belly, black body paint, same hairstyle as everyone else. She moves in a way that suggests she's almost at the term of her pregnancy. She shoves a handful of meat in my face as if I'm a nuisance. Even in the failing light, the red flesh stands out.

Don't eat it!

I cover my mouth with my hand.

She shouts a few incomprehensible words before jerking the meat closer to my face. Samuel had warned me refusing food is a sign of disrespect, so I take it from her and eat it so fast, imagining it to be chicken because, hell, everything is supposed to taste like bloody chicken. I refuse to think of the possibilities of the source and signal again for more water.

My stomach growls, and not long after, I'm hit with sharp jabs of pain.

Sliding my arm through the dirt, I lay my head on my arm, and close my eyes, praying when I next wake, it will be sunlight.

At least I would have survived another day.

9

EDEN

IT'S NOT the sun that wakes me.

I throw myself onto all fours with an excruciating spasm in my gut.

"Please, no. Not my baby," I whimper.

The Watache shaman's quiet snores alert me to where I am.

Oh God, I need a toilet. If I don't find a bush and fast, I'll make a mess of myself.

Enough moonlight shines into the hut to see him curled on his side. He seems younger or perhaps vulnerable in his sleep.

The stench of poop hits me, and it's not mine. I heave then cover my mouth. The pong comes from his corner of the hut like something is dead, and I have to get out before I lose control. On my first step, I stumble, then stop to steady my balance and take a deep breath when the room spins. I must have moaned because the Watache shaman springs to his feet and yells out to me. I jab a finger at my bum because I have no idea how to say toilet. I doubt he even knows what a restroom is. He grabs my arm, and I yank it out of his grip and groan, clutching my gut. He stares down at my abdomen as if for the first time understanding the roundness. He follows me out, shouting. Deep murmurs come from near the fire as people stir from sleep.

The full moon casts enough light where the central fire lags. There are two large, open-walled huts on either side of the fire. I keep walking past the women and children in one hut. In the other hut, the men lie huddled, side by side. Legs and arms are wrapped around each other, and abdomens are used as pillows. All lay close and not a woman among them.

Movement catches my eye. Thrusts in sync. Gentle moans of pleasure. I look away and turn to the opposite side, where women sleep peacefully with their children. Many of them are pregnant, yet the men find pleasure and comfort with each other. There's no sign of a family huddled together.

The shaman shouts again, and this time, some men spring to their feet. I make my way to the closest edge of the jungle, one hand clutching my stomach, the other flexed straight in warning not to follow me. I rush forward with faint awareness they didn't stop me.

When I reach the closest tree, I lower in a wide squat, one hand on the trunk for support. The flatulence alone is enough warning for no one to come close until the pain has tears falling from my eyes. I blink the tears away, hearing sniggers from the men on the other side of the tree.

When I immerse from the dark jungle, the men chuckle and point to the shaman, making a circle shape with their hands. "Sano, sano," they repeat.

Mother.

The shaman's expression sours, and he yells before gripping my hair, and again, I'm stumbling behind him. Did he think I was going into labor? Hopefully, he believes I'm a well-fed white woman with a gastric bug.

Inside his hut, he releases his grip, yells more words, and points to the corner.

Does he expect me to poop in the corner?

It explains the stench coming from his side of the hut.

When I lower myself to the ground, I'm coated with dirt as it adheres to my limbs. There's no regard to hygiene, and it's only a matter of time before microbes will feast on me.

The odds of survival are stacking against me.

Faint light fills the hut.

Soft sounds drift in from the village coming to life—hushed voices, not threats of fierce cannibals I imagine them to be in my mind. I survived one night, although not from the mosquitoes. The itch from the bites covering my arms and back drove me half mad through the night.

I ache all over. Lethargy weighs down every part of my body, and I'm losing the will to fight for what seems like an inevitable ending. I close my eyes and wait for *him* to summon me.

The Ularan shaman would be in the medicinal garden at the break of dawn. He cared for every Ularan as if they were his responsibility. While this man sleeps the morning away, it seems he only cares for himself.

Ugh, my dry, scratchy throat is on fire. I'm not convinced water is the cure. I recall coughing through the night—hard coughing capable of cracking a rib.

This isn't how I want to die.

I feel so helpless, lost in my mind about how to save myself. An urge to sob, really sob, overwhelms me. Holding it back has my throat burning. I squeeze my eyes shut to stop the tears and push out every scary thought of death because the hysteria is clawing at my chest. A shiver washes over me and then another. I open my eyes and interlace my fingers to stop my hands from shaking, and the terror taking over my thoughts.

Block it out. Think of our baby.

I can't let the Watache shaman see my fear.

Closing my eyes, I focus on the forest, the trees, and many months ago when I connected with a jungle spirit in an ayahuasca ceremony.

Breathe.

Slowly, in for a count to seven and release for a count of seven.

Clear my mind.

Close down the chatter and negative thoughts.

The voice telling me this is all for nothing.

I. Am. Not. Going. To. Die.

Clear my mind.

Breathe.

I envisage my third eye seeking guidance from the unseen spirits surrounding us. At night, the decaying leaves are moist under my feet as I pad through the pulsing dark forest. Walking blind toward a presence, something draws me closer. Not a bright light as one would describe death but another soul—one that can provide protection.

A pair of eyes shine through the trees. They're not yellow or white like other animals. These are blue and mesmerizing, bewitching me to come closer. As I move closer, the dark silhouette morphs into a cat—a black jaguar. My heart lurches out of my chest only to be lulled into quietness, and a serene calmness surrounds me. The animal pads toward me and then circles not as though I'm prey, more in warning for anything lurking beyond the trees to stay away. The jaguar is protecting me.

Breathe.

Hold the image.

I allow the vision to wrap around me like a protective cloak.

Slowly, I open my eyes.

The Watache shaman is squatting, staring at me. God knows how long he's been doing it. His eyes hold suspicion, as though I could magically disappear at any moment.

The whole magic thing has me weighing up what to do. Should I take the I-am-powerful path or prove I'm not a threat?

I push up, change my position, and signal for some water to soothe the burn even though the cloudy water could be the source of my abdominal pain. He stills, eyes fixed on me. Suspicion evaporates, and there's no fear in his eyes. Instead, lust glimmers in his eyes, a universal longing recognized in all humans. His bamboo pipe bobs around his waist. I glance down to my exposed breasts, full and round unlike those of the women in the village.

Sex is carefree and permissible whenever and with whoever. I witnessed that last night.

I point to the water and mime drinking from a cup. He brings it to me, and as I drink, he flicks my hair over my shoulders and takes his fill. I keep drinking despite the cup being empty rather than meet his dark eyes. He squeezes both breasts. Sandpaper hands roll over my skin. I gulp air in revolt and fear.

I bow my head and hand him the glass, afraid to look him in the eye. I point to my mouth and hope he gets the message. He stands, his erection obvious even hidden in the bamboo.

He scoops water and brings it to me, turns to yell at the two women standing in the doorway holding fruit. He takes it from them and pushes on their backs to shoo them away. Then he squats directly in front of me. A long pointy nail pierces the skin of the passionfruit. He sucks out half of the fruit and then hands it to me.

My head screams *no* with his filthy nail and his black teeth sucking on it first.

I suck the remaining pulp greedily. One taste and I'm craving more. I point to the other fruits, and he hands me a banana, and we eat, him watching my every move. He peels the entire banana and holds the fruit in dirt-covered fingers. I stick to what I know and handle less with my hands, though, at this point, it all seems pointless.

My thoughts wander, and I can't help imagining my heart being offered as a sacrifice to the others to eat and ingest my spirit power.

A spine-tingling scream comes from outside. I freeze. What now? The shaman's face glares at me as though he doesn't trust me enough to leave. The screaming continues, and he dashes through the doorway. I move to get a better view. A woman bounces with a small child limp in her arms. My thoughts tick over to the cause of the child's illness, but damn, it could be anything, including last night's meal.

"Iwoi. Iwoi," she wallows. *Snake.*

Behind her, a young boy holds a limp green snake, killed too late. Her cries of loss fill my heart. She refuses to hand over her limp child, his head now dangling from her arms. Beyond the cries of the other women, the men shout, "Tamu'ne woryi mawarí," jutting their spears to the sky. *White woman spirit.*

Painted red faces turn in my direction, their eyes as venomous as the snake. There's more yelling, and I don't need to comprehend the meaning. It turns into a chant and continues long enough for panic to build until a woman explodes from the jungle, screaming and pointing. The attention falls from me as the men dash into the tangle of green vines. The shaman spins, comes at me, and shoves my shoulder.

I stumble back and retreat to my side of the hut. He stands over me, machete in hand. "Not now," I rasp, my throat still on fire. God, I no longer have the energy to resist.

I fall to my knees and bow my head. "Tamu'ne woryi wakü." *White woman good.*

My last words.

I close my eyes and picture the ones I love. Samuel's voice cries out to me. I sigh even though the shouting sounds real.

"Eden."

The shaman and I turn to the doorway, and I see a flash of white hair. *Please let it be him.*

"Tamu'ne woryi wakü," I repeat louder, hoping to be heard. *White woman good.*

The shaman spins toward me. His gaze is fixed, watching me carefully. A low hum rolls over the village, a song of low monotonous notes. The machete hangs low in the shaman's grip.

Samuel rushes to the door panting with every breath.

"Eden," he shouts in a combination of relief and panic.

Samuel's presence doesn't concern him. His gaze doesn't falter.

I don't look at Samuel in fear of taking my eyes off the shaman.

When the shaman sneaks a sideways glance, so do I.

Stupid because I witnessed the fear on his face, glimpsed the spears pointed at him and the Ularan warriors.

I fall apart piece by piece. Quiet sobs choke every breath. I don't have to hold on any longer because Samuel *is* here.

In a low, calm voice, Samuel speaks to him. I recognize some words. "Wakiipe-küruman, upetoy." *Thanks, friend.* He lurches with an outstretched arm, something shiny dangling from his fingertips.

"Are you hurt?" His gentle words help to calm me even though he hasn't risked taking his eyes from the shaman as he takes slow, deliberate steps closer to him.

"No," I manage. I hurt everywhere, but *no* was the easiest word to say.

Samuel demonstrates how to wear the watch, vying for the shaman's attention. Pulling rolled paper from the twine around his waist tie, he reveals a map. He unfolds it and lays it on the ground. "Here," Samuel commands and points to an area on the map. The shaman speaks to Samuel, and they both hover over the map, pointing and shaking their heads.

"Samuel," I wail, my breath becoming weaker.

"Breathe," he rasps out the instruction without looking at me.

He holds out a hand and sidesteps slowly until he can touch me. With his legs bent like he's balancing on a surfboard, he passes me a bottle of water, keeping both the shaman and me in his line of sight.

I don't have the energy to twist the lid or hold the bottle to my lips. So I just hold it and focus on trying not to pass out.

"I'm sorry." The strain in his voice comes from his chest. "Wayara," he calls to the Ularan warrior.

He takes the bottle from me and holds it to my mouth. I swallow each mouthful slowly, allowing my stomach to adjust.

“Oh, Eden,” Samuel croaks, as though he too is hanging on by thread. He strokes my hair. “Are you in pain?” He lifts a finger to catch my tears with his fingertips.

“My throat is closing up.” I fall into his arms, my face on his shoulder to stifle further sobs so as not to alarm the Watache shaman.

“I’m so sorry,” he says into my hair. My shoulders slump, the tenderness wrapping around me with each gentle stroke of my tangled mane. “You’re alive. You’re safe now, and I’m getting you out of here.”

10

SAMUEL

Shit. Shit. Shit. Samuel has mere seconds to think.

Thank God, he found her, but her strength is fading, and time isn't on his side. His heart is racing as quick as his thoughts because he has no clue if their plan will work. He can't panic, not now when Eden needs him to get her out of here. Before they do anything, he has to first assess her and determine what she needs to stay alive.

"You're going to be okay," he tells her and kisses the top of her head. Eden is limp in his arms, and he needs to get her somewhere safe.

Wayara is puffing when he enters the doorway. Samuel asks Wayara to speak to the shaman, as he is a better communicator—calm and powerful. He listens for the right moment to make his exit. Samuel stands with Eden in his arms, and Wayara explains to the shaman that Samuel is tending to her wounds.

He carries Eden to a stream close to the village, and he assumes it's why they chose this location. Several Watache warriors maintain a safe distance behind them, all with spears pointed and primed to kill. The small stream is the Watache's water source since the main river is a half-mile from their makeshift village. Hidden under palms and with no crops, he assumes they plan to move on since these huts won't last the next rainy season.

"We're at a stream, and I'm going to carry you in," he tells Eden.

She hasn't opened her eyes since he lifted her into his arms. The water takes her weight so he releases one hand and strokes her cheek to calm her. "You're going to be okay, my love. Just hold on a little longer." He can't lose her. He just can't.

She clutches the water bottle as though it's a lifeline. It is for now. One reason he didn't want her to stay in Ulara was the high risk of dehydration when he had no adequate place to store intravenous fluids. He's thankful Asoo delivered extra water bottles last week, the ones he ordered in case of an emergency. Before rushing into the jungle, he packed antibiotics and other drugs in his small backpack. He was prepared for the worst. Now he's counting on Wayara's negotiating skills, so when he returns, they can get the hell out of here.

"Tilt your head back," he whispers to wash the funky smell from her hair. She has slept in the dirt and God knows what else. He needs to clean her skin to treat her bites and inspect her for possible skin infections. It's what he can't see that stirs concern. Gastroenteritis, he expects—a possible cause of her dehydration. There's the risk of mosquito-transmitted diseases other than the ones for which she is vaccinated. The list grows. His thoughts wander to their baby and her mindset. Eden's life has to come first, and much of it relies on Wayara getting them out safe and fast. He's aware they are being watched and prays nothing spooks the warriors to react and come charging while he attends to Eden.

Samuel assists her up onto the rocky bank and sits her on a boulder, so he can retrieve the leaves from a nearby plant. The foliage soothes the skin and acts as a natural repellent. In gentle swirls, he massages her back, arms, and shoulders in the sap. "Thank you," she murmurs. "I didn't think I'd see you again."

"Of course, I'd find you." His voice finds strength within his fear. "I had Wayara to guide me."

Her lips curl. It's slight, yet he sees it. She opens her eyes, and a single tear falls to her cheek. "I don't think I'll make it home," she croaks. "I can't walk. I'm too weak... and my throat." Her hands go to her neck.

"Open your mouth." He angles her chin and notices the yellow dots at the back of her mouth.

He ruffles through his waist pouch, grabs a high-energy bar, and rips open the wrapper. "Little bites, Eden. You'll feel better soon. And you won't have to do anything because we'll help you." He has one antibiotic blister pack in his pouch. Punching out two tablets, he holds them in front of her face. "Can you swallow these?"

"What is it?" she croaks.

"Penicillin. Take them, and then we can get out of here."

Her brow furrows. "I don't want to go back there," she says in a stronger voice.

Only now he hears the chants and turns to the trees where bodies camouflaged in paint hold their spears like javelins. "No one is going to hurt you." Regardless of the underlying threat, she's in his arms, and he's not letting her go.

"We have to go back. You're with me and are safe."

She pushes up, and he helps her to stand. Together, they inch their way back to the village. By the time they reach the shaman's hut, Eden has slumped forward.

"I can't..." she moans, "... take another step."

"Wayara," Samuel shouts.

Wayara steps out of the hut, the shaman keeping watch.

Samuel tells him they need to get Eden out of the village.

Wayara has negotiated a trade and calls to Tïmenneng. "Bring the wild pig and Samuel's hammock," he says in Ularan.

"What's happening?" Eden groans. "I'm scared," she whispers.

Samuel tightens his arms around her shoulders. "There's no need to be afraid. Focus your energy on you. Just rest, my love."

"I can't relax here. I'm tired. So tired, but I'm scared to fall asleep. What if—"

"No what-ifs, okay?" He kisses the top of her head and understands her fear as his heart is still racing in his chest. "We killed a wild pig near the river." Despite the Ularans craving meat themselves, the pig's purpose is to use it as a bargain for Eden's safety. "It is a..." he refrains from mentioning the word trade, "... a gift."

Tïmenneng went into the jungle with another warrior and three Watache men in tow.

"Please hurry," he whispers, aware every minute is crucial. "Hey." Samuel strokes Eden's face. "Are you still with me?"

She nods once. It's slight, yet it's enough.

Wayara exits the hut. He announces the shaman has commanded Samuel to explain the map. He wants to know the magic of the pictures. Wayara enlightens him on the Watache plan and how fire destroyed their home. Wayara explains the Watache are searching for a new place to live. Years ago, they found one by the river, but illegal mining nearby had poisoned the water and their food source. The elderly remained too tired to walk any further, including the shaman's father. Divided, hungry, and tired, they need to keep searching.

But there's more. The shaman remains bitter about his cousin being raised by the Ularans. Eye for an eye, they were taking the woman with his cousin's child. Then Eden stumbled into the scene, and they thought she was the ultimate sacrifice to the Mawarí spirits.

Wayara stops speaking when Samuel's shoulders slump. He stares down at Eden and hopes she doesn't feel his heart racing in his chest.

The shaman likes Eden, which is why Wayara sent for the pig. Another gift along with Samuel's wristwatch and the map. She's alive because she was going to become another wife to the shaman.

Samuel tells Wayara he's not taking Eden inside the hut. Wayara tells him to use his *Paranakyry pyjai.*

White-European medicine.

Everything in his pack is for Eden.

"Wayara will stay with you, okay. I won't be long." Panic rises in his gut as she falls into Wayara's arms without caring. She needs medical assistance now. "Hold the water bottle for her to drink," he tells Wayara in Ularan before striding into the hut.

Samuel clears his mind to negotiate with the man that has nearly killed the love of his life. The bitterness is bubbling inside of him like a volcano ready to explode. He has to keep calm and save his energy because Eden needs him. Now isn't the time to do something rash or revengeful. Samuel inhales a deep breath and points to their location. He tells the shaman they took the picture from the heavens. He points out the tepuis and the rivers and circles the place where the Watache elders remain—the place Wayara was leading them and why they almost didn't find Eden. They had no choice but to move on when the elders held no clue to their descendants' whereabouts. They were at peace and prepared to die, unable to continue to wander the forest. On the return journey in the curiara, Tïmenneng spied smoke rising above the trees.

He leans close to point out the places where illegal gold mines dotted the rivers. He jerks back when the sharp sticks protruding from the shaman's cheek prick his nose. The shaman grins, believing he still has the upper hand. Ignoring the glare from red-painted eyes, Samuel continues to reveal all his knowledge of the river and jungle and the caves that could lead the Watache through the tepui to the other side.

The shaman's eyes narrow in suspicion. He suggests certain parts of the jungle where they would be safe and says they should remain close to the Peruvian border. He tells them to stay out of the sight of the miners and metal birds that fly in the sky.

Cheering comes from beyond the hut. Samuel's head dips, and he takes a moment to offer thanks to the gods. Both men stand to see the pig —legs tied to bamboo—carried into the village and placed over the fire.

Samuel shows the shaman how to fold the map. He drops it in the corner along with his other prized collections, including Samuel's wristwatch.

The shaman leaves him to inspect the pig. The Watache are hungry and distracted, allowing the Ularans to creep to the edge of the jungle. From here, they secure Eden in the hammock and carry her through the jungle without saying goodbye. In minutes, they reach the curiara parked under a tree on the narrow sandy bank.

Samuel barks instructions to Tïmenneng. He pushes the curiara off the bank and then hurls himself into the canoe. Wayara paddles with the strength of an Olympian with three other warriors paddling up front. Wooden paddles hit the water with loud *thwaps*, each nudging the canoe further from the bank. Shouting comes from the shore.

"Faster," Samuel says, only in panic he yells in English instead of Ularan. He points to the trees where painted bodies sprint out with spears over the shoulders. Several spears fly, whizzing on the descent. "Noo," Samuel calls out, then springs up to blanket Eden with his body, hovering on his knees. He leans his forehead on hers and squeezes his eyes closed for a moment. "Please, no," he moans in a raspy cry. The curiara tilts sideways with everyone scrambling to dodge a spear when it lands inches from the boat. He lifts his head to maintain his balance and not fall sideways and expose Eden to the danger. Spears spiral into the mud-colored river in a series of *tink, tink, tink sounds*. They steer the nose toward the middle of the stream until the current surges the curiara away.

Samuel glances down at Eden. "Are you okay?" He wipes matted hair away from Eden's eyes. She's already asleep. He places a finger on the pulse in her neck. Fast yet thready.

She's leaving him.

The walls of the green jungle close in around them like a green jail cell offering reassurance they are on their way home.

The torment eats at him. Every breath is a step closer to her going home. The river current takes control of his thoughts when he imagines her caught in the rapids and being swept away—far away to another world, one where she belongs.

Home, safe with her family.

11

EDEN

"I'M OKAY," I whisper as I blink away the haze. My throat is dry, and it burns when I speak. I tilt the bottle again, taking small sips as Samuel instructed.

"Shh." The tips of his fingers stroke my cheek.

"Thank you," I croak, again. Every time I've opened my eyes, they're the only words I've whispered before slipping back into sleep.

"I want you to remain here," he tells me. "I'll grab our bags, and we're heading straight to Canaima. I'll stabilize you there before we fly out to Ciudad."

I didn't argue. My body aches and my head hurts as though someone has hit me with a hammer. The last thing I want to do is be upright.

I keep my eyes open and stare at the blue sky with ribbons of white clouds. Yet experience has taught me not to be tricked, for in minutes, Mother Nature will sucker-punch you with violent wind and rain. The walls of the dense jungle canopy pass by. A small amount of me bursts with pride how I can now identify the coral trees, wild cashew, and my favorite white and orange flowers of the beauty leaf. Even from here, her brilliant leaves stand out against other foliage.

The Ularan warriors stand with perfected balance, the canoe steady beneath their feet. One push of the paddle and it hits the bottom, so we coast into a turn. The other men row and steer us toward the familiar sandy banks of Ulara.

Shouts sound from the bank. I lift my head to a dozen men and Kaikare.

"I won't be long." Samuel hurdles the edge of the canoe and speaks to Kaikare. She points to our quarantine camp. Asoo stands away from everyone else. They speak, and then Samuel takes off in a sprint, and in seconds, I lose him to the trees.

Kaikare boards the curiara. It rocks gently as she kneels before me. She strokes my face, and I manage a weak smile. She speaks to me, although I'm too exhausted to comprehend any words. Two hands cup my belly, and she closes her eyes as though she's listening for a sign or concentrating on touching. She opens her eyes, her face serious. "Wakü." *Good.*

"My baby is okay?"

She nods, yet I sense she means, *for now*.

Asoo stands at the nose of the curiara. "I sorry, Eden. When I visit yesterday, Kaikare tell me. So I stay in your camp and wait." He points to the makeshift campsite. "I take you to Canaima."

"Thank you." It's all I can manage for now, yet in my daze, I comprehend the enormity of him staying here the night.

My eyelids flutter with the weight of lead forcing them to close while Kaikare squeezes my hand. I fight to stay awake, afraid of seeing the Watache shaman's face when trapped in a feverish dream. A battle I'm losing for the red faces with sticks protruding like animal whiskers take over my thoughts.

Lost to the dreams and reliving the nightmare, I know I'm lucky as it could've been worse. Much worse.

The canoe rocks with Samuel loading our bags onto the other curiara. "You're back," I say and smile.

He leans over me and brushes my cheek. Sweat beads dot his forehead. Hot air caresses my face with every pant passing his lips.

Asoo speaks to Samuel, and they switch back to talking in Spanish. Kaikare squeezes my hand one last time before she jumps ashore. Samuel tilts the bottle for me to take another sip, then helps reposition me at the front of Asoo's curiara with our bags placed around me for support. I close my eyes and allow the sound of the motor to lull me into sleep.

The next time I open my eyes, the jungle is no longer a dense wall. It takes a moment to come around. I'm lying between Samuel's legs, my head in his lap.

I stare up at his beautiful face—dirt-smeared cheeks, hair tangled into knots, the lines near his eyes etched deeper on his thinning face, and still beautiful in a masculine way.

"Where are we?" I murmur.

Bloodshot eyes hold my gaze. "Hey. We're not far out of Canaima." He hands me another two tablets. "Can you swallow these?"

"Sure." I attempt to push up. Samuel takes my weight and supports me while I drink several mouthfuls of water.

I clutch my stomach as I drink. Everything is an effort. Everything hurts.

I close my eyes—then open them when I hear a helicopter overhead.

"They're flying closer to the river and closer to Ulara," Samuel says without checking if I'm listening. He watches its path as it heads for the opposite side of the tepui to Angel Falls.

"Why?" I rasp.

"More explorers are coming here seeking adventure. Looking for the caves or attempting to climb the tepui or even search for gold." He shakes his head. "Flying low enough for the Ularans to see them. The shaman asked me about the metal birds and if they were our Mawarí."

"Did you explain it couldn't hurt them?" I murmur.

His eyes meet mine. He strokes my jawline several times. "Yes, but the reality is if they see the village, the repercussions could hurt the Ularans. Years ago, no one flew close to the mountain range near that part of the jungle, but only now people are seeking their own adventure, dare devils taking bigger risks."

"You hear the aircraft before you see it, so you teach the Ularans to hide," I whisper, clutching my throat.

"They're going to have to find somewhere new," he says. "In the opposite direction to where we're sending the Watache."

"Where would they go?"

"Southwest and deeper into the rainforest. I'm sorry, I'm talking out loud, and it's not important right now." His fingers rest on my pulse. "I'll head straight to Victor and arrange a flight for you. I can check how long a medical flight will take to get here. If you can cope sitting up, then we can take one of the Cessnas, and I'll pay the pilot double."

"My throat is a little better."

"The antibiotics are working, but you're going to need a series of tests for the sake of you and our baby."

"Meaning?"

"Expect to be in the hospital for some time," he says it as though it's a difficult thing to endure.

"It has to be better than my last accommodation."

Samuel offers a weak smile, then pushes the hair out of my eyes. "Some hospitals have fewer supplies than I do in Ulara. They can't afford soap to clean, some don't have drugs like antibiotics or clean running water."

"What?" I croak.

"I'm taking you to a private one where I have briefly worked. It's well funded, and I've met many of the specialists."

Shades of pink streak across the eastern sky. A golden crown glows behind the resort creating a shimmer as if glitter has been sprinkled over the buildings. It's a fairy castle compared to where I spent the previous night.

Samuel carries me to his room while Asoo dashes to reception to alert Victor of our plans. Samuel runs a bath, and while I soak, he showers, then steps into the bedroom to use his cell.

The bubble foam cleanses the surface of my body. Beneath the skin, my joints ache. It's deep, as though the goodness in my bones is being drenched of nutrients for my deprived body to stay alive. My legs are heavy like steel. I barely have enough energy to lift my arms to wash my hair. In the other room, the bed calls for me to climb onto its softness and sleep for a thousand hours.

Samuel's voice turns deeper, engaged in a battle of words in Spanish. Before I move a single muscle, the bathroom door swings open.

"We have a problem." Samuel lowers to his knees and takes my hand. He circles his fingers over my skin to calm me. "There's no pilot to fly the plane until morning. I tried to arrange an emergency—"

"It's fine, and I'm feeling much better. I'll survive another night." I smile at him, trying humor to lighten his mood.

He rests a hand on my stomach as though he's holding our baby. His eyes meet mine, and I'm not prepared for the anguish building inside of him. "The health system has changed. Many hospitals are closed or, if open, there are no doctors. There are stories of women giving birth out in the parking lot and waiting rooms. Now there are limited supplies of the treatment you need—"

"What do you want me to do?" I rasp.

"I'm failing you. I—"

I reach for his hand and squeeze it. "None of this was your fault."

"I'm sorry." His expression falters, then he scrubs his hands over his face, although the pained mask remains. "I know a guy in Guyana... Georgetown, and you'll have good private care. We need to get to Ciudad Guayana first, then fly to Guyana, so you'll need your passport."

"Everything is in the small bag that I left with Victor."

"We'll fly out first thing in the morning and then catch a connecting flight to Georgetown. For now, I'll get us some food, and then you need to rest."

Samuel helps me out of the bath, dabs the towel over me, tenderly drying my skin, and then helps me onto the bed. He kisses my cheek before he leaves. "You're going to be fine," he whispers.

I need to believe him, for the way my muscles hurt, it feels like I'm slowly letting go. Every bruise is ingrained deep. Beyond the surface, my soul is scarred. Each scar has torn at my faith in surviving out here and keeping my baby safe.

I'm hanging on to my own life by a thread.

12

SAMUEL

A STEADY *BEEP* comes from the monitor beside Eden's bed. Her blood pressure and blood oxygen levels remain stable. He stands to check out the intravenous infusion pump even though the nurse left the room mere minutes ago. Medication and intravenous fluids have treated her dehydration and bacterial infections, and yet it hasn't stopped him from worrying and analysing the slightest change in her blood pressure.

The chair by her bed is where he's slept in short bursts, too afraid to close his eyes for long periods in case she needs him. How she has gotten through the ordeal is beyond him.

Dr. Jagdeo closes the door with a slight click. Samuel gives him an appreciative nod for not disturbing Eden.

"I'll let you know when her blood results are back. The obstetrician will be here soon to take an ultrasound of the baby. From there, we'll decide if further tests are necessary. As for Eden—"

"Can you write up some forms for fecal samples? I want to cover all bases," Samuel says impatiently.

Dr. Jagdeo places a hand on Samuel's shoulder. "Patience, Samuel, you know some blood results take longer than others. We'll cover everything on your list." Dr. Jagdeo pauses and meets Samuel's gaze. "Do you want her to speak to a psychologist when she wakes?"

Samuel had told his friend every detail, as he's one of the few medical specialists aware of Samuel living with the Ularans. He was working with Samuel when he voiced his desire to do voluntary work with the remote Indigenous communities.

"I'll assess her first. She's stronger than anyone I know." Samuel turns to the woman who has captured his heart and soul. Lord knows what he'd do if he lost her. Watching her battle through the fever was difficult, but he knows something more sinister could be swirling in the depths of her mind. He's barely held onto his own sanity through the ordeal, not knowing what they did to her and if he was ever going to find her. Waiting for the tests is torture. His mind grows silent with panic as though he's trapped in a car as it plunges into a river, the water immersing the space. Every minute drags him closer to drowning.

Opening her bag, he retrieves her photocopied travel papers and finds copies of the yellow fever certificate and vaccinations she had before her venture with her girlfriends. If only he could rewind time and stay the hell away from her. He was the worst thing to happen to her, and yet she was the very best thing that's happened to him. She thinks he's strong, and yet time and time again, she has proven her resilience and love with an open heart without fear.

"I think this is everything." He hands the documents to Dr. Jagdeo.

"Thank you. I'll come back and check on Eden soon."

Samuel releases a long breath when the door thuds closed.

His eyes sweep over the bones of her face. She's a beautiful woman, only he notices the gaunt cheeks, her chapped lips, and slight scratches above her brow. He clamps his eyes shut, knowing what has to be done. He has to protect the two most precious loves in his life.

"I'm going to miss you every day," he whispers.

A squeaky wheel disturbs him. He opens his eyes and greets the doctor in a white coat pushing the machine on a trolley.

"Eden," Samuel says gently to wake her.

Her eyes flutter open. "Hi," she says wearily.

The obstetrician checks her identification wristband. "I'm Dr. Vásquez. I won't disturb you for long. We need to check on your baby."

"Thank you." She pushes up onto her elbows and groans, gripping her abdomen. "Argh. This pain... I keep getting these contractions." She stares up at Samuel and grimaces.

"I assume she's having Braxton Hicks contractions," he tells Dr. Vásquez.

“Have you learned breathing techniques at antenatal classes?” Dr. Vásquez asks.

“No,” she murmurs.

“I can teach her,” Samuel adds. He squeezes her hand reassuringly and then counts with her as she takes some deep breaths.

“Thank you,” she says and rolls closer for Dr. Vásquez to examine her.

The doctor squeezes gel over Eden’s abdomen and prepares the wand.

She giggles. “It’s cold.”

Samuel grips Eden’s hand when a soft whoosh echoes from the monitor. He bows his head and sighs in relief at the beautiful sound of their baby’s heartbeat.

“There,” Dr. Vásquez turns the screen so both parents can view the image of their baby.

"Oh, wow,” Eden says and gasps. She swipes tears from her eyes and then meets Samuel’s gaze.

He shakes his head in wonder. For years he believed he was destined to live out his life alone. Seeing their baby for the first time is similar to an out-of-body experience with a sensation of floating from the pure joy pumping through his body. He leans down and kisses Eden’s lips, the woman who has saved him. “I love you,” he whispers.

Her happiness bubbles through muffled sobs. “I love you too.”

Dr. Vásquez focuses on hitting buttons. “I’ll print a sonogram for you to keep.”

“You’re the bravest mother in the world,” he tells Eden.

Her gaze returns to the screen. “It’s our baby.” The light burns bright in her eyes, reminding him of dawn, a time of day when the best is yet to come.

“You estimate the baby to be twenty-eight weeks?”

Eden’s brow pinches as she tries to gather her thoughts.

“Yes,” Samuel answers for Eden.

“By the scan, your baby has grown remarkably, and I’d work with a possible mid-January date.”

“Oh.” Eden’s eyes widen. “So, can you see the sex of our baby?” she asks. She glances at Samuel. “Do you want to know?”

“I... well, yes, if that’s what you want?”

Dr. Vásquez’s lips pull tight into a smile. “It’s a girl.”

"A girl," Eden says in a high-pitched voice. "Oh, Samuel."

Samuel chuckles. "I imagine she's going to be as beautiful as her mother." He shakes his head. "And yeah, I can't believe it." The thought of him almost losing both of his girls triggers the demons inside of him.

A voice he has fought hard to ignore.

You're a failure.

Dr. Vásquez's phone dings. "Excuse me a moment." He exits the room to take a call, leaving Eden and Samuel alone.

Samuel stands and walks to the window, only he can't open it for the fresh air he urgently needs. The last two days have played over in his mind again and again. He was dangerously close to losing Eden and their child. He doesn't have the stamina to fight the guilt. His eyes well as the emotion takes hold of his body. Eden can't see him like this when she needs his support more than ever.

"Are you okay?"

Samuel dips his chin, takes a deep breath, and looks over his shoulder. "Do you know how amazing you are?"

She tilts her head. "What's wrong?"

Samuel shakes his head. "I could've lost you."

"But you didn't."

"No." His voice cuts out as his demeanor cracks. One sob escapes him. He strides to her, collapses to his knees, and rests his head on the bed.

She runs her fingers through his hair to soothe him. "I'm fine. We're going to be okay."

His past and present collide, every thought undoing him until his entire body shakes. Every painful memory of his life is sucked into a vortex as the tornado rips out his heart.

"I'm so sorry," he weeps. "I almost failed you too."

"You saved me," she says gently.

Samuel shakes his head. "I saw everything I care about slipping away." He shakes his head. "You were out there alone, and I wanted to trade places with you. I kept thinking back to our time in Brazil. I wanted to go back to that day on the beach and not leave my room. I wish you never found me. Because of me, you almost died."

"Stop. Finding you was the best thing that's happened to me," she croaks and squeezes his fingers. "You can't blame yourself for what happened. I shouldn't have ventured out alone."

Wiping tears from his face, he then dots her fingers with kisses. "And you can't blame yourself when you had to pee. Something we all do."

A single laugh burst from her. She pats the bed beside her. "Lay with me."

Samuel slides on his side and lays beside her, taking up the smallest amount of room on the single bed. Everything has changed, and there's no going back to how things were before. They have days to contemplate what to do.

She runs her feeble fingers over his chin, catching on his stubble. "What are you thinking?"

"Sorry for interrupting," Dr. Vásquez chirps. "I'll let you rest, and we'll do another check in the morning."

Samuel walks the doctor out of the room to discuss further treatment and finds Dr. Jagdeo at the nurses' station. "I'm grateful to have Eden in a private room," he tells him. "It's a smaller hospital than in Venezuela. My concern here is if Eden went into premature labor, do you have enough incubators?"

"My friend, much has changed over the years. The medical system was failing in Venezuela, so I packed up my family and came to Guyana. This hospital is small, but we're better off here."

"How bad did it get?"

Dr. Jagdeo scratches his jawline. "I was told about a young girl who went into labor in her village. A friend took her on the motorbike across three rivers, then she caught two buses to get to a hospital. No one would see her as they had no incubators, and her baby was coming early. She tried several others. She slept on the street, cried for her baby as her labor pains worsened. Eventually, she banged on one hospital door and then passed out. They admitted her, and she gave birth to a little girl. The baby died hours later as she didn't have insurance, and they did not have an incubator in this particular hospital, but the young lady lived. She left the baby in the morgue as they didn't issue a death certificate, and she had no money for a burial. Maternal deaths rose, and infant mortality increased in that year. So, my friend, I'm glad you brought your special lady to me."

For a moment, Samuel has no words. His thoughts had jumped into overdrive thinking ahead to what they'll need. "When we leave, I'll require more sterilized products. Can I buy them through you?"

Dr. Jagdeo smiles. "I know of someone who can help."

Samuel gives a knowing nod. "I knew I could count on you."

13

EDEN

"Nooo," I wail with nothing left to give.

My heartbeat fills the dark space around me. It's all I hear, and every pulse is becoming weaker and slower.

Icy fingers claw at my chest. Cold tentacles spread the chill through my body. My arms are heavy as if a slab of steel restricts my movement, and I can't escape.

"Samuel," I rasp. He's not here. I'd feel him if he were here. I'm going to die alone. I'm so fucking scared.

I suck air in like it's my last breath.

"Where are you?" I shout to Samuel, only my throat constricts, and no sound comes out. "Please, Samuel."

He's the one person I need by my side to hold my hand even if I'm not okay, and the thought of him not with me scares me more than death itself. I imagine I'm home, safe with my family, yet my heart still yearns for a man who shares my heart. Through time and space, I'm searching for his soul, knowing we are one. Despite the short time we spent together, it was our destiny to find one another.

The air thins. My gut wrenches knowing I'm slipping away, and Samuel is completely unaware.

"Samuel," I rasp to the dark, empty space.

The life inside of me dies, and in those seconds, every face of those I love flashes before me. Faith, on her wedding day. Mum and Dad at Christmas lunch with my father making his traditional toast to our family. My girlfriends when we were on the beach in Rio. The darkness envelops me, and I'm among the stars, aware of another presence.

Gran.

Her gentle blue eyes hold an enormous amount of love for me. Her soft hand takes mine as she walks along the beachfront talking about what home means to your heart. How I'm about to give life to a new soul. She smiles, and a light shines around her.

The intense brightness forces my eyes to open.

A light reflects from the monitor.

My heart pounds with enough force to break a rib. Not a weak pulse.

A dream.

I'm cold and alone. Every part of me is trembling. It's the closest I've come to death despite it being a dream. It felt real, like a part of my subconscious the ayahuasca had accessed.

A warning.

Or a vision telling me not to leave him.

THE FOLLOWING DAY, I'm discharged from the hospital, and we book into a hotel overlooking the Demerara River and the Atlantic Ocean while I recuperate, and we wait for the remaining blood results.

Sweeping the curtain aside, I take a moment to enjoy the view and inhale a deep, cleansing breath of fresh ocean air.

The seaside city reminds me of home.

I close my eyes with the ache in my chest of missing my family and friends.

I glance over my shoulder to where Samuel had placed my phone on the table to call them, only I don't have the strength to speak to anyone without my voice cracking. Especially if they ask how I am because I'm too weak to fake a strong voice, and they'll see straight through me.

I lift the hem of my long blue dress that Samuel bought for me at the nearby Stabroek Market. He purchased new T-shirts for himself and some loose dresses that flare for me, bright-colored Boho dresses with beautiful patterns to lift my spirit.

It worked.

I'm still weak but don't want to be cooped up in a room after four long days in a hospital bed, especially after my dream. I cup my stomach and whisper, "We both need sunshine."

Taking a seat on the balcony, I inhale the fresh ocean air and gaze down to the sparkling blue hotel pool where Samuel swims lap after lap.

My gaze moves back to the beach. "You're going to love the beach," I tell my daughter. The beach is one of my most favorite places in the world. The ocean is the place I've missed the most, knowing the warm months in Adelaide are when my friends are having fun.

God, I can almost feel the sand between my toes.

The door behind me creaks. I turn to Samuel entering our room with a towel draped around his waist.

Good God.

I see his bare chest every day, but today, droplets glisten on his golden shoulders where light streams through the window highlighting his sculpted physique.

We meet in the center of the room.

"You look..."

"I've washed and dried my hair." I grin at him, knowing he doesn't understand how one small thing can do wonders for my morale.

"That's not it. Your cheeks are flushed."

"It's the effect you have on me." I take his face in my hands and taste the pool water on his lips. I taste more until our tongues collide with love and silent apology. "I need you," I say against his lips with an overwhelming desire to be adored by the one person who can destroy me and put me back together all by his love.

"Eden..." He pulls away and shakes his head.

"I need to feel again," I plead. Love will heal me quicker than any drug. "We haven't been intimate for a long time. Let's not waste another day where we don't put a comfortable bed to good use."

He lifts and carries me to the mattress. "Give me a moment."

It's the quickest shower for I've barely stripped my clothes before he's back, hair dripping and body glistening with moisture. His lips meet mine in gentle kisses, bathing my skin from my neck to my shoulders and then to my lips. He hovers over me with far too much space between our bodies. Every minute, he slowly eases closer as though not trusting himself not to break me.

My vagina works just fine, I want to tell him even though slow and gentle is all I can cope with right now. He's not only worried about the parts of my anatomy, it's the bruises to my heart, my soul, and the hurt deep in my mind where the demons hide.

If only he was aware how his lips are like heaven, and every touch has me floating on the clouds above as he breathes new life into my bones. His love awakens me and makes me truly feel alive.

THE AFTERNOON SUN beats down on my bare shoulders as I take tender steps toward the ocean. Samuel has a tight hold on my hand as though he's ready if I stumble.

Small steps.

Deep breaths.

"Let's just sit," I say. He assists me to lower until my rear lands in the sand. "It's beautiful in Adelaide at this time of year. I can't wait for you to visit then." I'm aware it won't be this year. "A hot, dry Christmas by the beach." I smile, hoping he can imagine our future like I do. "Dad has a spread of seafood, although Mum still likes to have some roast meats and vegetables. There are too many choices considering Faith and Jake don't stay for dinner. They share themselves between families and go to his parents for the evening."

"It's how I imagined you spending your Christmas with your family." His tone is off, and I know what he's about to say.

"By coming here, I chose not to have Christmas with my family," I say firmly. "I wanted to be with you and then leave before the airlines refuse my travel."

Samuel stares at the ocean. "Everything is different now. Christmas is a month away, and you're thirty weeks pregnant. We need to talk about what's best for you and the baby, not what is best for us."

"What about us?" I wait for him to look at me. "I need to know we have a future together and where that will be. Our baby will have grandparents in two different countries." His gaze drifts back to the ocean the moment I mention his parents. "We need to talk about many things," I whisper. "It's time you level up and be honest not only with me but to yourself."

He stands, brushes the sand from his rear, and offers me a hand.

"Let's start by you making some phone calls home. I'm sure everyone is worried about you."

"I'll make the phone calls if you promise to talk later." I don't give him my hand until he nods. When I'm upright, I kiss him on the cheek. "We promised each other *no secrets*," I remind him. "Some of your painful memories might be before my time, but we can't move forward unless you share them with me."

WHILE DRINKING a glass of ice water, I make my way through the long list of text messages from my family and friends. Most are updating me with their lives with 'stay safe' at the end of the message.

I start with the easiest call to build the strength to speak to the others. I sigh in relief when Bree's phone switches to voice mail. I expected it, considering the long hours she works.

"Hey, Bree. Hope you're shaking it up in Sydney's most prestigious hospital. I know you're doing great and just wanted to leave a message to let you know that I'm okay. Love you and can't wait to kiss ya face."

The screen goes blank, and I wait a moment before calling Yasmine. Again, it goes to voicemail.

"Yas, it's Eden. Just wanted to check in and let you know I'm okay." My throat turns dry, thinking back to only a few days ago. A ghost of the woman she knows. "I'm so jealous thinking about you all partying at night at The Bay and hanging out at the beach on weekends. And I can't wait to hear about your new job. Love you, babe."

I sink onto the bed and hug the pillow before I call Amy. *Hey, remember when...* is how she starts each message. I do, Amy. I remember all the fun times we had together.

"Finally," she says on the other end.

I smile as though we're in Adelaide, and she's been nagging me to come out on a Saturday night with her. "It's good to hear your voice."

"Is everything okay? With you, the baby, and how's Samuel?"

"We're g-good." I swallow a few mouthfuls of water. "I had an ultrasound. Do you want to know what I'm having?"

"Fuck, yeah," she yells, and my shoulders relax.

My cracked lips stretch into a big smile, only it hurts, so I try not to smile so hard. "A girl."

"I knew it!"

We both laugh. "You'd say that if I said it's a boy."

Amy chuckles. "It's good to hear your voice."

"Same." I close my eyes and imagine us in the same room together. If we were, Amy would see right through me. "I hear Yasmine has a new job."

"She does, and she's been working weekends, so we haven't caught up in weeks. Trust me, you haven't missed out on much here. It's been bloody cold."

"Serious?"

"It's shit and not at all spring weather. I want to come back to South America. I don't suppose you're allowed another visitor?"

The reality of where I am hits me. "Amy, I told you it's complicated —" A sob escapes, and I cough to cover the sound.

"What's going on, Edes?"

"Nothing, I'm fine," I blurt.

Silence.

"You're keeping something from me."

"Oh, Amy, I was so fucking scared. I almost died." I let out another sob until the tears keep coming.

"Fuck, what?"

"I'm okay now," I rasp out. Even though I still have a long way to go because my thoughts are messed up. I wish Amy was here to hug me and tell me I'm doing the right thing because after what happened, I'm feeling shitty with myself.

"Hey. I'm here, babe. Tell me what happened."

I nod even though she can't see me. "I wish you were really here."

I tell her what happened and how I'm now in Georgetown, Guyana.

Amy cries with me.

"Come home," she croaks.

In my heart, I know it's what I need to do, but I also don't have the strength to leave Samuel.

"Have you booked your flight?"

"There's no way I could sit on a plane and be at airports for the next thirty-odd hours. I haven't got the strength."

"Samuel would accompany you, right?"

"He can't right now."

"Bull... shiiit," she draws out. "That's it. I'm coming to you."

"You can't." My shoulders slump. "When the time is right, I'll come home. Samuel will make sure I'm safe, only it can't be now. When I know, then I'll let you know."

"You'd better, Edes. And he better be doing the right thing by you."

"He is," I whisper. I knew of Samuel's commitment before I returned, and I don't expect anyone else to understand him as I do. "I have to go, Ames. I still need to call Mum, Dad and Faith."

"Text me soon," she demands.

"I will."

"Love you."

"I love you too."

"Eden—"

"Yeah?" I say, placing the phone back to my ear.

"Please be careful."

"I will."

I end the call. My fingers tremble as though I've run ten miles and sprinted to the finish. I close my eyes with my phone in my hand. I need to rest before talking to my family.

14

SAMUEL

"You should call your parents," Samuel says after returning from the market with fresh food for lunch.

Eden shakes her head. "It's too late with the time difference. I'm lucky Amy was awake. I sent a text and intend to call them tomorrow."

Samuel gives her a look as though he'll keep her to that promise.

"What do you think my parents will say?"

The question throws him. "I expect your father to say—"

"Come home?" she finishes. "Why is it you're concerned about my parents, and yet you skip over any details for yours?"

"I'm not the one who was hospitalized, so my parents have no need for concern." He places the paper bag on the table and unpacks apples, bananas, strawberries, and oranges.

"They should be concerned." Eden slides onto the chair at the other end of the table. "You've been living in the jungle for years on your own."

"On my own?" Samuel arches his brow. "Last time I checked, I was living in a community."

"It's not a normal community." Eden folds her arms over her chest. "And I bet they are concerned because when was the last time you spoke to them?"

"Normal. What's normal, Eden?" He shakes his head. "Talking about *normal,* most of your tests have come back, and all are within acceptable limits except your iron levels are low. Although I may need to challenge the pathology on your iron levels. You don't sound tired at all."

"You're not funny."

A laugh escapes him. "I could debate with you all day. On a serious note, I'll find a pharmacy to fill your prescription."

"Explains why I'm craving a steak."

He takes a plate of fresh fruit and places it in front of her.

"I eat *this* every day," she moans.

"*This* is what's good for your body, and it's just a starter. If you're up to it, I'll take you out for dinner tomorrow night."

"On a date?"

"Yes, Eden, a date. It's what *normal* couples do."

"We're not a normal couple." She takes a handful of strawberries and nibbles on one. "It's not a bad thing, but I know we can't do what other couples do."

His hand stills with a knife, ready to cut the orange in half. "We can." He drops the knife and sits beside Eden, taking both her hands in his. "You want to go out?"

"My God, yes. It's like prison has released me on probation, and there's so much to see—"

"Prison?" he chokes. "No one has forced you to stay in Ulara." Her words hurt, for it's the place where he feels free, and he thought she understood him.

"When we're there, we aren't free to do what we choose."

"Every society has rules."

Her eyes flick over his face. "Right."

"You know Dr. Jagdeo asked me if you wanted to speak to someone confidentially."

"Like a psychologist?" She pulls her hands from his and wraps them over her pregnant belly.

"I said I'd run it by you. The option is there."

"What do I tell them? Cannibals kidnapped me? They'll think I'm delusional."

"It's for you to decide what to tell them."

"You know I'd feel a lot better if my, my... what are you to me? A boyfriend?"

"What? No. We're more than..." He stops himself and runs his fingers up and down her arms before looking up to meet her gaze. "You mean everything to me. *Everything*. You know that, right?"

She holds his gaze but doesn't answer him.

"Before you, I barely lived. I had no idea how I survived in the dark until that sunny day on the beach in Salvador when the light radiating from you almost blinded me. You're the sun and the moon together, and I need your light, your warmth, and your magnetic energy to survive every day."

Eden caresses his face, pushes long strands of hair out of his eyes. "And yet you're about to send me home, aren't you?"

He understands why she was defensive in their conversation. "It's the safest option."

"No. What I need is to be with the father of my baby. I have another month to decide what to do. I want to be with you."

He pulls her onto his lap. "Let's get something straight. I never considered our commitment to each other to be decided by a piece of paper or a ring on your finger, but I can arrange for it to happen tomorrow."

Her eyes pop. "Just like that, you would marry me?"

Taking her chin between his fingers, he raises her face until she's looking him in the eye. "Yes." He kisses her cheek and wraps his arms around her.

"You're right. Paper and rings aren't a symbol of our love, and if I'm honest, if we were to be married, I'd want it to be in front of our family and friends."

"If we do this now, it would be for you and me. We could have another celebration later."

She takes his hand and places it over her heart. "It's reckless for you to have my heart racing after all it's been through."

Samuel slides down onto one knee. "Eden. You steal my breath, and I'm often lost for words just by the sight of you. I know what I feel in my heart, and it beats only for you." He takes her hand and places it over his heart in the same gesture. "I want to spend the rest of my life with you. Will you marry me?"

She kisses him again and again. "A thousand times, yes."

Samuel assists Eden from the taxi and takes her hand as they enter the hotel foyer. Dinner at a romantic restaurant is what Eden had needed. They chatted about her family and friends while dodging the topic of her return home. Tonight, he'll gently coax her into doing what's right, and it's not returning to Ulara with him.

He expects she'll be tired and want to fall asleep. The remaining pathology results should be back tomorrow, so he'll arrange for her to go home in the next week.

While Eden sleeps, he can research flights. He had overlooked the effort for her to come to him. Her flight to Sydney was a couple of hours. Then she took an international flight to Santiago, Chile, which was almost eighteen hours in duration. It took several flights from Santiago to reach him in Venezuela, all before boarding the curiara for the boat ride.

Their baby is growing. Flying for many hours can be problematic and not only for comfort. He's concerned about deep vein thrombosis.

Eden showers before bed, and he smiles at how she's showering at least three times a day while she can.

He opens his phone and scrolls through the news. Eden has forced his hand to face what's happening in the world. He has only answered to the shaman for several years and thought every country's leader insignificant to his chosen lifestyle. There's political unrest *everywhere.* He had researched what his friend told him about Venezuela and was shocked to read how thousands of physicians had fled the country. Even in Chile, people sleep in airports where flights have been delayed because of an imposed curfew. He'll fly as far as he can with her to Santiago before returning to Ulara to his quarantine camp. He doesn't want to think about Eden leaving, the lonely nights and the days blending as one.

Every day she has chipped away at his armor, leaving his life and love exposed and his heart vulnerable. He wants nothing more than to be with her, spend the rest of his days with her, and until then, it's his responsibility to keep her safe.

Samuel closes his phone when Eden exits the bathroom with a towel on her head and one draped over her breasts. The swell of her stomach gives the most beautiful shape to her curves, one he never expected to see on a woman who had captured his heart.

He falls to his knees where she stands, opens the towels and kisses her thighs, the dark line of her linea nigra, and turns his head as though listening to their baby.

Eden runs her fingers over his scalp. “You’ll only hear my belly complaining I ate far too much.”

He gazes up at her. “Do you mind if I have a word?”

Eden tilts her head and smiles.

“I’m yet to meet you, and already you have fulfilled my life in a way you’ll never know. As your father, I vow to do what’s best for you and your mother, even if it means sacrificing what’s best for me. So forgive me for sending you away when all I want is to be there when you come into the world. Your mother will take care of you until we can be a family.”

Eden clutches his hair and tilts his head until their eyes meet. A single tear rolls down her cheek. “No,” she murmurs. “Please don’t do this.”

“I need you to be safe.”

Eden backs away, so his hands fall to his sides. “No.”

“I’m doing this for us.”

“Then come with us. Come with us now, and be with me in Australia when I have our baby.”

15

EDEN

"In Australia…"

Samuel remains on his knees, head bowed.

I wait for an apology, a confession.

"I can't," he whispers. "Not yet."

Gah.

I storm to the minibar and shake the bottle of whiskey. "You know this is when I miss drinking."

He's beside me, and I didn't hear him move. "I have to finish up my work, complete my contract, and then I'll be on the first flight to you."

"It concerns me how you don't want to be there when I have our baby. I mean, what if things go wrong, and I can't contact you—"

"Don't. Don't do that." He places both hands on her shoulders and leans, so his forehead touches hers.

"And it's not just me." God, he has unleashed the bitch inside of me. I can't control my voice to discuss anything calmly with the urge to yell at him until he gives in. Only he won't. I know it's the part he struggles with —a side of him hung up on failure. And I'm destroying him by allowing him to think he's failing me when he's doing his best to keep us safe. "Your parents. Why haven't you told them they are going to be grandparents?"

"I can email them now."

"Christ, Samuel, listen to yourself. *Email.* When was the last time you spoke to them?"

He backs away from me until his legs hit the bed, and he sits on the edge. He slouches so his elbows rest on his knees. "We don't have that sort of relationship, but if it's what you want, I'll do it."

"I have to call my parents," I tell him. "We'll do it together. I'll call from the bathroom, and you do it from here." I check the world clock. It's nine at night, so it's around five in the afternoon in LA and nine in the morning in Adelaide. His face turns ghostly white, yet I stand my ground waiting for him to pick up the phone.

"Are you going to police the call?" he asks. I ignore it because these are all steps to melting the armor to why he believes his life is in Ulara.

"Only until they answer, and then I'll make my calls."

I wait until he presses buttons, then he turns the screen.

Mom.

A woman's voice answers.

"Samuel?" Her voice sounds excited yet confused.

His free hand supports his forehead. "Hey. I'm sorry it's taken this long to call..."

I leave him and head into the bathroom to call my parents. I decide to buzz Mum in case Dad's in a work meeting.

"Eden."

The warmth of her voice wraps around me like a blanket comforting and protecting in equal measures.

"Hi, Mum."

"It's good to hear your voice. I'm at Faith's now helping her with the baby. Seb, stop. Mummy can't do that while she's holding the baby. Come here, and Nanna will do it for you. Wait, love, I'll put you on speaker. Say hello to Aunty Eden."

She doesn't question my safety, so it makes it easy to account for my well-being. I love hearing her interact with her grandchildren and look forward to the day she'll have a special relationship with my baby.

"Seb." I focus on my nephew. "Aunty Eden misses you. Do you want me to bring home a surprise?"

"Tell Eden you miss her. He's showing you his dinosaur figurine. Darling, Eden can't see it. Growl, growl, roarrr. Yes, that's right, darling. Oh, now we have a lion toy."

"Hi, Eden," Faith calls out from the background. "Welcome to my madhouse."

"How are you, Faith? And baby James?"

"I'm good. Busy coping with a two-year-old and a two-month-old. Wait, no he's ten weeks now."

I never knew why mothers counted in weeks.

"Great. Well, I just wanted to check in. Everything is wonderful here. I thought I'd call while I have internet. Sometimes it's hard, and the weather has changed, so it just rains nonstop." I hold my tongue, not wanting them to panic about any little thing. "It's annoying, that's all. Makes for a boring day sitting in the hut. I'll check in soon, okay? Oh, and I had a scan..."

"Is everything okay?" Mum asks quickly.

"Of course. But I wanted to let you all know I'm having a little girl, and everything is fine." I'm amazed by my acting skills and how together I sound.

"Oh, Eden, that's wonderful. I'm so happy for you. When are you coming home?" Mum asks.

"I'm not sure, Mum. In a month or less. I'm working out Christmas festivities with Samuel now. I love you. I'll talk soon, okay."

"Stay safe, Edes," Faith says quickly.

"Bye." I end the call and take a deep, healing breath. The hardest call is to Dad, and I'm waiting for tomorrow to speak to him. Beyond the door, I hear the murmur of Samuel's voice. He's still on the phone. So I stay in the bathroom to give him the privacy he needs and scroll through the few photos on my phone. There are some of the jungle and others on the curiara with Asoo and Samuel. I send them to Amy, then to Faith with a text asking her to show them to Mum and Dad.

I open up Instagram. Scroll. Close it. Facebook. Scroll. I feel out of touch with everything I'm reading. An unsettling sensation creeps over my skin as though I'm lost in another dimension, and the world keeps spinning without me. I open up the Netflix app. Damn, there are so many shows I haven't seen. If I were home, I wouldn't have missed them. Did I watch half the shows so I felt like part of the mob and excited?

Everything I did then seems insignificant when compared to my life here.

The room next door is silent. I open the door enough to see out a gap. Samuel is lying on his back with his arm over his eyes.

"Are you okay?" I ask in a gentle voice.

"Y-Yeah." His voice cracks, and his arm remains over his face.

I slide onto the bed next to him. "Were they glad to hear your voice?"

"They want to meet you."

I smile even though he can't see it and remain quiet, hoping he'll say more.

"They want to know when I'm coming home. The conversation started well until they berated me for not having a career and a home for you and the baby. They questioned my sanity as to why I'm here and putting you in danger. It made sense, and yet it opened up a gaping hole of emptiness at the thought of going home to live the same life as them. Always living to their standards and never being enough."

"You're enough. You're an amazing man, and I'm proud of what you're doing. Your work makes a difference to many lives." Holding my stomach, I roll onto my side so I can look at him, touch him. I rest my hand over his heart. "I know how big your heart is for all of us."

We haven't resolved some issues, and yet he took some steps in reassessing what he needs in his life. I know it's my baby and me. And it might not be his home in LA, which is fine by me. I'd like to think he was on good terms with his parents so they would want to come and visit us. I'm yet to find out what really pushed him to come to the jungle, and I know it had something to do with his parents and a girl while he was at college.

But this is enough for one day. I'm exhausted, and we both need to call it a night.

"Eden."

I open my eyes and try to focus. Is it morning already?

Samuel hands me his phone. "It's Dr. Jagdeo." He's dressed, showered, and shaved. I'm still in bed.

"What time is it?"

"Eight thirty."

And I have an overwhelming urgency. I wave my hand at him to take the phone. "I have to pee."

Samuel chuckles before he speaks. "She needs to pee."

Argh. Did he have to tell him?

"Sure, I'll pass on her results."

My bladder hasn't been the same this past week. I'm sure our daughter takes pleasure dancing on my organs.

When I exit the bathroom, Samuel has ended the call. "Did you want to talk to him because you can call him back?"

"Do I need to?"

"Your bloods are fine, and your fecal samples have come back negative for blood or any worms."

"Worms?" I cough.

"There are worse things than worms. He wants you to stay on the iron tablets until you have the baby."

"Those tablets make my…"

"No need to explain." Samuel grins at me. "It's best for now. You should have a repeat blood test in another month to compare."

Another month. For now, I'm not sure where that will be. All I know is I want to be wherever Samuel is and not *alone*. "Hey, can we go out for coffee?" It's a luxury to do these things with him, and I'm trying to show him what our future could look like."

"I'll do whatever you want since it's our last day here."

"Are all my results back?"

He nods once.

I'm not discussing anything right now. "Book a taxi for an hour. Maybe we can eat lunch in a quirky café."

"Quirky…" He shakes his head.

"And maybe you can get a haircut," I tell him.

The look on his face has me giggling as I head to the shower.

"I need a date, Eden." He taps away on his phone. "We're booking your flight home today."

The smile has evaporated from my lips. "No." I shake my head several times. "You promised me one month."

"Okay. One month. Give me a day." His steely eyes fix on me.

"Fine. Two days after Christmas so we get to celebrate together."

"Eden." He lowers the phone from his face. "You are required to fly before you're thirty-six weeks pregnant. Now that your date is mid-January—"

“But the authorities don’t know that. They still have my January 30 date from my gynecologist. Please, give me Christmas.”

It gives me the extra time to convince him to make the journey home with me.

16

SAMUEL

Two Days Later...

Eden had convinced Samuel to stay in Canaima for a week to quarantine in his room, yet not so far from a Cessna if she needs to fly out. He was also comforted knowing his order of supplies will arrive, and he'd have enough medication and sterile instruments on hand.

"Samuel."

He turns to his friend who's calling his name outside the room. Eden is asleep on the bed, so he sneaks out to speak with Asoo, remaining a few yards apart.

"The miners you speak of along the Carrao River. They talk of burning forests and building mines, look for hidden gold in river. In tepui. Garimpeiros will come work. Everyone needs money."

"Mine near the tepui?"

"Yes, my friend."

"Christ. Where did you hear this?"

Asoo points to the restaurant. "They stay here. They eat here."

"When?"

"Three days ago." He holds up four fingers.

"Where are they now?"

"Getting chain saws and guns."

"You need to warn your friends, all the Pemón communities, not to work for these men. Ask the elders to explain the damage and how they'd be slaves."

He assumes it will be months before the mine opens, yet he knows the shaman has to be notified. The mine will be on the opposite side of the tepui, but the mine leaders will risk Pemón lives with no regard to Indian values and destroy everything that's sacred.

"Asoo, please bring me a map of the area from reception."

Asoo nods before heading to the office building.

It's time the chief and shaman saw his paper map.

He returns to his room and sits on the bed where Eden sleeps, opening the news app on his phone. Many countries remain hostile, and civilization is still competing to be the most beautiful, the most famous, or the biggest jerk. There's a part of him that vowed never to return to society, and it creates an internal battle with his love for Eden.

She makes a sound from her throat. A sharp sob. Is she dreaming?

Samuel takes hold of her hand and gives a gentle squeeze to indicate she's safe. It's enough to rouse her, and she opens her eyes, closes them as though relieved to be with him.

"What are you dreaming about?" he asks gently.

"Their faces," she murmurs. "I keep seeing the sticks in their cheeks, mouth, and nose and the way his dark eyes stared at me as though I was an animal."

Sliding down the covers to be closer, he pulls her to his side. "Appearances are measured differently in every society. What you find beautiful, they may find offensive. The Indians are in tune with the jungle. She's a source of life and not feared or considered a hostile place."

"I don't think the jungle is hostile. I just... don't know it well, so it's dangerous in that respect."

"I know, and you're looking more relaxed with every week you stay. I'm explaining how the Watache respect all creatures of the jungle, including the most venomous. Those sticks in the shaman's face? It's his way of dressing like a cat. He believes it helps him to hunt more effectively and move quietly through the jungle."

"Like the jaguar."

He strokes her long white tresses, now tamed after days of brushing and repeated washes. "Your hair would've freaked them out. A white-haired woman would be sent from the spirits. You would be equally disturbing to them as they were to you."

"I've never been more flattered to be called ugly," she murmurs.

He offers a weak smile, knowing her nightmares may go on and cause her other grief.

"The jaguar... I see it too. It's in my dreams only I'm not afraid, which is weird," she murmurs.

"Why is it weird?"

"It's the one animal the Indians fear even though they respect everything about the jungle. My brain must work backward because I'm afraid of the things you mention can help, and what everyone else fears, I'm like... meh."

"Dreams and reality are two different things. There must be something about it that's talking to you," he prompts.

"It has the most hypnotizing blue eyes. It watches me. It's not like I'm its next meal or anything, it's more like..." she shrugs, "... it sounds crazy but as though it's protecting me."

"Not crazy," he says. Samuel thought her grandmother's spirit might look out for her granddaughter. "The jungle speaks to us in many forms."

"It's another reason I want to stay. There's a voice calling me, and I feel like the jungle isn't done with me yet. I hope it's not the Mawarí enticing me back to seek revenge." She holds his gaze. "I've made mistakes before, but this feels different."

"It's not the Mawarí." He kisses the top of her head. "I have something to tell you. While you were sleeping, I emailed the pharmaceutical company's HR explaining I won't be renewing my contract for another year. One more journey to the tepui to retrieve the flower along with the roots, and once I've sent the samples to Caracas, my contract can be terminated."

"What about your duty to the Ularans?"

"You and our baby will be my responsibility."

For a long moment, Eden stares at him. "You'll struggle to say goodbye."

"I will," he says, his throat suddenly tight. Fear runs along his spine at the thought of returning to society to the place that caused him years of unhappiness. Back then, he had no soul. He's no longer that man, thanks to the beautiful woman beside him. Yet that dark voice whispers to him, reminding him of his past.

A failure.

And Eden is better off without him.

He has built a life in Ulara. A life he loves.

Now it comes down to a choice.

And he'll always choose her.

Regardless of the consequences on him.

17

EDEN

THE FOLLOWING MORNING, Samuel left to meet with Asoo. He says they need to discuss business and to call him if I need him. I have a couple of hours to spare, so I wander out to the gardens and stroll a short distance along the path.

It's truly paradise, and the postcard view lifts my spirits. Closing my eyes, I visualize the animals and their sounds echoing from the rainforest. Howler monkeys high in the treetops. The macaws deathly screech. The constant clicking of insects, and now the buzzing above my head. I head back to Samuel's room intending to nap. If only I had a book to read.

It's been a couple of weeks since I opened Gran's diary. I retrieve it from my backpack and slide onto the bed with a piece of chikoo fruit. Samuel insists this fruit should be part of my daily diet because it's a super food that has everything our daughter and I need. He also emphasized that it will help my body heal quicker than most drugs people have been shoving at me. Since it tastes similar to a pear, I'm not objecting, and it's easier to eat than some foods I've been offered in Ulara.

Relaxing with a book feels much like home.

The thought comforts me.

Until I clasp my chest and burp out air. Ugh, this heartburn is annoying.

Another thing, when did I stop being a lady? Because at night, I giggle, thinking how air just sneaks out of me.

"What are you doing to me?" I say affectionately to our baby. A smile stretches my lips, knowing we're going to be okay. Staring at Gran's diary, I wonder about her pregnancy and what support she had from the shaman because she didn't have someone like Samuel to guide and support her through it. I imagine my Gran being strong like the other Ularan women. I have her blood pumping through my veins. Her strength is with my spirit, and she'll help and guide me while I'm in the jungle, doing what she did decades ago.

Mum said she had blessed me when I was born. Maybe she had some power to see my future and visualize this moment where we'd connect even though times separate our journey. A different level of consciousness unites us.

15TH MAY 1961

What's wrong with me?

I'm a nurse, for God's sake, and I can't even cope with a baby. I know my skills. I have the knowledge only the black hole keeps threatening to swallow me up every night. Every night I'm scared to close my eyes. It is not the fear of dying. It's the demons waiting for me, whispering that it is all a lie. It shouldn't bother me, but no sooner do I close my eyes and Winston starts crying, I'm up pacing the floor with him in my arms.

Last night I was so tired I walked around in zombie form, and I almost dropped him. There was a moment I wished I did because then all the crying would stop. And I've hated myself since because it's not how I feel. I love my baby. I've just stopped loving myself because I'm trying to find that mother-baby connection.

It's not there.

My heart is empty.

I tried to talk to Albert this morning.

He brushed me off and said all mothers are tired, and I'm going through a stage. He didn't even offer to help.

19th May 1961

I haven't showered in two days, and I'm wearing the same pajamas.
Winston isn't crying as much, so I can't even blame the colic.
What sort of life can I offer him when I can't even manage to change my clothes? I see the sideways glances from Albert. He notices, yet he doesn't say anything. I know he thinks I'm a terrible mother.

3rd June 1961

Brenda is getting married. I'm thrilled for her as it's her dream, and she wants babies more than anyone.
I showered before she came to visit me and pinned my hair to the top of my head in a classic roll. The guilt stops me from telling her the truth.
I wanted to share in her happiness. When she asked me to be her Maid of Honor, I cried. She thought it was tears of joy. How am I going to pull myself together in three months?
I need a miracle to get me out of this cave.

"Gran." I wipe a single tear before it cascades over my cheek. I don't want to keep reading, only I need to know she got through this and found her way out of the darkness because it's the darkness that scares me too.

I remember the day Gran died. It was the same time we heard of the Haiti earthquake in January 2010. I remember the devastation of Dad telling Faith and me that Gran had passed in her sleep from a heart attack. Then the world grieved with the devastation of Mother Nature's wrath. I was around fifteen at the time, and I couldn't fathom life without Gran.

She had never mentioned being in the jungle, although her stories of life lessons made sense, especially her love of nature and every creature on earth. I got my spider phobia from my mum's side of the family because Gran loved to keep the huntsman spiders in her house.

"*Henry is eating the flies and mosquitoes for me*," she'd say.

I lean up on my elbow and look around the stunning vista surrounding me. *God, she must have loved this place.*

My stomach tightens, and I groan before breathing through the Braxton Hicks contraction. "You can practice all you like," I tell my daughter. "I'm not ready for you to make any surprise appearances just yet."

23RD SEPTEMBER 1961

It's Brenda's wedding day. I'm so excited for her. Albert bought me the dress for the wedding, and I feel excited to finally wear it.

I have had time to think and consider the guilt that cripples my thoughts. It is not being a mother that I struggle with most, and it's not working and being financially independent. I miss caring for my patients, knowing I'm doing some good in the world. Winston doesn't need someone like me. Anyone can feed him and change a nappy. He'll appreciate his mother when he's older.

I'm going to ask Albert if I can at least take on the bookkeeping for the hotel. He'll need to teach me. Then he could care for Winston while I do a day's work.

I'm going to ask him tonight after the wedding when he's in a good mood.

28TH SEPTEMBER 1961

Albert told me he didn't need my help to run the hotel. I should just do what I'm good at and be a mother for Winston and cook his dinner every night.

I've cried myself to sleep the past five nights.

I don't have a purpose. There has to be more to life than this.

After completing my nursing, I have so much to offer. Why do I have to act like it no longer matters? Albert said my role is to be a good wife and obey my husband.

We have one shot at life, and this isn't the life I choose.

I'm an awful person.

I should be happy. I have a home, a husband who loves and cares for me, and a beautiful son.

When did I become ungrateful?

Date: 10th October 1961

Today I received a letter from Dr. Anderson.
I hid it from Albert and waited until he was in the office until I read it.
I can't stop shaking.
It's the best news to feel valued. Only it is pointless. I can't go.
There's no way I can leave Winston and Albert to do something like volunteer in an indigenous community in Venezuela. He'd call me selfish.
And it's true. Only I can't stop dreaming about it.
I'll keep the letter as a reminder someone values my work and me.

I'm holding my breath. Despite my heart breaking for the pain she's suffering through, I'm struck with the realization this is the letter that invites her to come here fifty-eight years ago.

My whole body tingles. I hold the diary to my chest.

I want to feel the excitement and sense of adventure my Gran would've experienced. Mum mentioned her time in the jungle is documented in a journal, which her friend Brenda knows about. I vaguely remember Brenda at Gran's funeral, dressed in black with red shoes and handbag. I remember thinking why red?

Our advances in medicine have come a long way since the 1960s. Yet, she endured the hardship. She survived for a couple of years as I'm not sure of her time volunteering before she discovered Ulara. In that time, she gave birth to a baby in the jungle with more than likely no help from anyone. Remembering Gran as a strong-minded lady and slightly stubborn, her determination to be included in the community and be as one with Ularans with no special benefits isn't surprising. The energy explodes within me with the lightbulb moment. This is my destiny. Gran lives in me, her spirit has remained here, and if Gran could give birth in the jungle like many other women, it's not outrageous for me to have my baby here with my daughter's father by my side. Apart from the improvement in medicine and having extra supplies on hand, Samuel *is* a doctor, and he'll be with me during the birth—an advantage over Gran who would've wandered from the village, squatted over a hole, and delivered Kaikare herself, going by their tradition. Maybe some women were there to help.

Nonetheless, I'm in a far better position than her.

I'll have the baby here—in Ulara.

18

SAMUEL

SAMUEL TOOK commitment as serious as a vow.

Years ago, he took an oath to keep the location of Ulara a secret. The people's safety was of utmost importance, and he promised the shaman he'd work alongside him to provide medicine and advise him on the science Samuel had learned in his medical studies. Although science isn't a word he could use, and it came down to his people, where he was born. Now *his people* are about to illegally mine an area close to the tepuis—a dangerous undertaking for those workers with the unpredictability of the tepui formation and how those in command treat the workers. He hopes his fear of the mine affecting Ulara is only that—a fear. Other mines have poisoned the local river systems with mercury leaching into the water and soil. It not only destroys the environment and water surrounding the mine but thanks to the poisoned fish, all the communities further down the river have been known to fall ill. He prays the government hears about the illegal mine and stops it before it destroys the surrounding ecosystem.

Overbearing all other fears is someone stumbling across Ulara. Their primitive minds and ways of life will be mocked, and he understands the mindset of outsiders. Other tribes have been bullied into change and tried to be saved with the way of God.

Their beliefs, lifestyle, and superior connection to the jungle would be perceived as being crazy, and they'd be thought of as inferior beings.

The thought of bullying and enforcing change, then the suffering of the people he loves, has his chest tightening in fear. Especially knowing the Ularans have no immunity to many diseases outsiders will bring.

Even though the sun has barely encroached the horizon, he makes out Asoo throwing a bag into the curiara.

"Buenos días," Samuel greets Asoo. He leaps into the curiara and distributes the waterproofed bags evenly under the seats. "What happened here?" He points to a section where several planked seats have been removed.

"Eden to rest," he says, as though Samuel should understand. "Eden in pain last time."

Samuel hesitates, wanting to tell him Eden will not be traveling in the curiara. She's resting in Canaima before traveling home. The gut feeling she'll fight him on this halts his words. For now, she is healthy and safe. Victor will check on her during the day while Samuel investigates the location of the proposed mine with Asoo. He doesn't expect any complications. However, he left instructions with Victor on who to call if there's an emergency.

The risk holds more danger than he cares to contemplate. Both men are aware their presence needs to be hidden at all costs. They have fishing lines and bait to use as an alibi in case they are questioned.

To further strengthen their camouflage as hunters searching for food, the men have no phones or cameras. An action to prove they aren't spying so as not to cause a reaction if they are caught out or anything untoward happens, Victor is the sole person aware of their venture, and they have no means of contacting any other authority.

Samuel opens the map and spreads it out on the wooden seat. He marks the location of the small Pemón communities dotted along the river. With the latest rainfall, another tributary formed with the overflow of surplus water from the tepui, and it snaked a path to join the Carrao River. The tributary is their destination. Some of these smaller offshoots disappear in the dry season. It is a risk yet perfect for the mine to be invisible since barely anyone would know the location unless they are planning to dam the water supply from another source.

"You have sent word?" Samuel says as they sail along Canaima lagoon.

"Everyone want money," Asoo says, his expression serious.

Samuel understands the difficulty in convincing the communities the small pay for slave labor isn't worth risking their lives. Money is survival to these communities as many have forgotten the way of their ancestors by relying on the land for survival. Western lifestyle has influenced their lives, and money controls their life. It's no longer simply hard work and toil in the fields to sustain their well-being.

They sail along the Carrao River, navigating the Mayupa rapids and onto Orchid Island. They pass the fork to the Churun River, which leads them to Angel Falls and Ulara. Instead, they continue east, then north on the Carrao River, and when the sun is high in the sky, they pass the first curiara anchored to the bank with a makeshift tent onboard, supported by poles. A long rope secures the temporary barge to nearby trees. Three hammocks hang beneath the canopy as well as a line with towels drying. Between the trees is a small opening leading into the jungle.

Asoo shakes his head, and they continue their journey. Several of these unsafe barges dot the shores of the river. The water is a dull caramel color, and there's evidence of sedimentation from the mines.

The curiara hits something hard in the river, and Samuel's body slams forward. Asoo kills the engine and leans over the edge to investigate the cause. Closer to the shore, there are artificial sand mounds caused by the mine drenching the riverbed searching for gold. Not far ahead along the river edge is a barge constructed of ropes and plastic bottles acting as a flotation device supporting the machines that do the damage.

Asoo hands Samuel a paddle, and the men steer the curiara toward the shore. They drag their curiara onto the sand and creep toward the sound of a clicking motor.

They barely make it one hundred yards before a bare-chested man wearing long shorts calls out to Asoo.

"Stay here," Asoo tells Samuel.

Samuel watches as the two men talk for a few minutes until the other raises his voice and uses his arms to dramatize his response. Although Samuel is fluent in Spanish and Pemón, the men are speaking fast and over each other. The dark-haired man turns and glares at Samuel, halting Samuel from taking a further step. Instead, he leaves the men to speak in private and takes shade under a tree. He reaches to lean a weary arm on the trunk and, in a reflex action, snaps his arm away. From the ground to the canopy, organized lines of bullet ants carry leaves in their pinchers. Samuel springs back, checking the ground for the nest. He dusts himself and stamps his feet, then glances up to both men smiling in his direction. Ten days away from the rainforest, and he has forgotten the ways.

Asoo weaves around the wild cashew trees and waves Samuel toward the curiara.

"We go now," he says with underlying urgency.

"What did you see?" Samuel pushes the curiara into the water while Asoo mans the motor.

"Nothing." When they are in the middle of the river, Asoo speaks over the sound of the engine. "Other bad men. Diego do nothing wrong. He say he Pemón and this our land. We mine our own land so he not..." he pauses a moment, "... breaking law."

"I'm aware many people break the law, but this isn't about the law. It's about the damage to the environment and poisoning the water. You've seen first-hand what the mercury does, and we don't want radioactive green lagoons that will kill the fish, your primary source of protein." Samuel curses under his breath. Asoo isn't the person to lecture.

"He's earning six American dollars a month. He has to feed his family."

"He is risking his life and destroying his water system for a mere six bucks a month?"

"It good money, my friend. Most earn two dollars."

Samuel shakes his head. "The younger generation needs to be educated about the benefits of living off the land. We don't want them to think this is what they have to do to survive."

Asoo's shoulders slump. "His wife coming to cook for men. His children will help sift. He get more money in gold."

"Where will they live? On those makeshift barges on the river? If the government finds out—"

"He tells me I no understand. I have job. The government made him broke. This our land. He needs to feed his family."

"So the children's education will cease?"

"We fight another way, my friend. If we stay and his boss return, we all die."

"I'm guessing his boss isn't Pemón?"

"No."

Asoo remains quiet for a while. Both men are aware the dry season is when more mines will pop up, and operation will be at night under the lights of gasoline burners.

This fight is bigger than one or two men. Samuel hopes Asoo can warn the communities not to fall prey to these mines. He needs him to directly influence other employment using their farming skills or even their craft work including basket weaving for the tourists—if tourists return. Only with no tourists...

Samuel focuses on the impact to the Ularan people. In time, their migration to find another home is inevitable.

West.

That's the way he'd have to send them. It's the only safe direction. It's the same direction he sent the Watache, only deeper into the jungle.

A journey the shaman would expect him to do with them.

But would he find his way out alone?

19

EDEN

I'M ALMOST asleep when there's a bang on the door.

I jump up, expecting Samuel.

"Oh, Victor." I lean a hand into my lower back and stretch out.

"Sorry, Miss Eden. I hope I didn't disturb you?"

I shake my head, not wanting to admit he got me out of bed. I saw him before dinner, and he wasn't this pale. "No, I'm just resting."

"Is Samuel here?" He moves his weight side to side while waiting for an answer.

"Sorry, no. Wait, you haven't seen them either? I expected them to be here by now."

Victor scratches his ear without looking at me. "Please ask Samuel to speak to me when they get back."

"Should I be concerned about something?"

"No, Miss Eden." He waves both hands at me as though to erase any stress. "Everything fine. Samuel will be back soon."

He takes off along the garden path and disappears into the night. Beyond the lodge, Canaima Lake is still peaceful. There's no sound of a motor, only the constant croak of frogs and chirping insects. A buzzing at my ear has me swatting the air, then pushing the door closed. I adjust the mosquito net and climb into bed even though I'm no longer tired.

This is what it will be like when we're apart—Samuel out trying to save everyone, me worrying about the danger and whether he'll even return. It's why I begged him not to go until he explained the reason, and I understood his concern. Only I know this isn't something he and Asoo can fix in one day.

Pressing fingertips to my temples, I massage tiny circles. I can't allow my mind to jump into a negative cycle and think the worst. There's strength in optimism. Samuel is an intelligent man, and Asoo knows the river like the back of his hand.

Positive thoughts. I rub my hand over my baby bump. *Everything will be fine*.

Eventually, I fall asleep, but I'm woken with the discomfort of gas. I am learning the many discomforts associated with being pregnant. When I rise to head to the bathroom, I notice the space beside me is still empty. I check the time on my phone—two o'clock in the morning.

Damn you, Samuel.

How am I to sleep knowing he's out there somewhere and possibly in the hands of criminals.

I switch on the light and pad to the bathroom. Then I climb back into bed, and before I switch off the bedside lamp, a sound chimes from my phone, and it's not the usual ringtone.

I dive on it, thinking it could be Samuel when, in reality, where he's traveling doesn't have connection service.

Snapchat?

I swipe the screen to accept the group Snapchat video call. One by one, my friends' faces appear on the screen.

"You answered," Amy screams. I can't help the smirk in reaction to her big, bright smile.

"Hi, girls," I sing. "Checking in on me?"

"Damn right," Yasmine says and blows me a kiss. "When Amy said you could still be in Canaima, we thought let's do a group chat."

"Where are you?"

"Having a late lunch at Yasmine's," Amy responds. "What time is it there?"

"After two."

"Shit, tell Samuel we're sorry," Yasmine says. "Hi, Samuel." She waves.

"He's not here." Before I explain, Yasmine's brows tighten.

"He's left you alone, again?"

"He's supposed to be back by now. He is with Asoo looking into..." I decide not to explain the situation to my friends. I shake my head. "It's not important. He'll be home soon. Hey, do you want to see my baby bump?"

"Hell, yes," Amy says.

I stand and tug up my tank top and angle the camera for my friends to see the swell of my abdomen.

"You're huge." Amy laughs.

"You look beautiful," Yasmine says in a gentle voice. "I wish you were here so we could experience it with you."

"Yeah... I miss you both." I take a breath and force the emotion from building in my chest. "One good thing, I haven't had to spend a shitload of money on an entire new maternity wardrobe while in the jungle."

Amy chuckles. "No fun in that."

"How are you really?" Yasmine asks.

I fake a sincere smile. "I'm good. We're both healthy. The time has passed so quickly, and it won't be long until I'm home again."

"I miss us," Amy says. "I miss going to the Shores, just the three of us for cocktail Fridays."

"Even if I were there—"

"I know, I know," Amy says quickly. "Stay safe and hurry home." She wipes an eye, and my stomach drops to my feet.

"Soon, the three of us will be taking long walks along the beach behind a carriage," Yasmine chimes in.

I can picture it clearly and smile at the thought. "We have plenty of good times ahead of us with a plus one."

"You mean plus two," Amy corrects.

"I'm still working on him," I reply honestly.

Yasmine's eyes widen.

"He has some work to do first but hopes to make it back to Australia in time for the birth," I lie.

Yasmine's lips press thin. As though she senses my apprehension, she smiles at Amy. "Have you told her about your new guy?"

"No, he's not my new guy. He's my guy for now."

Yasmine and I both chuckle.

"Yet you have a date in an hour," Yasmine adds.

"Get ready, Ames." I smile at my friends. "When I'm next in Canaima, we'll do this again."

"Do you know when that will be?" Yasmine frowns at me.

This time, I opt for the truth. "No."

AT FIRST LIGHT, I push out of bed, ignoring the lethargy weighing down my legs. I refuse to lay here while Samuel could be in danger. My first instinct is to pull back the blind and peer out to the vast green jungle bordered by prehistoric mountains to where Samuel could be. I move the blind aside, and my God, there's a body curled up in the hammock on my porch.

I creep out despite only wearing a tank top and panties and lift the mosquito net to touch his shoulder.

Dirt smears his face, bare arms, and legs, and it reminds me of our life in Ulara. Sliding my fingers through his already unruly hair, my nails catch in knotted ends. "Samuel," I whisper. "Come inside."

"I need to shower," he mumbles. "I didn't want to disturb you."

"Well, I didn't sleep well without you, so please come inside." I take his hand and tug lightly.

He lets out a groan, swings his legs over the side, and rubs his dirty hands over his face. "Is it dawn already?"

"How long have you been here?"

"A couple of hours."

I take his hand to pull him up, and there's smeared blood over his shins. "What happened to you?"

"I'll shower first. Then sleep. Then we'll talk."

With his hand on my shoulder, I walk with him to the shower realizing how much the trip took everything out of him. He rips off his T-shirt and cargo shorts. "These can go in the trash," he grunts.

I pull my tank top over my head and toss it aside. I slide off my panties and step into the shower with him. "Here." I place both his hands on the wall and then lather soap to wash over his back, arms, and shoulders. I miss these sensual moments. Even if he's exhausted, I'm not passing up an opportunity to run my hands over the smooth muscles of his body. After filling the palm of my hand with shampoo, I lather it into his hair. "Can you bend down so I can massage your scalp?"

"God, that feels good."

A soft laugh comes from me. "It's nice to reverse the roles. You can rinse it now."

Eyes closed, he tilts his head and pushes the last of the shampoo out of his hair. I focus on his face. His expression is a combination of pleasure and relief. The bones of his cheek are more prominent than they were when we first met. Lines are etched deeper near his eyes. The slight stubble of fair hair dots his chin. I prefer him without a beard, but I'll take Samuel any way I can.

He rubs both hands over his face and opens his eyes. I gasp. So many emotions roll off him—so much pain. Even though his love for me is there, I sense more.

A man seeking understanding.

A man crumbling with the walls of his demeanor cracking.

A heart that wants to give and give until...

"What happened yesterday?"

His eyes flick over my face.

"Don't give me an edited version. I can handle it."

"I know you can." He places a hand on my cheek. "But you've been through enough."

"Apart from going crazy last night knowing you could be in danger, I'm fine," I emphasize. "You don't have to carry the burden alone." I take his hands and place them on the swell of my body. "Talk to me because we're here for you."

His gaze fixes on my ever-growing stomach. He lowers to his knees and kisses my stomach before placing his ear to the mound. "Yes," he whispers. "I know your mother can be stubborn. I agree." His gaze lifts and meets mine, and he's smirking. "We're both tired, and we need to sleep."

I smile at his effort to distract me. I turn off the tap and hand him a towel. While I dry off, I keep a close eye on him. He groans when he bends to run the towel along his long limbs. I push up to my toes and ruffle his hair with a towel. "I'm going to cut your hair before we leave."

"When you say we leave, where do you think we're going to go?"

I take his hand and lead him back to the bed. "Ulara."

He says nothing, yet I feel the tension in him.

"Another thing to discuss after you sleep," I add.

I climb under the sheet with him and roll, so my head is close to his, although my stomach keeps us apart.

He edges closer to kiss me on the lips. "Let me sleep so at least I can put up some argument about keeping you safe."

It doesn't take long for Samuel to fall asleep. While he rests, I think more and more about the future. Our future. How far we have come as a couple.

Thinking back to the times I was with Ethan, there was an element of flirtation, a lot of sexting, and every weekend we went out, drank a lot, which led to drunk sex. Yet during the night, he remained with the guys and I with my friends until it was time to go home.

In a short time, I've learned what love is while being with Samuel. We don't need the flirting. Take everything away, his touch, his kisses, the sex, and still that deep feeling of what he means to me remains.

How far I will go for him.

It will be tough when we're apart. I'll give it my all to convince him to come home with me after the baby is born, although already I know there are certain tasks he needs to fulfill, including another trip to the tepui. The thought of him making the journey and leaving me alone in the village again freaks me out. So I accept he'll do the trip when I'm gone. After everything we have been through, I believe we can overcome any obstacle thrown at us. It will take time, and thankfully, I'm learning to be a patient person.

Except while we're here in Canaima with my erratic hormones controlling my thoughts. My fingers skim over his muscled abs, stalling at the dent of the 'V' pointing down to where the sheet sits on his naked hips. I slip one finger under the edge of the sheet.

I want all the sex while we're here because admittedly, there's a lot to be said for a comfortable bed and having access to a shower. As much as I want to wake him and throw my leg over his hips so I'm strategically placed to arouse him, I have to focus on relaxing him so he'll talk to me.

Perhaps there's a point to having sex first.

Allowing him time to sleep, I roll onto my side, close my eyes, and relax alongside him.

"EDEN," Samuel whispers.

My eyes flutter open.

Warm breath blows in my ear. "You were talking in your sleep," he says in a low, sexy voice.

"What did I say?" I murmur, rolling with one hand to cover my eyes.

"It's not what you were saying but more the noises you were making."

Noises. I wipe my mouth. "Was I snoring?"

"Were you dreaming?"

I know what I was dreaming about. I open my eyes, and the way his gaze heats, he knows.

"You..."

"Was I doing this?" He flips onto all fours and trails kisses from my shoulder to my breast. My breath hitches the moment he takes my breast in his mouth, and his tongue toys with my already hard nipple.

"Maybe..." I rasp.

"Or this?" His fingers slide to my hips and then to my legs. He gently prises my thighs apart and finds me ready for him.

My breath comes hard. "More," I manage to say between breaths.

He leans close to my ear while his fingers keep building me to climax. "Let's get one thing straight. For you, I'll give everything and more. At the very least, you have the whole of me." His kisses dot over the swell of my stomach and lower.

"Oh," I murmur when his kisses my clit, then slides his tongue over my labia. I buck my hips. Large hands rest gently on my thighs. I look up to catch a glimpse of Samuel's beautiful face between my legs before I flop back on the pillow, my abs too weak. His fingers find the delicious spot while his mouth teases my clit. He sucks, flicks and licks, and I moan through the rapture.

I cry out when the colors of ecstasy fill my mind. It's more beautiful than ayahuasca's kaleidoscope.

Samuel gives me a moment to catch my breath. I place a hand on his cheek. "I want you," I tell him. "Now and always."

He turns his head and kisses the palm of my hand. "You owned me from the moment I laid eyes on you."

20

SAMUEL

SAMUEL'S HEART doesn't want to slow.

His body calls to hers, the boom vibrating in his ear as loud as the 125 decibels of the white bellbird's mating call. No matter how many times they make love, how close her body lies to his, he'll never get enough of Eden.

For years, he embraced his safety in loneliness. He appreciates those years of being alone to truly experience the pleasure of Eden in his life.

The old Samuel still lives within him, and the same instincts of understanding a woman's needs haven't been lost.

When he used to go out to bars and nightclubs, he could spot the woman needing extra attention from across the room—a woman dragged out by her friends. Tell-tale signs included the way she had to hold something in her hands. Her gaze would flit around the room as though she was assessing her surroundings, and she'd nervously chug down her drink.

Those women craved to be like their friends, and he gave them the confidence to be more in tune with their bodies. Rarely did a woman say no to him. As a young man, Samuel's good looks bewitched women. His friends also possessed unique talents. Michael spoke in French or Spanish, and the ladies became putty in his hands. Given the opportunity, Harrison would remove his shirt to bare his football-muscled body, and women flocked to him.

"What is it?" he asks when Eden winces, a hand reaching beneath her abdomen.

"Braxton Hicks contractions, I assume. Ugh. They burn." Rolling onto her side, she brings her legs to her stomach.

His gut tightens, and his thoughts roll over to all the possibilities that could cause her discomfort. He'll do what he can to reduce her suffering since her pain can bring him to his knees. Sliding her hands away, he gently massages the tight muscles of her abdomen. "Breathe through it."

"I know it's going to get a damn sight worst," she mumbles. "But, ugh."

"It is, and the days are passing fast. We need to discuss—"

Pushing his hands away, she uncurls. The movement is slow. "I've already thought it through." Eden repositions herself to meet his gaze. "I'm going to stay and extend my visa."

He closes his eyes momentarily while images flash through his mind of the worst possible outcome.

"Samuel." Her hand brushes his cheek. "I need to be with you. If you can't return to Australia with me, then I'm staying here with you."

Are the antimalarial drugs clouding her thoughts? "It's no longer safe."

"Really? Is it more dangerous than the time you left me in the jungle to fend on my own when I first found you? Or when I was captured by the cannibals?" Her brow pinches, and she lets out an exasperated sound.

"Yes," he murmurs. "These people are by far more dangerous than the Watache. There's no reasoning with them. They'd rather shoot first and think after."

"Well, I won't be anywhere near those mines, which brings me back to my second part of the argument. If you're in danger, then I don't want you here. You should accompany me back to Australia so you can be with our daughter and me."

Samuel's gut tightens. Eden is even more stubborn than when they first met. Does he have to place her on the damn plane himself to keep her safe?

"I'm going to book your flight, and I don't want to hear another word." He gives her a stern look, but she meets him with a glare reflecting equal determination.

"And if you're not stepping onto that plane with me, you don't have a flying fuck of a chance of sending me away."

He flinches at her words and her tone.

"Take my blood pressure now, I bloody dare you." She awkwardly pushes up from the bed with both hands on her lower back to stretch out her spine. Throwing another glare over her shoulder, she opens her mouth. Closes it. Changes her mind. "It seems I'm the only one committed in this relationship. I gave up everything for you. However, you're still trying to save the bloody world and be the hero to everyone else but me. It's so easy for you to send me home. Keep me safe so you can go about doing whatever it is you're trying to prove to yourself to some... some bloody ghost." She throws her hand in the air to make a point.

His heartbeat thuds behind his ears, and like her, his temper is rising despite years of training to withhold emotion.

She walks to the door and yanks it open, then slams it so hard behind her that the window rattles with the bang. The small print hanging above his dresser slides down the wall and hits the wood with a thud.

Maybe this is what's best for Eden. He can handle her anger if it's what it takes to convince her the safest place for her and their daughter is far away from him.

For how long?

Without her in his life, he'll barely survive. Yet, living in a society where he no longer fits scares him.

Does she expect him to don a shirt, tie, and pants and continue to work as a doctor in the very way he needed to escape?

Samuel closes his eyes and tries to imagine his future with Eden in a world where he doesn't belong. But he has to try for her and their baby.

An hour has passed, and Eden hasn't returned.

There's no perfect solution for either of them. He leaves his room and takes the path toward the restaurant. The vista of the tepuis and Canaima Lake is one of his favorite places, and he smiles, appreciating the place he calls home. Her voice echoes ahead. She's on a bench seat under a tree, looking out to the lake. She is talking on her cell. He approaches cautiously, not wanting to overhear a conversation not intended for him.

Eden turns as if sensing him and holds his gaze. "Yes, I'm fine." She pauses. "Of course. I love you too. I'll speak to you soon." She lowers the cell from her ear. "I have informed my family I'm safe and staying longer."

"What do they think of me?"

Eden tilts her head. "What do you mean?"

"Only a selfish man would keep his pregnant wife in a place that's not safe. So, I can only imagine what their opinion is."

"I told them the decision is mine and that you want me to leave." She pushes up from the seat. "I want more time here. I don't know when I'll see Kaikare again, so please give me this. Yes, I want to stay with you, but there are also other reasons why I'm not leaving yet."

He takes her hand and guides her back down to the seat.

"How long? I'll be comforted if we can book your flight home and work with a date. If we have to change it, then fine, but I don't want to risk not getting on all the connecting flights in time."

Eden nods, and he's relieved she has not fought him on this. She looks out to the lake before responding. "I want to spend Christmas with you."

"Christmas will be more enjoyable with your family." Her head snaps back to meet his gaze. "Only because it will be just another day in the village. The Ularans know nothing of Christmas, and I have never tried to explain our celebrations to them."

"Of course." She takes his hand and rests it on her lap. "But we'd know. We would be together, and that means something, right? I mean, when was the last time you spent Christmas with someone you cared about?"

"I care about the Ularan people even though I don't celebrate what our society has taught us. The gesture is appreciated, but please understand, I want you to be surrounded by family celebrating something *you* believe in."

"When was the last time?" she asks again.

He ponders the question. "Five years. Longer away from family."

She exhales loud enough for him to hear. "I refuse to allow you to spend another Christmas alone."

"Eden."

"No. It's unnecessary, and you no longer *have to* be alone."

Samuel remains quiet so as not to fuel her contention. "What if we have our own Christmas celebration before you leave, so you're home to celebrate with your family?"

Eden remains quiet. At least she doesn't object.

"I'll agree to book a flight if you promise to tell me everything."

He gives her a sideways glance.

"Everything about what happened yesterday at the mines and why it's so dangerous and about the girl you promised to give up your life for."

Samuel's stomach hits the grass beneath his feet. "The mines yesterday," he begins on the subject that doesn't rip his soul apart. "Asoo's friend was shot for talking to us. He's okay," he adds when she stiffens beside him. "His blood was on me. We applied pressure on his wound in the boat until we arrived back in his community. The doctor on site treated him. Luckily, it was a surface wound, yet the warning was clear... keep your mouth shut. He's being blackmailed and has to return to the mines to work. Otherwise, they'll go after his family."

She nods. "That's horrible. Why can't you call the police?"

"Victor informed us gold is being smuggled out on the planes. We're in way over our heads to try to stop this, and we don't know who's involved, including corrupt police and government officials. If we stop this mine, then another will appear elsewhere along the river system. Everyone wants to make money fast. It's getting to a point..." he swallows down the lump of truth at the back of his throat, "... the Ularans will have to migrate west, toward Colombia, only it's where I sent the Watache."

Eden makes an exasperated sound, and he can see the concern in her eyes.

"They should travel toward northern Brazil until they are closer to the Peruvian jungle."

"You have given this considerable thought."

"I have." Samuel hesitates on disclosing more—especially the part where when the time comes, he feels obligated to accompany the Ularans on a safe voyage since he has maps and a satellite cell.

"They are lucky to have you looking out for them. I know they're like your family now..." Something stops Eden from continuing.

He lifts her hand to his lips.

"But now you have us."

"I do. And I'm thankful for it every day."

"But it's not enough for you to return to Australia with me yet, is it?"

He takes her face in his hands and kisses her. "That day is close, only it isn't for Christmas as you hoped."

She nods slowly as though she understands. "Okay. Book my flight for three and a half weeks so that I'm under the thirty-six-week deadline. And I want you to book a flight as well. A date where you promise to return to me."

21

EDEN

LAST NIGHT I slept the best I have in weeks.

Whether it was knowing it was my last night in a comfortable bed for a while or whether Samuel and I came to some agreement about our future, it was the most relaxed I have felt in a long time. All I know is I'm sitting on the curiara heading back to Ulara with Samuel and Asoo, and I'm as excited as if I'm on a luxury cruiser sailing the Mediterranean.

Samuel and Asoo fall into easy conversation. I have no clue what about since they are conversing in Spanish, but the tone is calm.

The forest curtain surrounding me reminds me of green lava pouring out of the tepuis and covering everything it touches. It's familiar and comforting. I close my eyes and snuggle into the cushions Asoo has provided for me.

The journey must be uneventful as I don't wake again until we're gliding into the sandy embankment of Ulara.

Samuel hoists me up from behind, and it's awkward with a bulging stomach. We wave goodbye to Asoo, and Samuel makes arrangements for his next visit.

"We'll quarantine in my hut," he tells me as we stroll toward Ulara. "Or at least try to keep some distance from everyone. I'll get Kaikare to make you some purifying tea after I speak to the chief and Shaman."

"Please tell Kaikare I'll see her soon."

"Of course, she'll be looking forward to seeing you."

We remain quiet as we pass the village, and as soon as we reach his hut, he plops our bags down and grabs our skirts and beads before taking my hand and leading me to the stream.

"You know we haven't discussed names. Do you have a preference?"

"Whatever you like." He smiles at me.

"No, that isn't how this works. We decide on a name together."

"Please don't think I haven't considered names. I want to run something by you." Samuel places our skirts on a rounded boulder. He pulls his T-shirt over his head. I gather up my long dress and pull it up and over my head. It will be weeks before I wear it again, which is a pity because I love the bright colors and the printed mandala swirls. He pushes his shorts down his thighs and steps out, giving me a moment to appreciate all of him. I kick my panties aside, and before I have time to respond, he has swept me up in his arms, and we meander into the water as though he's dancing with me in his arms.

I giggle and loop my arms around his neck before we both plunge into the cold water up to our necks. I can't help but yelp in shock at the change of temperature on my skin. It only takes seconds for me to relax in his arms. He's smiling as he wades through the gentle current, and instinctively, I kiss him. Samuel glances down at me, the desire he has for me swirls behind those beautiful blue hues. Today the color has specks of hyacinth blue, and it reminds me of the macaw's feathers, and if it's his jungle spirit, now he's *home*.

"What did you want to run past me?" I murmur and then kiss him again.

The moment he breaks the kiss, his eyes hold mine captive. "Do you remember how I told you in Ulara you're given two names? The first is a traditional Ularan name the parents and the shaman and child acknowledge, not to be shared with anyone else. I've been thinking about this name and the personal meaning, rather than a name everyone else will know our daughter by. And you Aussies..." he smiles at me, "... will more than likely change it, abbreviate it, right? So regardless of what name we give our daughter, family and friends will change it."

"Are you referring to my friends calling me Edes instead of Eden or Monts instead of Monteford?"

"Exactly, and I heard an Aussie call me Macca after a few hours of meeting me."

I giggle loudly as Macca does not suit him. "Okay, Doctor McMahon, what names are you considering for our daughter?"

Samuel takes hold of my hand. "Float on your back," he says. "It's therapeutic with the water supporting your weight." He guides my head to rest on his shoulder, and my body rises to the surface. "Stretch out your arms and close your eyes."

I do what he asks, and it feels almost sensual. With my eyes closed, the surrounding sounds are amplified—the trickle of water over boulders and the birdlife in the trees.

"Arukuma Turùpo," he whispers close to my ear. "Star of our heart."

With my eyes remaining closed, I picture the stars, a tiny bundle of warmth in my arms, and my heart lost forever to our unborn child.

"Her name is only for us and our daughter's ears. Our secret, her private treasure."

"I think it's perfect," I whisper. Reaching behind me, I feel for his head and guide his lips to mine.

"It tastes rank," I tell Samuel after one mouthful of the tonic or the tea, as he describes it, used to purify our immune system. I understand the need for it, but it doesn't make it any easier to swallow.

Samuel chuckles.

"No, seriously. How long did it take for you to drink it without shuddering?"

Samuel shrugs. "It never bothered me. I visualize the good it does for my body, and it's enough to block out the unusual taste."

"*Unusual.*" I roll my eyes. "Well, I guess my visualization skills suck balls."

Samuel coughs and chokes on his last mouthful of tea.

I laugh at his reaction. "Did I shock you, Macca?"

His brows pinch. "Eden, I'm warning you—"

"Eden, I'm warning you," I parrot in a deep voice.

In a flash, he's beside me, mouth close to my ear, hands around my waist. "In another world, I'd silence you in another way, one where my mouth is on yours until you slowly give in to lust."

"Another world? That's my world every damn day. I live for your kisses, your touch." Suddenly, my tea is placed on the ground, and I'm whisked up into the hammock. Thankfully, with us in quarantine, the Ularans will keep their distance from us tonight.

Four days later, Samuel walks with me to the stream. I'm swimming twice daily, especially to ease the pressure in my back and to move a little in the water. I compare it to hydrotherapy as one would indulge in back home.

When we return to the village, the women have gathered around the fire, along with the men.

"What's happening?" I ask Samuel and tighten my hand in his.

"I don't know." He lets go of me and steps into the circle with the men. Kaikare turns and comes to me. She wraps her arms around my neck and lays her cheek on my shoulder. I pat her back affectionately. It's the best way for us to communicate the family love between us.

"Wakü," I tell her. *Good.*

She lifts her head and stares into my eyes as though she needs to assess my well-being herself. Her hands press to my bulging stomach as though she's holding a glass ball and can foresee the future. She glances up at me and smiles.

I'm relieved to see her smile. Kaikare and her father both have a divine presence about them, and I trust her unique wisdom.

Samuel asks me to mentally take notes when the baby moves. It's something I have to monitor every day, and Samuel has to take my blood pressure.

We talk about keeping the fluid down in my ankles by resting in the hammock frequently. And, of course, he has banned me from wandering into the forest alone. Even to pee—last night he stood a good distance away to give me some privacy but also to keep guard. I'm not going to object because I've vowed never to wander off on my own again.

The memory hits me at the same time I lock eyes with Kapeá Tapire. *Red Moon.* Her stomach is more pronounced since I was last in the village. I can still picture her strung to the bamboo like a wild animal ready to be carted away. It's like an understanding passes between us, one where I saved her life.

She smiles at me, and I give her a subtle nod in return.

Kaikare turns to where my focus is and smiles. She takes my hand and leads me to Kapeá Tapire. Kaikare speaks to her, and then the young girl, like Kaikare, wraps her arms around my neck and lays her cheek on my shoulder. This is now our universal way of showing gratitude.

When she releases me, I reach out and touch her stomach with one hand. She mirrors my action on my stomach. "Wakü?"

She nods once and smiles at Kaikare, then at me.

"During our absence, the shaman granted Mari' Iwoi permission to move his hammock to her family hut," Samuel announces.

"So Dancing Snake is free to... well, literally do that," I say and giggle.

Samuel shakes his head at me. "Do you reference everything to sex?"

"Says Väi Uarati Kún-imá," I say and laugh again. "Seriously, how can I not with some of these names. At least you kept our daughter's name clean."

"Eden," he says in a reprimanding tone. "The discussions with the men are serious. Someone passed along the river while we were gone. They hope the intruders didn't see the smoke rising above the trees from the cooking fires. There's tension in the village, and you're giggling with Kaikare and Kapeá Tapire."

"To be fair, nobody informed me about the discussions. And both ladies are happy to see me so, of course, we're going to be smiling."

"I understand." He takes my hand and leads me to the fire where the women are frying bread. Kaikare steps ahead and picks up some flat bread and hands it to me.

"Oo?"

"Waküpe-küruman," I tell her. *Thank you.*

Samuel takes me aside and sits me away from everyone else. "My fear is the people cruising the river in boats are those working for the mines and that they're finding secret places along the river too. It also means they'll carry guns and disease, and even if they set up camp further along the river, the mine will poison the water in these parts. I need to get word to Asoo. Some of the nearby communities have inside information. We need to know if Ulara is on their map to mine.

22

EDEN

THE FOLLOWING MORNING, I search my bag for my antimalarial tablets as I only take them once a week. That way, it's less harmful to the fetus—that's how my doctor described the medication. Cupping my hand under my belly, I consider my baby as already real and not a medical term. I'm yet to decide on a name that suits her, although I want it to reflect my grandmother, so maybe her middle name should be Ivy as in hindsight, that also signifies the jungle. My name is also connected to the jungle in the sense of a biblical garden or paradise. I smile with memories of my gran, and with that, I pull out the diary and open it to the page where I last read.

24TH OCTOBER 1961

Albert and I have fought every day for the last two weeks.
Tonight, in anger, I told him about my letter and how I wish I hadn't met him and wish I was going to volunteer and help people who needed me, people who were genuinely poor and sick and in desperate need of medical help.
He got upset and told me that he and Winston needed my help in other ways and why I couldn't see it. Why must I keep fighting him on this? Why do I find it hard to just be his wife and a mother?
It opened up a can of worms, and now I'm doubting my ability to be both. I'm a terrible mother and wife.
In the end, we went to bed crying and made love. It's the first time in months that he has touched me.
I promised him I'd try harder.

I turn the page.

24TH NOVEMBER 1961

I'm trying.
Every day I try to be who they want me to be.
I love them. Deep in my heart, I know I do, yet I'm fighting a dark, empty space inside of me that keeps clawing at my confidence, telling me I am worthless.
Maybe Albert should've married someone who could be a better wife to him than I could ever be. Not a woman who's more interested in caring for visitors if they are stung by jellyfish or have a fishing hook in their finger.
I'm not going to drown in the black ocean threatening to swallow me whole. All I can do is keep swimming and hold my face above the water.

There it is. Her postnatal depression just like Faith had told me.

20TH DECEMBER 1961

Tonight, Albert took Winston and me on a picnic by the water.
Thankfully, we didn't have far to walk.
I stayed with Winston while he walked up the stairs to our apartment and carried down the picnic basket and wine glasses. We snuck in some wine while the sun set over the ocean. Albert asked me to make a wish, and then he asked what I'd like for Christmas.
I couldn't honestly tell him what my heart craved. Instead, I told him I didn't want anything because I was thankful to have a loving husband, a healthy baby boy, and a beautiful home that also was our livelihood as a business.
It's how I should think and be grateful for my blessings.
Not cry myself to sleep like I do every other night.

25th December 1961

My hand is shaking while I'm writing this entry.
I can't believe it.
Albert gave me my gift after I put Winston in his crib.
It was a note.
One that told me he knew I needed to go away and finish the part of my nursing that still lived inside of me. Until I 'got it out of my system,' I'd never be entirely happy.
He wants me to reply to the letter from Dr. Anderson and tell him I can volunteer for twelve months, then return to him hopefully more settled and ready to be a good wife and mother.
I said no.
I couldn't possibly leave him and Winston for twelve months.
Albert insisted as he couldn't handle hearing me cry at night anymore.
My heart sunk. When I let go at night, I thought he was asleep.
He reassured me he and Winston would be fine, and his parents would help while I'm away.
No wonder his Mum has barely spoken to me. Albert must have told her his plan, and she must think of me as an awful mother. Can't blame her.
I am.
But he's right.
This is a yearning my heart won't let go of, and it's as though a strange force is pulling me away from my family.
I promised I'd do anything he asked.
Is this a dream? I still can't believe it.
But I'm writing the letter to Dr. Anderson tonight before Albert changes his mind.

So that's how my grandfather agreed to let Gran go.

The rest is all history.

I flip the pages, and there are only a couple of more entries, and then there's a wad of blank pages now a creamier color, tarnished over time.

Resting her diary on my chest, I close my eyes and imagine what it was like here fifty-eight years ago.

I need to find Brenda when I return home and ask for Gran's journal of when she was in the jungle.

The burden of the secret no longer has to be Brenda's alone. I wonder how much she knows and whether she too was sworn to secrecy.

A DARK BLANKET has fallen over the village, and the deafening chatter of insects and creatures is enough to keep me awake. My heartbeat refuses to slow, despite my efforts to remain calm. I'm no longer naïve. I'm aware of the predators lurking beyond the village boundary. Even though I've convinced myself the Watache have moved on in the direction on the map where Samuel has sent them, my thoughts snowball with the possibilities of potential threats. Beyond the doorway of our hut, the darkness pulsates with life, death to preserve life, and a hunger by every species to survive.

I'm just a number.

A statistic.

No more important than any other individual or animal in surviving what life throws at us.

Why am I still alive?

What purpose do I hold?

What good can I do besides feed my selfish need to be with Samuel?

It's the first time I've been alone in the village at night since my ordeal, and my subconscious is playing havoc with my mind.

I wouldn't even know if something or someone were sneaking up on me or even outside the hut because the bloody monkeys and insects are deafening right now.

The clicking and mindless chatter stops. My hearing pricks and thoughts sharpen. I listen intently as it usually means there's a predator close by.

When the raucous returns, my shoulders slump, and I let out a long breath, hoping the danger has passed.

I need to pee, and I'm struggling to wait any longer for Samuel to return from the waipa.

Stepping carefully down the few steps of his hut, I pad toward the green web enticing me closer. Spinning in a full circle, I assess no one is around, so I squat the best I can, and as far as my stomach will allow, and simply pee.

Nothing is simple, and I pass the loudest fart ever.

"That wasn't me. That was you," I whisper to my daughter.

"It makes finding you easy with flatulence like an elephant." Samuel's voice comes from behind me.

"Oh God, did you hear that?"

"I think every animal in a mile radius heard. You stunned the jungle into silence for a brief second."

I stand and cover my face with my hands even though Samuel can't see me. "I tried to hang on as long as I could waiting for you to come home."

"I'm sorry." His silhouette is before me. "The ceremony took longer than the shaman expected."

"Did he find the answers he's searching for?"

"Yes and no. He's not sharing much at the moment, so I fear it's not all good news." He places an arm around my waist and leads me back to his hut. "The shaman mentioned more rain is on the horizon."

"More?" I moan.

"He said the Mawarí's cooking pots on the tepui are full and will overflow."

"Are you concerned about the village flooding?" We reach his hut, and I kick off my sneakers and slide into the hammock. Samuel secures the netting around us.

"Yes. Tomorrow we continue to build more huts in the trees. The crops will be harvested, so we have plenty of food for now. The canoes are for getting around in the upcoming wet season. He believes it will be the most rainfall in decades. What concerns me is if it begins early and while you're still here, there's a risk of disease to you and the baby, and returning to Canaima will not be as easy."

It never was.

THE FOLLOWING MORNING, Samuel lifts my arm and inspects the skin. His fingers trail lightly over it, and I moan, savoring his touch even though I want to scratch. He lifts my hair and touches my neck, and I shiver. He plants a kiss on my shoulder.

"I hope you don't do this to all your patients?" I ask.

He chuckles lightly.

“We have three weeks to decide how we’re going to celebrate Christmas,” I say to lighten his mood. “My creative skills will be tested, but I can decorate the room with acai berries and use flowers like monkey brush, orchids, passionflower, and heliconias,” I say dreamily. “The ferns are no mistletoe, but… well, there’s an abundance of ivy.” I smile at him, hoping he’s the least bit excited, but he’s distracted by something on the side of my abdomen.

With a gentle touch, he runs his fingertips over the skin to the side of my ribs. “How long have you had these?”

“Ouch.” I scratch where he touches. “I’m not sure what it is, but it’s itchy and a little tender.”

“It’s some sort of bite. There’s no inflammation, but I’ll monitor it.” He grabs the stethoscope and listens to my heart. “Take some deep breaths.”

I do so and scratch an itch near my eye. His gaze follows where I scratch. He stops listening and pushes strands of hair out of my eyes.

His brow pinches together. “And how long has this been itchy?”

For a few seconds, I scrutinize his tight expression. “I’m not sure. I have a rash almost all over me and thought it was just a heat rash, but now you’re touching it, I want to squint because it’s tender.”

“I only hope it’s not triatomine bugs, known as kissing bugs.”

“So, you did hear me when I mentioned mistletoe.” I chuckle. “Or maybe you bit me?”

“Eden, it’s serious.” He stretches my skin, studying the bite. “Kissing bugs cause Chagas disease.”

“And that can do what?”

He leans back and meets my gaze. He hesitates, and I assume he screens his response. “Do you have any fatigue, headaches, a fever, or body aches?”

“Really? Of course, I do. I’m carrying a baby, and I’m living in the damn jungle.” I ignore his frown. “My back hurts because of obvious reasons, my hips ache because things are expanding around there, and I’m permanently bloody hot, so I wouldn’t know if it’s a mild fever. And tick the headaches as well, as I think I kinked my neck sleeping in the hammock. What were the other symptoms? Oh yes, fatigue… what do you think?”

His expression is unreadable.

“What?” I snap.

"I understand how you're feeling, but there are hundreds of symptoms I'm looking out for. I hope none lead to serious disease."

"I've had vaccinations for—"

"I'm aware. Don't assume because you've had vaccinations against yellow fever and others, and you're taking antimalarial meds that you're safe. Many other diseases are caused by fungal pathogens and parasites as well as the bacterial and viral ones you're vaccinated against. There's a risk of Chagas disease, adiaspiromycosis, and now leishmaniasis, especially with the surrounding mines clogging the waterways." Taking my chin in his hand, he tilts my head slightly and peers closely into my eyes. "Onchocerciasis, an eye disease," he whispers while concentrating before releasing me and scooping up my foot. He brushes away dried mud before angling my foot to inspect it.

"I swear you're trying to scare me."

He releases my foot and then cages me in, leaning both arms on either side of the treatment table so we're nose to nose. "Eden."

I swallow hard, acknowledging the seriousness in his eyes.

"You scare me by merely being here, especially with the wet weather coming. Everything is exacerbated in my mind, and you and our baby are my responsibility."

23

SAMUEL

"ASOO IS BRINGING YOUR CELL," Samuel informs Eden. "I asked him to pack it every trip to check your messages and send word back to your family. You need to account for your safety."

"Of course," Eden says.

Eden has been quiet for the last couple of days. He hopes he has educated her on the dangers other than the visible ones she may face.

"He's also bringing more medical supplies."

"For me or you?"

"Both. I'm heading there now to meet him. Do you feel well enough to join me?"

"As long as you can handle my slower pace." She takes his hand, and they meander through the village.

"Did I mention there's a ceremony tonight?"

"No. What type of ceremony?"

He holds her hand while she balances to step over an exposed root. "I know how you worry when I take ayahuasca, only tonight is special. I'm drinking the tea *with* the shaman. Together we hope to find answers."

Eden stops walking. "Have you done this before? I mean with the shaman. He usually guides you, right? Will your minds be locked together in, I don't know, some weird dimension?"

"I haven't, still it's not necessary to worry." Samuel rests his hand on her cheek. "I won't be far away. Kaikare is overseeing the ceremony."

"Don't for one minute assume I'll be sleeping while you're puking your guts up and stuck in some universe. I'll be there with you, at least physically and emotionally."

"Eden, I—"

"No. Don't tell me not to come. I. Will. Be. There."

"It could go well into the early hours of the morning."

"I expect it will."

For now, there's no changing her mind. He takes her hand and continues toward the river. "Is there anything you want to request from Asoo? Cushions? Even pillows to sleep with in the hammock? Do you need support under your stomach or between your legs for comfort?"

"Is it hygienic to have those things here? I didn't think the Ularans used anything like that from the Western world."

"No, they don't."

"Then neither will I. You know I want to do this like the other ladies in the village and my Gran."

"Is that what this is about? To prove you're as strong as your grandmother? I understand you're trying to connect with her on some level, but you need to remember everyone's journey is different. Every pregnancy is different. What do you need to support you through the next few weeks?"

"You."

It's all Eden says before turning on her heel and striding to the river bank without Samuel.

He jogs to catch up, and the *putt-putt* of a motor echoes from the trees on the riverbend. The sharp point of the curiara appears first, then Asoo's smiling face comes into view.

"Samuel. Miss Eden." Asoo waves his hand in a large rainbow arc.

Samuel stands aside when the point of the curiara rams onto the embankment. Wading into the water, Samuel takes the packages Asoo hands him and lays them on the sand.

Eden wanders out and stands near the edge. "Is there anything I can help you with?"

"I have mail." Asoo scurries through his backpack and retrieves a wad of envelopes and hands it to Eden.

"One is for me," she says with an elevated voice. She tucks the papers under her arm while she tears open the envelope. "Oh, Amy wrote to me."

Out of the corner of his eye, Samuel observes her body language. When she giggles loudly, his stomach relaxes.

"Wait here while I deliver some of the boxes to the village. Chat with Asoo and read your messages. Prepare more texts to send for when Asoo reaches Canaima." Samuel packs up several boxes to carry back to the village and leaves Eden with Asoo.

When he reaches his hut, he piles the boxes in the corner then breaks into a jog toward the river. Closer, the motor of the curiara purrs in the distance. Asoo must be eager to leave. He picks up speed, and before he steps beyond the trees, another curiara is cruising by, the driver looking at Asoo's boat.

He darts backward and searches for Eden and Asoo. Fifty feet away, they both crouch behind trees and bromeliads, well hidden from the driver. The man steers toward the sandy beach—Samuel assumes it's to inspect Asoo's curiara. The hiss of a spear whirls out into the water and lands several feet from the boat.

A warning.

The driver curses and jumps to the side, ready to turn the boat in an arc. Another spear whizzes closer this time. Samuel turns to his right. Tïmenneng prepares another. Samuel waves his hand, slamming it to his side in a chopping action.

Tïmenneng places the spear at his side, then turns his focus to the imposter.

In a scurry, the Caucasian man turns the curiara, revs the motor, and then disappears around the bend.

Asoo uncurls and straightens. He yanks Eden to stand. Bent at the waist, they creep out from the ferns and myrtles and peek when they get to the opening on the sandy embankment.

This could've been another situation where Eden's safety was compromised. A sense of urgency grows inside of him to keep Eden safe and to get her out of here as soon as possible. Samuel jogs over to them and wraps his arms around Eden. "Are you okay?"

"Of course."

"Did you recognize him?" he asks Asoo.

"No." He shakes his head vehemently. "My friends will know. I ask them."

Samuel holds Eden to his chest. "We need to get you back to my hut."

"Wait. I threw the mail in the boat when Asoo told me to run. I'm sorry it's probably important, but I panicked."

"It's fine, Eden. Nothing is more important than your safety."

Conversing in Pémon, Samuel instructs Asoo to be careful in his travels back to Canaima and to find out as much as possible without being obvious he's prying. He collects the remainder of his parcels from Caracas while Eden carries the mail, and they head back to Ulara.

She doesn't say anything.

Yet, he assumes the silence stems from fear.

THE CHIEF IS unhappy with the intruders being close to Ulara. He's aware no one is at fault except those who survive on greed with no knowledge of the land. The gods will punish everyone surrounding the tepui, and Samuel assumes the upcoming rain season, predicted as torrential, will be the act of unhappy gods.

He sprints back to his hut, to Eden. If the situation worsens, he'll send her home immediately regardless of her stubborn desire to stay.

Back in his hut, he tears open his mail.

A letter from Caracas catches his eye.

The pharmaceutical company has commenced testing his plant—the purple flower, and they're now requesting more. His hope was for the shaman to speak to the trees and be guided on how to prepare the flower for health benefits for the Ularan people. The Western world is jumping at the opportunity to study the benefits, especially in healing diseases like diabetes and blood cancer. The request stands out like blood drops on white paper.

More samples required.

They are successfully growing the flower here, although it has not grown enough to cut the flower for samples without possibly killing it.

The only way is for another trek to the tepui, which he refuses to commit to while Eden is in the village.

His contract with the pharmaceutical company is ending.

He promised Eden he'd not sign on for another year.

The Ularans need to migrate west, especially after today's threat. If the thugs come back with semi-automatic weapons, then it will end badly for both parties. The Ularans are camouflaged, and their blowpipes with poison-tipped darts kill in seconds. Never has he seen darts hit their target as they do with the precision of the Ularans.

The major threat is guns. To his knowledge, the Ularans have not witnessed the firing of bullets or the intimidating roar of a gun, and it could have devastating results.

He gazes up to the universe, closes his eyes, and prays for nothing to happen while Eden is here.

At twilight, Samuel sits beside Eden while she eats fish, oo bread, and a berry paste dip.

"Is the fish satisfactory?"

She nods.

"I see you've acquired a taste for the ants."

Eden shrugs. "I couldn't be bothered picking them off."

Samuel slides closer to her to wrap his arm around her waist. "You're afraid. I understand," he whispers.

"I'm only tired," she murmurs.

He assumed she'd deny it. "If you want to vent to me, then go ahead."

"No need. I'm good." She pushes the palm leaf aside with her meal only half-finished. "Can we go? I want to drink some water before I accompany you to the waipa."

"There's no rush. Finish your meal first. The shaman is still to tell his story."

Samuel sips his tea while waiting for Eden. It must spur her to eat more as she finishes the meal quickly.

"Let's leave," she says and stands before the shaman has started his story.

Samuel gets to his feet and brushes the dirt from the back of his thighs. He bows at the shaman and chief before leading Eden to his hut.

He pulls Eden into his arms and mashes his lips with hers. "You don't have to be brave all the time," he says against her lips.

"Neither do you." She pulls away from him and steps to the table holding their water bowl. Eden scoops out a cup and chugs it down. She drinks another three cups before placing the clay mug aside. "Do you want any?"

"No, thank you. I'll have Wayara go to the stream and refill it for you."

"Thanks. I'll need it when we return in the early hours of the morning."

"Lay with me," he says and tugs her gently until he's sitting on the edge of the hammock. "We have time to close our eyes and just be present with each other."

Samuel senses her resistance and assumes she's tired enough to fall asleep if she stops moving. It's what he wants—for her to rest.

"Five minutes." She clambers in with him with even less grace than she did when she first arrived in the village.

"Here. Allow me." He springs up, grabs her feet, and swings her legs around while taking her weight. "Your feet will thank you in a few hours."

Clambering into the hammock beside her, Samuel stretches his arm behind her head and listens to her breaths as they slow. He places a gentle kiss on her forehead so as not to disturb her, then his fingers trail lightly up and down her arms until her head is heavy on his chest.

The jungle choir has lifted a notch with darkness around the village. His eyes adjust to the darkness and the faint moonlight streaming into the doorway of the hut. He cups Eden's stomach with his free hand and sends a silent message to his unborn child.

I WANT you to know I love you with every fiber of my being.

It may be months before I get to see you, and I'll struggle with the thought every day.

You'll be surrounded by love and safe in a beautiful country.

I'll count the days until we meet, but I'm blessed to watch you grow inside your mother and feel your presence within her.

I'll be forever your father and will love you always.

SAMUEL PICTURES the day when Eden is holding their baby in her arms, smiling and full of joy. She'll make a wonderful mother, and he can't wait for the day he will join them.

A steady drumbeat brings him out of his thoughts.

It's time.

24

EDEN

KNEELING beside Samuel in the waipa, I'm reminded of many months ago when I was here.

The round hut holds an ethereal essence—a calming sensation with the small fires dotted around it, flickering like candles providing an ambience similar to what I'd indulge in when I was home taking a relaxing bath.

It feels spiritual. I don't doubt there's a *presence* here since the shaman began his prayers calling to the forest before we even arrived. The shaman is taking the tea with Samuel, and to be honest, the notion of two great minds connecting simultaneously with the spirits freaks me out. Yet, in the gentle breeze, there's an aroma of herbs and an earthy scent wafting in from the rainforest.

I turn and look to the green cavern, unusually quiet and still at present.

Samuel touches my knee, and I turn back to the shaman blessing the tea. He hums a tune, the same syllables over and over.

From a bamboo pipe, he sucks in smoke, blows it over the tea, and continues chanting.

Much of the preparation was completed before our arrival since the shaman himself isn't overseeing the ceremony.

Kaikare is.

It strikes me that Kaikare is in charge and the enormity of the responsibility for her to lead two of the most powerful and influential men in the community. Kaikare is preparing to be a shaman and has studied all her life to follow in her father's footsteps. My stomach drops, knowing what could've been.

Kaikare is my aunty.

Her life might have been very different if my gran had brought her back to Australia. She'd have grown up alongside my father in a world different from this.

I imagine all the places we could've traveled together—attended football games, visited shopping centers, and—

Kaikare snaps her head in my direction as though she senses my thoughts. I give her a tight smile, trying to empty my mind and focus on what's happening, but maybe it's in here where our world collides with the spiritual one that *what if* is challenged.

Is it my ego talking? Is my selfishness surfacing with wanting Kaikare to be part of my world and not part of her father's where she was born?

Would she be any happier in my world?

The point is, she's happy here. She knows of nothing else.

Her world lured Samuel to leave society—the selfish, material world where money rules. A world where happiness is more about wealth, what you own, and power in the form of stardom.

I bow my head and concentrate on letting go of my ego, superiority, privileged upbringing, and just be in the moment.

Who am I to say one way of living is more prestigious than the other, especially for happiness and our purpose?

I glance at Samuel and see him for who he really is. Not my lover or the father of my baby, but the doctor. The man who heals and cares for other humans. The man who has given up everything I know to be important in our world to live here in what I initially thought was a substandard way. Only now, I know the Ularan way is far more superior.

The Ularans understand life, live with nature, and protect the earth only taking what they need without destroying their surroundings. They have a social set of rules like we do, only it's obeyed, knowing it brings happiness and harmony within the community. They are peaceful, spiritual beings in tune with the universe and who wouldn't hurt a soul. Well, unless the Watache kidnapped someone, but even then, they didn't want to harm anyone. A peaceful resolution was their first approach.

The Watache.

I'm scarred by those memories. Yet when I think back on those moments, they acted out by what they knew, and now I question if their shaman would've hurt me. After hearing about their village being burned to the ground by Caucasian men, no wonder they were afraid and reacted the way they did.

If I weren't pregnant or a privileged white girl, my body may have coped better with their food. The Watache shaman gave me food and water and treated me similarly to everyone else. I just wasn't used to sleeping on dirt, eating raw meat, or pooping right in front of everyone. Their ways are different from mine, but does that make them wrong or of less importance?

We all do what we need to survive in this world.

We're given one chance at life, and we have to make the most of it.

I came to South America hoping to find myself, and although I did, I also found Samuel. Could the shaman, or even Gran, have influenced destiny?

It's something we'll never know.

Only now, I'm questioning whether I have the right to pressure Samuel into making a choice—whether the baby and I should have priority over his life here. My ego says it's the right thing for him to do—be a responsible father and be with us.

Here in the waipa, my ego is silenced even without taking ayahuasca. We're two people compared to a village. He was happy and content before he met me. He has tried to explain—without falling apart—why he preferred to be here. I understand we all have secrets locked away in the back of our mind to stop the memories from crushing our souls.

Maybe it's this life. The sense of purpose. The happiness of life and nature and living in harmony with the earth. Maybe my world truly scares Samuel. He has tried to explain how unhappy he is in our society, and I assumed by being with me, all would be okay.

Shit.

Who the hell do I think I am?

"Eden, you don't have to be here," Samuel says softly and places a hand on my knee.

What?

Are they mind readers?

Realizing he's referring to the ceremony, I straighten my shoulders and bow my head. "Sorry. I'll focus now. It's just baby brain." Or is it a spiritual power here, surrounding us in the waipa, questioning my motivation?

He offers a slight smile before bowing his head once more, and we're both charmed by the shaman's prayers.

Samuel takes the tea from Kaikare and swallows the entire cup in one go. He wipes his mouth and bows his head.

He didn't flinch.

Ugh, I remember the vile taste. Earthy and bitter.

Kaikare hands another bowl to her father, then to Samuel. The shaman bows his head, raises the bowl high, and continues with the chant before swallowing the tea. Neither Samuel nor the shaman shudder or react.

Wow.

Many bowls later, the shaman holds up his hand to Kaikare.

Joining our circle, she lowers to her knees and bows her head. Her eyes now closed, the shaman continues to sing. He sways gently side to side, chanting the same syllables over and over.

What I'd give to know what he's visualizing.

Samuel also has his eyes closed and his brow is pinched. I place a hand on his knee yet say nothing, not wanting to distract his thoughts. We remain like this for some time for the tea to infuse their blood and brain. Kaikare pushes up to her feet, retrieves a cane mat, and rolls it out for her father. I follow her lead and lay out a mat beside Samuel. We gather empty bowls, much larger than those served with the tea, and place them beside the men.

Now we wait.

SAMUEL REMAINS ON ALL FOURS, panting, waiting for his fifth purge.

I'm aware it's to expel negative energy and the pathways of our past lives to lead the way into the next stage of the ceremony. Only it seems brutal to me. I mean, who likes puking?

Kaikare breaks out into song—a harmonic tune that speaks to my heart.

To my surprise, the shaman has puked only once. Then again, this is something he practices regularly, and it's part of their culture. And I assume the rituals provide him with cleansed, purified energy pathways.

I leave Samuel to empty the bowl outside the round hut and return to sit beside him. He curls up onto the mat, and I move away so my presence doesn't interfere with his aura and energy.

Homing in on Kaikare's beautiful voice, I allow the repeated syllables to infiltrate my mind, absorb the song of healing into my cells just as Samuel and the shaman do. Even without the presence of ayahuasca, my entire self feels present, and I close my eyes and allow the serenity to envelop my aura.

There's no light show, no kaleidoscope of color in my mind, and yet I detect a powerful presence around us.

There is a pull from beyond the waipa, a pulsing life, energy, and growth. Life seeks more life to be as one. The rainforest calls to all of us to understand what we need to survive, and now the shaman is calling to the trees in the most powerful way known to man.

Samuel's heavy breaths jolt me out of the trance.

Light flickers from the fire and casts an eery shadow around the room. Yet I make out his pain. His eyes are tightly closed, and deep lines highlight his brow. He pants quick breaths like one would in labor.

Samuel groans. At first, I believe it's from nausea or his stomach twisting in pain from the tea. I know that feeling—he doesn't know which part of his body will try to eject the poison next. Only the way Samuel's fingers grip his long locks makes me freeze. Could there be more to his pain?

His breaths amplify into grunts with sounds of fear and panic equally mixed. I shoot Kaikare a questioning look, asking whether I should do something, at the very least touch him and whisper consoling words?

Only her eyes are closed, her song continues without alarm. Are her visions within our space as strong as the shaman's?

Breathe.

Be patient.

The minutes pass, and Samuel is moaning, yelling incomprehensible words. To me, it's clear something is wrong, but neither the shaman nor Kaikare flinch at Samuel's reaction.

I have to do something.

What if he's in trouble, and they're both—I don't know—maybe in another dimension, another realm and are beyond helping him?

His breaths come faster. His chest is racing. I place my fingers over his pulse point on his wrist just like he does to me. His pulse is pounding. It's so fast I can barely keep up.

Shit, now he's hyperventilating!

Think.

Shit. Shit. Shit.

What the hell is happening?

25

EDEN

KAIKARE STOPS SINGING.

She creeps over to where Samuel lies in the fetal position and places a hand on his shoulder. Her father remains in a trance. With his legs crossed, his seated position reminds me of a buddha, only his eyes are open, staring out to the forest.

Kaikare shoots me a look and then gently shakes Samuel's shoulder.

A single second, and yet in the flickering light, her eyes communicate concern. When she uncurls and stands, I lean over and whisper in his ear, "I'm here, Samuel. You're not alone."

Kaikare raises her arms and sings to the jungle. She doesn't stop me, so I take it as a green light.

"You're safe, my love. I'm here. And your daughter, Arukuma Turùpo, is with you."

He twitches—the reaction I hoped for. Whispering our daughter's name over and over is my way of penetrating any walls the spirits have constructed to keep me out. I glance up to Kaikare.

She gives me a nod. She leans over and places a hand on his shoulder. "Piriki'ki," she says firmly. "Piriki'ki," she repeats. She looks to the jungle. A rumbling growl overpowers the sound of every other creature—every hunter. Did it come from the dark, pulsating wilderness or the space around us?

Eyes. I see a pair of eyes, blue and unblinking on the ground. I turn to

Kaikare, unmoving. Is she frozen in fear that it's a jaguar and our men's minds are temporarily paralyzed from the tea? The creature's eyes convey emotion, and I feel it with every fiber of my being. Anger? No, frustration.

What's Kaikare waiting for?

Moving onto all fours, I remain in front of Samuel, protecting him from whatever it is out there.

Kaikare breaks into another song, and it tricks my mind into relaxing. She nods to the trees. There's another set of eyes staring back at us. It hoots a soft sound.

"An owl?" I ask.

She nods. "Piriki'ki."

Right.

A flapping of winds comes from behind me, and I duck my head as I catch a flash of red, blue, and yellow before it disappears in the dark. Yet, it was enough time for me to realize the macaw is heading toward the owl.

"Kawak," Kaikare states. *Macaw.*

I nod. *Kawak.*

Kaikare bends down, touches Samuel's shoulder, and points toward the trees. "Kawak, Piriki'ki, Väi Uarati Kún-imá."

Wait. Väi Uarati Kún-imá is Samuel's name. I shake my head for my thoughts to unravel. Is she telling me Samuel is the macaw and the owl? I stroke his beautiful face. His eyes remain closed only now there's a peacefulness surrounding him.

Yet we have overlooked there is a jaguar crouched beyond the dense foliage.

I point. "Tïmenneng." *Jaguar.* Recently, I learned the warrior and friend Tïmenneng's name is the word for jaguar, and he's the most fearless of all the Ularan young men.

"Tykaraije Tïmenneng." *Black jaguar.*

My chest tightens with every breath.

Another set of fierce eyes, this time yellow in color, join the black jaguar, and a growl echoes through the trees. A clear warning these powerful cats are a threat to every creature. The noise of the jungle fades into the distance as the throb of my racing heart echoes behind my ears.

What's happening?

A smaller feline springs out from the ferns. Wild, with the same frustration reflected in its blue eyes. The larger jaguar roars, and it tumbles and retreats to crouch at their sides.

What the hell have we done?

I can't breathe. My chest heaves with each breath as though the forest is angered and has sucked all the oxygen out of the waipa.

"Kaikare," I murmur with my hand on my chest until I can't take anymore.

I lay alongside Samuel, my lover, close my eyes, and will my heart to slow.

26

SAMUEL

A LOW HUM sounds from the jungle. The first light of dawn breaks through the trees and into the waipa.

Samuel opens his eyes.

Eden.

She lies beside him. She has a hand under her cheek with a peaceful expression on her face. There's not a hint of distress evident from the previous night.

Flashes come back to him. He pushes up onto his elbow. The dotted fires around the waipa have been reduced to nothing but glowing embers. The shaman sleeps. Kaikare rises from her mat as though sensing his presence.

She creeps over to him and places a hand on his shoulder. Kaikare stares at Eden, her eyes reflecting compassion and love. When her gaze meets Samuel's, his memory jolts again.

"Mawari? Kanaima?" he whispers.

Kaikare tells him a negative entity had entered the waipa while the shaman's spirit was deep in the forest. Kaikare's spirit was there in the waipa preventing it from taking hold of him, although she wasn't strong enough yet.

She smiles and bows her head. Kaikare explains her mother returned to protect Samuel, the shaman, and Eden.

"Eden?" he whispers.

Kaikare nods, confirming her danger. She explains the shaman's spirit returned from the forest and stood beside Eden, but he couldn't enter the waipa. Eden unconsciously released her spirit, a young jaguar. Eden passed out, and it was the moment her spirit entered the waipa and stood alongside Kaikare. Together they were powerful enough to force the entity back into the jungle to where her father and mother awaited.

My god.

He had no idea of her power

Samuel reaches down and caresses Eden's beautiful face.

Will she remember?

Kaikare's grip tightens on his shoulder. He turns away from Eden and meets Kaikare's insistent gaze. "Inesa."

He closes his eyes slowly and inhales a deep breath. He nods in understanding. His negative thoughts surfaced during the ceremony allowing the entity an opening to enter his thoughts and cripple his progression. But it didn't have time to attach to Samuel's soul.

"Inesa arukuma," she says. *Inesa stars.*

Samuel nods, acknowledging Inesa's soul is with the stars.

"Inesa, tuna." She moves her hand in a snake-like action like running water, "tuna." *Water.* Kaikare lightly taps her heart. "Turùpo wakü." *Heart good.*

Samuel nods. He has to release his thoughts of Inesa to the river. Let it go so his heart will be good. For as long as he can remember, he has held onto the past and locked it away. He is a better man and has changed his life for Inesa, yet it means nothing if he's not honest with Eden.

Everything in his life has led to being with Eden. Would he have found her if every event of his past didn't exist? His friends' poor treatment of Inesa, him leaving society to live in the jungle, then stumbling across Ulara. Ivy upsetting her family and doing what was considered outrageous for her time—leaving her husband and young son to volunteer in the jungle. Finding Ulara much like he did, maybe.

Had the shaman seen them all coming?

Be it fate or destiny, where's it leading them now that their souls have met?

Eden groans, and her hand wraps under her stomach.

"I'm here," Samuel whispers. He leans down and kisses her cheek. "I'm here, my love. What do you need?"

"Water," she murmurs without opening her eyes. Samuel signals to Kaikare a drinking action, and she scoops water from the bowl and hands Samuel the mug.

"Let me help you." With a hand under her back, he assists her head so it's high enough for her to sip the water.

Her eyes widen. She looks around the room as though awakened by her memory. Rolling onto her side, she pushes up into a seated position with her legs tucked to one side and her other hand pressed to the ground to support her. "Are you okay?"

Samuel smiles. "I'm fine, thanks to you. I'm more concerned about you and your exhaustion. Do you want me to carry you to our hut? You can sleep in the hammock all day."

"Why would I do that? I'm fine."

"Last night was difficult. I understand—"

"I know what to expect now. I'm seriously fine. Though I'm surprised we slept here."

"You don't remember passing out?"

"I passed out," she gasps. "Did I fall?"

Samuel asks Kaikare to tell him what happened step by step. He translates the night to Eden, what happened in his visions and the moments after she passed out.

"I remember seeing the eyes in the forest and..." She clutches her throat.

"Do you need more to drink?"

"No. I mean, yes, but I remembered something, and it spooked me a little."

"About your spirit?"

"No. I have no recollection of myself in another form." Her brow pinches, and there's a hint of doubt in her words. "Kaikare said you were an owl and a macaw."

Samuel stares up at Kaikare. He asks her what happened for her to tell Eden his sacred birth name. Kaikare explains his spirit was scaring her, and she sensed your energy leaving your body. Eden was afraid of losing Samuel, and Kaikare reassured her his spirits were watching over him.

"Wakü Turùpo," he says to Kaikare. *Good heart*. He touches Eden's cheek. "It's time we talked about something I have kept from you." He takes her hand and assists her to stand. “First, you need to eat, and then my day is yours.”

“I’M TIRED.” Eden cradles her head on Samuel’s shoulder as they sit on a boulder near the stream. “I think I’ll take that nap later.”

“And you didn’t eat enough. I’ll gather more berries for you.”

“It’s weird as I’m always hungry, but lately, I’ve lost my appetite. I’m sure after a nap, I’ll be fine. You should also rest. Even the shaman slept until late morning.”

Samuel stares into the forest while he decides what to tell Eden. “The shaman’s visions are complex and multidimensional. He travels to the future and the past while the forest delivers a message.”

“Did he receive answers last night?”

“I haven’t had a chance to speak with him. It can wait until tomorrow.”

Eden kisses his cheek. “I told you I’m having a nap. You don’t need to stay with me while I’m sleeping. Go and speak with the shaman.”

“He’ll summon me.”

“Of course, he will,” she snaps.

Samuel chuckles and scoops her up in his arms and wades with her into the water.

“Wait! My skirt and beads,” she exclaims.

“Will dry quickly.” Samuel chuckles. He drops onto his knees with Eden in his arms until the water comes to their necks.

“It’s freezing,” she shouts.

“Refreshing,” he corrects. With wet fingers, he wipes the dirt from her face and then from his own.

“You know...” she swipes her tongue over her teeth, “... I could do with a good toothpaste and a new toothbrush. The plants and my worn brush ain’t cutting it at the moment.”

“Ain’t cutting it,” he repeats and laughs at her Aussie accent.

Eden thumps his shoulder.

He chuckles again. “I’ll have Asoo bring you some more supplies. Anything else?”

“Yes. What did you want to discuss with me?”

He leans his forehead against hers. “Remember the time I spoke of Inesa?”

Eden nods. Her eyes widen, and in them he senses her compassion and relief that he’s finally opening up to her.

“It’s time I told you what happened.”

Taking his cheeks in her soft palms, she kisses him in a way to remind him she’s here for him, always.

27

EDEN

"It's a long story, but I'll keep it brief," Samuel says as he climbs into the hammock beside me. Lying on his back, he lifts an arm for me to lay my head on his shoulder. He stares up to the pointed ceiling, the bamboo angling to the sky.

"I don't mind," I whisper.

"It began in high school. A girl called Inesa took the brunt of our heckling. I later found out Sean had been sleeping with her but never spoke to her outside the bedroom.

"Looking back, I realize Brant secretly liked her, but she was, in his eyes, not at his level. He was top dog of the social status ladder, and Inesa was the girl next door." He rubs the side of his jaw slowly as though he's considering his next words.

"I didn't participate in the bullying, but I didn't stop it either. In time, she developed severe depression, and it took a toll. Years later, she ended her own life.

"Two days before..." he clears his throat, "... I bumped into her at a bar in Santa Monica. I was home on a short break. She'd been drinking and wasn't herself. She told me how much she had loathed me because although I did nothing, she knew I was weak." He taps his chest over his heart. "And for that, she never forgave me for not condemning my friends' behavior. When I told her they wouldn't listen to me, she didn't believe me and then broke down. If only I spoke up just once and made her feel worthy of respect.

"When her tears stopped, she lectured me more, telling me to do something constructive with my life. Do something for the greater good, for the underprivileged. She pointed out studying medicine isn't for the greater good because I gained a monetary reward.

"I had status and an ego and thought I had the power of life and death in my hands. In her words, if I were truly a decent human being, I would give and seek nothing as repayment... a kindness to others without remuneration. I didn't know what she was talking about until dark thoughts consumed me, and realized what society stood for and the part I was playing... power."

"It wasn't your fault," I whisper.

"No? But I wasn't an innocent bystander, and I should've seen between the lines and told her she was worthy. Stopped her..."

I take his hand in mine and squeeze it. His face screws up with the burden he has carried all these years. "You weren't to know."

His Adam's apple bobs as he swallows. "I attended her funeral. None of my friends bothered. Watching her heartbroken family sob at the graveside ripped open my heart. I knew I couldn't continue on the same path, only I didn't know where to turn or start. All I knew was from that day, my life had to change. Standing by her grave, I made a promise to be a better person and do good in a world without relying on compensation. That's when I applied to volunteer in a remote area as far down the socio-economic ladder as possible. The rest is history."

I stroke his beautiful face. "All these years you've been too hard on yourself."

"No. I'm glad I found Ulara. Even more delighted that I found you."

"I'm glad you found me too." I lean up and kiss his cheek. "You'll always be the kindest man I've ever met."

He meets my gaze and stares, really stares.

"I see you," I murmur. "And I'll always love you."

"And I love you," he croaks. "You're now my reason for life." His brow crinkles.

"What is it?"

Lifting his arm from behind my head, he pushes up. "I've just remembered something." Throwing his legs over the edge of the hammock, he springs to the floor. "I'll be back soon."

A moan comes from my throat with him leaving me. Only I'm too tired to object. One thing I'm certain of is now nothing will hold us back from a future with our daughter. He has taken steps to face his past. The next step is to return to society with me.

28

EDEN

SUPPORTING the swell of my abdomen, I roll over in the hammock.

"Bloody hell," I groan. Now I need to pee. How long have I even slept?

I sit for a moment on the edge of the hammock to gather my balance.

With a hand resting under my abdomen, I push up to stand. I wander out to the jungle border to do my business. I check the ground and the tree close to where I choose to relieve myself because it's huge and helps hide me from people and creatures. Checking for creepy crawlies is all second nature now.

I feel better already.

Pushing the palm leaves aside, I head back to the hut. Before I reach the edge of the forest, I stare through the fronds at a woman standing outside Samuel's hut.

Kaikare.

I smile and call out to her.

She comes to me and wraps her arms around my back with a gentle squeeze. "Waküperö?" she asks gently. *How are you?*

"Wakü." *Good*

She releases me and checks me over. She places both hands on my abdomen and closes her eyes.

I stare at her face, searching for clues. Her eyes remain closed.

There's no pinching of her brow in concern or smile of joy dancing on her lips.

Nothing.

She pulls her hand away. "Senneka Awarö."

Senneka is a word the Ularans use for activities like work. Awarö means bad. I rub my stomach. "Wakü?" I repeat in a tone she understands. *Good?*

Kaikare smiles, and I let out a sigh of relief.

Glancing over my shoulder, she peers into Samuel's hut. When her eyes meet mine, I sense torment. Shit, do I need some of his medicine?

"Fff-o-to," she pronounces.

It takes a moment for my thoughts to align and not think her concern is about my unborn child.

"Photo?" I repeat.

Kaikare replies with one curt nod.

I take the lead, and she follows me to the steps of the hut. I point to my hammock. She sits on the edge while I rummage through my backpack to retrieve the tightly wrapped package containing my grandmother's past.

"Here we go." I pull out the brush first and hand it to her while I unwrap the photographs. Kaikare lightly brushes her hair, and I smile, imagining her sitting in front of a mirror doing just that, only with my grandmother standing behind her. Dammit. I swipe a tear that forms quickly. These bloody hormones.

I envision them fifty years ago. My gran's long blonde hair was cut after returning from Ulara. I imagine her with her newly styled bob cut with a curl at the ends, in a way reminding me of Marilyn Monroe. She smiles down at her daughter, brushing the length of her wavy, long brown hair. The gorgeous girl with brown eyes and ochre skin like her father, although she has her mother's kind heart. I witness the twinkle of compassion and love of my grandmother in Kaikare's eyes every day. Taking every step slowly so as not to break the precious time these two have together, even if it's a figment of my imaginings, I hand the photographs to Kaikare.

I take a few steps back to give Kaikare the space to absorb the memories of her mother, her brother—another life.

A tear cascades down her cheek, and the sight has air catching in my lungs. "Turùpo," she whispers and lifts her hand to her chest. *Heart*

“My heart hurts for you as well,” I murmur. I sit and wrap my hand around her waist while she slowly peruses the photographs. “And look, this one is of us in the curiara.” I smile at her. “Ina.” *We*. I circle my finger between us.

Kaikare’s lips curl up, and I’m glad our photo gave her some joy.

A warm feeling sweeps down my neck and spine to my abdomen. Shit, I have to pee again.

I push up and point to the forest.

Something in Kaikare’s expression changes, and there’s now a seriousness in her eyes that concerns me. She shoves the photographs to me as though the reminiscing session is over. I wrap them in the waterproof packaging and hand them to her. “Amäre.” *You.* They are here for her when she’s ready.

A few steps before I reach the jungle, water gushes down my legs.

I gasp and spin to Kaikare.

She strides to me and assesses the small area of wet dirt between my feet. I’m mortified at the thought of peeing myself only I know I didn’t. “No,” I wail. “It can’t be. Not yet,” I beg to the universe.

Kaikare takes my hand and leads me through the village. My thoughts are in overdrive. I can’t have my baby here. In a moment of panic, I assess how to get to the nearest hospital. While my mind unravels, I allow her to guide me, assuming she’s taking me to find Samuel.

When we reach the village center, Kaikare speaks to the women cooking over the fires. Three elders stand and gather sticks and leaves in a pile before speaking to Kaikare in calm words. I spin toward the shaman and chief’s huts, only they look deserted, and there’s an eerie silence descending over the village.

She holds up a hand, and I know I’m to wait. She rushes to her hut and returns without the photographs. Taking my hand, she leads me in the direction of a stream. Not to Samuel. The three women push the wayward branches and fronds aside to make a path for us to follow.

“Kaikare, I need to find Samuel,” I blurt. “Väi Uarati Kún-imá,” I say his Ularan name. *Sun man with long leg.*

The women ahead of me shout something over their shoulder while Kaikare remains tight-lipped. Oh God, I can’t have my baby alone out here and not without Samuel.

“Argh.” Wrenching my hand from Kaikare’s, I stop and grab my stomach as a contraction rips over my abdomen. Shit, this is real. The practice is over. "Väi Uarati Kún-imá," I repeat with a sob. *Sun man with long leg.*

Kaikare places a hand on my shoulder. She smiles and moves aside and points to a tree where the women are busying themselves. The tree is enormous with a massive hole cut out of the base, making it appear like a wooden cave.

"I'm not going in there," I tell her.

The women have already created a smoking fire, placing long branches with a mass of leaves around it. Woven twine dangles from a branch as a noose.

What the hell?

"Awarö," I say sternly and bring my hand down in a fast swat. *Bad.*

"Ahh," I cry out again with another contraction. I'm not well-educated on the matter. I thought I had more time. I thought contractions started slowly, like thirty minutes apart. This one is a couple of minutes from the last. I grab my stomach and hobble over toward the ladies because right now, they are my only help.

If ever I have agreed to some stupid things in my life, this has to be the dumbest.

Two of the women disappear while the other has a sheet of bark. She waves the bark over the little fire sending smoky clouds toward me, causing me to splutter and cough.

This can't be good.

"Samuel," I call out, only it's more of a croaky sob. Where is he? I'm so bloody scared something will go wrong, and he's not here to help me. I stare through the smoke with more clarity. These women have aided birth without medical help or assistance from the outside world, but Samuel has told me repeatedly that I'm not like them.

Kaikare cares for me. I have to trust she'd do everything in her power not to allow harm, physical or spiritual, to come to me. She lifts the beads over my head and places them on the ground. Then she unties my skirt and lays it alongside the beads.

Here I am, in the middle of the bloody jungle, butt naked in front of three strange women about to smoke my baby out of me.

My heart is pounding against my ribcage. I can't think straight.

I have gone mad.

Kaikare takes my hand and leads me closer to the fire. She pushes up on her toes and kisses my cheek, left then right. She wipes the tears from my eyes. Reaching up, I grab her hands and give a gentle squeeze.

"I trust you," I whisper. "I'm bloody scared, but I trust *you*."

Kaikare stands with her legs wide apart and points for me to do the same.

Mortified and frightened, I do it. The smoke is wafted closer between my legs, and I close my eyes and pray to my god and the forest gods that I'm doing the right thing.

"Ahhh," I groan and bend in pain. Kaikare rubs my back until the pain eases a short time later. When I straighten, more smoke wafts my way, blurring my vision. The two elder ladies have returned, and one is placing leaves over the fire. The leaves sizzle and produce an aroma that makes me somewhat lightheaded. It could be the desired drug effect. The other *wise-woman* has a residue-like sapling mixed with a fatty substance. She and Kaikare rub it over the leaves in a fast action. I assume the friction and heat from the fire does something to the leaves. At this point, I don't care as long as it helps with the pain and assures a safe delivery.

They spread warm emollient over their hands, then massage my stomach and lower back, and damn, it feels amazing.

My breath catches when two hands go between my thighs and near my private area. I glance down to Kaikare—a little less embarrassing since it's her—rubbing the fatty substance over my inner thigh and groin.

"Argh," I shout out when a contraction is stronger than the last. I lean over to catch my breath. Placing one hand on Kaikare's shoulder, I lean my weight on her. Kaikare places both hands on my stomach and closes her eyes.

Her face is unreadable. I search for a crinkle, a sign to know what she's thinking. "Please tell me she is okay," I whisper.

The women break into a song, one that has them pointing to the heavens and trees.

They prepare paint on a small banana palm, dot my face with white and red paint and then decorate each other's faces.

"Nooo," I scream out when the contraction rips through me again, ceasing all curiosity about the paintwork. What the hell was in that balm? Now the pain is tenfold. With my eyes closed, I pant through the agony of my cervix twisting like a rope.

I can do this.

I can do this.

Nearby, movement has my eyes shooting open. One woman rushes away and returns moments later with more sheets of soft bark.

They take the smoked palm and lay it at my feet. In front of me, Kaikare drops to a squat, encouraging me to do the same. Slowly, I ease my way down in an unladylike manner and cringe when all eyes focus on my vagina.

Even I know the baby's head isn't crowning. I shove two fingers inside of myself to verify and hunch a little in relief when I feel nothing but soft flesh.

"Nooo," I scream out when the contraction has me thrusting forward onto my hands. It feels almost natural to be on all fours. Focusing on a controlled breathing rhythm to get me through the pain, I rock back and forth in a gentle sway. Keeping my eyes closed, I remain like this—rocking and breathing, my thoughts drifting to the beach with calm, clear water where I can visualize the seashells in the sand at my feet. For a few minutes, it calms my mind until the next contraction is so intense, my head could spin like in the *Exorcist* as the pain takes control of my body.

"Samuel," I shout at the top of my lungs. "I'm not having this baby alone with a piece of bloody bark to catch our daughter!"

As one contraction rolls into the other, I pant my way to some sort of sanity, then screech his name again.

"Samuel!" This time my screams are loud enough to silence the monkeys. The birds nesting overhead squawk, then scatter through the trees for cover.

As more pain hurtles through my body, I hope and pray that Samuel comes soon.

Please, Samuel.

Be here for me.

29

SAMUEL

SAMUEL ASKS Itariru to repeat her answer.

He understood her words as *Tamu'ne Akare is with Kaikare and the elder ladies, preparing Eden at the birthing tree.*

She says the same words again.

He has only been away a couple of hours.

Maybe Kaikare is teaching her their ways as practice. Even more of a reason why he needs Eden to leave Ulara and be safe in her home country. He can't allow the tribe to have a claim over their child.

A scream from the jungle has him spinning in the direction of the stream. His heartbeat leaps to his throat. He sprints without further question toward the sacred birthing tree.

Samuel lopes through the jungle thrashing the palms and low-lying branches aside with no medical supplies on hand. A week ago, he prepared an emergency pack hoping his worst fear didn't come to fruition.

There's no time. I have to get to Eden now.

In his next breath, he gets a whiff of smoke from the birthing ritual. If Eden is too far along in her contractions, even he might not be able to save their daughter. What if her lungs are underdeveloped, and she's unable to breathe unaided? The rainforest might be known as the lungs of the world, but it's no oxygen tent.

Another minute passes. The stench of smoke is stronger. He's close. He falls into the clearing, stumbling to gain his balance.

Eden is naked and on all fours. His breath catches. Panic builds in his chest. His thoughts race as he battles to calm himself, calm his heart and mind.

Kaikare crouches beside her and lifts Eden's head to meet Samuel's gaze, a look telling him he doesn't belong here.

"Airö," the eldest woman shouts. *Goodbye.* She tells him to wait until he's summoned.

"Make no mistake, I'm now in control," he tells them in Ularan.

"Hey," he pants, crouching down beside Eden.

Her eyes meet his. "You're here," she sniffles. Tears stream down her cheeks, and it rips at his heart.

Samuel gently places a hand on her shoulder. "Yes, and no matter what, I'm not leaving you. How is your pain?"

"My bloody vagina is on fire. I don't know if there's smoke coming out of it or if it's from the friggin' fire."

"It's not on fire," he assures her. Even without assessing her, he can tell she's closer to dilation than he assumed. The eucalyptus and citrus aromas alert him to the balm already covering her body. "What the women have prepared for you is safe and quickens the birth, so you're not in pain for long."

Blue eyes brimming with tears peer back at him. It crushes him to see her in pain and trying to brave. "You don't have to do any of this *their* way. I have medication back in my hut. Only some I can't give you. Depending on how far you have dilated will influence what drugs I can administer. Do you mind if I examine your cervix? It will be uncomfortable."

"Do what you have to-oo—" she screams out the last word and pants through the next contraction. "Just hurry."

"You're doing great, Eden," he tells her. "Let's focus on you, okay?"

"What do you mean on me? Jesus mother of all hell," she curses at him when his fingers slide inside of her. She bucks a little. And he quickly whips an arm beneath her to support her weight. His thoughts tick over.

He can feel the baby's head.

There isn't much time.

"Kaikare." He tells her to go to his hut to retrieve his emergency pack.

Kaikare shoots a hand down in a swift axe-like action. She says the other women will fetch it for him as she's not leaving Tamu'ne Akare. He doesn't have time to worry about the women rummaging through his belongings or his private work.

Kaikare asks Týkire to run to his hut, and Samuel explains the special case for her to bring to him.

Týkire's name means yellow—they gave her the name after she was jaundiced at birth. It's a trigger for his brain, and he races over the possible implications of having a premature birth, including the complications Eden could suffer.

Bile rises to the back of his throat. He struggles to think clearly.

Eden is his priority.

His focus has to be on stabilizing her. What if she hemorrhages?

Eden screams out, and it breaks his control.

"I'm sorry," he tells her. "I didn't wish for you to have your baby here like this."

"Too late now," she growls. "Just get our daughter out of me."

"Do you need to push?"

"No. Oh God, did I just pee myself?"

"It happens," Samuel shifts for Kaikare to remove the bark from beneath Eden's legs and flips it to empty the urine onto the ground. She gathers more bark from near the fire and replaces it between her legs.

"Is my baby supposed to land on that? Please tell me you'll catch her," she moans.

Samuel rubs her lower back. "If the women need to lay the baby somewhere to attend to you, that's where they place her. The smokey aroma mixed with the bark can help the process. And don't worry about Arukuma Turùpo," he says for her ears only. "I'll be here for her."

"Promise me you'll do what you can to save her," Eden pleads through a muffled sob.

How can he promise when he doesn't know the extent of their baby's premature birthing complications? "I need you to focus."

"No, Samuel. I'm serious. Promise me," Eden rasps.

He meets her gaze before her eyes clamp shut with another contraction. "Yes," he whispers, hoping his word to be true.

"Argh, I need to move. I think I want to push now."

He assists her to squat, and he asks Chirké to come and sit behind Eden to take her weight.

"I want you," she croaks. "I want you to hold me."

"Then I won't be able to assess you. Give me a moment, and if I'm satisfied, then I'll allow Kaikare to observe your progress."

"I'm scared," she rasps.

He strokes her forehead. "It's okay to be, but Kaikare has assisted in childbirth for many years."

She reaches out and grabs his hand. "Do you think this is how my gran gave birth to her?"

He leans in and kisses her damp cheek. "There's a high chance it was here under this tree. She'd be proud of you. Like her ancestors, Kaikare has learned much of her practice over the years in the same technique used for your Gran." She smiles at him, and her joy in the smallest thing gives him a reprieve.

Eden squeezes his hand. "It hurts so much," she wails and curls in on herself.

"You're doing great, my love. I'm so proud of you." Samuel maintains a serious expression when the baby's head crowns and slides back. "I want you to push on your next contraction," he gently urges.

"Okay." She pants a few times, then groans loudly. Holding her knees, Eden grunts hard while pushing for as long as her breath allows. She falls back into Chirké's arms. "I'm spent. I can't push like this," she sobs.

"Eden. Eden, look at me," he demands. He waits for her bloodshot eyes to meet his. "See that twine hanging in a loop?"

"God, what's it for?"

"To help you push. You squat while hanging onto that and use it to help push. We can carry you over there."

"No, I'm not moving. Please don't make me move. The pain is unbearable."

"It's okay." He offers her his balled hands. "Use me to help bear down."

Curling her back into a C-shape, Eden gives three more pushes. Samuel lets go of her hands to assess her progress. "Pant through the next contraction."

"Why? What's wrong?"

He uses his fingers to help stretch her labia around the head. "I'm giving you time to adjust so you don't tear."

"Tear? Ugh, great."

Kaikare tells Samuel she's preparing the twine and pipe and walks to the fire.

"Okay, push when you're ready."

On the next contraction, Eden pushes with all her energy, groaning until the end of her breath. "Good," he tells her. Pure joy pumps through his body, his head feeling light with excitement and fear. "The baby's head is free. One more push." Eden isn't out of the woods yet.

She clenches her teeth and bears down again. The baby slides out, and Kaikare is beside him with her pipe and twine.

Eden screams in relief as Samuel eases their daughter's feet out. "Let me see her," Eden cries as she slumps back. Only their daughter has not made a sound.

Samuel rubs her back. He tries not to panic. He hopes the quick labor has left their baby a little stunned. She's limp in his arms, and he's suddenly nauseous.

"Samuel, what's wrong with her?" Eden rasps.

"Tamy mïta," Kaikare directs. *Tobacco mouth.*

"Give her to me," Eden wails.

If he does, the baby might not take its first breath. He has no suction equipment, and Týkire hasn't returned with his pack of small instruments. There's a tiny hand pump that could help. He searches the nearby shrubbery. There's no sign of movement.

"Samuel," Eden's voice demands, her arms outstretched.

Samuel nods at Kaikare and holds the baby closer. Kaikare sucks in a breath through the pipe and blows smoke over the baby's face. Their daughter lifts her arms in the startle reflex and cries a beautiful sound. Kaikare meets Samuel's gaze, and her eyes are brimming with joy. She gives him a curt nod.

Their beautiful daughter wiggles, and a tiny scream bursts from her. He lays her on Eden's chest. "She's perfect like her mother."

"You're perfect," Eden whispers to their daughter and kisses her cheek. Her soft cries quiet down as her mother comforts her.

While Eden gushes over their daughter, Kaikare and Samuel use the heated twine to tie off the umbilical cord, and Kaikare cuts the cord with a piranha tooth.

Panting comes from the bushes, then Týkire springs out of the forest. She hands him his box, and he scurries through it searching for his stethoscope and sphygmomanometer.

Kaikare presses lightly on Eden's abdomen.

"Can you hold her with one arm?" Eden holds out her arm for Samuel to apply the cuff. "It's Ularan tradition to gently press and massage your stomach to help pass your placenta. Are you okay with this?"

"Fine." Eden is too preoccupied with their daughter to care what they are doing. As soon as he establishes her health as stable, he'll be right by Eden's side, cuddling them both.

"Your arm will feel tight with the pressure." She shoots him a look, one telling him it's nothing compared to the pain she has endured.

The reading is low.

Shit.

Emotion comprises his decision-making. His throat is tight, and his heart is racing with the realization of everything that could possibly go wrong. He's unprepared for an emergency in an unsterile environment with limited instruments.

"Look." The joy in Eden's voice brings him back. Their daughter is sucking from her breast.

Their baby doesn't suckle long. "She's beautiful," he purrs.

Eden stares longingly at their tiny bundle curled into a ball. She runs a finger along her spine. "I think I'm going to spend the rest of my life gazing at her." She looks up at him, eyes twinkling. "Do you want to hold her? I know you have already held her, but you didn't cuddle our angel."

His heart still thumps like he's being chased by a leopard. He is afraid to get attached to their daughter. His heart couldn't bear losing the two loves of his life. Until he has them both safely in a hospital, his guard will remain in place.

Eden's eyes flick over his face.

"Of course," he whispers. Samuel lifts their tiny bundle and cradles her to his chest. He closes his eyes as a wave of emotion washes over him. He allows himself to feel the love of being a father, a partner, and having his daughter nestling close to his heart. So, this was what it was like to belong, to have your own family. His demeanor cracks, and with it, a tear of joy cascades down his cheek.

"What do you want to name her?"

Samuel can't take his eyes from their daughter. "Rose," he whispers. "She's my Rose, a rare flower only found high on a tepui determined my belonging and commitment to Ulara. Our little Rose has stolen my heart, and my vision is for her, and…" he meets Eden's gaze, "… her beautiful mother."

Eden's eyes hold the warmth and love that fills his heart. "Rose, it is." Her expression changes and her brows pull tight. "Oh, what's that?" she moans loudly, and Kaikare is there to assist with the placenta.

"Give me a minute." Samuel carefully passes Rose back to Eden and moves so he can assess the organ for tears in its entirety. He passes the organ to Kaikare and moves to trade places with Chirké so Eden is leaning against his chest.

"Where are they going?" she whispers.

"To bury your placenta. They believe we come from the earth, so they give back to the earth. The placenta gives life, and the nutrients will be returned to the soil to sustain more life."

"You know I thought they might ask me to eat it," she says seriously.

"It makes sense. It would help with your iron levels."

"If it meant survival, I would. If you had asked me a year ago, I'd have said no. But I'm not that same girl. I'm braver and wiser and would do anything for the two people I love the most."

Samuel kisses the hair on her crown. With one hand, he holds the love of his life while his left hand strokes the shoulder of their baby asleep on Eden's chest. Neither Eden nor Rose are clear of medical complications, and until both can be assessed, only then will his mind relax.

At the bottom of his medical pack, he pulls out the satellite phone and fires it up. In the past, he'd never have used it in front of the Ularans. The circumstances have changed. He hopes to the gods it has coverage and reception isn't blocked by the towering tepuis encasing them in the jungle.

It beeps, and he lets out a sigh.

He taps in Asoo's number and smiles when he answers.

"I have little time to speak. Eden has had the baby. How soon can you get here?"

30

EDEN

I WAS MORE exhausted than I realized as I slept between feeds. Yet, there was awareness of Samuel remaining awake. In the dark of night, he touched my skin and took my pulse. Telling him to rest was pointless. And now he's moving through the hut with the sun's light breaking through the trees.

"Morning, beautiful." A soft kiss lands on my cheek, stirring me from a deep sleep.

"Is it morning already?" I moan, my eyes fluttering open. Samuel stands beside my hammock with our daughter pressed to his chest. "Oh, I didn't hear her cry. Is she hungry?" I adjust myself in the hammock and hold out my arms for Rose.

"She was stirring, and it was an opportunity to cuddle her before her mother does." He gives me a guilty smile. "Once you have her in your arms, you never want to let her go." Samuel kisses her cheek before passing her to me to feed. "And you need to prompt her to suckle."

Caressing her cheek with my nipple, Rose turns her face and opens her tiny mouth. "She's doing fine," I boast.

Samuel smiles, although the concern is still there by the way his forehead wrinkles. "Asoo is on his way. When we arrive in Canaima, your case will be at the reception. We're not stopping." He gives me a pointed look. "We'll take a flight to Ciudad Guayana. I have covered your health insurance, and we'll remain there until your condition has stabilized."

"Well, I feel stabile." I return the pointed look he shot at me. "Although, I feel gross," I mumble. All night I wanted to wash. With only a few pairs of underpants and limited sanitary pads Samuel had in his pack, I'm making do hygiene-wise. Up until now, I've never menstruated in the jungle, and I have a newfound respect for how the ladies deal with discharge naturally.

"I'll wash quickly," I tell him even though the distance I have to walk is something I can't hurry. How the women are back in the fields working a few days after childbirth is damn amazing.

Samuel takes Rose from me. "If Mommy wants to bathe, then we bathe," he says to Rose.

"Don't make it sound like I'm the boss," I mock as I clamber out of the hammock.

He gives me a look, and I can't help giggle. "You bend rules or make your own, and everyone around you allows you to do it."

"You make me sound like I'm a bully."

"No." He takes my hand and leads me out of the hut. "You merely charm those you meet. The moment I first saw you, I was under your spell."

"It's not the way I recall it. You wouldn't speak to me." I bump his hip with mine.

"I was lost for words."

Samuel rubs his nose over Rose's mouth. She opens her mouth ready to suckle.

"Stop teasing her."

"I'm encouraging her suck reflex."

"Stop worrying. We're going to be fine." Only I know he won't relax until we have been checked over in a hospital. "How difficult is the process of applying for a birth certificate?"

"I'll see that it happens quickly."

"Okay." He seems to have contacts everywhere, yet something is bothering him as his expression has tightened, and he's back to his closed thoughts and tight expression like he expects nothing but doom. "We're going to be fine. I know it, so please relax."

"I will tomorrow," he says. "When you get your test results."

Samuel's concern remains with him the entire time I bathe and packed up my belongings. He has been like this since he returned last night after speaking with the chief and shaman. All he told me was they granted us leave, but the shaman thought it unnecessary as we aren't unwell.

Packing the remainder of my belongings gives me a sense of déjà vu. Samuel insisted I bring everything in case I need it, yet it reminds me of my first time here, preparing to go home. I inhale a sharp breath and turn in a full circle, imprinting our *home* into my brain. I have to face the realization it might be one of the last times I stay here.

"I think that's it," Samuel announces as he places his sack on the bench. He lifts Rose from the twine basket where she's swaddled in banana palms.

Kaikare appears at our doorway. "Oh, you're here." I take each step carefully, and then wrap my arms around her neck and lay my head on her shoulder. "Thank you for yesterday," I whisper.

Samuel translates my words, and both her hands rest on my back. I take an extra second to feel my aunt's love before I release her.

Kaikare sidesteps me when Samuel comes to my side. He leans and positions Rose in his arms for Kaikare to get a better view. A smile stretches his lips from almost ear to ear. Lifting a finger, she trails a path over her forehead and down her nose in one straight line. She whispers strange words as she does. Then she makes an invisible line from her temple to the opposite cheek and repeats it on the opposite side. It's the Ularan's symbol—an 'X' with a straight line through the center.

Was it a blessing?

Samuel lifts Rose and kisses her cheek. His gaze lifts and meets mine. There's a sense of apprehension, and then he closes it down. "Ready?"

I nod and take Kaikare's hand as we all meander the trail toward the river. We reach the sandy beach with no sign of Asoo.

"I'm going to miss you," I say and hug her. "I'll see you soon."

Samuel translates my words.

She takes both of my hands and squeezes affectionately. Her dark eyes flick over my face. There's a sense of sadness and appreciation. "Waküpe-küruman," she whispers. *Thank you.*

I squeeze her hands back and nod my head. "Samuel, I need you to translate for me. Please tell Kaikare I'm grateful to have met her and forever thankful for all she has done for me. And our daughter will know how her aunt loves her." I'm not counting on this being the very last time I'll see her, but I have an overwhelming urge to express my gratitude and love.

We hold each other's gaze while he does. Her eyes brim with tears, and then I can't help it, a sob shoots from my throat. We hug each other again, and her warmth and love seep into my heart. She then releases me and steps to Samuel. She opens her arms, and Samuel hands Rose to her. Kaikare lifts Rose close to her face, and she rubs her nose over her cheek. The sweet moment only lasts seconds as the putt-putt sound of the motor divides our attention.

She hands Rose to him, and in seconds, disappears into the forest before Asoo steers the curiara onto the riverbank. If she's more upset than she was displaying, I hope there's someone in the village to comfort her. I wipe my eyes and steel myself for the journey ahead.

"My friends." Asoo waves out to us. "I happy to see you."

Both Samuel and Asoo assist me in boarding before Samuel steps in gracefully even with Rose in his arms.

Asoo leans closer to see our daughter while maintaining a respectful distance. "A beautiful girl," he says. "I have your packages." He points to the pack wrapped in plastic.

"Please pass it to Eden." Samuel nods at me. "There are diapers and some clothes for Rose."

I can't help but frown. We haven't even left the riverbank of Ulara, and he's wanting to clothe Rose.

He catches my scowl and shakes his head. "She's yet to pass her first stool. I don't think Asoo would appreciate meconium covering the seat of his curiara."

"Me-con-ee-um?" Asoo repeats.

"Poo," Samuel translates. "It has no aroma, but it's thick and sticky, a little like tar."

Without further question, I take the pack and retrieve a nappy, or a diaper, as Samuel calls it.

"Please no tar on seats," Asoo says as he steers us toward Canaima.

Samuel sits beside me in the cut-out area Asoo has created for me. He unwraps the banana palms swaddling Rose's arms, and she gives herself a fright lifting her arms when she's set free. Samuel has the nappy under her rear and secured in seconds. I've had experience with my nephew, but I've forgotten so much from when he was a newborn. I barely saw him until he was a few months old. Rose is so tiny, and neither Samuel nor I were prepared for her sudden entrance to the world.

She's barely made a sound since birth, and I know it concerns him. She has suckled which is a positive sign, although I'm aware my milk won't come in for a few more days.

For the rest of the journey, I settle back with Rose in my arms and enjoy the view of the jungle caging us on the river as we slowly leave the towering tepuis behind us.

SITTING ABOARD THE SMALL AIRCRAFT, I'm more afraid of being up here in the clouds than in the green wilderness below us. Every turbulent bump has me clinging to Rose.

For the short time we were in Canaima, I wasn't allowed to hug Victor or Asoo. Samuel's concern is now on Rose's immunity, and we both need to keep our distance from people. I thanked them for all they did for me and hoped to see them soon.

My rear then leaves the seat, and I let out a little scream.

"Are you okay?" he asks.

"Yes," I say quickly. It's a short flight, and I'm counting the minutes until we're back on the ground.

The small Cessna aircraft touches down, and no sooner are we inside the terminal than Samuel is on his cell, pacing the floor. I remain on a chair nursing Rose with our luggage by my feet. I told him I didn't need my entire case considering we'd only be gone a week, but he told me to bring it for extra packages like diapers and clothing for Rose because his case is small and barely the size of an overnight bag.

Rose pulls a face as though she's unsettled. I don't have a maternity dress and can't breastfeed in public when I'm unsure of the rules or what society accepts here.

"Samuel," I say loud enough to get his attention. He stops pacing and stares at me. "I need to feed Rose. Where should I go?"

He speaks quickly in Spanish and ends the call. "We'll go to a feeding room." He slings his case over his shoulder, then wheels my bag, leading us along a corridor until a baby on a sign indicates we're heading in the right direction. Inside, there's a cubicle, and he locks the door.

"Wait." He pulls antibacterial wipes from his bag and wipes down the vinyl chair and armrests before we sit. The antibacterial wipes are one of many items he ordered and had Asoo store in Canaima. He assists me in pulling my arm out of my dress so I can feed Rose. He waits until I'm feeding before he speaks. "We have a change of plans. We're heading back to Georgetown in Guyana. You'll need your passport. Dr. Vásquez has verified our passports with the authorities and that Rose is ours. We have a private flight booked in an hour."

"A private flight?"

"There are risks flying with a newborn, and many airlines forbid it. I'm transferring money to a company I have worked with over the years so we can get there hassle-free."

"Hassle-free." I roll my eyes.

He ignores me and continues listing the items we need to purchase. "If Rose requires formula milk, we'll need a bottle sterilizer as well."

"She's feeding from me," I state.

"Your milk hasn't come in. You're thinner, and your diet has been lacking. I'm thinking of Rose and whether she'll need to be topped up with formula milk."

"My God, stop. You're worrying unnecessarily."

His brow pulls tighter. "We have a few days to organize everything. I can do most of it while you're in the hospital."

"Wait. I only need tests. I shouldn't have to stay. I could come back to the hotel with you."

"I'll be staying at the hospital with you since I'm paying extra insurance."

My shoulders slump. Here I am telling him to stop worrying, yet I'm a burden with hospitalization in a foreign country. "I'm sorry. I'm sure my medical insurance will cover it."

"We're not claiming your insurance. It's easier for me to pay and get the best service, and besides, I have contacts."

I release a sigh.

Life in Ulara was simple.

Everyone did what they had to and got on with business working the fields and cooking the meals. Everyone ate what they needed, and the hunt was merely for meat once a month—maybe even less. Money didn't guarantee a better service or divide social classes.

Everyone had a role.

Everyone contributed.

Right now, I feel lost, and I understand why Samuel didn't want to leave.

THE ULTRASOUND BEEPS, and it reminds me of my time here in the same hospital when I was dehydrated and ill. I was afraid of losing Rose and wanted to go *home*. Now she's safe with me, and they are checking my uterus for retained placenta as a precaution. Samuel has ordered every test possible even though Dr. Vásquez has reassured him some are unnecessary. The amount of blood the nurse took from my arm was incredible. I shook my head and gave Samuel a dark look. I know he's going to send me home when ironically, I now want to stay.

Last night, he finally opened up and told me that Asoo had mentioned more drones are flying closer to Ulara, scoping out the land. He assumes illegal mining is to blame, but they can't point blame until they have facts. Samuel's concern is for the Ularans' safety, and I understand that. When I asked him what the solution will be, he merely shrugged.

Samuel doesn't shrug.

Even though he opened up by telling me this, he's still avoiding matters that concern both of us.

Like now—his gaze is fixed to the screen while he's speaking in Spanish.

Dr. Vásquez turns to me. "Everything is clear. There's no evidence of placenta. Are you clotting at all?"

I shake my head.

"We'll take some swabs and make sure there's nothing untoward, and then you're free to leave when your blood results have returned. Over the next day or two, we'll observe Rose for jaundice, keep a check on her feeding and urine output. Has she passed a stool?"

"Yes," Samuel says quickly. "On the flight." He looks at me and grins. It was a moment we both laughed as we tried to remove the revolting sticky stools from her little buttocks. Thank goodness it didn't stink out the cabin of the plane.

Rose cries out, and Samuel brings her to me so I can feed her. Dr. Vásquez leaves us to take my samples to pathology.

Samuel lowers Rose to my lap after I have adjusted my clothes. "The colostrum will help with her immunity, and it's satisfying. Tomorrow she's likely to be unsettled right before your milk comes in."

I raise my brows at him. "Unsettled?"

"I just thought you should know."

"Is this how it's going to be between us?" I ask in a direct voice. "You, always aware of the possible problems and alerting me to what I *should* expect. I mean, motherhood I can handle. Being in the jungle and not knowing what to expect is a time you shouldn't have left me to discover my way. It's one extreme to the other."

"I'm only trying to help."

"Help, yes. Having yourself in a constant state of worry and watching over me like I could be obliterated in seconds isn't comforting. I want you to be with me, Samuel, the man I love. Not Samuel, the doctor."

He lowers his gaze and rubs his thumb over my hand. "I'm sorry. I guess old habits die hard."

"Old habits? Or are you hiding something from me?"

"Hiding?" He raises his hand to rest it on the back of his neck.

"Keeping something from me. It's like you have to be with me every second. I'm not complaining, but we have the rest of our lives to be together."

His lips tighten, and I sense I've hit the nail on the head.

"What? Tell me what you've planned?"

"I don't have a plan." He massages the back of his neck as though ironing out the kinks. "I'm continually changing my course of action, and I don't want to concern you with matters that won't affect you."

"If they don't affect me, then they shouldn't affect you."

"I have charged your cell." He pulls it from his case. "You can call your family and friends to inform them you're safe and announce the birth."

"Don't change the subject." He holds my gaze momentarily, then places my phone on the table beside the bed.

"I also have my own calls to make." He heads to the door and closes it behind him.

Shit. I want to know who he's calling because we both know it's not his parents.

31

SAMUEL

"SAMUEL?"

"Hi, Mom." Samuel paces the length of the garden outside the hospital. This is a phone call that has taken a hit on his dignity and something he can't do sitting down. "Is Dad with you?" Samuel raises his arm to check his wristwatch—the one his father gave him when he graduated from medical school. It's not something he wears often considering the value, only it keeps exceptional time, and he has used it to track Eden's pulse rate. After giving his other watch to the Watache as a gift of goodwill, when he arrived in Canaima, he retrieved the watch his father had given him that he had locked in a safe. In Guyana, it's lunchtime. In LA, it's morning, and he assumes his father has already commenced work for the day.

"Are you okay?" she blurts.

"Yes, I'm fine."

"And Eden?"

"I need a favor. It concerns Eden."

"Wait, I'll put you on speaker. Christopher..." she says, "...it's Samuel. Okay, we can both hear you. You may need to repeat yourself as your father isn't well, which is why he's home on a Monday. His ears are blocked from an upper respiratory infection."

Samuel's throat thickens. "Are you okay?"

"Yes, son. It's just not something I can afford to spread to my patients."

Samuel understands the need for caution. He glances up to the third-floor window to Eden's room. "I'll just get to the purpose of my call. Congratulations. You're both grandparents to a little girl."

His mother gasps. "Oh my."

"Rose is well." His voice is filled with pride. "And thankfully, so is Eden. We're in Georgetown, Guyana, having tests for precautionary measures."

"Precautionary. Were there complications with her labor?" his father asks in a stern voice.

Honesty is best. "She delivered in the village where I work—"

"Heavens," his mother says in a breathy sigh. He can visualize her with a hand on her chest.

There's a moment of silence.

"Eden did amazingly well, and I arranged transport immediately to a hospital where I know the physicians who'll give her the best care. Rose is almost seven weeks premature and doing well considering her size."

"Rose?" his father repeats.

"Yes, Rose. We're yet to give her a middle name and will decide tonight for the authorization of the birth certificate."

"This is wonderful news. We're thrilled you called and can't wait to see our granddaughter. Please send some photos."

"I will."

"Now, you mentioned a favor?"

"My work here isn't complete."

"You can terminate the contract with the pharmaceutical company, son. I can call—"

"Dad," Samuel interrupts. "I have another commitment in which I have never expected you to understand or support. I intend to join Eden in Australia soon. *When* I do, I hope you can come to visit. We'd also like to make a trip to LA, but my priority is getting her home as soon as possible. Eden wants to support me and remain by my side. Don't worry yourself as I'll not allow it and prefer if she were home with family and safe in her country."

"At least you're thinking straight regarding your... partner."

Samuel withholds the urge to cuss. Instead, he focuses on the garden bed of red geraniums lining the paved path.

"I intend to marry Eden when we're in Australia. Dad, please don't make this about doing the right thing by Eden in the time-honored way you conceive as respectable. We love each other and plan to spend the rest of our lives together. Eden understands my commitment, and when upheld, I will, in your words, do *what's right*. My phone call isn't to discuss moral obligation. I need Eden home, and I don't have the funds to fly her on a private jet home to Australia without having to first arrange an appointment with a bank in another country. I don't have the time to fly to Colombia."

"You want us to fund the flight?"

"No. Consider it a loan. You know I have the funds since I barely touch my salary given my lifestyle. The protocol in accessing it is difficult. Years ago, I set up steps to prevent theft. Please understand time isn't on my side."

His parents murmur quietly between themselves.

"You understand the risk of a newborn flying?"

"It's why I need a private jet to minimize human contact for Rose's immunity."

"Eden and Rose will require clearances from the hospital."

"It goes without saying. I won't put my family at risk. The arrangement is to safeguard them." He almost added *from me* only he held his words, knowing it could incite an argument. Instead, he offers words of peace. "I'm sending the photos of Rose to your email now. I know Mom will gush. She's truly my little princess."

"Consider it done, son. Just do the *right thing*."

Samuel closes his eyes and slowly opens them with his father's words opening wounds of the past. "It's my intention. I'll email you the details of payment. Thank you. This is generous, especially considering the short notice. I'll be in contact soon."

"I'll email you when the funds are ready."

"Thanks, Dad. Bye."

Holding the phone to his chest, Samuel assesses his next move. He has a mental list to tick off before he can arrange the flight for Eden. With no time to waste, he calls the private jet company to secure flight dates. He glances up to the window where Eden waits and inhales deeply. They promised each other no more secrets. Only he can't share his plan to keep her safe, for without a doubt, she'll fight him on it until her last breath.

Samuel bows his head and prays she understands he's doing it all for her.

THE LONG, white-walled hallways of the hospital ward remind him of where he studied. There are fond memories mixed with bad. In his final years of medical school, he decided he had to be a better person after Inesa asked him to promise not to follow the same path he was on.

He hopes he has made her proud.

Hopes he has fulfilled his obligation.

There's one more matter to uphold before he can move on with his life.

He opens the door to where his future awaits and hears her on the phone. Their eyes meet. She laughs, and a twinkle lights up her blue hues.

"I can't wait for you to meet her, too... I'll send more photos... I know, I know. I'll tell him he has to look after me." She grins at Samuel. "Love you all. Bye."

Pulling the AirPods out of her ears, she says, "My friends say hi."

He nods. "Have you sent photos?"

"I have, and they want more." She giggles lightly as though still high on happiness, and it's a moment of reassurance that sending her home is the right thing to do.

"Have you called your parents?"

"They are next on my list." Her eyes narrow. "Did you call yours?"

"I did. They send their regards to Rose and you and can't wait to meet you both. I also need to send photos, so I'll compose an email now."

"Okay... while you *compose your email*, I'll call my parents."

His phone vibrates before he does so. It's the private jet company. "I'll give you some privacy," he tells her. "I have to take this."

Samuel opens the door and says, "Samuel McMahon," and then closes the door behind him.

32

EDEN

I CAN'T BELIEVE he called his parents.

I take a moment to absorb the steps he's taking for Rose and me. I wish he had given me the chance to speak with them but given their history, I understand he has to smooth out some personal issues first.

Inserting the AirPods in my ears, I glance to Rose, still sleeping in her crib, and dial my father's number. It's close to midnight in Australia so I disconnect the call. Dad will be sleeping. The only reason my friends called is because they received the photos I sent and were out late at the Shores nightclub celebrating Yasmine's achievements in her new job. I miss them, but if I had a chance to go back in time, I wouldn't change a thing. My future is with Rose and Samuel, wherever they lead me.

I type out separate messages to Mum, Dad, and Faith with images of Rose attached. At least they are aware we're safe and well. Before I place my phone on the table, it sounds with an incoming call from Faith.

"Hey, you're awake?"

She makes an exasperated sound. "I'm nocturnal and barely sleep, something you'll know about soon enough. It's great to hear your voice. I can't lie and pretend I haven't worried about you."

"I'm fine, I promise. Did you get my message?"

"Yes. It came through in good timing since I'm feeding James. Oh, honey, Rose is just adorable."

"She is," I coo. "I'm sorry my messages were scarce, but you know I had limited internet in the village."

"Yeah, I understood. Bloody hell, you had her seven weeks early. Is she okay? Where are you now?"

"In a hospital in Guyana. I'm not sure for how long. Everything is fine, so I assume we'll be discharged soon. Not to mention beds are scarce, and I don't want to take a bed from someone who needs it more than me."

"Your baby was born premature. There are steps and precautions you need to follow. I guess they can discharge the mother, and you can visit."

"What? I can't leave Rose. If she stays, I stay."

"Does your insurance cover you?"

"Samuel is paying. He won't even tell me how much or anything. He said to just concentrate on Rose. Seriously, he worries more than our father."

Silence.

"Faith, are you there?"

"Yeah. If Samuel is worried about something, then I think you should be as well."

"He's worried about many things and not only for Rose and me. Her sucking reflex is good, and she has no jaundice. Her breathing is fine, and her blood-oxygen level is great. Yet Samuel wants me to fly home soon. He has some loose ends to tie up here before he can join us."

"That's good news. When is your flight?"

A wave of nausea hits me. I shake my head as my thoughts mesh into a jumble as though I'm blocking out the idea of leaving him. "There are matters to organize first... Rose's birth certificate, and we have to be cleared to fly."

"So... three to four weeks? How quickly can Samuel make it happen?"

I chuckle lightly. "He somehow pulls strings in the medical world, only I presume this is a government department so it may take longer."

"Where will you stay?"

"To be honest, I'm not sure. Wherever Samuel thinks is best. It may be here in Guyana close to the hospital. The next step is to make sure Rose thrives from my breast milk." I hesitate in telling my sister I hope to return to Ulara to say goodbye to my friends one last time. I glance over to my bag and see Gran's diary sitting on top. "I have so much to tell you, even more about Gran."

"Gran?"

"Yeah. While here, I started reading her diary. When I return, I'm going to look up her friend, Brenda, and ask for the diary she gave to her for safekeeping. I think it's an account of her stay in the jungle."

"Whoa, do you think that's a good idea? Seriously, it's all in the past, and people have moved on."

My hand rests on my chest thinking about Gran's life. "She did some wonderful things, and we should be proud of her." Tiny grunts come from Rose's crib. "Sorry, I have to go. Rose is waking. We'll talk soon, okay."

"Eden, keep me up to date with what's happening."

"I will."

"Stay safe, sis."

"I will. Love you."

With an overbearing need to sigh, I allow my shoulders to drop. There's one more phone call to make, but I'll have to wait until morning to speak to my parents. Shuffling off the bed, I go to Rose and peer down at my daughter. She has the purest pale skin with light hair on her crown, and her eyebrows are barely noticeable. Tiny lips pucker, and she stretches out her back.

Oh my. I could watch her sleep for hours.

"Are you ready to feed?" I whisper. I inhale a sharp breath, and my hand rises to my right breast. Suddenly, a tingling sensation in my breasts is followed by a feeling of fullness. I think my milk just came in. Rose gives a little whimper, so I pick her up and cradle her until I'm in a chair. Adjusting my clothing almost comes naturally, and I position her on my breast. Her little eyes open as she sucks slower and stronger. "That's it, my Rose. Good girl," I whisper.

"That's truly a sight to behold."

I glance up at Samuel standing in the doorway. He comes to us and brushes a long finger over her little head.

"My milk came down," I say proudly as though it's an achievement.

His lips curl into a smile. "A few days of her getting the extra rest to grow and feed without complication, and you'll be on track to going home."

"Home? I thought I'd remain here for at least another month. I mean, you're the one who's over the top about her immune system."

My phone vibrates on the table, and Rose pulls off my breast with a scowl. I help her reattach, and before I can say anything, Samuel has picked up my phone.

"It's your father."

"Right. I sent him a message and thought he'd be asleep."

Samuel swipes the screen. "Evening, Mr. Monteford. This is Samuel."

I hold out my hand, but he walks away from me.

"No," I say firmly. "Let me speak first." My heart pounds in my chest. My father will be concerned, and I wanted to calm him down first. "Samuel, you're so frustrating."

He stops and turns to me. His gaze locks with mine, equally determined. Suddenly, his expression softens. "Eden is feeding our beautiful daughter. She's almost finished and excited to tell you about her. I'll hand her cell to her to speak first."

He gives the phone to me and mouths, "I also want to speak to him."

"Hey, Dad. Congratulations, you're a grandfather again."

"Are you okay, sweet pea?"

"Yes, I'm great. I'm in a hospital in Guyana. We're all well. I'm sorry to wake you, so we can chat tomorrow if you like."

"It's fine. I'm relieved to hear your voice. And now I can't wait to meet my beautiful granddaughter. When are you coming home?"

He has jumped to this subject quickly. Doing my best to ignore Samuel's serious expression, I steel myself to answer calmly. "Oh, you know, whenever the birth certificate arrives, and it's safe for Rose to fly."

Rose pulls off my breast and has a little vomit. "Oh, honey."

"May I speak to him while you care for Rose?" Samuel holds out his hand.

"Dad, I'm handing you over to Samuel for a moment. I need to attend to Rose."

"Okay, love. Mum is also here, and she wants to ask you questions about the birth."

Samuel takes the phone.

I don't fight him because Rose is squirming.

"Can you put it on speaker," I ask.

Only it's too late.

He has closed the door behind him.

33

SAMUEL

"IT'S a pleasure to finally speak with you. Eden talks highly of you."

"I have to admit I didn't approve of my daughter traveling to a part of the world I considered unsafe while pregnant to be with a man I have never met."

"I understand, and I want to apologize for any worry we have caused you. During her time with me, I have done my utmost to protect her and keep her safe in the village." Samuel rests a hand behind his neck and stares at a spot on the ceiling.

"Thank you for taking care of Eden. Please tell me she didn't give birth in the bloody jungle!"

Samuel swallows hard and closes his eyes at the harshness in Mr. Monteford's tone. "Sir, the baby came early, and we didn't expect—"

"That's the thing about babies. I thought as a physician, you, for one, would understand the spontaneity."

Samuel's eyes flash open. "Yes, sir. I acted swiftly, and Eden and Rose are now safe in the Georgetown hospital in Guyana."

"Where the hell is that?"

Samuel opens his mouth and closes it again, realizing Eden's father isn't really interested in the answer. His comment is to emphasize his concern at his lack of knowledge of her whereabouts.

"I'm aware you want to speak more to your daughter, but I hoped to have a quick word first." When Mr. Monteford doesn't respond, Samuel continues to speak.

"Eden and Rose are my priority. I love your daughter more than anything and refuse to allow harm to come to her." He blocks out the time the Watache kidnapped her and how many times he has failed her. If her father knew the truth, he'd probably ban Samuel from having anything to do with his daughter. And Samuel would accept it and understand.

"Eden loves me, and she wears her heart on her sleeve more than any woman I know." There's a light chuckle of understanding on the other end. "So, I have had to take extra measures to protect her. There are a few matters that prevent me from returning to Australia with Eden. If given a choice, she would, without a doubt, choose to return to my place of work and be by my side. This isn't something I want for her, and since she's as stubborn as she is, I have gone behind her back and arranged a private jet through my father's company to transport Eden and Rose safely back to Australia. This can happen in the next two weeks, depending on two things. The first is Rose's birth certificate and whether it's processed in time. The second is my daughter's health. We need the doctor to clear both Rose and Eden as being fit to fly. From my end, the private jet will be ready when they are. The biggest hurdle is getting Eden to agree to this. She's not aware, and I'm afraid she'll object. So, I hope to have your support in convincing your daughter this is the right decision for everyone. I promise I'll be with her as soon as I can." Samuel inhales a deep breath and waits for Mr. Monteford to respond.

"You've organized that? For her?" Mr. Monteford's voice is loaded with caution.

"Yes. There's nothing I wouldn't do for your daughter."

"That's... that's very good to hear." Could Eden's father be crying? Something cracks in his voice as he says the words, but he clears his throat and continues, "I certainly agree the best place for Eden is home with her family. What can I do to help?"

34

EDEN

Christmas Day

After leaving the hospital, Samuel and I checked into the Ramada Hotel.

He had his reasons not to leave Georgetown, and he agreed to stay here and celebrate Christmas together.

"Morning," I say and roll over in bed and kiss Samuel. "Merry Christmas."

Samuel lifts an arm, and I snuggle into his side. "Merry Christmas, Eden." He kisses me and then kisses me again.

Rose whimpers. We both turn to the crib, our focus no longer on each other.

"Stay," he says. "I'll get her." He passes Rose to me and sits on the edge, stroking Rose's back while she feeds. "She's so precious."

I smile lovingly. "Our little miracle."

"I'll order in breakfast as the dining room will be busy."

"Sure, but not much. I don't want to spoil our lunch." I grin at him. Samuel stands and opens his bag and pulls out a box tied with ribbon.

"You said no presents," I blurt.

Samuel smiles and places the box on the bed beside us. "I didn't want you shopping in the crowds. I ordered this and had it delivered."

"And I could've shopped online as well if I'd known you were breaking the rules."

He chuckles and pats my leg. "I'll shower first, and then I'll burp Rose."

Staring at the box, I'm tempted to untie the red ribbon and take a peek. It's a small rectangular box, and it's not as small as one that holds a ring. Besides, we agreed to buy my engagement ring together. And that won't be until Rose can be in public with a stronger immune system.

Rose pulls off my breast, her lips pursing as she makes a contented sound. "Did we drink too much?" I say and giggle at her adorable facial expressions.

The bathroom door swings open, and a freshly showered Samuel emerges. He towel-dries his sexy blond hair. "Is she finished?"

"Yes. I think she overdid it."

He takes Rose from my arms. "Okay, baby girl, no puking on Daddy." He places a hand towel on his shoulder and moves around the room while gently patting her back.

"Can I open this now?" I hold the box in my hands.

"Go ahead." He beams a smile at me.

I untie the ribbon and lift the lid. "Oh, Samuel." My hand rests at the base of my neck. "It's beautiful." I can't take my eyes off the intricate gold heart on a chain. The design is a 3D heart with smaller hearts on vines to make the shape. Inside the cage are three diamond-encrusted hearts.

Samuel sits on the bed beside me. "The vines and hearts represent *love grows*. And the three smaller hearts—"

"Represent the three of us," I say enthusiastically.

Balancing Rose on his lap, he leans in and kisses me. "I love you."

Taking his face in both my hands, I hold his lips to mine and show him how much I adore him.

"I'm sorry I don't have anything for you."

Samuel shakes his head. "I have you and Rose. I don't need anything else."

I kiss him again and then head to the shower. I take my time washing my hair and lathering the fruity-scented soap over my body. Taking the bathrobe from the hook, I wrap it around me before opening the door. Our breakfast platter is on the table. "Oh, did I take a long time?"

Samuel chuckles. Rose is asleep in his arms. "Take all the time you need." He places Rose in the crib and joins me at the table. Besides the usual fruit Samuel insists I eat for my health, there's a plate of scrambled eggs, toast, and fruit juice.

"I'm not sure if this qualifies as a light breakfast."

He hands me a glass of camu camu juice. "No, but you need nourishment."

"We," I add with a smile.

He stands and finds my gift, then he clips the necklace around my neck. I lightly touch the heart hanging between my breasts and close to my heart. "I'll treasure it always."

"Ready?" Samuel asks with Rose secured in a wrap around his shoulder and tied at the waist. He's wearing a white button-up short-sleeved shirt and navy shorts.

Brushing my hair for the last time, I check myself in the mirror, admiring my forest green dress, then take the elevator to the ground floor. Tinsel and sparkly Christmas decorations line the hallway and foyer. I smile, thankful to be sharing this day with Samuel.

A waiter directs us to a table with a red umbrella to protect us from the sun. The sapphire blue pool has floating tables all decked with candles, tinsel, and angel statues.

"It's so pretty," I tell him.

Samuel pulls out a chair for me to sit. I can imagine him as the perfect gentleman in society.

"Thank you." I sit opposite him and Rose, then take in the colorful ornaments surrounding us.

"I love Christmas."

After our meal, we retreat to our room, and I nap for an hour until Rose wakes me ready to feed.

Samuel is sitting on the balcony. Lifting Rose from her crib, I walk out onto the balcony to feed her in the chair beside him.

Below us, the pool hums with revelers still celebrating.

"Do you think we could take another drive tonight and find more Christmas lights? I'd love to see the huge Christmas tree in Rahaman Park."

"Of course," he says and strokes Rose's crown. "I hope to discuss something with you." His eyebrows pull together, and there's a seriousness in his eyes.

Oh no.

His expression is scaring me, so I glance down and focus on Rose feeding. "What is it?" I murmur.

"You know I love you and Rose and only want what's best for you both," he says in a level voice.

"Just tell me, Samuel."

"I need you to go home and be safe with your family."

I nod, still not looking at him. "And you'll eventually join me?"

I look up when he takes my hand between both of his. "I promise I will. As soon as possible."

I scan his face. "But that's not what you want to discuss with me, is it?"

Samuel holds my gaze before speaking. "Tomorrow, there's a jet flying directly to Adelaide with a stopover in New Zealand. I'd like you on it."

My heart goes to my throat. "And if I say no?" I rasp.

"Please, Eden. I needed to take the extra measures to keep you both safe."

"So, I don't have a choice?" I croak. "Why now? Why not wait until the new year?"

Samuel bows his head.

A sob escapes my throat, and I can't control it. I sniff loudly. "No." I shake my head. "I'm staying here with you!"

35

EDEN

The Following Day...

"We're ready to board," the flight attendant says to me.

"So, this is it." I swipe a tear before it trails down my cheek.

Samuel's bloodshot eyes portray his sadness, but unlike me, he has been stiff-lipped the past twenty-four hours and not shed a tear in front of me. We're the only ones standing in the private hangar with the two pilots already boarded and two other flight attendants.

"Call me when you arrive in New Zealand." His large hand cups Rose's cheek.

I nod quickly. "I will and again when we touch down in Adelaide."

He pulls me close, careful not to smother Rose, who's cuddled into my chest. My bones are weak, the sadness seeps deep, and the littlest pressure could send me to my knees. God, I wanted to drop to my knees several times and beg him not to send us away.

"Ask Asoo to keep me updated. I know time gets away from you, but every minute will feel like days to me," I croak.

"And me. I don't want to go around in circles, but it's for the best. I'll be with you in a month or so." He kisses the side of my cheek, and I grab his arm to stop him from pulling away.

"It's too long. How quickly can you speed up the final documents in Caracas to end your contract?" I reach up with my spare hand and cup his neck, so his lips lower closer to mine. I kiss him through the tears and the burn in my throat, so he knows he's my everything, and I hate being apart from him for a second, let alone weeks.

"Sir," the flight attendant interrupts. "They have given us clearance, and we need to get the plane on the runway."

Our lips break away, and Samuel leans his forehead against mine. "You're the love of my life, Eden." A sob escapes my throat. "My heart will be with you and Rose. Take care of it until I can be with you both again."

I can't stop my face from squishing when an ugly cry threatens to undo every inch of composure I have left. Tears roll down Samuel's cheeks. His demeanor cracks. "Go," he rasps. "Please go." His voice breaks, and like me, his face screws up in pain.

"One month," I say to confirm our separation. "I'll see you in one month."

The flight attendant takes the bags at my feet. Samuel waves to me and turns, then keeps walking. He doesn't look back. Not once. Head down, long strides, he walks out of the hangar and around the back to where a black Audi awaits him. His father ensured Samuel had enough money to cover us for a quick departure, and now Samuel can drive himself back to the international departures section and catch a flight to Venezuela.

"I'm Daryl," the attendant says with a Spanish accent. He walks beside me holding my three carry-on bags filled with what I need for the next twenty hours for Rose.

"Jenna is a nurse and will assist you with any needs on board." Daryl offers a warm smile, only right now, I doubt anything will help with the gaping hole in my chest. The neckband of my shirt is wet from the tears spilling off my chin and onto my chest.

I climb the stairs and take the first step into the luxurious furnishings of the jet. There are white leather lounge chairs wide enough to transform into beds. To the side are lacquered wooden tables. Lush carpet runs the length of the plane. Up front, a glass bar catches my eye with stools strategically placed in an arc for guests. Samuel and his father must have paid a mint for this. The thought makes me angry. Normally, Samuel lives a simplified life and places no value on money. If we'd waited, I could've flown using my return ticket and not wasted a shitload of money unnecessarily just to get me home early. Rose's immunity is the point he emphasized in his reasoning for the private jet. Yet, for the sake of a few weeks, he could've saved himself at least one hundred thousand dollars. The thought of him going behind my back angers me, and right now, I'm using the anger to stop the tears.

Jenna points to a seat that's more like a luxurious lounge suite. I force a smile. "Ms. Monteford, I need you to adjust your seat belt until we're in the air. I'm here if you need anything after take-off, including assisting you with feeding and minding Rose when you use the restroom and to make sure you get adequate sleep. I'll monitor Rose for any signs of distress, including difficulty in breathing. The lower air pressure may be problematic, and the changing cabin pressure may cause her to have some ear pain. As soon as you're settled, I'll get you to feed her, so she's sucking during take-off and again on each descent."

I undo the clip under my right armpit, so my top falls away to reveal my right breast—quite the invention for feeding mothers. I unclip the cup of my maternity bra, which would have to be the ugliest bra I have ever worn, and tease Rose's mouth with my nipple. Apparently, my nipple isn't enticing. "Rose," I whisper. I run my fingers over her cheek so she turns her head. A few more attempts, and she opens her mouth to attach. I nod at Jenna. "She has been slow attaching the last week."

"It's not unusual in premature babies." Her hand rubs my arm. She wraps an additional strap over Rose and attaches it to my belt. "This is just until we're in the air."

Jenna signals to Daryl we are ready, and the plane crawls along a path as we head toward the runway.

When the nose is pointed upward to the sky, I lean my head back and close my eyes, wishing it didn't have to be this way. I swallow the lump in my throat to even out the pressure in my ears. The plane levels, and I look out my window to the city disappearing below. Within minutes, the view turns green with the vast rainforest covering much of the country. A world where I belonged. A world so far from the one where I live.

Tears fill my eyes like wells and fall onto my cheeks. I can't fight the gnawing pain in my chest any longer. But my tears aren't only for Samuel. This was probably my last visit to Ulara—the last time I'll see my friends again. I screw up my eyes, knowing Kaikare will expect me to return with Samuel. What will she think?

Samuel told me they were to migrate soon. If they do, we will never know their whereabouts—only that they were heading closer to the

Colombian jungle and then south to the Peruvian jungle. A journey that could take months—even years. Kaikare may never meet my father, nor will she see me or her niece again. In those last weeks together, I'm glad I gave her a photo of us even though Samuel warned me against it. I smile. Kaikare and I are family, and we did secretive things so the men didn't get upset. Her eagerness to know more reflected she had some of my grandmother's blood flowing through her veins.

In Ulara, I was brave and free.

My Gran, Kaikare, and I may be wild at heart, yet we're courageous, strong women. Now Rose will join our legacy. I wonder if she'll have the same drive to return to where she was born to find her jungle spirit?

Wiping away the tears that land on Rose's head, I look back to the window and watch as the vivid green fades and the clouds block out my view.

Through the heartache and frustration, I can't help my concern for Samuel. Not only for his safety. How will the shaman react to him for sending us away?

"We have begun our descent into New Zealand," Jenna whispers. "Do you want me to take Rose for you?"

I stretch out the kinks in my neck and force my eyes to open. Despite the comfort of a bed on a jet, I barely slept with my thoughts whirling about the future. "No, it's fine," I murmur. Pushing up onto my elbows, I reach for Rose sleeping in a small crib beside me.

"Let me help you." Jenna lifts Rose and waits for me to sit up. After adjusting the pillows behind my back, I then hold out my arms for my daughter.

"Take your time," Jenna says softly. "I don't mind holding her." She gazes down with a contented look in her eyes.

I adjust my top and bra. "Thank you. I can manage now." I lift the window blind to dark skies and the sun peeking over the horizon.

"We should land around six o'clock. It will give us time to refuel. Then when the tower clears us, we'll be in the air and on our way to Adelaide." She gives me a warm smile as though this is reassuring. It only confirms the distance separating Samuel and me is increasing by the hour.

"Thank you," I say quickly and gaze out the window once more. I can't look at her because I'm holding myself together by a mere thread, and the slightest comment could unravel me in seconds.

It's only when the plane jolts as the wheels hit the runway do I notice Rose has detached and is asleep in my arms. She didn't cry. Not once. I shake my head and curse under my breath for not realizing this sooner. I have to snap out this haze of self-pity and focus on my daughter.

Jenna unclips her belt and comes to me. "She's a remarkable little girl." She pushes her dark hair behind her ears, then leans for the antibacterial hand sterilizer and applies it to her hands. God knows how many times she has used it on the flight. I can only imagine Samuel's instruction to the crew.

"Allow me to hold her while you freshen up. There's a private restroom just outside the hangar. You can use it as we all have to disembark while the plane refuels. Unfortunately, we can't venture any further because of our visas. Airport customs staff are waiting, and they'll monitor us even though we're a private company."

"Right. Do you think I could make some phone calls?"

"Yes, you'll have time."

Jenna remains with me while the customs staff asks questions about our travel. "Let me care for her while you make your calls," she says.

God, I must look miserable.

"I'll change Rose first, and then I'll shower. Do you mind taking Rose while I do?"

"Of course. But you go, and I'll change Rose's diaper."

"Thank you."

As much as I want to remain under the water spray, it doesn't relieve the tension the way I had hoped. Eager to call Samuel, I dress quickly and head back to the lounge area.

"I really appreciate your help," I tell Jenna. I bag up my dirty clothes and head to a quiet corner of the room, then bring out my phone.

"Eden." I smile at the affection and relief in Dad's tone. "Are you in New Zealand?"

"Yes, it's a quick stopover to refuel. We should be there in around five hours, but I'll need to go through customs." I gaze down to my new gray sneakers, the ones I bought after throwing out the old ones. "Did you get the list of things we need? I'm sorry it's short notice. I can't believe how unorganized I am."

"It's fine, my girl. James is using a larger car seat now, so we have his smaller seat for the car for you to use for Rose. We have everything you need. We've done it all before. Only I'm not used to seeing so much pink again." He chuckles, and I can't help but smile at the sound of it. I'm looking forward to seeing my family, only I hoped Samuel would be with me to greet them and show them *our* beautiful daughter together.

"It will be good to see you all." I look up in the direction where Jenna is taking slow steps with Rose in her arms. She's not bouncing her, but she sways like the camu camu leaves moving in the breeze.

"I can't wait, love. It's been too long."

I nod to myself. "I better go. I think Rose may be a little unsettled. I'll call you when I land."

"We'll be waiting at the airport for you," he says enthusiastically.

"Bye, Dad." I end the call and rush over to Jenna. Rose isn't crying, and she's still sleeping. "Is everything okay?"

"Yes. She started to pull a face, so I thought if I moved around the room slowly, it would help her to settle."

"She already has us wrapped around her tiny finger," I joke. "I have one more call to make." The hardest of all.

I call Samuel's phone, and it goes to his voicemail. "Dammit." I hope this isn't how it's going to be between us. Samuel was aware of my flight details and what time I'd call him. I pace in the corner of the room thinking of what to text him when the phone vibrates in my hand.

Thank God.

"Samuel, I was beginning to worry."

"How was your flight? How is Rose?"

"Good. We're fine. How could we not be? It's a beautiful plane. Rose has barely cried, which is good, and she has fed regularly."

"The staff has assisted you?"

"Yes. Wonderfully."

"Good."

We pause, and I sense he's hiding something with the formalities. "I miss you," I say, and my throat dries with the pain in my chest.

"I miss you too."

"Did you send your email to Caracas?"

"Eden." He hesitates a moment, and my heart goes to my throat.

"Asoo called me. There were more drones flying near Ulara, and this time, he followed a boat. When they realized he was behind them, they didn't take the secret turn down the river. They continued on, and the boat was more powerful than Asoo's curiara."

"They had boats… what are you telling me?" I croak.

"Asoo believes they are scoping the area, and it's putting the village in danger."

"And?" I whisper.

"When I return to Ulara, I'll have a meeting with the chief. I think it's time they considered migrating deeper into the jungle."

"And?" I repeat.

"Eden, please don't read into this. Allow me to return and assess the situation. I'm in Canaima now. I feel obligated to keep them safe."

"They're not your responsibility anymore," I whisper. I glance up as Jenna strolls toward me. Daryl is collecting my bags, and everyone is heading toward the jet. "I have to go. Please don't make any rash decisions. I'll call you when I'm in Adelaide. I love you."

"I love you too. I'll speak to you when you're safely at home. Look after our precious Rose."

I nod and end the call as Jenna reaches me and blink away the tears. "Is it time?" I fake a smile.

"Yes, we're cleared now."

I follow Jenna toward the plane and hope to hell Samuel doesn't leave for Ulara before I have a chance to speak to him again.

On board the jet, I settle back into the seat for the final leg of the journey. I glance down at Rose sleeping in my arms. "We're going home," I whisper. "You're going to meet your grandparents, your aunty and uncles, and your cousins. You'll love your new home."

It's weird to think Ulara was her first home, one she'll never know. Maybe a home she would have loved, like Kaikare, as she'd be ignorant to what lies beyond the jungle, the privileged world that relies on money as power rather than survival skills.

I promise to teach you to respect the land, all creatures, and people just as you would if you lived in Ulara. Money will not rule our egos or happiness.

Leaning forward, I kiss her cheek, and her little lips purse in the sweetest duck face I've ever seen.

Once the plane is in the air, I unclip my belt and the strap over Rose and place her in the crib. Digging into my bag, I pull out Gran's diary, ready to embrace the last of her words before she begins her journey.

DATE: 15th November 1962

The journey by boat has been long.

The nausea never leaves me. Most days, I vomit. I intended to write in the diary every day on the boat, but it's dragging on, and after being surrounded by nothing but blue, it has affected my mood.

So this is my last entry in my diary. I have bought a new leather diary for my volunteering journey, and I can't wait!

HER ADVENTURE IS about to begin just as mine has come to an end.

36

SAMUEL

"ESTAS SEGURO?" Samuel asks Asoo. *Are you sure?*

"Sí." *Yes.*

Asoo explains to Samuel the men in the powerful boats were near the riverbend when their drones flew over Ulara. The Ularans are in immediate danger, and Asoo races to get Samuel back to the village. Samuel is a mess of emotion. He has gone from deep sorrow saying goodbye to Eden to a clustered mess of anger and fear, knowing the Ularans safety is at risk. He has raced off to help, yet he has no gun or any weapon if it comes down to fighting these men. He's fast if he needs to run, but he hopes his negotiating skills will be his best defense. Either way, if someone enters the village, their secret is lost and their immunity compromised. Who knows where these men have been and who they have associated with?

In the back of his mind, he has accepted the inevitable. In Canaima, he collected his phone, identity papers, passport, and important belongings that will fit in a backpack. He left everything else with Victor. Most of it is replaceable. He has another two backpacks in Ulara for notebooks, long accounts of his work, and other medication and first-aid.

His phone and charger are wrapped in plastic. He's sent his last message to Eden, and he has no idea when he'll be able to contact her again.

They turn the final bend, and Samuel squints to make out the boat moored on the bank of Ulara.

"Apaga el motor," he says. *Cut the motor.*

They glide into the embankment near Samuel's makeshift campsite. The imposter's boat is thirty yards away. Both men spring from the boat and dash to the thick shrubbery to take cover. Samuel scouts the area, inspecting the ground for footprints or freshly broken twigs or palm leaves. There's no evidence of anyone around his campsite, but he fears the worst. The men could be in the village. It's a ten-minute walk, less if he runs. He tells Asoo to leave now, otherwise they'll discover his curiara.

"Esconde la curiara," Asoo suggests. *Hide the curiara.*

They sprint back to the river and drag the curiara into the bushes, then snap palm leaves to cover it. It's not completely covered, although it's obscured enough not to be obvious.

"Te vas a quedar?" *Stay?*

Asoo shakes his head. Both men take off through the jungle, slapping palm leaves aside, careful to avoid the prickly vines. When they near the village, they slow to a walk. Pushing a low-lying branch aside, Samuel assesses the situation, yet everyone is going about their business. The women are cooking over the fires, the children kick a coconut in a small clearing, and the older men sit cross-legged weaving baskets.

"Quédate." *Stay.* This time, it's an order. Samuel walks past the ladies and holds a finger to his lips. They give him a subtle nod, yet there's an uneasiness in their eyes. Kapeá Tapire is now around six months pregnant herself, and she's not working in the fields today. He squats next to her and observes her cooking a broth in a clay pot. He looks to the chief's hut and then to the shaman's hut. Only now do English words carry in the air. He asks her how many men are in the shaman's hut.

"Oko." *Two.*

"Jopoto?" *Chief.*

Kapeá Tapire nods.

"Pyjai?" *Shaman.*

She nods again.

"Kaikare?"

Kapeá Tapire shakes her head. She points to the other side of the village. Crouched beyond the trees are several figures. From here, he can make out Kaikare and Tïmenneng.

"Waküpe-küruman," he says. *Thank you.* Samuel instructs her to tell the ladies to remain calm. While monitoring the doorway of the shaman's hut, he darts to the other side of the village and speaks to three warriors and Kaikare.

"Tamusi areku." *Old man angry*. Kaikare points and shows more distress than the others. She explains how the men pushed her father into the hut and demanded his gold.

Samuel asks her to remain calm and says he'll try to negotiate with the men. He doesn't know if it will help, but at least he can communicate in English.

Standing outside the shaman's hut, he signals his approach. "I'm a physician, and I work in the village. Is there anything I can do to help?"

"C'mon in, doc," a gruff voice demands, a voice sounding raspy as though he has chain-smoked for fifty years. The chesty cough confirms it.

Samuel ducks his head to enter the doorway, and no sooner than he's inside, a gun is shoved near his face.

"Take a seat. Perhaps you can translate what we want because your chief here has no clue." The two Caucasian men have fair hair. This one speaks with an American accent. The odor reeking from their khaki shirts and the dirt smeared over the sweaty arms and shins indicates they haven't showered for days. He assesses their clothing—matching khaki shorts and worn leather boots with the clay mud coating the exterior. No belts carrying knives or ammunition.

Samuel shifts his attention to the chief and then to the shaman to assess their well-being. Both men have fresh bruises on their brow and scratches to their cheeks, shoulders, and arms, as though their faces have been pushed into the ground. The shaman's eyes reflect sorrow and disappointment. The chief has a defiant look, and it concerns Samuel.

"They have something I want." The gun waves between the chief and the shaman. "Tell them to give me the gifts other travelers have left for them."

"I have no clue to what you're referring, but I'll ask," Samuel says. Samuel asks both men if they have something of value from people who visited the village before Samuel. The chief tells Samuel the stone mountains are unhappy that he took Rose without a formal blessing. And now they are being punished. Ignoring the comment, he asks the shaman again. The shaman meets his gaze and gives a curt nod.

Samuel speaks to the shaman in their native tongue, so the outsiders don't understand their conversation. Samuel asks him what's of value and who gave it to him.

The shaman explains there was a man before Ivy, but since Ivy, there were no visitors until Samuel. He stands and walks to the back wall. He reaches into a twine basket and retrieves a brass vase. Samuel has not had the privilege of seeing this vase. The shaman tips it, and a chain falls into his hand. On it dangles a huge gold nugget. He tips the vase again, and a strand of pearls lands over the nugget. He tells Samuel the pearls were Ivy's.

Samuel explains this is all the shaman has, but the pearls aren't authentic, hoping the travelers disregard them.

The gun fires.

Samuel, the chief, and the shaman drop to their knees in response to the explosion. Samuel uncurls his body and checks the chief beside him who's hunched with his hands over his ears.

"Wakü?" *Good?*

The chief's eyes are wide, and beyond the fear, he gives a curt nod. The shaman moans. Like him, he has fallen to his knees. A hand rests over the left side of his abdomen. He flops backward. His brow pulls tight, then he lowers his gaze and lifts his hand. Dark blood cascades between his fingers and down his stomach toward the band of his skirt.

Fuck. He shot him!

"Don't take me for a fool." He angles the gun at Samuel. "Don't tell me lies."

The other guy pushes the chief, and he falls to the dirt. Samuel's heartbeat thumps behind his ears. He wills his panicked thoughts to calm, but he can't take his eyes off the shaman. Mentally, he's assessing the puncture wound and his blood loss.

"Bring me the box and chain." The man's sinister expression turns into a smirk as though he's enjoying the power. "And no tricks because the next time will be you."

Suddenly the gunman's face turns gray before he falls flat on his face, the gun spinning from his grasp. His eyes are wide with instant death. A small dart in his back is to blame. Samuel and the other low-life turn to the doorway. Another dart hits the accomplice in the chest. Tïmenneng lowers his poison blowpipe.

It takes a moment for Samuel's thoughts to catch up. "Shit," he shouts and rushes to the shaman. He rips his T-shirt over his head and presses it to the wound. With his free hand, he lifts the shaman's head so he rests on his lap. Behind him, the men's bodies are dragged from the hut by the young warriors, and the chief is rushed away. Terrified screams come from outside the hut and then Kaikare appears in the doorway. Through the silence, there's quiet panic in her eyes.

"Pyjai," Samuel tells her. *Medicine.* He explains he needs her to go to his hut and get *his* medicines. Without question, she does what he asks.

Seconds later, Asoo appears at the doorway, his eyes as round as a full moon.

"Kaikare is getting the first-aid box. I need the women to concoct some heated leaves to stop the bleeding and help with the pain. Can you go to the ladies cooking over the fire and give my request?"

Samuel looks down at the shaman. He hums a harmonic tune as though he's singing to the forest. He can't give up. It isn't his time. Samuel's chest tightens with panic. The musky rust scent of blood fills his nostrils. Samuel adjusts his T-shirt, and with the pressure, the material soaks up blood faster than Samuel can manage to control it. He needs emergency surgery. Something he can't perform here. Major blood vessels and organs are damaged, and without medical equipment to scan the shaman's wound, the extent of the damage is unknown. Managing blood loss, shock, blood pressure, and infection are his priority, and one T-shirt will not be effective in saving his friend's life.

Samuel tells the shaman he's getting his white man's medicine.

The shaman lightly shakes his head. He explains to Samuel the forest calls him.

Samuel keeps the conversation positive, telling the shaman his medicine will act quickly. Samuel looks to the door wishing for Kaikare to appear.

"Come on, Kaikare. Please hurry," he murmurs.

The shaman's breathing becomes heavy, labored, and sweat beads over his forehead and face. Blood streams from beneath the material and pools on the dirt. He's suffering, and yet the shaman's expression remains stoic. With one hand, he reaches up, and a rough skinned palm cups Samuel's cheek.

"Airö, upetoy." *Goodbye, friend.* "Wewe pyjai," he rasps. *Trees call the shaman.*

Samuel shakes his head in a desperate attempt to remain positive.

"Mosìpe nono oma." *Long earth path.* The shaman lifts a weak finger and points to Samuel. "Urekon." *We.* "Aina," he murmurs. *Hand.*

Samuel takes his hand and squeezes it. Is it his way of giving his word in the Western world in the form of a handshake? Samuel stares into the shaman's eyes. His lifeforce is fading. Samuel's chest tightens knowing there is nothing he can do. The realization is a dagger to his heart.

He has the knowledge of both world's medicine and yet he feels helpless, a failure again.

Panting in the doorway diverts his attention. Kaikare is out of breath as she runs toward them.

"Thank God," he rasps.

She bends down and places the case beside Samuel. He asks her to unclip the lid. He points to the dressings and tape, and he swaps places with her so she's cradling her father's head in her lap and hands. Her sad eyes hold his gaze as he peers up to her apologetically. They whisper to each other while Samuel washes the wound and presses clean dressings to the area. The shaman doesn't flinch—not once. Instantly, bright blood soaks the white bandages, and Samuel catches the fear in Kaikare's eyes before turning her focus back to her father. He tells her it's her time. She lets out a quiet sob. He asks her to be strong, no tears, as his journey is complete.

Samuel works as fast as he can. His hands freeze hearing Ivy and Dawn's words, and Samuel realizes the shaman is talking about Kaikare's mother and their time together. The shaman's eyes shutter closed and slowly open again. He's losing consciousness and soon will not be alert enough to know what's happening around him.

Samuel tells the shaman coming to Ulara was the highlight of his life. Through him he found a father figure, a mentor, and a friend. Samuel sniffs and wipes his nose with his forearm. The shaman has taught him many things about life and himself, and he's proud to call Ulara home.

The shaman mutters, "Areku," he asks them not to be *angry*. He closes his eyes and asks for Samuel to help him. Samuel assumes he means with his treatment, only he mumbles. "Mosìpe nono oma." *Long earth path.* He opens his eyes long enough for Samuel to nod. Then his hand softens in Kaikare's palm, his eyes closing in peace.

Samuel removes the dressing. The blood loss has slowed. Taking

Kaikare's hand, he closes his eyes. He doesn't need to touch his neck to know the shaman's heart has stopped beating.

Kaikare curls over her father's limp body and whimpers. Gently, Samuel rests a hand on her back. Her whimpers turn to wails as she mourns her father. His heart aches feeling her loss. She is now alone without family and he has sent Eden, her blood relative away.

"I'm sorry," he murmurs and rubs her back. "So, so sorry." He understands the need to grieve before Kaikare steps up to be their leader. She squeezes Samuel's hand, her bloodshot eyes begging for support.

"I'll stay with you as long as you need me," he tells her in their native tongue. He then quietly stands and leaves her to have the final time with her father, alone.

As soon as he exits the hut, he's hit with chaos. The men run and shout, shock etched into their expression. Asoo rushes to him.

"The men throw bodies into boat," he says in a shaky voice.

"We need to dispose of it now. Remove all the evidence they were here."

"How?" Asoo covers his eyes with his hands. "This will end bad."

"Can you retrieve my bags from the curiara?"

"Si." Asoo scampers toward the river.

"Tïmenneng," Samuel shouts. When Samuel catches up, he asks him to dispose of the boat. Tïmenneng nods and then gathers the warriors.

Samuel finds Chirké, one of the elder ladies, crouched by the fire. He asks for her help to calm the women. The younger women sob, not yet controlling their emotions like the elders, and it's scaring the children. Samuel doesn't want to deny the Ularans a sense of mourning. His heart has splintered into a million pieces, but now isn't the time. They need to support one another and keep noise to a minimum in case other intruders are sailing nearby, searching for their friends. He places a hand on the back of a young lady and tells her it will be fine. He then heads to the chief, ready to inform him of the shaman's wishes and his insight.

It's time to move on. Take the great earth path and find another home.

Kaikare will become the shaman, and Samuel will be by her side until they settle deep in the jungle where no man ventures.

He has made promises to the people he loves.

Eden.

The shaman.

But a promise to a dying man's wish to save his Ularan family when Samuel's family is safe in Australia is important to him. Samuel has the paper maps that only he can read and Western medication and knowledge to assist the Ularans in their voyage. He'll help with replanting vines and other medicinal herbs until more can be discovered. In the coming weeks and months, they'll need him more than Eden. In fact, the entire civilization depends on him for their safety.

His gut twists in pain. How will he survive without her? Will she forgive him? Without her by his side, the journey ahead will be torturous, but he *will* return to her again, only much later than he promised.

Asoo returns carrying Samuel's packs. "Two more I not manage."

"It's fine, my friend. It's time for you to go. The Ularans will move on from this site as it has become too dangerous for everyone. I need you to leave now before anyone recognizes you and associates you to what went down here today."

Asoo tilts his head. "Samuel come with Asoo?"

"No, my friend." He lays a hand on his shoulder. "I'll travel with the Ularans until they find peace and safety deeper in the jungle. Their migration was inevitable... the timing, unfortunate. I made a promise to the shaman to remain with Kaikare and assist her on a safe journey. I need your phone to send a message to Eden. Please let her know I'm safe, and I'll be with her soon. I'll type out a message for you to send in Canaima. She'll call you, so please just reinforce I'm safe so she doesn't worry."

"Where you go?" he asks, his voice thick.

Samuel exhales loudly. His words will not be reassuring. "Southwest toward Colombia and Brazil. Preferably closer to Peru."

Asoo groans. "No, friend. Brazilian Garimpeiros and Colombian Guerrilla control much of the land."

Samuel bows his head momentarily before meeting Asoo's wary gaze. "I'll keep away from towns and stay close to the river. My map will guide us."

Asoo shakes his head as he reaches down to his pocket, pulls out his phone, and hands it to Samuel.

Samuel types a message to Eden. With every word typed, he endeavors to remain positive as he knows she'll consider his journey a death wish.

He can't help thinking she's right.

He hands the phone back to Asoo. "Send it when you're in Canaima."

"Miss Eden will be sad."

"And I'll need you to reassure her I'll be fine." Before Asoo replies, Samuel hugs him and pats his back several times. "Thank you, my friend. You have helped me more than I can ever repay. One day we will meet again."

When they break, Asoo wipes his eyes filled with fear. "I'll tell Miss Eden you a good man."

Samuel smiles and bows his head, hoping she sees it that way.

Asoo and Samuel strain to push the curiara from the riverbank into the water. Asoo turns and gives his friend one final salute before revving the motor and guiding his curiara to safety.

Samuel drops to one knee as the sound of the motor fades as it reaches the bend in the river. He bows his head when Asoo disappears behind the thick, overgrowth overhanging into the murky water.

Samuel's demeanor cracks. Asoo will not return here for weeks. Realization sets in. His chest burns as though a knife has ripped down his sternum and someone has pried his ribs apart.

Alone, the tears come and blot the sand beneath his feet. He allows himself this moment until he can breathe again without pain.

A roar of a motor in the opposite direction catches his attention. The intruder's boat is alight as it sails across the river. It explodes into a fireball before reaching the trees on the opposite side. Smoke billows toward the sky, a tell-tale sign to anyone searching for the men.

Samuel pushes to his feet.

He'll stress the urgency to move on to the chief before more men come searching. He sprints in the direction of the village for possibly the last time. The next path Samuel treads is toward the stream and deeper into the jungle.

Deeper and away from any form of civilization.

And.

Eden.

37

EDEN

WHEELING my case behind me and holding Rose in my other arm, I exit through the customs gate in Adelaide with the other passengers. Peering through the glass barrier, I spot Mum and Dad chatting to each other. To Dad's left is Faith. She is holding James in her arms, and she's distracted by Seb running around.

"Eden," Mum screams as I exit through customs. She pushes past a young couple in front of her and rushes toward the arrival gate. "Oh, darling." She wraps one arm around me despite the grumbling of those travelers behind us trying to exit and meet their families.

"It's great to be home," I tell her and move aside so people can pass us.

"My girl." Dad hugs me.

"Hi, Dad." We exchange brief smiles before their focus switches to Rose.

"Oh, Eden," Mum coos. "She's just delightful."

"Hey," Faith says, pushing past Mum. "Let me give her a hug." With her free hand, she embraces me.

I kiss her cheek and then kiss James. "Where's the rascal?"

Faith stops James from poking a finger at Rose's cheek, and while holding his tiny hand, she swivels and calls out to her son.

A moment later, Seb is pulling at my skirt. "Let me see."

"Where are your manners, Seb?" Faith rouses. Dad lifts him so he can see Rose. "What about a kiss for your favorite aunty?"

Faith chuckles as he leans in and gives me a sloppy kiss.

"Do you want to meet your new cousin?" Faith asks. He stares at Rose as though she's made of china, and he knows he's not allowed to touch.

"Give Rose to me, darling. You must be tired." Mum takes Rose from my arms and stares down at her admiringly. A pang of sadness rises inside me in a weird way with Rose being taken from my arms.

This is it.

The start of our new life outside of Ulara.

"Let's get home, so we can all hear about your adventure," Dad says. In the months I've been gone, he must have had time to digest my reasons for traveling into the jungle. He takes my case from my hand and then grabs hold of Seb's hand.

Faith and I fall in behind them.

"You look exhausted," she says.

I give her a sideways glance and smirk. "So do you."

Faith rolls her eyes. "I've barely slept the last two years. Rose is only three weeks old. I want to know *everything*."

"And I'll tell you. But what's with Dad showing interest in the jungle?"

She smiles warmly. "He has done a complete circle while you've been away. He didn't want to lose you, so he'd rather support you. I may have mentioned his secret sister."

"What? He knows?" I whisper.

She nods. "Pick your words. He's still fragile."

"Understandably." Though I doubt us all sitting around and bonding over a cup of tea and cake will be enough to prepare him for what I'm about to say.

While away, Faith has updated to an SUV with more seats, so we all file into her new car fitted with two car seats and a baby carrier for Rose.

"This is nice," I tell her as I buckle my belt. I wiggle Rose's belt to ensure she's safe. Her little eyes are wide open as if she's listening to the unfamiliar noises surrounding her.

During the drive home, I check my phone for a message from Samuel.

When none register, I drop it into my bag. The last thing I want is for my parents to see me pining for Samuel. It might alert them that something isn't right, and I don't want anyone to assume anything.

When we reach the esplanade, I'm distracted by the blue ocean, a beautiful azure color that I love this time of year. I've missed celebrating Christmas by a few days, but the decorations still twinkle all around us.

We pull up in the driveway of our apartment complex. The white façade looks different, and yet it's the same. I guess it's what time away does to your memory.

"Walk, don't run," Faith says to Seb as he dashes toward the stairwell. "You would think he doesn't know how to walk."

He holds up his foot to show me his sneaker. "I got new shoes, and they make me run fast."

I laugh at my nephew. "I bet they can make you superfast."

Inside my parents' penthouse, Dad follows me to my room. I haven't decided where I intend to live with Rose, but for now, home with my parents is best. "We have Rose's crib set up beside your bed. I assumed you would want her in with you for a while."

I open the door and admire the new set of pale pink water-colored paintings donning the wall near the crib and a mobile fixed to the side of the crib.

"Thank you. This is great, and I appreciate what you have done for me on such short notice."

"Anything for my girl." Dad places a gentle hand on my shoulder. "Now, are you tired? Do you want to rest, or do you want something to eat or drink?"

"I think I'll eat first and then feed Rose before I take a nap."

"Okay, then." Dad parks my case in the corner of the room. Then we head out to the kitchen to Mum still cradling Rose and Faith chastising Seb.

"May I?" Dad takes Rose from Mum's arms. "Eden is hungry, so we'll sit for a while before she takes a nap."

"Great. Mum has baked you a cake that has sustenance for when you're feeding. It's loaded with carbs, and I'm not sure *I* should have any, but damn, it looks delicious." Faith closes the refrigerator door with her foot as she balances the cake with both hands.

"Gosh, it will take me a month to eat it."

"Not with your father and sister around." Mum giggles. "It's a carrot and banana cake mixed with walnuts, raisins, cashews, and almond meal."

"Topped with the best cream cheese icing you'll ever taste," Faith adds. She slides her finger over the edge and sucks the tip of her pointer finger. "Yep. I'm not denying myself this pleasure."

"I can't remember the last time I've eaten cake. Well, any sugar, actually," I say. My family all turn and stare at me as though I've arrived from another planet. I'm unsure whether it was my tone or my choice of words.

"Yeah, about that," Faith finally breaks the silence. "Do you want to tell us more about where you've been the past few months?"

I smile warily. "Where do you want me to start?"

"The beginning." Dad gives me a firm look and then nods. "I want to know everything."

"You mightn't like all I have to say," I murmur.

"It's fine, Eden. We need to hear the truth. You have arrived home safely, and I want to hear about your journey and what you have learned about..." Dad's voice cracks on the last words.

"Your half-sister?" I ask gently.

He bows his head as though ashamed. "Yes. I'm sorry I didn't trust your instinct before. I'm not going to lie and say I wasn't worried, as there were days I was beside myself and cursed you for not being in contact. But you've arrived home safely, God willing, and achieved more in finding out about Mum's life than I cared to know. But I respect what you did, and I'd like to hear about it."

"Okay. But I'm going to need a cup of tea, weak maybe, but something to moisten my mouth as it's a long story."

For an entire hour, I speak about the shaman, Kaikare, my life in the jungle, and, of course, Samuel and how amazing he is doing the work he does. I'm careful to omit the kidnapping story as I'm not sure any of them are ready to hear it.

"Well, I think you're amazing," Mum says quickly. "Having your baby in the jungle with minimal help—"

"I had help. The women were skilled. They supported me and knew what to do. They were like any midwife here and had decades of experience delivering babies in the village."

"That may be so, but you were far from any hospital or medical service if you needed emergency surgery." Faith raises one brow, challenging me.

"Yes, but I had to be positive and hope everything would go well. Other mothers have done this for hundreds of years. To panic wouldn't have benefitted Rose or me."

"It was wise to leave the worrying to us." Dad stares down into his cup of tea.

"Yes, you told me several times how you worried." I reach over and pat his hand. "But it's all okay. I'm home and not going anywhere."

"Which brings us to Samuel. When does he arrive?"

It takes an effort to keep a poker face and not think about what's currently happening in Ulara with illegal mines threatening the Ularans' quiet existence and the safety of the people I love.

"He has resigned from his contract. He has a few things to tie up before he can join me. I assume he needs to sort out his visas, etcetera, before he can apply for work here." I stall as not once did we discuss him working here and if he'd continue as a physician.

Shit.

He hasn't worked in society for six years. Is this even what he wants? My bottom lip quivers, and I take a mouthful of lukewarm tea to disguise my stress.

"We're looking forward to meeting him," Dad reassures me.

"Yes, I hoped the circumstances had changed so he could make the journey with you." Mum tilts her head, and her eyes fail to hide the disappointment behind them.

Maybe my stoic expression needs work because Faith is out of her chair, arms outstretched to take Rose from Mum. "Eden is looking tired. I think she should feed Rose and then take a nap."

Faith holds Rose close to her chest and waits for me to stand.

"If I'm still asleep in two hours, please wake me. Otherwise, I won't be able to sleep tonight."

"Honey, you might sleep through."

"Mum, she has to feed Rose."

"Oh, of course. Well, if you need help, just wake me."

Faith chuckles low.

The moment we get to my room, she closes the door behind us. "What's Mum going to do? Help Rose attach to your breast?" She rolls her eyes. "She never offered to help me during the night. Not even with James."

"I guess she thought you had Jake to help you," I murmur with fatigue setting into every crevice of my body.

"And you should have Samuel here to help you." She raises one eyebrow. "So when—"

"Not now, Faith." I shake my head. "I'll tell you about it tomorrow."

Faith sits quietly on my bed while I settle into the pale-pink faux-leather armchair in the corner of the room.

"You have both made a beautiful baby," she tells me genuinely.

"Thank you." I stroke the fine layer of fair hair on Rose's crown. "We think so too."

"Which is why I don't get why he didn't return with you."

I close my eyes momentarily and inhale a deep breath. "I'm struggling." I meet her gaze, and the moment her understanding sets in, it triggers tears to my eyes. "I begged him to come with me. But he promised he'd come as soon as he ties up a few things. And one of those things..." I say before she interrupts, "... is eating away at my ability to stay strong. If Dad knew, then he'd have reason to worry."

"What? Tell me," she demands with her serious gaze. The one I'm sure she uses in a court of law.

"It has to do with the illegal mines. Some groups are seeking new sites close to the Ularan community. Samuel is doing all he can so their safety isn't threatened."

"Bloody hell." Her face pales. "Eden. I have been reading up on these mines because I was tracking what was happening in Venezuela.

Of course, she was.

"I never filled Dad in, but I knew it wasn't good. What's happening to the land and the Amazon rainforest is shocking. The damage they are doing is just heartbreaking. They are destroying not only the flora and fauna but poisoning the waters with gold and mercury. The Ularans' future and that of many tribes in the Amazon looks bleak."

"I know." I pull a face to stop myself from bursting into tears.

"Oh, honey. Here, let me take Rose and burp her."

"Thank you." Wiping my eyes, I try to pull myself together so I don't fall into a blubbering heap. “Samuel thinks the Ularans are his responsibility, so he’ll do anything to keep them safe.”

“But they’ve survived hundreds of years before he began living with them.”

“Ugh. Yes, but he’s a loyalist, and the reason he remained there stems back to honoring someone he knew in school and college after she died.”

“Honor? How is living primitively honoring someone?”

I focus on how Faith rolls the cup of her hand in small circles over Rose’s back. Her tiny face falls to the side with her chin supported in Faith’s other hand. She makes motherhood look easy while I’m still fumbling my way through the first few weeks of Rose’s life.

“She asked him to be a better person and to do something worthwhile in the world where he didn’t achieve the accolades. To do something purely for the good and not for the benefit.”

“But there are many—”

“I know. Can we talk about this tomorrow? I do need to take that nap.”

Faith places Rose in the crib and then comes to kiss my cheek. “Rest up, sis. I’ll see you tomorrow.”

The moment my head hits the pillow, my eyes flutter closed.

THE SOUND of my phone vibrating with a message alert on the table beside me is enough for me to open my eyes. The time on the screen shows I have been asleep for two hours. At least with daylight savings, the room is still light. And I have woken covered in sweat with the late afternoon sun beating down on my bedroom window. I groan loudly and rub my eyes, then reach for the air conditioning remote. I switch it on to cool the room at a comfortable temperature. After months in the stifling humidity of the jungle, I’m not going to deny myself modern-day comforts. I thought I’d be mentally tougher and not bothered by the dry heat. I need more sleep, that’s all.

Assuming the message to be from my friends asking when they can see me, I casually raise my phone to read the text.

Asoo:

Eden, it's Samuel.

Three words, and it's enough for me to sit straight up in the bed. Mentally, I prepare myself for the words to follow as Samuel's track record with messages and notes usually brings heartbreak.

There was an incident. Drones located Ulara, and two men who worked at a nearby illegal mine assumed treasure was hidden in the village. They expected previous travelers would have left gifts for the shaman to assist them on their travels. A gesture by explorers from earlier days if lost and then taken sick. Some indigenous communities helped these explorers until well enough to travel again. At first, I thought someone had given them false information. But it seems there was someone before your grandmother, as the shaman had a gold chain with a massive nugget hidden in a brass vase. The vase was disguised easily as a clay sculpture, the tarnished metal so old.

With my hand on my chest, I close my eyes and remember Kaikare's tarnished mirror from Gran.

These American men were looking to get rich quick. The shaman was shot and killed.

I gasp. My stomach flips, and my eyes burn as the sadness engulfs me.

The men are no longer a concern. Their boat exploded on the river, and the billowing smoke was a tell-tale for the village location. We expect more men will come, and it will jeopardize the Ularans' safety. There's no other choice than to migrate deeper into the jungle. The shaman foresaw the migration in his last ceremony. The timing is now imminent with increasing danger.

I'm so, so sorry.

"Please no," I murmur.

I promised the shaman I'd guide them with paper maps and head southwest toward the Colombian and Brazilian border, away from those areas controlled by Guerrillas and Garimpeiros. When they are safe, I'll come home to you. I will come home to you. In the meantime, please message Asoo if you need to speak with someone. I'll not be in contact with him, but there may be a way for me to get a message to Canaima.

"How? With smoke signals?"

Please don't worry about me. I'll find my way out as you are home, the beacon to my heart. Think of it as a minor setback—our future together delayed by a few months. In the big picture, we will look back with only a memory of our short time apart. I love you. Please kiss Rose and tell her I love and miss her like I do you. I'll come back to you. I promise. Samuel xx

"Don't worry. You have got to be bloody kidding me." My bottom lip quivers all too easily, fragile emotion like a pendulum swinging from fear for the safety of Samuel and my friends to relief at being safe at home with my family. As much as I want to be with him, this journey isn't something Rose and I could endure.

Reality sinks in.

Covering my face with both hands, I sob and sob, releasing the fear of never seeing him again. "Why?" I croak through the tears. "Why would you do this?"

The shaman was shot and killed.

Clamping my eyes shut, the sadness turns to pain and it seeps bone-deep. The emotional weight fills my legs with what feels like lead, and I sink into the bed. Now paralyzed with overwhelming grief, I don't want to open my eyes and see the world as it truly is. I fail, and my thoughts fill with the possibility of Samuel dying in the jungle. If not from hunger and dehydration along with exhaustion, from a bullet like the shaman as they head into an unknown country.

Poor Kaikare. She has lost her father, her mentor, and best friend. The village has lost its healer and the man who decides its future. The future is dire for all of us, and I can't help it—I fall apart, one tear at a time.

When I can breathe again, I swipe the screen to send my sister a message.

> What do you know about the Colombian Guerrilla and the Brazilian Garimpeiros working near the borders?

Seconds later, my phone vibrates in my hand.

"Hi. I just received a message from Samuel," I say before she fires the first question. "He's not coming here until he finds the Ularan people a new place to live and build a new village."

"Um, what? And you're telling me this is going to be in the heart of where F.A.R.C and Guerrilla Garimpeiros own the land, and by own, I mean control?"

"To be honest, I have no clue exactly where he's going, but he said he'd avoid those areas."

Faith snorts. "Yeah, like he'll even know if they have recently gained control of a new community."

"You're not helping," I rasp. Closing my eyes, I will the tears to stop rolling down my cheeks. "How will I ever get a message to him or know if something bad has happened to him?"

For a moment, Faith remains silent.

Then she rallies, her voice calm and confident as always. "Eden, you need to remain optimistic. Your positive attitude has gotten you this far when we thought you'd gone mad. You're home. Samuel *will* come back to you."

I smile even though I know she truly doesn't believe it. But she's right —it's all I have—the belief that he'll do whatever it takes to get out alive. If I convince myself it will happen, then hopefully, the universe will continue to look out for me.

"At least I know Gran's spirit will protect him in the jungle."

"What?"

I let out a sigh. "Another story for tomorrow..."

38

EDEN

My thoughts home in on the ticktock of the kitchen clock on the wall before me, a grandfather clock handed down by my grandfather. The swinging time-keeping element is hypnotic in the silence.

Seb calls out to Faith to help him go to the bathroom, and like dominoes, our shoulders fall in relief to the ending silence.

"No wonder you didn't sleep well," Mum says gently. "I thought you must have been awake because of Rose."

"No." I shake my head. "Rose was great. Fed and went back to sleep. But I do need to make an appointment to see a pediatrician to check she's on par with her development. I don't want to assume her quiet behavior is that of a good baby."

Dad nods, but his expression is blank, and I assume his thoughts are fixed on the news I just relayed to them all. "Part of me despises the man..." he says in a low voice, "... although it also saddens me knowing the shaman was part of Mum's life." Dad dips his chin and rubs a hand over his jaw. "Questions about Mum's life in the jungle is now lost."

"Your sister is out there." Mum rubs his shoulder. "Answers may be lost, but she's alive."

"Mum," Faith interjects as she returns to the table. She hands her phone to Seb to watch a child's program.

"*Bluey*," he sings and jumps up and down to the theme song.

"Apart from the sadness of the shaman and the whole new sister thing for Dad, Eden's main concern is Samuel. He may never get out alive. She just told us that she doesn't know how to contact him, and if something tragic happens, she may never know about it," Faith says.

A whimper sounds from James in the playpen set up in the corner. He throws a toy train aside. Faith pushes up from her chair and lifts him over the barrier. She places him on her lap and raises her top to feed him.

Dad rubs his hands over his face. "How long did he give you? How many weeks did he calculate it would take him to find a new home for them?"

"Months." I bow my head, unable to look at them with a wave of dread washing over me. "He then has to find his way out of wherever they are hiding, *alone*. If he does, then I assume he'll need to return to LA and organize his visas to come to Australia." Every time I weigh it up, I find it more difficult to remain optimistic.

Faith's serious expression conveys her concern. "And he's heading into areas controlled by the Colombian Guerrilla or the Brazilian Garimpeiros." She pushes dark locks away from her face before gazing down at her son.

"Can we do anything to help? Anything at all?" Dad's gaze meets mine, and his eyes brim with fear.

"Distract me." I force a smile.

"All these years, I had a sister, and now I may never meet her," he mutters. "I barely know anything about her."

"I'll tell you about her." I smile. "I'll remember more when I'm not so emotional. I intend to find Brenda and ask for the diary Gran kept while she was in the jungle. I know Grandpa forbade her to keep it, but it might help us understand some things."

Dad nods once, and it's in slow motion, as though he's absorbing what I'm telling him. "Can you print off those photos you have of Dawn... I mean Kaikare? I can't get her face out of my head. I can see a little of Mum in her."

"I know. From the moment I arrived, I sensed there was something about Kaikare. And the way we connected was different to everybody else." I shrug. "I'm going to miss her." My voice is hoarse, and I stop myself from saying more. "I'll send the photos I have on my phone to you."

Dad peers up at me and smiles. "What's done is done," he says, putting on a brave face. “We have to get on with our lives. Let me know how you do finding Brenda. If you meet a dead end, I might be able to help.”

“Thank you. I’m heading out to see Yasmine and Amy tonight. So I won’t need any dinner.”

“Before I leave, I can help you fit the baby seat from my car to yours,” Faith says and stands. “Mum, can you watch the boys for me?”

“Sure.” Mum takes James into the lounge where Seb is lying with Faith’s phone.

“I can help Faith,” Dad says.

“It’s fine. If you could watch Rose, I’ll go since I need to learn how to do these things.”

Dad takes Rose from my arms. “Hello, my princess,” he whispers.

I wait a few seconds to absorb the moment, the loving relationship between my dad and daughter to help heal my pain before I follow Faith down the stairs.

As soon as the door opens, I’m hit with the salty clean air. I inhale a deep breath. “I’ve missed the scent of the sea. I’ve missed the vista, everything about the beach. Only when I was with him, I didn’t care. I could’ve been living in a dark hole and loved every minute because we were together.”

Faith wraps an arm around me as we take the last step before the parking lot. She squeezes my side and says nothing. Right now, her support is enough.

By the time dinner time comes around, I can barely control the anxiety consuming me. The one thing keeping me from losing my mind is Rose. Babies can pick up on emotions, so I’m doing my best to control the fear. The thirteen-hour time difference between Adelaide and Canaima has been frustrating, as I wait for a reasonable time to call Asoo. I’m due at Yasmine’s at six thirty, so I hope he’s awake.

I call his number and pray he answers.

Just when I’m about to give up, a voice answers the call.

“Hello? Asoo?”

A woman speaks in Spanish.

"Si."

A moment passes, and then my shoulders relax on hearing Asoo's voice in the background.

"Hola."

"Asoo, it's Eden," I blurt.

"Oh, Miss Eden. You home now? You safe?"

"Yes." I close my eyes and exhale. "I'm in Australia. I received your message. My heart breaks."

"Si. It sad. My heart break too. The shaman..." He makes a tsk sound. "Bad men still come, Miss Eden. We afraid. We can't go near Ulara as they have men in the area."

I swallow the lump in my throat. The one that has grown to the size of a small apple and refuses to go away, a lump that burns every time I think of Samuel and try not to burst into tears. "And Samuel?" I rasp. "When did you last see him?"

"After those men shot shaman, Samuel told me to leave and not come back. He tell me they are walking into the jungle when the moon rises."

"They're walking at night? That's insane. It's the most dangerous time."

"Men won't find them. They follow maps and walk night, then day. Rest on the second night. Samuel took men's guns. Bad. Bad. I know nothing more."

"I understand." He has to be careful as someone may be listening to our conversation. "If you hear anything, please message me," I plead. "I'll then call for you to tell me any news."

"Si."

"I'm scared." My lip quivers. "Scared he'll never make it out of the jungle, never make it home to me."

"Samuel have maps. Samuel good man."

A sob escapes my lips. I want to say his merit will not save him. Instead, I say, "He is. I hope he knows what he's doing."

"Samuel loves you, Miss Eden. He'll come to you."

"Thanks, Asoo. Stay in touch, please. You're the only person I can contact."

The line goes silent. Holding the phone to my chest, I take a moment to compose myself, willing all the tears cascading over my cheeks to stop.

I'm none the wiser about Samuel's safety—I only know that people believe in him. With no other choice, I pray for him to be safe and get out of the jungle alive.

I strap Rose into her baby seat and drive the ten minutes it takes to reach Yasmine's apartment.

Before I reach the front door, it swings open, and both girls scream with excitement. I giggle and check they haven't startled Rose. Yasmine gives me a quick hug, then takes Rose from my arms.

"She's just gorgeous," she coos and heads inside. "Let's get you out of this heat."

"She was born in the jungle. It's the winter months I'm worried about." I hug Amy and almost have to pry her arms from my neck.

"I missed you," she whispers. "So damn much. I can't say I'm sorry you're home even though I know you wanted to stay with him."

"Before."

She steps back and gives me a quizzical look. "What happened?"

"Shit went down." We both follow Yasmine inside and sit on the couch beside her. For the next ten minutes, I give them a rundown of my last days, the latest shitstorm, and how Samuel is now wandering the rainforest with a bloody paper map. The more I repeat the story, the more frustrated I become. "So now I just wait and hope he comes out alive."

Both girls' eyes bulge.

"You're kidding me." Amy shakes her head. "Does he want to die a fucking hero?"

I shrug one shoulder. "His loyalty is something else. I haven't told you the story yet of how he ended up there."

"We're eating first," Yasmine quips. "You need your sustenance for this little princess." She stares down at Rose as though she's the most beautiful thing she has ever seen.

"I do. And I have several appointments in the next few days for us both to be checked over."

"Well, she's perfect." Yasmine smiles at Rose. "I can't wait for you to move in with Aunty Yas."

"We can discuss that when I'm back at work and earning money again."

"Which is why you're not paying for dinner." Yasmine eyeballs me.

"Thank you."

Amy sits sideways on the couch, so she's facing me. "Surely, you don't have to go back to work for a while. I mean, *Ethan* is still there. You could look for something else now like you originally planned."

"I haven't thought about anything. The paperwork is being processed, and then I have to apply for maternity leave. It's on my long list for this week, although I'll probably work one day here and there to get back in the swing of things and as they need me. As for changing careers, being a new mum is challenging enough for now. Until life calms down, I'm not considering anything else. I want things to be easy and to do what I know, so it doesn't take time away from Rose."

"Absolutely." Yas runs her nose over Rose's cheek. "I love how Rose just stares as though she knows who we are. Already knows her *aunties*."

We all chuckle.

It feels good to be home with my girls.

39

EDEN

One Week Later...

On Saturday morning, I bathe Rose then dress her in a cute little summer dress before placing her in the stroller to wander along the esplanade on my way to meet Yasmine and Amy at our favorite café in Glenelg.

I'm grateful I didn't have to rush off for clothes suitable for feeding in since Faith gave me most of the clothes she wore after Seb's birth. She gained more weight with James and bought freer-flowing styles. My family has thought of everything, and I'll only need to buy more clothes for Rose when she grows into the next size.

I pull the stroller cover down to protect Rose from the sun's rays as I head outside. A slight breeze with a hint of jasmine mixed in the salty air hits my senses, and I smile.

Home.

My thoughts shift straight to Samuel. I hope he loves it here as much as I do.

The optimism remains, and yet there's always underlying doubt. After all the effort it would take for him to come to me, it could all go pear-shaped if he hates living not only in a strange country and knowing a handful of people but living in society in general.

I stop walking the esplanade path. A man behind me grumbles as he walks around the stroller.

"Sorry," I murmur.

It hit me why Samuel's gone into the jungle.

Is it his intention to get lost and never come out so he doesn't have to return to society?

I shake my head to dispel the thought.

No.

No, he wouldn't do that to us. He'd *try*.

My own bloody thoughts are going to be my undoing.

Instead, I smile at everyone sitting on the grass enjoying the morning sunshine. Yet it's hot enough that I'm eager to get Rose and me inside the café and out of the heat.

A woman greets me at the door. "Welcome. I'm Deanne. Do you have a booking for a table?" She has short brown hair and the kindest eyes, maybe because they are the same color as Kaikare's.

"My friends should be here." In the corner of the café by a window, Yasmine is chatting with Amy. "There they are."

"Yas and Amy. Oh, you must be Eden. I feel like I know you already."

"I hate to think what they have said about me."

Deanne laughs once. "All good, I promise. They are here at least once a week. Today they requested a larger area to fit the stroller by the table." I follow Deanne, and I'm surprised when she introduces me like she's part of our little group. "Eden is here."

Yasmine's expression tells me I've interrupted a serious conversation, but a smile soon grows on her lips when she acknowledges me.

"We thought Rose might be napping." She stands and peers into the stroller before hugging me.

"I'll come back in five and grab your order," Deanne says, leaving us alone.

"Thanks, babe," Yasmine shoots over her shoulder.

Babe.

"Deanne is new here," I say.

"She started working the week you left," Amy says. "We were both upset one day, and she sat down and comforted us."

"By giving us brownies and extra caffeine on the house," Yasmine adds. "We became friends, and she meets us at the Shores if we're in the mood for cocktails."

"Is that code for she enjoys getting wasted with you?" I take a seat beside Amy.

"Pretty much." She chuckles. "She's one of the most interesting people I've met. Besides helping us out when we were missing you, she reassured us you would be okay."

I frown at Amy. "How could she when she knows nothing about me?"

"Dee has been to Brazil and then did a week in Venezuela, including time at Angel Falls." Amy lifts her brow to emphasize her trust in Deanne.

"Right. I'm curious to know what tour she did and her take on what's happening to the ecosystem."

"You'll have time to ask her as she's meeting us on the weekend… if you're up to it?"

Yasmine rolls her eyes. "Don't, Amy. Eden has Rose to consider."

"It's fine. I can pop down for an hour but count me out for any big nights for at least the next few months."

Amy wraps her arm around my shoulder. "To be honest, I'm getting sick of going out all the time."

Yasmine laughs. "Whatever. I'll remind you of that tonight."

"We know it's too early for you to come out with us. But in a few months…" Amy smiles. "Everything will settle down for you."

In a few months, I hope Samuel has found his way back to me.

Yasmine peers down at Rose sleeping in the stroller. "We'll have our own special days just for you and Rose."

"She still looks so tiny." Amy looks adoringly at my daughter.

"She does, but we've had several appointments this week, and she's on track in her development."

"Is that your sister?" Amy nods to the doorway.

"Yeah," Yasmine confirms. "Cleo is the physiotherapist for The Thunder football team. They've commenced pre-season training. They just had a beach recovery session."

Amy twists to check out the shirtless men filing through the café. "Does she need any volunteers to help?"

Yasmine rolls her eyes. "She gets that a lot." Her expression changes. "Actually, she's also just started working at Lombardi's Restaurant in the city on weekends, and I want to celebrate my birthday there. The owner, Oliver, has turned the front section into a cocktail bar at night, and Cleo said it's attracting some famous people."

It takes a moment for my mind to catch up. "In two weeks. Are you celebrating on your actual birthday or the weekend?"

"The Saturday night. Is Rose okay?"

Leaning forward, I check on Rose. It's unusual for her brow to be pinched.

Oh no. She only pulls that face when she—

"Oh wow." Yasmine's eyes widen.

"Rose," I say, pretending to chastise her for passing gas loud enough for the people on the table next to us to stop mid-conversation. "I think that's my cue to leave. If she follows through, then she'll also be hungry, and I'll need to change her nappy."

"Yeah, I'm not ready to help with that," Amy apologizes and shrugs.

"Is anyone ever ready for poopy nappies?"

"No, except when you don't have a choice." I push up from the table. "It's the first time I'm leaving without coffee, and I have a feeling it won't be my last."

In one short week, I've realized my life here will not be the same as it was before I left. I have come home a different person, and I need to adapt to my new life.

ON MONDAY, with Rose in my arms, I slowly pad the stairs of our apartment complex to the office located on the ground floor. It's time for me to show Dana my daughter. I'm filled with guilt because I didn't take her last week. I know Dana has been waiting for me to visit the office. Only Ethan will be there, and I didn't want to be emotionally vulnerable around him after everything that's happened.

I hate that I need to be strong around Ethan, prove to myself I'm the bigger person and forgive him for treating me like shit.

Pushing the door open, I find Dana alone in the office. She gives a little squeal and rushes around her desk toward me. "Finally," she says, smiling, her arms outstretched toward me.

I give Rose to her for a cuddle and turn toward my father's empty office. "Dad's out?"

"Yeah, he and Ethan are in the city for an appointment with a construction company."

"About the pool renos?"

"Yeah."

Damn, now I want to know what they are planning as this was my project—the Bali-inspired resort pool.

"When are you coming back to work?" Dana's eyes remain on Rose, although her tone is a little desperate.

"I have four months leave, although I could pop down and help when you need me."

Her eyes lift to meet mine. "Between you and me, Ethan isn't covering your work. He's paving his way to assist your father and leaving me to pick up his slack."

"Help Dad? In what way?"

Rose whimpers, so Dana places her on her shoulder and pats her back. "No idea. Your father thinks rainbows shoot out of his ass."

I chuckle. "I can come in for a couple of hours when Rose takes a nap during the day."

"Thank you. And seeing both of your faces here will help to cheer me up." Dana smiles. "What else have you been doing to keep busy?"

"Just trying to be a mum." I shrug. "And I'm trying to get in touch with Brenda, a friend of Gran's. But I'm not having much luck."

"I remember Brenda. Was she the one at your Gran's funeral that wore the—"

"Red shoes. Yes."

"Good luck with that." She hands Rose to me, then reaches for a tissue to wipe her forehead. "I can't wait to hear about your adventure. Your dad has already announced Samuel might not return."

"He said that to Ethan?"

Dana nods.

"That's not entirely true. He's just going to take longer to come here."

"The sooner he arrives, the better."

I smile at Dana. I need to be around her more. "I have a story to tell you about Gran too. I'll feed Rose in here while Dad and Ethan are out, and I'll fill you in."

"Let me make a coffee since it's my lunch break. I want you to tell me everything."

40

EDEN

Two Weeks Later...

SHUTTING MY LAPTOP, I close my eyes and hope I've done the right thing. Emailing Samuel's parents with an update as to his whereabouts was a precursor in case things go pear-shaped. At least they know now, and if they want to alert any authorities, they have more power than me to do so. I also attached photos of Rose as they wanted to be updated on her progress. It's the least I can do for them.

It's mid-morning, and I promised Dana I'd assist her for a couple of hours. After feeding Rose, I place her in the stroller and walk along the esplanade until she falls asleep. It doesn't take long, so we turn back and head to the office. The moment the door opens, Ethan is on his feet and walking around the table to greet us.

"Eden," he says affectionately. "It's good to see you again." He leans to get a closer look at Rose. "She's beautiful. The image of her mother."

"Thank you. I think she's beautiful, but I'm biased." I look around the office. "Where's Dana and Dad?"

"Dana is in the restroom, and your father is in the city meeting with some lawyers."

"Right."

Brown eyes meet mine, the ones that used to turn my legs to jelly.

God, his eyes are still beautiful, but he no longer affects me that way. "I've missed you." He takes a step closer and rests a hand on my back. "Come and take a seat. I'd love to hear your stories?"

His comment throws me off-kilter because I find it hard to believe he wants to hear about Samuel. Maybe he's trying at being a friend. "I can't right now. I'm here to help Dana."

Dana strolls into the room. "You're early."

"Yeah. Rose settled quickly, so I came here while she was sleeping. What do you need me to do?"

Dragging over another chair to her table, I take a seat while she runs through a list that I could complete in an hour—if Rose remains asleep. If I get more time, then it's a bonus.

Ten minutes later, Rose wakes and screams at top volume. "Sorry, she started screaming like this two days ago. It's only after she feeds." Scooping her into my arms, I lay her on my shoulder, patting her back as I walk around the room. "If she doesn't settle, then I'll get you to email anything you need me to complete, and I'll do it from my room."

"I can help," Ethan says. He watches me closely as I pad around the room. "Give Rose to me so you and Dana can work together."

"Are you sure? Do you even know how to hold a baby?"

"I'm an uncle now. Know all the tricks." He winks at me.

"What? Harry has children?"

"No, Myles." He grins.

"No way," I say. "When did he get a girlfriend?"

"This time last year. They keep to themselves. There were a few surprise pregnancies last year." He holds my gaze for a moment, and there's a touch of sadness behind those chocolate eyes. "Anton is two months old."

"Okay, here you are." I hold up Rose, and he lifts her over his shoulder and then paces the room. Within minutes, she stops crying, opens her beautiful eyes, and watches us as Ethan circles the office.

"You're a natural," I tell him.

"Yeah, yeah. Now get busy as I don't know how long my magic touch will hold out."

I laugh and head back to Dana's table. She's eyeing him, and from where I stand, it's obvious she still doesn't trust him.

“Is Rose okay?” Mum asks me as I pace behind the kitchen table with Rose over my shoulder. “What age do they develop colic?”

“James had reflux, and he was so much harder to settle than Seb. After endless sleepless nights, I had him checked, and they diagnosed him at around one month old. It might be worth getting her checked out.” Faith stands and comes behind me to assess Rose. “She appears happy enough now.”

“I know. After every feed, I have to do this until she calms. Some nights it’s two hours of pacing the room.”

“She looks tired, dear.” Mum stands and pours herself another wine. “If you need me, just come and wake me up.” After a glass full of wine, she won’t feel like getting up at two in the morning to help me.

“I wish Samuel was here.” On my next lap around the table, I sense everyone’s eyes on me. Shit, did I say that aloud?

“Still nothing?” Dad sits back in his chair and folds his arms.

I’m only days away from being home for a month. It’s too short a time to have heard anything from Samuel. The early days will be the hardest for the tribe to remain hidden and reach the jungle beyond the tepui. A journey many of the Ularans will struggle to complete, especially with the pace having to suit the women, the children, the elders and the men.

“I don’t expect to hear anything for at least another month.” I close my eyes, determined not to get upset because Dad isn’t convinced Samuel will do the right thing by us. He hasn’t said it in so many words, but his eyes and demeanor tell me the truth.

“Do you expect him at my sixtieth birthday celebrations?” His brows arch before he reaches for the red wine and half fills his glass.

Dad’s birthday is this weekend, but he has postponed the party to the end of March when Will returns from college, and his friends in Sydney, who are tied up with business, can get away. They have planned not only the party but a men’s weekend including an AFL football game and five days holidaying at Victor Harbour, fishing, and then touring the McLaren Vale wineries.

“I hope so, but...”

“So do we,” Faith says. “I’m looking forward to meeting him. As for Rose, book an appointment with the doctor, and I’ll come with you.”

"Thank you. I appreciate it." With Jake working all day and late into the night, I'm grateful to spend more time with Faith.

"See if you can get it on a Thursday when the kids are in daycare."

"So where are we going for dinner?" I ask.

"Lombardi's. It serves the best Italian food in the city," Mum says.

"Yasmine's sister, Cleo, works there."

"The physiotherapist?" Faith asks.

"Yes. She's saving to travel, so she is working two jobs."

"I saw Yasmine at the health shop on Jetty Road," Mum says. "How long has she worked there?"

"A while now. She's studying naturopathy and is an influencer on Instagram. She uploads videos of her special shakes and herbal snacks and now has two hundred thousand followers."

"Is that impressive?" Dad says, obviously clueless.

"If you checked our hotel's Instagram profile at all, then you would know it is. I have to say Ethan has done a great job marketing Monte Hotels while I've been away."

"He has. I hope he stays with us, but I think our HR role isn't the challenge Ethan wants."

"But he's also doing the marketing, and he's involved in the recent development." I'm not sure if Dad was hinting at something else.

"Yes. I think Ethan is ready to take on an assistant managerial position."

The room falls quiet.

I stop walking, and Faith's eyes meet mine. In the silence, there's an understanding passing between us.

"Don't you think it's premature to be promoting him in our *family* company?" Faith says seriously.

"Ethan's been working with us for a year now. He has demonstrated his capabilities, and I see his potential through his commitment. And he works late almost every night."

"What about Dana?" I interrupt. "She has been with us for decades. I think it's an insult not to promote her first."

"These are two different roles. Besides, I think Dana's husband is looking to transfer interstate. I really don't know how long she'll continue working with us. I hope a while longer. Otherwise, I'll need to find more admin staff to assist you when you return to work."

"Me?" I look at Faith to get a gauge if she knew about any of this. She rolls her eyes. "I can help for now, but I don't know what my future holds. I haven't ruled out studying nursing either. It will depend on Samuel when he returns and on his work as well. I mean, we may need to move to the country for him to get a job."

Dad huffs. "Every damn hospital is crying out for doctors. He'll get work here. Besides, you don't know when and if this will happen. In the meantime, you need to work and secure a future for you and Rose."

"For one, Eden will have maternity payments from the government for a few more months," Faith argues. "And I think it's up to her to decide what her future holds." She holds up a hand when Dad attempts to interrupt. "And don't speak like she's going to be alone for the rest of her life."

Standing behind Dad where he can't see me, I mouth to Faith, "Thank you."

"Thank you for a lovely dinner, Mum. I'll try to settle Rose in her crib while she's quiet." I walk around the table and kiss Faith goodnight. Then I meet Dad's gaze. "I understand what you're saying about Monte Hotels, and it concerns you how Faith and I aren't there to work, especially when it's our family business. Please be careful, that's all. Will hasn't even finished college yet. Give him a chance to decide. What I'm saying is, I don't want you to hand it over to someone who isn't family." His expression changes, and I know exactly what he's thinking—what he hopes for Ethan and me. "When you meet Samuel, I think you'll understand why I'm holding out with every drop of hope I have inside of me that he'll return to me safely. He truly is the best man for me and the best father to Rose. I just have to be patient."

I head to bed thinking about what Dad said. The notion of Samuel not returning sticks in my head.

Alone.

A life without him.

Until this point, I believed I was strong and had grown into a confident woman. Without Samuel by my side, I'm not sure she exists. All I can envision is an empty shell of the person I had become, even less of my former self, and I can't and won't go back to being her.

As I'm laying Rose in her crib, she opens her eyes and stares at me before closing them again. My heart melts. She was created from love, and I see Samuel in her every day. I have to be strong for her. For us.

"Daddy will come home soon," I whisper.

I lean in and kiss her cheek before flopping onto my bed.

Beside me, the phone screen lights up with an alert. One new email from Christopher McMahon.

Dear Eden,

Thank you for your email concerning Samuel's safety.

Despite the alarming reference to him finding a new location, we appreciated you reaching out and keeping us updated. We especially appreciated you taking the time to send photos of beautiful Rose.

She has grown at just six weeks old.

Rose reminds Caroline of Samuel when he was a baby.

It has cheered us somewhat to see the photos. Please keep in touch, and one day we hope to meet you and Rose.

As for Samuel, I'm disappointed in his decision not to return home and be with you as soon as he could. His place is with you, not with some primitive tribe that doesn't need his help as much as you do.

Please don't worry. This is nothing new to us. For years, we suffered with the fear of losing our son and not knowing what he's doing or where he is. In previous years, he had disappeared for eighteen months at a time with no contact. For some reason, he loves his work and is smart enough to find his way out of trouble. He'll do it again.

We know how much he loves you, and he'll do what it takes to come find you.

Please stay in touch.

Yours sincerely,

Christopher and Caroline McMahon.

Without responding, I set my phone aside and close my eyes. His parents have no idea how dangerous this journey is, how it's nothing like Ulara. When I think about it, Ulara is the people, and wherever they settle, Ulara will be. It's not a place or a river, it's a state of heart and people being as one to form a close community.

But if anything happens to Samuel, they'll not notify his parents or me. As time passes, we will just have to assume the worst. I can't imagine the gut-wrenching pain that will consume me if he fails.

He can't.

He has to do this.

It's been years since I prayed, but tonight I close my palms together, bow my head, and ask for Samuel to be guided through the jungle and then return safely to me.

41

EDEN

Two Months Later...

"THE DECORATIONS ARE FABULOUS," I tell Cleo.

Yasmine's dusky pink lips stretch into an admiring smile. "I didn't think you had a creative flair. Honestly, I always believed you were science, science, science, but your artistic skill is next level. Seems like we have similar genes."

Cleo beams a proud smile at her sister. Her skin is makeup-free. She's every bit as beautiful as her sister with dark skin and eyes and high cheekbones. I envy their model-like appearance. "The colors are of the Thunder Football Club, at your father's request. Teal and white and black with balloons and other decorations. The silver makes the teal pop."

"Even the dried flower arrangement on the wall with ribbons and balloons looks every bit as masculine as it does feminine and perfect for your dad," Yasmine says as she continues to peruse the room.

My father's hearty laughter breaks through our conversation, even from the far corner of the restaurant where he stands in a circle with his mates. "It's going to be a big night for him. I don't think Mum will see much of him after tonight." I tell my friends about his plans for a celebratory week with his mates. "More than likely, it will take another week for him to recover, and I don't think we'll see much of him in the office. He'll probably work from home," I joke since the office building is part of our home. "Walking three levels of stairs might be a bit much for him."

"Why is Ethan with them?" Amy asks. "Surely, he's not staying with the men the entire week?"

I shake my head. Ethan's youth stands out among them yet equally distinguished with his dark hair slicked back and Gatsby-like. "I really don't know."

"Has he hit on you yet?" Amy's brows pull tight as though she expects me to admit to it.

"No. He's been supportive while I'm working. He takes Rose for strolls in the stroller and holds her as he reads through emails while I'm caught up in meetings with Dana."

Amy makes a humph sound. "I still don't trust him."

"He's trying… we're friends. That's all."

"Are you defending him?" she asks in a higher voice.

"I'm giving him a chance at being nice. Being supportive as a friend. And he hasn't tried to get me between the sheets."

"Anyway," Yasmine says. "There's a glass of champagne with my name on it." She takes one from the tray as the server walks by.

We all do the same.

"Cheers," we say in unison and clink the crystal.

"To forever friends," Yasmine chimes.

We all turn and agree, watching my father belly laugh and almost spill his glass of beer.

Cleo's dark spiral curls bounce as she rushes away, leaving Amy, Yasmine, and me alone.

"This is the first time since Rio that we're dressed in ballgowns and drinking champagne." Yasmine looks up to the starry lights dotting the ceiling, and the memory of the night I first spoke to Samuel has me smiling.

"Please take me back," Amy says. "It feels like a lifetime ago."

"Over a year." Yasmine makes a sad face.

"The white gown I wore to the ball at the Copacabana Palace Hotel will never be repeated until Rose is at school," I say and run my finger over the navy material of my long, snug-fitting dress. I wouldn't be wearing a strapless dress a month ago with the feeding bra limiting my daily attire. Unfortunately, my breast milk didn't last, and Rose has settled on baby formula. I'm not sure what I'd have done if we were in the jungle. Eight weeks old and no breast milk... would other mothers feed her? Filled with guilt, I wondered what Samuel would say, yet I blamed it on the stress of worrying constantly about him. At least tonight, I can have a few drinks and not wear a bra.

"Hi, ladies." Ava, Cleo's friend and part-owner of Lombardi's, joins our group. Her long brown hair is swept off her face and pinned in curls around her crown. A long black gown hugs her petite figure.

"Hi," we all say in unison.

"It's been years since I've seen you," I say and smile.

"Right. I hear congratulations are in order."

"Thank you," I say proudly.

"Jardine and I are trying for another baby, though I'm not keen for those sleepless nights again."

I laugh. "Yeah, some nights are tougher than others." I admire Ava as she is two years younger than us, and running a business with children must be tough. And her husband is a famous cricket player.

"How is Jardine?" I ask. Cleo supported Ava through their messy breakup after she had their first child, and now that she has her happily ever after, it gives me some hope.

"Good. He's in Sydney playing in the World Cup finals."

"So, he's away a lot?"

She nods. "It's okay, though. It's not forever, and I have support here with Louis." She smiles as though she understands. "Enjoy the night, ladies. If you need anything, let me know. I'm overseeing to make sure everything runs smoothly tonight and hope it's a fabulous celebration for your father," she says before striding toward the kitchen.

Lifting my chest and pulling my shoulders back, I inhale a deep breath.

Stop feeling sorry for yourself.

Faith waltzes through the door with Jake fashionably late and looking like a million dollars in a red ball gown.

"Hey," she says, joining our circle. "What have I missed?"

"Ladies," Jake says and gives us a nod. "You all look beautiful tonight."

"I've always liked your brother-in-law," Amy says and smiles at Jake.

"Nothing. Although Will still hasn't arrived."

Faith checks her cell for the time. "He should be here soon."

Will's flight was canceled last night, and the next available flight was six o'clock from Melbourne.

We both turn to the entrance, and instead of seeing Will, a group of tall men donning stylish tuxes enter the doors.

"Why is Rhett Williams here?" I say aloud.

Cleo spins toward the entrance. "Good, they've arrived. I asked them to pop in and surprise your father. The majority are players from The Thunder, but I also asked Rhett and a few players from the Blackbirds to come along to spur him on." She stares at me. "Do you know him?"

"Yes, we spent some time together when I had a short stint at university after school. I had to do a subject as part of business studies. Most of it was online, but some required attendance. It was only six months, but he made an impression."

"Sounds like Rhett." Cleo smiles. "I better send them toward your dad. Hope he's ready for a surprise." She gives us a wave. "I'll come say goodbye before I leave."

"Why didn't I know about this?" I ask Yasmine.

"Because I didn't know about it. Cleo takes her work seriously, and the players are part of her work circle. She has a clique, and I'm sure all the girls want to be friends with her just to get inside information. She never reveals confidential player information, and I guess she classified your father's surprise as being confidential."

Laughter erupts from the other side of the room, where Dad is the center of attention.

"Shall we see what's going on?" We all head over until we're standing close enough to hear the conversation between the players and Dad.

Rhett turns around, and when he recognizes me, he comes over. "Cleo tells me it's *your* dad's birthday."

I smile at him, his blue eyes reminding me of Samuel's. "Yes. And I didn't expect to see you here."

He grins and straightens his bowtie. "Did it brighten your evening?"

"Knowing the effort you went to for him? Well, yes."

He picks up my hand and kisses it. "How are you really?"

I shrug. "I have a baby daughter and a partner who remains in South America."

His eyes widen. "Stuck because of his visa?"

I smile and bow my head. "Something like that."

"Hey." He gently lifts my chin until I'm looking him in the eye. "Dance with me. It will cheer you up."

"God, you're still full of confidence."

I'm suddenly whisked away with Rhett, twirling and swaying as though we're professional dancers. He's right. Within minutes, I'm laughing and enjoying myself.

When the song ends, we're still laughing until Ethan comes to join us.

"Excuse me, do you mind if I cut in? I'd like to dance with Eden."

What's happening? I have two handsome men vying to dance with me. And Ethan rarely danced with me when we were together, so his gesture surprises me even more.

"Of course," Rhett says politely and leaves Ethan and me alone on the dance floor.

Ethan's feet slide in a slower rhythm, and it's more sensual than fun. I keep my gaze fixed over his shoulder with a quick check now and then to read his expression. When I do catch him staring at me, our eyes meet, connecting, before I look away.

"Did I tell you how beautiful you look tonight?" he whispers close to my ear.

"No. This is the first time we've spoken."

He leans back and grins. "That's because you're far more stunning than just beautiful. I can barely take my eyes off you."

"Ethan," I whisper and bow my head. "I can't—"

"I know. I just want to compliment a beautiful woman because compliments are good for the soul."

"They are," I admit. "Is this the part where I tell you that you also look handsome?"

"I think it is." He smirks.

He spins me, and when I land closer to him, I steady myself by gripping his shoulder and waist tightly, so I don't overbalance. After months in the jungle, it's taken me a while to get used to wearing heels again. I glance up to the footballers talking to Cleo, Yasmine, and Amy. Only Amy isn't listening. She's glaring at me. Or is it Ethan? I'm not sure Amy will ever let go of the animosity she has for Ethan.

"Thank you for the dance," I tell him when the music stops. "And for the compliment."

"The pleasure is all mine." Ethan grips my elbow and leads me back to my friends.

Before I say anything to Amy, I'm overcome with déjà vu. And how life is panning out.

The server walks by, and Amy takes a champagne glass from the tray in a swift action, downing half of it in one go. "You two were looking cozy."

"I just realized how easily I have slipped back to my old life, my old ways," I tell her.

"Too easily," she says and takes another sip without looking at me.

"It's not what I want. I don't want to be complimented on my fake dress and makeup that has transformed me to look desirable. I don't want this. I want Samuel... wherever he is. Until he's out of the jungle and can contact me, I need you to stop me from falling further down the rabbit hole of normality."

Amy looks me straight in the eye. "Challenge accepted."

"Will is here," Faith announces.

We turn to the doorway, where Will rushes in and makes a beeline for our father. With champagne in hand, both Faith and I walk over to my father.

"Happy birthday, Dad," Will says in a deep voice and holds out his hand.

Dad spins and ignores his hand, instead taking his son and hugging him in a warm embrace. They both pat each other's back before breaking apart. Dad holds Will by his shoulders and looks him up and down. "You look well, s-son." His voice cracks on the last word.

My dad is turning into a big softie.

And I couldn't be happier about it.

"Hey, bro, what about a hug for your sisters," I say.

Will turns to Faith and me and waggles his eyebrows. "Don't you both scrub up well, especially you, jungle girl," he says and winks.

42

EDEN

Four Months Later...

I'M SITTING at home on a Saturday afternoon, a scarf wrapped around my neck and a blanket hugging my shoulders.

Rose lies on the carpet, a safe distance from the fire. "C'mon," I prompt her. "You can do it." I crawl to her right, and she rolls onto her belly. She slowly pushes up on all fours and takes the first few movements to crawl. "Yay." I clap my hands, and she beams her cheeky smile with the cutest two front teeth. "Daddy is going to be so proud of you."

Daddy.

It's now mid-July, and I haven't received any messages from Samuel. And my birthday is one month away, and I hoped he'd be here to celebrate with me. My heart aches for him.

Rose makes a cute sound, saving me from my dark thoughts. She rocks back and forth on all fours—something she has been doing for weeks—but today is the first time she has attempted to move her chubby limbs.

I wipe the drool from the corner of her mouth and assume at seven months old, more teeth will appear soon, especially since her cheeks have a red glow. As I take her hands, she pushes up onto her feet while holding my fingers for support. A giggle erupts from her as she bobs up and down. "You're too cute," I tell her and kiss her cheek.

Letting go of my finger, she balances with only one hand for support while I reach for my phone and pull up a photo of Samuel. I hold the image in front of her face. "Dada," I repeat. She giggles, and I say the word like a mantra. "He'll come to us soon," I tell her. But with every passing day, hope fades a little more, and I face the reality that we may never see him again.

My throat dries and burns. I do my best to shut the emotion down. "Dammit." I open my phone and send Asoo a message.

> Hi Asoo. I know it's a long shot, but have you heard anything from Samuel?

> Every day I worry. Every day I watch Rose grow, and I hate he's not here to see how beautiful she is. Is he dead or alive? Sick or healthy? Does he even want to leave and come find us?

NAUSEA HITS ME.

> I don't want to think the worst, but if something were to happen, I doubt I'd ever find out. If they died of starvation in the middle of the jungle, then no one would know. If they ran into trouble with mafia-type gangs and were held hostage or shot, would we ever find out?I'm lost and have no one to turn to for help because everything about the Ularans is secretive.

I swipe my cheek. I have shed so many for Samuel. I can't believe I have tears left to cry for him. In my heart, I want to believe he's alive and trying to get home to us. Only so many months have passed without a single word.

I have to face the truth that he may never come. I don't want a future without him, but the universe has set him on a dangerous journey, and all I can do is hope and pray he's still alive.

Even his parents don't act concerned, and they remind me he has done this before. They won't file a missing person report and told me to wait as he sometimes remains silent for eighteen months.

I hope everything is good with you, and I miss you all. I miss Canaima. Below is a picture of Rose. Love to all xxx

I attach a photo of Rose in a pretty pink dress with a big smile on her face.

"Darling," Mum says as she enters the room. "Would you like to go out for dinner with me? Dad said he'd look after Rose."

I glance up from my phone and wipe my eyes.

"Honey, what is it?"

"Samuel." I shrug. "I just wish he'd send a message somehow so I know he's okay."

She lowers herself to the carpet and crosses her legs with ease, thanks to years of yoga. "It was around this time last year that I told you about Ivy." I nod. "Look how far you have come. We're so proud of you. You're a wonderful mother, and you work full-time." She gives me a serious look, and I'm unsure what her point is. "Last year you told me you wanted to study nursing."

"My circumstances have changed."

"They did, but I can see you have your life on hold, working a convenient job you're not completely happy doing to support you and Rose. You are waiting and hoping for the love of your life to return to you and *save* you."

Everything Mum has said is true, and every day it's easier to continue along the same path. I close my eyes slowly and open them to give myself a moment.

"Don't settle for second best." She rests her hand on mine. "You deserve more, and you don't need saving. You found yourself in the jungle. You can do it here too. Maybe you have to reinvent yourself or simply embrace the new you... the person you discovered hidden inside." She pushes strands of hair behind my ear. "You're beautiful and strong. Talented and passionate. You have learned so much from Ivy. Don't let it go to waste."

Chocolate brown eyes meet mine, showing me the warmth of an adoring mother. "I want you to promise me starting tomorrow, you'll focus on you. Take steps forward to secure a happy future for both your daughter and yourself. And before you say anything, I hope as much as you do that Samuel is safe and will come home to you. But whatever fate delivers, make sure you're prepared because Rose needs you more than ever."

I glance at my daughter as the words of advice sink in. "Yeah, she does."

"Those first days on arriving home, you said you were going to look for Brenda to find Gran's diary. Did you find her?"

"I hit some dead ends. And life became busy, so I stopped." I bow my head, realizing the promises I made to myself have slipped by.

"I might be able to help. Her husband's brother came into the esplanade café this morning where I meet Kate. Even though I haven't seen him for around ten years, I recognized him immediately. I asked about Brenda's health, and he said she's in a new care facility as her dementia has progressed. It's only ten minutes away. If you want to visit, I'll give you the name of the facility. If you'd rather let it go, then that's okay."

I need to act now in case something happens to Brenda.

"I want to see her," I say enthusiastically. After everything I read in Gran's diary, I now feel closer to Brenda.

Mum smiles as though I responded correctly. "Good. I can come with you for support."

Scooping Rose onto my shoulder, I hug Mum with my other arm. Rose coos with the delight of being in a group hug with her mother and grandmother. "This is for your great grandmother," I tell her. But I have a feeling their spirits have already met.

AFTER ARRIVING HOME from a dinner date with my mother, we hang our coats on the wall hooks before heading into the lounge to stand by the fire. Dad is sitting by the fire, his legs raised on a footstool with an empty red wine glass beside him.

"Is Rose asleep?"

"She fell asleep only half an hour ago. We had a fun night. Did you know she can now say, Pa?'"

"No way," I tease as I unwrap the woolen scarf from my neck.

Dad chuckles. "I knew she'd say it before Nan."

Mum rolls her eyes, and I can't help but giggle. "It's not a competition."

"Ah, but it is," he jokes.

"I'm going to join her because I'm beat. Night."

"Night, sweetheart. We're in for a storm, so I hope the thunder doesn't upset her."

"Me too. More the reason to get some sleep now."

After closing the bedroom door, I place my phone on the side table and then settle into bed. Minutes later, the screen lights up with a notification. A message from Asoo.

> Hello Miss Eden. Thank you for photo of Rose. Very beautiful. We not hear from Samuel. I sorry. We hear nothing. There is now a mine in Ulara. They knock down huts. Burn trees. So sad. We stay away. I know nothing more. I sorry I no help. I hope to see you one day. Not this day. This day not good. I hope you hear from Samuel soon. Your friend, Asoo.

Holding my phone to my chest, I'm lost for what to think. Is no news good news? Not in my mind when I need hope to keep going.

I send a message to Amy and Yasmine, although I expect Amy to be asleep since she has an early start teaching tomorrow morning.

The phone vibrates with an incoming call from Yasmine.

"I've been speaking to Michael. I asked him by chance if he has heard anything from Samuel. He hasn't."

I let out a sigh. "Thank you for asking. I know you care."

"I do. And wish I could help more."

"It's okay. I'll be fine," I murmur. "I just hate not knowing."

"I know, babe. But I need to tell you something. Tonight, I decided I'm going to meet Michael in Peru to do the ceremony like I've always wanted."

Now upright in bed, I blurt out, "What?"

"I'm wiser and smarter, and he knows he's on his last chance. We've been talking regularly, and in my mind, I need to do it."

"Yasmine," I croak. "I don't want you to go alone."

"You're not coming with me," she stresses. "You need to stay here with Rose. Besides, someone might know something of Samuel. Michael speaks Spanish, so we can let you know if we hear anything."

"Thank you," I whisper and close my eyes. "That's kind of you, but I'm still not convinced you should travel alone. Group rules."

She chuckles. "Cute. You know I love you, right?"

"Yes. And I love you too."

"I have to go. We'll talk soon, Edes."

Placing my phone on the bedside table, I consider the possibility of traveling with her. Only I'm not prepared to take Rose with me or leave her alone.

The best solution is to remain here patiently and hope every day I'm doing the right thing by not searching for the man I love.

Only my patience is measured equally by my stubbornness. Opening my laptop, I type out an email to the USA embassy in Colombia and explain my fiancé, Samuel McMahon, is in the Colombian jungle, and I'm afraid for his safety. I provide dates he was last in Canaima and how he's trekking through the jungle.

I'm sure they would be thinking, *WTF*?

I comment further, explaining I don't expect to hear from him, but I'm concerned he could be unwell or injured. Then I ask if they could check if he has been hospitalized or arrested as I can't communicate with him.

Being I'm in Australia and his parents are in the USA, I expect they'll be notified first of any news. I'm okay with that, but my point is the embassy needs to be alerted that he's a possible missing person.

43

EDEN

Four Weeks Later...

THE UNOPENED EMAIL in my inbox from Samuel's parents offers hope. They are my closest link to Samuel since every place and person we know has led to nothing.

DEAREST EDEN,

Thank you for the photos of Rose. We'd like to Skype so we can see Rose, and she may come to recognize our faces until we can meet her in person.

One particular photo of you and Rose concerned us. You look exhausted. If there's anything we can do to help until Samuel comes to Australia, please let us know. If you need any finance for Rose's needs, please don't be embarrassed to ask for our help.

Samuel would want us to offer support.

Regards,

Christopher and Caroline McMahon

FOR A MOMENT, I don't respond. Why are they not concerned when their son's life is at risk? And *Samuel would want them to offer support.* Seriously? Wouldn't they want to offer support to their only grandchild?

I type out a reply.

Hello from Downunder,

I'm glad you enjoyed the photos of Rose.

Please don't be concerned. I assure you we're fine and don't need any financial aid.

Regards,

Eden and Rose

No photo is attached because their email has left me disgruntled.

Maybe it's why Samuel lost contact with them over the years.

Pulling on my coat, I head out to the lounge room to where Mum and Dad are playing with Rose. She's walking sideways around the room, holding onto the furniture and periodically plopping onto her rear until she pulls herself up again.

"It won't be long before she's walking," Dad boasts.

Mum wraps a scarf around her neck. "I hope it's not soon because you'll be chasing her from room to room."

"I know, right." I watch her crawl to the barrier across the stairway and peer down. "No, Rose," I say gently like I do every other time, hoping she understands it's an out-of-bounds area.

"Good luck," Dad says and then scoops Rose into his arms. "I'll distract her while you two make a getaway."

Placing a hand on Dad's arm, I give it a gentle squeeze. "I love you."

His eyes meet mine with an understanding and appreciation of what Mum and I are about to do.

"We'll be back after lunch," Mum tells him and kisses him on the cheek.

We dash down the stairs to her navy Mercedes parked in the basement and crank the heating too high. Mum gives me one last look before reversing the car. "Are you ready?"

"Yes, so ready." Then I pull up the directions to the care facility to visit Gran's friend, Brenda.

The drive is mostly in silence until I direct Mum through a gated driveway and into a parking lot designated for visitors.

I pull my taupe woolen coat around my chest. We sign in and wait for someone to assist us.

After explaining the reason for our visit, the receptionist almost sent us away until she located a note from Thomas, Brenda's brother-in-law, alerting the staff we'd be visiting.

After assigning us sticky visitor badges, she leads us through two sets of glass doors and punches a code into the facility's locked doors.

We walk along a hallway and turn into another until we come across a large lounge area where families and friends are spread out on a dozen sets of lounges.

"If you head outside, you'll find Thomas sitting with Brenda under a shaded tree. She loves the garden, so we take her outside every day."

"Her friend also loved the garden," Mum replies, and the receptionist nods even though she's clueless as to who Mum is referring.

We make our way across the freshly mowed grass to a garden brimming with colorful flowers lined with lavender. The aroma is delightful as is the rainbow of color. No wonder Brenda likes to come outside.

A bald man makes eye contact and then smiles. "Brenda, you have visitors. Remember Ivy's daughter-in-law and granddaughter?"

Brenda's gaze meets Mum's, and even from here, I can tell she doesn't recognize her. A lap blanket covers her legs, and a navy cardigan hanging loose over her shoulders and arms outlines her thin limbs. In a steady rhythm, Brenda picks at a loose thread in the blanket, her gaze fixed in the distance.

Thomas stands to greet us. "Ladies." He nods.

Mum hugs Thomas. "I'm not sure if you remember my daughter, Eden."

"Nice to meet you, Thomas. Thank you for allowing us to see Brenda," I say.

Thomas smiles. "Last time I saw you was when I was visiting Brenda and my brother, and Ivy called in with you and your sister. You were both under ten years old," he says affectionately.

"It's been a long time," Mum says and rubs my shoulder.

"Take a seat," he says and pulls two more plastic chairs into the circle. "Thanks for visiting Bren. There are days where she sees nobody. Both her children are interstate and visit once, maybe twice a year. She barely recognizes them, and her grandchildren are strangers to her."

"That's sad for her." Instead of sitting, Mum squats in front of her covered knees. "Hi, Brenda. Do you remember Ivy? I'm her daughter-in-law." Brenda hums a tune, seeming unaware Mum is even speaking to her. "We know how close you both were. You had some grand adventures nursing together."

Brenda's eyes flick over Mum's face before focusing on the blanket.

"I'm sorry. I thought there was a slight chance she might remember, but her dementia has progressed. She doesn't recognize anyone." Thomas pats Brenda's hand. "I try to visit once or twice a week. I can't handle that no one is here for her. But when you reached out, I wanted to see if she'd recognize you. For so many years, Ivy and Mum caught up. Mum would tell Ivy stories of her time nursing after Ivy had stopped."

"Yes, Ivy never continued nursing after returning from volunteering overseas. She focused on her husband and her son," Mum says.

I look at Mum, knowing it not to be entirely true since Grandpa forbade her from nursing when she came home from Ulara.

"Brenda," Mum says gently. "Ivy gave you a little notepad. Do you remember? It was a diary of her travels."

Brenda continues to hum, and I doubt she even knows we're visiting. A magpie's fluty song catches her attention. She stares at the branches of the gum tree and then fixes her gaze on me. For a moment, she stares at me, and then something crosses her expression, and she blinks slowly.

"Where have you been?" she asks me.

I hesitate before answering. "Umm, I've been shopping."

"Not to buy him more beer, I hope."

I give Mum a quick look, and she nods for me to continue. Is she talking about my grandfather? "No beer. Just some milk and bread." I shrug my shoulder at Mum.

"Talk about the diary," Mum prompts.

"I needed to buy more pens as I ran out of ink to write in the diary." I bend down so we're at eye level. "Did I give you a diary about the jungle?"

"You gave it to me the other day, remember?" She smiles at me. "Told me never to show anyone."

Shit.

I sneak a glance at Thomas and Mum, and they nod for me to continue prompting her.

"Yes, but I need to write some more. I have remembered what happened in Ulara when I had Dawn."

She reaches out for my hand. She squeezes it and gives me an empathetic glance. "My heart hurts for you. I'm sorry I wasn't there to help you through it."

With my other hand, I pat her arm. "I know. You're a good friend. Can you remember where you hid my diary?"

"Of course. In the bottom of my jewelry box is a secret compartment. Turn it over and push the two buttons together. The base will fling open. No one ever found it. Your secret is safe with me."

Air stills in my chest.

Double shit.

"Thank you. I'm going to borrow it, okay?"

She nods, and then her focus is back on the wayward thread of the blanket.

"Well done," Mum whispers.

"Guess we should see if it is really there," Thomas says.

"I'll stay here with Brenda," I say. Thomas and Mum stroll across the grass and disappear behind the double doors.

"I'm Eden," I tell her. "Ivy's granddaughter. Do you remember me?" Her eyes glaze over. "I loved hearing about your adventures when you and Ivy used to climb out of windows and sneak off to meet Albert and Jonathon." Pretending I'm Gran didn't feel right, and I don't want to confuse her. At the very least, I hope my words trigger fond memories.

"Ivy loved you," I tell her. "You were a great friend." I pat her hand again. "I saw Ivy's spirit in the jungle and got to meet Dawn, her daughter, although her name is now Kaikare. You would like her," I whisper.

The double doors open, and Mum steps out with Thomas. They scamper across the grass until they join us.

"Got it." Mum holds up an old tan leather-covered diary. The writing etched on the front is faint.

"Thank you," I tell Brenda. "I'll come and visit again soon and share stories of the jungle."

"Thank you again," Mum says to Thomas. "We appreciate it."

"If you don't mind, I'd like to come back and visit Brenda and perhaps remind her of the good times she and Ivy had together." I smile at Thomas.

“I think I’d like to hear those stories myself,” Thomas says and laughs. “You know she saved my life. I had a heart attack at fifty-five, and she performed CPR until the ambulance arrived. It’s why I visit regularly. After all she did for so many people, she doesn’t deserve to be alone at the end of her life.”

“Perhaps we can all meet here once a month,” Mum suggests. “It will give Eden some time to read and absorb what Ivy wrote.”

“And since I have read her other diary, I can remind Brenda of all the fun times they had together,” I say affectionately.

Mum and I say our goodbyes and head back to the car.

Holding the diary in my hands, I flick the tainted pages like a deck of cards and close it again. “Now I have it, I’m not sure I’m ready to read it.”

“It’s there for you whenever you are ready.” Mum turns her head and gives a quick smile before focusing on the road ahead. “You need to be first to read it even before your father. If some details need screening, then I’ll leave it to your discretion whether to tell him.”

“I think he’s ready to know everything. He has to, for Gran’s sake. I need Dad to be proud of the work she did and not think of her stay in the jungle as time lost with him as a toddler. There were many positives of her going to Ulara, and I hope Dad can also come to understand the importance of her journey.”

44

EDEN

Most people loathe working on their birthday.

I'm no exception.

"Have a good day," Mum says and kisses me on the cheek. Rose whimpers. She's aware I'm leaving for the day, and I'm thankful today is a day she gets to spend with Mum. Mum lifts her onto her hip and leans in so Rose can kiss me.

"Mwa," I emphasize the sound. "Have fun with Nanna, gorgeous girl."

"We'll leave here around six and walk to The Shores. I've booked ahead to ensure your favorite seafood dish is available," Mum says. Rose holds her hands out for me, and I pretend to kiss each one. She giggles, and it's the best sound to warm my heart.

"Have you done something different with your hair? You look different today."

I shrug my shoulders. "Spent a little more time on my makeup trying to make myself feel special."

"My darling, you are special. I like it and think it makes you look..." Mum hesitates. "You always look beautiful, but there's a glow about you today."

"Ha. That's because I was running around after missy here between finishing my makeup."

We both chuckle, knowing how Rose likes to have us chasing after her.

"It's your birthday. Accept compliments without blushing and feeling you don't deserve them." Mum smiles. "I know you, Eden. Say thank you and smile."

"Thank you and smile," I repeat, mocking her because we both know it will not happen. I laugh when she shakes her head and heads down the stairs.

I open the office door and, "Happy birthday to you," is playing from the computer's speaker.

"Seriously?" I laugh and can't wipe the smile from my face at the dozen pink helium balloons floating from the ceiling.

"Happy birthday," Dana sings and wraps her arms around me. "We have cake for morning tea so bring on ten o'clock."

"Ha, you're always thinking about food." My arms tighten around her back. "Thank you for cheering me up."

"You're welcome." She kisses my cheek. "I think we need to order in lunch for a proper celebration and have a bottle of bubbles."

"You sound like my friends."

"Happy birthday, honey." Dad squeezes me in an almost bear hug. "Your mum has everything under control for tonight."

The second he releases me, Ethan is hugging me tightly. "Happy birthday, Eden. Now you have caught up to me. I can verify twenty-six isn't so bad."

I groan loudly.

"Oh, please." Dana rolls her eyes. "Listen to you spring chickens." She claps her hands and almost stands between Ethan and me. "Let's get this work done so we can celebrate."

Picking up my coat, I place it on the back of my chair and fire up the computer for the day. I set my phone on silent and then scroll through my emails. My heart jumps at an email from Christopher McMahon, and attached is a response from the Colombian Embassy. "Finally," I breathe out the word, my hand touching the heart necklace on my chest, the one Samuel gave me. Only it's the shortest email stating that Samuel's visa is registered in Venezuela, and he hasn't left the country as far as they know.

It was dated only days after their last email.

I wonder why they waited to send it?

Below the attachment is a short response from his parents.

PLEASE DON'T WORRY about Samuel. He's fine.

Is it polite to reply with *FFS, listen to me!*

Ugh. I move on to the next email.

Today is a stress-free day. I'll not spend it worrying about Samuel and whether he's alive or freaking dead because I need a day of peace. Head down, I focus on work and not the future.

Dana comes out of the kitchen area and leans her hands on my desk. "It's time."

"What?" I gape at her.

"C'mon, birthday girl, it's cake time." She runs her fingers over the material of her navy skirt as she stands and looks around.

Ethan strolls in with an oversized chocolate glazed birthday cake. The top is alight with as many candles as could fit. The office door swings open, and along with a gust of air, Yasmine and Amy stumble in as though they're blown in by the wind.

"What the?" I say and laugh.

"Dana said to bring bubbles." Amy holds up two bottles and grins at me.

"Dad is allowing this?"

As if summoned, Dad comes out of his office and checks his wristwatch. "Your mum, Faith, and Rose should be here any minute."

"Faith is just parking the car," Yasmine tells us.

I shake my head in surprise at my family and friends who are like family. "Thank you. I feel so special to have you take time out of your day to celebrate with me. I really didn't expect it."

"We know." Amy places a hand around my waist. "But we wanted to."

I lower my gaze. "I'm sorry I've been no fun for a while. But..." I meet all their gazes, "... it will change from today. It's not your job to cheer me up, but I'm so grateful because I can't keep going on like this." I convey an apology with my eyes. "Today is special, so thank you, and from now, my misery ends. I mean, I've been drearier than the damn weather."

Yasmine chuckles.

Everyone is smiling except Ethan. He is staring as though he's hanging off my every word, and my every word holds a silver lining. I'm not sure what to think, but I can feel his eyes beyond my skin to where he once owned a piece of my heart.

The door swings open, and everyone spins and laughs at how my sister and Mum, holding Rose, are swept inside by the wintery August wind. "What did I miss?" Mum asks.

"Eden's speech that she's going to be cheerier than the weather," Dana replies.

"Well, that's easy. It's mad out there."

"Is that a bad omen on my birthday?" I ask Mum. She looks at me blankly.

"Is it bad luck?" I question Dad.

"You have Gran's diary," Faith says, finger-combing her hair away from her face. "Start reading it because I'm sure she'd reference her superstition." She hugs me. "Happy birthday, sis."

"Thank you." I lean my head on her shoulder. "Thank you for coming."

"It was all Dana," she whispers. "She's one of a kind."

Dana comes to me and hands me a knife. "Time to cut the cake."

I make my way to the table, and before I slice the chocolate, she calls out, "Make a wish."

My first instinct is to wish for Samuel's safe voyage home. Only I stop myself and find my daughter now in my father's arms. I close my eyes as I slice through the cake.

I wish to have a long and happy life with my daughter.

Pop. One champagne bottle.

Pop. Another bottle and then laughter.

I turn to my father. "Have we clocked off for the day?"

"Yes." He raises his arm in the air.

"Happy birthday to me," I cheer.

AFTER THREE HOURS of sitting around the office and celebrating my birthday, Mum and Faith leave. Yasmine and Amy had left only moments before them.

"Well, I'm heading off," Dana says and wraps her scarf around her neck. “Your father rarely does this, so I’m taking advantage of his generosity.” She winks at me and then kisses my cheek. “See you tomorrow. Enjoy the rest of your day.”

Dad’s office door is closed.

Ethan is packing up his desk, so I do the same, hitting the buttons and closing the drawers a little too hard because the bubbles have gone straight to my head.

I lean down to get my bag and freeze when Ethan is beside my desk.

“Hey,” he says and smiles.

“Hey.”

“I bought you something but didn’t want to give it to you in front of everyone.”

“Oh. Okay.” I sit then stand again when he doesn’t move.

“I want you to trust me.” He takes my hand and holds it like it’s made of porcelain. He strokes my fingers, and even though I know I should yank my hand away, I don’t.

“I do trust you.” I mightn’t want to, but I do.

“I like you, Eden.”

I pull a face probably more dramatically than I should because of said bubbles. “I like you too.”

“No. I *really* like you. Haven’t stopped. I want you to give me a chance.” His chocolate eyes filled with emotion meet mine. I’m vaguely aware I’m gaping. “I’m not trying to spook you. If we could start with... say a dinner date, a picnic. Get to know each other again. I know we could make it work.”

“It’s too soon,” I mumble. I go to pull away, only he grips my hand and turns it over. With his other hand, he places a box in my palm.

“Open it.” He lets go and adjusts his tie, undoing the top button of his shirt.

Pulling at the ribbon, I flip open the box to reveal a sparkling diamond ring. Seven to be exact in the gold band.

“It’s a friendship ring.” He shoves both hands in his trouser pockets.

“With diamonds? I can’t accept this.” I close the box and hold it out for him to take.

Both his hands remain in his pockets, and he rocks gently back on his heels. Ethan shakes his head. “It’s yours. Take it and leave it in the box. Think about it. You don’t have to wear it. It’s just a gesture of our friendship to show how much you mean to me. If you feel the time is right, then wear it. Then I'll know and might get the guts to ask you out on a date."

I gawk at him.

He's afraid to ask me out.

Since when?

"Happy birthday, Eden." He kisses my cheek and scoops up his suit jacket with his fingers, holds it over his shoulder for it to drape down his back.

He gives me a nod before stepping outside.

The door clangs shut with a gust of wind.

I flop back in my chair and flip open the box.

Do I say no because I'm still praying for Samuel to come to me?

No. I promised myself I'd stop.

I pick up the ring, turn it side to side. The diamonds sparkle under the light.

How does something so tiny cause my chest to tighten like I'm wearing a corset?

45

EDEN

It is not a commitment.

The following morning I'm holding the ring between my fingers, afraid to slide it on in fear, like *Frodo,* I'll disappear. Not my physical self but the person I've become—the person I'm finally content to be because of Samuel. I'll never forget him, but I can't hold out for a man who wants to live in another world. One that doesn't include me.

"It's not a commitment," I murmur for the tenth time.

A symbol of friendship, but the moment I slide the diamonds on my finger, it's a green light for Ethan to ask me on a date.

Is it what I want?

No.

But I'm refusing to dwell any longer.

For months, I have waited and waited and hoped and prayed Samuel would come out of this alive and then be so overjoyed he'd head straight back to LA and sort out his visas to come to me.

What fairy tale am I living in?

There are many scenarios, and as much as I want to think of him alive, my hope is fading every day. In one of the last honest conversations we shared, he told me he didn't want to return to society. He's miserable living a privileged life, and by my own foolishness, I believed that would change, and he'd be happy if Rose and I were with him.

Every day my vision clears and shows me Rose and I aren't enough.

He loves us, but to do so, *he* forfeits happiness. Then there's that loyalty to the Ularans he can't let go of. Only now do I realize giving up all that he worked for, all that he believed in, could break him and send him into a depression like he was in years ago.

For a year, I have compromised my happiness to do what's right by Samuel. I have changed for the better. I'm a better person for knowing him, learning from him, and being with him. Now the anxiety from fear of hearing they can't find him is destroying me. I can't continue to beat myself around any longer.

I need to be prepared mentally for any news.

Gran's leather diary is by my bedside table, and yet, I haven't opened it in fear it will completely undo me when I'm already hanging on by a thread. I expect the truth about Kaikare will be revealed. Already I can picture Gran in our jungle home—Rose's first home.

I thought I'd run out of tears by now.

We'll never see Ulara again.

Never see our friends.

Samuel.

Squeezing my eyes shut, I try to stop the tears believing Rose will never see her father again.

The real possibility I'll never see the love of my life again.

Stop.

I have to focus on new beginnings.

Keeping my eyes closed, I hold my breath and take a giant leap and pray to the universe that, like Froddo, I don't disappear.

GRABBING MY COAT AND SCARF, I head into the kitchen and say goodbye to my mother, then head down the stairs without waking Rose.

Inside our office, I fire up my computer and wait.

Ethan should arrive any minute.

Reaching for the glass of water, I knock over the container of pens and groan when they scatter across the floor.

What's wrong with me?

The door closes with a thud, and I jump. On my hands and knees, I peer up at Ethan grinning at me. In a brief second, I'm admiring the blue printed shirt and navy tie with his beige pants. His hair is styled, and those big brown eyes find me.

He raises his hands, and he's still wearing that damn smirk. "I'm not saying anything."

"Good." I gather the pens one by one.

He chuckles loudly. "Why?"

"Why what?" I stand and adjust my pencil skirt and white shirt that has come a little untucked.

"Were you on all fours? I'm not complaining. You looked bloody hot down there." His brown hues bore into me, telling me exactly what he's thinking.

"I was picking up the pens I knocked off the desk," I blurt out.

"What has spooked you?" His expression changes, and his gaze lowers to my hand. When his eyes meet mine, recognition settles in. We stand in silence, considering each other, and I'm aware of my heart thumping against my chest.

So, this is it.

My new beginning.

Not knowing what to say next, I say, "Hi."

In two quick seconds, he's beside me, lifting my hand and bringing it to his lips. "Hi, you."

I smile. "Little steps." It's all I can manage for now.

He nods, his eyes not wavering from mine. Keeping hold of my hand, he says, "To friendship."

"Well, we better get back to work before Dad walks in." I pull out my chair and scroll through my emails, doing my best to concentrate on the screen in front of me.

The moment Ethan logs onto his computer, the door swings open, and Dad closes it behind him with a little extra force. "Damn wind," he grumbles. He glances at Ethan and then at me. "Morning."

"Morning," we both chime together.

Ugh, could we make it any more awkward?

His brow raises enough for me to notice before he turns his back, and then his office door closes behind him.

I let out a breath as though I am a kid hiding a chocolate bar under the table. Unclasping my fingers, I lift them from my lap and continue to type.

"I cc'd you in an email to the city council," Ethan says without looking at me. “And I have three quotes from three construction companies I’ll forward to you.”

Glad it’s business as usual.

Dad’s door squeaks as it opens. He stands so the door conceals half his body. “Dana has called in sick. She said to check your email.”

“Right. Thanks.”

Dad begins to close his door until a noise has his head jerking toward the office entrance door. The wind blasts it open along with my mother hanging onto the handle and stumbling inside.

“Grace?” Dad’s eyes widen as Mum swipes hair out of her eyes.

“Eden,” she says out of breath.

I jump up out of my chair and freeze, seeing Mum’s frazzled face.

“Is it Rose?” I snap. Every second feels like minutes anticipating her answer.

She shakes her head.

“Close the damn door, Grace,” Dad grunts just as the wind blows loose sheets of paper over my desk. “There’s a damn storm brewing over the ocean.”

Mum spins toward the door but doesn’t close it. A man with a buzz cut is bent over as he stumbles inside. He straightens, and I realize he was protecting a bundle in his arms.

Rose.

He looks down, admiring her. Rose has her arms out for me. My legs become weak, and I lean on the desk, unable to take another breath.

“He knocked on the apartment door looking for you,” Mum blurts out and pushes the door closed.

Blue eyes meet mine. Even more beautiful without the blond hair framing his face. A face gaunter than the last time I saw him, and yet still as handsome as it was the day we met.

My legs find the strength to move, and he opens one arm for me to collapse into his side. Burrowing my face into his chest, I sob uncontrollably. “I’m so mad at you. I didn’t think I’d see you again.” I lightly thump his chest without lifting my head from the wet patch I’ve created against his tailored black suit jacket.

Then my arm is around his back, squeezing him so I know I’m not dreaming, and he really is alive.

“Mumma,” Rose babbles and taps on my head.

I manage a single laugh and lift my face.

Samuel wipes tears from my eyes, then taking my chin, he lifts my face so he can lean in and kiss me. "I promised I'd come find you," he says against my lips. Then he kisses me again.

He smells woody as though the scent of the forest is ingrained into his skin. His minty breath mingles with the salt from the tears that have streamed down my face and onto my lips.

"I've missed you so much," I whimper.

Leaning my head against his chest, I hug him again. Realizing we have an audience, I straighten and lightly dab my cheeks.

I focus on my father. "In case you don't realize... this is Samuel," I rasp.

"I met your mother when I went upstairs," he tells me. He nods at Mum, and she has the goofiest expression as though Samuel's charm has already bewitched her.

Dad strides over to Samuel. "I'm Winston Monteford. Glad you finally found your way here."

Samuel unravels his arm from my waist and takes my father's hand to shake. "Samuel McMahon, and it's good to finally meet you."

Samuel turns to Ethan with his hand outstretched.

Ethan's gaze flicks to mine, and I smile through happy tears. He gives the slightest nod, and I take it as an understanding between us. "Ethan. I'm a friend of Eden's."

Thankfully, I can't see Samuel's face.

From my position, there's a quick handshake before the men step apart.

Samuel turns to my father. "Sir, I'm exhausted after flying over twenty hours to get here. Do you mind if I whisk my fiancée away for a couple of hours before I fall asleep?"

Dad's eyes widen, and then he clears his throat. "Certainly."

I'm tucked under Samuel's arm. He guides me to the door, where Mum has a permanent smile etched into her expression like she's the joker. She pulls open the door.

"Ready to face the storm?" Samuel asks.

In here or outside, I don't care because right now, my body is warmed as though it's the middle of summer.

"Yes. Always yes, as long as it's with you."

PERFECTLY WILD

PROLOGUE

EDEN

THE ENERGY of waves flows through the ocean from one side of the globe to the other.

Wind whips over the surface, carrying droplets in the icy atmosphere. The blustery force encircles my body with the power of a tsunami crushing ribs and forbidding air to my lungs. A usual winter's day, only it's exacerbated after Samuel bursts through the office door.

The door slams closed.

I suck air into my lungs, needing a moment before taking the stairs to my parents' penthouse.

Samuel tightens his hold on my hand. "Hey, are you okay?"

I stare deeply into those blue eyes for the first time now we're alone. The hues of his eyes remind me of the sea in summer, unlike the stormy, gray Southern Indian Ocean mere feet from the back door. There are many questions loaded on my tongue, only I need to focus on breathing, and all I want to do is feel *him*.

"Not really," I murmur. "You're so calm, and I feel electrified from the shock." I shake my head still in disbelief.

"I'm not calm, Eden," he says gently. "My heart is racing, and I'm trembling internally not knowing how this would go down."

He tilts his head, and for a second, I see sadness in his eyes. Just as quick, his expression changes, distracted by Rose touching his shaven head. His face lights up, and he kisses Rose's cheek, then leans in, and his lips crush mine. I touch him, taste him, and inhale his forest scent. He may have escaped the jungle, yet the aroma surrounds him as though ingrained into his skin.

Our lips part, he leans his forehead to mine, his eyes close, and I sense this is painful as is the overwhelming joy of us being together after what has passed.

"Let's get upstairs," I whisper. "I need to feel you."

He spins, not letting go of my hand. Each step feels like twenty when all I want to do is fall into his arms and never let him go. I let go of his hand to unlock the door and shove it open, the impatience building. I make a beeline for the couch before my shaky legs give way. Samuel balances Rose on his hip and slides next to me, kissing my neck and cheek. Tiny kisses and then his mouth is on mine, reminding me how much I have missed him.

Rose slaps our cheeks as though it's a game, and I laugh, breaking the kiss.

As much as he wants me, he's not letting go of his daughter. She stands on his thighs, and he balances her with the other arm that's not curled around my shoulders.

"Dad-da needs to kiss Mommy," he coos at her.

Resting my forehead on his shoulder, I can't hold it in any longer.

I burst into tears.

Tears of happiness.

Tears of relief.

My stomach clenches.

The happiness I have longed for hurts, an ache deep in my chest. A surge of emotions streams through me. "Why didn't you tell me you were coming?" I croak. "At least I could have prepared to not be a mess."

"I'm sorry." He pulls me closer and kisses my forehead. "But I'd still be a mess."

I reach for his shaky hand draped over my shoulder. His body trembles against mine. Silent tears stream down his cheeks. He rests his forehead against mine while we take a moment to simply breathe and allow our bodies to calm some.

Mum walks into the room and finger-combs her windswept hair. "Here, let me take Rose."

"I don't want to let her go," Samuel rasps.

"You both need time together," Mum insists. "Get some rest. Rose isn't going anywhere."

I squeeze his thigh, the boniness prominent beneath the material of his trousers. His face is gaunt. The reality of him fighting to survive the past eight months hits me with the force of a wrecking ball.

"I think that's a good idea." My thoughts scramble. A long road of healing—physically and mentally—lie ahead of us. I stand and hold out my hands for Rose and kiss her cheek before giving her to Mum. "Thanks. We appreciate it."

I lead Samuel to my room and pull him onto the bed with me. For a few seconds, we simply stare. For me, I'm still somewhat in disbelief.

"So, this is where you spent your nights," he whispers. Rolling onto his back, Samuel looks around the room and then stares at the ceiling. "Every night I tried to imagine you sleeping. What you saw from your bed. Your room. You..." He kisses me again, and his hands roam, lightly scratching my skin.

"My room is basic. I'm not one for clutter." I follow his gaze to an oil painting on my wall—a palm tree and the ocean. A snapshot of serenity. On my bedside table is a framed photograph of us taken while we were in Brazil.

Taking his hand between mine, I study his fingers. Scaly skin peels around his nails. Every nail is short and cracked. His palm has a callous beneath every joint.

"How long were you home before coming here?" I whisper.

His gaze darts over my face then his lip quivers, and his demeanor cracks. His body shakes, and as much as I want to hold him, heal him, he's scaring me. "Hey, you're here, and we're all safe and together," I say gently. He's never cried like this. Not even when I was in the hospital, those were tears of a man stricken with worry. Before me is a broken man, and I can't let go of the feeling *I did this to him*.

I cry with him. Our bodies are entangled together. The physical bond is not enough to stop the pain of our broken hearts.

He needs time to heal.

Inesa's tragedy broke Samuel. He abandoned society, hid in the jungle, and denied himself love. His mission was to be a better man by helping others, a physician working for free. His promise to prove he's a good man. That promise transformed into a commitment to the people he called family.

His loyalty is second to none.

He vowed to come home to me.

It almost killed him.

I make a silent promise to help him pick up the pieces and show him he's worthy.

Prove my love for him is everything he'll ever need.

For right now, I feel unworthy of this man's love.

1

EDEN

Two weeks later...

Happiness.

Many define it as the emotion of feeling extreme joy.

I'm now wiser in understanding I had to go through a period of complete sadness to experience the bliss, and I'm now riding the happiness wave every single day. From the moment I open my eyes, I feel only contentment waking up beside Samuel.

For months, I worried he might not come out of the jungle alive. If he survived the arduous trek through the jungle, finding seclusion for the Ularans' safety came with a cost—the impossibility of finding his way out.

It's been two weeks since he surprised me and burst through the office door, returning to me. A week where I cried, overwhelmed with many emotions. We've made love every single day, hugged each other, and sobbed or sat in silence simply to be together.

He's still not ready to talk, only mentioning how the journey took every fiber of his being to find his way out.

Instead, he asked for time.

Time to heal.

Time to forget.

The thought of him traumatized by a dark memory fills me with terror—a silent scream slicing through my brain. The pain is an unforgotten memory of how I suffered when he was unconscious and almost lost to an unexplainable entity. In the dark of night, my anxiety heightens, reminding me of what I could lose.

For now, he's content to be with Rose and me, and already his spirit has been lifted by being reunited as a family.

To help him focus on each day and not the past, I undertook a personal role as his tour host and showed Samuel around Adelaide. I was so relieved to see him smile and enjoy the coastal city I call my home, even if it's significantly colder than what he's used to.

The cracks are there.

Even in the way he holds Rose or takes her hand while she sleeps. His love for her warms my heart, yet something isn't right, and it shows in his eyes. Beyond love is a flicker of uncertainty and fear. Here, he's not the powerful man I knew in Ulara. Considering the trauma he has suffered, he needs to heal, and Rose and I may not be enough.

It's why *I need* to see his smile and hear his laughter. Even now, while lying on his side on the beige carpet of the living room helping Rose build a tower with her blocks, the joy on his face is comforting. After taking him on a winery tour and a weekend away to a secluded beach house, it turns out he's happiest here, playing with Rose. By focusing on activities so he'd fall in love with my city as much as me, I didn't consider the toll on Samuel's body during those initial weeks at home. He's still awfully thin, and given he has not consumed alcohol for years, the two glasses of wine made him sick and drunk.

It was my first fail.

The second was buying clothes too big. He told me not to take them back as he'd fit into a medium size soon.

Soon.

Time to Samuel differs to the rest of us.

For years, he lived by morning time, noon time, night time, and moon phases. Not by the clock or calendar days of the year.

For the past two weeks, he has managed small healthy meals mainly of fruits and raw vegetables with some fish for protein. If he overeats, he vomits.

He refuses medical help and says he'll be fine in a matter of time.

It's hard to argue with a doctor.

When he first arrived, exhausted and gaunt, I went through a checklist, including private health and insurance options. In the few weeks he stayed in Los Angeles, his parents arranged the initial medical assessments and then helped him set up a financial plan to come to us. Even though I have not met his father, I understand good deeds come at a price, and Samuel has promised him to do the *right thing*. Working and supporting us doesn't sound like a bad deal, only I know it holds more than meets the eye.

Rose knocks the blocks, the castle tumbles, and the pieces scatter across the carpet. She bursts into laughter, and I can't help but chuckle at the sound.

Samuel notices me. His eyes flick over my face and then travel down to where I'm wearing an olive-green jumpsuit. "You look lovely. Are you going somewhere?"

"Lunch, I hoped. It's the last weekend of freedom," I emphasize the last word as my holiday is over. "My friends are hanging out to see you again, and Faith is coming over tomorrow. So, I was thinking lunch today, just you and me."

My phone buzzes, and seeing my sister's name, I read the message.

> Can we come over today and meet Samuel?
> We're all out of quarantine, and I can't wait
> another day.

"Faith wants to come over today."

Samuel looks up from where he's playing with Rose. "I'm looking forward to meeting her." He smiles at me. "And since you're dressed, I could take you out to dinner tonight?" He glances at Mum. "If you don't mind watching Rose for us, Grace?"

"Of course, it's fine. Knowing you two are moving out upsets me that I won't see our angel all the time."

"You can see her whenever you want, Mum." I kneel beside Samuel. "Ready for the thousand and one questions?" His gaze meets mine. I sense his nervousness and pat his back. "I got you, and I'm only telling you this because I know Faith, and it's her thing. She drags information out of you like a suction tube."

His eyes round as though he's pondering the situation. "Fine. I better shower and prepare myself for the onslaught." His gaze meets mine in warning. "I'm not ready for hard questions, Eden. You know that. I'm happy to discuss minor things, especially about your aunt." He then pushes up and heads to the bathroom.

I send a reply as I stride into the kitchen.

Samuel is looking forward to meeting you too!

"What do you want me to get for lunch?"

"All good, honey. I have a lasagna in the freezer."

"How about salads? I can pop out and grab some fresh stuff?" Lasagna is Faith's favorite meal. Samuel will struggle.

Mum gives me one of her trademark frowns. "I have it covered, Eden."

"Thank you." I don't have the same confidence in my sister, so I send her another text.

Eden: *Please go easy on Samuel today. He's not ready to discuss his journey with anyone.*

Faith and I have different ideas about the meaning of easy.

AN HOUR LATER, Faith and her boys burst through the door. The boys call "Nanna" with excited screams. "Eden," Seb yells as soon as the front door closes. His tiny feet pound the floor, sounding more like an elephant as he sprints toward me. "I got pox," he says excitedly.

We break into laughter.

Seb sprints to the kitchen and leaps into Mum's arms to kiss her. "Nanna, I got pox."

"I know, darling," she says with an empathetic expression. "Mummy told us all about it." He wiggles to get down. Sometimes I wish I possessed the energy of Faith's boys. James crawls after Seb. He uses the cupboards to rise to wobbly feet, peers up at Mum, and touches his chest. "You too, darling," she says and lifts him to plant a loud kiss on his cheek. "Are you better now?" James lifts his top to show Mum the few spots on his belly.

Rose turns on hearing her cousins' voices, and she babbles, not to be left out. I love she recognizes them.

Faith drops her bags inside the door and hangs her coat on the wall hook before pulling me into a tight hug. "Where is he?" she asks and steps back to peruse the room.

"In the bathroom."

"That jumpsuit is gorgeous on you. Are you heading out?" She pushes unruly strands of hair out of her eyes. Only now do I notice the dark rings around Faith's eyes.

"Thank you. We were heading out to lunch. It's now a dinner date." I wink.

"God, I'm sorry. I've been dying to meet him and can't believe I've had to wait because of isolation. Some blisters have scabbed. James didn't have many spots. Seb's stomach was covered in them. There's even one on his penis, and it was a challenge to stop him from scratching. He wouldn't stop crying," she moans.

The way Faith is rambling, it's evident the isolation has affected her. "I can remember having chicken pox as a kid. It's horrid."

Samuel walks into the room, looking as handsome as ever wearing denim jeans and a blue T-shirt. The sky-blue shirt highlights his eyes, larger and more beautiful with his buzz cut. It's all I see as those eyes tell a story. Right now, he's deep in thought. "Did you try the oatmeal and chamomile baths?"

Faith's face lights up. I understand because although he's handsome in pictures, his presence demands attention in the room in a good way, as he'll enlighten us with knowledge while being mesmerized by his good looks. "I did, and thanks for the tip because it eased the scratching in his sleep."

"Did you apply coconut oil and a drop of lavender and tea tree oil?" She nods, staring at him. Faith is lost for words. "If you have an aloe vera plant, you should continue rubbing it on their skin." He beams his beautiful smile, and his big, blue eyes hold her captive. "It's nice to finally meet you, Faith."

"Oh, the pleasure's all mine," she says, shaking his hand and reaching in for a hug. "I've waited years to meet you, and I have to say my sister didn't exaggerate your good looks." He pats three gentle taps on her back before breaking apart.

"You're taller than I imagined."

"I'll take it as a compliment." He grins at Faith, and I now assume he spent time in the shower mentally preparing himself.

"Shall we?" I tilt my head toward the kitchen where Seb is running in circles around the dining table in a game of chase with himself.

"Enough," Faith demands. "Find a chair and sit on it or get a toy and play quietly in the lounge room."

Rose screams with no attention on her and crawls after us. Faith scoops her up before her son crashes into her. "And no toys with small parts. Only Duplo blocks or your cars, okay?" She turns to Samuel. "One day I'd like some quiet time with you because I'm not the crazy woman I am now."

Seb stops running and notices Samuel. "Eden, I got pox," he says as he leans into my thigh, staring at Samuel.

"Are you better now?" I lift him into my arms and rub his little back.

He exaggerates a nod. "Mummy said you have a boyfriend." He's still eyeing Samuel curiously.

Samuel's brow pulls together as he mouths, *boyfriend*.

A giggle erupts from me.

"Thanks for throwing me under the bus." Faith huffs. She rounds the table and takes James from me. She lowers him to the floor to stand. He immediately plops onto his bottom before crawling back to the chair, pulling himself up.

"Ugh, I swear this kid hates walking. At this rate, Rose is going to be running around before him."

"Give him time," Mum cuts in. "Your father walked late. At eighteen months, actually."

When Mum tells us things about Dad's childhood, I often wonder if it's because Gran wasn't there to help Pop raise him."

"At thirteen months, he could be walking. He chooses not to and would rather crawl." She blows dark strands of hair from her eyes and then adjusts her long ponytail off her shoulders.

I place the salad and serving utensils in the middle of the table.

"Is there anything I can do to help?" Samuel asks in his polite American accent.

Faith beams the biggest smile. "I love your accent." She turns to me and winks, then takes a seat beside Samuel. She coughs to clear her voice. "I'm sorry for your loss."

He eyes me momentarily before turning to Faith. "I appreciate your kindness."

I warned him.

“Take a seat.” Mum slips on her oven gloves. “The lasagna is ready.” James crawls up onto Faith’s lap, and I place Rose in the highchair beside me. Seb slides onto a chair between Mum and Samuel.

The aroma of Italian herbs and the strong lasagna sauce fill the room. Out of the corner of my eye, I notice how Samuel’s hand casually covers his mouth and nose until he adjusts to the strong scent. I’m not sure what does or doesn’t make him nauseous, and currently, everything is a trial.

“Eden told us how much you loved the jungle. To be honest, when you were trekking toward Colombia and the notion of you being close to the Brazilian border, well, I was freaking out with her. You had us worried for months.” She places her hand on his shoulder. “We’re glad you’re back here with Eden and Rose, yet understand how hard it must have been to leave the people you love. And when she told us about the shaman...” She shakes her head. “I’m so sorry. It must have been traumatic for all of you.”

Samuel lowers his gaze to his hands. “Yes, it was extremely sad.”

She waits a while, only he doesn’t say another word.

“Please pass the salad,” Mum says to Faith.

Faith scoops out some for herself and then passes the bowl to Samuel.

“Eden falling in love with you has been a blessing. She has never been happier, and you have also given us the gift of an aunty we never knew. So, thank you.”

My sister could seriously speak underwater.

Mum points her knife at the lasagna. “Faith, could you please serve since you’re closest.” One by one, we pass Faith our plates. She holds her hand out for Samuel’s plate.

He waves a hand. “I’m fine with salad, thank you.”

Faith looks at me, then at Mum, and I know she’s bursting with more questions, especially because she hugged him and would’ve felt his skeletal frame.

“Faith, please eat,” Mum says casually without giving her a second glance.

2

EDEN

Later that night, I read the menu out loud.

I stop speaking when Samuel looks around the restaurant. His brow has a slight dent.

Something concerns him so I reach out and take his hand. “Relax, babe.”

His beautiful eyes meet mine.

“What is it?”

He shakes his head. “Nothing. I’m merely assessing the situation.”

“We don’t have a situation. Tonight is our alone time to simply be together and enjoy a meal.” I squeeze his hand, and when he squeezes mine back, it offers hope he’ll lower his guard.

“Technically, we’re not alone. There’s always potential for a situation, especially in a crowded space with people moving about.” His gaze roams over the crowd. “It’s ingrained into me to assess.”

He’s not talking as a doctor. It’s about his time in Ulara and being mindful of transmitting disease when they have no immunity to certain diseases. Except he doesn’t have to be concerned for the Ularan community in this Italian restaurant.

I watch him for a while before I speak again, “What are you not telling me?” I whisper.

His eyes meet mine, and we hold each other’s gaze for a few seconds. His brow softens. It’s something I’ve noticed since he’s returned like he's composing what he's going to say before he speaks to me.

"I haven't told you many things. I will, in time. It's taking a bit to adapt to the people and the noise." He picks up the menu and reads it for several seconds before placing it aside.

"Have you decided already?"

"There are few salads to choose from." He smiles at me. "What's your favorite dish?"

It didn't click before, probably because I focused on showing him the best places around the city. Samuel is concerned for his own immunity, and it's why he evaluates every place we visit.

"Well, I'm also full, so I'm happy to go with a salad." I place the menu aside and try to snag the server's attention to order our food.

I thought a date night would be fun, but now I know I need to stop pushing him into doing normal couple things. He's not ready even though he agrees to do whatever I suggest.

It's taken me until tonight to see through him, and a wave of disappointment hits me that I didn't see it before.

He'll say yes to everything I ask to make *me* happy, even at a cost to him.

And now his charade is over.

THE FOLLOWING AFTERNOON, Samuel and I make our way from the front of our apartment to the green grass of the esplanade. There's barely a cloud in the sky.

I collapse onto the lawn, laying my forearm over my eyes to block the sun's glare. Samuel lowers to sit beside me, legs bent to his chest and arms wrapped around his knees. He still moves in stealth mode and if I weren't peeking, I wouldn't know he was there.

"I'm exhausted," I whine.

"Last night too much for you, princess?"

I take his arm and slightly pull until his face is close to mine. "Making love to you is never too much."

His lips find mine, and in seconds, his kiss turns passionate yet still gentle. He licks over the contour of my lips. "You're sweet and addictive."

He stretches out alongside me and kisses me again. "*I can never get enough of you*," he whispers against my mouth.

Caught in the moment of a deep kiss, children laughing in the distance remind us we're not alone. Other couples and families enjoy the early spring weather and take in the beach view.

I push up onto my elbows. The blue-green ocean meets a baby-blue sky. The scent of salt fills the air, and I catch a hint of lavender wafting from a nearby garden. We remain silent, taking in the scenery or closing our eyes and simply being.

His words play over in my head.

I can never get enough of you.

"Samuel," I whisper and wait to get his attention. "I've never felt the relief and happiness I did when you waltzed through the door holding Rose. The journey out of the jungle," I shake my head. "I won't pretend to understand how hard it was or the suffering to help the Ularans and then to find your way out to be with us." I let out a long sigh. "I get you need time to process everything. And I'm sorry if I'm pushing you to show you my favorite places to visit, only I'm scared you're going to change your mind. So if I show you the best places—" I stall.

"I appreciate what you're doing, Eden. Admittedly, I did the same in Ulara by wanting you to fall in love with the place I loved and called home. I wanted you to stay and tried to convince you it was paradise before realizing my selfishness and the danger I placed you in when you weren't equipped to survive in the jungle."

"Yet I did."

He smiles. Samuel lies back, his elbows supporting his weight. "Yes, you did. I knew you couldn't stay. It was for a short time. I could protect and teach you, yet I'd never ask you to live out your life in the jungle like I'd chosen."

I knew you couldn't stay, I replay his words and brace myself for what he's about to say.

His eyes rise to meet mine. "There's much to tell you—" His voice cuts out, and he coughs to clear his throat. "All I can do is focus on each day as it comes. When good days become good weeks, we can talk about the future." He takes a piece of hair and tucks it into my ponytail. "Be assured I can never leave you as I can't suffer like that again." He kisses my forehead. "My heart is bound to yours, and I'm only whole when I'm with you. So, you don't need to impress me with your pretty city. I'll go wherever if I'm with you. One day at a time."

Glancing down at our linked fingers, I squeeze his hand.

"We're a little closer to nature by the beach, and it does something to my heartbeat and blood pressure, and everything around us slows." He takes me in his arms, and I place my head on his chest. Closing my eyes, I concentrate on his heartbeat. It's a steady rhythm, yet I understand he's not at peace even though he has found Rose and me.

3

EDEN

WAVES ROLL in over the white sand, the sound hypnotic. At dawn, the ocean is a dark gray, and for a few minutes, the stillness of life surrounds us—a calm presence until the seagulls squawk, alerted to the break of light.

"I enjoy this time of the morning," I say to Samuel as we meander along the esplanade. Rose woke early to feed, so she came with us in the stroller, enjoying the first minutes of a new day. Samuel is at peace here though I'd rather stay in bed and cuddle up close to him. Only today is my first day back at work.

"What's on your agenda today?" Samuel steers the stroller, ready to cross the road to home. We wait for several dedicated cyclists to pass before stepping onto the narrow street.

"I'm following up on the construction dates for a pool on the northern garden bed. We have a garden storage structure that must be removed first."

"A pool, yet you have an amazing body of water a mere fifty feet from your door." He gives me a sideways glance as we step onto the path.

"Not all our guests like the ocean," I remind him. "And the pool will be heated so visitors can swim in the colder months as well. The sea is damn freezing in winter with the wind blowing up from Antarctica."

He grins at me and tilts his head toward the ocean. "Yet swimmers are braving it now."

I chuckle. "The Icebergs. They're a dedicated group. Only the thought of drying off in the icy wind isn't for me."

He grins at me. "The Icebergs. Does everything have a nickname in Australia?"

"Almost." My phone beeps with a message.

"Are you on the clock already?"

"Not yet." It's a message from Dana. "I'm following up on something since Dana has resigned." I let out a sigh. "She has been part of our business and family since I was a teenager, and I can't believe she's leaving."

"Has something happened for her to want to leave?" He sits on one of the outdoor cane chairs and signals for me to sit beside him.

"Her husband has a new position in Queensland. They have always wanted to retire up north, so they're setting themselves up for a few years before they do."

He nods slowly. "Is your father replacing her?"

"Eventually. I'll take over her work until he creates a new role."

His eyes meet mine. "Is this what you want? In Ulara, you spoke about returning to university to study nursing."

"Circumstances have changed, Samuel. I now have Rose to consider."

"*We* have Rose to consider," he emphasizes. "I'm not questioning your decision. I only want you to be happy."

Me to be happy. What about him?

"I'll care for Rose while you work the extra hours until your father finds a new employee." He drops an arm over my shoulder. "Although, anytime now, the paperwork will be approved for me to work."

Samuel sat for an exam the first week he arrived in Adelaide and passed. My man has a photographic memory, not forgetting his former training.

"Until then, I'm free." He kisses the side of my head, his lips lingering longer than a normal kiss.

I want to ask him if this makes *him* happy, except I can't because I know it doesn't, and it scares me, especially since he must begin his specialist training from scratch. He's here for us, and in this society, we all need to work.

LATER IN THE MORNING, I get off the phone from the construction company and toss it across my desk. "Why do we have to jump through hoops to get something done?" I moan into my hands. "Seriously." I stand and meet Dana's gaze.

She stops tapping on her keyboard. "Anything I can help with?"

I shake my head and glance at Ethan, who's typing away, unaffected by my outburst. With pods in his ears, I assume the music is cranked.

"Yes. Do you want to get coffee?"

"Thought you'd never ask." Dana stands and signs out of her computer. She picks up her handbag and wraps her signature hot pink silk scarf around her neck. It's bright like Dana, and I need people like her in my life.

We move past Ethan's desk.

He glances up, taking out one pod from his ear. "Everything okay?"

"We'll be back in five," Dana says quickly before I invite him.

He's barely talked to me since Samuel burst into the office a few weeks ago. Today, I need time to chat with Dana.

When we're out on the footpath, the salt-infused air hits us, and I inhale a deep breath and let out a sigh.

"Is it that bad?" she asks.

"It'll work out. The resort pool would never be smooth sailing past all the fine print." I shrug.

"Not what I meant." She bumps my elbow. "You don't want to be here. I can see it. You're only staying to please your father, and it's... easy. Not easy work. It's what you know, so it's comfortable."

Dana has always understood me.

We turn the next corner and head straight to the café.

Deanne greets us with a wide grin. "Morning, ladies. A table for two?"

"Yes, please. How are you, Dee?"

"Awesome," she sings and leads us to my favorite table by a window. "I hear your man is back."

"He is." The mere mention of Samuel's name radiates heat through my chest. I take a seat. "I want to introduce you, and perhaps you could talk to him about your time in Brazil."

She pauses. "Be happy to, since it's one of the best times of my life."

We order coffee, and moments later, Dana stares out the window as though she's deep in thought.

"I'm going to miss you," I whisper.

Her gaze falls to the table as if she's aligned her thoughts before she looks up. She fiddles with her short ponytail before her brown eyes meet mine. She swipes at the tears, leaving a smear of mascara beneath her lashes.

"Not going to lie, it's gonna be tough. I've been part of your family for as long as I can remember."

"I know." My mouth dries thinking about the time when Dana leaves us.

She picks up a glass of water from the table and guzzles a few mouthfuls. Then she lets out a long audible sigh. "For years, we've dreamed of retiring somewhere warmer. Escape these damn winters." She laughs once as if the idea is silly. She wipes her nose, then picks up the glass of water and drinks more. "When Kerry requested an interstate transfer, it excited us about the next phase of our lives. The grass is always greener on the other side, right?"

I sense regret, yet say nothing.

"You. Well, you were making plans to leave. You have this new incredible life." She frowns. "Please remember those plans because it's a whole other can of worms I want to discuss with you."

"O-kay."

"Ethan—" she shakes her head. "I'm not sure what he's up to. But I won't stick around while he walks all over me when he's only been at Monte for seventeen months. The Montefords are *my* family."

I reach across and squeeze her hand. "You are family. I've always considered you to be more, so I was surprised when..." My throat tightens on the last word, and I also need to take a few sips of water. "You've always been there through the good times and the bad," I croak.

Dana makes a strangled noise. "The bad times." She shakes her head. "The absolute worst time wasn't business related, and my heart ripped open for you like you were my own daughter. I remember everything he did to you. And yet you have easily forgiven him."

I swipe tears before they fall. "Forgiven but not forgotten." I hold her gaze. "There's a difference, and it was easier to do after I found happiness. It cleared my head, and I realized..." I remember my time in Ulara, especially my first holiday, when I discovered more about myself in a couple of months than in the past ten years. "It took more energy to resent him." I glance down. "Trust." I meet her eyes. "I have a new team, and you're my main gal."

She smiles and shakes her head, and I laugh once through my tears. "Where's the damn coffee?"

"No matter what, you're only a phone call away," I murmur.

"And a short flight," she adds. "So please come and visit me in Brisbane."

"I promise I will."

WHEN I LEAVE the office to find Samuel sitting on a deck chair with Rose asleep in his arms. He's wearing his jeans and a black tee, and to me, he looks as hot as he did in Ulara half-naked.

"Hey, you." I lean over and kiss him, one that lingers. His tongue finds mine, and I groan when he deepens the kiss.

He chuckles lightly. "How was your day?"

"Better now I'm with you," I gush.

"Are you ready to resign yet?" he murmurs.

"What?" I straighten.

With his free hand, he runs it over the snug material of my skirt along the contour of my hip. "Let's take a walk." He pushes up with Rose in his arms.

"Here, let me." I take Rose and kiss her cheek. "How long has she been asleep because we'll never get her to sleep tonight?"

He runs a gentle hand over her fair hair. "Only ten minutes. After half an hour, I'll wake her. It's why I want a quick chat while we can."

Samuel places a hand on my lower back as we head toward the beach. The sun is low on the horizon. Twilight on the foreshore is nature's gift to enjoy. I have Samuel and my time in the rainforest to thank for my gratitude, including the strength to weather the storms.

"How was your day?" he murmurs.

"You already asked me."

"And you didn't answer. I have approximately half an hour to make it better."

"You already did," I say. "Just by being here fixes everything."

We take a seat on a boulder by the sand. "I'd like to believe it, only I don't have the power to wield happiness."

"No." I stare down at Rose. "You both do."

"Eden, as reassuring your words are to me, we should discuss our future."

I assume it's the promise he made to his father and how being a workaholic is his foreseeable future. It's what his father believes taking care of us and his responsibility entails.

"I bought a house. It's nearby. You could walk to work."

"Like a block away? Wait. You bought one without me?"

"I wanted to wait, only it happened so fast. After lunch, I was perusing the real estate app and found this house. It was open for inspection within the hour and before the auction. I thought, why not?"

"You bought a house," I repeat more in surprise, not anger. In fact, I'm delighted he wants to take the next step to stay here with us and build a life in a family home.

"It ticked all the boxes. On the esplanade and with a modern Scandinavian interior design. It reflected your style."

"My style? I didn't know I had a certain style since I haven't designed a place of my own yet."

"When the bidding commenced, something came over me, and I had to have this house for you. For us."

I nod, slowly taking it all in.

"It's only three blocks away on the beach." He points in the house's direction, the opposite way we usually walk.

"I'm familiar with the house." I shake my head. "I can't believe you bought it.

"The cost is not what concerns me. I received a phone call and email to say I can start working in a week."

I shake my head again to find sense in all the news he's sharing with me. "Are you concerned about Rose? Because Mum is happy to mind her until I find a childcare facility."

"Our life together will be nothing like the one we had in Ulara. I'll be on a rotating roster and—"

"Hey, I understand," I murmur, knowing it's inevitable.

"If we're planning for our future, I want you to consider what you want. Do you want to continue working for your father's business?"

I let out a sigh. "Dana mentioned the same thing today."

“I want you to reflect on what it is you want for yourself at this time of your life?”

I shake my head, unsure of what he’s asking me. “Do you want me to stop working and care for Rose?”

“Is that what you want?”

I stare out to the golden horizon, searching for answers. The breeze has picked up. Loose strands of hair blow around my face, and I don’t brush them away. Instead, I hide my face behind a curtain of hair. “I want to spend more time with my daughter. I also want to focus on something for me. I enjoy working, not every day, as I want time with Rose.”

“So don’t work. Study part-time,” he says to the sunset as though it offers new hope. “You can spend some time studying at home as well. Simply choose something that interests you and you’ll enjoy because it’s an ideal time to change. Life may only get harder to make a big career change.”

“Is it how you feel? Do you believe it’s too late for you to change?”

He frowns before meeting my gaze. “The promise I made to my parents before coming here was I’d do the right thing by Rose and you... continue with my medical studies, support you both, and be responsible. This all translates to resuming my residency at a hospital.”

“I understood oncology wasn’t the right path for you. I recall you saying how finding a cure made you happy. Patients dying and sick children tore your heart out.”

He looks to the sand, where the waves crash close to the rocks. His eyes glaze over, deep in thought. I know he misses Ulara, the people, his friends, and his adopted family.

The shaman.

“I assumed you’d continue in medical research. You enjoyed working —” I stop myself from saying more. He puts his hand in mine and squeezes it. I’m thankful he’s discussing our future and wish he’d talk about what happened on his journey with the Ularans because until he does, he’s not really here with me. Only physically while he silently mourns.

“Honestly, I’m happy to continue working at Monte for a while longer. I have plans and renovations I want to see come to fruition. You should find a new career or work that makes you happy since money isn’t a problem.” This deal he has made with his father seems to be tied up with a monetary bow. "You're an intelligent man, so study something of interest to you. You're in a new country, a new city, appreciating a different ocean. Tomorrow is a new day. Make it yours."

He turns and kisses me. "I wish it was that easy. I made a promise, and I need to honor it."

Are you bloody kidding me?

We barely finished discussing how he's free to choose his own path.

His parents aren't here.

We're in control of our future.

He thinks my father has a hold over me. Well, his parents are next level. I study his face, only he is wearing his unreadable professional expression.

Twenty months ago, I fell in love with this beautiful, honorable man. His morals impressed me, and I knew he was someone I could trust. I have faith in us, only we have a long way to go before *he* is happy.

All I can do is keep chipping away at his armor and hope I don't break him in doing so.

4

SAMUEL

On Friday, Samuel waits outside Eden's office. Sitting on a cane chair, he takes in the ocean view. The ocean offers him a sense of peace. He closes his eyes and simply listens to the waves breaking, the gulls squawking, and distant laughter.

A door slams and he snaps out of it when the king of douchebags walks out of the office.

"Ethan." Jaw clenched, Samuel gives a curt nod of his head. He despises Ethan for breaking Eden's heart, yet he should be thankful as it led her directly to him.

Ethan gives Samuel a sideways glance, throws his key ring in the air, and catches it while whistling to himself as he walks over to his sports car.

His gaze lingers momentarily, weighing him up.

If he owns the latest dang BMW, why is he working for Eden's small family business? And why is she driving around in an at least ten-year old beat-up Holden?

Ethan revs the motor, a sound demanding attention.

Samuel looks away and focuses on the ocean.

"Hey." He turns in the direction of the voice to the woman who's his world.

"Evening." He stands and kisses Eden. The loud motor beside them has her pulling away for the attention-seeking douchebag.

"Hey, Edes. We're heading to The Shores for Friday night drinks. After the week we've had, I thought you might want to come along?"

Samuel glares at the asshole. It doesn't have any impact because Ethan only has eyes for Eden.

"Sorry. We have plans. Please say hello for me." She waves and then turns to Samuel. "Where's Rose?"

Glancing over Eden's shoulder, Samuel waits until the black car disappears from his sight.

Ethan's words sink in.

He takes her hand and links his fingers between her delicate ones. "You haven't mentioned having a terrible week."

"It hasn't been all bad," Eden says in her sweet voice. "Especially since I came up with the brilliant idea to get away for the weekend. Just the three of us, then Sunday night the girls have asked to catch up."

"With you."

"No. With us." She smiles. "Where did you say Rose is?"

"With your mother, shopping." For the past six months, his emotions have been in turmoil, and everything he learned in Ulara about shutting down emotions, being a better man, is lost in a matter of months. Even more so with men like Ethan who have no respect. A part of Samuel's past from when he was at college finds its way back into his thoughts, wanting to teach the asshole a lesson. Then Eden kisses him, and the bitterness evaporates. She makes everything better, and he understands Ethan wanting her back in his life because Eden makes us all better men.

Only Ethan blew his chance. Big time.

He may understand the need to want Eden, yet there's no changing Samuel's opinion of the douchebag.

"Only the three of us?" He pulls her into a hug. "Where did you have in mind?"

She smiles as if he doesn't understand her. Her eyes widen playfully. "It's a surprise."

"Now, I'm afraid."

"You should be," she says and laughs.

"Do I need to buy more clothes? I haven't really been shopping—"

"No." She reaches up on her tiptoes to whisper close to his ear, "When Rose is sleeping, we'll be naked."

Samuel's grin broadens. "Now, you should be afraid."

"WE COME HERE every winter to watch the whales," Eden says, standing on the sandy beach in front of their holiday house at Victor Harbor. They have built sandcastles with Rose for the past hour. It may be springtime, but Victor Harbor is south of Adelaide, and the wind is considerably colder.

"The sharks don't bother them?" Samuel asks and wraps his arms over his chest, thankful for the sweater Eden suggested he pack. He feels the cold even more after living in the rainforest for almost a decade. His thoughts wander to the fact he has minimal fat on his frame, but he pushes it out of his mind.

"Does the ocean scare you?"

He wants to say no and be the man Eden knew in Ulara, only his anxiety has attributed to fearing things that normally wouldn't concern him. "Everything in your sea has the potential to kill." He knows as he did extensive research before boarding his flight.

Eden's eyebrows arch above her beautiful eyes. "You find the ocean more of a threat than living in the jungle?"

"Hmm... sharks, bluebottles, blue-ringed octopus, box jellyfish, white stinging sea ferns, flower urchins, stonefish, and let's not forget stingrays. Then if I avoid the ocean for safety sake, I'm met with some of the most poisonous snakes in the world... the redback spider, funnel web spider, crocodiles, cassowaries, which I've recently learned about, and..." he emphasizes, "... a sunburned country with one of the highest rates of skin cancer in the world." He shakes his head. "I must have been delusional to leave the safety of the jungle."

"The jungle is hardly safe, Samuel."

Samuel widens his eyes. "Will you protect me?"

"Please, most of those creatures are on the East Coast or up north. I squish redback spiders all the time, and I never swim deep enough to be shark bait."

"Shark bait," he mumbles. "God, please don't tell me you stomp redback spiders with your bare feet?"

"No. At least they're not hairy like tarantulas, and we don't *eat* them." She cups his cheek with her hand. "You have nothing to fear." She winks at him. "I've got your back."

"I wish it to be true," he murmurs.

She gives him a puzzled look.

How can he be honest with Eden when he's not being truthful with himself?

"Come on, let's go up and shower before dinner. I hope Rose goes to sleep early so you and I can have some fun."

"Fun is why I came to Australia. The country of fun."

Eden chuckles at his response.

They both take Rose's hands and give her a chance to walk aided before he scoops her up in his arms.

"Dad-da." She taps his chin, and he pretends to bite her fingers. Rose giggles, and the sound warms his heart.

"How long have you been searching for poisonous animals on the internet?" she whispers.

"Too long," he mutters. "I was looking for something to amuse myself while you were at work."

"You surprise me, considering how fearless you were in Ulara." Samuel gives her a sideways glance, and her face drops. "Sorry. I know you're not yourself since..."

"I'm orientating myself to the surroundings as I did in the rainforest. And I'll need to treat patients if they're bitten by one of the hundred thousand killer creatures lurking," he adds quickly.

"So, you're being proactive in your research."

"Right."

Eden jumps in front of him before he can respond. "Tonight, I'll remind you why you're here."

EDEN GENTLY CLOSES the door to where Rose sleeps. A quiet click is the only noise he hears. Closing the magazine where he was blindly flipping pages, he moves so Eden can sit beside him on the couch. Only she straddles him, her mouth covers his, and the kiss escalates quickly. "Let's take this to the bedroom," she murmurs against his lips.

He should carry her.

One of the many things he finds himself incapable of performing in his current condition.

His failures disappear from his mind when they're on the bed, clothes stripped, and under the covers. He fists her hair, giving her neck the perfect angle, kissing every inch of her neckline down to her perfect breasts. Sucking and flicking her nipple with his tongue, her moans of pleasure guide him, tracing his fingers along her stomach, lower, and between her legs. She arches her back and whispers his name, a desperate plea from her lips. She takes his shoulders and encourages his lips to meet hers once more. Her hands wrap around his body, running her fingers over a thin frame. Lining himself, he eases inside her, takes both of her hands, and holds them beside her head. Eden's pleasure is all he wants to see without her eyes portraying worrying thoughts as fingertips trace over every rib.

"I love you," she whispers.

Samuel thrusts harder and faster, and Eden cries out, her legs wrapping around his thighs, her heels pressing into his muscles. Every skin cell tingled, every neuron fired, he's lost to her. Every right or wrong decision has led to this moment, to this joy he feels with Eden, all concern evaporating from his thoughts.

The discipline he learned in Ulara is lost to animal instinct, even from the moment he saw her on the beach in Salvador. For months, he ignored the pull she created like the moon's gravitational force on the ocean. With the certainty of the tide rolling onto the shore every day, Eden wasn't going away. She affected his life.

She's his weakness and heart source in one. She terrified and excited him equally. There's no getting the upper hand. Eden rules his heart, and he'd do anything to be with her, the one constant in his life.

She calls out, and he smothers her mouth with his, kissing her as he thrusts until the high of his orgasm blinds him. A shudder rips through him, his muscles burn with pain, and he collapses over her. Easing his grasp on her hands, she pulls away, wrapping her arms tightly around his body.

After a few minutes, his breathing slows. "I love you," he finally responds when the fatigue fades. "More than anything." It sounds lame, only he's unable to focus, and all he wants to feel is her. Like most nights, exhaustion sets in quickly. Like a drain, energy gushes out of him. He positions himself beside her, wraps an arm around her waist, and closes his eyes. He drifts into sleep, aware of her hands moving over his skin as though she's making an invisible map, touching his hips and every rib before coming to rest on his chest over his heart.

Naturally, she's concerned about his weight loss. If it were her, he'd also be worried. He can't afford to be vulnerable. He needs the upper hand, and proving he's fine helps him to believe it to be true.

Masking the truth isn't a lie.

His throat tightens when he cries out.

A strangled noise.

He can't breathe.

Lifting blood-stained hands, he looks around, terrified. What happened? His heart pounds hard against his ribs. "Eden," he yells again, only she's lying on the ground lifeless.

The shaman beside her.

"Nooo," he wails. "Please, no."

"Samuel."

Gentle shaking.

"Samuel," a beautiful voice calls to him. "It's okay, honey."

His chest weighs heavy as though a crate of lead is on top of him, and he can't take a breath.

"You're safe."

His eyes flutter open and search the darkness. His vision adjusts to her silhouette leaning over him.

"It's just a bad dream. You're fine."

He attempts to swallow and moisten his dry throat. "Sorry." He blinks several times. What time is it? "Did I wake you?"

Soft fingers stroke his forehead. "You were having a nightmare."

Samuel closes his eyes to allow his head to clear.

"Do you have them often?" she whispers.

"No." The first here in Australia. Every second night when he was in the jungle—lost—afraid he'd never see her again.

"Here." She takes his hand so it touches a glass. "Have a drink."

His shaky hand takes it. “Thank you.” The water cools his throat. “Did I wake Rose?”

“No.” She places her hand on his forehead.

“I’m not sick, Eden. I need a moment.” He places the glass on the table and slides down the bed. Eden rests her head on his shoulder and wraps an arm around his body, holding him tight.

“I worry about you.” She kisses his chest.

Weak and vulnerable. It’s not how Samuel wants her to see him. She has enough to worry about, and he doesn’t want to be another thing added to her list.

Running his fingers over her soft hair calms him, lying this close more so. “It can happen when you’ve suffered a shock,” he tells her. “It’s nothing for you to be concerned about.” He kisses the top of her head. “I’ll be fine.”

In the dark, Samuel stares at the ceiling, afraid to close his eyes again. He senses her awake, not moving or making a sound, simply listening while holding him close. Neither of them speaks, yet his mind is far from quiet.

Closing his eyes, he focuses on the steps to calm his mind and eliminate the thoughts that cripple every part of him—thoughts of how his world has stopped making sense.

A BRIGHT LIGHT burns Samuel’s eyelids. He remembers watching the sun rise and the gentle warmth shining through the blinds. He intended to get up and attend to Rose. The comfort of daylight must have lulled him into sleep.

A soft melody comes from the other room where Eden is singing. He rolls over to check the time on his cell—half the morning is lost. He leaps out of bed and strides to the kitchen. “I overslept.” He runs his fingers over his head.

She chuckles as her eyes wander to his boxers. “Good morning to you, Mr. McMahon.”

He glances down at what has her amused.

“Dad-da.” Rose holds out her arms for him.

“Give Daddy a moment.” Eden grins at him.

After changing into jeans, he walks back into the kitchen. "Have you both eaten?"

"Almost ready for lunch. I didn't wake you, not when you looked so peaceful."

Samuel appreciates the gesture. "I had full intentions of getting up to Rose while you slept."

"I'm fine, Samuel. Please don't worry about me." She wraps her arms around his waist and leans back to look him in the eye. "If you don't want to work as a doctor, then don't. We make our own rules, and the last thing I want is for it to exacerbate anxiety."

"I don't have anxiety," he murmurs.

"Samuel." She lets out a sigh. "Don't pretend with me. I'm here to help you through it. You have experienced some horrific things and lost someone you loved. Grieve. Don't hold it in, and stop trying to be so damn brave."

"Brave is the last thing I feel," he mutters under his breath.

"And stop googling the shit out of this country." She rests her cheek on his chest. "You need time to adjust to a new life with me."

His woman is so wise.

"You're working in the wrong field." He kisses the top of her head and tightens his arms around her back.

"And so are you if you settle for anything less than what your heart wants you to do."

5

EDEN

"You finally made it here, my favorite monkey man." Amy hugs Samuel. It's his first time at The Shores cocktail bar. "You had us worried."

"Monkey man?"

"Tarzan. King of the Apes," she continues. "Lives in the jungle."

Samuel's brow tightens.

"He gets it, Ames." God, she's blonde. I shake my head. *Not helping.*

"We've missed him, that's all." She hugs him again, and by Samuel's expression, he doesn't know how much my friends adore him because they have listened to me for months. They know what it means to have him *home.*

We find a table by the window overlooking the ocean.

"It's good to see you again," Yasmine chimes. "How are you enjoying Adelaide so far?"

He glances at me. "It's a pretty city... only I asked Eden to slow down. She was adamant about showing me every sight in a single week."

My friends chuckle.

"It's not the jungle, but it's nice." Yasmine smiles at Samuel and tucks a dark ringlet behind her ear. "Have you heard from Michael recently?"

Oh shit. They're diving straight into questions.

I signal to the server and ask for a bottle of rosé. "No, not for many months."

He glances at me.

I give a subtle nod to go on.

"I know he was an asshole in Peru..." She turns in her seat so she's facing Samuel. "We've been chatting again. I'm going to meet up with him in a few months."

Samuel's eyes widen. "To do what?"

The server returns and fills our glasses. Samuel refills his glass with water.

"Ayahuasca. You know I've always wanted to try it," she says more to me.

My eyes meet Samuel's, and I signal for him to intervene.

"Then you need to prepare in the long term. For a start..." he inclines his head to her glass of wine, "... can you give up alcohol?"

Yasmine slides her glass toward me. "Done."

Samuel folds his arms over his chest and straightens his back. "If you're serious, I have a diet to follow. You need to adhere to it to give your body a chance to prepare. It's like a detox and promotes the benefits of the tea because you've already cleansed."

"You were going to advise her not to take it," I whisper.

"Yasmine is a strong woman. No matter what we say, her heart desires this. Her spirit calls to her. I can offer the best advice to keep her safe. With or without our approval, she'll do this."

"With Michael," Amy mumbles.

Yasmine's eyes sparkle. "You know he's apologized to me several times. He's back to the same guy I met in Rio."

Samuel's expression remains reserved. "Michael... has a big heart. Occasionally, a selfish side of him surfaces. Unfortunately, poor decisions highlight that side."

"I surprised him when I mentioned you were here. I didn't give him details of what had happened," she says gently. "Only how you reconsidered and decided to give Australia a go."

Samuel stares at Yasmine, and no one speaks for a few seconds, which feels like minutes.

"What did he say?" Samuel's legs move beside mine. I don't want him to feel uncomfortable, especially when we haven't discussed what happened in any detail.

Yasmine removes the scarf from around her neck. She rolls it up and stuffs it in her handbag. "He said he'd like to visit here, but it depends on how *we* get on in Peru."

Amy rolls her eyes.

She still hasn't forgiven Michael. I remember how distraught she was when alone, and Michael took a sick Yasmine into the jungle.

This was supposed to be a fun night of simple conversation, yet tension weighs heavy in the air around us.

The patrons on the opposite table have ordered food, and an herbal aroma wafts toward me.

"Do you want to order?" I ask Samuel. "Some bread?" I change the subject. "Samuel hasn't tried Lombardi's yet."

Samuel smiles at me. "Is your social life all about where to go for the best food?"

"Abso-bloody-lutely," Amy sings.

CUDDLING INTO HIS SIDE, Samuel pulls the bedsheet over my shoulder and my eyes flicker closed. An uneasiness surrounds me, but I focus on the positives, the wonder of Samuel being with us until my thoughts slow.

Then a light is bright enough to disturb me so I pry open one eye.

Samuel is awake and reading his phone in the dark.

"Is everything all right?" I murmur.

"It's an email from my parents."

I haven't expressed my frustration to him about how they wouldn't listen to me when he was lost and in danger.

"Are they okay?"

"It's an update on the position Dad secured for me. He knows a professor and is asking about my working visa." He continues to stare at the screen. "They want to come out here for Christmas," he says in a lower tone. "Meet you and Rose. And then tour some."

"That's great. Rose needs to know her grandparents." He says nothing, so I rub his chest in small circles. "I can do an itinerary for Adelaide and the wineries. It will keep them busy for weeks."

Samuel chuckles and places his phone on the table before turning to face me. He strokes my face, pushing strands of hair away from my eyes.

"How desperate are you for money? I mean, is it why he's hurrying your visa?"

A grin creeps along Samuel's lips. Then it drops away. "Eden, don't ever feel afraid about money. Ever. Rose and you will always be looked after."

I push up onto one elbow. "How so?"

Samuel pulls me so I'm lying on top of him. He kisses me hard. "I've told you before that money isn't an issue, and if you want to quit work, you can."

"Then why are you hurrying back to work? Why are you proceeding in a career that makes you miserable?"

Even in the dim light, I make out his furrowed expression. "My father has expectations. My grandfather also possessed expectations, and to continue receiving his inheritance each year, I need to adhere to some rules elaborated in his will."

"What? If you don't, are you cut off?" He remains quiet, and I take it as a yes. "Why haven't we spoken about this before? Anyways, we don't need the extra money. We have what we need, and I want you to be happy. Do anything as long as you're happy."

He kisses my forehead. "Touché."

"I don't need a flashy house or the best car and clothes. I only need you." And all this news of his family and inheritance doesn't make me secure knowing I'm cared for. My stomach churns, understanding there's someone else controlling our decisions and happiness.

Warm fingers stroke my back. "It's not that I don't enjoy my work. It's more where I work."

I open my mouth to say you don't have to work in a hospital and then realize he's talking about society. The city.

My thoughts race.

"Why don't you convert to naturopathy, and we could buy a property in the hills away from everyone, and clients could drive to you? We could have a room out the back and—"

His kiss silences me. "It sounds wonderful. Only I need to uphold a promise, and I'll continue to work as my father sees fit."

I let out a long sigh.

"This week I need to find a car for us."

"I have a car." I attempt to roll off him, and he stops me, adjusting my legs. His mouth comes within my breathing space. His face hovers, his eyes caress my face, and God, I feel it like fingertips tracing over every contour. His lips skim along my cheek to my mouth. I'm lost to his kiss, his touch, and his passion as Samuel shows me his perfect love.

THE FOLLOWING MORNING, Rose is having breakfast and talking gibberish to Mum while eating her scrambled egg. I have minutes before I dash out the door. Samuel is still asleep. "He had a restless night," I tell Mum. I recall periods of his phone light disturbing me.

"I'll watch Rose until he wakes." She has maintained a distance, allowing us to be a couple while we're all living together.

"Dana has been asking to see Rose, so I'll take her down with me for a while. I'll bring her back in an hour. Samuel should be awake then."

"If not, I'll watch over her." Mum smiles at me. "I miss our special time together."

"Well, you'll get plenty of it when Samuel begins work." I lift Rose from her highchair. "Let's get you cleaned up."

After changing her into a cute lemon-colored dress, we walk down the stairs to the office. The space is quiet. Ethan's head lowers as he reads over something on his desk while Dana focuses on her computer screen.

"Morning," I chime.

"Morning," they both murmur back and then do a doubletake.

"And a fine morning it is." Dana pushes out of her chair and is by my side in a flash, regardless of her tight pencil skirt and pointy two-inch heels. "Come to Aunty Dana." She holds her hands out, and Rose goes to her, all timidness lost. Rose has the sweetest smile, and then she touches Dana's red lips. "Do you like the color red?" she asks against her finger, making Rose giggle. The sound has us all grinning. Dana takes her to her desk and sits Rose on her knee. She gets out her phone and plays something to keep her entertained while she continues to read her screen. It gives me a moment to start up my computer and begin reading the long list of emails. A particular email has my attention. "Construction is starting tomorrow?" I stare at Ethan wide-eyed.

Ethan smiles as though he was waiting for me to see the email. "We'll finish it within a month. Then it's the landscaping, and the pool will be ready at the end of spring."

"Oh wow. Our summer guests are going to be thrilled." Most come to enjoy the beach and swim in the ocean, yet there are always some who dislike the ocean and prefer a pool.

My thoughts race to Samuel and what he said to me. This is the one project I wanted to see through. And it's going to be complete in a matter of months. I spoke to him about the freedom of choosing his own career, and I'm struck with the reality of freedom for myself.

Rose whimpers, and I turn to check on her.

"Oh, honey, Aunty Dana is almost done."

"Let me take her for five," Ethan offers. He stands and goes to Dana. "I'll hold her until you finish, and Eden can respond to the email." He takes Rose, then turns and smiles at me. "I purposely didn't respond as I assumed you'd like the honors."

"Thank you." I immediately tap out a response on the keyboard, my lips taut with a smile.

I'm vaguely aware of Ethan walking around the office pointing out things to Rose. He says each word to her as though teaching her to talk. *How cute.* I don't have time to dwell as I'm attaching the last of the files to my email when the office door swings open. Samuel is standing there in his board shorts. My eyes wander over his bare tanned chest and broad shoulders. He remains thin, yet every muscle is visible, and when he lifts his arms, his biceps contract. He mesmerizes me until I see his pinched brow and realize what's irritating him.

He strides over to Ethan. "I apologize. My alarm failed this morning."

Ethan looks at me, then back to Samuel. "It's fine, man. Rose is a delight to babysit." He hands Rose to Samuel and watches as he walks away with her.

"Honey, it's fine," I tell him. "I was going to bring her to you soon." I move around the table to walk him to the door. "Are you doing anything today?" His brow pulls tight. I wasn't implying laziness. "I thought maybe I could bring Rose down on my lunch break so Dana could spend time with her."

Samuel dips his head slightly, leans in, and kisses my cheek. "I'll see you then."

I close the door behind him, and the click of the switch is like a finger snap in my brain. He didn't have a good night, and I can only imagine what he's thinking.

6

SAMUEL

Samuel arrives in the city by mid-morning.

After tipping the cab driver, he folds Rose's stroller and secures her straps. He stands on the footpath and takes a deep breath, preparing his mind to be the man he used to be when he negotiated business in LA.

In a mere thirty seconds, the Porsche salesperson is beside him. "Are you looking for any style in particular, sir?"

Samuel stares down at him momentarily before perusing the room. "Sporty, classy, and also family-friendly."

"I see." He holds out a hand. "I'm Gerard, and can definitely help you."

Samuel shakes a hand. "I'm Samuel. If you have what I want, then I'll make it worth your while to process the paperwork quickly as my daughter's patience won't last all day."

Samuel loosens the top button of his white shirt.

"Come this way, sir."

Gerard and Samuel weave around several cars and stop by the glass window beside a sparkling black 911.

"We offer our own child seats to fit." Gerard smirks as though he has won the lotto. Maybe he has as it piques Samuel's interest. "Take it for a drive, and you won't need any more convincing."

"Can you fit a child seat now?"

Gerard's hands go to his hips. "You seem like a man who knows what you want. And I'm the man who can make it happen."

"Stop boasting, Gerard, and show me how good you are."

Gerard scratches his jaw. "So, you want to take it now?"

"Do I appear the type to mess you around?" They eye each other momentarily.

Samuel slips into the driver's seat and wraps his fingers around the sporty steering wheel. He closes his eyes and imagines the smooth sound of the turbo engine and how it easily slips up a gear with his fingers controlling every move. A powerful and intelligent car. He remembers it well when driving his father's car mere weeks ago. He remembers how a small part of him could easily slip back into the past where wealth and power had defined him.

Gerard appears by the open door, standing beside Rose's stroller. She looks up at him and smiles. "My assistant will fit the child seat now."

"Perfect. Lead the way to your office, and we'll settle the paperwork."

Gerard's brow pulls tight. "I understood you wanted to take a test drive?"

"No need. I drove the car a few weeks ago."

Gerard's smile is almost ear to ear. "All right then. Do you have a color preference?"

"Gerard." Samuel steps from the car and stands over him. "You must have misunderstood. I want you to fit the child seat immediately so we can tick off the paperwork, and I can take my daughter somewhere fun."

"I'm sorry, sir, but this car..."

"... will be mine in a matter of hours. I told you I'd make it worth your time. If it's not done by the time my daughter is bored, then I walk."

7

EDEN

A NOTIFICATION FLASHES across my screen with a text message from Samuel.

What time are you finishing work?

I glance up. It's already five o'clock.

I booked a table at a Greek restaurant for 6:30 p.m. Is that okay?

It sounds wonderful.

Although an early night sounds good right now because I could fall asleep sitting upright. I scan through my emails for any late replies. We're ready for tomorrow's demolition of the old buildings and the commencement of new foundations.

"I'll see you in the morning." Ethan tucks his satchel under his arm.

"Yeah, I'm signing off now as well." Everything else can wait for the morning. Dana clocked off an hour ago, and Dad's been in Sydney and Melbourne for the past two weeks on business. He visited my brother, Will, in Melbourne, and seeing Will always cheers Dad up.

After logging off, I follow Ethan out of the office. A horn sounds while I'm locking the door. A black sports car cruises into the soon-to-be-demolished parking lot. I'm about to warn them not to park here overnight. We forewarned guests to park on the street until construction is complete. The expensive car stops beside me, and it's not any car, it's a Porsche. The tinted window slowly lowers.

"Samuel?"

"Jump in, beautiful."

Rose squeals, and I peer in to see her excited face in the car's rear. "Did you buy this?"

I close the door and note his attire. Navy pants and a white button-up shirt. "Cars are significantly more expensive in Australia."

"Is this your idea of a *family* car?"

He steers to where Ethan has parked, quickly reversing the car. "No, this is my car."

My window remains lowered, and I give Ethan a quick wave. His eyes round, and then he gives a curt nod before Samuel reverses quickly.

"The family car that's yours arrives next month."

I gasp. "Which is?"

"A Range Rover. If you want to show me this beautiful country, we'll need a four-wheel drive."

Material things have never appealed to him, so why is he spending a hell of a lot of money on things we don't need?

"Is this a work car?"

He gives me a sideways glance and grins. "Do you like it?"

Cars are meh to me, and why I didn't care about driving an old car. Yet, I take in the dark, sleek interior with touch-screen prompts. How can I not? "I do. Dad has always driven a BMW, and—"

"So does Ethan," he finishes. He's smiling smugly.

"Are you showing off?"

"Me?" he asks incredulously.

"It's not your style to be flashy, and I don't want you to change from who you are because you're here."

"Here, as in Adelaide?"

I don't want to say 'society' because he told me many times about how he didn't want to return, and it's played on my mind ever since. "You know what I mean."

He veers onto the street and my thoughts race to why he needs these expensive cars. Is he trying to impress me? "Is it rude of me to ask how much you have spent on cars today even though it's your money and none of my business?"

"Our money," he adds. He gives me another sideways glance. "It's *our* money, Eden." Taking my hand, he raises my fingers to his lips. "And we need to go shopping for a ring."

I pull my hand away and stare out the window to gather the right words, then shake my head. "What the hell is going on? It's like I'm talking to another man. And where the hell is all this money coming from?"

"I told you about the inheritance. It was on hold while I was in Ulara. A sizable sum of money is sitting in my bank that really needs to be spent so the government doesn't take it. So please, don't feel guilty. And I haven't changed. I need to spend the money on whatever makes life comfortable for us. I've never told you before because I didn't want it to define who I am. I'm still the same man, and I don't need these material things in my life." He places a hand on my leg in an attempt to soothe me. "I have the money, and it needs to be spent. That's all. I'll be investing in other areas. I'll always take care of Rose and you."

"You're missing the point. We don't need all this to be cared for. We only need you, and, more than anything, for *you* to be happy. And while I can see you're enjoying the car and spoiling me, it's not you and not us. And if it means giving up work and doing what your heart craves, and yes, losing your inheritance and upsetting your father, so be it. We only answer to each other."

"For me to come to Australia and get a working visa quickly after being out of the workforce for some time, my father managed to pull a few strings. And I made him a promise. In two years, we can reassess our lives to where we want to be."

There's my answer.

He has given himself two years in society.

I have two years to help him be happy living in my hometown. If not, I'm not sure where we'd go because even his ultimate home in Ulara is no longer possible. And it concerns me as to how it's affecting his mindset.

He steers into the restaurant parking lot.

I take his hand and squeeze it as I know he's trying. Restaurant dates are a big thing for him since he still can't eat much, and certain smells make him nauseous. "Have you ever been to Greece?"

"I have in my teens. What do you call spring break here… schoolies?"

"You went to Greece for schoolies?" I shake my head. "Where we stayed last weekend in Victor, well, that tiny coastal town is where we go, and I thought we were cool."

Samuel chuckles. "I only went to Mykonos to party and would gladly go on a family holiday to see the sights."

"All this talk has me starving and craving Greek food."

WE ARRIVE HOME, and Samuel places Rose in her crib. I can hear him telling her a story. I open my bottom drawer and retrieve Gran's journal she wrote while in Ulara. Untying the string around it, I carefully flick a few pages. A small puff of dust blows up in my face. It all appears intact. Rubbing my nose to stop a sneeze, I then lift the journal and inhale. I envisage her scent, only I'm hit with a pungent, musky aroma.

The door clicks behind Samuel. "Why the frown?"

I hold up the journal. "Remember my gran's journal? Well, this is the one she wrote while in Ulara. I'm ready to read it and revisit Ulara with her."

His eyes widen as he lowers himself onto the bed beside me. "I realize it's private, except I'd like to read it as well. Imagine what it was like around fifty-plus years ago."

I offer a brief nod, thinking if I should keep it private for Gran. "Okay, but there might be parts I'll screen in case, you know."

"It was smart to document her journey, her thoughts, and life in the village." He removes his shirt. He's unbuttoning his trousers, and I'm distracted by him *and* the dusty book in my hands. "All her experiences aren't lost. I should do the same."

Samuel agrees.

Wow! I moan as he slides his boxers down his thighs. I want to toss the book aside when he strips down and slips under the covers. He kisses my neck, and I close my eyes, my stomach fluttering as he dots kisses over my skin. "Maybe you could write what happened to you. It might help you…" I fail to find the right words for *heal*.

"You're the only help I need," he says all breathy. He takes the journal out of my hands and places it on the bedside table. "Now, come here, and I'll show you why."

THE FOLLOWING MORNING, I wake early to a quiet house.

Samuel's breaths are steady and deep before I climb out of bed and check on Rose in the other room. In the cot, her head is down, and her bottom is up in the air. I have no idea how it's even comfortable to sleep in this position. Turning the door handle and holding it tight to minimize the click, I wander back to my room, take Gran's journal, head out to the living room, and curl up on the couch, ready to embrace the first chapter of her journey.

8

IVY

November 2, 1962

After walking the corridors of the ship for the last time, I was glad to leave the stench of vomit behind and embrace the extreme humidity introduced a few hours before docking. Passing the mess deck, where several broken chairs remained scattered across the floor, I remembered the fights that broke out each night due to the restless, bored, and drunk men. With every step, I gripped the handrail, unsure if my wobbly sea legs would carry me down the stairs to where land awaited.

Considering I only had a small case, most of my clothes needed a good wash, as did I.

Like sheep, they herded us off the ship in almost perfect lines. From here, I observed lovers hugging, kissing, and sobbing. The ship was far from full. Some were volunteers like me, and others were immigrants seeking work of promised treasure. The ship will be at capacity on the return trip with immigrants hoping for a better life in Australia. Almost three months at sea, and I don't want to think about the journey home while my stomach is unsettled. Some days were so bad I imagined the moment I'd sight land and considered disembarking regardless of where. I didn't care where I lived my life if I could get off the ship to stop the endless puking.

When I did, I'll never forget those first few hours of dealing with the heat.

Never had I dealt with humidity so extreme my rigid lace bra stuck to my skin within minutes of stepping outside. A shuffle on the wharf alerted me skin within minutes of stepping outside. A shuffle on the wharf alerted me to the large number of military present. It wasn't the guns that spooked me. More, the shouting in another language, and I couldn't understand their demands. If I didn't understand, how would I know if I was doing something wrong or even illegal? How could I reason with anyone? Not learning Spanish added to my long list of regrets as I stepped into a foreign world that will be my home for at least the next twelve months.

When I reached the wooden deck of the port, a woman, Maria Pérez, greeted me. She took me aside and after confirming my identity, led me past the military, shouting something in Spanish as we walked.

It took all my energy to keep up with her, especially since my sea legs were not cooperating. I asked her why people were shouting.

In her thick Spanish accent, she explained they were calling out Yankee interference about the Americans coming to work as they have a better tax system and can return with more money than if they stayed in the US.

Politics. I was clueless, so I asked her about our itinerary, and she spoke so quickly I could barely make out what flight we were to take to Venezuela. I caught her words 'visa' and 'passport,' and I already packed them in my small case. The plan was to then continue onto another flight to Canaima come morning. Diego will meet us for orientation for my medical role in the camp.

After months at sea, the four-hour flight didn't bother me, nor did the never-ending questions Maria had to translate at customs. The following morning, we were ready to board another flight to Canaima, a tiny, beat-up aircraft that barely appeared capable of leaving the ground. Only then I wanted to stomp my foot and say enough.

Until I remembered what I had given up on coming here to live my dream—Albert and Winston were back home, surviving without a mother and a wife. If I were to give up now...

No, I was stronger than that.

So, I boarded the plane and prayed we landed safely. And we did so in an hour of flight time.

As Maria promised, Diego was there to meet us at the flight strip and would drive us to the camp. He told me how appreciative they were to have someone like me with my expertise. They have volunteers only, and more are needed as most head to Africa or Europe. They would pay me well in gold, even as a volunteer.

If I were to reread this entry, I'm to remind myself of the ride in the jeep as the bumpiest I've ever experienced. Hence, the bad handwriting.

Only my thoughts are fresh, and I intend to document every part of my journey.
I'm about to be overwhelmed with emotion when we arrive at the base camp.
I hope to write about the most amazing adventure while helping those unable to receive the benefits of modern medicine like many of us in the modern world.

9

SAMUEL

SAMUEL'S DREAM seemed real as it's almost a recount of the past. With his people, they trudged against stems of thick leaves to forge their own path —a path into the unknown. Yet they trusted and relied on him to get them to safety wherever it may be.

He tosses and turns in the covers, his dream broken by the roar of modern heavy machinery that sounds like it's coming through his window.

Rubbing his face, he then clambers out of bed. Construction work has begun on the resort pool—the project Eden is determined to see through. Rose screams from the other room, so he dashes to her and swings open the door.

"Dad-da." She lifts her arms for him.

"Come here, my beautiful girl." Lifting her into his arms, he presses her head against his chest. "Dad-da is here. You're safe with me." A promise he'll uphold her entire life. He takes her to his bedroom and points down to the trucks.

Eden is standing nearby wearing an industrial yellow hard hat, looking every bit as sexy as the day they first met. "Mama," she coos.

"Yes, Mommy is down there," he says in his American accent to influence his daughter. He's curious about what accent she'll take when she learns to talk.

He turns and checks the time.

"It's breakfast time, cupcake." He heads toward the kitchen and notes Ivy's journal on the couch. He places Rose on the carpeted floor and examines the cover. The weight of the memories between the covers makes the book seem heavier than what it is. Memories of a place he still dreams of, a place he longs for but not without the two loves of his life.

A suffocating weight tightens his chest.

He closes his eyes and takes a moment to reel in his thoughts. Pressing the journal to his chest, he then places it on the table. Yesterday showed glimpses of the old Samuel. Money held power, and he remembered it as he stepped into the car dealership with the salesperson almost falling at his feet after realizing the commission he would receive.

He hated the man he was.

Hated his life of wealth and fake people.

He promised Rose a different life, yet he has fallen back into society and his old ways in a blink of an eye. Samuel draws his energy from the ocean, and being close to nature is his one requirement to stay.

The dreams have left him exhausted. He's mindful of eating healthy, yet it will take time for his body to adjust. The walks along the esplanade with Rose are therapeutic, although he's mindful not to burn energy and lose more weight.

Sitting on the couch, he takes Rose's hands, and she pushes up to her feet. She takes a few supported steps toward him then bounces up and down on her toes.

"You want to jump?" He lifts her, and the sound of her giggles is something he'd love to bottle. Rose is a needed distraction helping him get through each day. She melts away his dark thoughts, thoughts he knows he needs to explain to Eden. She wants to know what happened, only he's not ready to unleash his memories. Every night snippets creep out of the locked cupboard in his brain to terrorize him. Retelling his ordeal like a story to Eden will require more strength with the mountain of emotions unleashed from his memory.

His phone pings in the other room, and he leaves Rose on the floor to find it. When he returns, he finds Rose standing up alongside the couch, using it to balance and get around the room. Rose then reaches for the coffee table, and holding onto the furniture has expanded her walking space.

He sits on the couch to monitor her and opens his email. The hospital has received his paperwork, and orientation is arranged for the afternoon.

"There go our plans, baby girl," Samuel murmurs.

BEFORE LEAVING THE HOUSE, stomach cramps almost crippled him into postponing the appointment—a combination of nerves and stress exacerbated by his current health ailments. He felt numb like the clock had wound back, and he was no longer in control of his life. His life mapped out in a similar way before he escaped to Ulara.

The interview went smoothly.

He stayed for a tour and then was introduced to the staff. Thankfully, he slipped into a work mindset of familiarity.

On the drive home from the hospital, Samuel's nausea eases somewhat.

One day at a time.

When he walks into the apartment, Eden is on the couch with a glass of red wine. She turns and smiles at him.

"Did I tell you how sexy you look in a suit?" Her devilish grin has him thinking the suit isn't an entirely a bad thing.

He sits beside her. "Mum and Dad are out to dinner and staying the night in a fancy hotel in the city, so I thought we could get takeout?" She places her red wine on the table and plants a kiss on his cheek. "How was your interview?"

"I begin on Monday. I met some of the staff." He shrugs. "Everyone was pleasant."

"Okay, great." She takes his hand and squeezes.

"Not for Rose. I don't want your mother to care for her five days a week. She has her own life."

"I know. She said she doesn't mind in the interim." She lowers her gaze and smiles like she has a secret. "When the pool project ends, I'm going to resign. I'll be home with Rose until I work out what I want to do. Either study or a change of work or both."

He brings her in for a hug. "I'm proud of you. I'm sure this wasn't a simple decision to make."

“No, it wasn’t. I’m confident Dad will understand.” She lays her head on his shoulder and lets out a sigh.

“Maybe I should have a glass of wine with you to celebrate?”

Her eyebrows arch. “Is that wise?”

He understands her concern. His nausea comes and goes, yet he’s learning to live with it for now. “Only a small one as it seems we have much to celebrate. To add another thing to the list, the cooling-off period ended, and we’re now the proud owners of a new home.”

She smiles at him and takes his hand. “The one you bought *without* me.”

He strokes her face. “You’ll love it, I promise.”

“I’m sure I will.” She kisses his cheek. “In the future, big decisions are something we make together.” Eden opens her mouth and closes it, and he senses her holding back in not wanting to offend him. She desperately wants him to be happy living in her city. If only she knew he’d be happy anywhere if he’s with her. Spontaneity is unusual for him —only the house felt right. “You’re right. And if our home isn’t what you dreamed of, then we’ll sell and find something together.”

“Samuel, I trust you.” She curls into his side and wraps an arm around his waist.

Samuel rubs a hand over his heart. Her words weigh heavy on his chest, along with the other people in his life relying on him to ‘do the right thing,’ especially after what happened to the Ularan people.

He can’t fail again.

10

EDEN

"You were talking in your sleep last night."

Samuel stills. "Was I coherent?"

Pulling the bedcovers over my shoulder, I curl into Samuel. "Not really. I stroked you until you settled."

Samuel stares at the ceiling, and it frustrates me I can't help him. "It might help to talk about it."

He remains quiet. I wrap my arm around his waist and kiss his shoulder. I don't want to push, only he needs a gentle nudge. It's Saturday morning, and I'm grateful to have this time with him in the morning to lie with Samuel and hold him, even if it's in silence.

The quiet doesn't last as Rose calls out and continues to talk gibberish. At least she wakes happy.

I bring Rose into the bed with us, positioning her in the middle.

"Morning, princess." Samuel turns on his side to admire our daughter.

"Her little feet are weapons, so protect your balls." I laugh at Samuel's expression.

My phone vibrates with a text, and I read the message from Faith.

"Did you make plans for this morning?"

He frowns. "Should I have?"

I chuckle. "Maybe because Faith and her family are coming over for morning coffee."

"We better put a helmet on you, princess," he says to Rose.

I laugh. "Jake wants to meet you. It seems you're the flavor of the month."

"And you wonder why I went into hiding."

"NA-NA. NA-NA," James yells.

"Okay, buddy, you can have a banana." Faith stands and chops a banana and places it on a plate. She plops James in a seat beside Samuel and opposite me and puts the plate on the table before taking a seat.

"I do too," Seb yells out.

"Come and get it, Seb. You know how to peel and eat it."

Five minutes after formalities, Samuel's head is moving side to side like at a game of tennis, watching Faith's energetic boys.

Seb races in and jumps onto a chair to reach the fruit bowl on the counter. Then he runs back to the television.

"I'm usually monitoring their screen time, but since they were all sick, I allowed it for my sanity." Faith turns to Seb. "Half an hour, mate, then it's off."

I'm watching Samuel's expression and doing my best to withhold the flicker of a smile. He looks exhausted just sitting next to Faith. Beside me, Jake is also grinning.

"When are you both trying for a second baby?" Jake teases. "Eden said you have the patience of a priest."

Samuel's eyes widen at me, then he kicks his chair out from the table and stares down at his crotch.

"Oh, I'm sorry," Faith says quickly. "James, you can't squish banana onto people." Faith stands and wets paper towel.

"It's fine." Samuel takes the paper towel and wipes the mashed banana from his board shorts.

Rose passes wind, and it's so loud it even surprises me. "Oh, that doesn't smell good." I wave my hand in front of my face at the rotten egg odor coming from my daughter amid the giggles from around the table.

"Allow me." Samuel drops the paper towel and mashed banana in the trash before lifting Rose from her highchair. "We won't be long." He carries Rose out of the room.

Samuel calls my name.

I stare at Faith and tilt my head. *Weird because he's capable of changing a nappy.*

"Eden," Samuel shouts again.

I dash to the bedroom, believing something is wrong with Rose. Samuel is standing over the change table, Rose is kicking excitedly, and poop covers his outstretched hands all the way to his elbows.

"Oh my…" I step tentatively toward the table, poop covering it. When I meet his gaze, his eyes beg for help. I can't help it and burst out laughing. "I'm going for backup," I say and rush out of the room, laughing way too hard.

"Don't leave me," he calls out. "I can't touch anything."

"What's going on?" Faith asks with a coffee now in front of her.

"Samuel has poop to his elbows. Can someone help us?" I ask, trying to be serious.

"Jake, watch the kids." Faith jumps up to follow me.

"Gladly," he chimes.

"There has to be something wrong with her. It was like a projectile of feces," Samuel moans. His arms are stiff, and he's afraid to move.

Faith chuckles while pushing up the sleeves of her navy sweater. "We've all experienced days like this. It's funny when it's someone else."

He ignores Faith and stares at me. "Someone will have to turn on the faucets for me."

"Faith, take Samuel to the laundry room," I instruct. "I'll finish cleaning up Rose in the bathroom."

11

SAMUEL

Rose is the devil in disguise. Her pretty face was distorted as fecal matter blasted from her tiny sphincter covering everything in a one-foot radius. Immediately after emptying her gut to what appeared as the last week of stomach contents, she smiled at Samuel and kicked her legs in relief.

"Okay, doc, stick your hands under here," Faith says as she stands by the sink with one hand on the faucet. She turns the water on and stands back to avoid the splash. Matter washes away, and she squirts soap onto his hands.

"Thank you. I appreciate the help."

She makes a strangled noise. "Surely, you have experienced this in your day, doc? You're acting a little precious." She grins at him.

"Obviously, yes. In a hospital environment, there are vinyl floors and faucets I can turn on with either my foot or an elbow, not in someone's luxurious home. More soap, please."

"What about in the jungle? You didn't even have running water to wash your hands."

"It was different." A memory flashes into his head—excretory products landed on dirt and were covered quickly to absorb into the earth.

"Okay, you're good to go. I'll splash disinfectant around the basin to be sure."

"Don't bother," Eden says from the doorway. "Can you please take Rose, and I'll clean up after I'm finished."

"Allow me to wash my hands one more time," Samuel says.

Faith snorts and then grins at Eden. "He won't feel any cleaner for a while even if he scrubs the skin off the bone."

"You better take off your clothes so I can soak your T-shirt and shorts as well."

Samuel heads to the bedroom and changes his clothes. Faith is right. When did he become precious? His first reaction was to assess her condition because he's still not convinced this is normal.

"Are you okay?" Eden asks when he hands her his soiled clothing.

"I feel foolish. Thank you for helping me and for cleaning up the mess."

"It's fine, it happens. She has only done it once to me before, and thankfully, Mum was there to help." She offers him a warm smile. "Join the family. I won't be a minute."

"After I wash my hands one more time."

He hates to admit it, but Faith is right. No amount of soap, water, and meticulous scrubbing made him feel any cleaner.

He heads into the kitchen and takes his seat at the table. "I'm sorry for upsetting morning tea."

"You didn't upset me," Jake says and smiles.

"Sam, do you have photos or anything since I missed everything while in quarantine? I was so out of it."

"I do, but—"

"Faith gets to call you Sam?" Eden looks at me wide-eyed.

"And doc." He rolls his eyes. "She's not someone I'd correct."

His comment causes laughter around the table.

"Sam's a quick learner." Eden winks at me.

"Guys, I suffer from FOMO, and knowing you've been here for three weeks and I'm not sitting at the table hearing your stories and learning about my aunty has tortured me." She looks past Samuel to the lounge room. "Seb, turn the TV down. I'll not ask you again," she warns.

"I told you Samuel has barely discussed it yet." Eden reaches under the table and squeezes his hand.

"There were photographs, right?"

"It's fine," he murmurs. "I can get the photos and show Faith and Jake."

"I'd like to see them again," Eden adds.

Eden had promised her family to make extra copies, only it completely slipped her mind while showing Samuel around the city.

"He bought a house?" The surprise in Faith's voice projects to the bedroom, where Samuel is searching for the pictures. He heads back into the room and hands Faith the images.

"I hear congratulations are in order."

"Thank you."

"Eden is a better woman than me. No way would I allow Jake to buy a house without me checking first."

"Eden trusts my judgment, and I base my decisions on what's best for them."

Faith's gaze lowers to the first image. "Well, we know she trusts you after running away from home to live in the jungle while *pregnant*." She lifts her gaze to meet Samuel's momentarily before concentrating on the pictures.

"Faith," Eden says gently.

"I'm sorry. I know she trusts you." She turns the image around. "Can you tell me who this is?"

Samuel's throat tightens. "The shaman."

"I started reading Gran's journal," Eden says quickly, and he knows it's for his benefit. "Only the first entry, and it's when she gets off the ship. The way she describes the voyage, she must have endured some hardship for three months on a boat with everyone puking around her and feeling sick herself would have been horrid."

Faith meets Eden's gaze. "I'd like to hear about her travels. Can you tell me what happened after you read each entry *if* it's something she'd want us all to know? I'm still getting used to the notion you were supposed to find Samuel and find out about Dawn, and it's eerie, yet I want to know about Gran. She was so brave, and it helps us to understand her. I'm putting pieces together when I think about some memories."

Eden nods. "It does. I believe she'd want us *all* to know the truth and what she experienced so we can understand some of her past."

"And your father," Jake says and smiles. "We have Samuel to thank for leading you all closer to Ivy."

"Ah-hmm," Eden clears her throat. "Pretty sure I helped."

"This is true." Samuel pats Eden's back. He admires his beautiful partner in life. He pushes blonde hair away from her blue eyes, reminding him of the ocean mere yards from where they sit. "You and Faith are similar." He runs his fingers along her long ponytail. "You persuaded me to ask questions and bent every rule in Ulara."

"Oh, I don't bend rules, and I'm not a risk-taker," Faith says without looking up. "I may ask questions, but I follow protocol. Eden is more like our grandmother." Faith lifts her head and smiles warmly at her sister. "You have softened Dad in the last eighteen months. And I'm sure he'd like to know what's in the journal. That reminds me, when did you last visit Brenda?"

"Not for a while. My plan is to read more of the journal so I can talk to her about it because I'm sure she'd have read it or listened when Gran vented to her. And I know what you're thinking," Eden adds. "Her Alzheimer's prevents her from understanding, yet I hope talking about Gran might trigger some happy memories, even if it's only for a few seconds."

Faith agrees. "When are Mum and Dad due back?"

"Around lunch, I assume."

Faith's gaze homes in on Samuel. "Is it okay to ask you some questions, and then we'll put the photos away? I know Dad's accepting of all this, but it's still raw, and he needs time to process everything."

Don't we all?

AFTER FAITH, Jake, and her children leave, Samuel and Eden take a stroll past their new house. It's a spring day in September and not one to be indoors. They come to the three-story house on the esplanade and pause on the pavement to admire the frontage—a white-rendered home with floor-to-ceiling windows to capture the panoramic view.

From her stroller, Rose watches the seagulls fly overhead and looks everywhere except at her new home.

He points to a covered veranda on the second level. "I picture a telescope there for us to view the night sky. It's been some time since I've had the privilege of stargazing."

Eden wraps an arm around Samuel's waist and leans her head on his shoulder. “I picture us as a family, enjoying everything a seaside home offers.”

Samuel kisses the top of her head. “Thank you for trusting me.”

Rose whimpers and kicks her legs. “It’s time for an afternoon nap. We should get back.”

“I’m thinking I’ll take a nap with her,” he says.

“It’s been quite a morning already.”

After walking back and a half-hour later, Rose is asleep, and Samuel is drifting off on the bed, exhausted. He’s aware it will take time for his body to heal.

Long days working will take a further toll on his body. With no other choice, he’ll find other means to manage his health.

He has to, for her.

The dense canopy blocks out the last of the light before darkness falls. A thick, pungent aroma fills his nostrils—decaying leaves, moist air, and a never-ending buzz around his head. It has never felt more like home. Only there’s no familiarity, and his breath is laced with fear, a scent predators seek.

He has lost sight of the river, treading deeper into the unknown and further from any known points on his map. His satellite phone, an emergency source, was lost weeks ago in the Negro River. Survival weighs heavily on instinct, knowledge to avoid danger, and his awareness of the location of Colombian guerrillas.

The men spark a fire. The children string hammocks to trees and secure palm throngs overhead to protect them from the rain.

Some nights the downpour drenches the camp.

Come morning, everyone is tired, sick, and exhausted before they begin their trek south toward Peru.

Life has changed for the entire village.

Safety is compromised every step of the way.

In the months passed, they have lost souls—elderly and the young, depending on the disease and their fight to live.

Another four weeks before they stop walking.

Another four weeks will mean more loss of life.

Yet, they can’t stop. They’ll be safer in a denser part of the Colombian jungle with nearby waterways and mountains. From there, if threatened, they can travel south toward Peru.

Kaikare informs Samuel they must rest. They need time to heal. The men have agreed to build sturdier structures and set up a hunt for food.

The Ularans are unhappy, and if undermined, it could lead to them losing trust in his judgment. So, he agrees to resting for a week.

A decision he regrets as on the third night, gunshots wake them.

"Tïmenneng," he screams, hoping the warriors secured the boundary.

A gentle stroke to his forehead calms him.

The fire flickers, yet he's blinded beyond the trees.

Another gunshot.

"Nooo," he yells, only his voice chokes, and no one can hear him.

"SAMUEL, you're okay. I'm with you," a gentle, familiar voice reminds him. "I got you."

The safety in her voice pulls him out of his dream.

"It's okay, honey. It's only a bad dream."

Only a bad dream...

He wishes it were true because he'll never forget what happened next.

12

IVY

November 30, 1962

Venezuela

The days and nights have blurred from exhaustion.

My initial welcome was less than favorable from a corrupt group even though this country recognizes the Peace Corps.

The company I'm working for is somewhat smaller and less influential when bargaining with criminals. This particular group highjacked us the moment we pulled up in the jeep as though they were expecting my arrival. The moment I jumped out of the car, they grabbed and dragged me away, regardless of Maria screaming at them in Spanish. Looking back, I should have heeded the warning and got on the first ship back to Australia.

"They think you're a spy," Maria had yelled after me and not at all reassuring. "I'll have you released in no time."

Communication between the channels was poor, and for two days and nights, they kept me in a locked room, awaiting their decision on my fate. Each night seemed like an eternity when begging for the bathroom in a cockroach-infested derelict building.

It turned out these gang-like groups are everywhere and are not government-run. Regardless of any importance my visa and passport held, they were deciding if I could be of financial benefit to them.

Thankfully, Maria returned with the police before they decided my worth.

She told me I was lucky not to be kidnapped, taken away, and held for

She told me I was lucky not to be kidnapped, taken away, and held for ransom. I think the constant prayers to the universe helped with my fate, not so-called luck. And any investigation may have led them to believe I was a nobody.

Ever since, my nerves have been on edge after learning these raids happen at any time, and some villages live in terror.

It has taken a month for me to write about it.

On a positive note, it's been four weeks of doing what I came here to do.

There are no creature comforts in the indigenous village, and it has taken a while to adapt to sleeping in a hammock. Alongside the American and Brit volunteers, we spend nights by the fire discussing medical treatment if it's not raining. Apparently, the daily inch of rain is mild compared to what May will bring.

It has opened my mind and eyes as we practice without sterilization procedures or any hospital standards.

We sleep in thatched grass or mud structures. Every hammock is sheathed with mosquito netting, and along with a daily chloroquine tablet, I hope it's enough to ward off malaria.

After day one with Maria and the doctor, I realized there was no job description. I'm not sure of Diego's role, but he has done little to help me. If I can do something even if by Western standards it's considered doctor's work, then I attend to the patient as best I can.

In a matter of weeks, I have learned to suture a wound. It's more of a problem keeping the wound dry and clean so it can heal. Bandages are washed and boiled over a fire then laid over twine made into a makeshift line to dry before being reused. Resources are scarce, and if something can be reused, then its value is like mining gold.

Today, I have cared for babies with a fever. Measles broke out in the village, and although I contracted the disease as a child and have antibodies, I'm even more fortunate not to suffer from any serious side effects. Here, the treatment is difficult, and I'm relieved to learn about a vaccine. It's not available yet, however there are shipments going to major cities.

Our community isn't high on the list for distribution, and it angers me how the value of human life holds more importance in certain locations as can the color of your skin.

Racism is everywhere. I witnessed it in Australia with our own indigenous. Racism is one thing I'd love to see eradicated along with life-threatening diseases.

Over the years, I have watched the young and the old die. Another thing I hope to accomplish is to see vaccines offered to all, regardless of demography or social status. If supplies of the new measles vaccine were given to the indigenous, it could have a massive impact on survival rates and the spread, especially when it's often carried into communities by outsiders.

My time here is short, a year, maybe two. If I make it my mission to fight for this, then it's something I could be proud of when I return home to Albert.

For now, it's back to helping with basic hygiene, even assisting the dentist with oral care since no one even owns a toothbrush.

While we might be helping, Maria explained how many deaths in the community have occurred from respiratory infections. We're providing the care, yet the indigenous label us for bringing 'cough' diseases into their community, and the balance between remaining isolated or receiving help from the outside world swings on a pendulum.

Part of my duty is recording name, gender, date of birth, and estimated age in a registrar for our records. Not the work I signed up for, but at least I'm learning the names of some locals.

Once a fortnight, we get two days off, and Maria has already planned where she's taking me. Heading to one of the official holiday resorts in Canaima for a cold beer sounds good to me.

December 5, 1962
Camp Canaima

No experience or knowledge prepared me for tonight.

It's no surprise babies decide to come of their own accord. When a young girl who appeared no older than fifteen went into labor close to midnight, it's commonly perceived as a natural occurrence.

Maria translated the doctor's orders since most of the local volunteers communicated in Spanish or their native tongue.

Only the baby was breach and couldn't be turned.

With no definitive gestation date, the staff went by her size, and her stomach wasn't big. A rough estimation assessed her to be thirty weeks.

Regardless, she went into labor. We were concerned not only by the size of the baby but at thirty weeks implicated the probability of survival and multiple complications of the girl delivering a breach baby were highly likely.

For the next two hours, my stomach sat in my throat, and I wanted to puke with nerves. Extra help or emergency care wasn't available, as there's no nearby hospital and no roads lead to Canaima. By the time we got her on the canoe, then a plane, and to a city, it would be too late. And she owned no health insurance.

I'll never forget her screams as long as I live.

Never forget the way her eyes pleaded with mine.

Maria explained we were out of time to perform the ways of their labor rituals. The labor came on hard and fast.

She tried to squat, then the staff assisted her in lying down.

When dilated, the baby's bottom came into view. The doctor tried to maneuver the baby with his fingers, only the young mother's heart gave out first.

Maria and I performed CPR for half an hour.

The doctor delivered the baby, yet they pronounced him dead at birth.

It was the most heartbreaking and traumatic day of my life, and I experienced it in my first month of volunteering.

I wanted to mourn their deaths with her family.

So, I sat with them and cried and cried.

Me, the woman who had left her own child to be here to help them.

I need to make it all worth it after this devastation.

13

EDEN

PLACING Gran's journal on the side table, I swipe a tear from my eye. Samuel stirs beside me so I give him a moment to wake.

"Morning," I whisper. "Are you okay?"

He rolls onto his side and kisses me. "I am now."

"These dreams," I begin. "You're having them regularly. You need to talk to someone, if not me."

I stroke his face and wait for his eyes to open then he meets my gaze. "I'm not ready."

"Samuel."

"I'll talk to you eventually. It's not something I'm comfortable sharing, especially if questioned why I was there. I'm protecting the Ularans' location."

"I want you to talk to me. I'll listen to you any time, but I hate seeing you suffer." He doesn't respond. "Can you tell me what happened last night?"

He shakes his head. "It's not where I want to start. I'll tell you about Kaikare and her bravery during the hardest days. It's a positive memory, and it's best I start there."

I smile at my beautiful man. "Did she mention me?"

He kisses my lips. "Every day. She misses you, and said she tries to find your spirit when she takes the tea. She has connected with your Gran and hopes to connect with you too."

I gasp. "She visualizes Gran?"

He smiles reassuringly.

"Can she connect with me even though I'm not dead?"

"I've been thinking about this. If there's a time you could take ayahuasca safely, and if you connect with your Gran, which you already have, you could connect with Kaikare through your Gran's spirit."

This isn't the conversation I thought I'd be having with Samuel, yet it has offered some hope.

"Wow." I shake my head. "It's like in the movie *Ghost* when he's in Whoopi's body. She's a host or medium or something."

He chuckles lightly. "Or something."

I wanted to ask him more questions, except Rose has awakened, and he jumps out of bed to get her. He puts her in the middle for our morning time together, and I roll onto my side. I do love this part of the day when the three of us relax in bed as though there isn't a care in the world.

Tomorrow will be a different story.

This upcoming job could change him, and it scares me.

THE FOLLOWING night I'm sitting out front watching the golden orb sink slowly into the ocean. The crashing waves then the fizz of foam hypnotizes Rose and me until a noisy seagull squawks overhead and kills the moment. Rose screams in delight and reaches up to the bird.

"Don't, honey." I nuzzle her arm down. "It will think you're feeding it." I gaze out to the ocean to catch the last of the sunset along with walkers lining the foreshore, many with dogs on a leash.

I hear his car before I see it. It has a cacophony of sounds and is rocketlike when his foot is on the pedal. Even at a safe speed, as I know he's mindful of pedestrians, the sound is its essence. He pulls up beside me, and the window's dark glass lowers.

Rose's excited screams demand his attention. "Hey, baby girl. Daddy missed you." He stares at me. "How was your day?"

"Fine. Everything went according to plan. Mum said it was noisy, and we needed to apologize to the current guests." I shrug as we can't avoid it. "How was your day?"

"Different. Interesting. And yet the same." He glances down at the steering wheel. "Anything planned for dinner?"

Asking me this, I realize how food still consumes his thoughts, how it stresses his mind whether it makes him sick, and more so, why he isn't putting on weight.

"Mum has prepared a beef stir-fry."

A few hours later, I'm surprised when he finishes his meal.

Maybe he has turned a corner?

LATER, when Rose is asleep and we're ready for bed, he stoops over and grabs his stomach.

I go to him and place a tentative hand on his back. "What is it?"

"My stomach." He winces.

"You don't have to eat everything Mum offers." I rub his back. "You're not used to rich sauces."

"It's not it." A muscle ticks in his cheek.

I hate seeing him in pain.

"Something is wrong. Excuse me a moment." He rushes to the bathroom and closes the door. The distinct sound of puking comes from the other side.

I open it a little. "Are you okay? Do you want me to stay with you?"

"No, Eden. It's unpleasant," he moans.

I ignore him and burst in. "I can handle unpleasant." Kneeling beside him, I rub his back, unroll toilet paper, and give it to him to wipe his mouth. "Do you want me to wet a towel?"

He shakes his head and then lies on his side on the cool tiles.

"Honey, come to bed."

"I can't. I need to stay here a while," he whispers.

I leave him to fetch a pillow and then position the pillow under his head. I lay beside him and rub his back. "I'm not leaving you."

At two in the morning, we crawl back into bed, my back aching from spending hours on the cold bathroom floor. "Please get checked out," I murmur as I snuggle in beside him and he drifts off.

Only I can't sleep with my stomach in knots, so I research potential causes on my phone. Apart from food poisoning, indigestion, migraines, and gastroenteritis, other causes were from medication, excessive alcohol, motion sickness, or chemotherapy. God, I hope my mother hasn't poisoned him. No one else is sick, and he said it was more than indigestion.

I research some more and find encephalitis, appendicitis, meningitis, intestinal blockage, and brain tumors as likely causes. He had his appendix out as a child. I know he'll rule out everything I mention and shrug it off in the morning.

Researching on the internet makes me even more concerned for him.

And doctors can be the worst patients.

COME MORNING, I roll over to a space. Samuel is up and gone without disturbing me. I let out a long sigh. I hope he's okay for work today. Yesterday, he talked a little about his position and how he's still working his way around a new building.

My day was uneventful, and I sent a text to Samuel every hour, asking for an update. I received one reply at lunch saying he was fine.

We've barely seen Dad the last few weeks with business trips and a dinner in the city with clients last night, but tonight he hopes to chat with Samuel. When Faith called in for a quick visit and offered to take Rose for a sleepover, I said yes far too quickly, hoping for some alone time with Samuel.

I'm in the kitchen preparing fish and a leafy green salad for our dinner when Samuel walks in.

"Hey, you're just in time."

He comes to me and plants a kiss on my lips. "Sorry I'm late. Where's Rose?"

"Having a sleepover at Faith's."

His brow creases.

"She's fine," I murmur.

"Samuel, come and sit, and have a drink with us," Mum calls from the living room.

"Evening, Grace." He nods at Dad. "Sir." He shakes his hand.

"Please sit, son. How was your day?" Dad asks with his feet elevated in a recliner chair.

"Busy. Most of the day is at a computer reading material relative to the residency and reorientating myself, and then I'm on a ward with my supervisor."

"Dinner is ready," I call out. "You can have a drink after dinner."

I place Samuel's meal in front of him.

"Thank you. It looks delicious." He turns to my father. "How was Sydney?"

"Too busy for me." He chuckles. "Beach-side real estate is five to ten times more than what you pay here. We're blessed with one of the best sunset views in the world."

"This is true," Mum adds. "It's why our guests keep coming back."

The simple conversation continues until we finish cleaning the dishes. I'm distracted and hurrying to clear the table so I can get some quality time with Samuel.

"Samuel has some studying to finish, so I'll see you both tomorrow," I say to my parents.

"Eden," he says to me as we head to our bedroom. "I wanted time with your father."

"Not tonight." I take his hand. "You need to rest, and we need to talk."

After showering, I climb into bed, and before I say anything to Samuel, his face changes color. "Are you okay?"

He closes his eyes and winces. "No, not again." He races out the door toward the bathroom. I'm right behind him, sitting on the white tiles, stroking his back.

"It's not food related. The fish was grilled, and the salad contained nothing to upset your stomach. What's going on, honey?"

"I'm not sure," he mutters and wipes his mouth.

"Is it stress? Because you don't need to continue along this path?"

He leans over the toilet and bows his head. "It's not stress. I'm enjoying the work."

I shake my head. "Then you need to get checked."

He pukes again. "Go back to bed, Eden. I'll be fine."

"You're not fine. This isn't normal."

He closes his eyes and hunches his shoulders. "It's the next stage of grief. I'll be fine. It's simply a bodily response."

Grief?

What have I made him do?

THE FOLLOWING day I can't stop thinking about Samuel, so I call Yasmine for a chat. "Can grief cause disease? Because Samuel is vomiting, and it's the first symptom to come to the surface besides his nightmares. I'm wondering what else he's not telling me."

"He asked for time, right?"

"Yes."

"He knows he should talk about it, only I'm not sure his mind or body is ready. He's with you, and he's loved. Show him he's in a safe place," she says in a gentle tone.

"All he wants to do is give Rose and me financial security. New cars. A new house. He's talking about enrolling her in the best private school. This isn't him. It's not us. I'm not sure why he's doing it." I close my eyes and imagine the worst as if he is setting us up for when he's no longer around.

"He's lost. He's acting like he did back in LA. You need to put your foot down and stop him from spiraling downward. Tell him you don't need material things and find a balance between city life and his life in the rainforest."

"You're right." I pause for a moment. "I need a plan. Can you meet us this weekend?'

ON SATURDAY NIGHT, Samuel and I park in front of Yasmine's.

"I'm not staying." He kills the engine. "I need sleep, but you should stay and hang out with your friends."

I pat his leg. "It's a quick visit." My intention is for him to talk, have some fun, and maybe reminisce about Ulara with Yasmine for positive reasons.

"Deanne and Amy are on the front balcony," she says after letting us inside. "Do you mind if I steal Samuel for a moment?"

"Sure." I release his hand so he can follow Yasmine."

"Bubbles is in the fridge door," she shoots over her shoulder.

As I fill a crystal glass with sparkling wine, I overhear Yasmine from the bedroom.

"Lie on the yoga blocks for a few minutes. It will open your heart space."

"And why do I need to do this?" he asks. I imagine him with his arms crossed over his chest and a defiant expression.

"We've all had a broken heart, Samuel. This exercise will help."

I choke on the first mouthful. *God, I love my friend. She knew how to help him without my asking.* Trusting my man in her care, I head out to the balcony.

"Eden." Amy jumps up and gives a tight hug. "I've missed you."

Deanne stands and gives a lighter hug. "You've had a haircut."

Deanne shakes her head, and her brown tresses jiggle with the movement. "I wanted short and manageable since I'm thinking of traveling to Peru with Yasmine until she meets up with Michael. Then I'll do my thing. When she's ready to come home, I'll accompany her back."

We clink our drinks. "She'll appreciate that."

It's reassuring to know Yasmine will have a friend if she needs one.

"How's your week been?" I ask Amy.

The girls tell me about their week, and then finally Samuel emerges from the bedroom with Yasmine.

"Good evening, ladies." He sits down and looks west toward the ocean.

From Yasmine's apartment, we can see a sliver of ocean between the tall buildings, a perfect slice of heaven at sunset. Splashes of orange and pink line the horizon on a cloudless night.

"What are your plans for the evening? I assume you're not dressed like this for Eden's and my sake."

Amy points a finger and makes a clicking sound. "Very observant of you. We're heading to The Shores." She shrugs. "A standard Saturday night."

He turns to me. His brow pinches. "Did you do this every weekend?"

"Not always, but at least once a month."

He nods slowly as understanding crosses his face.

"Why?"

"Do you want to go out?"

"No. Why?"

He shakes his head. "Because I don't want to stop you from having fun with your friends."

"You're not."

"Samuel," Amy says, demanding his attention. She runs her hands along her long blonde ponytail to sit it over her shoulder. "If we had a man like you, then we wouldn't be heading out either."

"That's not completely true," Yasmine murmurs. "We'd be more selective on where we'd hang out."

Amy points to Yasmine. "Right, girlfriend." She turns back to Samuel. "Guys hang out at The Shores. Most we know and..." she rolls her eyes, "... we won't go there, but we hope to meet someone *nice*."

"Nice?" Samuel tightens his brow. "You mean perfect for you."

"Exactly."

"Never settle for anything less, Amy."

Amy sighs. "Eden, can we please take Samuel out with us? I need him to say, *not that guy*."

I laugh. "One day, Ames." I rub his leg and tilt my head toward my friends. "Deanne is heading to Peru with Yasmine. I told you she lived in Brazil for a year, right?"

Samuel asks Deanne some questions, and before long, Yasmine joins the conversation as it swings to Ayahuasca and its purpose. I overhear a few pointers and let out a long breath when he tells my friends it's not a 'fix-all tonic,' and you need to prepare. He explains how everyone reacts differently, and then he asks why they want to take it.

"Need a refill?" I ask Amy. She stands, and we head inside.

"I feel excluded, not wanting to drink the tea," she whispers once we're out of earshot. "You and Samuel... after seeing what Yasmine went through, it scared me. I don't understand her fascination with it?"

I hand Amy her glass of bubbles, and we sit on the couch to give the others some privacy. "She's heard stories. It's why I wanted Samuel to speak to her. He had a terrible experience and wants Yasmine to be aware because, like he said, it doesn't fix everything, especially only once. I was lucky." I shrug. "Although I was also in a different headspace. I don't want to do it again, but..." I shrug because after what Samuel told me about connecting with the spiritual world, I understand our world is more dimensional than what most of us believe. "I never say never to anything now."

She clinks my drink with hers. “Never say never to finding a perfect man at The Shores nightclub.” She raises her glass before taking a swig.

I smile at my gorgeous friend. “You’ll find someone when the universe says so. For now, the stars might want you to find yourself first.”

14

IVY

December 8, 1962

We sat around the fire tonight, all the volunteers sitting on fallen tree stumps. Each stump seated three or four people, and it's the time of night when we discussed our day. A long day, to say the least.

I haven't recovered from the young girl dying. My heart feels like it's been ripped out of my chest, stomped on, then thrown on the fire before being transplanted back into my body. My throat burns, and my mouth is dry. There never seems to be enough water, and although they have some sort of treatment for the well-water before boiling it in pots over the campfire, my stomach hasn't adjusted.

And the drop hole of a toilet isn't ideal.

Only our discussions are important to brainstorm what we feel is problematic in the village. Felix sat next to me and assumed he could educate me on infectious diseases. He's in his late twenties and from London. I like him, although his tone often sounds like he is talking down to me.

He alleged some symptoms could be from worms entering through your feet. He reflected on how he read up on it in the Australian indigenous community.

I informed him it's Strongyloidiasis, a parasitic worm. Although I didn't believe it to be the cause here, I know not to rule anything out.

Not to take any chances, I adjusted the strap on my dusty sandals since the

Not to take any chances, I adjusted the strap on my dusty sandals since the parasite enters through the feet. The symptoms of the parasite—cough and a wheeze, body rash, and abdominal cramps—are signs of many potential causes and diseases.

Our deliberation was interrupted when Jennifer, the American nurse, mentioned one child presented with symptoms of yellow fever, although it could be malaria. She asked me to assess him in the morning. Jennifer is twenty-one and came here as soon as she completed her nursing certificate. Her mother had also volunteered, and Jennifer wanted to do the same in her honor. Since I'm older than Jennifer, she valued my opinion in the few weeks we worked together.

Although Felix is older than me, he hadn't studied infectious diseases and seemed put out when Jennifer asked for my advice.

As much as it honored me that she valued my opinion, I suggested speaking to Dr. Leon and Maria, as they held more experience and authority than me.

Despite my exhaustion, I'm fulfilled by doing good deeds in my life.

My dream to volunteer centered around helping those with poor medical supplies and caring for the sick. Beneath the positive reinforcement, I struggled with the truth. It didn't prepare me for the heartache or the suffering, especially the children. Late at night, I second-guess my decision, especially when I have my child and husband at home without me.

Exhaustion plays a significant part in my mindset, yet I must do more than simply help with the symptoms or make people comfortable before they die. How can I prevent the diseases? An impossible feat with limited finances and supplies.

Everyone deserted the fire for an early night, allowing me to write entries in my journal in private.
Maria strolled by and suggested we go on a tour to Angel Falls on our day off. She told me I'd love it, and it would help me forget about the humidity, something I'm still not coping with, but it's the least of my worries.
Earlier tonight, Jennifer had complained about the rain. She said it's nothing like the rain in Minnesota because it's freezing and more likely to snow. She described it here as hot rain saturating us to our bones.
She made me laugh, and I enjoyed listening to her American accent.
Diego said we're due for a heavy wet season.
Few of the huts here are on stilts. Some are barely raised.
Do they frequently rebuild since these huts aren't built to last?
The rainy season...
What the hell was I thinking coming here?

December 14, 1962

Every letter I send to Albert, I finish it with the same words.

Miss you and love you both very much.
All my love,
Ivy xxx

I don't expect any letters in return. Although, in this letter I have given the Canaima Lodge address. I have wished for them to have a wonderful Christmas and asked for them to not miss me but make this Christmas one to celebrate together. Make happy memories with my son as I'll soon be home and have many more Christmas with them, and my time away will be forgotten.
I posted the letter at the main lodge in Canaima.
Tomorrow, we will travel by motorized canoe to Angel Falls.

December 15, 1962

It was a little after dawn when I met Maria, and we boarded what she called a curiara to travel along the river—a wooden canoe with planks for called a curiara to travel along the river – a wooden canoe with planks for seats and nothing but a motorcycle motor to propel it along the river.

I held onto the edge of my seat as we sailed along the river for five hours, only stopping when we ladies needed to find a shrub to pee behind. And it had to be strategic as the rainforest walled most of the river in. The guides knew where to stop, and I was amazed by the abundance of flowers and bird life surrounding us. In these pockets, the bird songs overpowered the screech of the monkeys, and it was refreshing to hear. Maria told me the rapids were okay to ride through as it's outside the wet season. It's why she urged me to take this trip sooner rather than later, as the waterfall slows to a drizzle soon and is not so impressive.

Nearer to the falls, we disembarked the canoes and trekked uphill through the rainforest. My fitness is shocking, and I struggled to keep up with the guides' pace. Thankfully, they stopped to show us macaws and a toucan in nearby trees. I was sure the monkeys were laughing at me.

I find them to be cute animals and also a menace when they steal our hats and bottles from the campsite.

I don't know how long we walked, yet it was worth it to see the majestic waterfall. I had to cover my eyes from looking up directly into the sun to see the beauty of the waterfall in its entirety. Maria mentioned it's the tallest in the world, and I simply stared for minutes at the rocky formation of the mountains surpassing the clouds in the sky. Thankfully, I snapped plenty of photographs on my camera.

The lagoon below the falls is one of the cleanest water pools I have ever swam in, and even here in the tropics, the cool water temperature surprised me. It was a much-needed dip before the return hike down the hill, only to stop to admire the various plants, orchids, and animal life.

On our trek back, Maria told me she had spotted a puma. I quickly caught up to the guide and remained by his side until we reached the river. She laughed at me and said it was a puma, not a jaguar. I told her wild cats don't roam freely where I'm from, well, not the kind that eats humans.

On the trip home in the curiara, we discussed the myths of Angel Falls and the surrounding flat-top mountains.

Tepui is the indigenous term. I believed the mythology to be all fairy tales until we came to a fork in the river, and the mood in the canoe changed. We sailed past the confluence in silence. Beyond the overhanging branches almost blocking the river opening, I could see a short distance ahead. There were children swimming in the river.

I pointed them out to Maria, she shook her head, and covered her lips with *one finger. The silence piqued my interest, especially when I sensed happy children. After studying science and nursing for years, surely, she'd understand I didn't believe in hoodoo.*

So, I waited many hours until we arrived safely at Canaima Lagoon, and I asked her why she couldn't talk about the people living along the secret river.

She spoke about tribes that missionaries haven't touched. These tribes refused to have contact with the outside world. Not influenced by modern man, they live solely off the land and use the jungle as their pantry. It's not unlike the community at our camp. It's not like we have a shop to buy groceries. The men hunt and fish and the women work the fields and cook the meals. In the few weeks I've been here, I've lost any excess weight I may have carried by comfort eating chocolate. Even on the boat trip over, I packed enough blocks of chocolate to ration over the months at sea. It helped with the nausea and gave me some energy when I couldn't stomach the ship's food.

When I asked more questions, she said a powerful shaman lived there, and the Pemón community respected their privacy. Many years ago, Caucasian religious missionaries breached the river opening and were shot at with poison arrows, so she emphasized we must not travel there. Ever.

It should have been a red flag.

A clear warning, yet it has sparked curiosity to see these people living in their native life. I don't want to interfere or make contact, simply observe. I'm not a religious missionary trying to convert their way of life to follow my god or behave a certain way in a modern world.

I merely want to sit on the bank on the opposite side of the river and observe from behind the trees.

No one will even see me.

Maria doesn't have to come with me.

I know the way and could borrow a canoe and be back by dinnertime in one day.

December 20, 1962

After giving another letter to the lovely man at reception, I walked the trail back to our camp. It was a five-mile walk each way, and it gave me time to reflect and understand the overwhelming emotion that keeps hitting me like a freight train from the moment I open my eyes.

Overnight, we lost three children to measles, a disease that spreads like wildfire. It could decimate this community as the people have no immunity. One child suffered respiratory complications, and sadly, I assumed pneumonia killed him in the end. The other two were from encephalitis. I believed both girls were recovering. One day, they were sitting up talking and eating. Their fevers had broken. Then their brains stopped communicating with the muscles. In a short time, they couldn't move, fell into a coma, and died.

I'd seen it before and should have known not to be complacent in the recovery window. Measles fools us all.

Measles didn't distinguish between the rich or the poor or the color of your skin.

We have developed some immunity from our society, yet I still fear for the young children back home. Here, the indigenous have no immunity from a disease transported to their community from Europe, America, and Australia.

Microbiologists in the United States are trialing the vaccine.

It can't come quickly enough.

15

SAMUEL

Dr. Tolley appears in the doorway of where Samuel is sitting at a desk finishing the notes of a patient he reviewed.

"Dr. McMahon, please come with me." She turns and heads out of the room, and he catches up to her in the long hallway. "Dr. Edwards is performing a lower leg amputation on an osteosarcoma patient. They cleared us to watch from the observation windows." She gives him a curious look, one questioning why Samuel has special status when he's only been at the hospital a few weeks.

He offers no explanation and instead walks in silence.

Dr. Tolley is a tall, dark-haired woman in her late thirties, he presumes. She has more clinical experience than him, yet she's only a few years older. He senses a drive in her that can't be taught, and he ponders if he could open her eyes to the wonder of treatment beyond these walls. Modern medicine saves lives, except Samuel believes there's a place for modern and natural medicine to work together side by side to complement and strengthen the other.

They scan their ID cards, and thick double doors open to another long hallway with multiple side doors. They pass radiology and the nuclear medicine departments before scanning their cards once more, and the large doors open to a smaller room void of any furniture. Dr. Tolley is required to scan her card and then punch in a pin to enter the next door.

“The pin changes daily…” she tells him, “… depending on the surgery and the surgeon.”

Samuel follows her along a wide passage with windows beginning from his hip and extending to the ceiling where seats are positioned behind the glass. It reminds him of his residency training in California, viewing surgeries from an upper level.

The staff, including his supervisor, Dr. Tolley, aren’t privy to Samuel’s background or his training in California. As far as they know, he has no experience in a specialty except for Professor Roxby, his father’s contact who could pull all the strings, including his clearance for today’s procedure. The professor passed Samuel to work as an intern for a year and then return to his oncology specialty training. Before his time in Ulara, Samuel was two years into his specialty training in California before deciding to quit and volunteer abroad, a decision that brought him a mountain of happiness and an equal amount of distress to his father.

Samuel has never been interested in performing surgery, only specializing as a physician. Only his past decisions landed him two steps backward in his training. And if he never went to South America, he’d never have changed and, more importantly, never met Eden.

Eden has led him on a path to finding genuine happiness. Hence, he has taken a full circle in his medical training. At the very least, he’s thankful he didn’t need to train from scratch.

Dr. Tolley brings up her iPad and opens the screen. “X-rays before and after chemotherapy are available to view. The patient insisted on the chemotherapy although amputation was inevitable.”

Samuel has seen a similar surgery performed many years ago. Yet he remains tight-lipped and listens to Dr. Tolley, awaiting new findings in modern technology to be mentioned. When she discusses the remaining muscles and skin form a cuff around the bone to fit in the end of a prosthesis and the new prosthetics available—all a vast improvement from what he remembers—she has his full attention.

He returns to the ward many hours later and is to work alongside Dr. Tolley for the rest of the day. Her stiff manner softens as the day progresses, and when in a room with a man in his forties and his two children are playing nosily by his bedside, Dr. Tolley surprises Samuel with her gentle approach.

“Dr. McMahon, this is Mr. O’Toole.” She turns to Samuel. “A MVA patient with multiple fractures, and after further blood tests and x-rays, they diagnosed Mr. O'Toole with leukemia," she says softly. "His wife is in labor in the maternity ward."

"Afternoon, Mr. O'Toole," Samuel introduces himself. He picks up the chart and assesses his medication. "Are you in any pain?"

"No pain," Mr. O'Toole grunts.

Dr. Tolley leans closer to Samuel to speak. "The problem we have..." she whispers, "... is he doesn't trust us. Believes we're creating more illness by having him here."

One boy plays with a car on the floor, and the older one has picture cards spread out on the floor. Dr. Tolley smiles at the boys. "Are we having fun?"

"Vroom, vroom," the child roars, and Dr. Tolley chuckles. "Their aunt should be here soon to collect them." She turns to Mr. O'Toole. "We'll keep you updated on your wife when we hear more."

"I should be there with her," he snaps. He turns to the tubes coming out of his arm. "If you could disconnect me, I could *walk there myself*," he roars. His head flops back onto the pillow, and his face pales as though he realizes he's incapable of walking the distance.

"As soon as your sister arrives to take the boys, we'll set you up in a wheelchair so you can be with her. She's only in the early stages," she reassures, then turns to Samuel. "It happened quickly. His wife went into labor while visiting him this morning and went to the labor ward from here. We're waiting for her sister to finish work to pick up the children."

A nurse joins them in the room. "Excuse me, I was just talking to your sister on the phone. She apologizes for being held up and will be here in five minutes." She places the call button closer to the patient. "Please call us if you need anything."

"A cuppa tea would be good, love." His voice softer for the nurse.

Dr. Tolley's phone buzzes.

"Attention, code blue in room 203. Code blue in 203," comes over the speaker.

"Follow me," Dr. Tolley instructs.

Samuel quickly matches her pace. His thoughts are racing quickly as he prepares himself for an emergency.

BY THE TIME Samuel arrives home, Eden and her family have finished dinner.

"I'm sorry I'm late," he says to Eden. He pulls her close and holds her for a few moments longer than usual.

"Are you okay?" She pats his back. "I just put Rose to sleep."

"Fine." He pulls away and kisses her lips. "Exhausted, that's all."

"Samuel." Mr. Monteford stands from the lounge and shakes his hand. "How was your day?"

Samuel does his best not to allow the exhaustion to surface. Mr. Monteford has wanted quality time with him when Samuel first arrived in Adelaide, only his busy schedule interfered with moments for meaningful conversation. Since Samuel began working, his thoughts have been associated around the hospital, and fatigue prevented him from spending time with Eden's family.

"Interesting and exhausting, yet I'm enjoying the work. I've missed the patient contact."

Eden frowns at him as though she doubts his words.

He enjoys the work, always the patient contact. It was the demands on his life, other aspects of how he was perceived, and the arrogance of his peers that wore him down. Along with Inesa's words, he viewed modern medicine in a whole different light. It's why he wanted to volunteer as a doctor and care for those who couldn't afford private insurance or more, to the point, they were not privy to any medical care beyond their community.

He bows his head with the memory.

"Are you hungry," Eden asks gently and takes his hand to lead him to the kitchen. "Are the long hours too much? You should wait until you're stronger."

"I'm fine," he murmurs. "Exhausted but fine." For the entire day, not once did a memory of Ulara come to mind, and he feels as though it's the perfect distraction.

Eden places a gentle hand on his back. "I'll warm up your dinner."

He sits at the table, and her father comes and takes a seat beside him. "I believe congratulations are in order with your new home and two new cars. If you need any help—"

"I'm fine, sir. It's the least I can do for Eden and Rose." Samuel is aware of table manners, yet he leans his elbow on the table to support some weight from his aching back.

"The least? This is extraordinarily generous of you, and please don't call me sir. You are my family."

Samuel stares at Mr. Monteford. He's not sure if it's a gentle prompt to make his relationship with Eden official or if he's being friendly. His blue eyes home in on Samuel, the intense color reminding him of his daughter's. "Thank you, I appreciate you saying that."

"Dad, do you mind if I have a quiet word with Samuel? You'll have time to chat when he's not so tired."

"I'm sorry if I imposed." He stands from his chair.

"Not at all, sir... I mean, Winston." Winston chuckles lightly. "I promise I'll be bubblier in a few days."

Winston presses a firm hand to Samuel's shoulder. "Of course."

Eden places a plate of roasted vegetables and a small piece of chicken in front of Samuel.

He grabs her hand. "Thank you. I know I haven't made our relationship official or set a date for a wedding, but I promise it's something we can discuss later."

She leans in and kisses the top of his head. "To be honest, it was the furthest thing from my mind. We both have a lot going on."

"Thank you for understanding. I really am the luckiest guy." Taking her face in his hands, he kisses her lips with the need to taste Eden more than any food. He dips his tongue and finds hers. God, she tastes good. If he had the strength, he'd carry her to their bedroom right now and lose himself inside her. His imagination shows, and his kiss turns into a wildfire burning on their lips.

"Samuel," she moans. "Eat first, okay?"

"I'd rather eat you," he whispers in her ear.

"When did you say we can move into our new home?" She bites his ear playfully. "I have so many plans for when we're in a bedroom with solid walls, and you can make me scream."

Her eyes drive him wild, weariness leaving his body with thoughts of tonight.

If only the happiness from Eden came in a tablet form Samuel could take every day. In the back of his mind, he knows even Eden can only heal him so much.

Now that the nightmares have returned, he's fighting something not even Eden can cure.

16

EDEN

IN THE DARK, I reach out to silence my phone on the bedside table. The high-pitch ringing sound brings me out of my sleep. Before I tap any buttons, I squint at the name on the screen.

Michael FaceTime Video

"Samuel," I whisper. "Michael is trying to FaceTime us?"

"What?" he murmurs. "How does he have your number?"

"Yasmine gave it to me a long time ago just in case. He's never tried to FaceTime. Something could be wrong. Is he trying to reach you?"

"What time is it?"

"Almost midnight." I sit up, flick on the light, adjust the covers, then swipe the screen. "Michael, is everything okay?"

"Morning," he says, all chirpy. In the background, the branches on the trees are swaying and a rustling noise comes through the speaker. Michael's face zooms closer as he takes a sip of coffee in a takeout cup. "I have no clue when an ideal time is to call." He hesitates. "Sorry if I've woken you."

Samuel pushes up and leans into me so his face appears on the screen. "Michael."

"Christ, you look like shit."

"It's the middle of the night, and I have work tomorrow, so what's up?" Samuel runs his hands up and down his face to wake himself.

"I know you're not in contact with anyone. Last night Brant was killed in a car accident."

I inhale a sharp breath. "Brant, who attended college with you both?"

On the screen, our faces are minimized in the corner. A dark shadow falls over his face, yet his expression is unreadable. It's how he processes emotion.

In Ulara, Samuel told me how Brant was not kind to Inesa, yet it doesn't make it any less sad.

"Right." Michael wipes an eye. "He'd reached out to me only a few weeks ago to say he got his shit together, and we planned to catch up. I put him off until next week." He looks into the phone and directly at Samuel. "We're not supposed to die at our age. And I've been waiting to tell you the same thing, that I have my shit together and finally working in a great accounting firm. Been promoted in less than a year."

This is what Yasmine has been trying to tell us.

"Michael, while I appreciate the call, I'm sorry about Brant, but I can't chat now. I have work in the morning, and so does Eden. We can do this on the weekend."

Samuel hits the end button and rolls onto his side. "Brant wouldn't have cared if I died in the middle of the fucking jungle." He pulls up the covers to his neck as I rest a gentle hand on his shoulder. "And I don't want to talk about it tonight."

I let out a sigh and switch off the light. The Samuel I know is compassionate and caring and, under the circumstances, would have given Michael the time to chat. I understand Samuel is stressed and exhausted. Only this isn't him. He was abrupt. Brant had changed. Michael is trying. The way Samuel is handling his stress concerns me. It's why he can't manage more emotion and sadness because his sanity is hanging on by a thread and could snap at any moment.

I slide down the bed and spoon him. Wrapping my arm around his waist, I simply hold him.

"I love you," I whisper.

For now, all he needs is love.

THE FOLLOWING MORNING, I don't recall Samuel kissing me, something he does before he leaves for work. I don't want to sound needy, yet I feel as though I've missed a step in my morning routine by not being woken by his lips.

My day is the same as the last few days with only a few hiccups in the pool construction. It's running smoothly, and I wish I could say that about Samuel's work. I can't stop thinking about last night and why he was terse, yet I know better than to bring it up with him again because I'm choosing my battles, and the bigger fight is for his health.

During my lunch break, I head down to Glenelg shopping district and wander through the bookstore. I stop perusing when I stroll past a table full of journals. One cover catches my eye. It has green vines and palm leaves in a jungle theme. I tuck it under my arm and notice another vivid white cover with the word GRATEFUL embellished in gold.

These past months, and after being inspired by Gran's journals, I decided to write anything that comes from my heart. And being grateful is a positive step. I purchase both journals before heading back to the office.

Ethan and Dana have other commitments after lunch, so I'm working alone in the office since Dad is at a meeting in the city.

Around three o'clock, I call it a day and head upstairs to see Mum and Rose.

After a quick cup of coffee with Mum, I set Rose in the stroller, and we head along the foreshore to inhale the fresh salted air. Steering the stroller down a path and onto the sand, I lift Rose out of the straps and let her feet touch the sand while I hold her hands. She smiles at me and stomps her little feet, giggling with the sensation. "This summer you'll be a little beach baby," I tell her.

She giggles again and looks up toward Monte's white building. "Dad-da?"

"No, honey. Dad-da won't be home early today."

It turns out Samuel hasn't made it home early all week and has not seen Rose since Sunday. *TGIF is all I'm thinking.* When Dad headed into the city for a meeting, he mentioned it would end up as dinner, and Mum would join them. With no idea what time Samuel will arrive home, I assume he won't get time with Rose until tomorrow morning.

After Rose tires of the sand play, we head back. With Rose on my hip, we walk past Mum's bedroom. The door is open, and she's sitting at the dresser applying the finishing touches of makeup.

"You look beautiful," I tell her.

She glances up at my reflection in the mirror. "Thank you, Eden." Her gaze moves to Rose. "Did you have fun at the beach?"

Rose squeals, wanting to play with Mum's makeup thinking it's paint.

"Not a chance." I reposition her on my hip to stop her squirming. "After I bathe Rose, I can drive you into the city. Then you'll only have one car, and if Dad has a few extra drinks..." I smile at her, "... it's one less car to worry about."

"Oh, honey, thank you, but it's unnecessary." Mum stares back at the mirror and smacks her red lips together. "I can catch a cab."

"Rose and I are visiting Aunty Yasmine anyway, so it's halfway there. It's the least I can do after what you have done for us. You deserve a fun night out."

Mum smiles at me. "I appreciate it. I assumed you'd be wanting some alone time with Samuel?"

"I do, although I doubt he'll be home early, so I've already messaged Yasmine to meet up with her."

As a teenager, Amy always had my back. If I worried and struggled with decisions, Yasmine was the one we both spoke to. Yasmine has a worldly instinct—she simply knows things, and she can see problems from multiple angles and help work out a puzzle.

Mum meets my gaze in the mirror. "It will do you good to chat with Yasmine."

She glances down at her nails. "Shoot. If your father gave me notice, I'd have had a manicure."

"You know what Dad's like with communicating his work schedule. I should have forewarned you."

JUST BEFORE SUNDOWN, I arrive at Yasmine's apartment.

Yasmine answers the door in a pink and green boho maxi dress. It looks great on her. She takes Rose from my hip, and I follow her to the lounge area. A lemongrass scent fills the air, and as we pass through her small kitchen, I spy a candle burning on the counter. She dots kisses on

Rose's cheek, then places her on the beige carpet and empties a small box of toys in front of Rose. Toys she's bought especially for my daughter.

"Thank you for letting us hang out here. I'm not sure when we'll hear from Samuel. He'll be relieved to find an empty house so he can go straight to bed." I place my bag on the counter and turn at the sound of a pop. "Have I missed a celebration?"

"No." She hands me a glass of sparkling wine. "You can have only one since you're driving. I can have more, although as we get closer to the flight date, I'll be abstaining from all alcohol."

"The date?" I take the crystal flute and have a long sip. I'm still scared for my friend.

Yasmine and I sit cross-legged on the carpet alongside Rose while she plays. She takes a sip of her sparkling wine before placing the glass on the coffee table. She picks up a toy and puts it in front of Rose.

Yasmine meets my gaze. Her brown eyes hold warmth, and her expression tells me she's not about to argue with me. "Michael and I will see a shaman, and then we'll meet with Deanne again. He's changed—"

"I know. He called Samuel the other night."

"I heard. He realized the timing was off, but he wanted to set up another time. He'd only just heard the news, and he rang Samuel before anyone else because he wasn't thinking straight."

"It was nice of him to reach out to Samuel, only his work..." I pause and take another sip of wine to cool my throat. "It's too early. He's exhausted from work. At this rate, in a couple of weeks, he'll be losing weight again from the stress." I meet Yasmine's gaze before saying what worries me most. "He hasn't given himself time to grieve."

"He could end up with PTSD," Yasmine whispers.

"At the very least." Pulling my phone from my jacket pocket, I check the screen for missed calls before dropping it back in my pocket. "I've bought him a journal and hope he'll make entries to ease the emotion he has inside. Of all the people, he knows how to handle grief, yet he continues to suffer and not share the burden with anyone."

Yasmine rests a hand on my arm. "You're waiting for him to break?"

An image of a waif-like Samuel flashes into my mind. He's withdrawn from society, and I feel his pain in a dark cave where he refuses to come out. "I keep seeing this image," I whisper.

"It's not real, Edes. That's *your* fear."

"I know. I can't even tell what stage of grief he's suffering. For the months after the shaman's death, I can't imagine him being in denial or anger as he bore a tremendous responsibility, and they were all close to dying. I sense guilt, and he's not going through the stages like other people, and it's a problem."

"How we cope is a personal journey. In Ulara, Samuel learned to view the world and deal with emotion differently than the rest of us. He needs time to process and adjust to his new life."

I sniff and wipe my eyes. I'm not crying, yet the tears fall on their own. Talking helps release the tension and the fear building inside me every day. "Part of his new life, going back to work in a hospital, is what will be his downfall. You know Samuel... he made a promise, and he'll never break it."

"Edes." She rubs my back. "Let it go. I know you want to protect him, but you have a battle on your hands that might end unfavorably for you. Give him the journal. Give him time. He'll find his way home." She offers a warm smile that reaches her brown eyes, knowing it's supposed to comfort me, yet I can't rid the gut feeling he won't be fine. "Find something to distract you."

"I've been reading Gran's journal, and it helps."

"Good. Go home and read some more but please stop stressing."

Rose stands and walks to the television then points to the screen. "Dogga. Dogga."

"Did you see that?" Yasmine's eyes widen.

"You walked by yourself," I sing. "She has taken a few steps, although she's all wobbly. To stand and walk, what a clever girl." I clap my hands, and Rose turns around. "You walked, Rose."

"And Aunty Yas got to see it first," Yasmine cheers.

I laugh at Yasmine. "She wants to watch *Bluey*."

"Anything for our angel." Yasmine turns on the television.

"You never told me the date of your flight?"

Yasmine pulls a throw blanket over her knees. "First weekend in November. I can't wait. It's the beginning of the wet season, but I hope it's not too heavy to visit Iquitos and do the ceremony straight up. We can tour later."

"Except you'll stay and prepare for a week?"

"Aha. I really can't wait, Edes. It's all I think about."

I reach for her hand. "Please listen to Samuel and follow his guidelines. You might see a vision, you might not. It's unpredictable. Whatever you choose, please stay safe."

"Of course." She brushes off my concern.

"When will you be home?"

"A few days before Christmas."

Christmas.

"You'll get to meet Samuel's parents. They intend on visiting."

"So, they'll stay with you in your new house?"

I hadn't thought that far ahead. "Now I know why Samuel is rushing into everything. He has an internal ticking time bomb to get his ducks in a line within the next three months to please his parents."

17

EDEN

LAST NIGHT I didn't hear Samuel come to bed.

Rose coos in the other room, so I creep out of bed, grab some clothes, and take them into Rose's room to dress. He needs rest, so I close all the doors in an endeavor not to wake him. After attending to Rose and changing out of my pajamas, I find Mum and Dad in the kitchen eating breakfast.

"Morning."

Rose holds her hands out for Dad. Like Samuel, she hadn't seen him for a few days.

"Good morning, our little angel. Do you want a banana?"

"Na-na," she repeats. Dad peels the banana, and Rose holds it while taking a little bite.

"How was your dinner last night?" I sit beside Dad and peel a banana for myself.

"Good. Dana and Kerry joined us. They're now moving before Christmas."

"What?" My heart sinks. "She said six months."

Dad inclines his head. "Circumstances have changed. Faith will work two days a week."

"Faith?" I choke. "At Monte?"

Mum chuckles. "I had the same reaction. It seems she now cares about what happens to the family business, and she'll be an asset in

HR." Mum is smiling as though it was all her idea. "We discussed one day of child care, and I'll look after her boys for the other."

"It's time for Rose to be in child care, mingling with children her own age." Here I was thinking about writing a resignation letter.

"Winston and I wanted to discuss this with you, especially about you working part-time."

"Really?" A weight lifts from my shoulders.

"Eden," Dad begins. "It's time. We'll hire a junior receptionist. If you and Faith work the same two days, it would be better for your mother and the business."

I'm smiling hard.

"I'll mind the three kids because they enjoy spending time together. I understand my limitations, and two days is reasonable," Mum adds. "Faith is insisting on one as she said childcare would be good for the boys."

"Finally, I get to work alongside Faith." I wink at Dad. "Could be dangerous."

He chuckles, and Mum laughs along with him.

Then I think about Dana. "I'll miss her," I whisper.

"We all will," Dad murmurs.

Are his eyes watering?

Mum pats his back. "Dana is excited for a new adventure but sad to leave Monte and us. They were notified yesterday Kerry's position is now in Cairns, not Brisbane as they assumed."

"It's a thousand-mile difference." I gasp.

Mum's nod seemed heavy. Final. "They're happy about it since Dana always wanted to live in the tropics."

"Morning." Samuel stumbles into the kitchen while rubbing a hand over his face. "I'm sorry I slept in."

"You didn't. It's only eight, and you had a late night."

"Emergency needed extra hands. Friday night is when everything turns nuts."

"Go back to bed." I offer an understanding smile. "You need the rest."

"Dad-da." Rose holds out her hands, and his face softens.

"Hello, beautiful girl." He takes her from Dad and swings her into the air. "Dad-da has missed you." He plants an exaggerated kiss on her cheek. "Do you want to go shopping?" He turns to me. "Have you found any furniture online?"

Furniture has been the furthest thought in my brain. At this point, I don't care if we sit on the floor. Can't he see his health is our main priority, not furniture shopping? "I thought we'd have a quiet day."

"We have a matter of weeks to organize furniture, and some can take months to be delivered."

"This is true," Mum adds.

The start of… getting his ducks in a row.

At least the three of us will be together.

We arrive home mid-afternoon, exhausted. While Samuel and Rose take an afternoon nap, I open Gran's journal.

Following Yasmine's advice, I'm distracting myself from worrying about Samuel. I understand he's on a path of recovery and finding a new purpose, and it's giving him a new direction and consistency. In consistency, he's finding security despite what he's doing to his health.

We are his responsibility.

His words, not mine.

He's stubborn in doing the right thing by us. The problem is his idea of doing right by us and working himself to the ground isn't what I want. It's his father's belief, and when we meet, I'll be giving Dr. McMahon, Sr. a piece of my mind.

Samuel mumbles in his sleep. I don't wake him, only listen. He sounds distressed. Anxious. Nothing he murmurs is comprehendible.

"Nooo." He gasps then rolls on his side.

For now, the nightmares may be the only way for him to deal with the trauma.

I don't wake him.

Instead, I distract myself as Yasmine suggested, and read the next page of Gran's journal.

18

IVY

January 5, 1963

Christmas came and went with minimal celebration.

I have received no letters from home, yet I'm unsure of the time a letter would take to find me, or it may even be confiscated somewhere between the Venezuelan shore and our camp. Every night, I hope and pray my husband and son are healthy and happy.

Are they missing me as much as I'm missing them?

Some of us celebrated in the new year when Jennifer brought bottles of alcohol from the Canaima resort. I'm not game to try the traditional alcoholic beverage after witnessing the women chewing yuca roots and spitting into a bowl. An enzyme in the saliva turns the starch into sugars, and it begins the fermentation process.

No thanks!

The volunteers love it. Jennifer and I prefer our beer in bottles, which is harder to come by, depending on who travels back to Canaima.

Today is my first day off in what feels like weeks.

One should be excited, yet considering I've seen nothing but death over the past seven days, I'd rather be working to distract my thoughts. I'm sinking into a mood pool of dark, murky quicksand.

It doesn't feel like enjoyable work when watching life drain away in a child's eyes. It's bloody torture, nothing less, and I'm not sure how much more I can take. And I can't spend my nights drinking beer to forget because there isn't enough pure water here to cure dehydration and hangovers. It's rained for ten days without a break, and I'm convinced it harbored the microbes which made saving the children more difficult. Maria told me it was unusual for this time of year. I'm thankful it's nothing but blue skies today, although the air still reeks of musty, rotten, decaying wet wood.

I need time on my own to reflect and recharge, so I asked to borrow the curiara and cruise the waters for a couple of hours. Dr. Leon was reluctant, especially with the lack of fuel for the motor. I reassured him I'd also use the paddles and not go far. He had listened to me cry night after night, and possibly it's the only reason he agreed.

My snacks are packed in my bag, and I'm ready for a few hours of peace.

How I feel in the jungle, the true essence of Mother Nature's heart...
After traveling the river for hours, I came to the river fork, killed the motor, and sailed beyond the long overhanging branches concealing the entrance. I paddled quietly, taking in the beautiful rainforest, untouched and full of animal life. I drifted closer to the shore and stopped to sketch the beautiful landscape before me. An eerie silence surrounded me. Today there was no laughter from children frolicking in the water. I sighted a sandy riverbank only a couple of hundred yards from the river fork, so I paddled to the bank, climbed out, and tied the canoe to a nearby tree trunk.
Sitting here, I'm surrounded by a sense of serenity. Apart from the mosquitoes continually buzzing above my head and the monkeys screeching in the treetops, there's no other life besides the plants, birds, and insects. Sitting in the sand watching the river current gives me a sense of contentment. Butterflies flutter past, and their beauty catches my eye. Their flight path is toward the trees where it lands on some berries, opening and shutting pretty blue wings.
Beyond the calm, I feel like I'm being watched. Only when I check, there's nothing. I can't ignore the tingles along my spine.
I'm rushing to write this last entry because I know I am being watched. I'm sure I saw a dark-haired man with equally dark eyes beyond the trees. Now he's gone.
I should return to the curiara and leave.

I'm back at our camp and writing this quickly before nightfall with no light in my hut.

My heart is still racing.

I want to write every little detail as I remember it.

When I turned back to the river, he was there, coming out of the water like a god rising from the river. Long, dark hair fell past his shoulders. He wore nothing except a twine skirt that didn't cover much, especially when wet. I dragged my eyes up his muscled, lean stomach and chest to those dark eyes that held me to a point I was incapable of moving. I stood so stiffly, if he touched me, I'd have fallen like a log to the ground. He stalked slowly toward me, and beyond his curiosity, he didn't look threatening. Because up close, he appeared to be a teenager, nineteen maybe. Only he had the body of a man, not a boy. Beautifully handsome for a wild man. For a few seconds, he stood there, staring. Then he reached out and caressed a strand of my hair, and I realized the source of his fascination. He didn't see me as a threat. Instead, my white hair confused him. And maybe my blue eyes because the way he stared sent shivers through my entire body. Voices sounded beyond the trees. He held up a hand and pointed to the river.

I didn't need words to comprehend what he was telling me. I fled in the curiara and paddled as fast as I could before any arrows reached me.

I keep telling myself I must never go back there again.

Yet, all I can think about is what would have happened next?

This place is messing with my sanity because what would have happened is his people would see me as a threat, and they wouldn't want an intruder observing them.

19

SAMUEL

THE GRAY HALLWAY of the hospital matches Samuel's mood. He has fallen into a routine like a robot.

Walking stiffly toward the meeting room, his life is no longer his own. He's back in society for her, for them both—acting responsibly, providing for his family, and doing the right thing. He'll do it for as long as he can, yet there are cracks in his façade.

Eden warned him it was too early.

He refuses to break a promise to his father.

In society, material things provide for more than love alone. And Eden deserves a luxurious house and car after what he put her through in Ulara. With the rest of his savings and inheritance now frozen, his wage is what will support them.

Yesterday he dreamed of Ulara.

Until it reminded him of his intrusion being the beginning of the end. How he failed half the people by the time they discovered a haven.

"Did you have a restful weekend, Dr. McMahon?" Dr. Tolley greets him and has already changed into scrubs.

"I did. Although we lost Saturday to shopping for furniture for our new house." He smiles because furniture was the furthest thing from his mind. In a small jewelry store, he found a perfect ring for Eden. A rose-colored diamond surrounded by smaller diamonds, the smaller diamonds embedded into the band.

Samuel went to hide it in the drawer as there was no ideal spot. They shared a space where Eden stashed scarves and gloves, and a drawer she wasn't using at this time of year. When he reached to the back, he found another box containing a ring with diamonds in the band. He considered it to be a gift, only the modern design wasn't an heirloom, and his thoughts drifted to one other person. The thought of how she came to be with it filled him with nausea.

"Dr. McMahon." Dr. Tolley's stern voice pulled him back into the room. "Are you okay?"

"Yes, I'm fine."

A lie.

He wasn't fine.

Not physically.

Not mentally.

Yet skilled enough to hide the truth from everyone.

20

EDEN

Six Weeks Later...

ON SATURDAY MORNING, I'm standing at the International terminal gate, and part of me wants to go on an adventure with my friends. With so many fond memories of our travels, I'm happy how Yasmine's following her dream and creating more memories.

People rush past making a dash for their gate. A buzz of excitement surrounds us with nervous and happy chatter. Looking around, there are mainly smiles and only the occasional wipe of an eye with loved ones saying goodbye. It opens a sad part of my heart, like a wound that hasn't healed completely when I remember saying goodbye to Samuel.

The second time was harder than the first. In hindsight, I'd have never gotten on the private jet without him if I knew what the future held for him.

"I'm going to miss you." I hug Yasmine one last time. "Please keep in contact."

"I will." Yasmine's eyes flick across my face. "Don't worry about me."

I feel happier knowing Michael and Samuel are talking again, chatting at least once a week. If Yasmine needed anything, I'm comforted knowing Michael would reach out to Samuel.

However, her expression hints at something else.

She hugs me again, only this time she leans in close and whispers,

"Samuel is having tests for his abdominal pain. He doesn't want to concern you." She leans back and looks me in the eye before her lips are close to my ear again. "You have known for a long time something isn't right. It's time you intervene."

"Ready, chickee?" Deanne comes in for a group hug. "See you at Christmas time, peeps."

Yasmine gives me one of her concerned looks then smiles at Deanne. I'm not about to rain on their happiness. "See you soon," I call out.

Wrapping my arms around my middle, I feel so alone watching my friends walk away and soon be in another country. Amy accepted a teaching contract in a country town for the rest of the year, and Dana leaves in a couple of weeks.

And now I find out Samuel is keeping a secret from me.

My chest is tight in an anxious way. Bit by bit I can feel my world crumbling around me. I need fresh air so I dash toward the exit.

After keeping my shit together on the drive home, I pull up in Monte's new undercover parking lot.

The pool is complete, and the accomplishment sends warmth through my chest. The car beeps with the security lock, and I stroll over to admire our design. The landscaping looks great with established palm trees and subtropical plants. It has the appeal of a resort along with covered street parking.

So much has happened in six weeks.

My brother, Will, came for a whirlwind weekend visit, and I'm glad he got to meet Samuel.

Samuel *is* making a life with us.

I need to focus on positives.

I'm working two days a week and spending more time with Rose.

We have moved into our new house. *Our* home, and I love it.

Life should be good.

Yet I feel dread in the pit of my stomach. And it's eating me up. Every time I try to speak to Samuel, he brushes me off.

And now I learn he has kept a secret from me regarding his health.

I head up the stairs slower than usual. Rose slept here last night as I stayed the night with Yasmine, her last night. I don't know if Samuel worked late. When Michael called Yasmine early this morning to confirm he had arrived in Iquitos, she went quiet on the phone.

It all makes sense now.

I swing open the door to Samuel playing on the carpet with Rose. "Oh, you're here?"

"Yes, I missed my girls, so I came for a stroll."

"He came for breakfast." Mum laughs. "Both have eaten blueberry pancakes."

"And now we have full tummies." Samuel tickles Rose's stomach, and she waddles away laughing.

Samuel jumps to his feet and comes to me. "I missed you last night." He pulls me in for a hug. "Are you okay?"

"Yeah. I just worry about her." I place a hand over his lower abdomen, glance at my hand and then look at him straight in the eye. "Like I worry about you."

His gaze flicks over my face. "She'll be home soon, and Michael has promised to watch out for both girls."

I decide not to quiz him further until we're alone.

"Did she sleep well last night?" I ask Mum.

"From seven to seven." Mum smiles. She packs up the last of Rose's toys and zips up her bag. "How was your night with Yasmine?"

"Fun. I'm happy for her, although I'm going to miss her."

"Perhaps you should make a trip to see Amy?" She hands me Rose's bag and smiles.

"You read my mind. I was going to call her tomorrow. Anyway, we'll get out of your hair as I'm sure you and Dad have plans."

"It's always a pleasure to have Rose. Dad popped out right before you got here, and when he returns, we're looking at some furniture stores. The couch is giving me a sore back so we're going shopping for a new one."

"Good luck. It took me weeks to decide." I grin at Samuel then pick up Rose and position her on my hip.

"Thank you for sharing your story of Dawn with Winston," Mum says to Samuel.

I look between Mum and Samuel. "Kaikare? What story?"

Mum places a hand on my arm as her eyes soften. "Samuel told us a few things about Kaikare... well, we like to think of her as Dawn."

"Nothing you don't already know, honey."

I bite my lip. He's finally opening to us, even if it's from years ago. It's a start.

Samuel walks Rose home, and I take the car. I drive into our underground garage and wait out front on our esplanade fence. In the distance, Samuel walks with Rose, holding her little hand. Then he lifts her onto his shoulders because at her snail's pace, it's going to take all day.

I pad the half-dozen steps to our double glass doors and press the code to unlock the doors. Rose takes each step by herself, screaming if Samuel tries to help her.

"Someone is quite independent." He laughs. "Shall we head to the beach for a picnic today?"

"You two go. I have washing to finish."

"No, Eden." He lifts my chin until I meet his beautiful blue eyes. "We're a family today. Everything else can wait." He kisses my lips, and I want to fall into his arms and beg him to tell me the truth.

On the kitchen island is a cane basket. Beside it is a large picnic blanket. "I have everything ready. All we have to do is apply sunscreen."

THE WAVES ROLL in one after the other and break along the foreshore. It's not hot enough to swim, and the water is cold on my feet. Rose jumps in the shallows then runs away as though playing with the waves in a game of chase.

"She loves the ocean, like you."

"Not as much as I love you." His gaze locks with mine, and there's a seriousness behind them, reminding me of our days in Ulara. "Rose, come here." She chases a seagull and attempts to waddle past Samuel. He scoops her up and swings her around in the air. He kneels and places her on one bent knee. Samuel whispers in her ear, and she giggles.

"Mum, Mum wing." She giggles again, and then he dips a hand into his pocket and gives Rose a box. Rose looks at me and holds it up.

"Not so quick." He laughs, taking the box and opening it. She screams, and he hands it back to her.

"Samuel." I gasp, realizing what's happening.

"I originally planned a candlelight dinner for the two of us. Only I wanted to include Rose as it really is the three of us, and I imagined no better place than here at our beach." He stands with Rose on his hip and her still holding the box in front of me.

With his free hand, he guides my hands away from my shocked face and takes my left hand in his. "All my life I have waited for you, and I never want to lose you again. I love you with all my heart and want to spend the rest of my life with you. Eden, will you marry me?"

I burst into happy tears as he slides the ring on my finger. "I said yes many months ago. A hundred times yes." There were times Samuel and I didn't need a ring to define our love. Nothing has changed, and yet my heart is full. It's a step forward to a future together.

"God, I'm glad it fits. When we went furniture shopping, I hid one of your other rings in my pocket and hoped I grabbed the right one."

"You're lucky I don't wear jewelry every day." I swipe the tears from my cheeks so I can admire my beautiful ring—a rose diamond. The significance to our daughter makes me choke out a sob. "I love you," I rasp. "You kept it a secret."

"A wonderful secret." He kisses me, holding my face to his. Rose giggles at our feet. He stoops to lift Rose and include her in our hug.

We continue playing along the shoreline until Rose whimpers so we pack up the picnic basket and cross the road to our home.

I wait until we are inside the house before I speak again, "Earlier, I was talking about *all* secrets." I hold his gaze and wait.

"Do you mean other rings as secrets?"

I freeze.

"I wasn't prying." His hand rests on my cheek. "When I was searching for a place to hide this box, I stumbled across another box. The only reason it concerned me is because it appeared new, and if you'd bought it, then I imagine it would be with your other jewelry."

Lowering his hand from my face, I take both his hands in mine. "You know I'm referring to you." I bow my head, knowing I should have told him about the ring Ethan gave me when he first came home, only it was the least of my concerns. "Yes, I should have told you." My eyes plead with his. "And I'll explain it, but first, I need to know about these tests you're having for abdominal pain."

"It's nothing to be concerned about." He lifts my hand, admires the new sparkly diamond, and kisses the palm of my hand. "I anticipated a parasite, which is of no surprise, or something else I contracted in the jungle. I'm having multiple tests for elimination's sake. I'm fine, so please don't be concerned."

"Easier said than done." I spring up onto the white marble counter and pull Samuel to stand between my legs.

His brow furrows. "Should I be concerned about the other ring?"

Oh, we're back to that. I let out a sigh. "You're changing the subject."

"Am I?" He leans in and kisses my neck. "And you're distracting me." He nips my skin.

"You also said to give you time," I murmur. He leans back, and his blue eyes turn dark, the same color when his mood becomes serious. "It's been ten weeks. Are you ready to tell me what happened?"

Samuel steps away and runs his fingers through his short hair. "I'm dealing with it in my own way," he mutters.

"By working yourself to the bone?" I croak out the last word as it holds more truth than anything. I reach for him so I can wrap my hands around his neck and stare into those beautiful eyes of his. "At least write in the journal. It helps. And then when you're ready for me to read it, it will be easier than you having to live it over again."

Samuel stares at me for several seconds. He nods, it's subtle, but I don't miss it. "Now, the other ring..."

"Dad-da," Rose trips and hits her head on the corner of the coffee table. She screams hysterically. Samuel grabs a clean dish towel and applies it to the cut while I hold her in my arms.

Blood is on her cheek and hands. "It's okay, baby," I whisper to soothe myself as much as her.

"Come here, munchkin." He takes her to the bathroom and sits her next to the basin. I help hold her hands while he cleans the blood away. She's still sobbing, and all I want to do is cuddle her.

"It's okay, Rose." I take her in my arms so she's at eye level for Samuel.

"It's close to her eye." He shakes his head. "She is lucky. I'll grab a surgical pack to clean it and then dress it."

"Does she need stitches?" I shout after him.

"No, I have special glue I can use."

I play games with Rose in the mirror to distract her until Samuel returns.

"I also have Moo-moo." He hands Rose her special pink fluffy toy she sleeps with or cuddles when she's upset.

Rose takes Moo-moo and squeezes it close to her chest. I lift her chin, and she watches Samuel's face closely as he assesses her. She stares at the glue as he applies it, and when it dries, he covers it with a tiny piece of dressing.

"How long will this last?" He winks at Rose.

"Were you seriously asking Rose?" I laugh.

He lifts her down and ruffles her hair. "Go slow, kiddo."

"I bought a round coffee table so we wouldn't have accidents like this." I follow behind Rose.

"It was impact, Eden. Her skin just split. Happens to kids all the time."

I settle on the lounge next to Rose and switch on the television for her to watch her favorite program. "Do you see a lot of kids at the hospital?"

"Some." Samuel comes and sits beside us. "You were about to tell me something before Rose fell."

I take his hand and envelop it in mine. "Before you came back, I felt lost. Afraid. Ethan was there for me and as a *friend*," I emphasize the friend part. "He was trying, and over eight months, I knew he'd changed." Samuel says nothing, yet I sense his contempt for Ethan. "On my birthday, he gave me a gift, a friendship ring."

"Eight diamonds as a friendship ring and no strings attached?" The lines on his forehead deepen. "Bullshit," he states. "He hoped for more."

"True," I say quickly, not wanting to lie. "He knew I wasn't ready. Two days later, you came home. I tried to give it back, but he said to keep it. A gift and nothing else."

"Did you ever wear it?"

"Twice. Before you..." I swallow hard.

Samuel gazes at the television, and I can't read his face. "You realize by keeping it he'll always think there's hope for you two."

"I told him there's not. You're the love of my life."

His brow furrows, and his gaze lowers but not to me.

"They're simply words to guys like Ethan." He turns and looks me in the eye. "It's best for both of you if you give it back. It's not just a friendship ring. Otherwise, he would've gifted you a candle or something less committal."

I let out a long sigh. "You're right. I didn't want to rock the boat. He's still a friend."

"And a friend would understand you'll never wear the ring. Please give it back."

Samuel's right. My concern isn't what he'll do with it. Because I'll never wear it. It's sitting there, a waste of money. If it's mine to do whatever, then I could sell it, except we don't need the money. He's never given Bree a ring like this, and he's closer to her as a *friend* than me.

It's true.

Keeping it gives Ethan hope.

"I'll take it to work on Monday."

21

SAMUEL

SAMUEL NEVER TOLD Eden the truth.

Not a lie as he has had every test, including those for parasites, and still no findings to indicate a reason for his extreme abdominal pain. He doesn't believe stress or grief is the cause. The nightmares are happening less. Yet his health isn't improving. The lethargy remains, and he's struggling by the end of the day, barely placing one foot in front of the other.

Sundays with his family are special. Soon, he'll be working weekends. Eden will be alone for longer periods, and after what she said about Ethan, he knows the douchebag will take every opportunity to win her back. He hated himself for insisting she gives the ring back. It's not in his makeup to be jealous, but when it came to *him*, Samuel isn't taking any risks.

He rolls over on the couch and stares at his beautiful fiancée. In his heart, they're already married, sealing their love in Ulara. Except society measures a couple in other ways. Family and friends have expectations. A shaman's ceremonial word will hardly convince Eden's father that Samuel is here for the long ride.

Eden's eyebrows pinch. He checks the book she's reading—her grandmother's journal. The words inside have opened a new world of understanding of her grandmother, and Eden wants Samuel to do the same. The journal she bought him is on the coffee table, a pen beside it.

He picks it up, and Eden's eyes meet his. No words, only understanding. Her gaze lowers to her grandmother's words of the past.

Samuel opens the first page of his journal.

His mind refuses to cooperate, so he acts as if he's at work and making initial notes.

December 2018

- *Eden is safely on a plane, and when I return to Ulara, everything has turned to crap.*
- *The shaman is shot.*
- *I make a promise to protect Kaikare and lead the Ularans to safety. The promise includes continuing Kaikare's training to be a healer. I deliberately avoid the word 'shaman' as I have taught her to incorporate some modern medicine practices.*
- *Convincing the elders to leave immediately didn't happen quickly enough. Kaikare stepped in, and I realized I had to earn their trust in my role as a leader.*
- *Many of the elderly knew they wouldn't make the journey, which is why they refused to leave and preferred to die in the only home they have known.*
- *When I couldn't convince them otherwise, it again divided the people as they knew I deserted them to their own fate. When I asked Asoo if he could investigate their well-being, he told me he already heard the miners had taken over the area, and the elders were gone. What or how he doesn't know, but it was too risky for him to ask further questions. I didn't want to implicate him in any way.*
- *For several weeks we walked and slept in makeshift camps, pacing ourselves for the elderly who attempted the journey. If I knew what I did now, I'd never have made them leave. They may have suffered less if death came by way of a bullet in Ulara.*
- *For months, my endeavors to save them led many to their fate. Some of them were aware and yet trusted me with their lives. The burden became heavier every passing week, especially when my survival looked bleak.*
- *Kaikare is the strongest person I know.*
- *People died because of me.*

22

IVY

January 6, 1963

I'm sitting by the river, trying to organize my thoughts.

I haven't been able to stop thinking about my encounter with the long, dark-haired man.

Had he seen people outside the village?

I saw nervousness in his brown eyes, but curiosity overruled any fear. He didn't see me as a threat.

Maria came and sat by my side and spoke quietly in case anyone overheard. A gang, or soldiers as she calls them, came to the camp yesterday. They were looking for me. They aren't military, more-independent military gangs. She used another word, only I struggle with the Spanish terms.

They held Dr. Leon and her at gunpoint in their hut and demanded to know about me. She thinks they're looking for ransom money and unsure when they'll come again. She told them I'm no one of importance and only want to help the sick. They told her I could be of use to them.

God, why me?

So now we must be cautious.

She told me I should go home

She told me I should go home.

Wise words.

I should listen.

Only I have a gut feeling my work here isn't done. I have some sort of purpose beyond helping the sick. And more importantly, I want to be here for the measles vaccine and give this community hope.

Safety measures have changed, and we require an escape plan if I need it. Maria is organizing a shelter for Jennifer and me in a nearby camp. So, if we need to leave fast, we can take the boat and go there, then she'll come back and get us when it's safe to do so. She said they won't be back for a while as Dr. Leon threatened them, so we should have a plan just in case.

I then told her about the young man I saw.

Maria became angry.

She told me not only did I place myself in danger as the Ularans forbid any contact beyond their village boundary, they also have a powerful shaman. She reminded me of the young man who was shot at with poison arrows. Her mood changed when she explained the Ularans have occupied the land before we created any government, and they have a right of ownership in her eyes. Their neighboring communities have welcomed outsiders to help, but they're survivors and wish to remain hidden from the rest of the world. To do this, they must resort to more forceful ways and only use weapons they make with their own hands. Guns and steel blades are foreign to them, and if we reveal their existence, they could be wiped out in seconds.

I now understand the need to protect their home, their land. The Europeans have converted some indigenous communities to the Catholic religion and a white person's way of life.

Promises of a better life...

It wasn't until she chastised my irresponsible actions of possibly transmitting diseases, even the common cold to them, I realized the result could be dire even though, in my mind, I was being careful.

My selfishness surfaced to satisfy my curiosity. I could have created the very thing I'm doing my utmost to prevent here—a viral outbreak with the potential to kill.

I apologized to Maria and promised not to return.

She went on to tell me why.

Some authorities believe there are no isolated indigenous communities in Venezuela. Only relative isolation and have been in contact with missionaries. Few people are aware of the Ularans, and we need to keep it that way and respect their community's rights. The more they're spoken of, and if other missionaries believe they need outside help, it becomes known, and logging and oil companies will believe they have the right to the land and invade the boundary. Currently, it's certified we care for that part of the river, even though we never go there. We do all we can to protect the people. Maria then said she's impressed how I came out of it unscathed. Blonde hair is fascinating to the Indians, although she really doesn't know how I returned without an arrow in my back.

JANUARY 30, 1963

When Brenda told me she was excited to study midwifery, I felt sorry for her. At the end of our training, there were many other courses and pathways I wanted to follow, and midwifery wasn't one of them. My subconscious may have considered babies and marriage a doom for my career, and staring at vaginas every day and listening to screaming babies was unappealing, at least to me. After giving birth to Winston, I understand it's much more. And now here, in an isolated community, I'm grateful to have some experience. A total of thirteen babies have been delivered since my arrival. Brenda would be proud.

Five newborns and three mothers have died. I understand why they breed quickly because a child's future is uncertain. Many deaths come from the children not surviving viral and bacterial infections, and most fatalities are from pneumonia.

We need more antibiotics.

Maria continues to tell us supplies are coming. She also told me in confidence how the gangs were intercepting and stealing supplies for their own. I don't blame them for wanting our supplies to help their community, so why can't we order more so there's stock for everyone? It may create more peace. Then Maria reminded me of our lack of funds and barely enough for the community here.

I suggested we call the police, only she told me the policía would not intervene. I asked more questions, then she insisted I stop talking and accept the ways while I'm here. Focus more on surviving.

She suggested we spend the next weekend in Canaima and hang out at the local bar and relax.

I'm not sure if she meant relax and forget or relax and get off her back?

Either way, I'm happy to have a night to ourselves with a few bottles of beer.

23

EDEN

I CLOSE GRAN'S JOURNAL.

Samuel has placed his journal on the side table.

We stare at each other for a long minute before he speaks, "It's difficult." An indent deepens between his brows. "I don't know where to begin and what to write. Nothing will ease the p-pain." His voice cracks on the last word. I glance at Rose. The Disney movie is more than halfway in, and she's sitting quietly on the carpet.

Grabbing the soft cushion from my back, I place it on my stomach and hug it. "How about you start at the beginning?"

He shakes his head, and I'm not sure if it's a no or whether he's trying to clear his thoughts. "You know what happened in the beginning. The shaman was shot, and it forced us to immediately evacuate before someone came to inspect the explosion."

"And what happened once you began your trek into the jungle?"

He drags a hand down his cheek, closes his eyes, and slowly opens them. Those eyes convey emotion and deep sadness. "When we were away from Ulara, we gained a sense of security. Most of the people were accustomed to walking and hiking. Yet I held onto guilt for leaving several elders behind. The ones too old to hike long distances. Everyone transported their belongings on their backs. The women carried baskets of food on their heads. Young warriors offered to carry those elders on their backs, but they were adamant they would die in their birthplace.

These elders had no family, their sons and daughters having died before them. Ulara is a sacred place, and they believed their loved ones' spirit remained." He glances up with tears welling in his eyes then he blinks and closes his eyes tightly, and I can see him fighting the pain. "It killed me to leave them to die."

I pull Samuel into my arms and hold him tight. "Did you hear any more about them?"

He shakes his head. "When I reached LA, I called Asoo. There's no way he could investigate without bringing attention to himself. Illegal miners had overrun the area, and if he approached, they became hostile."

"And you believe you could have saved them if they came with you?"

His arms wrap around my waist, and he clings to me before speaking. "No."

"So, it was beyond your power?"

"Remove me from the equation as though I was never a presence, and they would still be living in peace."

"And we wouldn't be together," I whisper. "I believe it's fate, Samuel. Even my grandmother being drawn to Ulara was fate. She risked her life to find destiny." I massage his back in slow, gentle strokes but his muscles tense beneath my fingertips. "And during your time in Ulara you saved many lives and formed wonderful friendships. The people were lucky to have you, and the shaman and you learned from each other. In doing this, you passed on modern medical knowledge to Kaikare. As the new shaman, Kaikare is wiser for knowing you."

He breaks into a sob. I offer silence for him to deal with the emotion bubbling out of him like a hot spring, small therapeutic bubbles releasing from deep inside his mind.

"In the beginning... were you able to hunt for plenty of food?"

Samuel swipes his eyes. "We'd ventured deeper into the rainforest, and wild pigs and fruits were plentiful, thanks to the Ularans knowing where to search for food. We stayed a few days at each site with makeshift beds in hammocks and secured palm leaves overhead to protect us. Everyone packed mosquito nets. We were near a river with a good water source, and fires burned day and night, depending on where we stayed. We'd walk solidly for one day, then rest for two." Samuel blows out air between his lips as though talking exhausts him.

"I imagine it to be difficult, although it sounded like it was going to plan."

He nods slowly. "For about a month, it's what I expected."

He remains silent for a few minutes. Even if he doesn't tell me more, we've made more progress in the last hour than in the past two months.

"The rain came early."

I let out a sigh. Already I know of the hardship in the rainy season without being lost in the jungle.

"It was difficult to see more than a few feet in front and blinded to a ravine with raging flood water. Four men tripped and slipped down the muddy slope with water gushing like a waterfall into a newly formed river. Two young men we never saw again. The other two, Mari' Iwoi and Wayara, followed our path from the other side. If we became separated, they had a chance with Wayara's swift survival skills. A small sense of hope, but among the people, I sensed their loss of faith in me after losing the other two men. Even though the Ularans were exceptional at hiding emotion, the cracks were showing, and Kapeá Tapire sobbed, cuddling her child." He stops talking, and his blue eyes meet mine. "She reminded me of you. And at that point, knowing you were probably feeling the same loss and fear as her, I had to do everything in my power to get back to you."

I squeezed his hand then patted the pillow, so he settled his head on my lap. I stroked his forehead, hoping to relax him enough to keep talking. "You had everyone else to consider as well as me."

He closes his eyes as though he's visualizing the memory. "We continued to hike for half the day, only we needed to get up high off the ground. Everyone's feet were suffering, so we couldn't walk as far each day. We needed to dry out before fungus infections took hold." He blows out a long breath. "Maybe the spirits helped us, for after a few days, we discovered a tree had fallen across the ravine, and Wayara and Mari' Iwoi crossed back to us."

"Kapeá Tapire would have been relieved," I whisper.

His eyes open. "It wasn't that simple. The log was unstable, and it took some time for one of them to cross. It was slippery, and they crossed on their hands and knees. Wayara went first to assess the log. When it came to Mari' Iwoi's turn, he slipped and went upside down, clinging onto the log, but his fingers were losing their grip. Thankfully, the men found a vine and secured it to a tree. Wayara tied it around his waist and ran and jumped, grabbing hold of Mari' Iwoi, and they both slammed into the mud slope. The men then pulled them to safety."

"How scary. What were you doing?" My choice of words insinuated he watched and did nothing which wasn't my intention.

"I carried the chief's wife on my back."

"Oh, Samuel." I stroked his head again. "How long did you carry her?"

"Until she died."

We remain silent for a few long seconds.

"I'm sorry," I whisper.

"Sore Dad-da," Rose says and points to the cut above her eye.

Samuel stands and scoops her up into his arms. "I'll get her some pain relief and check her pupils again."

Samuel had already told me she didn't have a concussion, although lately, he's second-guessing everything. It all adds to his stress, his choices, and not coping with his grief.

I keep asking myself what else I can do to help?

THIS WEEK I spent with Mum and Faith, either shopping for new items and furniture for our house or with our children building sandcastles on the beach. Every day is a cloudless sky, and the warm temperature indicates summer is almost here. It's a step closer to Christmas, and Samuel's family coming to stay. Last night, we chatted briefly about what tourist places we'll visit. Samuel hinted most responsibility will fall on me with his work commitments.

The conversation didn't please me, and it ended with him suggesting I use the days to better acquaint myself with his parents and allow them time to get to know their granddaughter. I'm not sure if he's avoiding them or proving to his father by working long hours, he is living up to his father's expectations and Samuel's part of the deal. He said his hours had increased at the hospital due to staff shortages on leave, so he couldn't possibly take leave.

He's always trying to prove his worth.

At least it's Friday afternoon, and he'll be mine for the weekend after barely seeing him all week.

It's the same thing every night.

After twelve-hour days, he eats dinner and heads to bed.

Rose has missed him and keeps asking for *Dad-da*.

Tonight is a date of sorts. Not the two of us. We're attending the Building Awards, and our builder invited Dad, Ethan, and me to attend the formal function. Dad couldn't attend as he's in Sydney on business until tomorrow. Dana is busy packing up her house so Dad suggested I take Samuel.

Mum arrives around three to pick up Rose.

"Thank you for looking after her tonight," I say while packing her pajamas into the bag.

"It's fine, love. Do you have her stroller?"

"It's in the garage. I'll grab it for you on your way out."

"I'll head home and wait for Faith and the boys to come for dinner." She says it as though it's the highlight of her week, having her three grandchildren together.

"Rose will enjoy that."

"It's easier if she sleeps at ours, and I'll bring her back in the morning." She glances at the lilac dress I borrowed from Faith hanging on the door. "What time will Samuel finish work?"

I shrug. "Hopefully, with enough time to catch a cab to the Convention Center, I'm going to take my time getting ready."

My phone beeps with a message from Samuel. "He must have heard us." I laugh.

> Working late again. I'm so sorry. Enjoy your evening x

I toss my phone on the table and can't help feeling annoyed with his work taking this night away from us. "Samuel can't make it." I tilt my head back and sigh.

"He mustn't be happy working late, knowing you'll be alongside Ethan."

"You've worked it out as well." Mum's blank expression has me wondering if I'm looking into it more than I should. "Although he also didn't want to be at the same table as him."

I pick up Rose from the floor and kiss her.

"There's a spare seat paid for by the company. I said I confirmed a plus one."

"Count Faith and me out." Mum takes Rose from my arms. "We have the night planned for the kids, and I can't disappoint them."

"You're a wonderful grandmother," I say warmly.

"I learned from an amazing lady." Mum smiles, and immediately Gran's smiling face flashes before me. "She was so good with us when we were young."

"I know. I believe she tried harder with Faith and you, even as toddlers, to make up for time lost with your father. It's a shame Will didn't get to know her like you girls did." She takes my left hand and looks admiringly at my rose diamond ring. "It's exquisite, Eden. He really loves you. Try to relax and enjoy the night."

"I know." I let out a sigh because I have never doubted his love. Yet the disappointment inside me stays.

My phone beeps with another message.

"Let's hope Samuel's situation has changed, and he can now make it. I was looking forward to having a night with him."

"Honestly, darling, he'll probably fall asleep during those mundane speeches."

I giggle at Mum because she used to love formal evenings and boring speeches.

"Nope, it's Amy," I say, reading the message. "She's back for the weekend and wants to catch up."

"And there's your plus one," Mum says and beams a smile at me.

24

EDEN

Fifteen building awards were presented before the renovation awards began. Amy and I have finished our second bottle of champagne. Admittedly, many images projected onto the large screen motivated my creativity to do more to our apartment complex, which I believe is the reason our builder invited us to the awards. He believes we could add more specifics and be in the running for next year's award in a category of renovations up to one million dollars.

"Gee-sus," Amy moans from beside me. "I can see myself waking up next to him."

"Amy," I chastise under my breath. But she's right. The guy on stage is remarkably good-looking—dark hair and tanned skin. Even from here, he has a face you can't help but admire and a voice that demands attention. A voice like Samuel's. One that has you stopping whatever you're doing and listening.

Samuel's voice still does this to me, and Amy is equally mesmerized by Mr. Builder on stage in the navy tuxedo.

"He's engaged," Ethan says from Amy's other side.

"Didn't stop you," she hisses.

"Amy," I repeat in a firm voice.

Oh God. It was Ethan who suggested we place Amy between us because he remembers all too well some of Amy's antics at parties after drinking too much. And the alcohol is free, so it acted as a double precaution rather than have her seated near any members of Spurlo Constructions. Except Anthony Spurlo is seated next to me and overhears, and laughs at Amy.

"Please don't encourage her," I whisper.

He gives me a playful nudge. "It's fine. I agree with her."

My eyes widen. "You want to sleep with him too?"

"No." He chuckles under his breath. "I've been to enough of these shows to know it can quickly get boring. And we also appreciate the free beer. All the awards complimenting your renovations are over, so if you want to slip out the door, do so now while dessert is served.

"Edes, I don't feel so good." Amy grabs her stomach.

"Thank you, Anthony. We'll be in contact, and I'll speak to Dad about your ideas." He shakes my hand, and then I place a hand under Amy's arm to help her to her feet.

On her other side, Ethan helps her to balance. "Okay, okay." She pulls away from us. "I can stand on my own." She pokes Ethan in the chest. "And I don't need help, especially from you."

Amy attempts her first step and her ankle buckles. Her ability to walk in her heels when sober is remarkable. However, being intoxicated could lead to her falling down the staircase. We assist her beyond the oversized wooden doors opening to a vast foyer.

"Stop." She stares at us incredulously. "Where are you taking me?" She stumbles to a long table where pre-dinner drinks were served, and thankfully, most of the crystal has been cleared away. "Oh no," she moans and leans over the table and heaves. A small amount of puke ends up on the table.

"A fast-track way to get us kicked out," Ethan says and chuckles lightly. It surprises me as I assumed he'd be repulsed.

"I'll grab a towel or something." I spin, and before I move, Ethan stops me. He rips off his designer suit jacket and mops it up.

I'm equally grossed out and impressed by his action.

"I'm sorry." Amy rests her head on her hands.

I place a hand on her forehead for support. "I love you, Ames, but dear god, please don't do this here."

"Why do I do this?" She moans. "Because I get overexcited thinking about the good times, and champagne is the common denominator."

Ethan glances over his shoulder. "Is she talking math?"

"And answering her own question." I rub her back.

With her head down, Amy's hand reaches out and touches mine. Her fingers rub over my engagement ring. "Did I ruin your diamonds?"

"No, Ames."

She lifts her head. "Did you see Eden's diamond ring, Ethan?" she says sarcastically.

"Yes, Amy." He glances at me and grins.

I shake my head. There's no knowing what she'll say next. "We need to keep her moving." I spin around and pray we can get her down the stairs.

"Is everything okay here?" The waitress' gaze flicks from Amy to Ethan, who is holding a soiled jacket, and she steps back. When he speaks, she meets his gaze and smiles. "Ethan, I'm Sienna's younger sister, Chloe."

Sienna.

Sienna, who I found pressed up against my bedroom wall with a butt-naked Ethan. Chloe's red hair should have given it away. Ethan didn't even blink an eye.

"Hey, Chloe. Good to see you. I need some help here. My friend is unwell. I hope it's not food poisoning. Could you dispose of this jacket for me?"

Chloe takes the soiled jacket without flinching. "It's good to see you," she calls after us before her eyes slowly lower to her hands.

Turning, I steal one last glance because she obviously didn't recognize me or maybe, like her sister, I'm invisible and insignificant when they see something they like. "Thanks, Chloe," I call back. "I'm Eden. Make sure you say hi to Sienna for me." Recognition dawns and her smile falls away.

"Was that necessary?" Ethan shoots me a sideways look, although he's more focused on holding Amy on both legs while her other hand swings loosely over his shoulder.

"Did someone say Sienna?" Amy mumbles.

"Come on the other side, Eden." Ethan gets a better hold on Amy while I press the button on the elevator and place Amy's other arm around my neck.

The doors slide open, and we stumble in.

"I'm the worst friend," Amy murmurs. Her head droops forward though her eyes remain closed. "After countless drunk times, you think I'd be a little more mature."

"You're our fun friend, honey. We love you for it." *I wish this elevator would hurry and the doors open.*

"The loser friend," she adds. "I'm sorry to be a pain."

"You're not." I tighten my hold around her waist. "You've had my back countless times, and I thank every day for having a friend like you."

"You know I can vouch for you," Ethan quips. "You're the friend everyone needs."

I'm taken aback by his kind words. Only I don't have time to dwell as the elevator door slides open, and we stumble out to the ground foyer and toward the exit.

With his spare hand, Ethan pulls his phone from his pocket.

"I'll take Amy to mine," I tell him. "She's only home for the weekend, and her mum gets funny when she's this intoxicated. It sets a poor example for her younger sisters."

"You can't stay when you have a baby, and with Sam's work hours, he wouldn't want to be disturbed."

I stare at Ethan. For months I have witnessed him become a better person. "Where do you suggest?"

"Mine, of course. I live alone, and sleep hasn't been my friend for months. It's overrated." He smiles, and it reminds me of the playful Ethan I knew back in high school.

"Is it why you're at work at the crack of dawn?"

"Nothing else to do."

The doors to the event center open, and we assist Amy outside. There's a slight breeze in the cool night air. Music, cheering, and the familiar sound of revelry come from further along Hindley Street.

"An Uber is five minutes away." He drops his phone into his trousers pocket.

"I can't let you watch over Amy alone. God knows what will happen when she wakes. Frankly, she'll probably assault you."

Ethan chuckles. "Nothing I don't deserve."

"We all make mistakes."

"Yet I don't sleep, reliving the times I messed up my life."

"Hey, you have a pretty good life now. A secure job and your own place to live. And—"

"Here it is."

We help Amy into the car first.

"If you vomit, you pay," the driver snaps.

"All good," Ethan replies. "I'll pay extra when we arrive because you're a good sport."

Amy is snoring by the time the Uber pulls up in the street behind Monte and not far from my home. *Why didn't I know this?*

"When did you move here?"

"Three weeks before you moved out of Monte."

"You didn't mention it."

He shrugs. "I had to move on with my life. And it's personal and nothing to do with business. Who knew I'd love the beach as much as you?" An amused expression quirks up the side of his mouth. "And I can walk to work. Beats driving in peak-hour traffic."

The streetlight shines bright enough to see Ethan has a relatively new gray-rendered brick townhouse on a small block of land yet close to the beach, which makes it prime real estate.

"This would have set you back," I remark.

While I'm balancing Amy, he scoops her into his arms and carries her as though she weighs nothing. His football days are beyond him, but it's obvious even in clothes covering his muscles, he still works out.

"Let's get her inside before she pukes in my new garden."

He punches a code into the door keypad, and I wait for him to step inside, then he says a command, and the lights turn on.

Fancy.

I head to the lounge, only he turns down a hallway.

"There's a spare room on this level where she can sleep. The laundry is the second door on the right. Grab me a bucket, and the towels are in the cupboard."

The laundry has black tiles from the floor to the ceiling and a white marble counter. Black cupboards line one wall, and a pot of green pothos vine cascades over the counter. It suits Ethan. All class. I grab the bucket and towels and dampen a washcloth. By the time I arrive in the bedroom, Ethan is fluffing the pillow under Amy's head.

He places her heels in the corner of the room along with her clutch purse. He moves to the other side of the bed and climbs on the bed on all fours. "I'll lift her head, and you place the towel underneath it." I do it so some of the towel hangs over the side to protect the bedding in case she pukes again.

Positioning the bucket on the side of the bed near her head, I watch Ethan position Amy on her side.

I admire his efforts.

He moves off the bed and stands, hands on his hips. "We should get her some water."

"You know she's going to be pissed to wake up here in your house, right?" I try to say it gently.

His gaze remains on Amy. "Yeah. She saw straight through me when I was an ass." His gaze flicks to mine. "Figure I could prove I'm not that guy anymore."

I snort. "By risking your life with Amy's wrath?"

He grins at me. "You monitor her, and I'll fetch some filtered water."

I sit on the bed and place the folded wet towel over Amy's forehead. "I'm apologizing now because you're going to be pissed off when you wake up." I use the other damp cloth to wipe makeup from her eyes and face. "Don't be too hard on him, okay? He really is trying to be a better guy."

"Okay," Ethan says as he enters the room. "I'll leave this here beside her." He places a glass and a jug by her bed. "Go. I'll keep a watch."

"All night?"

He shrugs, sits on the bed, then he stands again.

"Why are you really doing this?"

"I told you." He rests a knee on the edge of the bed. "Okay, I haven't forgotten that look."

"What look?"

"When you don't believe me." He pats Amy's leg. "A guy in my football team died after aspirating his vomit after a big night out with the boys." He shakes his head. "You didn't know him, and it happened while you were on your holiday."

"I'm sorry, I didn't know." God, I've never seen Ethan so anxious. He swipes his dark hair out of his eyes—his dark eyes convey his emotion, and I can't turn away.

"If one of us looked out for him, even kept him off his back, he might've lived. Ever since, I promised myself I'd never leave a mate if he was intoxicated and out of it."

"Shit, Ethan. Amy will be impressed you consider her your mate." I say it to lighten the conversation, but it doesn't work.

"We all used to be mates." His eyes meet mine, a pained look marring his face.

"You've gone through quite the transformation."

He smiles. "A little too late, yet I'm grateful we can still be friends."

"We will always be friends. Shit." I spring off the bed when Amy raises her head and heaves. I grab the bucket and secure her hair from falling forward. "And she better be grateful tomorrow," I joke.

Ethan wipes drool from her lips then offers the glass of water with a bamboo straw. "Have a drink, Amy." She does so without asking questions then her head falls back on the pillow, and she's out like a light.

"I'll go empty it." He's gone, returning a few minutes later with a clean bucket. "Do you mind waiting while I grab a few things?"

"Sure." I wipe Amy's mouth again.

Ethan walks through the door wearing a T-shirt and boxers. If I were into him, I'd be mush—I'm not blind to respect a beautiful male body when I see one. He places his water bottle on the other side table along with a book and slides onto the bed near Amy. "Go. I promise I won't fall asleep. If I need you, I'll let you know."

"I think she'll be fine. Honestly, she had bigger nights in Brazil," I murmur, not wanting to tone down his generosity. "But talking of friends..." I open my clutch and retrieve a tiny velvet box. "I've been carrying this with me trying to find the right moment."

Ethan sighs. His shoulders rise and fall. "There's never a right time."

"No," I murmur.

"If it makes it easier, I've been waiting for you to give it back even though I insisted you keep it as a friend."

"You weren't waiting in hope?"

He shrugs. "A guy always has a slither of hope. I knew you were happy, and it's all I wanted. If you weren't, then I'd be letting you know he wasn't the right guy for you."

My eyes widened. "Who are you, and what have you done with Ethan?"

He chuckles.

"I am happy," I say truthfully. "A little lonely at times, but I know it's not forever, and Samuel needs to do his required hours." I hand him the box. "I'll be your friend without substantiating it with a ring. And we both know my fiancé wouldn't appreciate me wearing it." He flips the lid open. "It's a beautiful ring."

Ethan pulls the ring out. "It's a friendship ring. Maybe it can be a sign of peace?" He holds up Amy's hand and slides the gold diamond ring on the middle finger of her right hand. “It held meaning when I bought it, but to be honest, it’s a peace offering, and I have no use for it. I hope Amy sees it that way. It’s too expensive to sit in a drawer.”

“And too beautiful.” I meet his gaze. “As a friend, I can tell you it’s exquisite.”

He smiles. “To friendship and getting the old gang back together again.”

“Talking of, have you heard from Bree lately?”

He shakes his head. “I’ve received the odd message. At least we get to see her during the two-week holiday she’s allowed.”

“I understand how busy she is now after living with Samuel. God knows how the extra leave was granted for her to come on vacation with us.”

Ethan leans over, places a hand on Amy’s forehead, and then replaces the towel. “She’s okay.”

“If she were sober and you tried that, you’d better protect your balls.”

Ethan chuckles. “You have a partner and a baby to care for tomorrow. Get some sleep.”

Opening the Uber app on my phone, I tap on a car only a few minutes away. I kiss Amy’s cheek. “I’ll call you in the morning because you’re going to want answers.” I glance at Ethan and wink while he walks me to the front door. Outside, the night air is still. The stars twinkle, and for once, it feels as though the universe is happy.

Ethan hugs me. “See you, Edes.”

His words feel like closure, but in a good way, and a fresh start between old friends.

Depending on Amy’s reaction in the morning...

25

SAMUEL

Samuel wakes around seven.

A sleep-in for him.

He was vaguely aware of Eden coming to bed last night yet too exhausted to wake and talk about the function. Guilt fills him knowing Eden was looking forward to a night out together. The gala awards was the last place he wanted to be, especially when time together is valuable. He'd have gone for her, though, until multiple motor vehicle accident cases arrived in the emergency room. Some were dead on arrival, but the children covered in blood sent him spiraling. He wasn't the only person who stayed back late to help. All he could think about was Rose and what he needed to do to save these children's lives.

He kisses Eden's shoulder and takes a moment to appreciate her beauty. She's an exquisite woman, and he's grateful she stumbled her way into his life. Eden changed his world, and everything he does is for her. He hopes she understands. Long work hours are a strain on all of them, especially him. He inhales a deep breath and forces himself to sit up in bed.

His body aches.

His head thumps with exhaustion.

Pushing up from the bed, he heads to the bathroom. His reflection in the arch mirror displeases him. His stomach clenches with disappointment and the onset of an anxiety attack. A heightened sense of mortality spikes fear. He tilts his head back and breathes slowly and deeply. The thought of food makes him nauseous. Yet he needs to regain weight to be healthy, at least visually because he's aware of her fingertips running gently over his ribs when she believes he sleeps.

Samuel gives himself a few minutes before showering. He avoids looking at his reflection until he's dressed. Running a hand over his hair, he likes the length, and growing it will deflect attention from his gaunt face.

Creeping around the room to allow Eden to sleep, he heads down the staircase and prepares a protein shake. He takes his healthy smoothy and sits on the balcony to admire the ocean view. Seagulls fly over calm waters while he inhales the salty, fresh air. He closes his eyes and listens to the waves gently breaking along the shoreline. Laughter comes from the beach, where children play in the sand. It's neither hot nor cold at this time of day and perfect T-shirt weather. It will be another story in a few weeks with packed beaches as they enter summer. His first Australian summer Christmas. Being here with Eden has ticked many firsts for him, and it brings back a youthful side in him. He wants a fresh start in life with Eden but forgetting some of the horror that traumatizes him will take time. He sips his drink and leaves the remaining third in the glass to finish later.

Locking the front door behind him, he strolls the esplanade path, smiling at walkers as they pass.

"Morning," he says to some familiar faces. He has spent many hours walking this path and recognizes the same people over the last couple of months. Many have dogs, and they congregate in groups discussing their breeds.

Samuel unlocks the front door of Monte Hotels and takes the stairs two at a time until he reaches the penthouse, where he uses another key to unlock the door.

"Here's Daddy," Grace sings when he closes the door behind him.

"Hello, princess." He scoops Rose from the floor playing with her toys, and showers her cheek with kisses. "Dad-da, missed you." Rose wraps her little arms around his neck, and it installs a calmness in him. He inhales her baby scent like he needs it more than air—the scent of *his* daughter.

"Is Eden still asleep?" Winston asks, not sounding surprised.

Samuel joins them at the kitchen table and places Rose on his lap.

"Your mommy is sleeping like a baby." He kisses the top of Rose's head. "Thanks for looking after her. I could have taken her home, although I appreciated the extra time to rest."

"We know the hours you're working, so think nothing of it. We love having Rose." Grace places some chopped fruit on a plate and slides it toward Samuel. "Did Eden tell you anything about last night?"

"No. I was sleeping when she arrived home, and she was in a deep sleep when I left."

Winston frowns. "Do you know what time she got in?"

"No, sir."

"Hmm... I spoke with Anthony, and he said they left at a reasonable time. And Eden's friend was tipsy."

Winston is concerned about his company's image, and Eden didn't get home at a reasonable time. His gut clenches at the notion of Eden with Ethan.

He forces the thought out as he trusts Eden. Samuel has made ground the past week in dealing with the past. No better time than the present to discuss with Winston what he has waited to hear since Samuel arrived in Adelaide.

"Eden bought me a journal," he says, changing the topic. "I've been writing in it, and I believe it's helped somewhat."

Winston inclines his head in a deep gesture.

"Let me get us a cup of tea." Grace stands and fills the kettle.

Samuel looks Winston in the eye. "You might need something stronger than tea."

"It's too early for shiraz, son." He turns to Grace. "Do you mind making me a double shot of coffee?"

Samuel continues, discussing his time in Ulara working alongside the shaman and Kaikare. He tells them about Kaikare's personality and how she defied the chief and her father if she strongly believed what they were doing was wrong, even if no other Ularan had her back. He told them how Ivy lived in her. Grace and Winston smiled as they sipped their coffee.

He continued to describe Eden and her influence over the village. Seeing the pride in Winston's eyes reflected what Samuel felt every day.

He relived the death of the shaman with him. Tears fell from his eyes, and when he glanced down, he found Rose asleep in his arms.

Grace patted his arm. "She's been asleep for a while, but I didn't want to interrupt your story. The sound of your voice soothes her." She gives an understanding smile. "Rose loves you."

Samuel wipes his eyes. The next half of his story is what Winston needs to hear, yet Samuel can only manage pieces at a time without crumpling to the floor in the pain of his past.

26

EDEN

MY HAND SHIPS TO pat the space in the bed.

Samuel isn't beside me.

My eyes flutter open, and I moan with a thumping headache. Pressing fingertips to my forehead, I stagger to the bathroom and shower in record time. A few minutes later, I'm throwing ibuprofen down my throat and guzzling water before almost running out the door.

Stepping out into the sunshine, I squint and curse for forgetting my sunglasses. I don't get far before my phone vibrates in my pocket.

Amy.

"Hey, babe, how are you?"

"You abandoned me at Ethan's?"

I stop walking, hearing the exasperation in her tone. "Are you okay?"

"Yes," she says harshly. "Well, no. My head is full of semi-trucks colliding, and I can't stop puking. Mum's pissed because we arranged a family breakfast, but I can't move, and Ethan is being *sooo* nice I feel like I'm in another universal dimension. I mean, what the hell is going on? Why am I here and not with you? And why is Ethan so freaking nice? I keep pinching myself like it's a dream. No... it's a freaking nightmare."

A giggle escapes me.

"Are you seriously laughing because I'm stressed and sick and ugh..."

"Do you need me to come over?"

"What are you doing?"

"Walking to Mum's. I assume Samuel is there with Rose. I woke up only minutes ago to an empty house."

There's a muffled sound. "Oh, thanks. You didn't have to."

I continue walking.

"Hey. Ethan has brought me breakfast in bed. I'll chat later."

"Be nice."

She's gone.

I'm grinning, and my body has a sense of weightlessness. She liked Ethan in the beginning, then toward the end of our relationship, something changed. She said something about him grating on her nerves, and she didn't trust him because he was a flirt. Amy has a good heart, and I feel bad for leaving her with him, and yet I hope it's a chance for my friends to make amends. They've known each other since school. The notion of them getting along gives me peace of mind. I have no animosity toward Ethan and need Amy to lay down her sword.

I open the penthouse door to Samuel speaking. He mentions Wayara. One word and I understand the seriousness of his tone.

"Morning," I say in a gentle tone to everyone. I lean to give Samuel a kiss and stroke Rose's cheek. She's peacefully sleeping in his arms. "Do you want me to hold her?"

Samuel shakes his head. By his anguished expression, she comforts him. "I'm telling your parents about my travels."

An unusual explanation, yet I say nothing. Mum and Dad are wearing the same shocked expression. "Can I make anyone a cup of tea?"

Everyone declines, and I sense the tension in the room.

Waiting for the kettle to boil seems like hours, not minutes.

"Excuse me." Samuel leaves the table and places Rose on the Disney Princess sofa bed. She doesn't stir at all.

"Did she sleep well for you last night?" I ask Mum.

"Yes, all night."

"Tell the truth, Grace," Dad quips. "She didn't go to bed until after nine when Faith and the kids left. She woke with me before dawn."

"Well, thank you again for letting her sleep over, but it sounds like both you and Rose need to have an early night."

"Same," Samuel says as he takes a seat.

"Can I get you something to eat?" I ask him.

"I already offered," Mum adds. She tilts her head at Samuel. "I can cook you eggs or anything you want."

"It's fine. I'm still full after my protein shake," he says convincingly.

I let it go and fail to mention I noticed some of it in the glass when I opened the refrigerator.

"I appreciate everything you have told us this morning." Dad's expression is genuinely grateful. "Eden told us stories of how they bonded together, and it warms my heart how Mum somehow brought my sister and my daughter together." He swipes a tear. "I only wish I got to know her and tell her how brave and wonderful our mother was in both of our worlds."

"Dad..." I choke up. I go stand behind him, wrapping my arms around him. "She knows."

"Is Dawn safe now?"

Samuel gives a subtle nod. His gaze lowers to the table.

"But?" I move around the table and sit beside him then place a hand on his shoulder. "Something is troubling you."

"When we stopped migrating, they set up a new camp. It wasn't until I sailed along the river a few miles that I found a remote Colombian community. We didn't make it to Peru. The risks outweighed the safety of stopping rather than crossing the border again." He glances at me. "We'd lost a few more men. At one stage, I ventured into a small town with a small amount of American cash on me and the gold nuggets Kaikare gave me. I bartered and purchased sneakers, medication, and food. It wasn't enough to sustain everyone. We'd traveled hundreds of miles by boat and just as many by foot."

"You had boats? It surprises me as I assumed you wanted to stay out of sight and deep in the jungle."

"We had no choice," he murmurs. "And I stole the motored curiaras."

Samuel could have murdered someone by his guilty expression. "I'm sure they understood." Resting my head on his shoulder, I then squeeze his hand.

"We'd already encountered thieves, and we handed over some other valuables Kaikare had hidden in her pack. She wisely grabbed them at the last minute. Rest assured..." he glances at Dad, "... Kaikare keeps Ivy's pearls hidden."

Dad lowers his gaze, and Samuel gives him a minute before

continuing. Interrupting Samuel is the last thing any of us want, and we don't want him to stop talking.

"We eventually abandoned the boats to trek through the jungle to avoid larger towns and any attention on us. Most of the river journey happened at night and the jungle trek on foot during the day. When we discovered the remote community, we set up a new camp, a new home, and the warriors built a makeshift raft only to get me to the next river community. It was no secret I intended to leave and find you when the Ularans decided on a place to settle. I didn't realize the closest community was only ten miles away. A volunteer doctor was working when I arrived. He helped me to find my way out. I told him about the Ularans and how they'll keep to themselves. If any of them venture close, he can explain he knows me and ask if he could check on them. Like in other communities, I explained their lack of immunity and minimal interaction with the outside world. He promised to keep in contact, only I didn't have a phone number to give him except my father's number as I'd lost my satellite phone in the river months ago." He kisses the top of my head. "It's why I couldn't contact you."

Something doesn't sound right. "You're worried because..."

He closes his eyes slowly and opens them again. "Guerrillas infiltrating the area." He shakes his head. "I don't know. I don't have the answers." Samuel bows his head. "The location isn't ideal, although I have to have faith in Dr. Jacques."

"You're a remarkable man. Never doubt it, son. The lengths you went to keep my sister safe and help the community are honorable."

Samuel drifts into silence. His expression turns skeptical as he bows his head. "I feel I failed them."

He's struggling, and an audience isn't what he needs if he breaks down. I sense he's still hiding something, and it's why the cracks are showing.

"No, you saved them," I say firmly.

My parents agree.

Raising my phone from the table, I make a point of checking the time. "We talked about taking Rose on a picnic today." Pushing up from the table, I place my cup in the sink, giving Samuel an opening to leave.

Late afternoon, Samuel naps at the same time as Rose. I decide to check in on Amy, so I head out onto the balcony and sit on the recliner and stare at the boats fishing at sea for a few minutes before calling.

"Hey, Edes." She sounds chirpy.

"Hey. Just wanted to make sure you made it home safe?"

Amy chuckles. "If you thought Ethan was a serial killer, why did you leave me with him?"

"It was his idea. Admittedly, I enjoyed watching him fuss, and he wanted to take care of you. And a little bit of me hoped you'd see how he's changed. I want my friends... well, to be friends."

Amy is silent for a moment.

"I thought you plotted it because he was *sooo* nice it was sickening. But you're right. He's changed. Although you need to make it up to me after pulling that stunt."

I laugh. "Sure. Name the place, and it will be my shout."

"Or maybe you could come and visit me?"

"What a great idea. If Samuel and Rose came, they could enjoy some fresh country air while I hang out with you."

"Sam would enjoy the slower country life. Maybe working as a rural GP would interest him?"

The more I thought about his work, the more I realized his stress and inability to gain weight related to his choice to continue working as a doctor in modern city hospitals.

"I'm not sure working as a doctor is right for him anymore. Or at least in a busy hospital. I'm still worried about him."

"Plan to visit me sooner. Just saying, it could be the best thing for him."

"Hey." Samuel sits on the chair beside me. "Sorry, I didn't mean to sleep for as long as I did."

"Ames, I must go. I'll call you later in the week."

"Think about what I said."

"I will."

Samuel stares out at the ocean, where the sun shines a bright column of light over the water. Light sparkles over the surface like a dance of minuscule firecrackers.

"Is Amy okay?" he asks softly.

"Yeah." I rest a hand on his leg. "She invited us to visit her in Berri on your next free weekend."

His expression falters. “You realize my parents will be here soon?”

I take his hand in mine. “Then we should go next weekend after Dana’s party.”

27

SAMUEL

SAMUEL LOCKS his bag in the locker and steps out of the staffroom into the hallway, almost colliding with Dr. Tolley.

"MVA in the emergency room," she says without looking at him.

Sliding his arms into a navy jacket as he walks, he falls into step alongside her. The distinct stench of hospital cleaning products assaults his nostrils. He begrudges taking the deep breath to prepare himself for the chaos awaiting them.

"Do we have numbers?"

"Eight." She checks the time on her wristwatch. "Two DOA. A provisional driver lost control on the freeway." She says it as if talking about what she ate for lunch. Her demeanor doesn't change. Motor vehicle accidents are part of their work life, and Dr. Tolley has seen her share of death.

He walks faster to keep up. Dr. Tolley is taller than him, and her long legs are used to walking at a faster pace.

"Two elderly patients are in radiology and being prepped for theater. The driver is also in radiology for query rib fractures. There was mention of a middle-aged woman with a possible ruptured spleen. She was driving to the hospital to receive adjuvant chemo post a double mastectomy."

"Is she in radiology?"

Dr. Tolley hands Samuel the spare pager from her coat pocket. "The message wasn't clear. She is being prepped for surgery." She holds her card against the black box on the wall and the double doors swing open. Staff is passing before them like a busy intersection in downtown LA. They slide between bodies without colliding and head to the main desk. Three doctors who have not been introduced to Samuel are in a deep discussion.

"Morning, Dr. Tolley and Dr. McMahon," the clinical nurse, Margaret, acknowledges their presence although she only gives a fleeting glance. Her head is down, and she's moving patient files to create a clearing on her desk. Managing an emergency ward demands respect, and within minutes, she reminds him of a bear going about her duties. If antagonized, you know to back the hell away.

Margaret appears to be in her mid-forties with a gray regrowth around the crown of her head, and when she catches him staring at her, she grumbles, "This is no place to be just a pretty face." She waggles her finger to her right. "Bed sixteen is waiting to be assessed."

"We were expecting to see the oncology patient," Dr. Tolley interrupts.

Margaret continues clicking on her computer as though we had disappeared. "Still in radiology. Dr. Tolley, can you please assess room seven? I'll inform you both when the patient has returned."

Dr. Tolley shrugs at Samuel, and they head to the assigned rooms. When he locates bed sixteen, he slides the curtain aside before closing it again. He picks up the notes at the end of the bed.

"Morning, Megan. I'm Dr. McMahon."

"Morning, doctor."

He flicks over her chart. "I believe you have difficulty in breathing and a cough on exertion."

"Yes. I had x-rays, and now I'm back here awaiting the results." She pulls the blue blanket up and over her shoulders. "It's freezing in here."

Megan is shaking under the blanket even though the room temperature is steady and not at all cool.

"What time were your x-rays?" He watches her breathing, noting the rise and fall of her chest is labored.

"Half-hour ago, but I was rushed out as there was another emergency."

He takes the stethoscope from his neck and asks Megan to sit forward. Inserting the ear tips in his ears, he then places it on her back and listens. Crackles are evident along with a dead space void of sound.

"Can you take some deep breaths in and out?"

No change, and then she erupts into a coughing fit.

He rests a hand on her shoulder. "Can I get you some water?"

She points to her bag on the chair. Retrieving a water bottle, she takes a few mouthfuls and tries to catch her breath.

He then hands her the call button. "I'm going to see if they have sent your results. Press the button if you need anything."

With the emergency demanding attention, Megan's results may have been overlooked. He assumes the results to be double pneumonia. So he signs a form for the nurse to take blood cultures, arterial blood gases, and a sputum specimen. Then he arranges for her to be admitted for monitoring overnight, along with pulse oximetry and further blood tests to eliminate other diseases.

He accesses her results on the computer. Dark shadows indicate pneumonia, the right side more prevalent than the left.

He finishes his notes and calls the medical ward for Megan to be an inpatient and for an orderly to transport her to the ward.

"We're not made of beds," Margaret says from behind him.

"Then you better find one for my patient." Samuel stands and returns to Megan to tell her she'll be spending at least one night in the hospital.

He could have sent her home with standard antibiotic therapy for pneumonia and Ventolin if she needed it. With her breathing unstable, he's not comfortable risking any more lives.

His hands have enough blood on them.

AT MIDDAY, Samuel seeks food.

He has little energy to continue working.

The last time he worked the wards he was in his twenties, and he's considerably thinner now. Before he makes it to the staff room, a queasy sensation overcomes him, and the hallway appears to move under his feet. He sways and then grabs the handrail for support, taking a moment to catch his breath.

A sharp pain stabs at his gut and his hand automatically presses for support.

"Dr. McMahon, are you okay?" He doesn't know who the nurse is but is grateful for her concern. He's about to brush her off and tell her he's fine, then he stumbles. Pulling the pager from his pocket, he hands it to her.

"Can you please call Dr. Tolley?" Samuel knows the warning signs for syncope.

"Sure, but let's get you to a bed first before you pass out."

Black dots join before his eyes.

She leads him to the side room of the medical staff quarters to rest if needed then assists him onto the bed, lifting his feet onto the covers.

"Do you want me to remove your shoes?"

Samuel holds an arm across his brow to block out the fluorescent light. "I'm fine. Thank you again," he says without opening his eyes. "I'll wait here for Dr. Tolley."

The door clicks closed.

Dang it. He should have asked her for food.

A short time passes before the door creaks as it opens.

"What happened?"

He opens his eyes at the sound of Dr. Tolley's voice.

"It's nothing. I just need food." He looks her in the eye, his expression solemn. "Can this please stay between us?"

28

EDEN

My hair is styled and makeup applied, ready for Dana's farewell.

A cab is booked for six o'clock to the city.

I've been anxious about today, and it's come too soon. Samuel promised he'd be home in time to go with me even though he hasn't arrived home before seven all week.

It's a family affair, and Faith's kids are sleeping the night at Jake's parents.

I booked Tiffany, Amy's cousin, to babysit, and I expect her to arrive within the hour. I'm also hoping to use Tiffany if I choose to follow the nursing pathway.

The decision needs to be mine without the influence or input of my family. I know Samuel will say to do it if it's what I want, though how can I when he's struggling mentally and physically?

I need to be here for him.

I *want* to be here for him.

Mum has told me I'd make a wonderful nurse like Gran.

My passion isn't as strong as hers. My dreams have already come true. Samuel is here with Rose and me.

Anything else is a bonus.

The thought of losing him makes me sick to my stomach. I'm not adding any stress to our lives until he shows signs of improvement. Only I feel like I'm not doing enough to help him. The contentment of him being by my side is now lost to constant nausea worrying about his well-being. His mindset has switched to survival mode. Slowly, his patience and strength are being stripped away.

It's time to step up and take control because I'm not losing him again.

The doorbell chimes and I check the camera at the front gate. "Hi, Tiffany." I press the button to release the gate. "Come in. I'll meet you at the door." Scooping Rose from the floor, I carry her on my hip down the stairs and then open our oversized, Italian wood front door. "Hey. This is Rose."

"Hi, Rose." She smiles at my daughter who plays coy and lays her head on my shoulder.

I stroke Rose's back. "She just needs a minute. Come upstairs, and I'll show you around."

"Wow," Tiffany exclaims as we ascend the staircase. "Your house is fabulous."

"It is, although I can't take any credit. We've only been here a few months, and I had no input on the architecture or interior design." We enter the kitchen, where Rose's dinner is on the stovetop. "She needs dinner, a bath, and then she might play awhile before bed. She goes down at seven. Just put her in the cot and walk out. I'm blessed she loves her sleep."

"Do you want me to do any cleaning?"

"Gosh, no. There's a spare bedroom for you in case we're late, and you're more than welcome to spend the night if you're too tired to drive home."

"Thanks, Eden. I'll see how the night pans out." She pushes long blonde strands of hair behind her ears, so many of her features and mannerisms remind me of Amy.

"I'll give you the tour of the house, and then I'll leave you so I can change. I expect Samuel to be home soon."

An hour later, I walk into Dana's party alone. A server strolls past with a tray of champagne flutes, and I take one before mingling with the crowd.

Seeing my family, I join the circle.

"Hi, everyone." I step between Faith and Mum.

Mum places a hand on my arm. "Darling, jade green has always looked good on you." She glances over my shoulder. "Where's Samuel?"

Faith's forehead wrinkles, and I know what she's thinking.

"He's working late," I explain. "He wants to meet me here, but I told him to go home. Since he's on call this weekend, he should rest." I scan the room. "I haven't found Dana yet."

My phone dings with a message so I hand Faith my glass and open my clutch.

Finally a message from Samuel.

Leaving now. I'll go home and shower and come immediately. I'm sorry xx

It's fine. Just stay home. Tell Tiffany to stay so you can get some rest. I was hoping you weren't on call this weekend as I wanted to take you to Berri for an overnight stay and see where Amy is living. Love you xx

...

Then the dots disappear.

...

Is he writing then deleting his comments?

I'll see you soon x

Does it mean he's coming, or he'll see me at home? Ugh. I drop my phone in my clutch.

Faith nudges my shoulder. "Everything okay?"

"For now." I force a smile then clink my glass with hers. "Bottoms up."

THREE HOURS LATER, most of the guests have departed. Dana's husband is entertaining old work colleagues and close friends by the bar. Dana, Faith, and I are at a table with a fresh bottle of champagne and are in a 'deep and meaningful' meeting.

"I'm glad you're working at Monte in HR?" Dana says to Faith. "When I leave and your dad employs a random, I assumed he'll groom Ethan to take over Monte." Dana glances at me and flutters her long lashes. "I know he's changed..." she draws out, "... but he's not family." She points a finger at me, then Faith. "You're family," she stammers.

I stare at Faith. "This is true."

"And why did you leave again?" It's a rhetorical question, and Faith sits back and folds her arms. "I agreed, and then you both resigned. Feed me to the wolves, why don't you?"

"The wolves," I say and giggle. "It's not a courtroom. Besides, I haven't resigned. I'm working part-time and with you."

"When are you both coming to visit me?" Dana whines. She snakes her arms over Faith and my shoulders and pulls us close.

"Whoa." I balance my drink from spilling over our designer gowns.

"You know the Daintree Rainforest is right on our doorstep.

Dana looks fuzzy, and I have trouble focusing. "On your doorstep? How?"

"We bought a house in Cow Bay in the Daintree and can stay on weekends. During the week, the small apartment in Cairns is for the convenience of work. Selling our house covered both mortgages."

I lean my head on her shoulder. "It sounds dreamy."

"I'll visit, except if there's any sign of snakes or a freaking spider, I'm out of there," Faith warns.

"I imagine it agreeing with Samuel," Dana murmurs.

There are hidden messages in her words.

The three of us remain silent in the unspoken words of Samuel's health.

After a few minutes, I say, "Yeah."

29

SAMUEL

"One night," Samuel says when they're on the open road driving toward Berri. "Tomorrow we get up and drive back so I get the day with Rose."

Eden smiles at him as if he gave her a million dollars. Being together on a road trip and exploring a new place is more exciting to her than a wad of cash.

Eden intended to bring Rose and have a mini family getaway until her mother suggested Rose stay with them overnight to give Eden and Samuel time together. Samuel is desperate to have quality time with Eden, only partying with Amy isn't what he had in mind.

"Thank you for doing this for me." Eden places a hand on his thigh.

With one hand, he releases the steering wheel and squeezes her hand. "As long as *we* get alone time."

"We will, I promise." Eden leans over and kisses his cheek.

He recognizes the gleam in her eyes.

"We could pull over here. Tinted windows." He winks.

Eden giggles. "Keep driving, Dr. McMahon."

On the outskirts of town, orchard farms line the road and toward the horizon.

Eden stares out the window. "The Riverina is best known for its citrus and stone fruit, and personally, I believe the best apricots in the world."

"The world?" Samuel repeats and chuckles. On the side of the road is a little tin shed with a hand-painted sign reading *Fruit for Sale.*

Samuel slows to veer the Porsche off the road at a safe speed where no loose stones flick up and damage his car's paint.

They wander over to a variety of fruits on display, including figs and homemade jam.

"Someone could steal everything," he says, wide-eyed.

"It's the country, and no doubt someone's keeping check from a distance. There might be a camera to snap your registration plate, and they could call ahead to the locals to watch out for you."

Samuel spins, looking around. "For real?"

"No." She grins. "Now pick some fruit." She picks up an orange and peels a piece, then takes a bite. "Seriously, this is good. We should buy some."

"And if it wasn't tasty?"

She bumps his hip. "You're too easy today."

They pack oranges, lemons, apricots, and plums into bags and then select apricot and fig jam. The honesty box has a lock so Samuel leaves a hundred-dollar bill.

Eden shakes her head. "It wouldn't even cost fifty dollars."

"It will make up for any missing fruit."

Eden kisses his cheek. "You're very generous, and it's a reason why I love you."

He holds her gaze. "Yeah? What are the other reasons?"

She takes his hand as they stroll back to the car. "Your good looks and your smile. It can change my mood in a second."

He presses her against the car and kisses her hard. "I could change your mood right now," he whispers against her lips.

"You always do." Eden links her arms around his neck. He kisses her nose then opens the car door, closing it behind her. Dropping the fruit on the floor in the back, he starts the engine and veers the car onto the road. Inside the safety of the car has opened a part of him to chat easily with Eden. "You said I didn't smile enough when we first met."

"You didn't." She places a hand on his thigh. "You intrigued me beyond the pull of attraction, despite your grumpiness," she jokes. "So, tell me, what first appealed to you about me?"

Samuel grins. "You, in that bathing suit on the beach in Salvador." He gives her a sideways glance and winks before looking back to the road. "I've seen thousands of chicks in tiny bikinis, yet you stole the air out of my lungs. I had to get a closer look, and everything about you appealed to me. My brain was like tick, tick, tick."

"You had a type?" she asks incredulously.

"I didn't know I had a type, and if you recall, I was also backing away, trying to put space between us. I wanted you, yet I knew we couldn't be together."

"And here I am proving you wrong."

Samuel shakes his head and chuckles. "It's your superpower."

"Hey, it's okay. You did the same to me. I remember wading out of the water trying to find you."

The cabin of the car falls quiet.

Samuel is only half the size compared to when she met him. He taps the steering wheel with one finger as though it's a distraction. "I'm trying, Eden."

She gives him a few seconds before answering, "I know."

THEY ARRIVE at Amy's quaint country rental in Berri. She gives them a quick tour before showing them to the spare bedroom.

"We'll head to the best bar in town tonight for dinner. You'll get to meet the locals."

"Great," Samuel says under his breath.

Eden gives a slight nudge with her elbow. "Sounds like fun, Ames."

"Get comfortable. I coached T-ball this morning and didn't get time to go to the shops, so I'll duck out now. I won't be long."

"I can come with you," Eden says quickly.

"No, it's fine. If you need to hang any clothes, there's free space in the closet. Besides, I want you to relax. It seriously will take me ten minutes." She flicks her ponytail over her shoulder as though shopping for groceries is exciting.

"Do you mind if I shower? I'm a little sweaty from the drive," Samuel asks with another motive.

"Yes, there are towels on your bed, and the bathroom is yours. I have an ensuite."

"It's a great little place."

"Thank you, I think so too."

She waves goodbye and almost skips out the door.

Eden places her small suitcase under the window and opens the lid. "I should hang my dress for tonight."

Samuel stands behind her and runs his hands over the rounded swell of her rear.

Eden freezes. "Samuel, it's—"

"Broad daylight and the window is obscured by grape vines. Can you stop yourself from screaming when I make you orgasm over and over?"

"Jee-sus, Amy said she'd be ten minutes."

"Exactly." He lifts her skirt and groans at the sight of her G-string panties revealing smooth skin. Sliding the thin material down her thighs, he bends to assist her in stepping out of them. He holds the satin strings in the air, and he smiles as she watches them fall to the floor. Samuel stands behind her, kissing her shoulders and neck. "Place your hands on the windowsill." His hands travel up her inner thigh and caress her slick creases. Eden sways her hips and moans with his touch. He adjusts her stance, pushing her feet wider with his and pulling her rear toward him. "You make me crazy."

She purrs at his words, moving her hips in a circular motion while his fingers bring her close to climax. Her reflection in the window is faint yet enough for him to catch the pleasure in her expression. Even better, he can't see his reflection except his face showing equal joy as Eden's. Before she comes, he slides his shorts down and finds her wet and ready for him. He pushes inside her, slowly, deeply. It's intimate, and she's all he feels. "I love you more than anything else in the world," he whispers.

"I love you too," Eden murmurs and then arches her back, seeking more.

Samuel leans back and lifts Eden's ass to perfect alignment with his hips and thrusts until she's gasping out of breath and whispering his name.

Samuel's body shudders, and for a moment, he can't stand, slumping over her, enjoying the thrill of his orgasm.

"Wow," she whispers.

Slowly, he comes out of the sexual haze while he dots kisses along her spine. "Now *that* was worth the trip."

She giggles. "You better get in the shower, doc, before Amy comes home."

He coughs. "Doc?"

"You can heal me in minutes." She smiles at him as they adjust their clothing.

"For you..." he kisses her nose, "... anytime."

"It could be the country air invigorating you."

Samuel doesn't respond, unsure if she's referring to him being unhappy in her hometown. Or does she believe he's simply unhappy?

What does he have to do to prove he'd move the earth just to be with her?

He has done everything possible to be here.

Does she now doubt his love for her?

30

EDEN

INSIDE THE TAVERN, a live band plays hits of the nineties, and the catchy beat has many patrons on the dance floor. In between songs, we talked quickly as we were almost shouting over the music. Amy secured a booth in the back near the bar, thinking we could have our own area, except it was a walkway, and she said hi to the locals almost every minute.

"You've made a lot of friends." My heart expands with pride.

She taps her glass several times before meeting my gaze. "Most say hello because I teach their kids or their friends' kids. You know how it is in a small town."

"Don't play it down. You're a magnet to people with your bubbly energy and beauty. And I noticed a couple of guys eyeing you off."

She waves a hand dismissing my words. "Oh, they're too young for me. A new face in the town has the appeal of a new toy." She winks. "I'm older and wiser not to fall for the hot guy with come-to-bed eyes and the smile to make you drop your panties."

Samuel chokes on his beer.

"I'm proud of you," I tell her, reaching out to squeeze her hand.

She squeezes mine back before releasing it. "Don't be too proud. I fucked a couple of hotties first before I realized small towns have a grapevine that's not only for wine."

I chuckle.

"Good for you," Samuel says. "As long as you're happy, Amy."

She smiles at him. “I am for now, but I’m a city girl, and I probably won’t stay long.”

We glance up at a guy staring at us.

“You know many a woman has said that *before* she falls in love with a hot country boy,” a deep voice says.

“Rhett,” Amy says and laughs before sliding across her seat. “You remember Eden, right?”

“No man would forget Eden.” He takes my hand and kisses it. “How’s your dad?”

“Rhett,” I say affectionately. “Still the charmer, I see. Dad is good.” I can’t help but smile at Rhett as he always has a starry-eyed effect on girls. “This is my fiancé, Samuel McMahon.”

Rhett stares at me, bewildered. “The doctor from the Amazon?”

I nod quickly as Samuel holds out his hand. “Good to meet you, Rhett. How do you two know each other?”

“Let me tell the story,” Amy pipes up.

“You’re quite the storyteller tonight,” I joke.

Amy’s gaze flicks between Rhett and Samuel. “Eden attended university for a short stint with Rhett when, what... you were around nineteen?”

“Yeah.”

“And they remained friends although we barely saw him as he played football and had superstar status until he got caught with drugs.”

Rhett moans. “You had to mention it.” His expression is serious when he addresses Samuel. “I was young and didn’t handle fame well, especially being a country boy. My father died, and I had two younger brothers who also relied on me. Leaving Mum alone on the farm while I bathed in the pleasure of football stardom got to me.” He glances at me and then Samuel. “I became an obnoxious prick.”

“Wow,” Amy says wide-eyed. “I wasn’t going to say all that. Anyway, he went on a reality show to clean up his image on national TV, or he’d lose his contract.”

Rhett stares up at the ceiling. “Not one of my finest moments.” He meets Samuel’s gaze. “Although I met my wife on the show.”

“Hang on,” Amy interrupts. She stares at Samuel. “She wasn’t a contestant. In typical Rhett style, he fell for his mentor.”

“Life puts us in extraordinary places so we can meet our soul mates.” He nudges Amy. “I keep telling her she’s going to fall for a local.”

Amy rolls her eyes. "Hang on. You jumped ahead. Rhett was one of the surprise football guests at Eden's Dad's sixtieth. And Rhett knows Cleo, Yasmine's sister."

"Small world," Samuel comments.

"I have heard about you, mate. I know Eden was concerned for your safety, and I'm glad you made it safely to Australia." Rhett turns his focus to me. "Weren't you talking about a charity for the indigenous in the Amazon when you first came back?"

"I was." I'm smiling, as out of the corner of my eye, I can see Samuel's surprise. "I wanted to do something to help until life got busy."

Rhett leans his elbows on the table. Long, tanned arms protrude from his polo sleeve. His thick muscles twitch with the slightest movement. It's obvious he's remained fit working on the farm. "If you get it up and running, let me know. I'm looking to be part of a unique charity."

"Samuel's the one to talk to. He has all the knowledge."

Samuel stares at me. "We haven't discussed this, but it's definitely something I'm interested in investing in."

Rhett stands and shakes Samuel's hand. "It's good to finally meet you. We should set up a business meeting in the future. Amy has my number, so call me any time."

Rhett walks away, and Samuel kisses my cheek. "You're full of surprises." He drops his arm over my shoulder. "Have I told you how much I love you?"

"Stop," Amy says and groans. "Get a room. Wait, no... because it's in my house!"

Samuel elbows me.

Then he groans. I assume he's reacting to Amy's comment until his expression falters. "I don't feel good."

I freeze.

His hand is on his stomach, and even in the dim light, his face has paled.

"Would you mind if I leave?"

"I'm coming with you." I slide out of the seat, ready to take his hand. "I've only had one wine, so I'll drive."

Amy is beside us. "Can I do anything? Buy a bottle of water?"

"I need to get him home fast," I whisper.

Amy understands as I vented my concern to her, and she checks in on Samuel regularly.

Samuel limps out to the car as though his hip is painful. My stomach is in knots. How severe is his abdominal pain to make him hobble like an old man? The benefit of small towns is we arrive at Amy's house within minutes. After helping him inside, he almost falls on the bed and curls up on his side. He reaches for his phone in his pocket.

"Do you want me to call anyone?"

He shakes his head. "I underwent some tests during the week. I'm messaging a colleague to see if the results are in."

I sit beside him on the bed. "What tests?"

"A few different ones. We'll talk about it later."

His phone dings, and he groans.

"What is it?"

"Mum and Dad have arrived in Sydney. They're staying a few days to tour and adjust to the time difference."

"That's a good idea." Because I know Samuel would not want to be like this when they arrive in Adelaide.

"There's medication in my bag. Can you please grab it for me?"

His eyes are closed. I don't move for a moment as the truth hits me. He hasn't shared any of this with me. I then rush to retrieve his small suitcase. "There are two types. What are they for?"

"Spasms. It should help my gut. The ones in a bottle are antiparasitic. I need the small box."

"You have a parasite?"

"Not that I know of," he murmurs. "It's precautionary."

I have so many questions, yet I let them go. *For now*. I head into the kitchen, and Amy is warming a hot pack. "How is he?"

"Okay." I shrug. "I wish I knew what's going on with him." I fill a bottle of water and take it to Samuel.

"Thank you," he says, downing his tablets.

"Is it something you ate? The chicken? And you had a beer," I emphasize.

"Maybe." He screws up his face.

I glance up at Amy in the doorway holding a hot pack. I wave her in. Samuel opens his eyes and smiles at her. "Thanks, Ames. Please, Eden, I'm fine. Go and spend time with Amy. It's a chance to be with each other. And by the sounds of it, you still have much to talk about." He winks at Amy.

I run my hand over his forehead. His skin is cool with no sign of a fever. "Okay, but if you need anything, just call out."

Amy gets us bottles of water, and we head into the lounge room. It takes a while for us to fall into easy conversation.

"I almost forgot." She jumps up and heads to her room, and returns seconds later holding a small, wrapped box. She hands it to me. "I saw this in a local shop and thought of you."

It's a ring with turquoise cut into a heart shape. I slide it onto my finger. "Amy, it's exquisite. Thank you."

"The lady said turquoise is a calming stone and represents wisdom, love and tranquility, protection, good fortune, and hope. It's also the stone of communication." She shrugs. "It's pretty too, and the color matches your eyes, and I thought this has *Eden* written all over it."

I hug her tight. "You are so kind, babe."

"You deserve it."

Her kindness brings tears to my eyes.

On the coffee table, her phone makes a funny noise, and we jump apart. "It's Yasmine," Amy says excitedly and holds up the phone. "She knows you're here and wants to FaceTime."

Amy and I sit close together and wave when Yasmine's face appears on the screen.

"Hey, my girls," she sings.

"You look great," I tell her. Dark ringlets are pulled back into a small ponytail, and it's changed her face. Her cheekbones pop.

"Iquitos is steaming hot, and I need my hair off my neck. It's grown since being here. It also sticks straight out on the ends." She grins at us, and I want to hug her.

"We miss you," I tell her.

"You both look good. How's Berri?"

I grin at Amy. "Full of hot men."

Yasmine breaks into a hearty laugh. "Did she tell you about Chad?"

"No, she didn't."

"Oh, I can tell her later. I have another bone still to pick with her." Amy scowls at me.

Before we say it's Ethan, the image shakes, and Michael comes into view. "Hi, ladies, how are we?"

"Good, thanks."

"Has Yasmine told you tomorrow is the day?" He smiles at Yasmine, and the connection between them is obvious.

She drops her arm over his shoulder and pulls him closer. "We're doing Ayahuasca together." She kisses his cheek. "We've been on a strict diet and no alcohol, and we're prepared this time."

"I hope it's everything you're searching for," I tell her. "And I'll pass on to Samuel you have stuck to his diet."

She shoulder-bumps Michael as though coaxing him on.

"In a few days, we'll meet up with Deanne and... I'm coming to Australia with the girls."

Yasmine stares at us with a goofy expression.

"I'm so happy for you," I say louder than necessary, knowing this is what Yasmine wants.

"Is Samuel around?" Michael asks, leaning closer to the screen.

"He's asleep," I emphasize the disappointment. "He'll be excited to know you'll be here soon.

"We better go as we're catching the boat to the village where the shaman is located in about an hour." She smiles again, then she stares at Michael. "And you still haven't packed your case."

"It was great chatting with you," I say quickly.

"Talk in a couple of days, okay," Amy says more as a directive, still wary from the last time.

We end the call, stare at each other, and sigh.

"So. Michael is coming to Adelaide."

"Yeah. Not to change the subject... do you know Ethan has been messaging me every second day?"

I didn't, and I can't help the surprise creeping up my neck.

"And did you know he placed a certain ring on my finger?"

I place a hand on her shoulder. "I did. He emphasized it's about friendship."

"Hmm," she says and scowls at me. "Are you setting me up with him?"

I cough. "God, no. I wanted for peace and us all to be friends."

"Funny, it's what he said, except all this attention is weird."

I take a sip of water and consider my answer, "Don't think too much into it. And I'm glad he's trying."

Jumbled words and shouting come from the bedroom.

Then silence.

Amy stares at me wide-eyed before we both spring off the lounge and dash toward the room. The bedside lamp is on. Samuel is upright in the bed with his eyes closed. His fists swing at something, and then he falls back onto the pillow, mumbling and grunting. He flips from one side to the other.

Amy grabs hold of my forearm. A vicelike grip from concern. “What’s happening?”

“Nightmares. They started a few weeks after he arrived. The first time scared the crap out of me. Now I simply wait them out. I observe and make sure he’s safe. I used to hug him and tell him he’s okay and he’s with me. It didn’t help.”

She releases my arm and wraps her arms around her stomach. “He looks in pain and afraid.”

“He’s not the only one.”

31

SAMUEL

AFTER A WEEK of solid traveling along the river at night and then sleeping during the day, they had finally set up camp. Exhausted, everyone needed sleep. For diseased feet, he treated them with antifungal medications and a balm for healing. Remaining on the boats at night and only walking a few miles during the day helped rest their wounds.

The small convoy of boats meant overcrowding to get all the Ularan men, women, and children on board. Samuel convinced them to wear the T-shirts he purchased, thinking they would attract less attention than if they were almost naked. He also distributed caps with either baseball, football, or basketball emblems embroidered on the front. None of it made sense to the Ularan people, yet they did what he asked. Some women and children giggled. The men only stared back with serious expressions, and he sensed they felt mocked for wearing the outside world's clothing.

As the light of dawn fell upon the earth, their silhouettes were now visible from the shore.

The river had widened. The hats and T-shirts helped to obscure their identity. Bare legs and feet were concealed by the side of the boat, along with arrows, darts, pots of poison, food, and tweed bags of belongings lining the curiaras' floor.

Another night passes, sailing the water without being questioned. When they find an uninhabited section of a sandy riverbed, he leads them ashore, pulling the canoes on land and into the trees to be out of sight. A simple chore leaves the warriors weak.

Besides the fish captured in nets hanging over the edge of the canoes, Samuel needs to arrange food to sustain their energy. The fish serves as food for breakfast, or is it dinner since they'll sleep during the day?

The women set up camp by starting a fire, then tying hammocks to the trees, and untangling mosquito nets. The men grab their blowpipes and wander deeper into the jungle. Samuel remains with Kaikare. They roam the nearby jungle, picking leaves and berries to use as medicine. His natural medical stock is low, and most detest taking Western world medication.

A twig snaps. And Kaikare spins to see what's behind them. After staring at nothing but tree trunks and palm leaves, they're satisfied no danger is present and finish collecting enough plant food to provide the community for at least the day.

After transporting the clay pots off the curiaras, they collect water from the plants and stems of bamboo. Water is poured into the pot over the fire. Kaikare grinds the leaves and drops the pulped mash into another pot of water. Samuel speaks to each woman about her health and the well-being of her husband and children. Being informed helps with his decision on how to treat and what his next move will be. Most want to remain here as they feel safe.

The men arrive home with several monkeys and two snakes, enough food to get them through the day. The fish is being served as he speaks. Kaikare has the medicine boiling in the water. The women will serve the snakes and monkeys soon.

Everything looks promising.

They manage around five hours of sleep before the camp comes to life, and the men decide to go out in search of more food. Something larger is necessary to feed the community.

Dusk falls upon the camp, and the men haven't returned, so Samuel distributes the fruit and berries he and Kaikare had scavenged. Originally, the stock was for the hours sailing the river, but with food scarce, he needs to focus on the present day.

With daylight diminishing, the atmosphere in the camp becomes restless, with the men and warriors not returning to camp.

With barely enough light to guide them, Samuel grows concerned and asks the elders to whistle and make animal sounds for the warriors to recognize so the sound guides them back to camp. A sequence of coos and whistles erupt every fifteen seconds. In the distance, a faint whistle echoes, and more men belt out whistles to lead their people in the right direction. In this strange land, trees surround them like twenty-story buildings, and the thick undergrowth hinders sight of anything beyond several yards away.

He understands the warriors are trained hunters and marked tree trunks, slashed palm leaves to guide them 'home,' yet they're in another country and, if caught trespassing, their poison arrows might be useless against powerful guns.

Another whistle sounds closer to the camp.

The men push through the palm leaves. Subtle cheering erupts when the warriors appear with three peccaries, inverted with legs tied to a bamboo branch. They tell stories about their hunt as the women prepare the meal and spear each pig to be smoked over the fire while they sleep. The excitement is a relief knowing how forlorn the people have become, yet in the back of Samuel's mind, he's alerted to the killing of protected animals in an unfamiliar location. The Ularans view pigs as food and part of the circle of life. Eat what they need and give back to Mother Earth. Rules beyond their community and the Western world's law about animal protection is foreign knowledge. Samuel struggles to find the words they understand when explaining how their behavior could be dangerous at every step of their journey.

The smoke wafts around Samuel, and it helps to mull the continual buzz of mosquitoes circling his head. He misses the days where fires in Ulara continually burned, giving a distinct aroma to jolt his memories.

Memories of good times comfort him to sleep, disguising the terror expanding in the back of his mind.

Deep sleep never lasts.

A bright light burns through his eyelids. Samuel rolls over and squeezes his eyes shut, hoping the tightness will block out the light. His thoughts confuse him as they're unaccustomed to experiencing sunrise in the thickest part of the jungle. Something sharp pokes his back. He twitches.

Another poke to his shoulder, only this time he senses aggression.

Samuel flings himself forward in the hammock, the gentle sway of the hammock offering split seconds of relief from the light shining directly in his eyes. He lifts an arm to shield the brightness until his eyes adjust.

A flashlight.

Spanish words.

Clothed men.

Another light shines from behind, and metal reflects in the light.

Guns.

Hurling himself forward to his feet, the light follows him, and standing with his arms raised in front of his eyes is a disadvantage. The Ularan men and women are already standing, unmoving and silent. He's thankful they understand danger and don't do anything to be shot.

"¿Cómo puedo ayudarle?" How can I help you?

A deep voice tells him they're trespassing and on private land. A threatening tone indicates they aren't getting away without a form of payment. He ponders his position to bargain, although his resources are scarce. Tiny pieces of gold are all that remain beside his American dollars. One of the flashlights shines over his hammock and lands on his backpack. A man dressed in a khaki shirt scavenges through his bag. He pulls out medication packets and his notes wrapped in plastic.

"Quién eres tú?" Who are you?

Samuel explains he's an American doctor caring for the people in the community, and they are traveling to find a new home.

The guy asks for their passports and visas, and it tricks Samuel into believing they're a sub-group of the government military.

Before he has time to explain, a gunshot fires, and a body falls with a thump. Wails sound before him.

"Por favor, colega, deje que le explique la situación." Please, colleague, let me explain the situation.

A grunt sounds from behind the intruder. The flashlights leave Samuel and shine on the limp body of an intruder gasping for his last breath. It gives Samuel a chance to flee behind a thick tree trunk. Flashlights scan the Ularan faces, all squinting their eyes from the light. Multiple beams of light scan the area like a prison yard searching for an escapee.

Another body falls, and a flashlight rolls out of his hand along the ground. It shines momentarily on a figure holding a blow dart.

Tïmenneng.

He disappears into the darkness, and the hostile men yell and flash the lights in search of him. Except one. The leader shouts a threat warning he'll shoot the women.

Before Samuel surrenders, he needs a plan. Only his thoughts scramble, and he has no weapon in defense other than his voice to reason with the criminals.

"Tengo oro," Samuel shouts. I have gold.

Lights shine in his direction.

Snickers of triumph and footsteps stomp closer.

Suddenly, an arm is around his throat, a blade pressed to his jugular. The intruder came from behind with a hand around his waist, holding Samuel like a vice. One slight slip could be fatal. The light is back burning his eyes. There are fewer men to fight thanks to Tïmenneng's swift skills, and Samuel knows he must act fast. The familiar thump of a body hitting the ground, and simultaneously, the light falls away from him, another flashlight rolling over the ground pointing at Samuel's feet. The attacker grunts and wails behind Samuel, and his hold loosens. Samuel flings his arm off his neck and turns to see him curled over, holding his testicles.

Kaikare stands behind, and he makes out her defiant stance.

He doesn't think, only acts and swings a brutal uppercut punch to the attacker's nose at an angle where the nasal bones, with enough force, penetrate the brain.

Samuel yells out with the pain of smashed knuckles and a loud moan of knowing he killed, not saved a life.

"SAMUEL, YOU'RE FINE." The voice breaks through his pain.

He reaches for Kaikare to ensure she's safe, except her body shape is fading. He opens his eyes to nothing but black space.

A hand rests on his back.

"You're safe. You're with us, and everything will be okay."

Samuel scrunches his eyes closed with awareness of his surroundings. "I'm sorry," he murmurs. "It was just a dream."

"No, Samuel. You're experiencing nightmares, and it scares me," she whispers.

Nightmares are still dreams.

He wishes it was just that and not the truth of his dark past.

32

EDEN

On Monday morning, I awaken to a note from Samuel on my bedside table.

Morning Eden,
My parents have caught an earlier flight.
I'll pick them up from the hotel after work. Please don't worry yourself with my parents staying at our house.
Enjoy your day.
See you tonight.
Samuel x

For him to mention not to be concerned, I'm now thinking have I missed something, and should I be?

The house is clean.

There's plenty of food.

Are they fussy?

Do they have allergies?

Shit, we don't have fancy cutlery or crockery or—

Stop.

This is exactly what Samuel didn't want me to do.

Yesterday on the trip home, he didn't talk about his nightmare. Instead, he talked about his parents and the places they would like to see. When I brought up Rose's first birthday, he played it down, saying Rose won't remember anything and to keep the celebrations to family.

I intended to keep it to family, only I wanted to decorate the house.

And today I hoped to shop with Mum, but she has appointments all day. Faith is also busy with errands.

My friends are not here.

My thoughts go to Yasmine and how she's coping in the jungle.

Then I'm thinking about Gran and her journal.

Looking around the room, I find it on the coffee table stacked with other books. This isn't something I want on view when Samuel's parents arrive. I pick it up and start daydreaming about Gran.

And then I think of Brenda...

THE WHITE HALLWAYS of the care facility are empty.

I had called ahead to register my visit and confirm Brenda is up to visitors today. All the doors to the residents' rooms are closed, and something doesn't feel right.

A door swings open, and a nurse in a blue surgical gown appears. She stops with the door half ajar. "Can I help you?"

Flicking the brake latch on Rose's stroller, I stop in the hallway. "Have I come at an awkward time?"

She peels disposable gloves from her fingers and drops them in the waste. "And you are?"

"Eden Monteford. I've come to visit Brenda James."

She smiles at me. "Hi, Eden, I'm Lori. Come with me, and I'll show you where Brenda is having morning tea."

"If it's in the garden, then I know the way." I flick the brake latch off and rock Rose as she has fallen asleep. Hopefully, she'll stay asleep so I don't have to chase after her.

"She is. I'll follow you out as I need to lock the doors behind you for a few minutes."

I give her a blank look.

"One of our clients has passed. We need to wheel her out of the building, and we prefer all doors closed for privacy. It can upset the residents."

"Of course," I say quickly and hurry along because I'm not sure I'm ready to stumble across that scene.

The door clicks behind me when I step outside into the warm sunshine. Brenda is sitting in a wheelchair under the shade of her favorite tree.

It's the beginning of summer, yet a striped crocheted blanket drapes her knees. Closer, I recognize the nurse sitting beside her from my last visit. Still, I check her name badge to jolt my memory. "Hi, Sophie, I don't know if you remember me? I'm Eden."

"Hi. I do. And who do we have here?" She leans in to get a better view of Rose.

"This is my daughter, Rose. I hope she remains asleep so I can have time to chat with Brenda without her crying to get out of the stroller."

"For sure. Well, I'll leave you alone while I get Brenda her morning tea. Call out if you need anything. Enter through those doors, and it's the first room on your right." She points to another set of double doors on the other side of the lawn.

Positioning Rose's stroller under the shade, I sit beside Brenda. Her gaze is fixed across the grass, and I'm not sure it's on anything. "Hi, Brenda." I lightly pat her hand, hoping for some eye contact.

Brenda stares down at my hand and then looks at me. "Oh, you came back?"

"Yes, I promised I would." I'm relieved she remembers. "I have Gran's journal and would like to read some of it. Do you remember the good times with Ivy?"

"We shared some good times," she says in her husky voice as though she needs to cough.

"Are you unwell?"

She shakes her head.

I remove both journals from my handbag. I open to a section I marked when both ladies snuck out of the nursing home and met up with their boyfriends and soon-to-be husbands. When I finished reading the entry, I turned to Brenda. "You two were mischievous together."

Brenda blinks, and her brows crease. "I didn't know you wrote about us?"

"What? No, I didn't. I—" Her hand reaches for the other journal. The one Gran wrote while in the jungle.

"Tell me another one of your adventures." Her finger runs over the cover of the journal. Her swollen knuckles are twisted with arthritis. Her eyes are mere slits from the excess skin overhanging her lids. Yet there's a spark of life and excitement as her lips curl upward. "You had the best life, so don't feel bad. Stop beating yourself up about Dawn. You did what you needed to do… what was best for everyone. Albert will get over it one day. I mean, would he rather you be dead?"

She thinks I'm Gran. Her best friend, Ivy.

"Do you want me to read to you?"

She smiles. "Does the sun rise every morning?"

"Right." Good point.

I place Gran's first journal away and turn the page of the entry I last read.

33

IVY

MARCH 10, 1963

Last night Maria and I stayed up late after drinking a purifying tea. We giggled by the fire and under a full moon, surmising they gave us the wrong brew. Jennifer and Felix were in Canaima for the night. A deserved break.

The moon's beauty didn't last in our thoughts as it encourages creatures to hunt.

Only the sounds we heard were not animals.

I'm still struggling to comprehend what happened.

We heard the Spanish tones coming out of the darkness. My heart is still racing as I relive the past night's happenings.

Maria sensed evil, she grabbed my hand, and we took off to our hut. She insisted I pack my belongings. I told her not to panic, for these men had threatened us before. In my mind, it had been months since their last visit, and I assumed Dr. Leon could threaten them enough to deter them.

An important factor I'd forgotten was Maria spoke Spanish and understood the words yelled from a distance. She pushed my back, urging me to hurry, almost forcing me out the door before I managed to grab everything.

"Leave it," she said. "If you don't need it to survive, then just go." She yanked the netting from my hammock and rolled it into a ball before tucking it under her arm.

I had my passport and papers. A little cash. Some toiletries and a few

I had my passport and papers. A little cash. Some toiletries and a few clothes I stuffed in my bag. My suitcase needed to remain here. I opened it and grabbed my pearls. I did not know why I even packed them, but I wanted to keep them with me for luck. Then I found my brush and mirror, not that I bothered brushing my hair every day. It had become wilder with time, and now I was about to hide out like an escapee from prison.

Maria stood in the open doorway, peering out into the darkness, listening. She pressed a finger to her lips and then took my hand. We crept around the furthest side of the camp and reached the river as shouting broke out in the village. We ran, pushing past vines for a few hundred yards. She stopped and listened. Pressing long grass aside, she revealed a dugout canoe. Under the moonlight, I could make out the weathered wood. It contained two rows of seats, not large at all, and two wooden paddles.

"This is here for emergencies. Take it. Go."

Her words keep playing over in my head.

I couldn't help it.

I began to cry.

She helped push it into the water before throwing the netting aboard. She then hugged me and said, "Look after yourself, Ivy." I can still picture her bleak expression.

I asked her where I should go and when I should come back.

She told me to find my Ularan friend since I'd be safer there than here.

The place where she emphasized I was lucky not to leave without an arrow in my back.

She hugged me again then pushed my canoe away from the embankment.

She told me to stay close to the river's edge, then she dashed into the night toward the sound of gunfire.

I sailed throughout the night.

Part of me wanted to wake up from a horrible dream, the other part of my mind wanted to believe I was hallucinating from the tea.

This was no hallucination.

At night the river felt eerie, and I felt trapped, only to be catapulted onto the set of a horror movie.

Tree and vine shadows overhung close to the water's edge.

I stayed my distance in case something lurked near the shore. Yet close enough not to get caught up in the force of the current near the middle of the river.

I sailed through the fork leading me along the river toward Ulara.

Closer to where I ascertained the village to be, I found an embankment and went ashore to a small clearing beyond the sand. Then I went back and lugged the front of the canoe ashore as best I could so at least it wouldn't get washed away.

Light was breaking above the treetops.

Dawn was almost upon me.

I didn't want to venture into the jungle.

I curled up into a ball, wrapped the netting around me, and tried to sleep. Only my eyes opened with every crack of a stick and every unusual howl from a monkey, a warning to its family of danger lurking nearby.

Sleep is impossible, so I'm writing this entry to capture my fear.

I don't know what will happen next.

There's barely enough light to check my writing, although enough for me to feel safer so I might get a few more hours of sleep.

With the intrusion of sunlight blaring down on top of me, I came to. Then a figure blocked the light, and my vision cleared.

He was one of them.

I wrestled with the netting and sat up. Though my sudden movement unnerved him, he jumped back.

He walked away and found a fallen log and sat on it. He looked awfully like the same man I saw a few months ago.

I said hello several times and pointed to myself. "Ivy."

He ignored me and continued to stare.

I was also busting to pee.

I climbed out of the canoe and headed downstream a little and away from the strange man. He began to follow until I held up my hand, insisting on privacy. He didn't understand my words, yet the hand signal worked. He stopped when he realized what I was about to do, only he didn't turn away. So, I peed in front of him on the edge of the river, and not at all ladylike. I zipped up my shorts and then washed my hands, along with my legs because I might be wild, but I want to keep my last shred of hygiene.

When I'm closer, I signaled to him for a drink. Then I rubbed my throat. After watching my charade, he then turned and assessed the bamboo behind him. He waved me over and cracked the bamboo, which I drank out of it like a long cup.

He yanked down an overhead branch full of dark purple berries. I ate one then I couldn't stop.

then I couldn't stop.

I asked him if he was taking me to his people. He merely sat down again as though he was about to watch a show.

At this point, I knew he wasn't a threat.

Maybe an assessment of whether I'm a threat, and he'd not take a risk for now. I also reminded myself how outsiders were not welcome in his village.

I walked back and gathered my bag then sat on another log in the shade and out of the sun.

With not much else to do, I'm writing this entry like a scientist.

I still don't know if I can go back or what happened to my friends. Did Maria know they were looking specifically for me? I wasn't worth anything for a ransom, although I guess they didn't know anything except I was from another country, and as I learned from their theft, they were desperate people.

Now I'm the desperate one.

I left my son and husband, who love me, believing I was doing something valuable in the world.

Now I'm in a world where I don't belong.

And every day will be a miracle from this time forward.

I'll keep writing in this journal for as long as my two blue pens last.

It might be my only link to maintaining any sanity.

34

EDEN

ROSE WHIMPERS, and both Brenda and I glance up from the journal.

"It's him, isn't it," she says.

"I think so." I want to read more as I'm scared for Gran, only not now when Rose is awake. Dropping the journal in my bag, I unclip the safety belt and place Rose on my lap. She stares at Brenda in the way a one-year-old would to a stranger.

"This is Brenda," I say to Rose.

Brenda leans over and makes baby noises to Rose before I get the chance to add, "She's Gran's best friend." Rose wouldn't understand, only I wanted to say it for Brenda's sake.

"Oh, you're babysitting Eden again. Thank you for bringing her. You know how I love babies."

I'm stunned for a moment. Brenda still thinks I'm Gran.

Brenda's love of children hasn't waned, and I watch her connect with Rose in a special way for a few minutes. My thoughts drift back to the journal, but I can't become lost in Gran's world of the past when I must be organized in the present, and I'm already distracted by Samuel's parents' arrival.

Sophie interrupts us and says she needs to attend to Brenda and give her some meds with her morning tea.

I thank her for the wonderful care and promise to come back to visit soon. I kiss Brenda on her cheek and tell her I love her.

"I love you, too, dear," she says and smiles.

BEFORE GOING HOME, I do some last-minute shopping to prepare for Samuel's parents' arrival. I also send messages to Faith and Mum asking for ideas for Rose's first birthday. Samuel didn't want a fuss, and although one minute he's indulging in extravagant gifts for me like the car, house, and engagement ring, the next he is playing down society's cultural ways like not making a deal out of one-year-old birthday parties. Wanting quality time with his family is understandable. Now we have all our families together, and I want to make a deal about it—confetti, balloons, cake, and poppers.

Walking into the party shop with Rose confirms her delight. She screams with excitement at the balloons on the ceiling. She kicks her legs, demanding to get out of the stroller. "Okay, okay." I unclip her safety belt and follow her through the store wheeling an empty stroller. "Which one do you like?"

She points randomly, then stops at the pink balloons and the silver ones with pink confetti. After ordering several for Thursday night, I pay and take one balloon away with us and tie the ribbon to Rose's wrist. We leave the store, and I sit to order online all the food for Thursday while my daughter is obsessed with the balloon floating from her wrist.

After clicking the delivery time for the food, my phone vibrates with an incoming call from Samuel.

"Hey."

"Hey, is everything okay?" Samuel rarely calls me from work.

"I'm sorry. I must stay back to work. I'll be there for dinner only it won't be until after seven. My parents can get a ride to the house. I'm checking you'll be home to greet them."

"Honey, I can pick them up from the hotel. Rose and I could go now as we're looking forward to seeing them."

"Please don't feel like they expect it, and they're happy to meet us at the house."

I shake my head. *Aren't they excited to be here, and why is he playing it low-key?*

"Send me their cell numbers and the hotel."

"Eden, it's unnecessary."

"It is necessary. It's an exciting time. I'll see you at home. I love you."

"I love you too. And thank you."

I end the call and can't help a weird sensation building in my gut that the truth of Samuel's relationship with his parents might be revealed during this visit.

A few hours later, I arrive at a busy city hotel. I veer into the concierge area, give him the details, and moments later, a fair-haired couple emerges through the revolving door. I step out of the car, and the closer I get, the more their appearances remind me of Samuel. I can't help it, I almost pounce on his mother.

"I'm so happy to finally meet you in person." I give her a tight hug. Turning to his father, I embrace him with equal warmth. "I'm Eden, if you haven't already guessed."

Caroline chuckles. "It's lovely to meet you." A few words and her American accent is noted.

"I'm sorry the traffic is crazy this time of day. Have you been waiting long? Please get in. Rose is in the car." My face is tight from smiling so hard. Although they seem pleased to see me, their expressions are almost professional, and I'm not overcome by their excitement.

Caroline moves to the rear door while Christopher takes the front seat. The concierge places their bags in the trunk, and after thanking him, I take the driver's seat and find the McMahon's already engaging with Rose. My daughter's eyes are wide, watching these strangers dote on her. Finally, she mutters some words, looks at me, and says, "Dad-da."

"Yes, we'll see Dad-da soon. This is Gran and Grandpa."

I glance at Christopher before pulling out into the traffic, and I'm met with the same blue eyes holding the seriousness I see in Samuel's eyes. I then turn to Caroline, and although her eyes are also blue, they are not as vivid as her husband's and son's eyes. Her hair is pure gray and cut into a stylish bob cut. She smiles at me, and the lines around her eyes deepen.

Along the Glenelg esplanade, I point out my family's hotel and explain how it's been in my family since the mid-1950s and we have transformed it to be a popular holiday accommodation. I can't help boasting as we have come a long way from struggling with finances for many years, and over the last seven years, we have slowly become financially comfortable.

"I understand the appeal of the location," Christopher says.

"And here's our place," I say with equal pride. "Samuel fell in love with our home the moment he saw it."

"It's exquisite," Carolyn murmurs.

Christopher seems to take it all in.

The garage door opens to the basement level, and I veer the car inside.

After turning off the alarm, I help Christopher lug their suitcases to the second level. I realize the stairs aren't ideal with their luggage and why they probably preferred a hotel with an elevator. Caroline requested time to unpack some of their belongings, so Rose and I wait in the family lounge until they are ready. I prepare refreshments since we're ordering takeout for the evening meal.

"It's a beautiful home," Caroline says after descending the staircase in the same stylish dress. She has kept her heels on, and although not a stiletto heel, the clicking sound on the floor reflects importance in the way she walks. She looks around the room while waiting for Christopher, only a few steps behind her. He remains in dress pants, white shirt, and black tie. They move toward the floor-to-ceiling windows and stare out at the ocean, the sun now lower in the sky and shining directly into the room.

"I can close the external blinds if you prefer."

"It's the first month of winter in LA, so we're happy for the warmth. Although we can't complain about the California weather," Caroline states.

God, I hate small talk.

I bring out the refreshments and place the plate of cheeses and dips on the table. "Can I get you some wine or coffee or tea?"

"A green tea for me." Caroline stares at the plate. "Did Samuel mention I don't eat dairy?"

Shit. We won't be eating the quiche I bought for lunch tomorrow.

"He mentioned it, but since having Rose, my memory is terrible." I'm not throwing my husband under the bus to his parents when I know he's doing his utmost to impress them.

"Eden?"

My shoulder slumps at the sound of Samuel's voice coming from the lower level. "We're all up here, honey," I call back.

Samuel appears from the stairway wearing a white shirt, dark pants, and a navy tie.

"Samuel." His mother beams at him and almost falls into his arms, causing him to step backward.

"Mom," he says, stroking her hair. "I hope the trip was comfortable."

When she releases him for Christopher to shake his hand, her expression tells of the same concern as mine. When you hug Samuel, there's no hiding his thinning frame.

"Son." Christopher places a hand over Samuel's and then pulls him into a hug with three pats on the back. "You're looking mighty fine, son," he says, assessing his formal clothes.

I'm in a strappy top with a mid-length skirt and flip-flops. Only now do I realize how underdressed I am compared to the McMahon family.

"Dad-da," Rose calls out.

"Excuse me," Samuel says, his smile now for his daughter. He scoops her into his arms and places a loud kiss on her cheek. "Hello, beautiful girl. Have you met your grandparents?" He places Rose on his hip and returns to his parents while gushing over Rose.

I stand back and watch, a little bewildered as to why they didn't do this immediately when arriving home. I push the thought aside since they probably aren't thinking straight with time zones and probable exhaustion, then go about preparing glasses of cold water topped with ice along with Caroline's green tea.

There's more small talk, especially about their business-class flight and the sights of Sydney. Samuel also talks about the places he hopes to visit.

All news to me.

Samuel begins to boast about Rose. The conversation doesn't last before his father asks him about his work.

Our meal arrives, and we eat out on the balcony.

I carry Rose inside to bathe her and put her to bed.

By the time I return, Samuel is in the kitchen with his parents.

"Well, it's only Monday, and I have a big week ahead of me. I'll see you all tomorrow night." He smiles at me. "No doubt Eden has plans to show you around Adelaide."

"Is there anywhere in particular you wish to visit, or do you want me to take you on a mystery tour?"

"I recommend the mystery tour," Samuel jokes.

"We could discuss it in the morning," Caroline suggests. "Perhaps have one day with Rose before we roam the countryside."

Adelaide is hardly countryside. And only one day?

Samuel explains they have their own living area off the bedroom so if they can't sleep, they're welcome to use it as they won't disturb us. He gives them the code to our keyless front door. His father mentions how they have adapted to the time zone, thanks to sleeping comfortably on their flight.

"I have also arranged for our cleaner to visit daily," Samuel adds.

What? Since when do we have a cleaner?

He doesn't look at me.

"She has a code to the door and will visit around ten every morning."

My jaw drops.

I glance around the room. The house is clean and tidy—I manage it fine.

Samuel kisses his mother's cheek then places a hand on his father's shoulder. "I hope you're comfortable here. I'll see you tomorrow night."

Why wouldn't they be comfortable? It's a freaking amazing house.

"We have a wine fridge in the kitchen if you need a little something to help you sleep," he says mainly to his father.

"Rose has me up early in the morning, so I'll head to bed as well. Have a think about where you would like to visit. I recommend the wineries... only a short drive from here."

"I'm interested in seeing the hospital where my son works." Christopher turns to Caroline, and she agrees with him.

"Sure. Just prepare a list."

I follow Samuel up the stairs and into the bathroom. He squeezes toothpaste on his brush and ignores me standing beside him.

"Since when has my cleaning been insufficient?" I fold my arms over my chest.

"It's something you don't have to worry about. You have enough with Rose, especially now my parents are here." His gaze remains on his reflection while cleaning his teeth.

Leaning forward, I force him to meet my gaze. "You invited a stranger into our home and gave her the code to our door, and what, the security alarm?" I ask, disappointed.

Samuel leans over, rinses then wipes his mouth with the hand towel. "Joan isn't a stranger. She works at the hospital and needs more work as she's a young single parent."

"So, you can account for her because of a few conversations. Jesus, Samuel, this is our home."

"I can assure you she's of no danger to us." He unbuttons the top few buttons, checks himself in the mirror, and leaves the room.

I follow him. "It's our personal space. Our belongings. I'm happy to do it."

"All material things that can be replaced."

My jaw drops for the second time tonight. "We don't need a cleaner every day."

He stops and turns to me with an exasperated expression. "My mother has OCD. For peace and to comfort her tendency, it's easier to have Joan come every day while they're here. Then I told her we can plan something permanent even once a fortnight after I discuss it with you." He turns to finish unbuttoning his shirt and drops it into the laundry chute.

He hangs his trousers and then climbs into bed, pulling the bedcovers up to his neck.

Inhaling a deep breath, I try a different angle. "I guess there's much for me to learn about your mother, although I sensed her concern for you."

Samuel rolls onto his side. "Eden, I didn't have a good day, and I don't have the energy to talk about it tonight. I'm thankful for all you're doing, and I'm happy to chat tomorrow. But please, not tonight."

35

SAMUEL

THIRTY MINUTES of CPR and no sign of life.

Calling it never feels right.

When Dr. Tolley told Samuel to stop, he wanted to continue with compressions. The guilt of losing his friends never leaves him, and in a hospital with modern medicine, they still couldn't save the forty-year-old man, a father to three children.

Samuel squeezes his eyes tight and wills himself to get a decent night's sleep. *Please, no nightmares tonight*, he says in his head. The logical side of his brain kicks in, reminding him of the facts.

Death is inevitable. From the day we're born, we are destined to die. The preferable cause is aging after a quality life, yet the percentage of accidental deaths or lifestyle choices exacerbates premature death. Then he thinks of childhood diseases. Cancer. The very thing that drove him to search for a cure rather than treat the symptoms.

Samuel has done a full circle, and while he's not satisfied by his career choice, it's the only option to be here with Eden until he proves he'll not disappear and be reckless again.

Reckless.

If only his father knew the truth of how he came to stay in Ulara. And yet his journey to find a safer haven for the Ularan people was just that.

Reckless.

Many of them died in doing so with thoughtless consideration for his own health. Longevity is now in doubt after the stress he placed on his body. Modern medicine fails to find an explanation, yet in his heart, he knows it's a combination of physical and mental problems.

To make matters worse, the hospital has a shortage of staff and beds, and he understands why his employment got fast-tracked. He has committed to staying back and helping. What other choice does he have when he has taken a vow to heal? A vow where prevention is preferable to a cure.

Prevention must be a mindset in society.

He lets out a sigh.

He needs to get off the merry-go-round.

Set a plan and work toward it.

Ayahuasca can help him do this.

A place where he can clear his head and fight the demons threatening to undo him.

Visualizing the vivid colors of ayahuasca in his mind, he imagines the kaleidoscope of neon lights and changing patterns before fingers flick through the filing cabinet of thoughts and memories before dissecting each piece of emotion.

Hopefully, it's enough to lull him into sleep.

Every day is unchanging.

He wakes early and is out the door before his family rises. He returns after they have eaten dinner. His father chats to him briefly, asking about his day—standard conversation. Yesterday, his father's demeanor had changed. His eyes flicked with concern before he smoothed his expression to a trained poker face—a skill of their profession.

Samuel feels bad leaving Eden to entertain his parents without him. She told him not to worry as they are spending time with their granddaughter, and she's showing them all the sights. His heart warms, knowing she's trying. Eden is an amazing woman, and it's why he is here because he knows he can't lose her again.

He unlocks the door, relieved it's Friday night and walks the stairs to the living room and hears the low hum of conversation.

"We enjoyed Victor Harbor and considered staying a week," his mother says to Eden.

Interesting.

It's a small coastal town south of Adelaide, and he assumed it wouldn't appeal to his parents when they're used to the bustle of Los Angeles.

"Evening," he says as he enters the room.

Eden is the first to hug him, and it's tighter than usual.

"Are you okay?" he whispers.

She nods quickly. "I've missed you."

If something upset her, he trusts she'll tell him later when they're alone.

His mother also hugs him.

His dad comes in for a handshake. "How was your day, son?"

It's the same conversation as every night.

Tonight, he won't be in bed early.

After Samuel has eaten dinner and they have discussed their plans for the weekend, Eden heads to bed, leaving Samuel to have time with his parents. Alone.

After hearing about his parents' adventures over the past few days, his mother kisses his cheek and takes the stairs to the bedroom.

"Rose is exhausting her." His father's lips curl, hinting at a smile. "And she loves every minute." Christopher looks at the dark ocean as if he's enjoying a memory.

"Rose has that effect on you," Samuel replies. He lifts his feet onto the balcony's railing and leans back in his chair, crossing his fingers and placing them behind his head. Elbows wide, he relaxes into the deck chair and stares at the stars in the night sky. "By now, I assume you've grasped why I rushed to get here. I couldn't let another minute pass without seeing my two girls."

"Yes, it's clear you love your family, and they love you. Only I wished you remained in LA to have a few more tests, son. Eden would have waited. You might have found more answers." He stalls. "Am I correct in observing you have lost more weight?"

Samuel closes his eyes and opens them to focus on the moonlight dancing over the ocean. "I have it under control."

"You're pushing yourself too hard. I, for one, understand a sign of burnout."

Samuel looks at his father. His eyes hold an understanding he's never witnessed before. "I've only just started working, and it's not burnout," he replies, in case he's testing his commitment.

His father nods slowly. "Please keep me up to date with your treatment. I want to be here for you." Lines in his forehead deepen with a frown. "I mean it. We have all made mistakes in the past. You have a bright future with a beautiful family, and I don't want you taking the same path as me."

Whoa. Samuel sits in silence, taking in his father's words. During his brief trip back to LA, he witnessed a change in his father, yet he was firm in making Samuel promise to uphold his responsibility.

What has given him a change of heart?

Samuel heads to bed and slips under the covers, careful not to wake Eden. He tosses and turns, unable to sleep even though he's exhausted. He closes his eyes and visualizes the future, seeing himself as a happy, healthier man with enough energy to keep up with his daughter. Picturing his family together relaxes his mind into sleep until images of his other family creep into his thoughts and his dreams.

The dreams start the same...

Walking. Slashing vine leaves to make a path for those following behind him. Tïmenneng leads the way, ensuring no poisonous thorny vines are on the path, as a brush with certain plants can lead to death in minutes. He is astute, but he's tiring, and Kaikare takes over in her assessment of the potential danger ahead. The wails begin from behind, then a messenger trots up to him. It's time to rest. The crying lasts a few hours as he has pushed them beyond their capabilities.

The alternative isn't what he wants to consider.

They can't stay in guerrilla territory.

They have lost lives along the way, and the responsibility is on him. His antibiotic supply is low, and with another infection where it's not treated by the jungle garden, it may be fatal. Two more weeks of walking will place them in safer territory.

Two more weeks.

Some of them can barely walk for two more hours.

Tïmenneng and some of the younger warriors carry the weak in hammocks strung between them. It gives those who suffer time to rest. Every day, the warriors continue to amaze him with the strength of their minds to continue without complaint.

Night falls, and they sit around a fire.

Kaikare has taken her father's role and tells a story of their ancestors. The underlying message is bravery in the face of hardship and talks about those who have died for them. He compares it to war and fighting for freedom. Death for others to live a better life.

He wants no further death on his hands tonight.

A woman cries out.

Kaikare goes to her.

She's in premature labor.

A sob escapes him as he realizes this is his fault. He has pushed the women too far. In a foreign country and at night, danger lurks, so searching the forest for plants to slow the birth is out of the question.

The women beg to search for the plants they can use in a smoking ceremony. The wails begin as they pray to their gods. Kaikare nods at Samuel, and the women rush into the darkness, hoping to find something close to camp. Mari' Iwoi follows to guide them back.

Chirké and Itariru stay with the young girl, dancing and singing around her. Arms folded, Kaikare watches Samuel, and when he waves her on, she goes to the group and takes charge. The decisions are out of his hands and into more capable ones.

The women return, and their ceremony begins. For hours, Samuel stares into the fire. The dry heat soothes his moist and swollen feet. The other men do the same, using the flames to heal their wounds.

Suddenly, the singing stops.

He can't see into the circle of women, especially with them away from the fire and closer to the jungle shadows. Kaikare emerges holding a bloodied baby, part of the umbilical cord dangling with the twine attached.

She asks him to give the baby a blessing, a blessing of the modern world as well as the Ularan world. They still believe his medicine holds magic, yet he can't save this tiny bundle. The baby girl doesn't cry. Watching her tiny chest, she's barely breathing, and he realizes she doesn't have long. Tears fall from his cheeks as he whispers to the baby. Dipping his finger in the ash from the fire, he marks the butterfly symbol on the baby's forehead.

Kaikare takes the baby from his hands and returns her to the mother. He stands and walks a few paces closer to the forest and looks into the dark shadows. The trees whispered their secrets to the shaman, telling him how to heal the people. Samuel doesn't have this power and only learns in the way of science and how the plants treat disease and save lives in the way he understands. If he could take ayahuasca, a light might direct them on their journey. For now, he needs to rely on a map he has inside his head and hope they find another river soon.

He snaps out of the daze when yellow eyes peer back at him. At first, he's caught in delirium wishing the eyes belonged to the shaman's spirit. The growl awakens him to the physical form. He doesn't have time to think before the jaguar has knocked him to the ground, its sharp claws tearing his skin. He rolls once, holding its head away from his face. In a second, his life flashes before him. In the moment, all he sees is Eden's beautiful face, her smile telling him she'll forever love him.

He yells a roar back to shock the jaguar, and then it rolls off him with the force of a blow. Dark hair catches his eye as the person rolls over the jaguar. Tïmenneng leaps and joins the wrestle until the jaguar's lifeless body is shoved off Kaikare. Samuel scrambles to her and pulls her to her feet. A bloodied knife in her hand. She may have stabbed its gut, but Tïmenneng slit its throat. Weapons from the intruders who tried to kill them. Blood trickles down his friends' faces and arms as he asks them if they're hurt.

They are more concerned for him.

Yet he can't stop thanking them over and over.

Kaikare told Samuel she could never live with herself if Eden lost both her grandmother and him. It's her duty to protect him as he's protecting everyone else.

Wrapping his arms around her, he allows the quiet sobs to erupt from his throat. A second longer and their fate may have taken a different path.

Behind them a chorus of cries begins. Fear of the jaguar among the people signifies they aren't safe here.

The mother carries into the circle the lifeless body of the baby. She drops to her knees at Samuel's feet.

What the hell has he done?

36

EDEN

Samuel moans, and it's loud enough to wake me from my sleep.

I force my eyes open and tap the bedside table several times, searching for my phone. The room is pitch black. I assume it's around two o'clock, the time he usually wakes me with his nightmares—2:20 a.m.

Sliding closer, I rest an arm on his chest and whisper, "You're safe."

Over the past few months, I have done this countless times while still half asleep.

I don't wake him. I'm sending a message to his subconscious to reassure he's with me and everything is going to be fine. Only tonight his moans were different.

And he's unusually cold.

Coming out of the daze, I palm his forehead. It's like he's been out in the snow. Reaching under the covers, I pat his inner thigh, a place of warmth only like the rest of him, there isn't enough flesh on his bones, and it raises a red flag.

I spring upright and switch on the bedside lamp.

Samuel is lying on his back, pale. Each breath comes with a low grunt.

The room tilts in a moment of panic, and I remind myself to breathe.

"Samuel," I say louder and press his shoulder.

No response.

"Samuel," I shout and shake him.

He groans yet doesn't wake.

I race out of the bedroom and bang on his parents' door.

"Christopher," I shout. "There's something wrong with Samuel. Please come and check on him."

I only make it a few steps before the door swings open to Christopher who's tying the cord of his robe around his waist. "I noticed he struggled with dinner." He runs a hand through his disheveled gray hair.

"It's not the food." I scurried toward our room, and he's right behind me.

He leans over Samuel and listens for a breath, then lays a finger on his neck pulse point.

"Call 911," he says in a low voice, even though I sense he's anything but calm.

"It's triple zero in Australia." I grab my phone.

"What emergency service are you requiring?" the operator asks.

"Ambulance," I blurt out.

It feels like an eternity before they connect. The medical operator asks me to describe his condition.

I emphasize how cold he is, and I can't wake him. I give my address and activate the speaker so Christopher can hear the directions.

Christopher arranges the bedding so more is covering Samuel.

"Does he have a pulse?"

"Yes. And he's breathing. Shallow breaths and moaning."

"A thready pulse," Christopher says, and I repeat it.

"An ambulance is on the way. Do you have stairs?"

"Yes, we do. Our bedroom is upstairs."

"Please switch on a front light and be ready to unlock the door. Do you want to stay on the phone in case he deteriorates?"

I glance at Christopher.

He shakes his head. "I can monitor him until an ambulance arrives."

Caroline appears and leans over Samuel. "What happened?" She touches his forehead. "Christopher, he's so cold."

Christopher looks up at me. "Does he have a stethoscope and blood pressure monitor?"

I turn toward the cupboard. "Yes, er—"

"Caroline, please bring mine." He looks at me. "I carry a wireless monitor and a stethoscope."

"Thank you," I say quickly.

I move to get out of the way and sit on my side of the bed, lost in how to help. My throat is dry. My thoughts are racing. I'll need to go to the hospital with Samuel. Only I don't want to leave Rose with Samuel's parents yet.

Caroline rushes into the room and hands Christopher the monitor. He places the strap around his arm and presses a button to inflate the bladder. A digital reading comes up. His silence speaks volumes. Placing the end of the stethoscope on Samuel's chest, Christopher closes his eyes and listens to Samuel's heart.

His eyes meet mine.

"Is he okay?" I croak.

"How has he been the past few months?"

I blow out air slowly as I consider my answer. "He is stressed. And he's lost more weight, not gained any. He has struggled with eating and..." I can feel my heart breaking knowing he never wanted to return to society, "... his nightmares are bad. I thought he was having one tonight when he made weird breathing noises. It happens a lot around this time."

"The nightmares? How long has he been having them?"

"Since he returned. I thought he was suffering from PTSD and suggested he seek help."

Christopher stares at his son as though he's seeing him in a different light.

"That damn jungle," he mutters.

In the distance, I hear a siren. I race down the stairs and call Mum while I wait at the door.

"Mum." I burst into tears.

"Is it Rose, dear?"

"No. It's Samuel. An ambulance is on the way. Could you please come and stay with Rose so I can go to the hospital?"

"Of course. I'll be there soon. Try to stay calm, honey. He'll be fine."

"His parents are here. I'm sorry. It's not the way I wanted you to meet them."

"Eden," she says gently. "Stay calm. We'll all manage. Focus on Samuel. I'll be there in a few minutes."

For weeks, I have been telling myself *he's not fine,* and Mum has watched me worry despite Samuel saying over and over he only needs time.

Fuck time.

I should have gone with my gut instinct and made him tell me about his ordeal so he could heal faster. This treading around like I'm on an icy lake thawing out is bullshit.

I take a deep breath and remind myself not to panic because my thoughts are mashing together, and it's pointless looking for blame.

The sirens stop when the van pulls into the driveway. I greet two male paramedics and lead them up the stairs. They assess Samuel, asking questions and discussing his condition with his father.

The sight of him like this crushes me. He's so pale he looks—I can't say the word.

Don't you dare leave me again.

Tears choke my throat.

Please, Samuel. Fight whatever it is because I need you.

They take his blood pressure, immediately place a mask over his face, and begin oxygen therapy.

One officer pulls out a silver foil blanket and wraps it over Samuel. The other inserts a cannula into his arm and sets up a fluid bag. They talk in medical terminology to Christopher, and although I can understand some, all I hear is my heartbeat thumping in my chest while watching them inject drugs into the cannula.

"Does Dr. McMahon suffer from anorexia nervosa?"

"No. His condition is unique," I say in a low voice because I've heard unconscious people can hear, and I don't want to talk about him as though he's not in the room. "My fiancé was lost in the South American jungle for some time." The paramedics and Christopher gape at me. "He was close to starvation and physically exhausted. He also suffers nightmares, and I assumed it was PTSD."

One officer makes a note while continuing to monitor his blood pressure.

"He'll require VPI," Christopher says quietly. "And more blood tests considering his environment over the past several years. I wanted him to undergo more testing on his brief visit to Los Angeles, our home, in early August, only he was determined to travel to Australia only a couple of weeks after emerging from the jungle."

The paramedics and Christopher continue talking in their own jargon. My vision blurs from tears. I never knew what happened when Samuel first arrived in LA and those vital few weeks after barely making it out alive.

Has he known all along he was unwell, and it's why he rushed here to see us instead of seeking medical treatment?

"He should wake," the taller paramedic tells me after administering drugs into the cannula.

Samuel moans and opens his eyes.

"Hey." I sit beside him and run my hand over his cheek.

He blinks several times and looks around the room as though trying to comprehend his whereabouts. "What happened?" he murmurs.

I shake my head. "I don't know." I swipe tears from my eyes.

"Did I pass out?"

I shake my head.

"Dr. McMahon," the tall officer begins. "You're hypotensive. We're unsure if it could be from an infection leading to sepsis. Although your temperature is dangerously low, so you may have suffered shock from a nightmare. Your partner informed us of your recent trip, and you may have suffered some trauma."

Samuel's gaze flicks to mine.

I'm not backing down this time.

Christopher speaks, and Samuel's gaze shoots to his father. He still looks disorientated. "You need the tests I suggested you undertake back home, son."

If I leave the room, he might talk to them.

I grab clothes and head to the bathroom to change. Leaning both hands on the basin, I inhale a few conscious breaths to clear my head. Then I quickly attend to my hair, wash my face, and spray under my arms. I change into a summer dress then go into Rose's bedroom to check on her. Thankfully, she hasn't woken and is curled up on her side. Tentatively, I place a hand on her head. She feels warm—normal warm. After creeping out, I return to our bedroom and gather a change of clothes for Samuel because he'll not want to remain in his boxer briefs and T-shirt.

The paramedic is talking. "We need to stabilize your temperature and blood pressure in the hospital, and you might need to remain in for a series of tests, especially on your heart. We have detected an arrhythmia. Possibly a response to what happened tonight."

His eyes find me from across the room. "I'm sorry," he mouths to me.

"Don't be." I shake my head, then go to him and squeeze his hand. "I'll follow the ambulance and be there soon. Everything will be fine."

"No rush. Hospital protocol and all." He forces a reassuring smile. "You'll be sitting around. Stay and rest and come up in the morning."

"It *is* morning, and I won't be able to rest." I turn to the paramedics. "Where are you taking him?

"To the Bedford Park hospital."

"Good. Samuel works there. I'll follow soon."

"We'll retrieve the ambulant chair so we can strap you in for the stairs," the tall medic says.

"I can manage the stairs." Samuel moves upright in the bed.

"Sir, we prefer you in the chair."

"Samuel, your blood pressure," his father reiterates sternly.

In perfect timing, Mum appears in the doorway. Her hair is unbrushed. I walk with her to Rose's room. "How is he?"

"Stable for now. They're concerned about his temperature and blood pressure." She wraps an arm around my waist and pulls me in close.

"He's in expert hands. He'll be okay."

"I'm sorry I panicked and called you. Rose is still asleep and will probably remain asleep until six. I didn't want to leave her because Samuel's parents are still strangers to her."

"It's fine. I'll chat with them, and when she wakes, they can call me. I'll come up and get her then rather than wake her now. It might be good for the three of them to have some alone time."

"What if Rose cries because she doesn't know them?"

Mum squeezes my hand. "I know you're worried, but you don't have to stress about this. Caroline is a mother." She smiles. "And if Rose doesn't settle, they can call me. You go in the ambulance, honey, and don't worry about Rose."

Samuel still feels cold, not the ice-cold sensation of when he was unconscious. I take his hand in mine, and his eyes flutter open.

"I'm sorry," he whispers for the hundredth time. It's all he says before his eyes close again, as though he's completely exhausted.

"After you get some treatment," I whisper. "You're not coming home until you have an appointment to speak to a psychologist."

His eyes search mine. He doesn't argue with me or simply doesn't have the energy.

I kiss his fingers wrapped in mine. "You scared me. We can make small talk and dance around this, yet nothing will help you heal except professional help."

His eyes well up. "I'm sorry I let you down."

Seeing him like this breaks me. "You didn't," I croak while shaking my head in disbelief.

"I tried to be strong." He slowly closes his eyes and opens them again.

My heart shatters with him being ashamed, as though it's a weakness on his behalf. "You're the strongest person I know." I lean and kiss his cheek. "You have superpowers to survive what you did."

Silent tears stream down his cheeks. "Many didn't."

I place his hand over my heart, my hand covering his. "No, it's to be expected. You tried. You can't save everyone. The alternative was they *all* died if they remained in Ulara." His eyes lower to our hands. "My heart beats for you, and it hurts for you. And right now, I'm hurting too."

Samuel turns his head and closes his eyes as though something is destroying his demeanor. Today isn't the time for him to deal with the past. I need him to focus his energy on healing himself so he can come home to me.

A doctor walks around the curtain. "Hello, Dr. McMahon, I'm Dr. Weeks." He glances at his chart and notes the machine beeping in the corner. Then he looks at me.

"Hi. I'm Eden, Samuel's fiancée. I'll pop out while you speak to Samuel."

Samuel eyeballs me, and his expression softens as though he understands what I'm doing—giving him space to discuss his condition honestly. "There's a café on the second floor, Eden. Grab a bite to eat, and you might need some caffeine to stay awake."

I'll need more than caffeine.

By mid-morning, Samuel is falling in and out of sleep. After speaking to Caroline and Christopher, they decide to visit after lunch, so I head home so Samuel can rest. They have the keys to his Porsche so they can use his car until the hospital discharges Samuel. Then I call Mum, and she insists on keeping Rose for the day, and I'm relieved. As much as I want Samuel's parents to see Rose, there's only so much I can handle.

After a brief conversation about his condition, I tell his parents I need to rest. Once my body touches our luxurious mattress, I melt into it. Only my mind can't shut down. My thoughts tear at my heart, and my gut churns.

Gran's journal is on the bedside table.

"Gran," I whisper as though she can hear me. I close my eyes and imagine her presence. "Please, help Samuel. I know you have touched him spiritually. Please, please heal him."

I open my eyes and reach for her words to heal my aching heart.

37

IVY

March 11, 1963

I survived another night sleeping in the canoe.

God, my back hurts.

My friend has given me a clay bowl of water from which I drink. No cup. I simply tip the bowl and drink from it. I'm clueless as to how the water is clear and thankful it's not scooped straight from the river. While sitting and watching me, which seems to be his new hobby, he refills it from the bamboo. A flower and leaves float on top. I sense it's not where it is sourced. Regardless, I'm grateful he's taking care of me during the day.

Last night I was afraid to close my eyes yet also exhausted from only a few hours' sleep the night before. Without seeing any of his people, I knew I was being watched. I could feel it. Sense it. It's hard to describe, but out here in the jungle, my senses are on high alert, and it's a new awareness I've developed—my body's adaptation to prevent death.

It's something I've thought about frequently, especially facing it every day. Will it be today or tomorrow? A few months from now? Will I make it back to Australia, to my family?

My friend is watching me cry. I can't help it. I'm extremely overwhelmed. If I'm to survive long enough to get back to Maria, I must make peace with these people hidden in the jungle and hopefully return without an arrow in my back.

There are more men standing beside my friend.

They speak, not Spanish, their own indigenous language.

One is walking toward me, and I keep my head down, writing.

March 18, 1963

A week has now passed since I arrived in Ulara.

My bag was confiscated and only returned to me today.

The women took my clothes and washed them, and although I have them back, they gave me a tweed skirt and beads to wear around my neck. I wear it to keep the peace, but it doesn't leave much to the imagination. My joggers are gone, replaced by my flat sandals. I'm not risking a parasite entering my feet, and yet I'm bathing in a stream with the ladies every morning. I'm also living in the village in my own hut, although everyone keeps a distance.

In the mornings after bathing in the stream with the other women, I walk down to the river's edge and listen for a sign that Maria has come looking for me. I check where I abandoned the canoe. Again, the area is absent of any sign of her presence. Footprints get washed away by the late afternoon rain, yet I hoped she'd call out for me or leave a note or something in the canoe.

The people in the village are gentle. Most of the women have shorter hair, except for the children. They have long hair, and some are plaited with beads. It appears the older women with gray hair may grow their hair as do the women with children. I'm not sure about hierarchy, although the hair signifies a rule within the village. The men's jet-black hair is cut around their faces in a bowl shape, except for my friend. His hair sits at his shoulders. Until this morning, I never knew why. Only minutes ago, the chief, and I assume a medicine man—the shaman—emerged from their respective huts and gathered in the circle, both with the same fashionable long hair with graying strands throughout. Only they wore a crown of feathers on their head and walked with sticks that jingled with beads and bones of dead animals.

It feels safer for me to keep my head down and keep writing than to stare at... I guess they're my new leaders. The bosses of Ulara.

April 1, 1963

Two weeks ago, my journal was taken from me. The chief and shaman perceived my writing, being the pen and paper, as some form of magic or a demon. I guess it's referred to as evil spirits here, and I was associated as one. When they held my journal over the fire, I screamed. I fell to my knees and begged for forgiveness, then crawled to them and held out my hands while sobbing like a baby. It wasn't my finest moment. Desperation controlled my emotions as my journal is a link to home or for my family to know what has happened to me if I don't make it out of this godforsaken country.

It all started when I took the shaman's hand and showed him how to use the pen, hoping to impress him. Only, he threw it aside in fear.

I shouldn't have touched him.

My friend collected my journal and took it away for safekeeping.

Today, my friend returned it to me, and I'm not sure if my journal has undergone some ceremony to rid the evil spirit away.

This isn't an April Fool's joke.

Much has happened in the past two weeks, and yet most days are the same. I'm now permitted to work in the fields with the women to earn my keep, so to speak. At night, I have the job of cooking the most basic vegetables.

The men hunt and fish. The women work the fields, prepare the meals, and are solely responsible for the children. Even in the fields, babies are carried in baskets on a woman's back. It's not like the men hunt all day, every day. I have found them sitting in the village making baskets from twine or fishing nets or hammocks. It's fascinating to watch.

The people are self-sufficient, surviving off the land with no running water or electricity. I'm quite amazed by their society.

There's still no sign of Maria, and until I receive something, I fear not to return and place myself or the other volunteers in the community at risk.

Some nights I wonder if any of them are even alive.

The thought makes me nauseous.

How did volunteering come to this?

Life or death.

For now, I'm happy to stay here while I'm still welcome and until it's safe to return.

38

EDEN

WITH A SIGH, I close the journal and set it aside. At this point, Gran focused on coming home. The reality of how she ended up in the village would have been traumatic, and I respect Gran's bravery even more. Before closing my eyes, I send a text to Samuel.

> I hope you're okay. I'll come back tonight to visit. I love you xx

> I'm like a pin cushion with the number of tests being conducted and out of every orifice. Please stay home with Rose and my parents today, and I'll see you in the morning. I love you x

I bring up his number on my phone to call, and it goes to his voicemail.

"I'm not waiting until tomorrow to see you," I say. "I'm worried about you. I'll put Rose to bed then come and see you tonight. I love you."

As soon as I finish my message, the phone vibrates with an incoming call.

"Hey. I'm sorry. The specialist was here. He just left."

"How are you?" My voice trembles with concern, hoping he doesn't push me away.

"I'm fine. A little embarrassed and sorry you had to see me go through this."

“Samuel, don’t. I’ve been expecting something to happen only I assumed it was PTSD and not something sinister. I could’ve helped somehow.”

“Edes, there was nothing you could do, and I’m sorry again I couldn’t hide it better.”

“The point is you shouldn’t have to hide it,” I murmur.

“It’s something only I could deal with and believed time would help. Unfortunately, I ignored too many signs indicating I wasn’t okay.”

I inhale a sharp breath. “Please don’t say that. You’re going to be okay.”

“I’ll be doing everything I can to get out of here, bar for now, I need rest, so I’ll see you in the morning?” His voice ends on a high note.

“I want to see you tonight.”

“Babe. It was a rough night. Get some rest. Look after Rose. You could take my parents out to dinner.”

“They’re as concerned for you as I am.”

“There’s nothing you can do. I’m having never-ending tests. Fecal, urine, blood, nasal. Seriously, tomorrow will be a better day.”

I let out an exasperated breath. “Okay, but please message me regularly so I know you’re fine.”

“I’m fine. There’s a nurse in my room every ten minutes. I’m already wanting to come home for a rest because the monitors beep constantly throughout the night.”

His reassuring words fail to ease my concern.

“Okay. I’ll see you in the morning. I love you.”

“I love you too.”

I end the call.

I find Samuel’s parents sitting on the balcony admiring the ocean view. If anywhere could alleviate worry, it’s this vista.

“How is Samuel?” Christopher asks.

“He’s okay, although he wants to rest tonight. We can see him tomorrow.”

I notice Caroline wipe a tear. I go to her and lay a hand on her shoulder. “He promised me everything will be fine. You know your son never breaks a promise.”

Caroline places her soft palm over my hand. “Thank you. For years I told myself he knew what he was doing and we shouldn’t interfere in his life. He’s an adult, and it’s no longer our responsibility to guide him. Yet I can no longer pretend everything is okay. It's not, and I wish I did more to help him."

His parents have surprised the hell out of me.

"The three of us love him unconditionally, and together, we'll make sure he comes out of this with answers because he can't go on without treatment."

A single sob escapes Caroline's throat.

Christopher places a gentle hand on her back. "I promise you both I have colleagues I can ask a favor of and have them help with his case. This isn't a clear-cut diagnosis, so the more doctors to brainstorm, the quicker we'll get answers."

"Thank you, Christopher." Caroline lifts her chin and wipes her eyes.

"Do you mind if I leave you for a bit unless you want to come for a stroll to my parents' house so I can get Rose?"

"I'd love to join you," Caroline says quickly.

"We could head out to dinner in Glenelg. It's a short stroll, and Rose loves sitting outside at the restaurants."

Christopher glances at his wife's heels. "Best we change our shoes first. Maybe I could adapt to you Aussies wearing flip-flops all the time."

Samuel's parents' visit to Australia may be the best thing to bring their family together.

THE FOLLOWING MORNING, we drive to the hospital to see Samuel. After kissing him and letting Rose crawl over him for a couple of minutes, I sit back and try to amuse her while his parents sit and chat. There are times when I see them making ground and showing concern for their son. No longer is there a stiff upper lip and the posh attitude I first witnessed. I don't want to let an opportunity pass, so I tell them I'm taking Rose out to the garden to buy her something from the café to allow them time to talk.

An hour later, I return to red eyes on all three of them. It's not a bad thing to cry, and it doesn't show any weakness if it's not in anger and they have worked out their problems.

"When we leave, would you like us to take Rose home?" Caroline asks.

I glance at Samuel, and he gives a subtle nod. "Sure. I'll let her cuddle her father one more time." I place Rose on the bed, and she sits on top of Samuel. He grunts and exaggerates her heaviness, and she giggles. He lifts her in the air and plants a smoochy kiss on her cheek.

"See you soon, princess."

"You know she's going to believe it's her name as you use it so often."

Samuel chuckles. "It's not a bad thing."

I roll my eyes and smile at Caroline. She stands and comes to hug me. "Thank you for giving us time to spend with Rose. We really appreciate it."

"It makes us happy you can spend time with Rose," I emphasize. I pack up her belongings and pluck a screaming Rose from Samuel and place her in the stroller. "I'll walk your parents down to the car," I tell him.

I slowly rock the stroller to calm Rose while his parents hug Samuel goodbye. We walk the long hallways of the hospital until we get to the parking lot. Rose is almost asleep by the time we get to my car.

"She'll only rest for an hour and then go down again after lunch."

Christopher lifts Rose and clips her into her car seat. "We'll let her sleep then take her down to the beach." He smiles at me as though he's excited to have time with Rose.

"If you have any trouble, let me know, and I'll come straight home. I can either uber it or Mum can come get me. I don't want you making another trip with Rose."

"We'll be fine. And thank you," Caroline chirps.

After waving goodbye, I use the time to mull over all the questions I want to ask Samuel, especially why he considered struggling through this alone.

After Samuel wakes, our conversation is trivial, starting with the details of our dinner last night and how his parents got on well with mine.

My questions start slowly and recount his dreams over the past few months.

"I didn't want to mention this," he says and looks warily at me. "And I know you'll object without consideration."

"What? Tell me, please."

"I've been contemplating returning to Peru and taking ayahuasca."

"Nooo," I whisper.

"It's a way for me to understand what's happening with my body. Find some answers."

"Have you forgotten what happened the last time? How a dark entity interfered, and it could have been disastrous."

"The circumstances were different. This will help me to find the answers within my body. Not to connect with another shaman as powerful as—" He stops and looks at me. His eyes turn sad, and then he looks up at the ceiling. "It's the only way."

"It's not the *only way*. You must have faith in modern medicine as much as you do the shaman. I know you miss him, but you must find the strength to get through this."

"Don't you think I've been trying?" he murmurs and not in anger, more in despair.

I stare at him. Until now, my gentle probes haven't worked so I cross my arms. "Then fucking try harder."

His eyes widen. "You don't know what I've been through."

"I have a fair idea by the details you have shared. You have a lot at stake here, and giving up isn't what we signed up for as a couple. So do what you must and stop trying to avoid the inevitable. I'll find another way... even find some herbalist here if we need to, but you aren't traveling back to Peru, so get that plan out of your goddamn head."

His nostrils flare. I sit on the edge of the bed and hold his hand, ignoring the stubborn anger rolling off him in waves.

"Get mad. Be sad. We're in this together, and we're not leaving Australia, at least not until you're a lot bloody stronger than you are now."

He shakes his head, and a tear rolls down his cheek. Then another. I want to weaken and hug him and let him do what he needs to do, only I can't. I need to be tough and help him get through this without ayahuasca because *I'll* never forget the last time.

"I thought I was going to die." He chokes up on the last word.

Oh god. I crawl up onto the bed and lie beside him. "I won't let it happen."

"In my mind, I had an out-of-body experience and sensed my soul with other souls. In the darkness, I was overwhelmed by the presence of others."

I wrap my arm around him and tighten my hold. "Yet you didn't die. There's a reason you're here. And I'm never allowing you to be alone like that again."

Samuel turns and kisses my cheek. "I thank the universe every day for sending you to me even though you're a pain in the ass."

I snuggle closer. "I'll be whatever it takes to never leave you again."

COME THURSDAY, Samuel is still in the hospital. I know it saddens him not to be home for Rose's birthday, especially with our families together to celebrate.

Helium balloons float over the family room ceiling. I can hear Faith, Caroline, and Mum chatting in one corner while Jake, Dad, and Christopher play noisily with the children. I FaceTime Samuel when we light the candles on the cake Mum made—a caterpillar topped with candy. He's smiling and chatting to Rose, telling her what a clever girl she is, although her efforts in blowing out the single candle resulted in her bangs receiving more air than anywhere else.

After everyone leaves, I take my tired one-year-old and read her a story in her crib. It's not long until her eyes flutter close. I creep out of her room and join Samuel's parents in the living room. The curtains remain open while the sun is near the ocean horizon, casting streaks of pink and orange color across the skies.

Christopher pours a whiskey on ice and stands at the glass admiring the view. Caroline is packing the last of the dishes into the dishwasher.

"Thank you." I place a hand on her back. "I appreciate your help."

She smiles up at me. "I'm glad to help. It's been many years since I've been able to help someone."

It's possible they have a housekeeper, and with only the two of them, I understand what she's saying. Yet I see satisfaction in her eyes and know we all can feel good about ourselves when we do the smallest of gestures to help someone else.

"Would you mind if I asked the cleaner not to come for the rest of the week?"

Caroline blinks at me as though she doesn't know what I'm implying.

"Our house doesn't need to be cleaned daily," I say gently. "And I enjoy cleaning. Once a week is adequate for a house cleaner. Is that okay with you?"

Caroline straightens. "Eden, it's none of my business how you manage your home."

I sit at the kitchen table and pour a glass of red wine from the bottle Faith brought over. "Would you like one?"

She comes to sit beside me. "I have taken a liking to Australian wine."

I chuckle lightly, pour a glass, and slide it to her. "I know we do things differently here, and I like things done my way. My home isn't dirty, and although it's large, it's a new home and easy to manage. I can keep it clean between a professional clean. The reason we have someone visiting daily is Samuel's concern about your OCD."

Caroline takes a sip then slowly her blue eyes meet mine. "I try hard not to let it affect me. Only when I'm somewhere foreign, for the first few days, I find it hard to control."

I place my hand on hers. "I understand. Our home is your home, too, and I want you to relax here."

She twirls the wine in her glass before taking a sip. "Thank you, and to be honest, I have relaxed considerably over the past few days. It's quite laid back here and surprisingly, I enjoy it."

Christopher comes and sits at the table, lightly shaking the ice in his glass to blend with the whiskey.

"I'm glad I have both of you here as I want to discuss Samuel. He's highly strung since leaving the jungle."

"Eden, we tried to make him stay with us in LA and receive all the tests when he first arrived. We were concerned and alerted the authorities to what happened, only our son is stubborn and refused to stay longer than necessary so he could come to you. It's why our last email omitted concern as he made us promise not to mention he was home."

I gasp. "Why would he do that?" He knew I'd go crazy worrying about him.

"He believed enough time had passed for you to have moved on. Or you assumed he wasn't returning to you and again moved on with your life. He intended to assess the situation, and if you chose to be with another man, then he'd understand, except he wanted to see with his own eyes rather than discuss it over the phone."

I shake my head in shock. *Did he really believe I could move on so quickly?*

"There's nothing I won't do for him," I blurt. "It's why I'm going to bring him home tomorrow regardless of what the hospital doctors say. They won't get answers. He's suffering from PTSD. You need to have a long chat with him about why he remained in the jungle for so many years. Some motive resulted from his relationship with you both. He also didn't cope after Inesa's suicide. But the main reason was his love of helping people without benefiting himself." I sip more wine. "He's the kindest and most unselfish man I know. Despite whatever it is destroying him inside, being with Rose and me is the one thing saving him. I need him home with us. I'll fight for him, do what's right for him regardless of who I offend."

Caroline smiles. "I'm so happy he found you, Eden."

Christopher's expression remains stoic. "Please allow me a little more time to talk to a colleague before you do. There might be one more thing I can do to help."

39

SAMUEL

ON FRIDAY MORNING, Dr. Tolley enters Samuel's private hospital room with a gentleman in a navy-striped suit and lemon-colored tie.

Samuel closes his eyes momentarily to prepare himself for the questions to follow. He's done repeating his answers to every specialist who has walked through the door. Every physician thinks they have missed something—a clue or a misdiagnosis—so questions are endless until they find a lead to his illness.

There are more viruses than stars in the universe.

A small percent invades our body to cause illness. Considering scientists have only discovered around one percent of the viruses that exist, Samuel's condition might be unknown and rare, considering the Amazon is one of the most biodiverse places on the planet. He had ventured deep into the jungle, barely survived, and watched those around him perish, despite bats flying overhead at night, their droppings landing on their food and belongings. Good hygiene was compromised while they trekked and hid away from civilization. In a perfect condition, viruses are waiting to leap from wild animals to humans. The characteristic of the microbes is a mystery. Another specialist probing into his life to seek answers is futile. Samuel knows the origin of his illness may never be known. The least information given about his journey and why he was 'lost' will help protect his Ularan family.

"Good morning, Samuel." Dr. Tolley comes to stand beside his bed.

"We have received more blood results. While we have found nothing significant, your levels suggest there's an infection and not bacterial related." She lifts her chin toward her co-worker. "Professor Mundy is visiting from Sydney and has an interest in your case."

Samuel glances at the professor. "My case isn't that difficult. All fecal and blood results are absent occult blood and known micro-organisms including parasites." He shrugs nonchalantly. "I have an undiscovered virus so the fact we know very little about it means treatment is trickier until my body works out a means to fight it."

"This is true." The professor sits beside Samuel's bed and pushes his glasses up his nose to read Samuel's notes. "Although your weight loss and digestion lead us to believe your body has been trying to fight the micro-organism for many months now, and unfortunately, you're losing. Unless we intervene and try to identify and familiarize ourselves with its behavior, you might not produce the antibodies to win this battle. First, we need to commence nasogastric fluids and gain some weight, so your body has the energy to boost your immune system."

"My knowledge of T-cell production is adequate, and I don't need a lecture." Samuel reaches for his glass of water, already tired of where the conversation is headed. "I merely need time and will not consent to gastric feeds when it will not help."

"Dr. McMahon..." Dr. Tolley gently presses, "... your father has been in contact with the professor to help us find answers."

Samuel crosses his arms defiantly. "I'll tell you what I know. The deforestation of farms and the logging industry is affecting the biodiverse balance. Add climate change to the equation, and we're playing with disaster.

"The rivers are being poisoned, the indigenous tribes are forced further into the jungle, and the safety and food sources are compromised by the greed of these industries. What's the world doing about this? If it continues, the entire planet will suffer. Almost one-fifth of the Amazon has burned or been cleared for these purposes. Between fifteen and thirty years, if it continues and we reach twenty-five percent, then the effect could be irreversible. The reduction of the jungle along with climate change could lead to the jungle creating more carbon than it can absorb. Not enough rain will fall to sustain the jungle, and it could become a hothouse. Not a great outlook, Professor."

The professor peers over the rim of his glasses. His gray hair grew in patches over his balding head. The lines around his eyes depicted years of experience. “Dr. McMahon, I understand you’re passionate about protecting the rainforest. This isn’t the reason I have been called in to view your case—”

“My *case* has everything to do with what’s currently happening in the rainforest as we’re awfully close to anthropogenic change. The changing conditions are ideal for pathogens to pass from animal to human. Pathogens we have no prior knowledge of or how it will mutate.”

Professor Mundy stares at Samuel before lowering his gaze and reading more of his notes. “Is it my understanding you believe this happened to you? That you were in an environment where you contracted an animal virus because of ideal conditions similar to high humidity and the trudging through mud and flooded terrain for months? Perhaps a mysterious virus survived in a natural balance until you appeared and somehow ingested it, or do you believe it to be mosquito-borne? Or inhaled like fungus or mold?”

Samuel glances at Dr. Tolley. “I presumed whatever I have is not contagious, and I’m doing all I can for my body to eradicate it.”

Dr. Tolley places a hand on his shoulder. “Of course. I know of your love for your family, and you wouldn’t place any of them or your work colleagues in jeopardy.”

“Or my patients. I took my oath seriously. I keep thinking back to SARS and HIV and how we could have managed the disease better if we gained information prior to outbreaks.” He turns to the professor. “I’m more than happy for blood tests to continue so you can observe how the pathogen behaves, and I’m happy to try certain medications. Although only for one month. If there’s no notable change, then I’ll manage the symptoms myself.”

“I think it’s a reasonable agreement.” The professor stands. “Although, I highly recommend you cease work to take a month of leave, so you’re available for certain tests and getting adequate rest.”

“I’m not sure it’s possible so early in my training.” Samuel looks to Dr. Tolley for confirmation.

She shakes her head, and brown strands of hair move slightly across her forehead. “You need to focus on your health first, work second.”

“Do you live far from the hospital?” the professor asks with his eyes lowered to his note-taking.

“Not far at all.”

"And I understand you would like to be home with your family?"

"Yes, sir."

"Family support is important. I recommend twice weekly tests, and hopefully, we can identify what's making you sick." He stands and straightens his lemon-colored tie.

"Can I be frank with you?"

"Any advice is helpful, Dr. McMahon."

Samuel's lip twitches at the professor's ability to recognize most of Samuel's comments classify as advice or feedback, be it with sarcasm. "This is just the beginning. The indigenous lived harmoniously in the forests and didn't leave a footprint. Human greed is massacring the Amazon, opening the way for a killer virus to emerge. It will be our next pandemic, one difficult to control as the consequences could be worse than SARS, Ebola, and HIV all combined as we'll have little to zero warning or knowledge about it."

The professor listens astutely. "Similar to an RNA virus? Possibly SARS-related coronavirus."

Samuel shrugs. "Scientists have been studying novel coronaviruses since the seventies, so at least we have some knowledge about them. The Amazon has the potential to create something far more deadly. We both know how quickly disease spreads, yet flights carry a killer around the world. Viruses kill more than any war, and they're always one step ahead of us."

The professor removes his glasses and holds them in his hand. He moves to the end of the bed. "When you're better, I hope you can join our research team. You'd fit in fine as something tells me you weren't in the jungle to simply admire Mother Nature."

Samuel's lips curl up slightly. "There's much to learn as there is to explore."

The professor gives a knowing, lopsided smile. "I can discharge you today. I'll be in contact next week after your first results are in. If you're feeling unwell or your symptoms change, please call, and we'll arrange for immediate admission."

"Of course, thank you." Samuel wants to spring out of bed and pack his bag immediately.

Before the doctors leave his room, his father enters and introduces himself. He is wearing trousers and a shirt and fits in with the other doctors on the ward. Even though he's on holiday, his father hasn't worn what Samuel considers casual clothing to relax in. Not even denim jeans.

"Dr. McMahon, I've heard quite a lot about you from Professor Roxby." They shake hands. "We are dining out tomorrow night. You should join us."

"Thanks for the invite, although we're flying out to Uluru, Kata Tjuta tonight. Perhaps on my return. How long is your visit?"

"I'd like to be involved in your son's case, so I'll have Professor Roxby's assistant get in contact with you."

The door closes, and Christopher takes a seat beside Samuel.

"Have we made any progress?"

Samuel is honest with his father. He tells him what he said to the professor and then goes into the gory detail of what happened during the months he almost died in the middle of the jungle, the very place he felt most alive.

After Samuel finishes retelling his story, his father takes him in his arms and hugs him. "I know we've had our differences, son. I'm proud how you tried to make a difference to a community and to the planet, but nothing is worth your life."

"No. And..." he hesitates, "... I'm not happy like I was back then when the village was peaceful."

"I can see that, son. It's something you must work out with Eden. Whatever you choose, we'll support you."

Samuel stares at his father. "Who are you, and what have you done with my father?"

Christopher chuckles. "Last night, I engaged in a long conversation with Eden. You're a lucky man to have her. All we want is for you to provide for your family and be responsible. I misunderstood why you remained in the middle of a dang jungle, but you have clarified questions and thoughts of it as *wild* or meaningless work." He pats Samuel's hand. "Our focus is to help you heal and ascertain what is causing your illness."

"Am I to thank you for getting Professor Mundy on the team?"

Christopher smiles. "It's the least I can do for my son."

Samuel swipes each photograph on his phone. Eden sent through the pictures this morning with a text saying she'll be there to pick him up soon. She's waiting for his father to return as his mother wanted to take Rose to the beach and build sandcastles. The quality time his parents have spent with his family means a lot and a positive outcome from his hospital stay. He'd have bent to their every command. Eden would set them straight to what she expected as grandparents. It saddened him to miss his daughter's birthday last night, although he'll make it up to her. More importantly, his parents celebrated it with his Australian family. His father recommended he rest, and it was unlike him to promote rest over work. He promised to tell Samuel all about the adventure on Tuesday and, although disappointed, understood why it was best for Samuel not to travel to Uluru with them. At least it will give him time with Eden to discuss his future as he knows the current path isn't the right one.

He imagines her feistiness, ready to argue with him before telling her she's right. Eden always knew what was best for him.

Several months ago, there was a time he believed he wouldn't survive and thought he'd never see Eden or Rose again until he imagined her holding their baby, pictured Eden's beautiful smile, and her kind voice telling him he'll be okay. Her image motivated him to not give up.

And he certainly isn't giving up now.

"Good morning." Eden walks through the door wearing a summer floral dress, so radiant it's as though sunshine follows her. She checks the Apple watch on her wrist. "My bad, it's lunchtime."

He chuckles. "Do you choose not to mention the hour, or do you prefer to reference time like the Ularans?" He waggles his eyebrows. "Some habits stick."

"Oh, you mean noontime?" She leans in and kisses him. "Some habits should never be lost, especially those that bring you joy."

"You bring me joy." He pulls her hand so she lands on the bed, and this time he gives her a long, lingering kiss, showing Eden how much he has missed her.

Eden breaks the kiss and places a hand on his cheek. "Are you ready to go home?"

He leans his forehead to hers. "Yes, please. I can't wait to get out of here."

"It's not fun being on the other side of your work, is it?" She squeezes his hand when he shakes his head. "To be honest, I was coming here to take you home regardless. You need to be with your family. So, they were going to have a fight on their hands today."

Samuel's body buzzes with pride at how Eden would fight his work colleagues to take him home. "Did you mention this to my father last night?"

"Oh, I mentioned quite a few things to your father. To my surprise, he listened, but I think he realized he'll inherit a stubborn daughter-in-law."

"Our wedding is something else I want to discuss. I hoped we could have a small wedding while my parents are still here."

"Samuel." She leans in and gives him another kiss. "All that matters is you focus on getting better. Our wedding can wait, and I'm sure your parents will return whenever we decide the time is right."

"The time is right. In fact, it's never been better."

40

EDEN

CONVINCING Samuel to rest is difficult.

All morning I'm reminding him to play with Rose and leave other things to me.

Caroline and Christopher arrived in Uluru and already sent through photographs. Samuel reads the comment under each like a documentary account of their experience.

My phone buzzes with a call from Dana.

"Hey."

"Hey, Edes. How are you? How is everyone?"

"All good." I glance at Samuel and decide not to mention his hospital stay right now. "Rose turned one during the week."

"I saw Faith's photos on Instagram. She's grown so much, I can't believe it."

"She has. I haven't forgotten to book a visit. I have a few things going on. How is Cairns?"

"Fabulous. I want to take you to the rainforest. It's so beautiful, and it reminds me of when you visited the Amazon."

"Right. I'm on my way," I joke, only I'm staring at Samuel thinking how he'd love it.

"There are homes set in the thick of it and a stone's throw to the beach."

"What?"

"Don't get too excited as you can't swim all year round because of the stingers and crocs."

I laugh.

"I thought it too good to be true. No, seriously, the Daintree is something you must experience because…" she pauses. "I noticed Samuel wasn't in the pictures on Instagram."

I lower my tone. "No, he was in the hospital having some tests. I'll tell you about it later. Could you please send me some links to the accommodations?"

"Sure, but please stay with us in Cairns, and I'll organize the accommodation in the Daintree. I'll send links so you can choose where you'd like to stay."

"I really appreciate it, Dana."

"Okay, we'll chat soon. I'm doing the rounds and now calling your mum and dad. Is it crazy that I miss his grumpiness in the mornings?"

"Not crazy. I miss those days with us all in the office. We've been so busy with other matters I rarely speak to Dad about work."

"Eden, we all understand you have a lot going on. Check out my photos on Instagram. If I were a gambling woman, I'd bet you'll be booking a flight soon," she says seriously. "I'll talk soon."

"I miss you," I say a little louder before she's gone.

I keep hold of my phone and open Instagram not only to see Dana's photographs but to view the pictures Faith shared.

The images of Rose's birthday have me smiling. The photographs of the kids with goofy expressions are cringeworthy, and I can't help giggling. Then I find Dana's profile, and my jaw drops. The house in the Daintree is on stilts and surrounded by beautiful rainforest gardens and an ocean view from the mountains. Inside the home are all comfort and modern furnishings.

It's better than I expected.

I keep scrolling and find images from Yasmine's trip. So many pictures in Peru, and it reminds me of what Samuel said and how he wants to return. Maybe there's someone who can help him in the Daintree rainforest?

I stop and read an inspirational post from Yasmine because her posts are always worth reading. There's an image of the stars, and it has a Milky Way feel so it hints at being thankful to the universe.

Remember our first love?
Do you ever look back and wonder what letter could I write to my younger self warning of the heartache and yet tell her to experience it all because it will shape you to being the best version of yourself? And you won't get there without the hurt and pain of a broken relationship to a douchebag you assumed you wanted to spend the rest of your life with.
I'd tell myself to be young, have fun, and don't worry about all the dumb mistakes because you're going to be okay. Despite the pain of lies, betrayal, and the emotional rollercoaster of getting through one day when your heart is shattered, it is worth knowing who you don't want as a partner and listening to your own heart, protect her first because you're worth it.
There will be mistakes.
And your forever partner will make them too.
Know the person who's your soul mate may not be rich, may not send you flowers, may not open car doors, and may not say yes to your every demand. But that person is here for you, especially in the tough times, and learns from mistakes. When they make a promise, they honor it.
Most of all, they treat you like you're the most important person in the world. When you stare into their eyes, you see a future together, and it feels so right. A balance of the sun rising and setting every day.
And you thank your younger version for being brave and riding the storm because the best is yet to come.

Yasmine is happy.
They have worked out their differences and are in a good place.
And now I miss my friend.

As I ROLL onto my side, I wrap my arm around Samuel. He's propped up on pillows while scrolling on his phone, his way of avoiding sleep.

"Dana wants us to visit her and make a trip to the Daintree Rainforest," I whisper.

He looks at me sideways. "When?"

"Whenever you want. I read some plants have medicinal properties and many other secrets known by the indigenous communities living in the area."

His eyes widen. "I feel like I'm being given hidden messages. Even Dad sent me some photos tonight and mentioned a conversation with an indigenous leader at Uluru and how some of their medicine might help."

"Your father said that?"

"Maybe, we could visit Dana after Christmas?" His eyes are wide and earnest. When he makes this expression, it highlights his gaunt face, and my stomach drops, knowing how he's struggling. Hurting for me.

"Check out Dana's Instagram," I gently prompt.

He opens his phone. "Wow, it's beautiful."

I peer over his shoulder, and he continues to search the area. "A wedding. Now that's an idea."

I rest my head on his shoulder as he peruses beach wedding images with the rich green rainforest as a backdrop.

Leaving him to get lost in his imagination, I open Gran's journal, ready to be transported back to Ulara with her.

41

IVY

May 20, 1963

It feels strange to put pen to paper.

It seems like months since I wrote my last entry. Yet it's only seven weeks.

I have marked the days on the bamboo posts in my hut and added the days to estimate the date.

Though I fear I'll soon lose track of the days. The rainy season is upon us, and I've been stuck inside alone for many days. With no protection from glass windows or doors, only a hammock, I sit and watch the never-ending waterfall flow from my thatched grass roof to the ground. When I need to eat, I trudge through the water at mid-calf to get to the central hut—Waipa—where the fires burn for our food. They string bananas and other fruits from the bamboo beams. Many of the huts are above water, built on a slope with trenches surrounding them so the runoff flows away, protecting the important huts. Others are on stilts. Mine is on low stilts at the front section of the village and close to the river. I have a great view, yet I'm still being observed and not trusted. It's why I stopped writing, as the disapproval in their expressions was clear. I don't want to do anything to upset these people who are feeding me and giving me a safe haven for now.

I have given up hope of Maria coming for me until the rainy season is over. Jennifer and Felix were volunteering for six months, so I assume they have vacated the camp if they're alive.

vacated the camp if they're alive.

I'm slowly learning some of the Ularan language. Previously, I didn't bother when sign language worked for most things, only I hoped to have been rescued by now.

Rescued because my canoe disappeared last month. I assume from the force of the river with the water gushing down from the tepui into other tributaries that feed into this part of the river.

My friend, Weju, comes and visits me daily to check on me. Lately, something has changed in his eyes, as though he knows a secret and can't share. I fear it has something to do with my fate.

Though some days, I feel it's easier to have died. Maybe then Albert would have been informed. They could have made it appear as an accident.

An unknown future scares me. I don't want to be stuck here forever. Yet how do I leave?

I can't simply walk out.

No trails. No canoe. I can't even follow the river as the rainforest consumes every space. I have no drinking container or anything to carry food. My sandals have frayed and are almost unwearable, although I still cover my feet when I walk around.

The stench. My skin. Sometimes I don't feel human.

But I'm alive, so I shouldn't complain. Right now, I wonder what I have to live for.

If there were a chance I could go home, I'd take it. If I could turn back time, I would, as my world was right in front of me in Adelaide, and I set off for an adventure and my selfish need to fulfill a dream.

A dream that has become a nightmare.

Writing this from the safety of my hut, it makes me think of home.

At least the rain has eased, and I can see some of the village.

Weju is with the shaman.

They're discussing something.

I remember teaching him to pronounce Eden since our phonics are quite different.

Here, everyone's name holds meaning, so I told him my name was of the rainforest, as in a way, it's their paradise. In the Ularan language, Weju is the sun. He certainly has been my ray of sunshine through these tough days, even now when the sun barely shines at all.

This is an exciting entry. Weju came and led me to another hut. A younger girl went into labor and became distressed. I don't know how long she's been like this, as she was tired and running out of time to deliver safely. When I examined her, the baby was breach, and all I could think about was the young girl back at the camp. I'd not lose another life if I could help it.

It was too late to turn the baby, and it came out breach. A miracle she survived it and the tiny baby too. Due dates were irrelevant here. The baby comes when the baby comes. Three ladies assisted me. One sung, be it close to yelling, in a distinct language. Another wafted smoke, almost choking me, but I ignored their custom and focused on getting the baby boy out.

I'd never witnessed the cord being cut by a piranha tooth and twine to tie the umbilical cord. The women carried the placenta in the rain and into the forest. I'm curious about what they did and why, yet not enough to do anything to offend them.

By the look on the shaman's face, I had proved some worth and not just another mouth to feed.

I also have a name. They refer to me as Tamu'ne Pupö. When I asked Weju, I made out his explanation to be white woman. Not very exciting or warrior worthy, yet it's a name.

June 1963

I have stopped counting the days, and enough time has passed for me to know it's June.

I stopped writing because of what I'm about to confess.

So, I'll simply write it, and hopefully, it will explain matters so if my journal is ever found, it might be understood.

I slept with Weju.

It just happened.

Like most nights, I was crying. I feel like a prisoner in a hut, and I may as well be in the middle of the bloody ocean for the amount of water I wade through just to pee. I'm always nauseated. Hungry. Thirsty. Dirty. I am beyond feeling unclean. Sometimes I feel like a trapped animal.

It's hard to fathom this is my new life.

I keep telling myself to focus on staying alive. Hope is always in the stars.

And then he appeared at the doorway, his silhouette unmoving in the dim light. He approached me cautiously as though my sobs terrified him. When close enough, he climbed into the hammock and curled himself into me. I needed to feel human. I needed to be touched. I wanted someone to tell me I was going to be okay. Instead, Weju showed me. And I had a moment of happiness.

Only he isn't allowed to have a partner as he's being groomed by the shaman to be the next medicine man. And they're like a priest with no partner and committed to healing the people and learning the secrets of the rainforest.

In his culture, I'm not sure if it's considered a sin for him to have sex, but it is for a married woman in my culture.

The guilt has overshadowed any happiness.

Not that I can be sent to a prison for my crime as I feel I'm already locked away.

September 1963

I now count the months by the full moon.

And it's three full moons since I menstruated.

It's no surprise.

Weju didn't stop coming to my hut. He came every night except when he left for brief hunting trips.

Some of the older women assume. Their eyes drift down to my belly and breasts.

They don't treat me any differently, I simply sense disappointment. But I don't have the energy to deal with judgment as I must cope with surviving here not only for myself but for my unborn child.

How do I explain myself to Albert?

Will I ever see him again?

Will my baby and I survive the birth?

If I could leave, I'd have this child in Australia. However, I don't think walking out with the future shaman's baby is as simple as it sounds.

Lonely nights are part of my existence. My debilitating thoughts surface through the constant chatter of creatures are the only noise I hear. When my mind calms, the panic returns, hearing the squeals of animals in the distance. It squashes any ideas of running away.

Weju comes for sex then sneaks back to the long hut he shares with the other men. Our relationship is dangerous as are my thoughts.

The moment he's gone, I'm back to silent tears.

I assume he knows I'm with child even though I have said nothing. The men here have little to do with their babies—it's all women's work. I have someone in my life, and I've never felt more alone.

It's like I'm reliving my post-natal depression with Winston.

NOVEMBER 1963

The second trimester has been kind to me.
I'm no longer nauseous.
I have also found a way to bring some happiness.
I taught Weju how to make love.
Instead of intercourse like animals with him behind me, I have showed him how to love in the missionary position, since our time is limited with my growing belly, or I straddle him. And by holding his hands, I have showed him how to caress and just hold me tight when I need him to make me feel human.

42

EDEN

I SLAM the journal closed and let out a long sigh.

I can't read anymore.

These are Gran's private times.

My heart is racing.

They called Gran Tamu'ne Pupö. *White woman*.

I recall how the shaman recognized me on the day he appeared from the rainforest like magic as if my spirit called to him. Not exactly my spirit but Gran's presence within me. In Ulara, my name was similar.

Tamu'ne Akare meaning white tortoise. At least they didn't consider Gran to be a slow learner like me. Still, my head is spinning, thinking about her time in the village as well as mine.

Samuel has fallen asleep, so I switch off my light and close my eyes ready to dream about Gran.

I WAKE BEFORE SAMUEL.

It's light enough for me to read, and I'm surprised Rose hasn't woken yet.

Last night my dreams were of Gran, and somehow, we were in the jungle together. In my subconscious, I wanted to help her. I'm scared for her as I know what happens in the end.

Placing another pillow behind my head, I open her journal and keep reading until my family stirs from their sleep.

43

IVY

December 1963

Last night when I ventured out of my hammock, there were stars above the trees, and I caught the light from the moon in the cloudless night sky. It was like seeing rolling green hills of endless countryside after spending months in a cave.

Again the rain has eased.

I'm beginning to feel half-human again.

The village has come to life.

Like ants, everyone is scurrying in the fields, reviving whatever they can and preparing the soil for more plants. It hasn't affected the banana palms. If anything, many of the plants here have thrived in the rain. The men and warriors have been gone for a week on a hunt. Weju has spent more time with me and stayed most nights. Today he moved his hammock into my hut.

I should be happy, only I know this has cemented my fate. I have observed a few of the younger couples. There's no wedding ceremony. The man moves his hammock into her family's hut. The guy becomes part of her family, and they all sleep in the one hut—the newly wedded couple, the in-laws, and all the sisters and brothers. Not quite the wedding night I imagined.

Permission is granted from the chief and shaman, and I have seen the father-in-law and the guy speak with the leaders.

father in law and the guy speak with the leaders.
So, I assume something has passed between Weju and the leaders. I'm surprised as I couldn't see the shaman giving up his young apprentice easily. The shaman and chief continue to keep their distance. I'm unsure what to do to prove I'm not a threat. Maybe the shaman can see through me and knows I'll leave at the first opportunity.
And flashes of new hope of getting out of the village have surfaced now the rain has eased.
At an estimate, I'm around seven months pregnant, give or take a few weeks. My stomach is smaller than when I had Winston, although it's to be expected with the change in lifestyle. With no doctor to check on me or the baby, I'm grateful to see my stomach swell and confirm we're doing okay. It's all I can assume for now.
The idea of giving birth here isn't ideal, and it scares me. I've witnessed many complications and aware help is minimal even compared to the camp where I volunteered. The camp now has the appeal of a modern hospital with trained doctors and nurses compared to Ulara.
I must look beyond my white privilege and recognize how the people here have survived over time with their own natural medicine and how they rely on Mother Nature and the rainforest for disease prevention and treatment. In my mind, I need to plan ways to make peace with the shaman as he could be the one person who decides on what care I receive.

I know why Weju moved his hammock into my hut.
Nothing could have prepared me for last night.
I'm still crying while writing this entry.
Weju escorted me to the special round hut where they perform their ceremonies or rituals. Until now, I haven't been allowed to be present or even observe.
The exception came when the ceremony was for me.
I was 'encouraged' to drink the tea despite my tears.
Awarö is a word for bad. I repeated it over and over through my sobs, afraid it would hurt my unborn child since I didn't know what was in the brew. All natural yet for medical sake, the leaves boiled in ayahuasca ceremonies cause the hallucinations. An effect similar to DMT and not ideal for a pregnant woman.
Weju very calmly told me Wakü, a word meaning good. His eyes pleaded

Weju very calmly told me Waku, a word meaning good. His eyes pleaded with mine, and he kept looking back at the shaman. It wasn't until I realized it was a test or an initiation to be accepted.

I can still feel the tingle of an alien intruder sifting through my thoughts.

And the images have remained with me. My thoughts connected to the shaman's beliefs, and I sensed his presence long after the effects left my body.

I was gifted a new warrior name. Itariru Enu Tykaraije, meaning blue-eyed jaguar.

When I finally stopped fighting the inevitable and allowed my body and mind to connect with the rainforest, I sprinted through the jungle and saw the forest through the eyes of a jaguar. I interpreted the vision as a dream or a hallucination which I expected from the tea. I felt no enlightenment, only a never-ending sprint. Not lost yet, no destination. Now I've learned it's my spirit and, I guess, a new identity.

I've never asked about Weju's other name. Yet I can't help feeling a sense of power by being connected to the jaguar.

Regardless, today I'm left exhausted and confused.

Angry yet relieved.

Scared.

Afraid of what the future holds for Weju and me.

What future will my baby have if the brew has harmed it? How will a baby with physical abnormalities be perceived? As an evil spirit? Be an outcast?

My thoughts are out of control, and I need to be optimistic for my own sanity, yet at the least, the effects of the tea could bring on birth and cause me to miscarry. Was it a test that my child was meant to be in this world?

The miscommunication and unknown will be my undoing.

How can they trust me if I don't trust them?

I guess time will tell how my story will end.

January 1964

Another full moon has passed.

At some point, Christmas and the new year have come and gone. The second without my beloved Albert and Winston.

I'm holding back tears since this month Winston turns three. What a big boy he'll be. What I would do to hold him one more time.

Will he even remember me?

Has Albert given up on me and met someone else?

I continue to pray for a future with my family. Yet I'm here, about to embark on a different life with a new family, and I'm worried my husband has found someone else. My selfishness sickens me, yet I must hold out for hope for this isn't my fate, and I have a life back in Australia because I can't imagine spending the rest of my life here.

Weju loves me in his own way. Only not the way I'm used to.

I see infatuation in his eyes. Yet there's shame in giving up his time with the shaman and no longer special in rank yet considered a warrior like the other young men. The shaman still eyes me as though he senses an evil within me despite his intrusive thoughts in my mind during the ayahuasca ceremony.

I'm grateful for Weju's support.

And he seems proud to have Itariru Enu Tykaraije for a wife. It's going to take a while to adapt to my new names.

If only he knew how much I wanted to go home.

44

EDEN

OH, Gran. I swipe a tear from my eye.

Her circumstances being in Ulara were vastly different than mine. I had a choice. Gran feared for her life. And the cheating on Pop which everyone believed stemmed from a survival aspect.

God, I want to read on, although right now, I'm not sure my heart can handle it with what's going on in my life.

"Are you okay," Samuel whispers and curls into me.

I shake my head. "Gran… I had no idea." I swipe tears from my cheek. "Did you know the shaman's name?"

Samuel shakes his head. "I knew him as the shaman or the Ularans called him Pyjai, meaning *medicine man*."

"His name is Weju," I whisper.

"The sun," he says as though it makes sense. He stares up at the ceiling as though he remembers something. Or simply the man who was his friend and mentor.

"You miss him," I say with understanding.

He kisses my forehead. "Everyone and everything. I keep visualizing how they are and hope they're safe."

"You did your part. It's more than anyone could do." I kiss the tip of his shoulder. "I often think about Kaikare. I miss her too. And wonder if there's a chance Dad and her could meet." I stop myself and shake my head. "It's too complicated."

Samuel's Adam's apple bobs. "I have an idea where they're located, only the idea of returning so soon..." He closes his eyes slowly. He opens them, and he's overcome with sadness. "I'm not ready, and it could compromise everything."

"And too dangerous."

Rose stirs from the other bedroom, and I go to jump up.

"Eden." Samuel places a hand on my shoulder. "I'll get her."

"Bring her back to bed while I'll shower," I tell him because I want to prepare him a nutritious shake. Something easy to digest. I'm committed to helping my man get well.

By mid-morning, I've finished my chores. Samuel and Rose are playing quietly on the floor with blocks.

My phone dings with a message and my heart does a little dance seeing Yasmine's name.

Can we FaceTime?

I find my iPad then press the video button rather than wait. "Yasmine wants to FaceTime," I call out to Samuel.

Her face comes into view with a broad smile. Her black curls are tangled and unkept, yet she looks the happiest I've seen her in months.

"Honey, is everything okay?" Her smile falls away.

I nod quickly. "I miss you." I cough to clear my throat as emotion boils up inside me. I wish she was here so I could chat with her.

"I miss you too. We're flying out in a couple of days and home in time for Christmas." I laugh and sob together because I can't wait to see her.

"How is your trip? Is everything okay?" I know it is by the joy on her face, but knowing she intended to try ayahuasca, I needed to check on her.

"Oh, it was a fabulous experience and everything I hoped for. It opened my mind, and I now know how I want to live my life."

"Oh." I cough. "That's great. I'm truly happy for you. And there were no complications?"

"We did everything Samuel suggested and drank lots of bottled water after we came to. And tell him we took our trash out of the jungle with us."

I smile at her still doing good deeds. "Is Deanne still with you?"

"Yes, we met up with her last night, and she'll be back with our pizza soon. It feels like forever since I've eaten anything other than fresh fruit and nuts."

Samuel comes to sit next to me and positions Rose on his lap. "Look, it's Aunty Yasmine," he says. He smiles at her. "Hello, Yas."

"Hi, Samuel." She waves enthusiastically at him and then blows a kiss to Rose. "And you have grown, princess."

Rose stares at the screen. "As," she says and points.

"Yes, it's Yas," I say, understanding her.

"I'm glad you had an enjoyable experience," Samuel says, sounding interested. "Who was your shaman?"

"Santino. Michael said you'd remember his brother, Juan."

Samuel smiles at Yasmine. Then Michael comes to sit next to her. "Hey, hey," Michael says. "How are the Aussies?"

Samuel grins at Michael. "Really?" He shakes his head, amused. "How's Iquitos?"

"Like old times." Michael gives Samuel an understanding look as though they both share a memory. I'm watching Samuel's expression on the screen, our faces minimized compared to Michael and Yasmine's, yet I don't miss how his smile fades and his brow pulls together. It's slight, still I see it. It's like he's hit with a sense of missing out as he's reminded of a happy memory.

"I'm looking forward to hearing all about it," he says genuinely.

She turns and plants a kiss on Michael's cheek.

Michael drops an arm around her shoulder. "Thought you could use a friend Down Under," he says to Samuel and grins.

"Is that right?" Samuel remarks. He's smiling, and despite our history, I know Michael used to be a good friend to him.

"I think it's wonderful."

Samuel is still smiling, and I let out a sigh of relief as this might be exactly what he needs.

ROSE IS HAVING her afternoon sleep, and I insist on Samuel taking a nap as well.

It allows me time to call Amy and catch up on her news. The school term ends on Friday, and she's traveling back for the Christmas break.

She mentioned she might not return to Berri even though she loves the country. Before I ask her what led her to the decision, she mentions Ethan has traveled on three occasions to visit her.

For a while, I'm gobsmacked. The last time we spoke, he was proving to her he was a decent guy and a good friend. I must have missed the signs he wanted more with Amy. I never considered them compatible and believed it would take a lot for Amy to forgive him. I never imagined either of them taking the next step toward a relationship.

I'm not sure what I feel, although a sense of relief is swirling in my gut. They are both my friends, and while I'll always bat for Amy as one of my besties, I'm happy if they're happy. I grin, imagining Amy keeping him on his toes. That girl won't hold back if something pisses her off.

The universe is finally aligning for my friends and me. I then send Bree a message.

Hi Bree, are you visiting Adelaide over the Christmas break? We all miss you, and it's time for a reunion.

Hey, Edes, I miss you all. Life has been hectic yet I do have time off over the holiday break. I'll be in Adelaide for a week and then on a cruise to Fiji with someone special. I can't wait for you to meet Benjamin.

I let out a little scream.

I'm so happy for you!! I can't wait to see you again, and I'm looking forward to meeting Benjamin!!

With a sense of contentment, I decide to rest on our bed beside Samuel.

Without waking him, I open Gran's journal.

45

IVY

February 1964

My abdomen has grown considerably, and I'm close to full term. Labor is on my mind, and I'm having nightmares of the worst possible outcome. I have been observing other pregnant women and noticed the younger women have the elder ladies to assist them. From a distance, I've watched their smoke ceremonies during the birth. The purpose of smoke isn't clear, although I don't see the benefit of smoke inhalation for the lungs of a newborn.

Last week, a heavily pregnant woman worked in the field near to me. I noticed her as she struggled with the work and would stop and place a hand on her lower back. It was like a future image of myself. After a few hours, she wandered off, so I followed her, keeping a safe distance. I watched as she dug a hole.

She moaned quietly, almost singing words over and over in a mumbled chant.

Another woman joined her, then she squatted and gave birth to a child over the hole. I wanted to go to them and offer my assistance. Only many don't see me as someone who cares for them. I still have a shadow of doubt surrounding my aura, and I didn't want to scare her.

Yet it was the most simple and stress-free childbirth I have ever witnessed.

The next day, she was back working in the field with her newborn on her back.

As much as I wish the same labor for me, I'm afraid, after my last labor, it will last for days, being my experience with giving birth to Winston.

Special ceremonies followed by a feast happens approximately once a month. The people dress up for the occasion. Feathers secured by twine fan out like wings from their upper arms. Bodies are painted with a sequence of lines and V's and dots over their limbs and torso. The men also paint their faces. Some prepare with tattoos inked into their skin by paint and a piranha tooth. It's when I noticed Weju's new facial tattoos. Dots and lines and a star to his cheeks. The lines join those down his neck to his chest, reminding me of a diagram of the night sky. I know the people follow sun and moon cycles, yet the astrological artwork on their bodies is remarkable. Like other feasts, last night began with song and dancing to celebrate a successful hunt of five wild boars. The men imitated other animals in their dance—birds, jaguars, caiman. The descriptive body movements are easy to decipher.

Smiles were big.

Stomachs were full.

The shaman told a story, and warriors were praised.

Then the mood changed.

Weju was standing beside the shaman. They called to me to join them. The circle of dancers surrounded me. The song started again, the dancing lifted a notch to hands waving at me, then up and down like the flapping of wings. The song was directed at me until the shaman's song rose above everyone else. He took my face in his and blew smoke into my face. I coughed and spluttered while he did the same action at my swollen stomach. Then I realized he was either purging the evil spirits out of me or protecting me from them.

Weju's eyes were closed, and his arms reached toward me. His expression was trance-like and being the center of a voodoo-like ceremony freaked me out. I wanted to run far away and ugly cry.

Thankfully, the ceremony didn't last, and when the dance finished, I walked back to my place, sitting on the ground at the back of the circle.

Today everyone is back to their normal routine.

And barely noticing me, which is a good thing.

I feel safer living in an invisible bubble.

A few nights after my last entry I went into labor.

I'm overjoyed to be writing this while my daughter suckles my breast.

It seems the shaman took no chances once my water broke. Many of the elder ladies assisted in the labor and performed that damn smoke ceremony.

The details remain blurry.

I recall pushing with the contractions, coaxing myself through my own thoughts while imagining an out-of-body experience to assess my progress.

As I pushed through the contractions, the women sang a harmonious chorus over and over as my daughter came into the world.

Daylight was breaking through the leaves, and the overwhelming relief deemed it appropriate to name her Dawn, especially with the meaning of her father's name being the sun.

I've monitored her vitals and checked her reflexes. So far, everything looks to be in order.

Dawn has stolen my heart and provided hope and happiness when I was struggling to find the strength to live another day.

Weju is smitten. He comes and stares at our daughter even while she sleeps. He's not like other men in the village, and I'm glad he has the love in his heart I hoped for our daughter.

He has given her another name.

Turùpo Kapu. He pointed to the sky then to our hearts. So her heart is as big as the sky. Or he loves her, I guess, for infinity. I'm not sure, nevertheless, I love the meaning. Yet this name is only between Dawn and us. A secret name. I'm yet to learn why it's a secret, but I assume it's one of honor.

Weju decided her name in the village is Kaikare. In few words, he likened our daughter to a tortoise and a black jaguar. Maybe the tortoise is a reference to me.

In my heart, she'll always be Dawn.

A new day full of hope.

46

EDEN

My mouth drops open, and I slam the journal closed to relish the beautiful feeling of love swirling inside me.

The noise startles Samuel from his sleep, and his eyes snap open with a fright.

"I'm sorry," I whisper and pat his shoulder. "Go back to sleep."

He's on the couch and rolls onto his side. "Are you okay?" he murmurs.

I'm sitting on the floor in front of him with my feet under the coffee table. I swivel to face him and bring my knees close to my chest. "Gran just gave birth to Kaikare."

He smiles, his eyes blink, trying to wake himself up.

"Go back to sleep," I coax. "I need a minute to feel all the feels. It's so beautiful. The shaman's name reflects the sun. Gran named Kaikare, Dawn, as she was born at daybreak, and she offers hope to Gran like the start of a new day." I shiver as tingles of happiness roll over me.

Samuel chuckles quietly, then rolls onto his back and closes his eyes. "You can tell me about it after."

I'm still smiling and want to continue reading her beautiful story, especially about Kaikare-Dawn as a baby.

If only Samuel knew about this. He could have told Kaikare how Gran felt.

I pick up the journal and continue reading where I left off.

47

IVY

APPROXIMATELY MAY 1964

For many months I didn't find the need to write.

Life was good.

We were happy.

Dawn brought joy to us in a special way, and my lonely days were few.

Dawn barely cried.

At first, I thought something could be wrong, especially since she slept through the night. I was getting sleep. Dawn was feeding well. I then considered the tea I drank and the smoke therapy during birth and wondered if any of these calmed her. I only hope the tea hasn't affected her brain. Around me, the children are fine, and everyone is calm most of the time. Still, learning by way of school and university is what concerns me, and if these natural remedies have hindered her learning capability, I'll never forgive myself. Because I do hold out hope of us leaving one day and Dawn having a future as an academic.

I now have time to try and assess her.

Because the damn rains are back. Over an inch every day. Sometimes more. Sometimes less. Either way, after several weeks, the ground is saturated, and there's nowhere for it to drain so the village becomes a swimming pool once more. The main huts are fine. My hut is surrounded by water. It makes bathing Dawn difficult, and the non-use of cloth nappies has been harder to manage. I'm not complaining as urine and feces nappies has been harder to manage. I'm not complaining as urine and feces has never bothered me if I can clean up the mess.

The musky stench surrounding the village is back. Food is scarce. At least I have plenty of fresh water to aid my breast milk. It's something I have focused on as it concerned me how to feed Dawn if I couldn't provide milk. It happens. I had problems breastfeeding Winston. Though I assume other mothers here would step up and feed her as the women all look out for each other. Once upon a time, I wouldn't have agreed to it. Now I understand and find the gesture rather beautiful. We must unite as the men have an authority here, which isn't surprising.

Except Weju. He's back learning from the shaman. And he comes to check on us every day.

Dawn is different.

Her hair is brown, not jet black like the other babies. And her eyes are almost a honey color, not the dark eyes of her father nor my blue eyes.

As expected, her skin is also lighter in color, although it's premature to determine what features will dominate.

I often imagine taking her home to Australia, except Albert's reaction scares me.

Would he welcome me home with open arms, welcome us both?

Or would his honor be tattered by my infidelity? Would he want to raise another man's child? I see a vision of Winston and imagine how happy he'd be to have a sister. I often daydream of my children playing together, sharing a swing together or playing chase on the grass.

Grass.

I've forgotten what it feels like under my feet.

It's when I put pen to paper my mind wanders, and the tears flow, missing my old life.

It's why my entries are few.

More importantly, my pen is considered a form of bad magic, so I do it in private. The pen didn't come naturally from the forest, so if not sourced from there, they have trouble comprehending between good and bad. It's why I need to take photos on my camera without anyone noticing. Unfortunately, I don't have many clicks remaining on my film wind. And I want to save some for Dawn.

Tonoro, a young girl, is wading toward my hut. She loves to come and help me.

I'm signing off for probably some time unless the rains get to me again. Like Tonoro, there's much for me to be grateful for.

And I'm still alive.
Alive with a beautiful daughter.

APPROXIMATELY AUGUST 1964

The rains have showed signs of easing. We have more sunny days, and it's a good sign.
Over the past couple of months, Weju has helped me to understand their language. I can comprehend the important things and talk with the other women.
I'm finally being accepted and considered equal.
Weju and I are closer than ever.
More surprising is his time with the shaman. I'm so proud of him and how the community respects him. He and the shaman work together most days, even their songs to the rainforest relax me. It's a beautiful harmonic tune with strange phonics. It doesn't always make sense. They repeat what the rainforest is telling them. Weju believes the trees whisper how to heal their people.
After my science training, I find it hard to comprehend, yet I wonder how they find the knowledge of what plants heal certain diseases and the process of using the plants for medicine. Boiled. Crushed. Drained and drank as tea. How did they know what to do when they have no contact with the outside world or with other indigenous communities?
Their spiritual world is fascinating, and I'm beginning to understand and respect their values as long as it doesn't affect Dawn and me.
I must stop calling her Dawn in private. I can't allow her to answer to the name I gave her. I don't want to upset anyone here when I'm making progress on friendship and my own happiness.

I stopped writing as Weju returned from the forest, so I hid my journal. He was a man on a mission, and we made love twice and in the middle of the day! The man knows how to make me feel alive. He told me it's what the spirits want.
I'm not going to argue.

. . .

It's only been a few weeks since my last post, but I have to write what happened today. Weju saved my life.

After bathing in the stream, I almost reached the village before being bitten on the leg by a snake. I guessed by its striped markings it was poisonous. I screamed loud and hard and fell to the ground with Dawn rolling from my back.

In seconds, Weju was by my side. After seeing the bite marks, he pulled a piranha tooth from his pouch and sliced the puncture wounds on my skin. One warrior cared for Dawn while another gave him twine, and he wrapped it below my knee like a tourniquet. He then sucked and spat. Sucked and spat. He drained most of the poison from my blood in a quick response I believe saved me.

I almost passed out during it all. I have been vomiting. I'm not sure if it's from the special tea the women have prepared for me or the poultice on the markings on my leg. I didn't have the energy to assess their treatment.

I only hope it works.

In hindsight, I needed to write this in case something happens and I don't make it.

If I do, it's because Weju saved my life.

Approximately October 1964

My life is good.

I had to write words of my contentment as I'm not sure how often I'll make new entries.

Weju and I are very happy. My old life now sits at the back of my mind because I need to think and behave like a Ularan.

My entries have been about remembering my old life and holding out hope to return home.

I can no longer visualize a life beyond the jungle walls.

I have accepted this is my future, and I'm now bonded to Weju for the rest of my days. We have a beautiful family, and considering how often we make love, I expect our family to grow very quickly.

I could even be pregnant now.

If the gods want me to be, I will be. It's only a matter of time before my stomach will swell. Until then, I'll enjoy every minute practicing with my amazing lover.

Approximately November 1964

I didn't expect to be writing another entry so soon after my last one.

Only I wanted to document that something is wrong with Dawn. She keeps crying and has endured a fever for days. Whatever medicine the shaman is providing isn't working, and I wish to hell I could take her to my practitioner because it could be any number of viruses or bacterial infections. I don't want her to be another statistic like many children in the jungle by lack of advanced medical help.

Weju said I need to drink the ayahuasca tea again so I can help her. Does he not realize I could be pregnant again?

For the first time in many, many months, I'm afraid.

48

SAMUEL

SAMUEL'S EYES flutter open at the sharp inhalation of breath beside him. Eden's hand clutches her throat.

"Is everything okay?" He pushes up onto his elbow.

Her eyes are wide with concern.

"What is it?"

"I've reached a point in Gran's journal that's going to upset me."

"Do you want me to read it with you?" He hooks an arm around her shoulders.

"Not today." She closes the journal. "Until now, Gran was really happy. She and Weju were..." she hesitates, "... *in love* even though she never stopped loving my grandfather."

Samuel nods slowly. "What happened?"

"Dawn... Kaikare is sick, and Gran thinks she might be pregnant again. Until now, she believed she'd live out her life in Ulara, only her words in the last entry said she was afraid." Eden looks up at Samuel, her eyes saddened by what she has read. "I felt happy, and so I kept reading about Gran's happy times, but I don't have the emotional energy to deal with something as heartbreaking as losing her baby."

"Are you sure she's pregnant?"

"No, but I can't read anymore today."

Eden rubs her hand over Samuel's stomach. "How are you feeling?"

He kisses the top of her head. "Don't worry about me." He taps the couch for her to lay beside him. Eden crawls up and stretches out alongside his body. His heartbeat shoots up in response. He kisses her neck and slips his hand under her tank top to find her breasts.

"You're all the nutrition I need," he says against her skin.

"I wish that were true." She muffles a laugh.

"I can show you it is," he murmurs and hooks his leg until he's between her thighs.

"See," he says in a deep voice. "A perfect fit." His kiss is long, passionate, and full of the love that has always been inside him waiting to come out.

MONDAY MORNING, Samuel drives into the hospital for routine tests. While in the waiting room, he flicks through a geographical magazine. An article on deforestation in the Amazon rainforest triggers emotion and his chest to tighten. He recalls his memory of the rainforest and pictures it with clarity after living there for eight years. He focuses on remembering the early years and the adventure before him. He met challenges with an open mind and heart, and what he did never seemed like work.

Providing medical care in places of need was gratifying, and he never wanted to be rewarded. His work transformed to be more of a biologist, and his interest in medicinal plants overtook his life.

Back in society, he's struggling to adapt. Eden sees it more than anyone. Yet there's no other alternative because he wants to be with her and Rose. This is now his life and as much as he's trying to get the job done and move on, it's like his body or some deep-seated psychological problem is holding him back.

Watching the medical staff around him reminds him of a colony of insects all working hard in a robotic way within the sterile walls of a lifeless building. Cures for disease come in packaging, not picked fresh from the garden. It seems backward and yet it's referred to as modern medicine. He's not ignorant of the power and lifesaving breakthroughs of advanced medication he'd love to take back to the jungle to his friends. Yet, for basic health and well-being, society has it back to front. Prevention is the key, and yet fast food and a sedentary lifestyle contribute more to cardiovascular disease than if people were hunters and gatherers. There's so much humanity could learn from their indigenous ancestors by surviving on the food you can grow.

He lets out a long sigh.

Despite all his effort and knowledge, the root of his ongoing illness is unknown. If he could take ayahuasca, he knows he could find answers. He closes his eyes and imagines connecting with the shaman and Ivy. He knows they'll protect him if another entity attempts to control him.

Eden remains skeptical about the benefits. She still considers it to be a dangerous psychedelic drug. She's right. Although Samuel understands the importance of preparation and is trained, so his thoughts lead him to seek the answers he needs, as his soul has already been infiltrated and cleansed by ayahuasca's probing fingers over many years.

He opens his phone and messages Michael.

I'm jealous of your travels. I miss the jungle. There are many things I miss so I'm eager to hear about your experiences with Santino. Did he learn from Juan? It's been years since I've seen either of them. Remember our first holiday in our early twenties when we discovered Iquitos and the shamanic ceremonies? We were like kids in a candy store. Behaved like it too. Yet I'd never change a thing, and we learned from our mistakes. I'm looking forward to seeing you soon. I have many questions to ask and hope we can keep this between us. My health has declined, and after eliminating the obvious causes, I believe ayahuasca will help me to find the problem and heal. Unfortunately, Eden doesn't hold the same view as me and still considers it dangerous. Time isn't on my side, and if I suffer further weight loss, I may develop chronic issues and irreparable damage to some organs. I'm waiting on more tests, and I highly doubt anything will come from all the internal probing. So far, I have convinced Eden I'm doing all I can to find answers. The doctors here are querying an unknown virus which is the obvious answer, except the damage it's causing is concerning, and furthermore, how to eradicate it is anyone's guess. A long flight to Peru isn't ideal, but I'm lost for alternative answers, especially when one session could save me months of mistreatment. In your opinion, could Santino help me, or should I simply seek out Juan? Do you have a contact number? See you soon, Mick. Or should I say mate or matey? You'll be learning the lingo here with me.

Hey, Samuel, good to hear from you, 'mate.' I'm looking forward to coming to Australia and catching up with you. It's been a long time, and I know I must rectify the crap decisions I made in the past. Yasmine has forgiven me, and I see her as the chick I want to be with. Something about her makes me want to be a better guy. Man, that sucks about your health. I'm surprised they haven't found answers after all these months. As for Santino, we had a good experience with him, and the brew was light, which I insisted on for Yasmine's benefit. Maybe it's best to seek out Juan. He's more experienced and knows you. I have Santino's contact number. As you know, he only gets coverage on his cell when he travels closer to Iquitos. His resort is five hours by boat on a tributary river. We fly to Argentina tomorrow and stay a night before flying out to Australia the following day. Sorry I can't be of any more help.

Samuel contemplates his next reply.

Send me his cell details so I can contact him before booking a flight. Safe travels.

A few moments later, Michael sends through the information.

"Samuel McMahon."

Samuel looks up to a nurse. He follows the nurse into a room where she has numerous vials ready to take his blood. She reads the form, and when their eyes meet, he senses the curiosity.

He prepares himself for a barrage of questions.

Later in the afternoon, Samuel is resting on the couch. Out of curiosity, he opens the browser window on his iPad and searches for flights to South America.

How quickly could he plan a return trip in the new year?

He checks Eden is still preoccupied with Rose.

She picks up the television remote. "Want to watch *The Wiggles*?" Rose nods her head, and the way she does it is slow and exaggerated as though it's a new thing and dang cute.

The Wiggles dancing and singing on the television could keep their daughter amused for hours.

"Okay. Mummy is going to rest now."

"Mommy," Samuel corrects and then receives an eye roll.

Eden turns on the lounge and places her feet on Samuel's lap before rearranging the pillows behind her head.

She opens Ivy's journal.

The last time she read, she closed it quickly before she became upset.

At least he knows and is prepared to comfort her if she needs it. Yet part of him would like to also understand Ivy's journey. He didn't know her, yet he feels connected to her. Not only through Eden but through their Ularan spirits.

He wonders if his next ayahuasca ceremony could bring her closer to him.

49

IVY

December 1964

I'm writing this entry while lying in a hospital bed.

Much has happened in the past few weeks.

After the last ceremony when I drank the tea, I became weaker, not stronger.

The good news is Dawn came out of the fever, although it was a close call as some days she was limp in my arms. I expected her to get sick since she's now crawling in the dirt and often putting things in her mouth before I stop her. It's what children her age do. Only the thought of losing her scared me.

In a turn of events, I had been vomiting for days, sweating profusely and extremely dehydrated. At first, I assumed I caught a stomach bug. Only the pain was different, like a knife in my lower gut, twisting and slicing. If it was an infection or a parasite feeding inside me, in the back of my mind, I understood if it turned to sepsis, I wouldn't survive.

Then I hallucinated, and in my dreams, I saw my death.

That morning, I strapped Dawn to my back, then grabbed my journal. I stumbled to the river. Like I was possessed, I had to get to the water and get there any way I could. I collapsed before I made it and crawled the rest of the way.

I questioned the thirst and why my body craved fluids. Drinking the murky river water could be even more detrimental.

By the river's edge, I splashed water on my face, moistened my mouth then spat it out. I sat back and ignored the soft grizzle coming from Kaikare on my back. She was safe, and I needed to clear my thoughts as everything blurred around me.

Looking over my shoulder, I spotted my journal and pen in the sand. I must have dropped them when I was close to fainting.

I didn't know what to do.

There was a fallen palm frond beside me.

I scrambled to my journal then wrote:

Help me.
From Ivy Monteford.

Sweat dripped off my chin and onto the page. Regardless, I tore out the page and wrapped it in a palm leaf. I tied it with twine to a small branch and was about to toss it into the river when I heard a motor.

I managed a croaky, "Help."

I waved the palm frond in the air to get attention. In a last effort, I screamed at the top of my lungs, "Maria."

screamed at the top of my lungs. "Maria."

Then I collapsed by the water, the side of my face in the sand as I struggled to keep my eyes open with the black dots joining before my eyes.

Lying and simply breathing must have been enough to stop me from passing out.

I could still hear the faint sound of a motor, and I wondered if I was hallucinating or wishing it to be true.

As I blinked through my tears, I lifted a hand to wave and only then heard the tears from my daughter still stuck on my back.

Maria jumped out of the boat and helped me to my feet.

"You came back." I just managed to say the words.

"Many times, but you were never here," she said quickly.

She kept repeating something in Spanish to the others.

"You're going to be okay, Ivy."

I clung to those words.

Until Weju yelled, "Tamu'ne Pupö." White hair. The name I'm known by in the village. He glowered at Maria and her colleagues and yelled, "Awarö itoto." Bad strangers or it could mean the enemy.

I was already in the curiara. Along with his threat, spears were raised in our direction. A hazy curtain fell over my eyes, and I was close to passing out. Maria panicked, pleading with me to convince them not to kill us.

In my mind, it happened in slow motion.

I'd never witnessed Weju's intense expression. The shaman whispered in his ear. Even through my delusional haze, I knew it wasn't good.

I managed to speak and begged him to let me go or I would die. I told him I needed white persons' magic medicine to heal, and then I'd come back to him. I kept repeating I was dying and also told him I was pregnant and needed to save our child. I made a vocal promise to the spirits I would return.

He yelled for Kaikare with open arms, but the motor was already pushing us away from the embankment. She was in another woman's arms.

My promise must have been enough.

Still, he looked furious.

I called out, "I love you," before collapsing into Maria's arms.

I have whispered those words to him in our special times, and he understood the words to be a secret bond between us.

What happened after that is a blur.

Maria radioed ahead to organize a flight from Canaima to Ciudad, Bolivia.

I had emergency surgery for a ruptured ectopic pregnancy and a

hysterectomy.
The weeks passed while in the hospital and allowed me time to heal and process the past and my future in a safe environment. Dawn received antibiotics for an ear infection and has commenced her childhood vaccinations.
Maria has alerted the authorities, and word has reached Albert I am safe but not up to talking yet.
I'm not sure I can even write anymore.
I am confused.
My heart is torn.
I almost died.
Why am I still alive?

JANUARY 1965

I have been in the hospital for almost two months and have finished extensive antibiotic therapy.
I anticipated writing in February, not January. In December 1963, there were two full moons. So, my journal dates were incorrect. Dawn was, in fact, born premature, only by a few weeks. During my stay, I have felt foolish not knowing the happenings of the outside world. My daughter doesn't even have an exact date of birth.
Going by my hazy memory, we predicted the middle of January. Maria said, pick a date. So I went with the same day as Winston's birthday, January 23, 1964. I'm not sure why, as I'd prefer to celebrate my children's birthdates apart, yet in a panic, his special day came to mind, and possibly a sign of how much I missed him.
I also gave her Albert's surname.
Dawn Monteford.
Not her father's because who knows what that is.
It was the right thing to do because Dawn will be part of our family in Australia, and her birth certificate will have the same surname as ours with the father listed as unknown.
There's also a process for sending me home since I was listed as missing for so long.
In my heart, I know I must return to Ulara first.
I need to retrieve my bag, especially my passport, visas, and camera

I need to retrieve my bag, especially my passport, visas, and camera.

I also made a promise to Weju and will uphold it to the gods, even if it's for him to see us one more time.

And for me to say I'll always love him and will never forget him.

I can already imagine the pain in his eyes and almost don't want to go as there's a slight chance I'll stay for love.

Until I think about our future.

What will happen the next time I become seriously ill?

What will happen to Dawn?

I'm thankful she has received her childhood vaccinations and soon the measles vaccine. Something I am extremely grateful for.

And will Weju still love me if I can no longer bear more children?

This is also the miracle I'd wished for not so long ago—a chance to return home to the family I've missed.

Albert told Maria he's thankful and only wants me home safe.

I'm yet to tell him I have another child.

I only hope the husband I'll be returning to will love me as much as the one I'm leaving behind.

Tonight, I spoke to Albert over a very bad telephone line. The crackling made it difficult to hear, but still we managed to talk a little and confirm I was okay.

I told him a lot has happened, and we'll need to talk first.

He said his prayers had come true as he never gave up hope I was still alive. He knew my strength and how I'd fight to come home to him and Winston.

I broke down when I heard Winston's voice.

I couldn't tell him about Dawn. Not yet.

He reinforced he wanted me home safe again.

I want to believe it to be true. I also know Albert is a proud man and may not accept Dawn.

If he loves me like he says, then I must believe him.

Our family deserves a second chance.

50

EDEN

Oh, Gran.

My throat burns from holding back tears.

I swallow hard, only my mouth is dry. I close my eyes and try to control the emotion and pain swirling inside me for my grandmother. I can't read anymore, partly because I already know the ending.

She returns to Australia alone.

Dawn, or should I say Kaikare, remains in Ulara.

What happened on her final visit?

Oh God, I can't help it, and the tears cascade down my cheeks. I want to ugly cry.

"Hey." Samuel's arm snakes around my waist.

I take a deep breath and shake my head. "Everything is making sense. Gran..." I shake my head again, trying to string my thoughts together. "Her trip wasn't an easy one. When she arrived home, people believed she was a little crazy, well, you know differently." A sob escapes my throat. "No one knows what she went through except for Brenda. Pop wasn't as forgiving as she'd hoped, yet she didn't simply cheat on him with another man because of physical attraction. She did it to survive. She believed she might not make it home. It was so much harder in the sixties, and a gang, it's not what they're called, but you understand when I say they were after her. They wanted to kidnap her, so she hid in Ulara, and there was no way she could escape on foot. It's more complicated than I can describe, and my heart is breaking for her."

Samuel pulls me into his side. "You've always loved her."

"I have." I sniff. "I miss her so much."

"I understand."

Samuel wraps himself around me, and we simply lay together without speaking, holding each other until Rose demands our attention.

THE FRIDAY after my friends arrive back in Adelaide, we arrange to all meet out at The Shores cocktail bar for old-time's sake.

After leaving Rose with Mum for the night, Samuel and I take a stroll along the esplanade, inhaling the fresh sea air. We haven't spoken any more about him wanting to return to South America, and I'm wondering if he'll bring it up when he sees Michael. They haven't seen each other in over a year, although it's not unusual for them. When I first met Samuel, he mentioned how his friends would make him take a holiday once a year to vouch for his sanity and to ensure his safety. So, the time apart never made a difference in their friendship. Samuel has been friends with him since school and vouched for him. The blackmail stunt with Yasmine was out of character, and I still don't understand why he did it. Yasmine has forgiven him, and Samuel is happy to see him, so I'll lower my guard for Yasmine.

Amy and Ethan have secured a booth by a window. It's weird to see them together, and strangely, it makes me happy. Ethan is not someone I'd pick for Amy, but if they're happy, so am I.

Ethan stands and adjusts his tie, then shakes Samuel's hand. "It's good to see you both." He leans and gives me a light hug. "Edes. I haven't seen you around the office for a while."

"No. We've quite a bit going on, especially with Samuel's parents being here. We're still recovering from playing tour hosts," I joke. After Samuel was admitted to the hospital, I only visited a few places with his parents. I made the remark as I don't want to focus on Samuel's health tonight.

"Amy," I say affectionately and step past Ethan to give her a tight hug. "I've missed you, girl."

"Me, too, babe. And I'm here to stay now. I've applied for teaching contracts in the city." She pats my back. "I have really, really missed you."

I take a seat and wait for Samuel to hug Amy before he sits beside me. "Have you ordered?" I ask and pick up the drinks menu.

"Waited for you," Amy says and winks. "Thought we'd start with a cocktail then get a bottle of wine."

The waitress arrives, and we place our order while waiting for our other friends to arrive.

"Ruby is an asset. I'm glad Dana recommended her before she left," Ethan begins with office talk.

"That's great," I say in a high voice. I should be interested in my family's business, only the happenings in the office are the furthest thing from my mind. "Talking of Dana, we're going to visit her." Before I say any more, coughing interrupts us.

"Am I intruding?" Yasmine stands at the end of the table with a goofy smile on her face. "This is Michael," she says and giggles. "I mean, can you believe Michael is here? What the actual heck? She grabs his shoulders and pulls him in for a hug. "You know everyone except Ethan."

Ethan stands and shakes his hand, then Michael hugs Amy and then me. Finally, he shakes Samuel's hand before pulling him in for a hug with a standard three pats on the back. "It's good to see you, man," he says in a thick American accent. "We have a buttload to talk about."

Samuel is smiling, really smiling as he moves over for Michael to sit beside him. They begin their own conversation before Yasmine has even sat beside Amy.

"So, are we going to address the elephant in the room?" Yasmine begins. I look at Michael, then Samuel. Is she talking about what happened the last time we all saw Michael?

"What the actual hell, guys?" Her arms reach out for emphasis toward Amy and Ethan. "When the fuck did this happen? And how?" Her eyes widen. "You two hated each other."

"Did you consider secretly we didn't," Ethan says and winks at Amy. "He drops an arm over her shoulder and plants a kiss on her cheek.

Amy laughs and rests her head on Ethan's chest. "Life's full of surprises."

Yasmine smirks at her. "It is, girl. Well, I'm very happy for both of you."

Our drinks arrive, and Yasmine gives her order. Michael is drinking water, which is surprising.

"Before I forget." Reaching into her bag, Yasmine reveals two wrapped gifts and hands one to Amy and then one to me. "I got you both a little something from Peru."

Amy gives a strangled scream and tears at the gift wrapping. My gift is soft and seems delicate, so I unwrap it carefully. On top is the colored geometric-shaped Inca cross. "Oh, wow! You knew I wanted one of these." The cross holds deep meaning and importance and it's the same one Yasmine wears around her neck.

Her fingers go to her chest, and she strokes the cross. "Now all three of us have one." Her gaze lowers to my present while I continue to unfold a braided band with feathers attached.

"It's a headband." She gives me a warm smile. "Wear it when you're at your happy place, be it physical or spiritual. It's about feeling at peace wherever you are."

I gently run my fingers over the unique band as though it holds magic. "Thank you, I love it." I lean to hug Yasmine and give her a squeeze. Her gifts always have a special meaning.

"Just what I need." Amy pulls a colorful chullo hat over her head then tugs on the earflaps before tying it under her chin. "I love these hats."

"We know," Yasmine and I both say in tune then laugh.

We pack our gifts away and then Amy clinks our glasses. "To love and friendship."

"Any special occasion?" At the end of the table, a tall, dark-haired, beautiful woman smiles at us. It took a moment to process it's Bree, as the guy standing beside her looks a little out of place in a suit. Screams erupt from our table as we spring out of our seats to hug Bree. It's been too long since we were all together.

The four of us have finally moved on with our lives and found partners who complement every one of us.

It's the night before Christmas, and we're home surrounded by our families. The Christmas tree is decorated, and lights flash on and off.

Presents are stacked under the tree. Caroline has made eggnog and pumpkin pie. She's in the kitchen because it's too loud in the family area with Rose and Faith's boys playing dramatically.

Jake, Samuel, Dad, and Christopher are on the balcony enjoying the sunset, each holding a crystal glass with their favorite alcoholic beverage on ice. Samuel, like his father, is drinking whiskey on the rocks. I doubt it's the best thing for Samuel's stomach, but it's the holidays.

Mum and Faith are sitting on the floor near the Christmas tree—the present police. Not one has been opened under their watch. My phone dings, and it's a message to unlock the door. I do so from the kitchen and wait for my brother to ascend the stairs.

Mum screams. Will is standing in the doorway wearing a black shirt and chino shorts, grinning because he loves making an entrance. Faith and I roll our eyes, and we joke about him being the favorite. Mum and Dad are the first by his side. They never admit it, but we know they miss Will terribly. Sometimes I wonder if he's a younger version of Dad with Gran's blonde hair and blue eyes like me.

If only our grandparents could see us now...

"Have you grown again?" Hands on hips, Faith chastises him like he's still our little brother. Younger brother, yes, only Will is far from little. He is now taller than Samuel.

"Hey, sis." He leans in and kisses Faith. "How are the rug rats?"

"Ha. If you babysit while you're here, you'll understand why I already have gray hairs." Faith tilts her head at him. "Come here, ya big teddy bear." She pulls him back for a hug and leans her head against his chest. "I've missed you."

"No one to boss around?" He pats her back. "Talking of being whipped, where's Jake?"

Jake emerges from the bathroom, and his face lights up when he sees Will. They shake hands. "Good to see you, Will."

For a few seconds, I watch Will chat while looking around, taking in my home and the people surrounding us. He rarely comes home these days, and my parents have made trips interstate to see him during university breaks. Making Melbourne his home, he rents a house with other friends and has part-time employment. He plays football for a local club and hopes to get drafted. With all his commitments, I understand why he can't come home whenever he wants. I should arrange to visit him with Samuel and take him to an Aussie football match at the Melbourne Cricket Ground. The atmosphere alone would be worth the trip.

Will turns his blue eyes on me and gives me a cheeky grin. "Here's my jungle girl. Where's Tarzan?"

I shake my head. "Your jokes are lame."

He leans down and squeezes me. "I do it to get a bite, but you're boring now you're a mum."

"Is that so? Then maybe I should tell you to get a haircut since *you* look as though you've emerged from the wild and not brushed your hair for a month."

"It's because I don't own a brush." He runs a hand over his head. "It's a certain look, sis. Only you wouldn't know because… boring."

"Ha. You didn't see me when I was in the jungle." I bump him in the stomach in a playful way. "Come and meet Samuel's parents."

After all the introductions are made, the night passes quickly, and I constantly refill my champagne glass because this mum is *not* boring.

"HOW'S THE HEAD?" Samuel asks as soon as I open my eyes.

"What time is it?" I lick my lips, only my mouth is dry.

"Almost eight. Rose is entertaining my parents."

"Oh shit. I better get up and get organized." I push up and cringe before flopping back and holding the side of my head. "It hurts."

Samuel chuckles. "So, it's a no to a champagne breakfast?"

The thought makes me want to heave. "Why do I do this to myself?"

"Hmm." He taps the side of his cheek as though he's thinking. "Word was someone called someone boring?"

"Ugh. Right."

Samuel chuckles. "Baby, you're far from boring and, at times, you were entertaining, although it's going to be a tough day."

I groan again.

"I'll get you some Tylenol and water. And perhaps something with electrolytes will help."

"Please do your magic." I moan again, then compel my ass out of bed and to the shower before attempting breakfast.

"Pesens," Rose screams as soon as she finishes her toast with vegemite. She claps her hands.

"Yes, honey, now we can open our presents."

Samuel gets on the floor with Rose. Pure joy sets in on her little face with every present she opens. "Bluey," she screams, pulls the soft toy to her chest, and hugs it.

Samuel whispers to Rose, and she pushes up and waddles over to Caroline and Christopher and hugs them

"You're welcome, beautiful girl," Caroline says.

She waddles back to Samuel, and he gives her a parcel to deliver to his parents. She carries it and helps them unwrap their gift. When they reveal a furry toy kangaroo, Rose claps her hands, then runs back to Samuel ready to deliver the next gift. "It's from Rose," he says and winks. "She chose it. Your real gift will be delivered when you return home. A dozen red wines from my favorite McLaren Vale winery."

His father beams a wide smile. "Thank you." He holds up the kangaroo. "We'll find a special place for this fellow."

Rose carries another present to Caroline. She pulls out a small furry koala. "Oh, I love it." Rose claps her hands again and giggles when Caroline rocks it like a baby.

"Okay, my turn." I hand a box to Rose. "Give this to Dad-da." I watch his face as he opens the lid and reads the card inside.

My gift to you is a chance for us to escape reality and immerse ourselves in the green, surrounded by Mother Nature, and discover each other again.
I love you xx

SAMUEL'S LIPS part in a grin. "I have a good feeling about this."

I push up and go over to Samuel, lean in, and kiss him on the lips. "So do I."

He grabs my hand and holds me so he can keep kissing me. Until Rose taps our faces. "Pesen."

Samuel laughs against my lips. "Mommy is distracting Daddy."

"Ha." I go to rise, and his hand holds me still.

"I haven't given you my gift." He picks up a small box topped with a bow and places it in my hand. "Merry Christmas, Eden."

Inside the box is diamond-encrusted heart earrings to match the special necklace he gave me last Christmas in Georgetown after being discharged from the hospital. It was our first Christmas as a family, and it came close to being the last. As I placed it around my neck this morning, the happy memories came flooding back to me. I wrap my arms around him and kiss his lips. "Thank you."

I thread the earrings in my ears and move to our framed wall mirror to admire my gift. The earrings and necklace are stunning. "Oh wow, honey. They are beautiful." Only I don't have time to dwell as I hear the door downstairs with our guests arriving.

Presents are unwrapped, and food is consumed. Popped Christmas poppers and streamers cover the table and floor.

Mum is in the kitchen preparing the pudding and custard for dessert. Faith has positioned her pavlova in the center of the table.

I'm so full I have no room for sweets, but it's Christmas, and our tradition is to eat dessert. Samuel has eaten small helpings of food that won't upset his stomach. He's trying.

Will is entertaining the kids like the big kid he is.

"Tell me..." Faith says to him, "... is there a girl we should be meeting soon?"

Will dips his head back and stares at the ceiling while letting out a loud sigh. He looks back to Faith. "I knew you would ask me this. The answer is the same. No. If there were a chick, I wouldn't be introducing her to you because I don't want to scare her away." He turns and messes James' hair. In retaliation, James wrestles with Will at the table.

Faith shakes her head. "We'd kiss any girl's feet to tolerate you."

"Ha-ha," he says without looking at Faith. "I'll keep you to that."

"Sorry I haven't been around the office," I whisper to Dad, seated beside me.

"It's what happens when you resign." He winks at me.

"Yes, although I want to check in occasionally and offer to help out."

Dad rolls up his shirt sleeves. "You've a lot going on, my girl. We're not going anywhere. When you have time, come by and say hello to everyone."

I pat his forearm and lean closer to lower my voice. "I wanted to let you know I almost finished Gran's journal." He stares at me, waiting, only I don't know what to say.

"You need to read it."

He runs a hand along his jawline. "I don't think I can."

"It's important. I wouldn't say it if I didn't believe you should. It will give you a better understanding as to what happened, and I can't express words for the respect I have for what she went through. My heart shatters into a million pieces with every page, which is why I can't tell you about it."

Dad stares at me for a few seconds. "Okay. I don't read much these days except the *Financial Times*, except I'll do it for you."

"Not for me, Dad. For Gran."

He nods politely and then turns away when Mum carries the pudding to the table.

It's after nine o'clock when everyone leaves, and I want to fall into bed. My feet ache, and I'm in pain from overeating. Caroline and Christopher thank us for an enjoyable day and head to bed.

I take Samuel's hand and lead him to the bedroom. "How are you feeling?"

He kisses my lips. "I'm fine. Everything is going to plan, and so far, there are no setbacks."

I nod, even though he isn't convincing. Minutes after I switch off the light, I hear the gentle sounds of Samuel sleeping.

I can't relax. Some nights I wait until after two-thirty in case he has another nightmare. Holding a pillow to my chest helps to calm me. Not tonight. I give up and reach for my iPad and open the E-book app. I'm not ready to read Gran's journal tonight.

A LOUD GRUNT jolts me awake.

I gather my bearings and realize it's labored breathing.

"Please not again," I murmur.

I check the time—4:23 a.m.

"No. No. No..." I groan.

I grab my phone, and with the light, I shine it so I can see his face and not directly on him to wake him.

His breaths are fast and shallow. I find myself counting, and the only thing I know about hyperventilation is I'll need to get a brown paper bag for him to breathe into.

Samuel's eyes remain closed, yet there's movement beneath his eyelids. His face is twitching as his head moves gently from side to side.

"Run," he croaks.

I hate the dreams where I scream at the top of my lungs for help, yet only a squeaky voice comes out. I imagine him feeling like this.

"Run." Jagged breath.

"Run." Sharp inhales.

"Jump." He flings himself forward, and his head flops.

I massage his shoulder to calm him. The last thing I should do is speak to him and spook him.

His eyes are closed.

"Nooo," he wails. *"I'm sorry. So sorry. Awarö itoto."* Bad stranger.

He falls on his back, and his head moves from side to side. He's mumbling, and it's difficult to comprehend until he cries out, *"I did this."*

"Samuel," I whisper. "You're safe."

It has no effect on him.

"I love you," he murmurs. *"Please forgive me."*

"Honey." I gently rub the length of his arm. Is he talking to me?

"You were like a father to me." He mumbles other words.

"This can't be happening. You were the best part of my life." Choking sounds in sobs erupt from him. I want to wake him. Only this could be his way of letting go of his pent-up emotion. The trauma of his past. Whether it's a new dream or he is reliving the nightmare that has haunted him for months, it must be progress, as he's never cried like this in his sleep.

"I'll always remember you." It comes out in a wail. *"Never forget you. I love you and promise to protect your people forever."*

Forever?

51

EDEN

Beautiful words not intended for me.

Lying beside Samuel, I stroke his shoulder. This wasn't like other nightmares. I assumed his dream included the shaman and maybe Kaikare. He could have been reliving the day the shaman was shot or...

I wrap my arms around his chest and wiggle closer to Samuel. His brow is heavy. His lips are moving like he's saying a silent prayer. A chant, maybe. Samuel has a wonderful, open mind, and there's a possibility he is connecting to the shaman in his dreams. Like he would after taking ayahuasca.

The idea of him taking the brew again scares me. I'm the one who helped save him the last time, and I never want to see that again. I understand certain plants can enhance the experience, and he promised it would be a light brew. Nevertheless, there must be another way. A safer way to help him heal. If it's spirituality he's seeking from a higher being, then he has many religions to pick from. He needs to choose one to facilitate his healing.

We have come too far as a couple, and I'm not giving up without a fight. I won't lose him. I can't. Samuel is a part of me, and my life would never be the same.

The first day I saw him on the beach in Salvador, I knew there was something special about him. Out of the thousands of people on the beach, our eyes met, and a spark of hope and excitement shot through me. Then he was gone. He admitted he felt it too, and it spooked him enough to retreat to the hotel. Thinking about his reaction should have been a flag that he's no ordinary man, that his life differed from mine, and our meeting would impact his life to a degree none of us ever imagined. I was a willing victim and would have done anything for this man even after knowing him for a short time.

Was it a coincidence? I don't believe so.

Somehow, we were meant to be.

Maybe from the time I was born, my Gran saw something in me and knew something about my future no one else could possibly know.

Regardless of how and why we came to meet, we did, and all I know is we are meant to spend the rest of our lives together—long happy lives. And no way in hell am I going to allow Samuel to weaken and think the only way for him to heal is through a damn *magic* tea.

Because he's better than that.

He is stronger than he realizes.

And so am I.

We're not broken.

When I met him, I was emotionally ruined and had given up on love.

Samuel saved me and offered hope.

Showed me a new life and happiness.

It's my turn to help him.

Grabbing my phone from the bedside table, I send Dana a text.

We're coming to visit you soon. Looking at accommodation and flights now!

Then I search for holiday homes in the Daintree Rainforest.

I'm lost to images in the rainforest when he stirs beside me.

"Morning," he whispers, then leans over and kisses me. "What time is it?"

"Almost six. Go back to sleep if you're still tired," I say gently.

"My parents fly out today. I should get up and spend time with them this morning." He glances at my phone. "What are you doing?"

"Looking for holiday homes in the Daintree." I give him a sideways glance to check his reaction.

There's a tell-tale dent between his brows. "For when?"

"As soon as possible. It will be good for you. Best you give me the dates between tests so I can arrange a private getaway."

He pushes up on his elbow. "Eden, I see what you're doing here, and as much as I appreciate it, I've made up my mind. I'm going to Peru for a couple of weeks. Then I'll be back. It's the only way for me to find answers."

"It's not the *only* way," I state. "You're not even considering new options or even another place where we could be happy."

He shakes his head as though I'm not making sense. "Another place?"

"Yes." I scramble to sit up and show him the houses on stilts perched on the side of a mountain and surrounded by rainforest, some overlooking the ocean. "How beautiful are these? I could imagine us living there."

"Living there?" His forehead furrows. "How? What do we do for income? And do you want to sell this house?" he asks, exasperated.

"No, of course not. Maybe we could divide our time. Or even have a home for getaways when you need a break." I shrug. "We'd find work. Please trust me on this. You'd love it there."

"I..." He shakes his head again. "I can't keep up, Eden. I thought you wanted me to live here with you and be close to your family and friends. If none of it matters, why did you want me to come here?"

"If you remember correctly, *you* bloody sent me home without a choice," I snap. "I was happy as long as I was with you. You're the one who emphasized the jungle was too dangerous for me. You were right, but it was also too dangerous for you. And this place doesn't have as many risks. The homes are surrounded by the beautiful rainforest as well as creature comforts for modern living. It's perfect."

Samuel rolls onto his back and covers his eyes with an arm. "What about work? Do I continue my studies from there? Is a hospital even close?"

"Do you want to continue your training?" I murmur. "Are you enjoying it? Because from where I'm standing, the night you collapsed also stemmed from overworking."

He stares at me for a few seconds with a look I've seen through his charade.

"Please trust me on this." I lean over and kiss his lips.

He wraps an arm around my waist and guides me on top of him. "I do trust you. It's part of loving you. But if we spend a few days there, and it doesn't resonate with me in the way you hope for, then you must trust my instinct and allow me to go to Iquitos and see a shaman. Alone."

"Alone?"

"I need to focus on healing and not be distracted by anything else." He takes my face in his hands. "I want to be the best husband I can for you." He then kisses me, and our tongues tease with the passion capable of turning me into liquid lust. My heart beats so fast and, in a way, beats only for him.

"After the last time, it scared me. Why are you so desperate to return?"

"You know why, Eden. I need extra help beyond what modern medicine can offer."

"Maybe, yet you've only seen a psychologist twice. You m-must give it time." My voice cracks, and rather than look at me, he closes his eyes as though some other thought is controlling him. Then it dawns on me. "It's not the healing part, is it? You want to connect with the shaman's spirit. You want to—" my voice cuts out.

"See them." He finishes for me. Samuel opens his eyes, and this time when our eyes lock, I find determination and hope. "I need to know they're okay."

"Jesus," I murmur. "That's not a light brew. You need…" I stop myself and swallow any more words. Saying the truth out loud doesn't make it better. Samuel always intended on taking a strong tea, and the last time he took ayahuasca, I almost lost him. God knows what could've happened to his mind.

This changes the perspective of this holiday, and I'll do everything to show him the Daintree is exactly what he needs because I can't risk losing him again.

SAMUEL and I spend the rest of the day with his parents. We head down to the beach for one last stroll before taking them to the airport.

The seagulls fly overhead, squawking in search of food scraps. The ocean breeze wraps around us like a silk blanket transporting us to her world where all we can see and smell is her. Nothing else matters when your feet touch the sand and salted air hits your senses. Like meditation, the unique sound of waves gently breaking along the shore caresses the mind. It's the best therapy and food for the soul, especially in summer.

Children frolic in the water or ride the waves on boards. Parents sit under the shade, relaxing in their own way. Lovers are in the water, hugging, kissing, and being swept up by the ocean charm. We all lose ourselves in her.

"I don't want to leave," Caroline says to us. "It's been a wonderful seaside holiday, especially with you all."

"Well, you always have a place to come and stay for however long you wish," I tell her. "And if you want to retire here…" I wink. "I'm sure it can be arranged."

"Please don't give her ideas," Christopher says and chuckles. "I'll never get her to the airport."

"We'll miss you both." Samuel looks at his father then his mother. "You can visit anytime and see your granddaughter, or like Eden suggested, you could almost retire here. Return to LA when you need to for your visas."

"Talking about visas," his father adds. "I'm not sure what you'll decide for your future regarding your medical training, but please be aware of the circumstances involving your work visa."

"I will. And I've already discussed a wedding with Eden. When we set a date, we'll let you know."

"Thank you, love." Caroline smiles at Christopher. "I'll need a mother-of-the-groom outfit."

"Mom." Samuel looks at his mother. "I'm considering a beach wedding."

"Oh." She ponders it for a minute. "Do you wear shoes?"

He chuckles. "I wouldn't recommend it on the sand for the ceremony. After, maybe."

Caroline nods slowly, taking it all in her classy stride.

THE MOMENT we arrive home after taking Samuel's parents to the airport, he retreats to the couch to take a nap. During Caroline and Christopher's time here, bridges were built and relationships mended. He wouldn't admit it after being independent for the past decade, but still, I think he's already missing them. Seeing him build a relationship with his parents warms my heart, and I hope he's finding some peace in his.

Rose curls up beside Samuel on the couch and, within five minutes, is also asleep.

I'm not one for daytime sleeps, so I head to the bedroom to find Gran's journal.

The last entry left me with an uneasy feeling in my stomach, so I want to be alone when I read what's to come.

52

IVY

February 11, 1965.

I'm beginning to feel human again.

I'm not sure I have enjoyed hearing the news of the world. It was certainly easier living in a bubble.

Maria witnessed my heart shattering into a million tiny pieces. Too many parts to heal. My heart will never be the same.

It's been weeks since my miscarriage, and I'm still grieving for my baby.

I was about to have two children with a man I loved, and now I'm returning to a man who misses me, only I'm not sure I'll ever receive the kind of love Weju gave me again.

Putting my emotions aside, I must decide in the next few days as the authorities said I need to return.

The cost of my health care is enough for me to leave the country. I'm thankful Albert has met the government and insurance companies halfway.

Albert doesn't know where I have been living or my story. Only I survived by living amongst an indigenous community.

My mind reminds me of how close I came to death.

My heart misses Weju.

Although after all these weeks of living in comfort, I know the rainforest isn't the lifestyle I want.

Maria warned me not to go back to Ulara.

I made a promise, and I have to say goodbye to Weju. After all, he saved my life. I remind her of my promise and that my passport and belongings still remain there.

She waved her hand at me to forget those things as they can arrange new ones. Only I don't want to wait weeks or months.

She told me I'd be stepping on dangerous ground and hoped I knew what I was doing.

Is a promise and saying goodbye to a man I have loved enough?

After living with the Ularans and following their spirituality for months, I know not to betray them now.

March 12, 1965

Tomorrow, I board the ship for my long journey home.

Last night I cried to Albert about how I can't wait to get home. Only he didn't know the truth behind my tears.

didn't know the truth behind my tears.

I need to recount the past two weeks and address the pain I'm suffering. I fear I'll never be the same woman again.

So this will be the last entry in this journal as it will forever be a part of my life that has broken me.

The authorities and Maria escorted me back to Ulara. Maria told them about the community and how they must never speak about it again and never return.

The many hours we sailed along the river, she warned me of a bad feeling.

I now wished I had listened and didn't act on the good faith of a promise.

As though they were expecting us, the shaman, warriors, and Weju were waiting on the riverbank. I had told him about the dangers of getting too close to outsiders and how they carry disease, so I was relieved when they were standing closer to the forest.

That alone made this visit problematic, and I knew I couldn't touch him even though my heart yearned to one more time.

When I disembarked the canoe, I held Dawn in my arms, and his face lit up. I told him he couldn't touch us as we were with the paranakyry, a word he understood as white people or Europeans.

Weju and the shaman's expressions hardened to anger.

Still, I didn't heed the warning.

I told him I'm still sick and need to leave but hope to return one day to see him.

The shaman then spoke with authority. He told Weju not to be angry. His wife—me— was always from another place. I never belonged in Ulara.

I sobbed and said it was untrue and how much I loved him.

The grief inside Weju surfaced, and I'll never forget the expression of my husband's tortured expression. A broken heart because he truly loved me.

And I had betrayed him.

My love wasn't enough to stay, and it was killing him in front of an audience.

His anger exploded, his eyes turned venomous. More warriors and the chief emerged from the trees. It was unusual behavior as I have rarely witnessed hostility among the Ularan people. His reaction shocked me into a panic.

I pleaded for my bag and belongings. To my surprise, Weju retreated to fetch them, except spears were raised, and Maria was begging me to leave.

I asked her to wait until Weju returned.

Minutes seemed like hours.

On his return, his calmness fooled me.

He handed me my bag and then asked to hold Kaikare one last time.

My tears fall as I write this entry, and with every word I continue to write, I want to vomit, acknowledging my ignorance of the warnings Maria had shouted at me from the curiara. Warnings of offending their culture.

I was a fool for love.

I passed Kaikare to him so he could cuddle his daughter one last time, even though I knew of the infection risk. I couldn't deny him. He dropped the bag at my feet. When I bent to pick up the bag, Weju had taken his position beside the shaman. The shaman palmed Dawn's forehead and sang a song. Stupidly, I assumed it to be a blessing, and it gave me a minute to check inside my bag for my passport and other important belongings, including my camera. I was blind in understanding what the exchange meant.

Weju's expression hardened. He announced to all how Kaikare has medicine magic and can't leave the village. The shaman confirmed it. Her future was there, and she, too, will grow up to become a shaman.

Overwhelmed with hysteria, I begged for my baby.

Weju asked me again to stay.

Maria's voice was in the background telling me we must leave now as it's our last chance.

But I couldn't leave without Dawn, so I continued begging for my baby.

Weju held out his hand for me to come to him, and for a moment, I caught a glimpse of the love we shared, yet in those few seconds, he realized I wasn't going to change my mind, and the chief gave a command.

Spears lifted.

Maria shouted as the motor roared. I had one last chance to stay or go.

A warning arrow missed us. The next might not.

Leave without Dawn or stay.

I could get sick again. So could Dawn. I'm fresh out of surgery and can't bear more children.

Albert and Winston expect me to come home.

The authorities might not give me another chance if I stay.

Can I undo the damage I have already caused within the village?

My sobs were uncontrollable, and I couldn't hear myself think, yet alone make a decision.

Until Maria yelled, "Ivy, now or never."

"Wait," I screamed.

Through my tears, I opened my bag and retrieved my decoupaged mirror and pearls and held them out. No one made a move toward me. So I placed them in the sand and backed away with my eyes still on my daughter, knowing this was the last time I'll ever see her. I climbed aboard the curiara, my heart shattering into a million tiny pieces.

As the curiara reversed, the shaman strode to the river's edge. Like a gatekeeper, he slammed his stick on the ground, and the beads and bones attached at the top rattled in warning.

The ferocity in his eyes will stay with me forever. Then his expression changed to fierce understanding. Not in pity, more that he knew the ending of my story.

I'm reminding myself to breathe as I write this entry.

Even the months aboard the ship will not be enough to heal my heart and wear a brave face for Albert.

I remind myself I have another family who's eagerly awaiting my return.

Another family who loves me.

My broken heart can't be revealed as I could ruin a chance of happiness with them.

Maria told me never to forget my daughter in my heart, but to my family, I must never speak of her if I want to move on. Only mention the hysterectomy and my baby died.

It's not a complete lie.

Only now, I mourn so much more.

March 23, 1965

I'm on the ship and in my quarters.
Out of the porthole, all I see is blue. For many months, green was the only color surrounding me.
Blue represents another chance at life.
Last night I dreamed about my two babies I have lost. Set in the future, Dawn was four and my baby, a boy I named Albert, Jr. was around two years of age, and they were playing in the rainforest. Then the rains came and along with it, sadness.
Did I have the mental or physical capacity to survive another rainy season with two children?
I'll never know.
Have I made the right choice leaving my husband and child for what many consider a better life?
What will my life become if Albert decides he no longer loves the woman I have become?
Will I ever forgive myself for the many bad decisions I have made to get me this far?
I should never have walked away from Albert and Winston to follow a stupid dream.
Because I'm no longer the same woman who left them all those years ago.

53

EDEN

Closing the journal, I curl up into a ball and allow the tears to flow down my cheeks. I keep swallowing the lump in the back of my throat, hoping to get control of the emotion soaring through me. My chest feels like it's been split open by an ax—a raw wound.

My dear grandmother...

I love her even more for what she went through, and respect explodes from my heart. Respect as she did live out her life the best way she could. I know Pops found out about her affair, and it led him to alcohol and eventually to become an alcoholic, but did he ever understand the position she was in and what she had to do to stay alive?

It's hard to imagine if you have never been deep in the heart of the Amazon rainforest. I'm still shocked by the hostility of the Ularans and wonder if it's why Weju exercised his right as a shaman with love, and if he promoted calmness in the people after the shellshock of Gran leaving him. He had Kaikare and eventually found peace and contentment in his life. He also connected with Gran's spirit during ayahuasca. Their spirits were reunited in another world, I know that now. I only hope she'd reconciled with Pop and found peace with the two men in her life.

Years ago, Mum mentioned how Gran had blessed me. It was a weird thing to say, and I can't help wondering if Gran possessed a sense of what my future held.

I take the journal and press it close to my heart, closing my eyes and visualizing Gran's smiling face. "I'll love you forever," I whisper.

The journal must remain in the family. Both journals do, and my family needs to read both. It will be hardest for Dad, as he remembers Gran's depression when he was a child and the arguments. He needs to know why, understand what Gran endured, and how his mother was a warrior.

Not crazy like people assumed.

"Are you okay?" Samuel sits on the bed. Rose is curled into his chest still half-asleep.

"I finished her journal," I murmur. "I'm still mulling over it all. Everything makes sense why Gran behaved the way she did when Dad was young and why Pop became an alcoholic. He was proud. I only wished he understood Gran better and shared some of that pride her way."

Samuel takes my hand and squeezes it. "Is it appropriate if I also read it?"

"I'd like you to as there are topics I need to discuss. And you can offer support when my family also reads it."

"Do you want me to read both before offering them to your family?"

"I think that's a good idea. And so you know, we're leaving for our holiday up north in a couple of weeks."

Samuel's expression softens as though he knows better than to argue with me.

He's not the only one desperate to reconnect with the rainforest. It's a place where I can feel closer to Gran.

Two days later, Samuel comes with me to say goodbye to Will. It feels strange ascending the stairs of our apartment complex when I used to do this several times a day.

"Do you mind if I stay for a bit, then leave?" Samuel asks before we enter the front door. "Michael messaged and wants to catch up since Yasmine is back at work."

"Sure. We're only going to hang out here for a few hours until it's time for Will to leave for the airport."

We open the door to cheering. Will runs to us, being chased by Faith's kids. "Look, it's Mowgli and Shanti." He points to Samuel and me. Faith's kids stop chasing him and stare at us.

"No, it's not. It's Aunty Eden and Sam," Sebastian corrects him. He continues to chase Will with James following and copying everything Seb does.

Rose squirms in Samuel's arms. "Did I hear him right?" he asks while lowering Rose to the floor so she can chase after them.

"Yep." I shake my head at Will.

"Stop." Will holds his arms out straight at Faith's boys. "We need to wait for King Louie." Rose tootles after them.

"Will," Samuel warns in a low deep voice.

"Just kidding, mate." Will chuckles, then jab steps and sidesteps away from the kids as though he's on the football field.

Samuel and I sit with the family at the dining table. "Morning."

We join in the conversation about the upcoming Autralian Football League season. I don't add much, considering I haven't paid attention for years, and Samuel is clueless, still he listens attentively. "We need to go to a game," I whisper to him.

"We should all travel to Melbourne for a game," Dad adds. "And Will could come along."

Will pulls a seat up at the table.

"Enough," Faith says firmly when her boys jump on Will. "Excuse me. I'll amuse them for a bit so we can talk." Faith switches on the television, and the three kids sit in front of it, ready to watch *Pokémon*. Rose isn't familiar with it, yet she'll copy whatever her cousins do.

Faith takes her seat again. "When are you two heading to Cairns because I seriously want to come?"

Jake chuckles beside her. "With us or on your own?"

She rolls her eyes. "Do I need to answer that?"

I laugh at my sister. "In two weeks. I've booked the flights, and we're staying in a hotel for a few days, then with Dana in her holiday home near the rainforest." I glance at Samuel and smile. "It will be good for all of us."

"Exactly. It's why I want to come in your suitcase."

"We can go another time," Jake adds. "I know we haven't been on a family holiday for some time, so maybe it's something we could plan."

“We should all try and get up and see Dana,” Dad says in a low voice. “Have to say I miss her bossing me around in the mornings.”

Samuel’s phone dings with a message. He reads it and pops it back into his shorts pocket. “Excuse me. I’m meeting a friend.” He stands and shakes Will’s hand. “Have a good flight. I’m looking forward to seeing you in Melbourne and at a possible football game.”

“Thanks, man. Look after my sis. And I’ll deck you out in the right colors for the game.” Will winks at him.

“Right colors are debatable,” I quip. “Will and I don’t root for the same team.”

“Maybe I need to choose my own team,” he jeers. I walk him to the door. “I’ll see you at home. Say hello to Michael for me.” I kiss him on the cheek and close the door behind him.

“I’ve mentioned to Dad about Gran’s journal,” I begin after I sit. “I know Will doesn’t remember much about Gran.” Will was only around eight years old when she died. “I’ve finished both journals and think you all should read them.”

The air around the table changes with the silence except for squeaky kids’ voices echoing from the television.

“It’s important you all understand what she went through, as I don’t believe Pop understood her trauma. If he’d read the journals, they may have experienced a better relationship. I’ll let you be the judge.” I stare at Mum and then Dad. “I have this heavy feeling in my heart that she suffered alone, and no one understood her except Brenda.”

Dad nods his head slowly. “Frankly, I didn’t want to relive any bad childhood memories or think of my father in a bad light. He did a great job caring for me.”

“No one is arguing that, Dad. The point is Gran wasn’t crazy.”

Dad lowers his gaze to the table. There’s anguish in his expression as though he’s remembering his past. “If you believe it’s something we need to understand, then I’ll read them.”

I let out a sigh. “I do. For everyone. We can chat about it after.”

“I’m keen to read both journals.” Faith smiles at me. “And I volunteer to go first.”

“You should read them too,” I say to Will. “I want you to know about our grandparents and how amazing they were.”

“Honey, maybe you should find the box Gran left for you. It’s been years since you opened it.”

We're all staring at Mum. "What box?"

"Gran, gifted you all something." She smiles at Faith and Will. "You both received photographs and a few of her trinkets." I have stored them in my cupboard for when you're ready. You didn't want yours yet," she reminded Faith.

"How did I forget this?" Faith shakes her head. "Can I take it home today?"

"Of course." She smiles at Will. "I assumed you didn't want yours until you came home."

"What about Dad's box? What's in it?"

Mum glances at Dad, and she waits for him to answer my question.

Dad's thumb rubs at a spot on his opposite hand. He stares at his hands for a moment before looking at Mum. "I don't know," he admits. "The first time I opened it, some things brought back memories of my childhood. Mum rarely discussed my childhood because we all got on with life after I had you kids."

Mum gives him a nod to continue.

"After she passed, I received everything I needed, only the boxes included contents I'd never seen. She kept them hidden until after her death." His shoulders rise and fall as he takes some deep breaths. "It was like opening Pandora's box, and sad memories poured in. I stuck it in a cupboard until the right time."

"Dad," I murmur. "The time is right."

Dad gazes at Mum, his eyes begging for support. I've never witnessed this side of him. "It's okay, Winston. We can go through it when you're ready. Then you can share what you need to with everyone."

I swallow hard. Should I offer to go through it first and screen things for him? I need to know what's in the box and what he doesn't want to share with us.

"Please," I say gently. "No more secrets.

54

SAMUEL

THE FRESH SEA air wafts around Samuel as he sits at an outside table near the Glenelg foreshore. It has a trendy vibe with its outdoor cafés. Many offer organic food, and yet he struggles to feel at home, even by the beach with the woman he loves. He'll stay and work and do everything he can to make his family work. Except the cost of his health has him second-guessing his decision. One trip to Peru could be life-changing for him.

Michael slides into a chair opposite him. "Sorry I'm late, mate."

They both chuckle at the way he says *mate.*

"Are you settling in okay?"

Michael grins. "I enjoy the laid-back lifestyle and how easily assessable everything is." He leans back in his chair and pushes some dark strands out of his eyes. "Yasmine is awesome, man. I'm not messing up this second chance."

"How long can you stay?"

"I'm still sorting visas and hope the accounting company I worked for can organize work for me here. Pass some regulations." He shrugs his shoulders. "If not, I'll make the trips back and forth until I know Yas is in for the long haul, and we can make it official."

"Official?" Samuel chokes out. "I knew you wanted to give it a go, but are you seriously thinking of moving here?"

"We're not sure. Yas suggested she could spend some time in LA. She'll give anything a shot."

"I'm happy for you both, and it would be nice to have a friend here."

Michael taps the table as though he wants to say something. "You know you barely have time for your family yet alone our catchups."

Samuel eyes him carefully. "I hope it's not the case for the long term."

He juts out his chin. "You don't plan on staying in the medical field? Because we both know nothing will change in the future."

His friend knows him well. "I devised a two-year plan for Eden and Rose to have financial security if—"

"You're planning on leaving them?" he asks incredulously.

"If something happened to me," he finishes. "Or..." he shakes his head, not knowing how to answer Michael. To say it out loud sounds selfish. How does he explain if he can't live in society, if he's not cut out physically and mentally to cope, and he can't continue like this? It would leave him with no other choice than to leave Eden with family and return to nature. He doesn't plan on living like a recluse, yet short visits to see them he could cope with. He can't ask her to leave her family and friends to be with him. He's different, he acknowledges it, but how different is yet to be seen after his tests are completed. The investigations won't reveal anything he doesn't already know.

"It's a time thing."

"Right." Michael leans his elbows on the table and leans closer. "You're going to break her heart."

"Not as much as if I were dead."

Michael eyes him carefully. "So you'll work something out? You know she'll travel to the other side of the globe to be with you."

"I do, and it's why I won't ask it of her. She has the support of her family here... I'm not really a people fan."

Michael laughs. "Not people, man. You're not a fan of entitlement and arrogance in society. You're a great doctor, and it's because you care for people. You've got to give yourself more credit. And stop running away from the very thing that scares you." He reaches out and lightly pats Samuel's shoulder. "You have to give her the choice."

"If it comes to that, I would. It's why I need to go to Peru. It might be the answer to everything."

Michael opens his phone. "It might not be either. To be honest, I didn't gain much knowledge this time. I also wanted to be there for

Yasmine and take care of her." He places his phone on the table. "I sent his number. If I can be frank, I'd be trying something else before rushing over there. If you don't get the answers you want, then what happens?"

Samuel hesitates because he doesn't want to consider his last option. *Leaving them.*

"What do you suggest?"

Michael raises both his hands defensively. "Hey, man, I'm not getting involved. But if it were me, I'd be seeking the advice of an indigenous healer. Ask around. Your doctor friends should know of someone."

"Funny, it's what my father suggested."

Michael grins. "Well, I'm starved. You want to get some food?"

SAMUEL WALKS the esplanade path and is surprised to see a message from Eden letting him know she's still at Monte apartments with her parents.

He takes the stairs and opens the door. Eden and her parents remain at the kitchen table and are deep in discussion.

"Is everything okay?"

Eden turns, wiping her red eyes. "Hey. We just got news."

His stomach tightens. "What happened?" He sits beside Eden and wraps an arm around her waist.

"Do you remember when I visited Brenda in the nursing home?" Samuel nods. "She passed away yesterday. Her brother-in-law called to let Mum know and to also tell her they found some photos in her belongings they suspected belonged to Gran."

Samuel looks to her father. His expression sags. Grace gives him a nod. "There are photos of a baby." Grace wipes a tear from her eyes. "We have so much history we never knew about, and it's hard to take it all in."

"Samuel," Eden says and touches his leg. "I told Dad about the baby Gran lost and how Kaikare ended up in Ulara. It's so sad to know how everything would have turned out if Gran didn't return to say goodbye to the shaman."

"What if…" Samuel murmurs, "… is one of the hardest things to accept in life."

He lives with speculation every day.

55

EDEN

BRENDA'S WAKE is small and intimate.

Mum is by my side under the shade of a gum tree near the door of a small service room in the same gardens where she's buried. Garden, I repeat, not cemetery—it's an ugly word in my head.

Gran and Pop were cremated and had asked for their remains to be released over the ocean near Monte Hotels, an ocean where they'd spent their lives pondering decisions and life choices. A place where we all connected as a family. Later, we celebrated Gran's life at the apartment with her close friends and our family.

I recall Brenda wearing red shoes when she attended Gran's funeral. It's the one thing that stuck in my mind. Another woman commented it was disrespectful and a sign of a festive vibe, not sadness. Brenda agreed and said to Mum it's how she remembered her friend and their good times together. She was celebrating Ivy's life.

I down the last of the champagne in my crystal flute.

"Would you like another?"

"I think I do."

"Come on," Mum urges. "We should go inside and give our condolences to the family."

"The last time I visited Brenda, she thought I was Gran. She said a few things to me as though she was reliving old times."

"Did she tell you anything believable?" Mum takes my flute, places it on the table, and grabs two more.

"Little things like Albert will come around. And I shouldn't feel guilty. I had a wonderful adventure. I'm not sure *almost dying* classifies as that, but she understood Gran and supported her one hundred percent."

"Here's to Brenda." Mum clinks my glass. She turns to a photograph propped on a stand of a younger Brenda as a nurse. "Their friendship was special."

"It's final, you know. A door for more information has closed."

"Oh, honey." Mum wraps an arm around my waist and pulls me closer. "Not closed. Brenda had Alzheimer's, and some of what she told you might not be true. Besides, your father is yet to open his box. He will. And Thomas is yet to give me the photos Brenda kept." Mum downs her champagne like a pro and takes my hand. "Let's speak to Thomas."

I wave at the staff I recognize from the nursing home before standing in the outer circle of Brenda's family. I assume some are children and grandchildren, and others might be related to her late husband.

Thomas comes to stand by Mum. "Thank you for coming," he says to both of us. He has aged since I last saw him. Maybe I didn't notice his gray hair until today.

"We're thankful for the invite." I let go of Mum's arm.

"I don't have the photos on me, although I can swing by your home and drop them off tomorrow."

Mum glances at me. "That would be great. Eden and I will be there." Mum gives Thomas a hug, and we say our goodbyes.

"You and I should both be there," she whispers. "Before your father has a breakdown if the photos are of Dawn."

Photos of Kaikare as a toddler fan out over the kitchen table.

There are patches of red where the images have faded, yet it doesn't take away from the enormity of seeing these for the first time. Gran captured moments of her crawling with the jungle as a backdrop and another of her sitting on the hammock, with her smile lighting up her little face framed by dark hair.

Ivy is written in cursive on the back of each image.

Mum places a picture of her as a baby, maybe a few months old, on the table, and she keeps staring at it.

"What is it?"

Mum glances up. "I can see features that remind me of you as a child."

"Really?"

She nods yet doesn't say anything.

I pick up the image of the shaman—Weju. He didn't know she was taking a shot. He was a handsome man—a sculpted jaw, high cheekbones, and dark hair to his shoulders, wearing a short, woven skirt hanging from his hips, his bare muscular chest and arms on display. He was looking up, which gave Gran time to take the picture from, I assume, her hut, yet I can see a gentleness in his eyes.

One image confused me as it was a group photograph. Gran held Kaikare in her arms, the shaman beside her, and other Ularans stood next to them.

"They don't like objects from our world, yet someone took the group photo." I show Mum the image. "I guess they didn't know what it did, so it was like a hard box to them that made clicky sounds."

"Why do you say that?"

"Because they wanted to burn her journal and pen, believing the pen was bad magic."

"I see." She holds the photograph closer. "This is like the one she left for you."

In my beautiful engraved wooden box, the images included herself and a similar group one, only it was taken further back and hard to identify anyone. This picture is closer so she must have asked the person to come forward. Thankfully, whoever peered through the lens wasn't spooked.

I pick up another image. "We're lucky to have these."

"We are," Mum murmurs, still engrossed in the photograph she's holding.

"Do you think Pop found them? Or is it why Gran gave them to Brenda for safekeeping?"

"If Gran had lived longer, I believe she'd have told us about Dawn. Only at the time of her sudden death, your father wasn't ready."

"Is he ready now?"

"It's hard for him as he feels a sense of responsibility to help Dawn now he knows Samuel tried to keep them safe."

"He can't," I emphasize. "He'd never find her, and she's with the only family she knows."

"He said he regrets not meeting his sister, and if given a chance, he'd do it."

Wow.

"That's a beautiful thing," I say gently. "But it might never happen."

"No. I'll sit with him while he goes through the photos and then keep them somewhere safe."

"Has he had a chance to look at his box?"

"No, love. We can't force him. He wants to know more about his mother and Dawn, but it's affecting him more than he's saying. Your father is a strong man, and when he allows emotions to break him, he often falls sick for weeks. When I see the signs, I protect him by spacing out whatever is causing him stress. It's why I'm not pushing him. The photos are enough for now."

56

EDEN

Ten Days Later...

SAMUEL SMILES as we sit at the base of a waterfall in the Daintree rainforest. He dives into the waterhole and surfaces, waving for Rose and me to join him. "It's too cold," I call out after dipping my toes in the freshwater.

Four days into our holiday, we have bathed in the cultural experience of North Queensland. While Dana works, we have snorkeled the Great Barrier Reef and traveled to Mossman Gorge, to fast-moving streams, and found organic cafés with tropical fruit that agrees with him. He's booked an Indigenous tour, a guided walk through the rainforest, and to learn about the medicinal plants. He can't contain his excitement.

"You know there could be crocs in the water," I call out to him.

He chuckles. Other people are swimming closer to the falls. It's unlikely crocs are in this part of the stream.

He wraps a towel around his waist then lifts Rose to his hip. He stops and points to a spider web. "Look, spider." I shudder at the sheer size—bigger than my palm—yet he's undeterred.

"Gross," I remark.

"They remain in the trees," he says as though spiders have never bothered him. They didn't in Ulara, but in the city, it's another matter. It doesn't make sense, yet I know this is where he thrives, so it's natural for his anxiety to subside.

By the time we arrive back at Dana's apartment, she has finished work for the day. We talk about our adventures, then head to bed, ready to do it all again tomorrow.

The following day, Samuel decides to do the indigenous tour alone. He borrows Dana's car, and it gives us time to catch up.

"Fishy pool. Fishy pool," Rose says in excitement.

"Yes, sweetie. We'll take you to the fishy pool." The kids swimming lagoon is on the Cairns esplanade. Large metal fish sculptures rise from the water and is something Rose identified with the pool.

Dana and I take a stroll with Rose to the esplanade lagoon. We sit with our feet in the shallow water while Rose splashes about to cool down.

I tell Dana about Gran's journal, how she came to be in Ulara, and why she was depressed at times. "I identify with Dawn as Kaikare. Mum and Dad like to call her Dawn, as it's the name Gran gave her. While in the village and knowing her personally, it's what I called her."

Dana adjusts a cap over her eyes. "And the photos?"

"We'll have the photos restored." I peer up at the fluffy white clouds in a blue sky. The humidity is extreme, and even Rose has adapted. She screams as she runs, falls in the ankle-deep water, then giggles to herself. I laugh at Rose's antics and imagine myself living here until my thoughts drift to my family and friends. My father...

"I worry about Dad. At first, he didn't want to know about the jungle. Then he accepted it all and wanted to know more, especially about Kaikare. Now he's guilt ridden about Gran. A complete misunderstanding and the secrets didn't help."

"Your Gran had a kind heart. She'd come into the office to say hi and see Winston. She'd take you girls out for the day when Grace cared for Will."

"It must have been when she took us to visit Brenda. At least she had a friend to confide in and not judge her."

"We all need friends like Brenda. I have one, only she lives in Bali. Thank God for FaceTime. Her photos are what inspired me to live in the tropics."

"Lucy?"

Dana nods. "She reminds me of Yasmine. All worldly and spiritual and looks at everything with positivity."

"I feel like I know her already," I joke.

"We should get this little one out of the sun." Dana scoops Rose from the water, and she kicks her legs in protest. She kisses her cheek. "You're like your mum. But Aunty Dana needs to go home and finish packing as we're taking you to the jungle."

I laugh. "It's not really the jungle."

"It's as close to it as I'm going to get."

SAMUEL IS quiet when he arrives home.

"How was it?" I ask when we're alone.

"Incredible. I'm still processing everything he told me. I might need to document some points he suggested."

"Sure. We're packed and need to get our bags in the car."

"I'll tell you about it later." Samuel sits on the end of the bed with a notebook and writes frantically as though his pen can't keep up with his trail of thoughts. It's a déjà vu moment from Ulara. He still likes to use a notepad over the computer.

The drive to the Daintree was as picturesque as I imagined. We lined up to get the cars on a ferry to cross a river. Then we followed a narrow road lined with palm trees and thick shrubbery, and I knew we were close. We stopped to get biodynamic organic ice cream, and the flavors were amazing.

Dana and Samuel point out the window telling Rose to keep watch for a cassowary. We turn off a side road and drive up a long driveaway fenced in by the rainforest. All I can see is green with the occasional pop of color of heliconia flowers and pink-leafed plants. Kerry parks the car under the house.

"We're here," Dana announces.

My phone rings, and I almost don't answer it as I'm excited to explore the house. Only it's Amy.

"Hey, Amy."

"Edes."

Something is off with her tone and my thoughts race to Ethan, but I rein in any accusations.

"Is everything okay?"

"No. I've been in a car accident."

"What?" I gasp.

"I'm okay. A few broken bones, that's all. Ethan is fine apart from whiplash."

"Oh, honey. What do you mean a few broken bones?"

Samuel stares, waiting to see if she's okay. I mouth for him to go inside with Rose.

"A few cracked ribs and a broken collarbone."

"Not a fun way to spend your holiday break, babe."

"No." She bursts into tears. "The other driver died at the scene. It was awful."

"Oh, honey. I'm sorry."

"I keep seeing her face. Apparently, she suffered a heart attack and crashed into us. I can't stop seeing her bloodied face."

I peer toward the house. I want to be here with Samuel, only I hate hearing my friend sound distressed. "I can come home. If you need a friend, I'll be there."

"It's okay," she sobs. "Ethan is here with me, and Yasmine is checking in. I'll see you when you come home in a week."

"Are you sure, Amy? Because if you want me to come home, I will."

"No. I'm fine. I might need to call, okay? Because you're the one I talk to when life is hard."

My chest tightens. "Call anytime, Ames. I love you, and I'll be home soon to give you a hug."

I end the call.

For years, my tight circle of friends has supported each other.

Standing on the elevated driveway, I stare out at the ocean bordered by the rainforest. There is something magical about this place. There's an energy surrounding us, pulling us closer to the rainforest's heart. A similar sensation I felt in Ulara with Samuel.

Maybe it's calling to him.

To us.

Amy's phone call highlights the important people I'll be leaving. Can I leave my family and friends?

57

SAMUEL

After an extensive tour of the grounds, Kerry and Dana retreat to their room, leaving Samuel alone with Eden. Eden unpacks their case and smiles at him.

"It's certainly a beautiful place. Almost enchanting." She moves her case aside, and he senses her watching him.

"Enchanted, yes. I felt something similar on the indigenous tour... a magnetic energy drawing me to the forest."

Her eyes widen. "You enjoyed it?"

He takes a deep breath. "I resonated more than I thought possible. Even from the beginning, there was a smoking ceremony, and we focused on leaving bad thoughts outside the forest."

Eden sits on the bed and gazes at him. "Tell me about it."

"The poisonous plants appear the same as the non-poisonous varieties, including figs. And creeper vines... if you touch them, you can break out in blisters. I'll be educating you in your own country," he jokes.

"Now you're showing off." She pats the space beside her on the bed. "Would you remember the plants if you saw them again?"

"Maybe some. The more I think about it, the more I'd like to learn the ways of the forest up here."

"What are you saying? Do you want to have a holiday house here?"

He's aware of how much Eden wants him to like this place as she sees it as the answer to him not taking ayahuasca. He's not convinced. Yet. "I'll let you know after a few days." Samuel takes her face in his hands and kisses her gently. "Thank you for bringing me here."

"It wasn't all for you." Eden winks at him. "I also wanted to come and visit Dana. Anyway, what was your favorite part of the tour?"

"The edible wild fruits and medicinal plants. Some of the kernels can be ground to a flour consistency to make bread." He shakes his head as though he's clearing his thoughts. "Even the sap of certain trees can be used to treat fever. I'd enjoy a night walk to observe the bioluminescence of the fungi growing on the plants. It might transport me to some happier times." He places a hand on my thigh and squeezes it. "Although I'd want to check out a path first to ensure there were no harmful plants in the area. The guide mentioned fine hairs on one of the heart-shaped leaves stinging plants having the effect of glass, and the pain can last from weeks to months." Hearing his own words, he has resonated with the Daintree rainforest more than he lets on.

"Oh." Eden averts her gaze. "I'd have to be watching Rose twenty-four-seven."

"Eden." He waits for her to meet his gaze. "If we were here, I'd do routine checks to ensure the forest around us was relatively safe."

She bites her lip. "Apart from the creatures because you can't control them."

He looks out the window to the sky-blue ocean. "Or Mother Nature, and we'd have a rainy season of different proportions here."

"Meaning?"

"Cyclones. There's no evading Mother Nature even in paradise."

A storm Samuel has weathered before.

He can't deny the energy swirling inside him, ready to meet his problems with new insight he has gained from the tour. Not only about the medicinal plants but how to use the strength of his mind when dreaming and to think about his memories in a different light before falling asleep.

To reset his brain and way of thinking through memories in his dreams.

The brain is powerful.

If his new friend is right, maybe he has the force to not only weather the storm but to become the storm.

58

EDEN

One Month Later...

MY EXPERIENCE in the jungle has taught me how fate tests the balance of life and to never become complacent.

It's hard not to be when every morning I open my eyes, and I wish for nothing more than what I have in front of me.

With Rose and Samuel by my side, I flourish effortlessly. The three of us together is my ultimate happiness.

Eudaimonia.

After arriving home, I made Samuel a promise. A beach wedding. My only condition, we wait until he's *happy*.

He has to find a new job that agrees with his health and become physically and spiritually happy.

Money or material things don't buy happiness. It's why he loved Ulara. And I have faith he can find the same inner peace without traveling to Peru to take ayahuasca.

Already, the nightmares have subsided.

He's dreaming more about Kaikare and his friends. What they're doing in their new home. I suggested he could be connecting with Kaikaire in his dreams.

Because anything is possible.

Samuel walks into the room after receiving a phone call.

"You'll never guess who called."

"Who?" I ask impatiently.

"Dr. Mundy. He wants me to be part of a project in the rainforest finding medicinal properties in the unique plants of the Daintree."

I throw my arms around his neck and kiss him hard. "All you had to do was ask the universe. If it's meant to be, then it will happen."

"Like magic?" he mocks.

"No. Like fate." I kiss him again.

"Ah." He glances down at me and grins. "Like you coming into my life."

"You're right. No point fighting it. I'm destined to be with you forever."

"Forever isn't long enough," he whispers against my lips. "I have no intention of fighting fate."

"Your best decision yet, Dr. McMahon." He leans and pulls me close to his body, the warmth radiating from him surrounds me like a calming blanket. He kisses me slow and meaningful, passionate yet gentle.

"Thank you for fighting for me," he whispers against my lips.

I pull back and stare into those blue eyes filled with love and contentment, and hold his beautiful face in my hands. "Honey, I knew from that first moment we were destined to be together. Nothing and no one will take you away from me."

He leans his forehead against mine and closes his eyes. "I'm ashamed to admit for a while, I thought I wasn't going to make it. Contemplated leaving and—"

I smother his words in a kiss.

Words I don't want to hear as I knew what Samuel was feeling.

He struggles to survive in society, and he didn't want to ask me to leave my family and friends when inside he was slowly dying.

I could see it.

I'm even more determined for a new life for both of us.

After all, I have the courage of my grandmother inside me.

For even fate has no idea what I would do or how far I would go for love.

EPILOGUE

EDEN

Ten Months Later…

Before I lock the door, I eye the huntsman spider in the corner of the kitchen ceiling.

"Keep the mosquitos and flies under control while we're gone, please, George."

"Bye, George," Rose says as though he's a pet. With a *Bluey* bag slung over her shoulder, she toddles out the door. Everything on our front deck is packed safely away in time for the wet season. I gaze out over the green forest canopy to the ocean meeting the horizon. I'm going to miss this view.

Disappointment dissipates in seconds with my body overheating in the extreme humidity. I take Rose's hand as we amble down the steps toward the car.

I head south along a road with walls of rainforest on either side until a queue of cars brings me to a stop.

After showing my pass, I press the car window button to shut out the heat. With the sun sitting directly above us, there's no shade from the towering trees. Putting the car in drive, we crawl forward until we're on the ferry, ready to cross the river.

From the back car seat, Rose eyes the water eagerly, searching for a crocodile sunning on the muddy banks. It's a game we play—the first one to find a croc. We have only spotted a small crocodile twice over the past few months, unlike 'Mo,' the resident crocodile near Port Douglas that captures tourists' attention as they cross the Mowbray River Bridge on the outskirts of the town.

"There." Rose points to her left.

I follow her gaze. "No, honey, it's a log."

She sighs in disappointment.

"Maybe next time."

It's extraordinary how my daughter is excited to see a crocodile. Over the months, she has become accustomed to a place many consider has the most-deadliest creatures on the planet. We have learned what's dangerous and what not to do, like swimming in the ocean in the summer months. The deadly Irukandji and box jellyfish bloom from around November to May, so if you're not looking out for a crocodile, the smaller creatures are a threat.

Thankfully, we have a swimming pool in the house we bought a few doors down from Dana's holiday home. And as for snakes, thankfully, I've only witnessed pythons in the garden.

Many things here remind me of Gran and my time in Ulara.

"I'm hun-gy," Rose moans.

I meet her blue eyes in the review mirror. At two years of age, she's a mini version of Samuel, although her eyes are bluer and more like mine.

"Seriously? We have not long left, and your snacks are for the plane."

She huffs and folds her arms. "Yes, sewios-ly."

I can't wait for the sassy two-year-old stage to end.

"Mooksy might have some wild figs for you to eat."

"Yuck."

I hide a smirk at her expressing the distaste of bush food. I imagine, over time, it will change with her father's encouragement and passion.

I press the button for my Spotify list to play a song list, especially for Rose, and it distracts her long enough until we reach Mossman.

Driving through the parking lot past rows of four-wheel drives, vans, and motorhomes, I stop in the staff zone. The gateway to the Daintree Rainforest. People visit here to learn about the culture of the Australian indigenous people and come from all over the world to experience the Dreamtime Walks. Among the trees boasts the biggest conifers in the world, almost as large as the statue of liberty.

Rose and I meander through the center and wave to the staff before heading outside to the bus waiting area. A group of tourists circle a guide. They listen intently to the guide talk about the plants and how they can treat certain diseases. Questions are answered with respect to the indigenous way of life and include his extensive medical knowledge. The guide with messy blond hair isn't indigenous but has studied and learned from the leaders here, and I'm proud how he's passionate about their culture.

The rainforest has much to offer us all.

"If you have further questions, please see Mooksy inside the center," Samuel says to the group. The circle breaks apart. A smile lights up his face as he shares a joke with one of the tourists. Samuel's cheeks are fuller, his body more muscular. His energy has returned, and so has his zest for life.

My chest expands with pride.

My heart is full.

Samuel raises a tanned arm and comes to join Rose and me. He lifts Rose into the air and plants a kiss on her cheek before taking my hand and leaning in for a kiss. He pulls me close to his body, our tongues entwine, and my insides flutter as warmth fills me with his lingering kiss.

"I've missed you," he murmurs against my lips.

"Eww." Rose squirms to get down.

He lowers her to the ground and takes her hand. "Are you excited to visit Nanna and Pop?"

"Yes, and my c'usins. I want to play on the beach," Rose says in a higher pitch.

"We'll have months of beach fun," I add. I hand Samuel a bag with a change of clothes from his khaki shorts and shirt. "We'll wait in the car while you change."

"Before I forget, I received a call from Asoo. He wants to bring his family out for a visit. I told him I could help pay for flights, after all he did for me in Ulara."

"Oh honey, that's wonderful news." He leans and kisses me on the lips, slow and enticing. "Go, and change," I murmur, breaking the kiss. He gives me a quick peck on the cheek before striding toward the office.

"He's takin' for-eva," Rose complains.

"We have time before the plane departs. And we're saying goodbye to Aunty Dana first."

One Day Later...

WE STAYED up late last night celebrating our return with the family. Even Amy and Yasmine popped in to see me. Apart from our time at the beach, the day has been about relaxing in our home on the esplanade.

We have committed to living in the Daintree from May to early December. Samuel works at the cultural center, teaching about the benefits of the rainforest. From mid-December to early May, we return to Adelaide, to our beachside home, where we can enjoy the dry summer months by the ocean while avoiding North Queensland's wet season. Since summer is Monte Hotel's busiest months, I help in the office three days a week while Samuel takes care of Rose.

Mum and Dad arrive, and I pour us a glass of wine before dinner. We share the stories of our new life, and then they talk to us about Gran's journal.

"I want to feel closer to my mother," Dad confesses. "After reading her journal, I found the box she left for me. There was another journal where she documented notes about Dawn and her memories of being in Ulara. Most were sad entries, but it's triggered an enormous amount of guilt. I wish I knew before."

Mum lays a gentle hand on Dad's shoulder, and I sense there's more to say.

"If there is a chance to meet my sister, then I want to try."

Samuel stares wide-eyed at my father. "Sir, I-I..." he stutters.

"Samuel isn't sure where they are?" I interject. "And it might not be safe."

"I could get a message to the nearby missionaries." He shrugs.

We both know it's risky to go into the jungle after getting his health back to some normality.

I have fought for his happiness so we can be *free*.

"You know how we talked about setting up a fundraiser?" Samuel rubs my thigh, and I know it's to calm me.

"Yes, but..."

"The missionaries close to where I left the Ularans welcome volunteers. I'm sure they'd be grateful for monetary donations or unwanted pharmaceutical products." He smiles at me. "I can't promise anything, although it might be a way to find Kaikare. She'd want to see you again and meet her brother."

"Oh, honey, I'll do anything to help," Mum adds. "I could help with the administration and set up of the account while you focus on marketing. We'd like to contribute to Dawn's community."

"Your friend, Rhett, has already offered to sponsor." He kisses my cheek. "It might be the answer to uniting your family."

"It's your family too," I say warmly.

"We can only try." Pride oozes from Dad. "Because it's what families do. My mother was brave, and I want to honor her memory and show the same courage in finding my sister."

I take Samuel's hand and gently squeeze. "Only if there's no danger to anyone."

"I'll get correspondence to Dr. Jacques. It's all I can do for now."

My father once thought of Gran as *wild.*

Brave and wild, maybe.

And he wants to venture on the same path as Gran to find answers. Maybe it is our destiny.

I glance around the table at my family.

Then to the man who is my world.

The man I once thought to also be wild.

To me, he will always be *perfectly wild.*

Thank you for reading Eden and Samuel's story. I hope you enjoyed it as much as I did writing their love story.

For any news on my new releases please sign up to my newsletter email.

Thank you again for reading the Beautifully Wild series. After many years of writing, this story is close to my heart.

ACKNOWLEDGMENTS

Twelve years is a long time to write a story, and there are many people to thank during this time.

First and foremost, to my husband, Lynden. Thank you for your encouragement, love, and support of my writing journey.

To my four beautiful daughters, Jamie-Lee, Shauni, Ashleigh, and Demi, for providing constant inspiration. To my wonderful parents, Pam and Vic, and my sister, Vickie, and her family for believing in me and helping in any way possible. A big shout-out to my friends and biggest fans. Mum, Deanne, and Helen, Dayna, and Alison for believing in me from the day I decided to give authoring a shot. Your love for my story gave me the confidence to take a giant step forward.

To Kaylene Osborn at Swish Design and Editing. Thank you for all your expertise, for answering endless questions, and for making my book shine. You are my rock! And a big thank you to Nicki!

My appreciation extends to my Facebook reader group, Leesa Bow's Lovelies, and all the blogging community for helping to get my book out to the world. You all make the book world a much better place.

To my author friends, who I've chatted with while writing this book. You have been with me from the day I decided I wanted to publish my story. I can't express enough gratitude for all your advice and inspiration. To Nina, Maggie, Jen, Beth, KE, and Jodi you always have my back, and I appreciate you all! To all the authors whom I've met at retreats and at signings, you are my writing family.

To Carol, Kellie, Robyn, and Megan, thank you for beta reading my story and helping me refine it. You are all awesome. And to Adriana for helping me with the Brazilian terms. And to Carla for all the information about Venezuela.

To my doctor friends who answered my medical questions, thank you.

To my readers. Thank you for your endless support, and most of all, for loving my stories. Some of you have been with me from the start of my author journey, and to others, I'm a new author. What I love most is you all embrace my characters and stories and love them as much as I do. Thank you for reading, reviewing, and talking about my books to your families and friends in book clubs and blogs.

I appreciate everything you do for me!

Finally, to my daughter, Shauni, and the special teenagers and parents, we met at the Royal Adelaide Children's Hospital—Gina and Jenna, Michael and Sue, Will and Sherie, and Shauni's oncologist, Dr. Tapp. Thank you for your friendship and for showing me what it is to truly embrace fear. Your strength is admirable, and I'll never forget the bond, the support, and love when faced with the battle of cancer. To all the children in the oncology wards around the world, some of you now live in the stars, but you are never forgotten. You are forever the real heroes of the world.

ALSO BY LEESA BOW

THE HENDRICKS BILLIONAIRES

The Wrong Proposal #1

The Wrong Move #2

The Wrong Promise #3

The Wrong Time #4

Beautifully Wild Series

Beautifully Wild

Hopelessly Wild

Perfectly Wild

WILD BOXSET

The Player Series

Winning the Player

Winning the Game

Playing for Time

Caught Out Series

Jardine

Caught Out

Standalones

Charming the Outback

www.leesabow.com

www.ingramcontent.com/pod-product-compliance
Lightning Source LLC
Chambersburg PA
CBHW060637310726
48982CB00003B/810

* 9 7 8 0 6 4 5 6 8 7 1 6 3 *